The Gods of Venice

The Gods of Venice

Alan J. Shannon

iUniverse, Inc.
New York Bloomington

The Gods of Venice

iUniverse books may be ordered through booksellers or by contacting:

iUniverse
1663 Liberty Drive
Bloomington, IN 47403
www.iuniverse.com
1-800-Authors (1-800-288-4677)

ISBN: 978-1-4401-7403-2 (pbk)
ISBN: 978-1-4401-7402-5 (ebk)
ISBN: 978-1-4401-7401-8 (hc)

Printed in the United States of America

iUniverse rev. date: 10/07/2009

To my parents, who taught me the art of traveling,
and to
Kathryn Heekin, who taught me how to be.

With thanks to Holly Enichen for insights and encouragement.
And to Scott, for far too many gifts to mention.

This being human is a guest house
Every morning a new arrival.

A joy, a depression, a meanness,
some momentary awareness comes
as an unexpected visitor.

Welcome and entertain them all!

The dark thought,
the shame, the malice,
meet them at the door laughing, and invite them in.

—Rumi

Chapter One

Venice, 1997

The air, infused with warm weather scents, smelled as alive as the trees. The bright sun warmed the earthen walls of the city's buildings, its little patches of dirt and gardens, and even the cobblestones. Having passed another winter, Venice was coming alive again.

Louis walked along a zigzagging via, nearly passing his destination. Lost in olfactory musings, the heavy, earthy smell of espresso filled his nostrils, and he looked up just as he passed the front window of Café Tramonta.

Claudia sat at a corner table, two empty espresso cups—rims marred with rosy lipstick—stood neglected, cast aside on her table. By the look of the ashtray, and her vacant gaze out the wide window onto the *calle*, she was having a crisis. He furtively glanced at the top of her table again. Cell phone, lighter, a plate with the remains of a *cornetto*, and a piece of correspondence tucked under the saucer. A letter. A handwritten one. So this is why she'd called him.

"Spy!" Claudia shouted, smiling crookedly, catching Louis observing her.

The clanging of spoons on saucers and the humming and hissing of the enormous idling espresso machine ceased momentarily. The whole place seemed to hear what was intended for Louis alone. Customers turned toward Claudia whose face grew crimson. Poor Claudia. Dabs of pink rose on her slender, patrician neck. Self-consciously she clasped her throat and pulled the collar of her blouse closer.

"*Ciao*, Louis, *ciao, ciao*!" she called meekly, attempting a casual tone though she was aware everyone was watching her.

Louis sometimes tried to return the singsong, multiple ciao, but it always sounded forced, stilted. How could something so seemingly simple to express and duplicate be so impossible?

Patrons turned back to their papers and coffees, and Louis smiled and waved. "*Un momentito*," he pantomimed, pointing toward the espresso bar. "*Il caffè*."

Claudia nodded too enthusiastically, thought Louis. She would wait, seemingly patient on the outside, but he knew, likely a ball of charged nerves in the inside. She wore an expression of implicit desperation, and disappointment. A pang of guilt stabbed Louis, but he needed his coffee. And by the look of things, he figured he'd better order it before going to her table.

He ordered two cappuccinos. One to take to the table and another to be delivered in fifteen minutes. The first time he'd done this the owner and barista hadn't understood. One for now, one for later. "I'm American," he'd explained, shrugging his shoulders. "We like to eat and drink a lot."

The barista suddenly seemed to understand, nodding and grinning, and thereafter, his order for two coffees was never questioned. And always—with the exception of one occasion when the flamboyant opera star Luciana Serra fluttered through the door after having decided to take her morning espresso and *vin santo* at the café, throwing the place into turmoil—the waiter or barista never forgot to bring his second coffee fifteen minutes after he'd received the first.

Louis glanced at Claudia again, who brushed trembling fingers along the rim of her espresso saucer. He couldn't guess the contents of the letter poking out from beneath the plate, but he was certain that it was from her mother. Who else could write and upset her so? She would cry and wonder what to do. And then Louis would comfort her by reminding her that there was always crazy, lost Venice, a city as odd, improbable, and lost as they were. And so, whatever her mother wrote, whatever would happen, they would still have Venice to hide in. The city would undoubtedly one day sink, but not in their lifetimes. For the near future, the city was *terra firma*, despite appearances and what the government said.

Balancing a cornetto and cappuccino, Louis maneuvered through the crowded café, nodding at his neighbor Giacomo and the postman, who should have begun delivering the mail already. The postman didn't appear to be in any hurry; in fact, he'd just begun sipping a second cappuccino.

Louis and Claudia kissed, the customary two cheeks, two-peck version that Americans find so affected. He kissed without thinking about it. One year in Venice and he'd already adopted the city's customs as his own.

"Not a good day?" he asked, feigning ignorance, pretending that he hadn't heard the tone of desperation in her voice less than an hour earlier when she'd called to ask him to meet.

She nodded, giving a pained expression. He followed her eyes to the letter under the empty espresso cup.

"*Carta di Mamma*?"

Claudia nodded again.

"Disownment?" he joked. "You know they'll never cut you off. A penniless Baggi makes the whole family look bad. Besides, you know they'd be accused of shirking family duties for no good reason—"

"No good reason? I don't know what to do. I can't hold a job, and I fear my time is up. The men interested in me are awful, and the ones I like are even more *brutti*. I'm only good at … well … shopping, and drinking, and talking. Only I can't get paid for doing these. I don't even remember what I like or what interests me."

"It's just a phase," Louis said, wondering what was in the letter that had prompted her to think about these things. He'd known Claudia for less than a year, but tended to agree with her self-assessment. Somewhere along the line, the young patrician exited from her intended path and she'd been lost ever since. While blue-blooded Italian parents sometimes indulged their children a year or two of irresponsibility, Bohemian living or all-out rebellion, a lifelong pursuit of either of the three—in any combination—wasn't typically tolerated, and certainly not for daughters. But more than this, he'd gathered that her mother, *Contessa* Baggi, had made so many decisions and controlled her daughter's life for so long, that now that Claudia had finally broken from her, she wasn't sure what do. All along, she'd feared that her mother would force her to leave Venice. Was that about to happen?

"It's been a phase now for a few years, maybe longer. I can't even remember when I stopped thinking for myself," she said quietly, reaching across the table to take a sip of his cappuccino. "But I felt like leaving New York and coming here was a first step."

"First step?" he asked, noticing that his cappuccino was nearly gone.

"Figuring it out. But I guess I've wasted the past year. And now what do I do?" she whimpered, nervously pushing at her cuticles.

Louis glanced at the bar, hoping the barista was making his next cappuccino. "What was in the letter, Claudia?" he asked, wondering if he really wanted to know. If this perfect, easy existence he'd finally found in this intriguing, maze-like city were ending, maybe it would be better if he didn't know.

She shrugged as if it didn't matter, but she was visibly shaken.

"What did your mother write?" he asked, feeling a little like he was intruding. She would tell him when she was ready, right? In the meantime, he could pretend that nothing had changed.

Sighing, she leaned back in her chair. "Things are complicated," she whimpered. "There's a lot I haven't told you."

"Okay," he said, his voice shaking.

"I've told you that my mother's always called all the shots, you already know that right?"

He nodded, his head beginning to spin. Just when it seemed

he'd found the right place and the perfect friend, things were going to unravel.

"I was pushed and prodded to do hundreds of things when I was a kid, whether I liked it or not. So I don't even know what it is to do something because you want to do it. I did everything because I was forced to or because it was simply easier to comply with my mother's schemes and ideas, none of which were really horrid or anything, but most of which weren't what I wanted to do."

"Is she so bad?" Louis thought of the occasional photos he'd seen of Contessa Baggi in newspapers and magazines. In photos, she seemed so perfect, so superhuman. She didn't look cruel.

"Well, she's not spiteful—she doesn't do things do be mean," Claudia explained, her cheeks turning pink. "She's not like some other powerful women I have met. With my mother, you eventually submit because it's the easier thing to do, the path of least resistance. Compliance brings peace and other things."

"Other things?" he asked, marveling that even now when her mother was yanking her chain yet again, she couldn't completely bring herself to rebuke her mother.

"Money. It brings you money," she sniffed. "Cooperate with my mother and you're able to do what you want—provided it's also what she wants." Claudia glanced down at the table embarrassed. She traced circles with her fingernails on the metal surface. "When I was young, I did what she wanted because I had to. Now I do what she wants because I choose to, because I want the money."

"Well, how were you able to live here doing nothing for a year? She let you do that?"

"She didn't know," Claudia said meekly, pretending to gaze out the window.

"Didn't know?" Louis asked, his voice louder than he'd intended. Her mother hadn't known she'd been living in Venice for the past year?

"No," she said nervously, running her fingers across her neck that had which turned pink and blotchy.

"What is it?" he asked. "Why are you cringing?"

"Am I cringing?" she asked, shaking her head with resignation. "If I am, it's because I feel bad, because I never told you."

Louis wondered if he should order a vin santo. The combination of their conversation and the caffeine from the cappuccino was making him shake.

"I've been worried about it since the day I arrived here, wondering when I would receive this letter, when my mother would figure things out," she said soberly, gazing at the letter ominously.

Louis suddenly realized that despite the fact that he considered Claudia his closest friend, there were fundamentals about her that he didn't know. Sometimes it was difficult to figure out Italians, though he'd wrongly concluded that Claudia was unlike typical Italians. She kept her secrets, too. Then, maybe everyone did. If he were truthful, he would have to admit that perhaps he even had his own.

"Still, how did you keep it from your mother all this time?"

Claudia cringed again, tracing more circles on the tabletop.

"If you'd rather not talk about it," Louis offered, not sure whether he should change the subject or push her to tell him everything. He wanted to know and he didn't want to know. He'd been so happy the night before, feeling as if things were finally going his way—now this.

"No, no, I want to tell you," she said slowly, nodding her head as if to convince herself. "It's just that I've been dancing around the edges of the truth for so long that I'm not even certain if I recognize what's real and what's not."

Claudia shivered and rubbed her arms as if she'd just felt a chill.

"Just tell me how it happened," Louis said, realizing there was far more about her that he hadn't guessed at. And it sounded like there were things about Claudia that she didn't even know about herself.

"Well … with cell phones … it's easy to do," she stammered. "And, my mother's busy, so I merely visited more often than usual, which was easy, of course, because I was traveling from Venice, not New York. Anytime she talked about visiting, I would claim that I needed to get out of the city and would come to Rome. And she doesn't like to fly, anyway, hates to go to America, so I could easily persuade her to stay put. Pietro expressed her letters to me, and I expressed mine to him, which he mailed to her."

"Your mother thought you were in New York this whole time?"

"She wouldn't listen when I told her that it wasn't working with Pietro," she said defensively, her voice rising. "She wanted us to have a trial separation, so she paid for a small apartment for me, very close to the condo Pietro and I shared. I think she honestly believed that I would come around, that I'd grow up and return to him. She thought that ultimately all the years of catechism and time spent with her priest, Father Angelo, would prevail, and I would do my churchly, familial duty and go back to my husband. I honestly believe I was sent there to have children, to have Pietro's children and nothing more. And I'm just realizing this now. "

"She knows that you're divorced, doesn't she?"

"She does now," she said, her voice dropping to a near whisper. "Without telling me, she jumped on a plane to New York, only to find that my apartment was empty. She went to see Pietro and got him to tell her where I was and to admit that we'd gotten a divorce six months ago."

"That's what she wrote?"

"Partly," Claudia said with a grimace, gesturing toward the barista.

Louis followed her gaze. The barista was just finishing pulling an espresso shot at the nearby bar. He deftly placed the filled cup on a saucer and with a flourish, tossed two cookies and a lemon rind beside the cup, and placed it before her. He didn't seem to be listening, but Louis knew better. In quiet Venice, void of the roar of cars, buses, or crowds, it was still possible to eavesdrop. Venetians seemed to practice it, an art as old as glassblowing.

"Why didn't she come directly here?" he asked.

Shaking her head before downing the shot of espresso, Claudia frowned.

"That's not my mother. I'm sure she returned to Rome beside

herself. It must have shocked her to find out I'd done this behind her back, and to learn I'd been here, so close, all this time. She needed time to think, and probably to talk to Father Angelo."

"So when did all of this occur?" Louis asked, trying not to sound hurt that she hadn't told him.

"Just a few weeks ago. Pietro must have been afraid to tell me because he didn't call or e-mail. And my mother must have waited a week or so before writing me," she said, her voice shaking as she waved again at the barista.

"*Prosecco*!" she called.

The bartender nodded, grabbed a glass, and turned to fetch a bottle of the local bubbly from the refrigerator beneath the counter. He poured the glass, filling it nearly to the top, and told his nephew to bring it to the table.

"Won't you make yourself sick?" Louis asked

"I don't care," Claudia moaned. "I need both."

When the beverage arrived, Claudia took a big sip and closed her eyes.

"That tastes good," she sighed. "After all that espresso, I need something to calm me down. I feel like throwing myself in a canal."

"Really?" Louis asked, leaning toward her.

"No," she said quietly. "I don't know. Everything's changed now, ruined. I don't know what to think."

"And why exactly is your mother so pissed?"

"Where do I begin?" she said, her eyes turning pink as if she might cry. "It goes back very far. Ultimately, as it's always been, it's because I haven't done what she wants. And this time, I've disobeyed her wishes more than I'd ever even imagined I could."

"By divorcing? Your mother is so convinced it's wrong?"

"It was a marriage that my mother wanted, and it wasn't the first thing I did for her that I shouldn't have," she explained, sipping greedily from her glass. "It became a habit after awhile."

"You haven't told me exactly how that happened," he said, leaning forward in his chair. "I know that she wanted you to marry Pietro, but how did she orchestrate that?"

"We were friends, we loved each other as friends, but that's not enough to base a marriage on. His parents liked the match, and of course, it was my mother's idea, so we married, both of us, for our parents. Silly, isn't it?" She looked at him.

"Maybe," he offered. "But maybe not that unusual, even for today."

"I don't think so many people would be so stupid today. I don't think I've ever met anyone quite as stupid as I am."

"How can you say that?" he asked. "You just let your mother run your life for a long time, but you're figuring things out now."

"Only just now," she cried, her voice cracking. "Why did it take me so long to figure it out, so long that I hardly know who I am?"

"It happens to lots of people," he said, watching an old woman slowly walk up the street outside the window. "It could happen to anyone."

"But how could I have been so clueless? I mean, I didn't even realize at first that my mother had orchestrated our whole meeting and Pietro's parents did the same. We both fell into their trap. And that was okay for a while, like I told you, but in the end it didn't work. I followed Pietro to New York where he works for some giant bank, but that was no life for me. I was happy to have my acting classes and the cinema—so many theaters and movies that I could always find something to watch to carry me away. Not that it was so bad, but I knew it wasn't working with Pietro, and so that made me unhappy. And I was in a different country, in that enormous city, and life suddenly scared me. I had nothing to do, and realized I didn't even know what to do with myself. So I left shortly afterward and got my own apartment."

"But you still talk to Pietro. Often."

"Of course. We're friends, which is what we were at the beginning. He was the one who told me to go. He knew it wasn't going to work either. We were both sad, but what do you do when it just can't work?"

"Some people go to counseling."

"That's so American," she shrugged. "If you're making a cake and you don't have the right ingredients, what point is there in continuing to make it?"

She wondered why he was trying to persuade her to give Pietro another chance when he knew from everything she'd said about them that there was no point. No, she was right that the marriage had been wrong from the start. Besides, didn't Louis need her in Venice just as they were?

Louis sighed, shifting in his chair.

"Did your mother suspect that things weren't going right before you told her?"

"Certainly. She knew something wasn't right almost from the beginning, maybe even before we were actually married. Thank God, she's afraid to fly or I'm sure she would have been visiting all the time. She wanted us to see a priest."

"A priest?"

"That's how I know she knew that something was going on. She never said why she thought we should go see one, but I suspect she knew."

"So what is she saying now?" he asked.

"She says it's time to stop hiding out, to get back to Rome, and move onto the next phase of my life."

"What's that?" he asked nervously.

"I don't know—but I have a feeling that I'll soon find out," she said, her voice shaking again.

She finished off her prosecco, the tip of her tongue darting to the corners of her mouth to collect the last drops.

"She sounds kind of modern to me," Louis said.

"My mother can be very modern when she wants. In some ways, she's very old-fashioned and in other ways, she's thoroughly modern. She asks my father permission to do nothing; yet, she arranged my marriage. She also places a lot of faith in the church—and in her Father

Angelo, who seems about as old as Rome itself. In that way, she's as old-fashioned as they come."

Louis started to panic, wondering if Claudia would actually leave Venice.

"You won't go, will you?" he asked. "I mean, wouldn't your mother let you stay?"

Her eyes scrunched up and her face puckered vaguely as if she'd eaten something sour.

"Going back to Rome would be going backward," she said. "That's where I grew up, but there's nothing there for me. The Vatican is everywhere, and my parents are there, of course. Mostly my mother. I would always be a Baggi in Rome. In Venice, a Baggi doesn't mean anything—"

"Well, I wouldn't say *anything*," Louis said, remembering the tabloid photos of her mother.

"Still, it's different. People are nosy here, but nosy about everyone and everything. And I don't belong in Venice. Nobody talks about me or watches me more than they watch or pay attention to any other person."

"You don't belong here?" he asked.

How had she come to be his unofficial partner and companion in this faraway city? He hadn't had such a close friend in years, possibly ever. Like no one he'd known, Claudia appeared lost, vaguely out of sorts and he liked that in her, he wanted to take care of her. It was easier to accept his own uncertain future, the feeling that he was unclear about what to do next when he had a friend more lost than he was.

Claudia half smiled, shaking her head.

"I simply meant, I'm not *from* here, not that I shouldn't *be* here," she said. "I swear you look more dour than I do. And I'm the one who's being forced to contemplate leaving, but I think I have to stay. I can think more clearly in this crumbling old city because there aren't so many distractions, just the canals rising and falling with the tides every day. Everything is predictable and I like that. Besides, I've always been drawn to Venice. For a short time, I had this art instructor at school, a curator at the Vatican Museums. She loved Venetian art and architecture, and she used to go on and on about the city, and I fell in love without ever having seen the place. It's everything she described and more."

In the year since meeting, the two friends had spent hours over many coffees, bottles of wine, bourbons, and cocktails and discussing the indescribable—reasons for feeling so at home in Venice. They never seemed to tire of the subject. And for Louis, it marked the first time he'd ever felt like he could stay in a place. He wasn't thinking about when he could leave for the next city. One didn't meet expats in Venice who were studying international relations, whose parents were political leaders or CEOs. No, in this city, foreigners who stayed more than a few days or a week studied art or architecture or bided their time hiding out.

Claudia sighed, but her face brightened at the sight of the barista's young nephew bringing Louis' second coffee and another glass of prosecco for her, even though she hadn't ordered it. She waved at the barista, her face half embarrassment, half pleasure.

"It's a bad day," she chirped, holding her glass up to toast him. "And I need something to calm me down."

The boy whisked away the empty espresso cups and replaced them with a small dish of glistening Marcona almonds coated in oil. Claudia picked up the letter and set it down again, smoothing it with her small hand.

"She's coming," she said, looking at Louis soberly.

"Is that what she wrote?"

"No," she answered, drumming her fingers on the table.

"Then what makes you think that?" he asked, feeling stupid when he realized that if he told his mother where he was she would track him down, too.

"That's my mother," she said with a weary shrug. "She'll wait a few weeks to calm down, to give me time to think, and then she'll be here—that's how it was when I went to school, when I did an internship in Geneva with my father at the UN, and when I was in New York. She shows up sooner or later."

"So you think she's coming here to take you back home?" he said, his voice sounding panicked.

"I'd guess so. She won't like it at all that I'm here. She's always had this irrational dislike of Venice. She never brought me when I was a child no matter how many times I had asked, and she never had a good thing to say about the city. She wouldn't even let me take a school trip here—her dislike of Venice is irrational."

"You couldn't be more different from your mother, I think."

"Yes, in most ways. And the way we feel about Venice is just one of many."

"And your father? What does he think?"

Claudia looked pensive.

"I love my *papà*," she whispered, as if her father might be able to hear. "But he's never been able to make decisions for me. He's had an influence, but my mother always decides what's done. He's always encouraged me, seeming to know that I'd come here someday. From the first time we talked about it, he encouraged me to come. In fact, when my mother wouldn't allow me to take the trip with my classmates, he was the one who told me that someday I'd make it here."

Suddenly frowning, she took a sloppy gulp of prosecco. "I've finally arrived where I want to be, and now maybe I have to leave—"

"You don't have to go," Louis interrupted, leaning across the table.

"I worry that she'll cut me off, Louis. And then what will I do?" she said, her shoulders drooping. "I've never supported myself and I wouldn't even know how."

"If you've got a reason to be here, then maybe she won't make you leave. Maybe she won't *want* you to leave," he said enthusiastically, trying to convince himself at the same time.

"But how can that happen?" she said staring absently at her glass. "She'll probably be here in a month, maybe even a few weeks. How can

I get something together in such a short amount of time? I don't even have a job; don't even know what I'd be qualified to do."

"Maybe you could be working toward something, have a plan, or something," he suggested. "Hey, why don't you open the film office you were talking about? You'd be perfect—scout locations, show location scouts around, assist with filming permits."

He knew the suggestion was useless, still, he felt as if he had to offer something. Just because Claudia enjoyed film didn't mean she could open a film office. But if she left, he knew he would have to go, too. He'd grown so accustomed to having her as a companion that Venice would be no fun without her. In fact, it would be lonely.

"I worry that it's too late," she said, shaking her head slowly, deliberately. She stared vacantly at the letter on the table.

"No, I'll help you," Louis said loudly, slapping the table.

What would he do if she took him up on his offer? He was an underemployed, unfocused American on the run. Their situations were similar, so what help could he possibly offer? He listened to the words tumble out of his mouth, realizing even as he was saying them that they were meaningless, a promise he couldn't keep. He wouldn't even know where to start. After all, he was far more of a foreigner in the city than she was, despite her insistence that Venice was as strange and different to Romans as it was to Americans.

"That sounds so impossible—improbable, too. I mean, there just aren't that many films made here," she said hopelessly.

Louis shrugged, as if that fact were trivial, his mind racing to stumble upon a viable solution.

"Why don't you open a store," he said suddenly.

Claudia grimaced, shaking her head solemnly.

"A high-end fashion store … what about that?" he offered. Gaining confidence, he continued. "But not all the typical stuff for the Japanese and Americans, but stuff that's made by local people. Small name, different stuff. Clothing, paintings, ceramics … all kinds of stuff!"

A crease formed on Claudia's forehead, marring her long, narrow face. He'd only seen the crease form a few other times, only when she'd been really upset or angry.

"I could write travel articles on it, do PR releases, and create a big buzz. I know how to do that!" he said, leaning toward her.

She studied her empty prosecco glass, then leaned across the table and delicately picked up his cappuccino and took a sip. Avoiding his eyes, she focused on the foam on top of the coffee, considering his proposal.

"Why does whatever you're drinking always taste better?" she asked, interrupting her thoughts.

"It just seems that way," he mused.

Claudia took another sip before sliding the cup and saucer back across the table. She picked up one of the lumpy brown, malformed sugar cubes and examined it before setting it down again. She sighed.

"You could help me do this?" she asked, her gaze rising from the table.

"Yes, of course."

It was only a half lie, of course. What did he know about opening a store? But he could help paint, maybe work there. And he could definitely do the PR work. He could promote the hell out of it.

"If I had someone helping me, maybe my parents would help me with it. Of course, I don't have enough money to do it myself, so I'd have to get some money from them," she said.

A shadow crossed her face, as if she'd realized that her idea wouldn't work. From the expression on her face and the hard look in her eyes, Louis realized that she wouldn't be asking her parents for any money.

"Why does your mother dislike Venice so much?" he asked, trying to change the subject. He felt like they were stuck in a corner, so maybe if they talked about something else a way out would become apparent.

Claudia squinted, the delicate features of her face forming a wince.

"Who knows? My father thinks it's strange, too, especially because the city has always been intriguing to me. Odd, isn't it, that I'm drawn to the city while she despises it?"

"Maybe that's how mothers and daughters are." He chuckled.

He could tell she no longer wanted to talk about it, that they'd gone too far as it was. Claudia studied the barista and her face brightened.

"Maybe I could open a bar or café. That's practical and not too hard. Even I could make cappuccino and pour drinks."

Louis frowned, but quickly smiled, not wanting to discourage any idea that might keep her in Venice.

"No," she said, shaking her head thoughtfully. "My mother would never let me do that either."

"Maybe you could tell your mother to take a hike?" Louis suggested, wondering if trying to persuade her to defy her mother was hopeless. It was as if Claudia knew that was the step to take but for some reason was unable to. *Some reason*? He knew the inconsequential reason was money.

"Easier said than done," she said, biting the insides of her mouth. "I … I'd really like to do that."

"Then do it," Louis said. "And we'll figure out some way to make it work."

Claudia looked down at the table again, picking up the sugar cube and rolling it in the palm of her hand.

They'd talked enough, and if Claudia was going to stand up to her mother, it was going to take some time for her to get used to the idea. At least she was thinking seriously about it, he could see that by her solemn expression.

Louis pulled what remained of the second coffee toward him, greedily drinking the tepid espresso and foamy milk. He needed the caffeine and had to get to work on a translation job that was due that evening. He should have done it the day before, but Claudia had talked him into seeing a Mondrian exhibit at L'Accademia. Once again, he would be completing a job at the last minute. He tapped his foot nervously; worried that he wouldn't have enough time to complete the assignment. If he could finish his work, then his mind would clear and he could help.

"When do you think she'll come?" he asked.

"Probably in a few weeks."

"So we've got a little bit of time, anyway. I can ask around—maybe my landlord knows of something. I'll talk to him, okay?"

His landlord, Sacci, seemed to know everyone, having been raised in the city. The man's aging mother had moved out of Venice years earlier and he'd taken over the management of the apartment building that Louis lived in. The man seemed thoughtful and well connected. Maybe he would have some ideas or know of a job for Claudia somewhere.

Finishing his lukewarm coffee, Louis scraped a spoonful of creamy froth into his mouth before timidly standing.

"Oh," Claudia gasped. "Don't tell me you have to go? I'm just getting started—I need a plan to show I'm doing something or my mother's going to force me back home to Rome."

"Don't worry," he encouraged her, patting her shoulder. "We'll think of something and we've got some time. Right now, though, I've got to get to work—really."

"I forget that you work," she said wistfully. "What are you working on?"

"A translation—the one I told you about yesterday. I have to finish it by tonight. The minute I'm finished I'll help you. I promise. And we'll figure out something, I just know it."

"*Dio*," she moaned, grasping the sides of the table as if steadying herself. "When can you meet again—tomorrow for lunch? I'm suddenly feeling very needy."

"Are you okay?" he asked, suddenly worried that the prosecco and coffee she drank may have made her sick.

"Oh, I'll be okay," she said wearily, sitting back into her seat. "I guess we can't come up with a plan in one day."

"I'll think about it and give you a call, okay?"

"Tomorrow? Will you call me tomorrow?" she pleaded, clutching his arm.

"Sure," he nodded, inching away from her. "If I finish early enough or I come up with something I'll call you tonight. Otherwise tomorrow for sure."

He kissed her cheeks and gave her a big hug. What must it be like to have parents still telling you what to do and relying on them to live? He couldn't imagine it with his parents so far away, not even knowing exactly where he was.

Louis left the café with Claudia hunched over another , and nervously toying with the sugar cube. He felt bad leaving, but what else could he say? He was fresh out of ideas and neither of them could think straight. It would be better to have some time to think about it, to talk to some people. And if he didn't get his work done then he'd have no money to help her.

Walking slowly alongside the serpentine canals, he could feel the growing warmth of the sun seeping into the stone and brick of the buildings, gently warming the city. Though he could hardly afford it, he'd rented a cheap, tiny studio in a building that was a good ten minutes walk from his apartment. Right after he decided to stay in Venice and started getting regular translation assignments, he took the studio knowing it would never work for him to be doing his writing in his apartment. And because the studio was cramped and steamy in the summer and cold and drafty in the winter, he paid only fifty-thousand lire a month for it.

An old woman, ankles thick as gondola mooring posts, walked ahead of him clutching a market basket overflowing with vegetables. He thought about the letter from Claudia's mother. What exactly had her mother written?

What would his mother do? She would be on a plane in a heartbeat, showing up on his doorstep (if she could find it). He'd abandoned her, fled his parents and his whole familiar life in Chicago, telling no one where he was. And he couldn't even articulate exactly why. He'd felt stifled, his family and neighborhood friends he grew up with crowded him. But if he had to tell them just how they'd done so, he wouldn't know how to explain it.

He'd always had an itch to move away, to live somewhere other than the old neighborhood or the gigantic city in which he'd grown up. In this way, he was pure American. He'd inherited the restless blood of American immigrants and pioneers passed on from parents that no longer understood the urge to move away.

He and Claudia's positions were alike in some ways, but dissimilar in others. While his parents didn't want to control his life, he felt their inexplicably heavy presence. It seemed the farther away he got from them, the more they invaded his thoughts and dreams. Claudia had different challenges. At least he was happy translating and editing. After so many years of having decisions made for her, she didn't even know what she wanted to do. At least he knew what he wanted to do, what he could do.

A strange memory appeared—a vision so unlike the street scene before him that he shook his head. In his memory, it was a warm summer day and he was a child and lay with his brother on a soft blanket in the shade of a towering, whispering elm. He was dreamily awake, watching the shadows cast by the sun through the swaying branches and listening to the desultory, soothing rustle of the leaves. Birds were silent, as if the world had slowed for an instant to savor the sublime summer's day. His mother tickled his back, a slow, gentle tickle that made him feel what? A feeling he hadn't experienced since he was a child. What was he feeling then, as a five or six year old, when the sleepy summer days seemed to unroll endlessly and he didn't worry about working or buying groceries? What had his worries been?

He started to cry as he walked down the narrow street, knowing that the old, precarious city perched on sinking marshes had seen plenty of tears. Did anyone before him though, cry for his reason, for the vague, inexplicable feeling that something wasn't fully formed, that his life felt half-lived?

He hated when he couldn't figure out things, when puzzles were unsolvable. He'd never been good at math or science because he'd been confronted with problems and equations. There was a formula to follow, a way to go from point A to point B, but he always got some little part of the formula wrong, so the answer nearly always remained foggy to him.

The toll of procrastination squeezed his chest, a more pleasant feeling to him than the indecipherable mystery of that just-recalled memory.

Calle Ponzi lay just ahead and he walked faster, passing a *pasticceria*. He glanced in the window where loaves of bread were stacked high, glistening with an olive oil glaze, and flecked with sea salt and granules of browned flour.

He walked quickly down Ponzi, past one of the phony glass studios, which sold a lot of so-called Venetian glass that was actually made in China. The bartender at Harry's told him that this neighborhood was once filled with glassblowers, but very few remained.

Who was left in the city but a few fishermen, gondoliers, and hotel staff? Venice was a city where people were leaving, which was why he enjoyed being there even more. Let them leave it, quiet and disintegrating, slowly sinking into the sea. He would love it even more for having been abandoned to the trampling tourists, to history, and to the ever-higher tides. Always a sucker for the underdog, for the neglected and abandoned, he found the city alluring.

At *passeggio* Piccolo, a passage so narrow it resembled a crack in the faded facades of ochre and russet buildings, he briskly turned, his memory of the flashback having left him completely. The passage, which dead-ended at a canal, had only four tiny, but towering buildings. Two leaned forward as if trying to butt cornices. He glanced at the second floor window of the first building and saw the feline-like Signora Crespi peering down at him. He waved, but she abruptly leaned back from the window.

Why must he always forget that in this city you were never to let on that you knew you were being watched? He could tell his wave had irritated the scowling old woman. He imagined that in the shadows of her darkened living room she wore a frown.

If she'd been leaning out of the window, peering toward calle Ponzi as she often did, he could have said hello, and then she would actually have responded. After the first month of coming to the studio and greeting her with a *buon giorno* or *buonasera*, the signora had finally acknowledged him with a nod of her egg-shaped, gray-haired head. But after a few months, she began returning his greetings with a high-pitched sì that reminded him of a cartoon character's voice. He was never certain whether she was echoing his greeting, or merely tolerating him, as if to say, yes, I see you, *cretino*.

Louis hurried down the passage past mullioned windows tightly closed or shuttered. Always he had the feeling he was being watched, that some window high above harbored spying eyes. He was an oddity, certainly, a young American renting a small studio, a shoebox really, in a working-class neighborhood. But he concluded that everyone in Venice was odd whether native, vagabond, or transplant, only the boatloads of tourists lived normal lives.

What did he consider himself? A vagabond, perhaps, but one who suspected that the world he'd left behind might one day catch up to him. In the meantime, he would enjoy the solitude, his lack of responsibility, and the feeling that he'd slipped into a time warp of sorts, falling backward in time. He could live simply, cheaply, with few demands and only himself and a best friend to consider. It was an easy enough life.

If he could keep the world at bay, out of the narrow, winding streets and rising and falling waters of the canals, maybe he would stay. For the first time since wandering around Europe, he'd found a place that felt right. While Claudia might have always known she wanted to come to Venice, he'd merely stumbled upon it. A college friend believed there were no coincidences in life, and he'd always doubted that could be true. But how to explain the small, gnawing urge to come to this corner of Europe only to discover he felt oddly at home here? Then there was the fact that he had somehow chosen to study Italian in high school and college, merely to be different. Everyone else studied Spanish and French, so what had prompted him to choose Italian?

As he placed his key into the door lock, a small boat with a whining outboard motor passed by on the canal at the end of the street pushing small waves of green water into the end of the passage. The sound of water lapping in the canal replaced the fading drone of the boat, as the tops of waves broke onto the street sloppily, eventually falling back into the canal.

The door springs opened loudly, creaking on giant hinges. Louis shuffled into the hallway, not wanting to mount the stairs and begin working. As he started up the stairs, he heard a tinny sounding radio coming from the first floor apartment on the left. The first time he had heard the crackling transmission; he had pressed his ear against the sweating wall and heard the swelling notes of a full orchestra, the warbling voice of an opera singer. He couldn't be certain where the music was coming from; was it on the other side of the wall in the apartment where a retired fisherman lived?

Passing the large door to the canal and the boat garage, which no one in the building used, Louis thought he heard crying, a muffled, and steady sob. Pressing his ear against the damp, thick door, he listened for the sound again but heard only a sorrowful cat that had probably sneaked into the boat garage.

As he climbed the stairs, he heard the crying again, but less faintly. This time the sound was unmistakable. Who was it? The fisherman, perhaps, or Signora Crespi on the next floor? He couldn't tell where the sound was coming from—farther up the stairway, or across the canal? He pressed his ear against the wall so he could hear better. Implausible as it seemed, maybe the source of the crying was the tough-looking, retired fisherman, Signore Toto, with ruddy cheeks and forearms as big as pier pilings. He seemed the last person who would cry, Louis thought. Didn't he live on the other side of the wall? And he was a widower, so that might explain it.

The sobbing just as quickly stopped and Louis stood silent with his ear cocked toward the wall. He balanced on the stair, each foot on a different step, trying to quiet a creak in the old wood. But there was no more crying, just the faint sound of disco coming from somewhere down the canal.

Louis never figured it out, and if he lingered much longer, he'd be sorry by midnight that he'd spent even these few moments standing idly in the hallway. He wondered if Claudia might cry the same way when she returned to the quiet of her apartment. Bounding up the remaining steps to the fourth floor as if to drive the thought from his head, he arrived in front of his studio door out of breath.

His studio was tiny, drafty, and completely Old World. He didn't believe in ghosts, but he could sense the presence of all the souls who had sat under this same roof. He prepped his desk and then opened the heavy curtains covering the giant windows overlooking the canal. The landlord claimed the room had once been part of a lesser *palazzo*, for why ever would such a small apartment have such enormous windows overlooking the canal?

Sitting down at his computer right away—even before pouring himself a glass of water—he picked up the translation where he'd left off and jumped into his work. The first few pages translated quickly and easily. The short story, by an American, took place in Tuscany and recounted her misadventures with some college friends. There would be the standard affair with some strapping Tuscan stud whose olive skin, dark eyes, wooing ways and earthiness left the women panting for more. The mysterious, slightly flirtatious *uomo* would make an appearance by page six, he wagered. The world seemed to have an insatiable appetite for bodice rippers, which was fine by him as it kept him employed.

But he stood corrected when he passed page six, then seven, then ten and still no uomo. Instead, the story took an unexpected turn when the protagonist's best friend confessed a love she had harbored and hidden for nearly twenty years. And that's where the story abruptly ended, to be continued in the following edition. The next installment would reveal all, or at least a little more. He didn't even know how many installments the story had or in which magazine it would appear. It didn't matter; he was paid well enough that he could remain in Venice.

He finished translating the piece in ten hours, two hours less than he'd anticipated. He hadn't noticed, but the sky outside had turned to swirling blackness punctuated by a few pinpricks of light in the distance and yellowy light escaping a window across the canal. It was only eight o'clock.

He would have time for a drink before dinner, and why not at his favorite off-season spot, Harry's Bar. During the summer, he spurned the place, except in the mornings or late afternoons, but in the off-season, the legendary bar and restaurant was quiet, patronized by only an occasional tourist and by a different sort: a combination of Venetians, passers-through, and squatters who seemed right at home at the establishment. He liked to think of himself as belonging there, at ease among the spirits of Hemingway and Picasso.

Closing a set of aged, thick wood-slatted blinds and the heavy, old curtains against the early spring chill seeping in through the windows, Louis switched off his desk lamp and grabbed his laptop as he walked across the creaking floor to the door. He had e-mailed the translation to the service along with an invoice. If he were lucky, he'd be paid in a few months.

If he were careful, he'd have enough money for another three weeks. And if the check didn't arrive then—or another from a job he'd sent off weeks earlier—then he'd ask his landlord if he could pay the rent late. When Louis arrived a year ago, he thought the rather young landlord a typical Italian. He looked a little like a handsome statesman, well dressed and mostly serious. But lately, as he observed him making rounds in the building with his pugs or running out for a coffee, he'd concluded that maybe the man wasn't as typical as he had thought.

Louis crept down the stairs listening for the crying he'd heard earlier. But there was only a faint sound of a piano. At the foot of the stairs, he paused, cocked his ear toward the wall, and stood still. There was no sobbing and no opera music. He shrugged his shoulders just as the light timer expired plunging the stairway and hall into darkness. A thin strip of muted light from the street spilled under the door. He reached for the doorknob, finding it out of habit.

As he walked outside, frozen bits of mist struck his cheeks, reminding him how unpredictable springtime could be in Venice. A cold front from the Alps had usurped the spring-like warmth from earlier in the day. He tied his scarf against the chill and walked at a brisk pace toward Harry's Bar.

"Buonasera," called Arturo, one of Harry's bartenders, as Louis stepped through the door.

Louis returned the greeting and noticed with dismay that the bar was crowded—with Americans. He hesitated, stopping his hands in midair as they began unwinding his neck scarf. Should he just go elsewhere? All he'd wanted was to relax after translating for so many hours without a lot of noisy American tourists around. But what were they doing here in late March? Shouldn't they be home dyeing Easter eggs? He supposed they could say the same of him, though he felt like he had more of a claim on the bar—and maybe the whole city.

He heard a voice, a voice that at first sounded familiar only because of the immediately recognizable Midwest accent, flat, friendly, and open.

"He hung out here," the man was saying, "along with Picasso and I think Jackie O even stopped by—with Onassis. Not when she was First Lady, of course. Anyone who was anyone who came to Venice in the sixties and seventies stopped in here."

"But it seems so plain—not at all what I'd imagined. It's not very jet-set, you know?" another voice said with disappointment.

Louis could see a rather plain woman speaking, playing with the collar of what looked to be a new trench coat—probably Armani, he thought. Of course she didn't want to remove it, though the bar was warm enough; it was a recent purchase and no doubt she was feeling very native.

"Well, it's very understated, sure. I suppose if you're looking for a jet set bar circa 1997—or even the eighties—this place doesn't fit the bill. But bars often had a nautical theme. There's something genuine about it, don't you think? It's not so contrived. It's a bar."

"I see what you mean, I guess," the woman responded, fingering a buttonhole on her coat. "But still, I'd like to have seen a more interesting place. I mean, I would never guess that Picasso or Hemingway hung out here if you hadn't told me. Not to mention movie stars. It just doesn't look that fancy or posh."

The man she was speaking to nodded and then turned toward the bar. His hair was just beginning to gray, which was the reason Louis hadn't immediately recognized him. It was Tad Tucker, a neighbor from up the street in Chicago. God, the world was too small. He turned his head quickly as if he'd been casually scanning the room, but he knew it wouldn't work. It was Tad, after all.

"Louis Howard!" a voice boomed, no longer sounding flat, open, or subdued. "I see you there!"

Heads turned, but because Louis was slow to react, no one seemed to be looking at him. He was instead scanning the room for someone to respond to the name of Louis Howard. Arturo, the only person there who knew his name, gazed in surprise.

"So you've been found out!" he whispered conspiratorially, grinning.

"Apparently," Louis whispered back, shaking his head.

And within a moment, the voice—and his childhood neighbor—were at his side.

"So this is where you've gotten off to!" he announced in a shrill tone. "A man of mystery. Won't even tell his mother where he went."

The woman in the trench coat, who'd followed her friend over to Louis, poked her head between them.

"You know this guy?"

"Sure do," he said. "He's a neighbor—well, was a neighbor. His parents live across the street from me. Holy cow, what a find—I can't believe I found you out!"

"You didn't *find me out*," Louis felt compelled to say, despite thinking that this was exactly what had happened. If a grown man wanted to go somewhere and not be bothered, not tell a soul where he was, wasn't he entitled to? And why was it considered hiding?

"Imagine!" the woman shouted, her hand running slowly along the lapel of her coat.

Arturo gave Louis a sympathetic look. Louis shrugged in response.

"You're from Chicago?" the woman asked, eyeing him suspiciously. "'Cause you look like a native. I'd have taken you for Italian." She patted her coat, allowing her fingers to linger on the material, almost as if she wanted Louis to notice it, waiting for him to compliment her.

"And that's exactly what he would like you to take him for, right, Lou?" Tad asked, squeezing Louis' shoulder.

"It's Louis," he responded, trying to appear unfazed as he slowly removed Tad's hand.

"Right. I'm always forgetting. So this is a major find for me," he said, turning to the woman. "This guy is MIA, *very* mysterious, and difficult to pin down, and here I walk into a bar in Venice and catch him in his lair. How fabulous is that?"

The woman started singing, gesturing with her champagne glass, and sloshing its contents up and over the rim.

"It's a small world, after all, it's a small world, after all …" she sang, her voice hardly able to carry the tune.

"So what are you doing here, Tad?" Louis quickly asked, in a louder voice than he'd ever used—anything to quiet the woman. "And how are my parents?"

"Just a little trip with a group from the university, a Mediterranean cruise. And your mother tells me that she corresponds with you, so you already know how your parents are. They're fine, but puzzled as to just where you are and why you won't come home."

The woman sized him up, holding her champagne glass and swirling its contents. "I've just met you, but I bet you've got a story to tell."

Louis stared at her blankly, wishing he could turn his back to her. Of course, she was drinking champagne, though she was in a region famous for its own version of bubbly wine, prosecco. She wouldn't have taken the time to read a little about where she was going or what she might find there. Instead, she'd be looking for spaghetti *carbonara*, lasagna, Chianti, and maybe gelato.

She grinned a little, swirling the champagne again and leveling her eyes at him. "Are you gay?" she asked.

Tad laughed a bellowing laugh as loud and as horrid as his call for Louis had been a moment before.

"Of course he is," Tad answered quickly. "But only marginally."

"What do you mean by that?" the woman asked.

Louis sensed Arturo eavesdropping as he mixed a martini, and wondered just how much English he understood.

"Well—" Tad started to say.

"Hey, can we talk about something else?" Louis interrupted. Who was this woman? And what bad luck to see Tad—one of the last people he'd hoped to see anywhere, let alone in Venice. His whereabouts would be broadcast within a day of Tad's homecoming—if he didn't hurry to an Internet café and send his parents an e-mail before he returned to the ship. And "marginally gay"? What the hell did that mean? Well, maybe he could guess, but he couldn't even think about it now. Right now, he just wanted them both to shut up.

Louis should have known he could count on the woman to begin blathering again. "When's the last time you were in Chicago, anyway?"

"He hasn't been back in the states—that his parents or anyone in Chicago knows about, anyway—for three years."

"Not even for Christmas?"

"I'm Jewish," he lied, resisting a smile as he noticed her blush and stammer.

"Oh, sorry, I didn't know," she said, sounding apologetic, almost as if she were sorry that he was Jewish.

"He's not Jewish, Irene. He's a wayward Christian, just like you," Tad explained, clucking his tongue.

"And a storyteller, too! Ha! Why did you say that?" she asked, tapping her finger against Louis' chest.

"I don't know, just for kicks, I suppose."

"He's a mystery, all right," Irene announced. "And a strange guy."

"Thanks, I know I can always count on my fellow Americans to be brutally honest."

If they would just go away, leave him to nurse his bourbon on the rocks and talk to the bartender and maybe some bar regular, he would be so much happier. Maybe he should say he needed to leave. What if he had to spend the rest of the night with them?

"What are you drinking?" Irene asked in a perky voice. "I'll buy you a drink. But I want to hear what you're doing here—*why* you're here. You're so intriguing!"

"I don't know if just one drink is worth all that—"

"I'll buy you two, then," she interrupted. "We've got the whole night!" Irene turned to the bar and called out loudly, "Bartender, bartender!"

Arturo, who had busied himself cleaning glasses, leaned over the bar and lit the cigarette of an older woman drinking a martini.

"Nasty Italians!" Irene said loudly. "You just know they hear you, but they pretend they don't. Everywhere I go. It's infuriating. Why are they like that?"

"No idea," Louis replied. "But a lot of them suffer from a loss of hearing—from the noise of Vespas."

"Really?" Irene jerked her head back and studied him. "Hmm," she murmured. "You are just like them—inscrutable. I can't tell if you're mocking me or not."

"Not," he lied. "I would never mock a compatriot."

"Ha!" Tad shouted. "Don't believe *that* line, anyway. This was the most sarcastic guy on our street."

"That's an exaggeration. I think *you* might be in the running for that—or, maybe I'm thinking of the title of greatest exaggerator."

"Bull, again! I am not an exaggerator."

"Okay, you're not." Louis just wanted to leave, to agree with anything they said and be on his way.

"Bartender, oh, bartender! Señor, ciao, señor!" Irene called in a singsong voice, tucking her hand under her coat and resting it on her hip.

Arturo finally looked up at the woman, unsmiling. He nodded, his eyes steely.

"No hurry," Irene muttered peevishly.

"Sounds like you're a bit sarcastic yourself," Louis observed.

"Enough about me," she laughed. "What's your story, anyway? I've got a drink coming for you momentarily and I'm a perfect stranger. What's it going to hurt for you to tell me?"

"Why do you want to know?"

"I can tell you his story," Tad interrupted, boastfully. "There's not much to tell, really. I mean, I can't tell you entirely what he's been doing the last three years, though I've heard plenty of things secondhand. But I can certainly fill you in on a lot. Then you can buy *me* drinks. How's that?"

"I'd rather hear it from the source," she scolded, shaking her finger.

"What … do you like this guy?" he frowned. "I told you, he's gay."

"I can *tell* he's gay—I just like him, I don't know why. He's interesting to me." She patted his shoulder a few times, smiling as if he would welcome reassurance.

"You just met him," Tad said testily, his voice rising.

"Who cares? You're gay, too, and I liked you when I met you. So there," she said, snorting a little.

"Maybe you two can carry on without me. I've got to be getting to my boyfriend's," Louis announced. The world really was growing too small. A person should be able to get lost in Venice in early spring, but things had changed. Why couldn't they have run into him when he was in Prague or Portugal? Why the one place he planned to stay?

"So you *do* have a boyfriend," Tad said, looking surprised.

"Why is that so surprising?" Louis said, quickly regretting that he'd told a lie that was likely to elicit more questions.

"You were always such a loner—not the type to have a relationship for more than half a year, right? Am I wrong about that?"

"Arturo," Louis called quietly, "*Un altro e qualcosa per la donna, eh? Spiace, ma ho bisogno di salvazione.*"

The bartender nodded and hurried over.

"Now he comes," Irene muttered. "They know you here, eh? You a regular?"

"Not really. Everyone in Venice knows everyone. It's really a small town. Like Peoria without Caterpillar."

"But with royalty, foreigners and *palazzi*, right?" Tad said. "So not really like Peoria at all."

"Okay, then. Nothing like Peoria," Louis admitted.

"Doesn't seem like Peoria to me," Irene added. "Nothing like Peoria. And you didn't answer Tad's question."

Irene smiled again, tapping her foot expectantly.

"I don't want to answer his question. I don't *have* to answer his question," Louis said testily, feeling his cheeks grow warm.

He returned Irene's gaze, trying not to glare.

"*Pronto*?" Arturo said arriving just in time, though Louis knew the two would be put off only momentarily.

"Give me one of those famous peach drinks," Irene said in a syrupy voice, emphasizing each word as if Arturo didn't understand English.

"Make that two," Tad said.

"They're not in season," Louis explained. "It's a summer drink."

He didn't want to explain because he knew how he sounded—like one of those detestable Americans who move to Europe and suddenly were expert about all cultural aspects of their adopted home. But he couldn't stop himself. Not with them, anyway.

She ought to be embarrassed, he thought.

"They can't get peach juice in March?" she groaned. "We've got peach juice in America year-round."

"Of course they can, but they're not fresh peaches and the owner won't serve them without fresh peach nectar because it tastes completely different."

"Who would know the difference?" Irene cackled. "I bet you I couldn't even tell the difference. I bet *you* couldn't tell the difference either!"

"And they could make money serving them all year. The tourists don't care," Tad said.

"They don't serve them for the tourists," Louis explained, frustrated that Irene didn't seem embarrassed.

"But they could make more money off the tourists," Tad said, exasperated.

"I'll talk to the owner about that, suggest it to him," Louis said sarcastically.

Arturo gazed at them expectantly.

"I'll order for you, if you don't mind," Louis offered. "It's busy tonight and we don't want to annoy them."

"Great, order me something very Venetian," Irene chirped.

Tad shrugged.

"*Prosecco per le due, e un altro* bourbon *con ghiaccio per me.*"

The bartender hurried away shooting Louis a sympathetic glance. If only Arturo had stayed and talked, enabling Louis to keep the topic of conversation safely off himself. But he could hardly blame the guy for not lingering. Bad enough he had to suffer these American fools in the summer and during *Carnivale*, but in the middle of the off-season?

"Who's your boyfriend? Is he from here?" Tad asked. "I can ask because we know each other, right? I'm not a perfect stranger."

"And I won't listen to the answer. Besides, what would it matter, anyway?" Irene held her champagne flute upright, tipping it nearly vertically in a desperate attempt to get the last drops lingering in the glass.

She looked asinine, Louis concluded. Maybe she would actually stick her tongue down the side of the glass seeking the last few drops of the champagne. He diverted his eyes as her tongue slipped over the rim of the glass, reminding him of an anteater. Out of the corner of his eye, he saw Arturo stop and look.

If only he could have so accurately predicted winning lottery numbers.

"You don't even know me, anyway, and I don't know anyone who knows you—except for Tad," she added, stabbing her tongue once more toward the bottom of her glass. "Mmmm," she murmured. "They serve good stuff here—if only they gave you a little more of it!"

"I'll tell you," Tad said grinning, unfazed by his friend's tongue darting down the side of the champagne flute. "Just feel free to interrupt if I get anything wrong, okay?"

It was maddening, but Louis was perversely curious to hear what Tad had to say. "Thanks for the generous offer," he said cautiously.

"Louis can't stand being gay. Hates himself," Tad said matter-of-factly.

"That's absurd," Louis countered, his voice defensive.

"Well, you were that way once, weren't you?"

"Who wasn't?"

Louis took a big gulp of the bourbon, wishing he were alone. Why couldn't his night have gone the way he'd planned? He'd just learned that his best friend might leave Venice, his family and friends back home were likely to become aware of his whereabouts within weeks, and he'd just completed hours of translating—and now this?

"You were always the type to run. That's what your mother says," Tad clucked as he shook his head.

Louis felt sick. Had his mother really said that, and to Tad whom they'd mocked for years as being the neighborhood busybody? He hadn't come all this way, given up so much along the way to face the very type of people he thought he'd left behind. Why did people think it was their God-given right to get to know you, to force you to spend time with them?

"I'm not feeling well," he said, pushing the bourbon away. "Really. I've got to go."

"But this was just getting fun!" Irene chirped, jerking her head like a bird.

"Maybe for you, but I'm not enjoying myself."

"Oh, come on, we're just having fun," Irene teased. "We don't even need to talk about any of that. I just think it's great that we've run into someone so interesting, a fellow American living in Venice. Let's just have a drink and then get some dinner. You can show us an authentic Venetian spot where no tourists go—and we'll pay. Hell, we can even go to a gay bar. Be a sport."

Irene picked up the glass of prosecco that Arturo had just set before her, swirling the liquid as if it were red wine.

"No, thanks," Louis sighed. "I'm not up for it. I've worked all day, and I just want to go home and go to bed. Just needed a nightcap to unwind."

"I thought you were going to meet your boyfriend?" Tad said, his eyebrows arched.

"Tad, don't tease—we want him to stay, right?" Irene scolded, punching Tad on the shoulder as she scowled.

"He won't stay—trust me."

"No, I won't. I'm tired and not feeling very sociable. I just want my bed."

"Any message for your parents?" Tad asked sarcastically.

"I'm in touch with my parents—I can deliver any message I'd like to send myself. You reminded me of that yourself."

He waved to Arturo, tossing some lire onto the bar.

"*Arrivederci*," he said to Irene and Tad. "Have a good cruise home."

Irene turned her scowl on him, but changed her mind, suddenly grinning. Tad reached out his hand and forced Louis to shake hands, leaning toward his ear.

"I'll keep it a secret if that's what you want, okay?" he whispered. "I won't tell anyone we ran into you."

He patted Louis on the back, smiling broadly. Louis pulled back abruptly, studying Tad's face. Maybe he was an okay guy. Maybe he'd grown up and wasn't the nosy troublemaker he'd been when they were teenagers on Alta Vista. If Tad had changed, maybe he had changed, too. Anything was possible with the passage of time, wasn't it?

"Thanks, Tad. I'd really appreciate that. I mean … I'll tell them … probably soon," he said, faltering. "But I'd rather they didn't know right now. I need just a little more time to sort things out, and then I'll let them know."

"No problem. I'm your man," Tad reassured, winking. "Let me know if I can do anything for you—or if you just need someone to talk to."

Louis had always wondered if Tad had a crush on him, if the way he teased and picked on him was an indication of something more.

Irene piped in, pushing up to his elbow. "I won't tell either, even though I don't know your parents or even Tad's parents. But you have to kiss me first." She laughed, closing her eyes as she puckered her lips.

"I told you he's gay," Tad said impatiently. "You're making a fool of yourself."

"And I told you, I don't care," she giggled, leaning closer toward Louis. Reaching into her coat, she pulled something shiny and purple out of the pocket. "Here I want you to have this—now close your eyes!" she slurred, pushing a long, hard object into his coat pocket. She laughed, covering her hand with her mouth.

Backing away, Louis gently, but firmly pushed at her elbow.

"I'll leave that for you," he said, pointing at his drink on the bar. "But no kiss."

"Awww," she cried. "You're not nice. I thought you were nice!"

"And I thought you were sober," he said, waving at them both as he hurried out of the crowded bar. When he got outside, he hesitated, fully expecting the door to spring open with the two of them spilling out after him in rapid pursuit. But the narrow street remained silent, except for the muffled sound of Duke Ellington drifting out of the bar, and the soft, rhythmic lapping of waves from the nearby canal.

Louis didn't think he'd ever been so happy to be out of Harry's, or maybe any bar. Satisfied that the two weren't going to follow him, he set off through the maze of streets that would take him to his apartment where he could drink bourbon without the risk of running into anyone.

The icy breeze he'd felt earlier had abruptly shifted. A kinder breeze from the south carried the smell of rain, the sea, and the promise of warmer weather. Crazy weather. It would be a perfect night for sipping bourbon at his window and watching the little lights of the sleepy city and its jumble of rooftops, chimneys, and towers. If he was lucky, there would be a sliver of moon or it would rain and the canal below his window would come alive.

As he turned a dark corner, a glowing, ancient portrait of the Madonna silently observed him from a dimly lit niche. He wondered if Tad would keep his mouth shut. And he worried about Claudia. If he'd been religious, he would have prayed.

But he wasn't.

Chapter Two

The late spring day in Venice was sublime. The benevolent warmth of the sun caressed, but didn't yet punish, and the canals didn't carry the fetid smell of heat and overuse. Anna Maledetto could live in this enchanting city, she thought to herself. With its soft, quiet nights, devoid of the sounds of automobiles or autobuses and the putrid, stinging smell of exhaust, the city possessed a winsome, timeless character that she found alluring. The city seemed to force its citizens to adapt an infectious, easy-going attitude. Its residents and visitors were going nowhere fast—not to the train station across town, or even across the neighborhood, so why fret? People walked nearly everywhere because that was the easiest way to get around. Sure, if one was hauling groceries, trunks, or furniture, one might take a boat or *vaporetto*, but mostly, everyone walked.

The Venetian women looked fit from all that walking, but not as stylish as the women in her native Rome. Thankfully, she'd arrived before the city's *ancien regime* had fled the heat and tourist crowds of summer for their villas on Como and in the distant, rolling hills of the Veneto that were visible from the tower in Piazza San Marco. Somehow, the old families of Venice seemed older than those of Rome, as if by being isolated and tucked into a quiet corner of Europe, the city had in some ways changed little, or at least less. Anna couldn't put her finger on it, but in some ways, the city and the Venetians seemed old-fashioned, as if the city still thought it was at the height of its power, its old families believing the rest of the world really cared what they had to say.

Ships no longer left its ports, and no one seemed to care anymore what was happening in the watery city. One went to Venice to see what *was*, not what *is*, she observed.

But these facts merely lent the place more amusement and charm. There was a decadence and world-weariness in Rome, as well as a pace, that could wear. People in Venice were less worried with wearing the latest fashions or what the rest of the world thought. The city seemed to survive—just barely in some ways, she thought—on its own.

And then it was true that Venetians had better survived the war, being tucked into a sleepy, less-industrial corner of Italy and boasting no resources but seafood, gondolas, and blown glass—all uninteresting to the Allied troops. At that point, the war had been over for ten years, its vestiges such as a scarcity of food or electricity that still existed in Rome were virtually nonexistent in Venice. The sea continued yielding langoustine, clams, mussels, fish, and oysters, and so the city still ate well. And if you could eat well, then life wasn't all-bad.

Despite its smugness and insularity, the place had won her over, gradually infecting her soul. She longed to walk every tiny *via*, explore every waterway, and gaze at every crumbling facade—common building and palazzo alike.

And Anna Maledetto could admit, as she was not one to be easily fooled by impressions and emotions that she was most in love with Venice because she was in love with a Venetian, Vittorio Lunardini.

Member of one of the oldest families of the city, and owning some of the finest and largest *palazzi* in the city, Vittorio possessed the pedigree that Anna had been taught to expect by her parents and by her *nonno* Pucci, in particular.

"You have the *disgrazia* of a name like Maledetto, but you are a Pucci, all the same," he used to lecture. "And you are deserving of a proper old name. It is your right and obligation to regain one."

In the years before his death, the old man grew obsessed with his mission of ensuring that she would not remain a Maledetto and would marry back into a family with a proper name. If he heard she had seen a movie with some boy in her school that didn't have the right name, he would seek her out, take her arm, and walk her into a private spot in one of the shady, boxwood-lined, fragrant lanes of his Renaissance garden. And then lecture her some more. By the time he died, she had promised a few dozen times that she would regain a proper name for his only offspring. When she thought of her grandfather, she remembered the earthy smell of the boxwoods, and the sweet scent of rosemary, lavender, mint, and freesia.

"It's a curse to have no male offspring," he would whisper. "But you can regain what's been lost."

He was always saying things about knowing that she had the gift, insight, and soul that made her see these things, understand their importance, and have the confidence to obtain them.

"You understand me," he used to say, gazing at her with the penetrating blue eyes of the Norman knights who had arrived there and served the popes and kings long before the Pucci family name was established. "You are Pucci, not Maledetto."

He correctly surmised that she'd been born with some comprehension, a sense for history, and what a name meant—particularly since she had to shoulder the name Maledetto all these years. At that point, though, she wasn't certain if she possessed them from his constant drilling, or if they'd truly been there all along. Regardless, she was thoroughly a Pucci, and that meant she could no sooner marry someone nameless than she could marry an American.

Her nonno Pucci could rest easy.

She could not. He haunted her.

The old man never said anything directly against her father or that he disapproved of his mother for marrying him, but Anna knew from piecing together stories, whispers, and overheard conversations, that nonno Pucci had never thought her father good enough for her mother, good enough for a Pucci. And so she carried her unlikely name, Maledetto, awkwardly like a giant Easter hat that didn't fit.

On that fine day, though, she thought about Vittorio and how her life would soon change. He would certainly ask to marry her—he made that abundantly clear by his behavior. He'd hinted strongly that on that trip to Venice, something significant would happen. And he didn't mean the private dinner he'd hosted for her at Harry's the night before. He had promised that Picasso or Hemingway would attend, but neither had shown. Still, a few glitterati had shown up—Peggy Guggenheim, the wealthy American art collector, who said hardly a word to her—and some painter she'd never heard of. (Vittorio assured her that she would recognize his name in the future, though.)

They were about to board a boat and head down the Grand Canal toward the lagoon from which they could watch the sun's amber, dying rays strike the magnificent dome of Santa Maria della Salute and the other churches and palazzi in the Dorsoduro *sestiero* that crowded the sides of the waterways.

"It's a new boat," she observed. "So *moderno*, but beautiful." The motorized boat with unusually high gunwales was constructed entirely of deeply grained wood stained a luminous honey color and polished until it shined. The boat reminded her of something that would go to the moon, and at the same time, it reminded her of an object Renaissance craftsmen would have made.

"It's American," he boasted, running his hand along its smooth wooden side.

On the back and on the front was a carefully painted design of a trident and porpoise. The painting style was dated, strange looking on such a modern boat, Anna thought.

"What are those?" she asked.

Vittorio shrugged. "Just some old designs from the Greeks and Romans. It's just an homage, just for fun."

Vittorio seemed proud of his purchase, proud that while others could scarcely afford the upkeep of their little boats, he had purchased a big new boat, something that conjured up a distant land and a brave new future. She'd wanted to remark that she thought Americans only considered functionality and never beauty, and that the attractiveness of the boat surprised her. She knew, though, that it would sound like a criticism, so she smiled and took his hand, jumping into the boat from the rickety pier outside the Lunardini palazzo.

Two bottles of prosecco stuck out of buckets of ice sitting on the floor of the boat. A picnic basket, with the sides of crisp white linen sticking out of the lid, lay beside it.

Venetians could be funny, Anna thought, always drinking their tasty but somewhat flat prosecco instead of champagne. But these were just the sort of things she liked about them—a lack of pretense and a respect for those traditions involving Venice and the Veneto.

"Tell me a secret about you," she said, realizing there was still so much about Vittorio that she didn't know.

He looked up at her, smiling, but quizzically.

"But I have no secrets," he insisted, his smile growing larger, revealing a row of perfectly straight white teeth.

She laughed. "I'm not conducting an investigation or an interview—I'm just curious. You can tell me an innocent one."

"Hmm. What kind of a secret? You know we Venetians are full of them … a family secret perhaps?"

"I've heard this about you Venetians and it's very intriguing. But I can't imagine that you have any really shocking secrets," she said, taking in the view of a grand palazzo rising before them.

"What gives you that impression?" he asked, his eyes twinkling.

"I don't know. Just a feeling I have."

On a nearby bridge, two boys peered down at them, admiring the boat. She'd always been a good judge of character. That was one of the first things that had attracted her to Vittorio. Sure, he was from a family who used to be called nobility, but unlike many other of his class, he was no *enfant terrible.* She felt like she could trust him.

"Okay, well here is a very good secret. One you'll have to take with you to the grave," he chuckled, checking the gauges on the boat before moving the picnic basket to the back of the boat.

"I promise to keep it," she said, leaning toward him.

"This may mean nothing to you, but for a Venetian, it is very strange, embarrassing even."

She couldn't imagine what he would say, but she smiled encouragingly, curious to hear what he would reveal.

"I cannot swim," he announced with a self-admonishing cluck of his tongue.

"I knew you didn't have any really bad secrets," she said, emitting a small laugh.

"But it is really something to be ashamed of," he muttered.

"Well, it is odd to be from Venice, to live surrounded by water and not be able to swim," she mused.

"That's why it's so ridiculous. And no one knows. Not even my parents have ever figured it out."

"Doesn't seem so shameful," she said. "Even if you're from Venice. Not everyone is a swimmer. I am from Rome and I don't like politics?"

He laughed, his eyes flashing. "Hardly the same thing, but okay."

Serious again, she watched him prepare the boat. "Aren't you afraid then to be out on the water?"

"I go on the water precisely for this reason. It keeps my fear in check."

"You're courageous to face down your fears," she said, glancing at the hem of her dress and wishing it were longer. She worried that while she sat in the boat too much of her legs would be revealed.

"As courageous as someone who is afraid of swimming can be," he answered, shrugging. "And somehow I feel protected," he added. He looked out across the bow of the boat, avoiding her eyes.

Was he superstitious?

She unpinned and removed her hat slowly and deliberately, while Vittorio settled himself behind the wheel and started the engine. The boat roared to life, sending a blue cloud of vapor over the canal. A few people had gathered on the bridge. They watched the couple and seemed to admire the boat. Anna wrapped a scarf over her head, carefully tying it under her chin and replacing her sunglasses.

She would never admit it, but she liked that people—total strangers—were watching. In some way, she felt like she was in a scene from a movie. The canal shone blue, and she sat in a beautiful boat pulling away from one of the grandest palazzi on the Grand Canal—a fact that she knew was not lost on anyone watching. Though her time in Venice had been limited, she'd already learned that Venetians knew who lived where, and who in the old city mattered. This city did not offer anonymity as she'd heard that New York or Paris did. Venice, in many ways, seemed to be a small city indeed.

"*Bella donna*, are you mine?" he called to her, raising his voice as he accelerated the boat. A wake followed them, sloppily splashing into the piers and into the sides of the *palazzi*. They attracted onlookers who stood on the large bridges spanning the canal.

She nodded suddenly shy. She'd been lucky, luckier than her wise, strong-willed *nonno* had predicted. She really did love her Vittorio. She would marry not only to regain a name that meant something, but also to gain a husband that aroused her passion. Not only did she find his small Venetian nose and light hair attractive, but also his love of art, artists, and writers, and his interest in all things modern, intrigued her. Here was a paradox, a scion, and a member of one of the oldest families in Venice who seemed to want to have one foot firmly planted in the future—wherever that might be.

"Why don't you sit next to me then?" he called, patting the seat next to his.

She rose unsteadily, taking quick, uneven steps and landing heavily onto the dark brown leather seat next to him.

"*Voila*," she announced, raising her thin hand into the balmy, sweet-smelling air.

He stood, and with one hand on the polished wooden wheel, rested his palm on her upper back for a moment before leaning down to kiss her. She kissed him back quickly, looking up worriedly to see if there were other boats in their path. He laughed, lightly touching her back again with the tips of his perfectly formed fingers.

"Don't worry; I wouldn't risk damaging two beautiful things. I can go slower if you like."

"It's fine," she lied. She'd never traveled so fast on a boat before, and especially on the crowded canal, with taxis, gondolas, and tourist boats plying the waters. She felt nervous.

She heard the strains of an accordion and violin. Toward the lagoon, a large, flat boat came into view.

"The Americans," Vittorio smiled. "There's a large group that arrived the other night. They must be going on a sunset cruise."

"They're so loud," she said sourly. "Why must they always be so loud?"

The cacophony of laughter and voices carried across the water. Even with the droning of the boat motor, she could hear them. And now she could see the passengers, men in suits and women in dresses—all clad in the latest fashions. She could see they were drinking mostly cocktails, and sat or stood with their arms casually draped over their companions' shoulders, singing and laughing. They wore sunglasses and acted as if they really belonged there, as if it were the most natural thing that they sat and stood on a purring boat plying the Grand Canal as the sun set on Venice. She resented their sense of *joie de vivre*, their seeming sense of entitlement and belonging, though they were thousands of miles from home.

"It's not the worst thing to be lighthearted and enjoy life, you know," Vittorio scolded good-naturedly.

She pursed her lips, though he was right, of course. Since the end of the war, Rome and all of Italy seemed overrun with carefree Americans. If they weren't buying up the shops—what little was available in them—they were acting more lord-like and less democratic than even the oldest of the country's blue blood families. She'd grown to resent them, dislike the soldiers who acted as if they owned the bars and street corners, and the businessmen who had descended on the city like scavengers.

The boat continued along the Grand Canal, past shuttered palazzi and some of the grand hotels. And then the waterway grew wider until they were in a broad, lagoon-like section of the canal with the dome of Santa Maria della Salute on one side of the water and the campanile and Piazza San Marco on the other. Vittorio cut the motor, slowing the boat until it nudged along only by the small waves gently lapping its sides.

"This is a good spot, no?" He smiled at her, swept his open arms at the extensive view surrounding them.

"Magnificent," she sighed, standing up to admire the vista.

"Then let's stay awhile," he said, throwing the anchor off the bow of the boat. "There's nothing better than watching the sun set on Venice. And no better place to see it."

"Not the campanile?" she asked, pointing toward the tower, which rose above every other structure in the city.

"No, because you're too high," he explained. "You can see more of the city from it, but not the water and buildings and the way everything turns amber and then pink and lavender."

"Sounds incredible."

"You'll see," he smiled, rubbing the palms of his hands together. "Just wait a few moments."

He walked to the back of the boat and removed two starched napkins from the top of the picnic basket.

"Are you hungry?" he asked teasingly, knowing she hadn't eaten since lunch.

"Enough."

"Thirsty?"

"Very. It's warm today," she nodded.

He pulled one of the bottles of prosecco from its icy nest.

"You Venetians love your prosecco, don't you?"

He looked offended, and she regretted she'd spoken a thought she had on her mind since her first visit. In Rome, on the rare occasion people drank *frizzante*, they had champagne—not prosecco. Maybe it was an affectation, but that was what she knew. Here people almost seemed to prefer the local prosecco to champagne, and she'd already sampled it on a number of occasions.

"Well, I like it, too," she added quickly. She could make up for saying something stupid, couldn't she?

"Do you really?" he asked, prying the cork out of one of the bottles. "This is one of the best—but I'm biased."

The cork popped, just like with a bottle of champagne, and he began pouring the bubbling liquid into two glasses. "Why are you biased?"

"These are from our estate in the Conegliano. My father oversees the vines and making the prosecco—it's under the label Volpe with our insignia on it—you must've seen it, heard of it."

She nodded vaguely, uncertain how to answer. The truth was, in Rome they rarely drank prosecco, so she really didn't know.

"It's one of the best. And these are bottles reserved just for family and friends. We take the best for ourselves," he said grinning and then held a finger to his lips. "Just don't tell the Communists. It's just the sort of behavior they resent."

She laughed, pleased that she understood his joke.

He handed her a glass, and sat next to her on the padded bench in the back of the boat. "Salute," he toasted, gently touching his glass against hers.

"Salute," she echoed, bringing the glass to her lips. Though she was no connoisseur, the prosecco was tasty—maybe as good as champagne. And she felt confident that this glass was the best she'd had.

"I hope you like Venice," he said, resting his arm behind her shoulder on the polished wooden back of the boat. "You are adjusting?"

"Yes, I'm coming to love it."

She felt no deception saying this—she really was coming to love it. Of course, here they were on a beautiful boat that made them the envy of the city, bobbing in the middle of the canal with a view as magnificent as any in the world. The campanile and domes of St. Mark's stood directly opposite, bathed in amber light while a few sailboats floated across the lagoon, heading to their moorings before the sun went down, and the wind died. Of course, she loved Venice. How could a person not?

"Could you live here?" he asked, his eyes hidden behind sunglasses. She wished she could see them, to know whether he was leading up to another question. But she saw only a reflection of herself and the lagoon and the sky in the lenses of his dark glasses. "I know how fond you are of your Rome," he added.

She nodded, trying not to appear too eager.

"I could," she answered. "There's something about this city that's so beguiling, fantastical. And I'm tired of Rome. It wears me out."

"Some of those feelings, the charms, and uniqueness of the city become less visible after you've lived here for a while. But it always retains some of its magic," he said.

"There's no other city like it," she sighed. "And it somehow persists, surviving despite its setting. The other morning it came to me that maybe the city is a statement about the supremacy of man over nature, of his dominance over the earth." She took a quick sip of her prosecco, suddenly worried that she was talking too much, that she thought too much for a woman.

Vittorio just laughed.

"You have thought about this a lot. Do you think so much and so seriously about other things?"

She shrugged. "It's my grandfather's influence."

"Yes, I've heard about him. He must have been a hard person to deal with," he said soberly.

What did he mean by that? She'd loved her grandfather and didn't know anyone who didn't. The only thing she'd ever done that had hurt him was to admit that she harbored doubts about the church, and she just couldn't accept everything she'd been taught. On that issue alone, she had disappointed him.

"I'm not sure what you mean," she said, looking at him quizzically.

"Just things I've heard," he said. "Maybe they don't mean anything. Sounds like he was a very religious man—and stern. Oh, I don't know," he said, seeing her vague frown. "Just rumors or jealous people. I don't mean to offend—you look bothered."

She drew her eyes toward the shore and the jumble of palazzi and buildings rising from the flat, dark blue water of the canal, just barely rippled by the dying breeze.

"He had high expectations. That's true. But he taught that this came with our name, who we are, and our history as a family."

"But you are a Maledetto—not a Pucci," he said skeptically.

She shrugged again. "My grandfather always taught me that I'm a Pucci despite the name."

"You don't like Maledetto?"

"I'm indifferent about it," she lied. She had inherited—or been given—her grandfather's prejudice. But how could she explain that to Vittorio? He still had a name. If he had known how important a name was to her and had been to her grandfather, would that make her unattractive? Or worse, make him think that was the only reason she wanted to marry him?

"So if someday you lose your name it won't bother you so much," he suggested, sipping some prosecco and looking at her through his big sunglasses.

Again, she wished she could see his eyes. What he said had to be a hint, or was he merely looking for her reaction? He hadn't asked her, but had made the statement as if it were an observation, a fact. What did he mean to imply?

"I look forward to losing the name," she said suddenly, deciding she could afford to tip her hand. Why not encourage him if that was what she wanted? Maybe exactly what he wanted, too?

"And maybe living in Venice? Would those two things make you happy?" he asked, leaning toward her.

She felt she could be certain of his intentions. Was everything falling into place? Even as a girl she'd hoped that things would happen in just such a way, and she'd correctly anticipated the near-overwhelming, joyous emotions swelling in her chest. She was not a fatalist, not believing like her religious friends that praying made a difference or that there was such a thing as divine intervention, but she felt certain that every day in her life had been leading inexorably to that very day—and to marrying Vittorio. So maybe she was irrational as a common Catholic, but somehow her belief was different. *She* was different, she honestly believed.

"That's exactly what would make me happy," she admitted, smiling shyly.

He smiled back, grabbed her hand, and leaned forward to kiss her again. As his face neared, she reached and removed his sunglasses. Hers was a petty complaint, she knew, but all the same, she needed to see his eyes.

He kissed her fully, his tongue gently parting her lips and exploring the inside of her mouth. His eyes were closed, so she still couldn't see the vivid, liquid blue color. But even closed, she could remember the unique shade, a vestige of an English or German interloper somewhere in his family tree. Maybe a pre-Renaissance, Norman knight such as could be found in her own Pucci ancestry. Searching his handsome face, she admired his slender nose, fair hair, and light olive skin.

The jarring sound of cheering and hooting intruded, the boatful of Americans interrupting the perfect, fully ripe moment. Had they no decency? If she and Vittorio had been kissing in the middle of a piazza or some public space, she could understand the jeering, but they were in the middle of the widest canal, far from the shore and removed from the regular route of the vaporetti and gondolas.

Vittorio pulled away, his eyes reflecting the remaining rays of the sun and the rich colors of sunset in Venice. He smiled again, stroking the side of her cheek with his thin, manicured fingers. She trembled, smiled, and sat back into her seat, content to study his eyes as if they held some mystery.

They sipped the prosecco, avoiding the Americans and their oversize boat, and focused instead on the fantastical domes of St. Mark's. The falling sun set the buildings aflame with pink and orange tones, the colors reflecting off the blues and browns of the little waves rippling across the darkening waters of the canal. The city seemed so much smaller than Rome, quieter. She hoped she wouldn't miss the buzz of her childhood city and that she would grow accustomed to the slower, mellow pace of Venice.

The waterway had cleared, the sailboats had dropped sail and docked, and the smaller boats had taken their berth at piers. Except for the boat of celebrating Americans, the city and the canal felt tranquil, nearly abandoned. She felt surprised that it could be like this in the middle of a city, though she knew that the piazza and the little streets surrounding it, as well as the Grand Canal and train station, were crowded and swarming with people. On the wide canal, though, it was as if they were on a country lake and not in the middle of a city.

The voices and laughter of the Americans grew closer still until she turned with a start to see the large boat headed straight toward them, not more than twenty feet distant. The Americans stood clustered around the boat's pilot, pouring him champagne while the women smoothed his collar and stroked his arm. Anna realized immediately that the distracted driver hadn't seen their much smaller boat directly in his path. With his hand gripping the top of the wheel, the laughing pilot, who appeared to be no older than Vittorio, sipped from a martini offered by a young woman.

"That boat!" Anna called hoarsely to Vittorio who quickly turned.

"Hey, hey!" he screamed, standing quickly, but the vessel was already upon them, striking the bow of their boat with a crash.

Anna heard screams, wood, and metal crushing, and then felt water striking her head and ears, enveloping her. She was underwater, the cold and the water taking her breath. In the distance she could hear screaming and the muffled sound of a motor. She didn't know which direction to swim, unable to figure out which direction was up. Was she upside down or sideways? She began to panic, hardly able to see light in the murky waters of the canal. There were dark forms—maybe the boat?—and smaller shadows spinning and swirling nearby. Other people? Fish?

She floated motionless before she began to kick her legs as if she were in a swimming class. Her head felt waterlogged, her ears plugged, and she could feel the harsh tang of saltwater on her tongue and in the back of her throat and nostrils. She tasted gasoline, which made her want to spit and gag.

She had no air and little energy left. Her lungs burned, her heart raged against her chest. Her mouth longed to open, to gulp a breath of sweet air, but she knew it would be only water. If only it had been noon when they had gone on this ride, if only it hadn't been sunset with the sky dark but for the distant horizon, which she recalled being aflame as she fell into the cold darkness of the canal.

Her legs kicked rhythmically, unconsciously. She might have gone farther into the depths, but she suddenly became aware of more light, the shadows subsiding as her head broke the surface.

"There's one!" a voice yelled.

She coughed, spit water, and started gagging so violently she feared she might slip back under the surface.

Where was Vittorio? She could make out a long, smooth object rising just above the surface of the lagoon not ten feet away. The boat? Was that the boat? She swam to it, trying to heave herself onto the gently arced surface, but its bottom was too slippery, too new. She rested one hand on its smooth hull to steady herself and she started kicking in place.

Someone was screaming. Who was screaming? A voice somewhere nearby in the water?

"Here, swim here," the voice called in English. From behind her, the sound of a boat's motor revved. She turned to see the looming shadow of the boat full of Americans heading toward her. Were they going to hit her? Did they see her? She waved her one arm frantically, keeping a tenuous grasp on the hull of the boat.

"*Veniamo*! *Veniamo*!" a man driving the boat called. "We see you!"

But, where was Vittorio?

"Vittorio! Vittorio?" She turned and peered over one shoulder and then over the other. Her voice shook as she realized she was shivering, the cold spring water of the canal, the sea, really, chilling her to the core.

A bobbing head, the back of a head and arms striking the water, was just barely visible in the distance.

"Vittorio!" she called, but the person swam for the boat of Americans, even as it headed in her direction.

"No, no," she called, pointing at the swimmer. "I'm okay, get the other!"

The Americans looked in the direction she pointed, spotted the swimmer, and then one of the men grabbed the arm of the boat driver. He stopped suddenly, turning the boat toward the person, toward Vittorio.

She could hold onto the smooth hull of the capsized boat, tread water if needed. Or she could even manage to swim to the boat with the Americans—it wasn't that far away. But what had happened to Vittorio? How had he gotten so far from her? He looked okay, swimming sloppily, but steadily toward the boat. Why, then, did she suffer a sinking feeling?

The seconds passed slowly, her dress brushing against her legs like seaweed. The feeling was haunting, like something from the deep grabbing at her with rough, calloused fingertips. She could stay there, despite the gathering darkness, for a few more minutes. For an hour if she had to. She started kicking her feet for warmth, and to remind herself that it was her dress floating across her thighs and calves, not fish or seaweed. The movement of her legs gave her warmth, got her heart pumping regularly instead of beating frantically, the nervous pulsating of the heart of a rabbit before its death.

She wondered what her grandfather would say. Had she been wrong, after all? Was this the punishment for nonbelievers and doubters, as taught by nuns, priests, and her parents? It was certainly a sign, the exact sort of thing she'd been warned about her whole life.

Ridiculous that such a thought would pop into her head at a moment like this. She treaded water in the Venetian canal, the detritus and wreckage of nearly two thousand years worth of wars, trade and travel rotting beneath her on the muddy bottom, and there she was worrying about her grandfather, dreading his judgment. She and Vittorio could have been killed. The boat full of Americans had crushed their wooden boat, rolling it over like a lopsided canoe. All she could remember—it had happened so quickly—was the boat's gunwales rising up, nearly striking her head before she flung into the cold, dark water. She didn't see seen what happened to Vittorio, but knew he'd been thrown from the boat, too.

Stupid thoughts. She kicked her legs again and nearly lost her grip on the hull of the boat she kicked so hard. She'd intended to kick the thought out of her head, to expel it with force. Here Vittorio wasn't even safe yet, hadn't even reached the boat, but he was still swimming to safety with just a few feet left to the boat.

Swimming.

Hands outstretched, a rope uselessly thrown to the swimmer.

Swimming.

Silly.

She had forgotten he couldn't swim. Of course, the person hoisted aboard the big, flat boat wasn't Vittorio.

They had saved one of their own who must have fallen off the bow of the boat when they'd hit their boat. So where was Vittorio?

"*I can't swim.*"

His words haunted her as she began breathing in short, shallow gasps, spinning around in hopes of catching sight of his head above the water. If she'd found the boat, why hadn't he?

"Vittorio?" she called across the water, her mouth only inches above the wavelets, which created a pattern of zigzags across the surface of the lagoon. The gentle arcs of water caught the last small bits of light reflected from the silvery, deepening blue sky to the west. In a few minutes, the canal would be dark except for shadows. Her voice sounded tinny, trembling. "Vittorio?" she called again.

The big boat's motor sounded, quickly passing over the feet and yards that had separated them. A feeble beam from a flashlight swept across the water striking the hull of the boat and then fixing on her face. She'd read about people seeing a white light before they died, and she wondered if this could be the light. But she didn't seem near dead, the feel of the coarse dress across her legs reminded her of that. The boat pulled nearby and there was suddenly splashing in the water beside her. Two of the Americans had jumped in.

They gently took her arms, supporting her back as they pushed her forward, away from the hull of the boat. She hated them. Hadn't they been the ones to ram their boat?

"Where's your husband?" one of the men asked, out of breath.

"He's not already on the boat?" Her voice shook as she asked, her teeth chattering. She knew it was a silly question, yet she hoped that somehow she'd missed his face among those peering over the side of the boat, trying to spot her. She didn't bother to correct the man.

"No, we haven't seen him. But he's got to be somewhere around here."

The man shivered, helping her along as she swam aside the boat. So many hands stretched down to lift her up, she didn't know which to grab. A few managed to grasp her upper arms, and then she was hoisted out of the water and onto the deck of the boat.

"*Dai, spiace, spiace, signora,*" the Italian who had been driving the boat gushed. "We didn't see your boat; it was so small and quiet. Was the motor turned off?"

"Yes, the motor was turned off. I don't understand how you didn't see us," she shouted, her voice shaking.

She accepted a towel offered by an outstretched hand and wrapped it loosely around her torso. Standing in front of complete strangers cloaked in a towel and dripping with water, made her feel indecent. And she trembled, feeling fragile as a wind-shaken leaf or a newborn.

The boat driver shrugged and muttered another apology. The passengers bit their lips and avoided her gaze. She couldn't scream, couldn't become overwhelmed and angry until they'd found Vittorio.

"Can you drive around?" Anna pleaded. "My fiancé …"

Though she was out of the cold water, her heart continued beating wildly, causing her fingers to shake, and her voice to tremble. And she'd said fiancé without even thinking of it.

"He doesn't swim," she added, trailing off.

The driver sat in front of the wheel and jerked the boat into gear with a fluid motion.

"Maybe he swam to shore? We can look for him, though."

For a moment, the scene resembled a dream. She didn't feel conscious, couldn't feel the cold or the way her soaked, ice-like clothes clung to her. She would always recall the boatload of Americans, all scanning the sides of the boats or stealing, rabbit-quick, sympathetic glances at her. She called for Vittorio, hearing the uncertainty in her voice as it carried across the water, eventually snuffed out by the evening breeze. Her eyes focused on the dark water, straining to spot an object, any object floating in the lagoon.

A lady with a kind face and moles that reminded her of a French woman brought her a small glass of dark-colored liquid.

"Drink it," she instructed, her eyes saucer-like. "You'll feel better. It'll take away the chill."

She drank the contents of the glass greedily, allowing the heat from the whiskey to warm her throat and stomach. Still, she trembled.

"You're Catholic?" the woman asked, pointing at the small crucifix, which hung from her neck.

Anna shrugged. How to answer that?

"Do you want me to pray with you?" she asked in a near whisper, leaning down until her eyes met Anna's.

Angered, she waved the woman away and moved her eyes to the sky. The sun had set, the light on the western horizon fading to a crystalline blue. It was the blue of the famous stained glass windows of Chartres her grandfather had taken her to see, a hue that couldn't be duplicated. She remembered an art instructor telling her that nobody knew how the medieval craftsman had created such vibrancy, what mysterious ingredient it was that had been mixed into the molten glass to make it transcendent. She'd never expected to see this blue again, let alone in the sky over Venice.

The driver zigzagged through the water, aiming toward the closest shore near the imposing dome of Santa Maria. When he went too close to the shore, she urged him back toward where the boat had capsized, suddenly certain that he was there, treading water, and hoping they would see him. And when they'd made a loop around the still visible hull of the boat, then she would urge the driver to head toward the shore again.

"He's over there!" she would call.

The pilot would nod and smoothly turn the wheel.

"There, over there!" she yelled at the driver again and again, pointing between the overturned boat and the more distant shoreline.

The grim-faced driver turned the boat, reacting to her instructions as soon as she'd uttered them, but he avoided her helpless gaze. And when they neared the shoreline, again she would have a feeling, a premonition that he was back near the boat, that they'd simply missed him in the darkness. The boat crept through the darkness slowly and deliberately with its passengers, the now eerily quiet and sober Americans, hanging out over the railings, scanning the murky water and breathing imperceptibly in the moist evening air.

"Back toward the boat!" Anna yelled. "He's there. He's somewhere right around there."

Again, they circled the small boat, still visible in the darkness and glowing preternaturally like some albino whale. On the bottom of the boat, she spied a mark, which she first took to be a grasping hand or a clump of seaweed. With a bit of light from the rising moon, she could see that it was actually another of the designs that had been on the front and back of the boat: a porpoise and trident.

She heard the long, slow caterwauling of a siren in the distance, the sound growing louder and suddenly entering the canal from the west. A police boat, lights flashing and with an enormous searchlight scanning the lagoon, sped toward them.

She gazed upward at the solemn cerulean sky, but it had already faded into the blackish-blue of evening, the gloaming having eased into night.

Now they would find him, she told herself.

Chapter Three

The phone was ringing, a raucous, old black telephone ring. The Venetians had given up their clunky old phones for cell phones, but Louis preferred the sturdiness of the old phone in his apartment. He found it in a junk shop, the owner shaking his head that he would want to buy such a thing for even a hundred lire.

"*Pronto*," he murmured. His mouth still tasted slightly of bourbon, and there was a lingering bitter taste, too, of the encounter the night before with his childhood neighbor. He remembered, though, that he drank most of the bourbon as he sat on his windowsill watching and listening to the spring rain striking the canal below his window.

"Louis!" Claudia gasped.

"Ciao, Claudia. What's the matter?" he asked, rubbing his eyes.

She spoke so fast and the phone was so old that he could hardly decipher what she said. Maybe that was the reason the old man had hesitated to sell him the phone. Whatever it was, she sounded excited, panicked even.

"What? I can't hear you."

"*Dio, Dio*," she shrieked. "My mother, my mother is *here*."

"In Venice?" he asked, surprised that he suddenly could understand her.

"Yes. She called this morning. She says she doesn't want to give me any time to hatch any preposterous excuses for why I should stay here."

"I thought you had a few weeks, at least, maybe longer."

Louis' head started to throb, and the aftertaste of bourbon on his tongue made him cringe. What had he been thinking? He should have gone right to bed after returning from Harry's—that would have been the best way to forget about his encounter there.

"I thought so, too. But, no. She's here now and I've run out of time," she moaned, speaking faster. "What the hell am I going to tell her? I've got nothing, no ideas, and no job."

"You're not going to give up?" he asked worriedly, sitting up in bed as his heart began to race.

Sometimes he wondered if Claudia wasn't much of a fighter, if she would always ultimately take the path of least resistance. Sometimes he'd seen a spark of defiance in her, and then sometimes she seemed timid and unsure of herself. Is that what comes from having been unable to make her own decisions for so long?

"That's the last thing I want to do. If I go back to Rome, I'll go nuts. There's nothing there for me. Old boyfriends, everyone watching my every move. My mother parading me in front of awful men or trying to get me back with Pietro. And she'll never accept that I despise the church, want nothing to do with it. No, returning there would be the end of my life, going back to an unhappy time in my life."

"Then you have to tell her no," he said, rubbing his forehead.

He made it sound so easy, he realized. He hadn't met Contessa Baggi, but something told him that telling her no wasn't as easy as he made it sound.

"What can I tell her?" she asked. "She already told me she thinks I'm hiding and that nothing good will come of my staying here. 'What ever will you do for work, operate a gondola?' she asked. I had nothing to tell her. I couldn't answer any of her questions. I never did work in New York, or nothing much because she didn't think I should and Pietro agreed, and I fooled around after university, too, helping my father with his UN work in Geneva. But he never taught me how to do anything; he just let me watch. Oh, God, I don't know how to do *any*thing!"

"But you're older now—hell, you're divorced," he advised, his head spinning trying to think how he could encourage her. What had she done? What could she do?

Claudia's heavy sigh crackled through the clunky earpiece of the old phone.

"I don't think I should remind her of that. The fact that I'm divorced won't do me any favors with my mother. Remember, she's very Catholic and in some ways very traditional. She still goes to Mass most days."

"So cloak it in other terms—without mentioning the divorce by name. Tell her that you've grown up a lot the past year or so, figured out what you want to do—"

"But I haven't—that's a total lie," she cried, her voice cracking. "The only thing I'm reasonably certain of is that I'm finally where I want to be. I just need a little more time to figure out what to do here."

"That's okay—you'll figure it out. That's exactly the thing. But you just need to buy more time—and you need her to buy it for you."

"You make it sound so easy," she said, accusingly.

"I'm good at that," he snickered, wondering why he couldn't put the same spin on his own situations.

Claudia didn't sound too sarcastic and was maybe even a little more hopeful. Maybe he could help her yet. To him, she seemed funny and bright, and she possessed an uncommon flair. The quirky, stylish way she dressed, along with how she noticed every little architectural detail and the way the clouds formed patterns in the sky, made him think there must be some perfect job for her where she could those skills. Certainly, she could do something, a job that would fit the creative impulse that he felt certain lay just below the surface of her skin.

"So what's this great opportunity, what's the thing that I want to do? You know she's going to ask. We've got to think of something."

"Christ. I don't know. I can't even think straight—"

"Oh, don't tell me that," she moaned, her voice cracking again.

"I just need some coffee—that's all," he lied. "Don't worry, we'll think of something. It can't be that difficult."

What he really needed was a head transplant.

"Hey, I've got an idea," she said, beginning to speak so fast he could barely understand her Italian. "I need to buy some time. Will you go with me to the hotel to meet her? If you're with me, she won't torment me. That's perfect, perfect. She won't bother me if there's a stranger there—she hates to argue, hates to make a scene in front of strangers."

It seemed a good idea, but the last thing he wanted was to have lunch—and secondly, to have lunch with a total stranger whom he feared was going to see right through him, and whom he'd learned to fear from everything he'd heard about her. At least, that's how the newspapers and magazines described Claudia's mother. But how could he say no to a simple lunch? And he felt desperate to help Claudia in some way.

"When does she want to meet?" he asked, trying to sound unfazed.

"For lunch—at noon. She's at the Rialto and wants to meet at Nettuno."

"That doesn't give us much time to come up with a plan. Should I meet you there early?"

How in the hell would he think of anything? He experienced a sinking feeling, fearing that the dread he felt meant that everything would change just as he'd found a quiet, little corner in a watery, ancient, has-been city.

And how would he act at lunch? He wanted to protest that he'd just rolled out of bed and that his head was throbbing, and all he wanted was to close his eyes for a little while longer. But he tried to sound chipper, completely capable of helping his friend.

He chided himself, realizing he needed to rally quickly. He would need to drink as much espresso as it took or she'd be gone. And if she left, then where would he go, and what would he do? When he imagined Venice without Claudia, he felt a pang of loneliness. Why didn't he have such feelings during his past three years of wandering, not in London, Prague, or Nazaré, that sleepy little fishing village in Portugal, which turned out to be too quiet? In some unromantic, platonic way, he'd fallen in love with her, started relying on her more than he had on anyone for years.

"No, she'll probably be prowling the corridors early," she explained, her voice sounding panicked. "Let's meet at the café. I could use some fortification before I meet her. And a little prosecco will help us think of something."

"*Perfetto*," Louis said with forced enthusiasm, the thought of prosecco making him feel queasy. "And what's the worst thing that would happen if you told her no, if you decided to do what you want to do instead of what she wants you to do?"

Claudia lapsed into silence on the other side of the phone, leading him to wonder if he'd made a mistake by reminding her of what she would be facing in only a few short hours. The earpiece felt hard and cold against his ear. He wondered if he should change the topic, pretending he hadn't asked the question. Before he could think of a more upbeat question, she spoke.

"She'll cut me off, I think," she said slowly. "I think she'll cut me off. And then my time here will be up. No money and no time."

She sounded hopeless again, frightened. Why had he asked her that question, hoping that somehow she would reassure him that there wasn't that much riding on the lunch? Instead, he began wondering if the happy year he'd spent with her was coming to an abrupt end.

"Things will work out," he announced brightly, feeling that out of necessity they would find some way to figure things out, that he could quiet the rising panic in her voice. Didn't they both need things to go their way so much that circumstances would mold themselves around their desires, if only they believed they would. He wasn't used to approaching anything so confidently, but then, maybe he'd never faced losing anything that meant that much to him.

"I'll meet you shortly," he said.

Louis hung up the phone, his mind feeling waterlogged from too many hours of sleep. Razor-thin shafts of light sliced through the blinds of the bedroom windows. His worst scheming was always done on too much sleep. Better to be hungover, buzzed, or over-caffeinated.

The sun was shining on a March day, typically one of the rainiest months in Italy, so maybe he could be hopeful. The winds from Africa were blowing across the Adriatic, bringing what, he wondered. He would need a little extra time to get ready and to think, but Claudia would forgive him. She was never on time herself.

When he chastised her once for always being late, she snapped at him, explaining that she'd had to be early or on time her entire life, and that for her adult life, for the life she was finally choosing for herself, she wanted to be late—just for a while to try it on, to see what it was like.

Whatever plan they hatched, he would need to be shaven and well dressed. If he'd learned anything about Italy in his relatively short time there, it was that appearances count. And Contessa Baggi, from what Claudia said, wasn't easily impressed. And right away, she wouldn't like that he wasn't Catholic. Claudia had intimated that much.

Shave, shower, and dress. Did he even have pressed pants and a starched shirt? Would a tie be overdoing it? These sorts of issues were part of the reason he'd chosen to hide in Venice. Dressing and doing for others made him lightheaded, seeming to constrict the flow of blood to his head and limbs. His mother always said that if he made a routine of shaving, showering, and dressing well, that those and the hundreds of other little habits practiced by "normal" people wouldn't be so onerous. He wouldn't ever have to think about doing them, they'd become as second nature as sitting, getting out of bed, or eating with a fork.

"If they're routine, you don't have to think about them," she used to prod. "Routines make life easier."

He couldn't imagine ever finding shaving routine or innocuous—it was always painful and annoying. Leading his simple life in Venice, with his little writing studio and few friends, gave him a freedom he savored, a lack of responsibility he hadn't encountered living in the states.

Louis picked up his clothes from the night before and felt something unwieldy in his coat. He reached into the pocket and pulled out a long, rubbery purple object. A *dildo*?

"What the hell?" he muttered aloud, remembering Irene pushing something into his pocket. Where did she get it, and why did she slip it into his pocket? He could remember Tad and Irene laughing after he left them at the bar, Irene covering her mouth she was giggling so uncontrollably. Why she had the thing in her pocket while touring Venice and visiting Harry's, he couldn't imagine. She was more odd and more annoying than he'd imagined.

Before he could get to the shower, there was a rapping on the enormous front door and someone calling, "Signore Louis, Signore Louis."

It had to be his landlord. Signore Sacci. The guy always made him nervous because *he* was nervous, always looking at his hands, the floor, his shoes, or out the window, but never in the eyes. What was it about him? He wouldn't look a person in the eye.

Of course, now Louis was running late and always when there was some urgency or crisis, a neighbor materialized at the door. It was as if Italians could sense the urgency, trying to subdue expat Americans' tendency always to hurry.

Tossing the dildo under his bed, he rushed down the hall. "Sì, sì?"

"*É signore* Sacci! Sacci."

"I'm just getting into the shower," Louis lied through the crack of the door. If he opened the door, he might never get the man out of his apartment. The man wouldn't say much, but would ask questions about America and what Louis thought of Venice. The guy, obviously lonely, would talk about anything. But now, Louis couldn't afford to spend any time with him. Claudia might already be facing her mother alone.

"I have an appointment. *Ho fretta*! *Urgente*!" Louis called through the door.

"*Un momento, solo un momento*," the voice from the other side of the door pleaded.

"*Spiace, ma sono nudo*," Louis lied.

There was silence, a shifting of feet and shoes brushing across the floor.

"*Un momento*," the voice said again, uncertainly. "I can wait a moment for you to dress," he said in English.

Louis stood fully dressed in front of the door, his head still foggy. He could run back to his room and pretend to dress, or wait where he was and hope the landlord didn't sense him standing there, awaiting the passage of a believable amount of time before he would feel comfortable opening the door. But what was he thinking? The landlord could probably hear him breathing, sense his presence.

Perhaps it was better to deal with him quickly and have it over with.

He vowed to be assertive, to force his landlord out if necessary. Louis released the long metal bolt and slowly opened the massive wooden door a crack. Signore Sacci's pugs—two black and one fawn—rushed through the opening, snorting and spinning in circles. Louis thought it was odd that the man had pugs. In so many ways, he seemed a typical Venetian, reticent, inscrutable, and observing everything with watchful eyes. He didn't appear the sort to have three crazy pugs that were as outgoing as Venetians were reserved.

"*Spiace*," he said, following his dogs into the room and clawing halfheartedly at their collars to grab them as they raced by. "But I have to leave town next weekend—it's my nephew's first communion in Trieste. My sister says no dogs—not in the house, and certainly not in the church. Can you watch them for me? I just need to know because my nephew can't come. We can talk later, but I just need to know."

"Signore—" Louis started to say.

"*Per favore*, you can call me just Sacci," he insisted, dropping the formal tense and speaking to Louis for the first time in the familiar tense. The man smiled, turning distractedly to look at an oil painting that Louis had recently hung just inside the hallway. Impulsively, Louis had purchased the abstract piece from a dusty gallery on Burano. The dogs gathered at their master's feet panting noisily, their bulging eyes moving between him and the oil painting he appeared to be studying.

"Next weekend?" Louis couldn't even think what he had going on the following day, let alone the next weekend. He would need to find his calendar planner, but couldn't recall where he'd put it. Living in Venice, he hardly needed it, but since he missed a few deadlines, he scrupulously recorded every appointment and date, and most particularly when his translations were due.

"I think so, that should be fine. But I'll need to check. Can I get back to you?" he asked, trying to corral Sacci toward the hallway.

"Sì, sì, sì," Sacci replied. Every time he said yes, he repeated it three times, never just once. "I'm not so busy like you. I understand you need to check first. Sì, sì, sì, check your schedule and let me know. But let me know as soon as possible. Maybe later today when you return from your appointment?"

"That shouldn't be a problem. Sure," Louis said, peering over his landlord's shoulder at the painting.

For a moment, there was complete silence as the two of them studied the painting, a green, brown, and ochre abstract.

"It's nice," Sacci mumbled. "Melodic, or very musical, don't you think?"

Louis ceased being surprised by Italians who appreciated art. It seemed that even an average Italian had an opinion and would stop to look. He wouldn't have guessed that his landlord ever even thought about art. Now he observed as the man stood back from the painting, appraising and viewing the piece with the eye of a critic. He smiled faintly, seeming to savor the canvas.

As Sacci studied the painting, Louis watched him. He noticed again that the man was handsome, despite wearing bland clothing. He'd made some effort to dress up that day, having put on a faded melon polo shirt and khaki pants that made his light olive skin appear lightly tanned.

Studying him, Louis wondered that he'd never noticed his slightly wavy, deep brown hair or his prominent nose, a feature that Louis always found attractive.

Was the man gay? Louis felt a stirring, a vague pull toward the man. Could the man possibly have been gay, he seemed so straight? And hadn't one of the neighbors told Louis that his landlord had a girlfriend in Trieste, the town where his mother lived?

Louis snapped to attention, remembering he was going to be late. He needed to go, and as much as he was suddenly interested in talking to his landlord, he had to meet Claudia. He wished the man had stopped by an hour earlier, or better yet, the day before.

Then one of the black pugs sighed and growled, pawing Sacci's shoe before darting down the hallway. When the dog reached the end of the echoing hall, nails tapping on the floor, he turned directly in front of Louis' open bedroom door.

"Ah, *cane*, no!" Sacci yelled, but the dog played deaf, shooting a bug-eyed glance at the two men before darting across the threshold. Sacci chased the dog down the hallway and burst into Louis' bedroom. The other dogs followed, pursued by Louis.

"Sorry," Sacci cried, dropping to his knees to root around under the bed where he could hear the dog growling. "They have a think of their own," he said, speaking English again, screwing up his face seemingly aware that he'd said something wrong.

The dog emerged with the enormous purple dildo, which he awkwardly dragged across the floor. Louis tried to get to the dog first, but Sacci leaped and already had his hands around the dildo, tugging at it. "*Dammela*!" he shouted at the dog. But the pug clenched the dildo like a toy, refusing to release it as he growled.

"*Lasciala*!" Sacci commanded.

"Let me," Louis said, struggling to edge the man away from the dog before the head of the giant dildo popped out of the dog's mouth. He could feel his cheeks grow hot as he wondered whether Sacci had figured out what was in the dog's mouth. The man didn't even know he was gay, so how would he explain that the dildo wasn't even his? And would Sacci even know what the thing was?

"What-choo got *cane*?" Sacci cooed in English. The man yanked desperately at the purple dildo. "*Damme*, give it to me!"

"I'll get it," Louis said, pushing Sacci gently at his elbow. "Let me."

The man wouldn't loosen his grip on the object, and he pulled harder as the dog growled more fiercely, his curly tail wagging with excitement. The other dogs pawed the wooden floor, staring bug-eyed and hungrily at the dildo, twirling in circles and growling playfully. The purple head suddenly popped out of the dog's mouth as Sacci fell back onto his haunches. The man examined the object as he held it up in front of his face, his brow wrinkling in confusion. "*Cosa* …?"

Louis seized the object with trembling hands and tossed it back under the bed without thinking. Before he could stop them, the dogs raced back under the bed, growling as their nails clicked on the floor. He dived under the bed after them, wrestling away the dildo. The dogs growled, locking their little jaws on the piece of rubber, which Louis struggled to pull away from them. When he had it once more, Louis stuffed the thing down his shirt, but the dogs scrambled up his chest, growling frantically and clawing.

"No more play, no more play," he commanded helplessly in Italian.

The dogs grew more excited, making frantic pirouettes and jumping on his chest. They pawed and nipped at the dildo through his shirt.

"Can I help?" Sacci asked, his head appearing at the side of the bed. Suddenly, the man had pushed his way under the bed next to Louis, calling the dogs off, though they continued to act as if they were all playing a game together.

Did Sacci know what that was, Louis wondered? He felt the same peculiar rush he'd experienced while watching Sacci studying the painting in his entryway. Was he developing a crush on his landlord?

And there he lay under the bed with him, the handsome man pushed up next to him in the shadows.

His face feeling hot and his heart beating frantically against his ribs, he wondered if he should make a joke of the dildo, acknowledge it, or pretend it was nothing. He was grateful to be in the darkness, which hid his reddened face. What was Sacci thinking? If he knew what the curved purple object was, suspected that Louis was gay, would he tell everyone like a typical Venetian?

The man began laughing, giggling really while Louis' face turned redder. The man must have recognized the object, realizing it was a dildo. Why else would he have been laughing, almost nervously? He called to the dogs breathlessly, "No, no! *Vai, vai, cani mali*," he choked out the words.

"Cani, cani!" Sacci giggled. "Bad dogs, bad dogs!"

Sacci grabbed at Louis' shirt and pulled at the dogs, but his hands slipped, striking Louis' chest. Suddenly he rolled on top of Louis, squeezing between the bottom of the raised bed and the dogs, which piled on top of Louis, still frantically growling and barking, trying to find the dildo hidden under his shirt. Sacci reached for the dogs, pushed them off Louis, and grabbed for their collars.

Sacci had always seemed so awkward and formal, but now he lay sprawled across Louis' chest, pressing into him as he lunged for the dogs. Louis' face was blazing and he shook. Had he fallen for the guy so quickly? Where the hell had the attraction come from?

But was Sacci even gay, or had Louis developed yet another crush on a straight man? Trembling, he awkwardly rolled out from under the man, but not before catching a whiff of something mildly sweet—cologne? Was his quiet, timid landlord wearing cologne? That the man wore any at all surprised him. Maybe he was in his mid-thirties, but so quiet and housebound, that Louis couldn't imagine him wearing cologne. The man was handsome—how had he not noticed before?

When Louis cleared the underside of the bed frame pursued by the three pugs leaping and pawing at his chest, he struggled to his feet. Darting as rapidly and smartly as one of the dogs, he removed the dildo from inside his shirt and tossed it in the top drawer of his dresser. As he slammed shut the drawer, he heard Sacci still snickering under the bed. The dogs' expectant gaze moved back and forth between the drawer containing the dildo and Louis. The giggling from beneath the bed slowed as Sacci slowly rolled out from under the bed.

"Spiace, spiace," he apologized, rising awkwardly as he brushed off his pants.

Sacci grinned, but Louis couldn't determine whether the man's amusement came from the whole peculiar scene under the bed or recognizing the purple play toy. Louis' face burned still. But stealing a glance at Sacci's, he saw that the other man was blushing, too.

It had to be unlikely that Sacci would know what he'd just handled, given that he'd lived his whole life in a quiet neighborhood of that quiet city. If there were any porn shops in Venice, they were well hidden. To Sacci, the dildo must have simply been a dog's play toy.

Laughing nervously, Louis rubbed his hands on his thighs, his eyes darting around the room alternately resting on one of the dogs, his empty walls, and the giant, open windows. Out of the corner of his eye, he noticed Sacci also seemingly avoiding his face, gazing instead at the floor and one of the pugs that pirouetted at his feet.

Somewhere deep down, he concluded, maybe his landlord had a gay bone in his body, could that be why the man wouldn't look at him or why Louis had that surge of emotion, a trembling in his chest? He could hear his friends in Chicago, accusing him again of thinking everyone were gay. But these Italians were different. Call them gay and they might fight you over the remark, but then the men he'd talk to admitted that so many of them had had homosexual experiences. So where did Sacci fit in? And from where arose the suspicions, his hunch that the quiet man might be gay?

"Sorry," Sacci said sheepishly, breaking the awkward silence. "You know these clownish dogs; they don't know to respect a person's privacy. They only like to play."

The man was handsome, so straight looking, though, that even if he had a gay bone in his body, would Louis ever recognize it? Claudia would chalk it up to wishful thinking. And Tad would probably tell him he was purposefully or perhaps unconsciously directing his affections toward someone who could never reciprocate.

"Better they enjoy playing than biting," Louis remarked, glancing at Sacci.

Sacci nodded, followed by another awkward silence. The two of them watched the dogs as if waiting for something or someone to appear.

Sacci suddenly grinned, glancing at Louis.

"Would you like to get a cappuccino?" he asked.

"Well … yes … but no," Louis stammered, his nerves jangling as he remembered Claudia. He wanted to talk to Sacci more, but it would have to wait.

"I understand," Sacci murmured, leaning over to grab one of the dogs as he stepped toward the door.

"No … I mean I'd like to," Louis stammered, trying to keep his voice from shaking. "But I've got that appointment with a friend that I told you about—it's urgent."

"Oh, Dio," Sacci exclaimed, herding the other two dogs toward the door. "I forgot—*sorry*."

Sacci clapped his hands and waved the dogs toward the door. "I've made you late, eh?"

"I think I can still be on time," Louis said, wondering if he should ask him if they could go the following day.

Before he could speak, Sacci turned. "Another time maybe?"

"Sure," Louis answered, trying to sound casual, but wondering if he should be more specific. Fearing he would sound too eager, he remained silent.

"Okay, I'll stop by then," Sacci said over his shoulder, hurrying down the hall with Louis and the dogs just behind him. When he reached the door, he turned.

"Who's the friend you're meeting?" he asked casually. "Is it Claudia Baggi?"

"Yes. I'm meeting her and her mother for lunch."

"Contessa Baggi, eh? I've read about her." Sacci set the dog back down on the floor. The dogs sat grouped at his feet, looking at him expectantly.

"I've seen her coming to your apartment and have seen the two of you at Café Tramonta. She seems very *gentile*."

"*É molta gentile*," he agreed, surprised that Sacci had noticed the two of them.

"Will you get married?"

"No," Louis blushed. "We won't get married. We're just friends."

"Just friends? Just! A good friend can often be better than a lover."

Europeans always made such philosophical comebacks. Did they do it to remind Americans that they were so inexperienced and uncouth at the art of living?

"I suppose you're right. She's a good friend, but not a lover. Does that make sense?"

"Sure. Now I understand."

Sacci smiled, looking as if he wanted to ask something else. Was he thinking again about the dildo, wondering about Louis?

"I should let you go, I'm making you late," Sacci murmured, hovering on the threshold.

"Yeah, I've got to be on time or Claudia won't be so *gentile*. But don't worry—I'm sure I can watch your dogs. I'll let you know later today—okay?"

"*Perfetto*," he said, backing slowly into the hallway. "And you'll be very careful with them, *sì*? I know it's strange, but I'm fond of these dogs and don't like to leave them."

"Yes, I know," Louis said, thinking of how much like children the man treated his dogs. He thought it strange that an Italian man would have pugs, but heard that Sacci had taken them reluctantly when an aunt died. Now he couldn't seem to part with them.

"I'm most worried they'll fall into the canal. They're not swimming dogs, and I hate to think of what would happen if one fell in," he explained, speaking quickly. "They run around rather fearlessly."

"I've noticed," Louis said, moving anxiously from one foot to the other. Was Claudia wondering where he was?

Why was Sacci so worried about his dogs drowning when most days they were in a tiny courtyard scratching at grass or peeing on giant terra-cotta pots of bougainvillea or geraniums—far from any canal?

"I'll watch them carefully," Louis assured.

"I know you will because you're good people," Sacci said. "I don't ask just anyone to watch my dogs because not everyone is *gentile*, careful. You know?"

Though Louis was anxious to meet Claudia and uncertain just what was transpiring with Sacci, he realized the man was trying to compliment him.

"I'm honored that you'd trust me with your dogs," he said. Sometimes he felt so formal speaking to Italians. He said things he would never say to anyone in America.

Sacci smiled, nodding. He was strikingly handsome in that way that only Italians could be handsome. His nose was a bit large; unusual for a Venetian, but he had large brown eyes and thick, shortly cropped hair. He'd been so business-like at first, requesting Louis' passport and two months' rent, that he hadn't even taken a good look at him. He'd even asked for paycheck stubs to ensure Louis had income. He'd seemed more like a banker than an owner of a converted palazzo, on a very average street in a very average part of town. Like so many Europeans, Sacci had a world-weary air about him. But now Louis had seen the man giggling, rolling under a bed chasing after his dogs, and grabbing a giant purple dildo—even if he'd had no idea what he'd held.

Strange how there were so many layers to a person and at first, especially in a place like Venice, a person saw only the papery veneer, like the brown skin of an onion hiding the flesh within.

Sacci hesitated, herding the dogs in half-motions into the hallway.

"I hope I haven't made you too late," he repeated, apologizing again. "And sorry again about the dogs, eh? They're nosy creatures. But you like them, too, I think."

"Sì, sì, sì," Louis insisted, his eyebrows rising as he heard himself. "No problem. I can still make it on time, and the dogs are no problem."

As he closed the door, smiling nervously at Sacci, a wave of déjà vu washed over him, as if he'd lived the whole scene before. But he knew that déjà vu could be explained—it was simply a hiccup in the unfolding of time, his mind—subconscious, maybe—racing ahead of reality. Déjà vu gave him the same feeling he'd had as a child when he first attended Mass and fervently believed in Christ, that he was safe from hell, saved, and whatever else that had meant to him at the time. Those ideas were long gone, but the same feelings sometimes welled up in him, precipitated by the oddest experiences—déjà vu being one. No, he couldn't put his finger on precisely what this latest déjà vu was about, but he wondered if his gut might be right for once, that maybe despite all appearances and odds, Sacci was gay.

But even if the man was gay, what did it mean?

Chapter Four

Louis hated being late. And to let Claudia down made him feel even worse. With Americans already possessing a reputation for being unreliable, he despised arriving late. And then it made him nervous about his own future, too, since his seemed wrapped up in Claudia's. If she could stay in Venice, maybe he could, too. Though they'd known each other not quite a year—she was nearly the first person he'd met in Venice—she was like one of the friends he'd imagined he would have when he grew up. She was spontaneous, inquisitive, stylish, and full of interesting stories. He liked her impetuous manner, the way she would grab his arm and force him inside a café for a shot of espresso, or maybe a glass of prosecco if it were a warm afternoon. And then they could talk for hours about what their lives had meant up to that point, the mistakes they'd made, and how they shared a sense that Venice offered the chance for something different.

As they explored the city, heading down different streets and passages often scarcely wider than a wheelbarrow, they spotted tucked away architectural treasures; sometimes a once-grand palazzo with a crumbling facade, or a lowly, medieval-looking house, fronted with worn stones and moss-covered gargoyle waterspouts.

They wondered what the inside of the buildings looked like, if they'd changed much in five hundred years or had been utterly transformed. Some were sure to be empty, inhabited by cats and mice, while others hid tapestries, frescoes, paintings, and elaborately carved furniture. In Venice, the exterior of a building was never a sure indicator of its interior, and even a seemingly lowly building, covered with worn, mossy stones and a scarred, rustic wooden door might be a retirement home of an expat artist from Paris, a Rockefeller, or perhaps someone who simply wanted a quiet city in which to hide.

They talked about houses that might be for sale one day and what they would do if they could ever buy one. It surprised them both that they'd discovered a city in which they felt so at home. Maybe Claudia had always suspected that Venice was where she belonged, but it seemed like he'd just ended up there, pulled by the invisible tide that had seemed to govern his life.

Was it the city, or merely the fact that they'd reached a point in their lives where they were ready for something different or prepared to look at things differently?

The cooler weather and the growing warmth of the March sun had lured his neighbors to their windows and doorways. These were the days Venice liked best, when a person could sit in the window—or better yet—behind drawn blinds or shutters and soak in all the conversation floating in from the narrow streets and canals.

He should have been panicking because he hadn't come up with one idea to help Claudia, not one thing to tell her mother. At such times, he wished Venice had taxis. He could still have been on time if only he hadn't had to walk the circuitous route to the café. If it had been the height of summer or Carnivale, he would have been hopelessly late. Not one street in Venice ran in a straight line for more than a few blocks.

Louis worked well under pressure, though, so what was there to worry about? The déjà vu that had washed over him earlier seemed a good omen. Sure, tucked in his chest there lingered a fear of Claudia's mother. What American wouldn't be intimidated to meet a contessa, let alone engage in a scheme designed to persuade her to continue supporting her lost daughter in Venice?

But the sun shone brightly and he felt optimistic. It was as if Venice were willing him to stay, offering a vague promise that things would work out.

He skipped over the worn stone and brick bridges, through the back passageways that passed for streets, heading toward the touristy section of town. It being early spring, there weren't likely to be too many tourists. But what if he ran into Tad and his annoying friend? It would take Louis an hour to extricate himself from a chance meeting with those two. Taking the smallest, twisting streets, he avoided Piazza San Marco and the major tourist avenues—just in case the two were lingering—and walked quickly toward the café.

When the strong aroma of coffee met him outside the oversize doors of Tramonta, he was only a few minutes late. Claudia would already have prosecco to calm her nerves, but he would need coffee first. Then perhaps a prosecco. Or even a grappa. Then again, he didn't want the contessa to think he was a lush, so maybe he'd need to be cautious. Who knew how perceptive the woman would be? Maybe she had one of those noses that could smell alcohol on someone a day later. He wondered if the bourbon he'd drunk the night before was still on his breath. What if the contessa smelled it?

He would likely need both coffee and a shot or drink of something. The coffee to blow the cobwebs out of his head, and the alcohol to give him a mellow glow, diminishing his anxiety. He could finish with a second coffee or mint tea to take the smell off his breath.

The café was crowded, full of faces he recognized from the neighborhood. The papers, *Il Corriere della Sera* and *Il Giornale* lay spread across the small, scratched marble tables like cloths. The air hung heavy with the strong scents of coffee, cigarette smoke, yeasty pastries, and sweet steamed milk. Cups knocked saucers, and teaspoons clinked, creating a pleasant background for the melodic breakfast conversations occurring all around him.

But where was Claudia? He scanned the room looking for her thin neck and dark, silken hair. Every table was full, and a cloud of blue smoke drifted along the ceiling, spilling outside when the door opened. But she wasn't at the counter or at any of the tables.

At such times, he wished he had a cell phone, a new device that he found annoying. What if she'd been delayed, or couldn't meet him or maybe her mother had already intercepted her. There'd be no way to reach him, short of calling the café.

"It's Claudia, the regular who comes in with the tall American," she could say, and the barista would hold up the phone and wave casually for him to take the call.

But she would have preferred that he have a cell phone, like she did. Claudia wanted always to be in touch, able to reach him whenever or wherever, whereas the exact opposite was true of him. Louis liked to get lost, to hide. He did not want to be found until he was ready to rejoin the world. The thought of anyone calling him at any time that he or she wanted gave him claustrophobia. Better that he talk to the person when he was in the mood. That's one of the reasons Venice appealed to him. A person couldn't easily be found in the old city, and a cell phone would remove one of the very pleasures of being there.

But this one time he wished he had one. He looked nervously at his watch again, wondering if he'd missed her. He realized that he'd grown as anxious as she was about coming up with something to tell her mother. What if Claudia had to leave Venice? For starters, he wouldn't be able to stand coming to Tramonta any longer. That would be too strange, too sad, after all the conversations they'd had there, the times they'd commiserated about bad dates or talked about unknown things, like where they'd be and what they'd be doing in ten years.

Approaching the busy counter, he ordered an espresso *doppio*. The caffeine would wash over him within a few minutes, followed by a flush of thinking and passion about everything from the headlines of the newspaper to hatching a plan for Claudia. Under the influence of caffeine, he could even get excited about returning to the states. Someday. Maybe it would be different after he'd been gone so long and things wouldn't feel so suffocating. He couldn't put his finger on how things might change, but the stubborn thought arose every once in awhile, irrational and unsubstantiated.

The barista, the owner's big-nosed cousin, nodded hello as he drew two steaming shots into a small ceramic cup. The cup of even this small café had a scrolling, substantial logo on it. When Louis first arrived in Italy, he quickly discovered that a café owner wouldn't dream of serving coffee in a generic cup—not a true coffee place, anyway. Even the smallest cafés spent money imprinting their logos on their espresso, cappuccino, and latte cups, and sometimes even on their glassware.

The barista worked efficiently, but mechanically. He may as well have been on an assembly line, but the espresso arrived on the bar in front of Louis picture-perfect, a rind of lemon and two cookies the size of gumballs sharing the saucer, and a swirl of *crema* crowning the surface.

As he took his first sip, the heavy wooden door creaked open and Claudia rushed in.

"Ciao, ciao!" she called, waving and rushing toward the bar. "I'm so sorry I'm late—again. I changed clothes multiple times. I washed my face, put on makeup, took off the makeup. How do I look?" She pushed her sunglasses to the top of her head.

She looked horrid. Normally placid and beautiful, Claudia's face was puffy and pink. Had she been crying?

"Dio, I look awful," she moaned, not waiting for him to answer. "I couldn't sleep last night, and I put a mask on this morning but I must have been allergic to it. Look at me!"

Claudia pointed to her puffy eyes, the light pink bumps that dotted her neck and cheeks.

"What?" Louis lied. "I can't tell at all—you look fine."

"Are you lying?" she snapped, stepping back to study his face.

"No," he answered, pretending to study the espresso before taking a sip.

"You must be lying because I look awful. My eyes are puffy and red. And my cheeks are pink. And you're not even looking at me."

"Oh, that," Louis offered, trying to appear honest and reliable, squinting at her eyes skeptically. "You can hardly see that. It's barely noticeable."

Claudia scrutinized him as she set her purse on the bar.

He nearly had her convinced, though perhaps she needed just a little more persuading. Normally he was such an awful liar, but on this day, he was properly motivated to lie like a pro.

"Really," he assured, raising the cup to his mouth, "You're always harder on yourself. It's a fact. Everyone is."

"My mother will think I'm in terrible shape. I should be looking happy, confident, and successful—though I don't do anything. Instead I look lost and tired, exactly as I really am."

"Maybe that's good—maybe she'll feel sorry for you instead."

"That's not my mother," she sighed. "She'll only grow more determined to take control of me if she thinks I'm unhappy. Always she's been fond of projects, fixing things. And she especially likes to play puppet master—*un momento*—I thought you said I looked okay, that it was hardly noticeable?"

Just in time, the barista approached. "*Si*?"

Claudia was distracted. *"Buon giorno. Un espresso. Un prosecco."*

The man nodded and turned quickly to the giant espresso machine, which hissed and clanked as he turned knobs and released one of the handles.

"That's the reason she's never very long on any project. Eventually, either everyone else on the committee quits, or they force her out. She's not an easy woman to deal with," she explained, biting her lip and leaning wearily on the counter.

"So what do we tell her?"

"I thought of something while walking over here," she said.

The barista approached, clearing their empty cups and glasses.

"*Un altro espresso*?" he asked, shifting his gaze toward Louis.

"Um, *un prosecco*," he said timidly. With the caffeine having brightened his mood, he was ready for some alcohol, which would counteract the anxious edge the coffee sometimes gave him.

The barista scurried off down the bar.

"What's your idea?"

"It's a little crazy, but it just might work."

"Yeah?"

"I'm embarrassed to say because it means you'll have to lie, too. And maybe it's humiliating for you."

"How bad can it be?" But automatically, he feared he would be asked to act as passionately (but more believably) than he did during his last, long-ago role in a high school play. An actress in the play had whispered to him *sotto voce*, on-stage in the middle of the play, "Stop hamming it up—you're overdoing it!" That's when Louis knew he hadn't received his mother's side of the family's acting gene—or its lying gene. However, when he thought about it, was there really much difference between the two? And certainly not when it came to Louis: he was both a lousy liar and a terrible actor.

"I met you in the U.S. and you want to marry me. You're writing and conducting research at the Getty Museum and L'Accademia. And you'll help me get set up in a small shop or somewhere doing something. It doesn't matter—what will matter to my mother is that I'm staying here for a man."

"But I'm an awful actor," Louis protested. "I mean, I'd like to help, but I don't know if I can pull it off."

"Sure you can. I'll do most of the talking—all you have to do is nod and smile."

"*Dio*, it makes me nervous. I don't know. And what happens when we don't marry?"

He drummed his fingers on the bar nervously, not wanting to disappoint her, but wondering how her idea could work.

Claudia's face darkened.

"It's not perfect, but I'm fresh out of other ideas. We're just buying time, that's all. I just need to persuade her to let me stay a while longer until I get something going. If I don't think of something, then I may as well give up and follow her back to Rome."

Then Louis would be alone again. If Claudia were forced to leave, would he be next? And Venice—perhaps all of Italy—would seem lonely. If he could help her, if somehow she did manage to stay, then maybe things would be set back in motion. If she could make it work, then maybe he could, too.

"Okay, I'll do it," he said, realizing it was their only option. "What else do I need to know? What else will you be telling her so we can get our story straight?"

The barista set down two more glasses of prosecco, pushing a demitasse of espresso toward Claudia.

"I think it's better not to make up any complicated schemes," she cautioned, picking up the espresso and pausing as she drank the shot in a few swallows. Moving her hand toward the prosecco, she gingerly wiped the corner of her mouth. "Maybe you just let me do the talking and defer to me if she asks questions. Or I'll just jump in and answer for you. I won't lie about anything I already know about you—well, except that you're gay, of course—but you'll be from Chicago, a writer, etcetera, etcetera, so that will all be easy and pretty much the truth so you can easily speak to her about that. But if we create a big complicated story, then I think we're more likely to slip up."

"Sure," he nodded, fighting the feeling that it wouldn't work, that Claudia's mother would smell a rat.

Got to think positively, he chided himself.

"Drink up," Claudia chirped, lifting the glass to her lips. "If we're late to see my mother she'll be in a foul mood. If she's not already."

Louis gulped the prosecco. After the bitterness of the coffee, the carbonation and sweetness give him a jolt. Maybe Claudia's plan could work after all. Why should her mother suspect them of lying? How could she possibly guess his motivation for playing along with the ruse? And perhaps in the end, her mother wouldn't be as obstinate as she'd been portrayed, and maybe, just maybe, Claudia had miscalculated. People changed, didn't they? So maybe the contessa would be different from what they'd imagined and their worrying was unfounded.

Thank God for both coffee and alcohol, he thought. Suddenly, he was optimistic. It might even be easier than he'd anticipated, and all of a sudden, he felt excited to meet Claudia's mother. She would be the first contessa he'd ever met, and he sensed a near-tangible current of optimism in the air.

"This'll be easy," he said, smiling. Setting his empty glass beside Claudia's, he pulled a 20,000 lire note out of his pocket and pushed it across the cool surface of the bar.

"I hope you're right," she said, pushing the lire back toward him and smiling. "I'm treating for this and my mother treats for lunch. And no argument, eh? I want you to act like hell, okay?"

He nodded, reluctantly pushing the lire back into his pocket.

"Okay," he agreed.

"Shall we go?" Claudia asked, her upper lip trembling slightly.

"Sure," Louis nodded, stepping away from the bar. After she picked up her purse, they headed out of the café and into the spring sunshine.

Walking through the crowded via toward the hotel, he noticed his stomach felt jumpy and his head was numbed from the prosecco. He followed Claudia up enormous, worn stone steps and through yawning doors into the heavy darkness of the old hotel. The smell of expensive perfume and cologne that he associated with any spot in Europe frequented by the rich overtook him. The doormen sang "buon giorno" as they passed, and the concierge who sat primly at an immense, gleaming table with grotesque claw-footed legs greeted Claudia by name. She waved at him distractedly as they walked past.

Did the concierge cast a disapproving look toward him?

They were past the sour-faced man in a moment and headed down a wide, dimly lit hallway. Claudia walked quickly, faster than Louis had ever known her to move. He could scarcely keep up with her, his legs seeming made of lead while hers, long and lean, seemed like those of an athlete.

In a blur, they passed the immense ornate, Venetian-style pillars outside Nettuno and they were inside the restaurant. Claudia nodded at the *maître d'* and pointed toward a poised, slender woman sitting in front of large French doors overlooking the Grand Canal. The heavy, burgundy-colored curtains pulled well away from the windows, allowed the hazy, late March sunlight to pour onto the scarred, gleaming parquet floor.

Claudia reached back toward Louis and grabbed his hand.

"Ciao, Mamma," she called, probably louder than she'd intended.

Louis saw little resemblance between mother and daughter as he approached Contessa Baggi, who rose slowly, pushing the chair behind her. Her eyes moved quickly from her daughter's face to Louis, and then lingered on their clasped hands before returning to Claudia. Claudia released Louis' hand and then embraced and kissed her mother. Their greeting seemed formal, stiff, not at all like he'd seen other Italians behave when greeting family.

"Mamma, this is Louis," she announced in English, gently nudging him forward.

Louis was suddenly uncertain whether he should kiss her cheeks or simply grasp her hand. He lacked time to decide, though, as the contessa grabbed his hand, making no move to offer a cheek for even a cold Teutonic kiss.

"I didn't realize that you were bringing someone, Claudia," her mother said flatly. Louis didn't think her voice betrayed any anger, but felt there was something in her gaze, a momentary, steely glance, that revealed annoyance.

"I thought you two should meet, *cara mamma*, because I'm seeing Louis now. *É mio ragazzo*."

"*É vero*?" her mother asked, her eyebrows arching.

Was it a statement of fact or aroused suspicion? Louis feared the latter. What fools they were to believe they would pull this over on the contessa, he realized. And to think merely fifteen minutes earlier he'd been so optimistic. Of course, that had been the caffeine and prosecco talking.

"I thought it would be a nice surprise," Claudia warbled. "And he's the reason I'm in Venice," she added, her voice sounding artificial, chirpy.

"I see," her mother responded. She smiled wanly.

"Not the only reason. Part of the reason … but … the *main* reason," Claudia stammered, smiling nervously at Louis.

"Sì," her mother said.

Was she torturing her daughter, toying with her to make her squirm? He could see a faint reddening of Claudia's cheeks.

"That's wonderful," the contessa said brightly. "And Louis what do you do in Venice?" she asked, turning to him.

"He's doing research on medieval Venice. And translating books," Claudia quickly answered, smiling at her mother, not even looking in his direction.

"Fascinating. You're a researcher and translator."

It was another of her statements that sounded vaguely like a question. He wasn't certain how to respond, what to say, though the contessa seemed to be waiting for him to say something. She didn't seem to look at Louis with any sarcasm or hostility, but he couldn't figure out what she was thinking.

"Yes, mostly a translator, though," he answered, his voice sounding uncertain, trailing, despite his attempt to sound confident.

Claudia cast him a glance that looked like a warning. He couldn't help it, though. He hated lying, perhaps most because he felt certain they would eventually be found out. And maybe it was that he felt helplessly inferior to the contessa, and didn't want to be proven a fool or liar. He'd never met any sort of blue blood before. Why did he suddenly want to be liked or at least accepted by her?

The contessa looked at him, smiling, and he had the sudden feeling that she might like him. She nodded slightly, turning quickly to her daughter.

"Claudia, I don't prefer to have this conversation with your boyfriend here, but if you brought him along and we must talk about things, then I guess we must talk about them." She turned again to Louis, saying matter-of-factly, "I hope it doesn't make you uncomfortable, but it's one of these issues that needs talking out. I hope you understand."

Louis nodded, wondering if he should get up and leave, suddenly uncertain about the woman again. Was she providing him an invitation to leave? He hated not knowing what he should do, how he should respond. It felt as if he were playing a game to which he didn't know the rules. Had Claudia miscalculated? What was the contessa about to say?

"What are you doing here, *carina*?" she snapped impatiently, her voice dripping with disapproval. "I think it's time you came home. Don't you think so, too?"

"Mamma," Claudia responded, her eyes shrinking and bird-like. "I've still got to take some time to think things over. And I really like Louis; I want to be with him."

Okay, Louis thought, what she'd said was not so much of a lie, even if they enjoyed being with each other in ways other than Claudia was leading her mother to believe.

"I just want another six months or so to get something started here. I like Venice—it's a good place for me."

"Venice is a good place for tourists and people who are hiding out. It's not where you go to start a new life. I'm not talking about you, *Louis*," she said, unconvincingly. "I know there are people here doing more than hiding out, but for Italians, in particular, it's not a good place to go. It's a place people go if they're hiding or have gotten into trouble. The whole of Italy knows this. Even Father Angelo says so—he asked what you're doing here, told me it's no good that you're here."

"But I'm not hiding," Claudia protested, her voice quavering. "And I haven't gotten into trouble. And there's not anything in Rome that I'm so interested in returning to. And they have plenty of churches here—if I thought there was a reason to go to one."

The contessa's eyes flashed as she pressed her lips together tightly.

Why did she have to say that, to antagonize her mother? Even Louis sensed that such a comment was likely to anger the woman.

"I'm not talking about you and Papà, you know," Claudia faltered. "Just my friends and jobs. I … I feel like I've spent enough time in Rome. I'm ready for a change."

"But you had a change in New York. And now you are doing

nothing here in Venice. I can sense it," the contessa said petulantly, smoothing the napkin on her lap.

"But I want to spend time with Louis. Right now that's enough for me," she countered, avoiding her mother's eyes.

With the lying begun in earnest, Louis started to blush.

"You've already been here long enough to figure that out, as I recently learned," the contessa said with a frown, shaking her head slightly. "And can't you two commute? Rome is not so far, eh? And Louis could study in Rome; it can't matter where he does translating, no? He could just as easily do that in Rome. They have mail and Internet service there, too, new as it is."

"No he has to be *here*—he should be here," Claudia said quickly, her voice trembling. "I mean, I don't want to make him move. And I'm just asking for six more months. That's all. I know I'll have some type of job by then. I know people here now. I have lots of opportunities. Really. It's better for me to be here than in Rome."

"You don't want to return to Rome because you're ashamed of the divorce? Or because there are certain expectations of you?" her mother asked.

"In some ways both," Claudia shrugged, twisting her mouth into a grimace.

"Then it's exactly as I figured—you're hiding out here," she said, clucking. "You're merely confirming my suspicions."

Louis felt his face getting hot. If he had to pick a winner, it would have been Contessa Baggi. He experienced a growing, sickening feeling that Claudia was not long for Venice.

"Just six months?" Claudia pleaded, her voice thin and high. "What's six months more, Mamma, eh? And I've known Louis for only six months. I just want a little more time."

Louis shuddered. Why did she have to sound so desperate, so plaintive?

"Why can't Louis support you then?" the contessa asked. "If this is serious, then you should both consider such an arrangement."

The conversation was taking an increasingly uncomfortable turn.

Louis squirmed in his chair, studying the menu. He could feel the contessa's eyes on him, compelling him to look up, but he gazed instead at Claudia whose cheeks had turned a deeper shade of pink. There seemed to be little hope. Maybe he should save the two of them the torture by simply telling the truth, and then they could all enjoy lunch, possibly getting pleasantly drunk. Louis' mind raced as he seriously began to ponder leaving Venice. Maybe every place was bound to be ruined after a certain amount of time, for things eventually and inevitably sour.

"Oh, Mamma," Claudia moaned, sounding unwilling to yield.

Louis shouldn't have given up so easily.

"That's ridiculous. I'm asking only for a little more time. How can it matter so much to you?" she said, slapping the table, the heavy white linen muffling the sound of her small hand.

"Of course it matters to me what you do—I'm your mother," she countered, her voice growing strident. "And you're a Baggi. I don't think it's right what you're doing—Father Angelo doesn't either. I'm a modern woman, you know, but I have my limits."

"Dio—is another six months in Venice going to change things so much?"

"I could ask the same of you," the contessa remarked, returning her gaze to the menu.

The woman suddenly turned and studied Louis with a heavy, penetrating gaze. He glanced down at his menu nervously before sneaking a glance at Claudia. She looked angry, desperate. And maybe angry with Louis, too. Did she sense that he'd given up? Was her mother sensing that it was all a lie?

"Why do you push me so often in ways that I don't care to go? I went to New York for you, I married for you, and now you want me to return to Rome. Can't I have merely six months in Venice to see if I can do something that I want to do?" she asked, her lower lip trembling.

The contessa pursed her lips disapprovingly and with an irritated, desultory wave, signaled the waiter.

Claudia shouldn't have said that last bit, thought Louis. Even he saw that saying such a thing wouldn't help, realizing that he could handle the contessa better than her daughter could. Maybe that's why there were so many problems between them. But weren't most people blind to the numerous and often undetectable landmines lying between themselves and a parent?

"*Del vino*," the contessa called before the waiter reached the table.

"Spiace, signora," he apologized. Why were waiters always absent when a person needed them, and pesky and persistent when they didn't?

Louis hoped the wine would quiet the conversation. In his family, a good meal or wine could completely sidetrack the conversation, which would never again return to the topic that had set off the argument. Food and wine, the great sedatives.

"What will you take, Louis?" the contessa asked, her expression brightening.

Louis felt forced to look at the woman who studied him, seemingly scrutinizing every detail of his face.

Though he'd been looking at the menu, he hadn't really been reading it and had no real idea what was on it. Instead, he'd been focusing on the slightly frayed sleeve of his shirt, a detail he was certain the contessa had noticed.

"I haven't decided yet," he said nervously, recognizing that he'd begun lying, too, albeit a tiny lie seemingly of no consequence. Still, he felt that the contessa knew, sensing that he hadn't been looking at the menu at all.

"Ah, well our conversation has probably been distracting, but we'll discuss this a little while later before Claudia gets too heated up. So let's have that wine the waiter is bringing now and then order lunch, no?"

Claudia glared at her mother and then quickly dropped her gaze to the menu sitting atop her plate. She opened the menu slowly and deliberately, as if unsure what she would find there.

There was an uncomfortable silence. Louis watched the two women study their menus with a focus and determination that reminded him of college entrance exams. He scrutinized the menu, but moments later, couldn't recall what he'd read. When the waiter arrived, Louis realized he would have to choose something hastily, something or anything.

Contessa Baggi gave the waiter a nod of approval, and like the first rain of spring, the sound of the red wine splashing in the glasses came as a relief. Louis thought the respite might be short-lived.

When the waiter turned to Louis, he read off the first item that caught his eye, *ravioli con formaggi dolci* in butter sage sauce. For his second, he ordered a simple salad, but he already knew he'd ordered like a common tourist. The contessa and Claudia both ordered Venetian specialties studded with creatures found in the nearby sea. They were at one of the best restaurants in the city, after all, but he had ordered a dish that had as little to do with Venice as pizza.

The waiter nodded and hurried off across the creaking parquet floor. At least he didn't grimace when Louis ordered. Did Claudia's mother? Louis grabbed for his wine, noticing that the eager arms of his two tablemates had shot forward at the same time. Were they all seeking distraction or stoking the fire?

"*A Venezia*," Claudia toasted, her cheeks still bright pink.

Her mother reacted not at all, but lifted her glass.

Glasses clinked, and Louis tried not to gulp the wine. He preferred to be doing a shot, drinking something with more punch than simple red wine. Still, he was grateful for something with alcohol in it, something that would calm his nerves. He hated lying and pretending, which was probably one of the reasons he had to leave home. In some ways, though, he wondered if he could ever completely escape it. Was the truth as much a part of life as myth? At times, the two seemed to intersect at a point where there was no telling the one from the other.

"*Allora*," the contessa said brightly, lightly smacking her lips after taking a long sip of the wine. "Where were we then?"

Louis' spirits sank. The Baggi family was apparently nothing like the Howard family. And he would be made to suffer.

"Mamma, I don't know what else to tell you. I need to stay here. I'm on the cusp of something different, something I can do on my own that feels right," Claudia said hastily, as if she'd mulled over the words since silence overtook the table. "I need to be in Venice now, not in school, or attending dinners in Rome. That's not what I want to do."

"And that is all? These are your reasons?" The mother stared at her daughter while she swirled the wine in her glass.

"And for Louis," Claudia lied, returning her mother's stare.

"You are certain?" The contessa asked, continuing to swirl her glass as if she were mixing paint.

"Of course. I want to see where it goes, to try it out."

The contessa sighed, shaking her head slowly while diverting her eyes from Claudia's face to the wine. "Then I regret that I have to tell you—and I'm sorry, Louis—but a mother must speak her mind. Under any other circumstances I would not be so rude, but I can tell you, *carissima*, that this man does not love you."

Oh, God, she knew. He hadn't acted well enough, had somehow given away Claudia, and let her down. And if Claudia were to have any chance, he would have to give the performance of his life, persuading the contessa that he truly loved Claudia. Only, he was certain that he couldn't do it, couldn't act his way out of a paper bag. He couldn't even look at the woman, staring instead at a commotion at the door to the restaurant.

A group of noisy tourists entered the massive doorway, most lingering outside in the hallway. The obstreperous Americans, which he recognized by their laughter and general loudness, followed the *maître d'* across the glowing, creaking parquet floor and to a large table just behind them. Louis wished he were with them, about to enjoy a painless, carefree lunch.

"Oh, my God," a shrill voice sounded from the group. "There's your friend from last night—what's his name—oh, Louis, that's right, Louis!"

Other diners gazed at the woman while the *maître d'* formed a frown of disapproval. Before Louis could differentiate the shrill woman from her fellow travelers, he'd already re-formed her image in his mind.

He couldn't recall her name, but she provided it as she marched up to the table.

"Irene!" she announced, looking him in the eye and smiling. "Irene Carney, from Harry's Bar, last night! Of course you remember me."

Oh, God, why right then? Louis scanned the other tourists, wondering if Tad was there, too. Given the how things were going with the contessa, though, he couldn't help feeling some relief.

"You shouldn't have hurried off last night—we would have had fun. Really. You're so mysterious, such a stranger. Tad filled me in on you, though, so you're less of a stranger than you were last night," she chirped.

Though Louis didn't turn his head to look at them, he sensed Claudia and her mother staring at Irene. Then Tad walked up behind Irene.

"You're everywhere in Venice and nowhere at all, Louis Howard." Tad extended his oversize hand, tightly clasping Louis' shoulder.

Louis was suddenly fearful, realizing that he would disappoint Claudia within minutes. Bad enough that her mother would have it confirmed that they were lying, but to have it proven before her by two strangers would undoubtedly provoke her. And just when she was preparing to tell her daughter to drop him. Though he felt some pleasure that she'd probably sensed something foul in the air, he also felt a vague disappointment and longing. While he certainly didn't want to marry or date Claudia, he liked to think that others might think him good enough to do so. Instead, he suddenly felt very uncouth, very American, and very gay. And a very bad liar.

Claudia would be forced to leave, wouldn't she? More than anyone else, she was the one he relied on, his one real connection in a city of comer's and goers', of furtive glances, and thick, old doors that clicked ominously when they closed.

And things would undoubtedly get worse in the following minutes. His tongue seemingly frozen in his mouth, he wasn't certain what to say. Should he introduce Tad and Irene to the Baggi's? If the two stayed any longer, he felt it would be necessary. But if he waited a moment, maybe they'd figure out they weren't welcome. As far as they knew, it could be a business lunch. He could help them figure it out by acting reserved; civil, but not overly friendly—but then, wasn't that how he'd acted the night before with little effect?

Irene didn't allow him the luxury of deciding, however.

"Hi, I'm Irene. Irene Carney," she announced breezily, leaning past Louis toward Claudia and her mother, extending her thin, bracelet-clad arm across the table and nearly colliding with the bottle of wine. She emitted a nervous giggle, acknowledging the near upset.

"Claudia Baggi. And this is my mother, Contessa Baggi."

Claudia acted nervous, irritated. He'd disappointed her, but what could he have done? He'd tried to tell her he wouldn't be any good at acting. And who knew what further disappointments lay ahead?

If Claudia appeared annoyed and impatient, her mother looked angry. Her brown eyes, which had seemed large, welcoming and seeking, if suspicious at first, now seemed leveled against the two intruders with what might have been a bit of the same mild disapproval Louis felt directed toward him after their introduction.

"*Piacere*," she replied evenly, the corners of her mouth dropping into a near frown.

Tad's head popped up over Irene's shoulder. "Ciao. I'm Tad."

Contessa Baggi nodded while Claudia barely echoed his greeting.

"I grew up with this guy—in Chicago," he said cheerily.

"I see," the contessa acknowledged politely. She leaned forward, suddenly smiling at Tad, as if to invite his confidence.

"He's hiding out in Venice, you know. Keeping a very low profile," he said, grinning conspiratorially.

"I've always said that Venice is a place where people hide," the contessa said with emphasis. "Did you know that that is precisely the reputation it has in Italy?"

"For some—but certainly not for all," Claudia interjected, her cheeks turning from pink to red.

How was Louis to salvage the meeting? If Tad and Irene stayed any longer, they'd undoubtedly say something that would ruin their story, even if it already appeared that the contessa didn't believe it. Maybe it would be possible to persuade her, but not with his two compatriots hovering over the table. He guessed that Claudia sensed it, too. He saw it in her worried-looking eyes and the way she clutched her throat. But once the two left, the topic of conversation would return to him and Claudia, and that thought made him nearly as nervous. Still, if they didn't somehow persuade the contessa, if they couldn't get her to agree to let Claudia stay, then she would leave. He regretted that they hadn't thought of a better plan. How had everything unraveled so quickly?

"What do people hide from?" Tad asked, as if on cue.

Was Claudia's mother paying him to say these things?

"Many things, I think. Families, fear, responsibility, love, oh, it can be many things," she said noncommittally. "Too many to list them all."

"What do you guess that Louis is hiding from?" Irene chirped loudly.

That was too much.

"Tad, Irene! I know you're having fun," Louis said, his voice strident. "But maybe some other time, okay? I'm having lunch with Claudia and her mother, and we've just met. You'll miss your lunch with your group, anyhow."

He glanced nervously at the contessa who observed him feline-like, while continuing to swirl the wine in her glass.

"Are we getting the brush-off again?" Irene moaned. "Do you need to take this hiding out thing so far? We found you. And we won't tell anyone—well, hardly anyone—where you are. So quit with the games, okay? Would it hurt to spend a few hours with some fellow Americans?"

"And a neighbor?" Tad chimed in, his eyebrows raised.

"It's just that I'm busy now. Work's busy and I'm having lunch."

"He doesn't even mention his boyfriend," Irene laughed. "That must take up a lot of your time, too, eh?" Irene winked knowingly, smiling broadly. "That's what the big hurry was *last* night, right?"

Shit. Louis felt like he'd been stabbed in the chest. Not surprising, though. Had Claudia's mother understood "boyfriend"? Was the game up? Maybe she thought Irene had meant a friend who happened to be male. He peered over at Claudia, who looked dejectedly at her empty plate. The contessa didn't seem to have reacted, though. In fact, she studied her menu distractedly, allowing them to have their conversation. She probably hadn't picked up on the significance of what that big mouth Irene had said, he decided.

"Look," Claudia explained, turning to Tad and Irene and sounding like the New Yorkers she once lived among, "It was nice to meet you both, but I'm afraid we're having a private lunch and have a lot to talk about." She then smiled, though her crimson cheeks and neck gave her away. "Would you mind excusing us?"

It was now Irene's turn to look exasperated. "Is everyone in Venice so … so *private*, so hurried? I thought Italians were laid back, easy-going, but so far it seems like everyone is uptight about something."

Tad laughed. "Don't let Louis Howard color your opinion of Italians. He's a Chicagoan remember."

"We'll let you go—*sorry* to interrupt," Irene muttered, but she hardly appeared contrite. "If you finish your business, we'll be over there." She gestured toward the long table set nearby. "But I'm quickly getting tired of begging you to let me buy you a drink."

She nodded at Claudia and her mother, waving carelessly at Louis before clasping Tad's arm and pulling him toward their table, away from the oversize square table placed next to the open French doors where the March sun shone serenely into the room. "I don't know why I'm always chasing men that I can't possibly have. I guess you were right—I'm just a silly fashion girl."

The table lapsed into silence which lasted until the waiter timidly approached. "Is everything okay?"

Claudia nodded at the waiter solemnly, grimacing. Her mother waved her hand dismissively. "*Tutto a posto*," she said.

The waiter gave a slight bow and left. Claudia's mother picked up her wine glass and took a long drink. "I am thinking, Claudia …"

Had she changed her mind? Did the commotion with Tad and Irene somehow work in their favor?

"Yes, Mamma?"

"I'm thinking now that I have seen you here and met you, that I was very wrong."

"Yes?" Claudia said, hope creeping into her voice.

"I wasn't sure that you knew what you were doing here, but I thought perhaps when I saw you, I would realize that you were sorting things out, as Americans say. Now I realize that isn't exactly the case."

"No?" Claudia said, looking perplexed.

"No. I don't think that's it at all." She took another long sip of her wine, smacking her lips softly and nearly without sound, as if to say "*voila*."

Louis moved unconsciously forward in his seat, hovering over his empty charger. When his lunch arrived, he wouldn't be able to eat it. He could drink wine, but his queasy stomach wouldn't handle food.

"What do you think it is? What are you trying to say?" Claudia stared at her mother, gripping her wine glass, her other hand fluttering around her collar.

Shaking her head disapprovingly, her mother frowned. "I think you're lying. And that is something new for you, a development that I don't like at all. I don't think you've ever lied to me. Argued, yes. Disagreed, certainly. But not deliberate lying."

"What?" Claudia's eyes opened wide, but Louis saw plainly that she was guilty.

"Please, *cara*, don't protest, you just make it worse. Don't," she said, placing her glass carefully back on the table.

Louis saw the contessa's hand trembling. Was she so angry with her daughter lying to her, or was it something else?

Claudia took a loud deep breath, looked at both her mother and Louis, then at her plate, and finally out the enormous, yawning doorway into the canal and the sky beyond. She nodded her head slowly. "So that is that?" she asked quietly.

"I think it has to be," her mother replied soberly, and went back to swirling the wine in her glass, though her trembling hand caused the wine to slosh unevenly against the sides of the glass.

"That's all then, that's the end of the discussion?" Claudia asked, her voice high and thin. Her small hand formed a fist, which lay next to the knife and fork sitting beside her empty plate.

"Sì," her mother nodded, sighing audibly.

Claudia sighed, too, staring out the doorway at the sky again. Her eyes might have been seeking cloudbanks or flying birds—Louis couldn't tell—but they moved around as silence fell heavily, enveloping the table. For his part, he decided he wouldn't speak, unable to think of what he might say to break the spell. He felt the imposter, wondering if either of the women even remembered he was still sitting there. Maybe he should get up quietly and leave. He observed Claudia again, who softly chewed the inside of her mouth, pulling her still-flushed cheek inward. She appeared lost, uncertain, but then she broke her faraway gaze, glanced at Louis, and gave him a quick wink. *What was she up to?*

"Okay, I understand, and I won't fight it, Mamma. That's the way it must be then."

The contessa smiled brightly, swirling the wine even faster. She brought the glass just below her nose, inhaling deeply. "That's good," she said with finality, smacking her lips quietly. "There's no reason to fight about it, after all."

"No. I really do understand," Claudia said evenly, her voice no longer trembling. "If I want your money, then I must follow your rules. It's always been that way, and there's no reason why it should change now that I'm an adult."

Her mother smiled again faintly, obviously pleased. "So, will you come to Rome right away then or do you need to get your things together before leaving? Tie up loose ends?"

"No," Claudia said, glancing again at Louis.

"No, what?" her mother asked.

"No, I'm not going to Rome."

Her mother set the glass on the table unevenly, the wine sloshing sloppily against its sides. "I'm confused. I thought we'd reached an understanding."

"We have," Claudia said, returning her mother's gaze.

"But you won't stay *here*? Please tell me that," the contessa asked, her bejeweled hand patting the table.

"No, I'll stay in Venice," Claudia answered.

"With no money?" her mother asked, her voice incredulous.

"I can make some money," she said timidly, her cheeks turning pink again. Then she shrugged.

"But life will be much harder for you. I don't think you realize."

"I realize. Maybe I won't enjoy the comedown so much, but I guess I have to do it this way if I want to stay." She reclined slightly, leaning her shoulder against the tall chair back.

"Are you trying to blackmail me?" the contessa asked, her expression hardening.

"No. You've let me know very plainly where you stand, and I'm merely doing the same. I don't want to return to Rome—I've already told you that. And I want to stay here, so to do that, I have to work and earn my own money. And use what I already have—"

"You won't use the small amount that *Babba* left you?"

"If I need to. It's *my* money."

"It would be so much easier, make so much more sense if you were reasonable and came back to Rome. Wouldn't it be so much easier?" she cajoled, slapping the table softly again, hitting the padded top with each point she made. "I told your *babba* it would be a mistake to leave you money and now I'm proven right."

"It's my money and I don't want to be in Rome. I already told you that. And Louis will help me out—he's already said he would."

Claudia's mother clucked her tongue, shaking her head sharply and jerkily. Picking up her wineglass, she took a large sip and then drank again. She didn't set the glass down, but glared across the table first at Louis, then at her daughter.

Louis felt himself moving back in his chair. He realized the woman was truly angry. Yes, he wanted more than anything that Claudia stay in Venice, but maybe he'd hurt her cause more than he'd helped it. He fidgeted uncomfortably under the harsh gaze of the contessa, waiting for her to speak.

"So, you prefer to stay in Venice away from your family with this *finocchio*?" she asked petulantly, gesturing condescendingly at Louis. "That's what you choose?"

"Mother, now you're sounding crazy. Don't act awful—"

Maybe he should leave. Of course, he knew the word finocchio, the locals' equivalent of faggot. Things were likely to get messier, so maybe he should just leave. So, the contessa had heard that big mouth Irene's comment. Well, Tad and his friend had certainly done enough damage during their short visit.

"I think I'm going now," he announced, standing up awkwardly, interrupting Claudia.

"Don't be ridiculous," Claudia fired back. "The food is coming right now. And it's just an argument."

The contessa didn't protest, but looked absently at her wineglass. Yes, he could see that she preferred he go.

"Please assure me that you're not in love with him," she said, turning to Louis. "I have nothing against you, really, but I am just looking after my daughter. She comes first for me. Certainly you understand."

So it was always, with all mothers everywhere. What would his mother have said about the situation? Likely, she would have told him to storm away from the table, accepting insults from no one, least of all a contessa who had created an unhappy, lost daughter.

Much as he wanted to stay for his friend, he couldn't. Things could get uglier, and he was only aggravating Claudia's mother. He quietly opened his wallet and pulled out a 50,000 lire note, which he set in the middle of the table. It was more than he could afford for a lunch, but more than anything he wanted to show the woman that she was no better than he was.

"Please don't insult me," Claudia's mother said, shaking her head.

"I'm just returning the favor," he said reflexively, then instantly regretted it. But Claudia's eyes smiled as he realized he'd insulted a contessa, an action that even a hundred years ago might have put him in prison.

"Signora." He nodded at the contessa from where he stood, making it clear that he didn't intend to kiss her or take her hand.

"Piacere," she answered dryly.

"Louis," the contessa called as he turned to walk away, saying his name as if she had known him for years. "One more thing."

He turned, overriding the temptation to continue walking, to ignore completely a calling contessa—now that would've gotten to her! But he wanted to hear what she had to say.

"There are things that you don't know, lots of things that play into my feelings about this situation. Far more than you can imagine. Claudia doesn't know either. They're not secrets, just history and even superstition, some would say. And I'm not a superstitious woman, but I know some things about this place and the people here."

"What do they have to do with me, with Claudia, or our friendship?" he asked.

"They say that Rome wasn't built in a day, yes? Well, Venice wasn't built in a day either. What do you know of Venice? Marco Polo? The palazzi? The Guggenheim? And you probably favor a regular visit to Harry's? Yes, these are all very typical *American* impressions of the city."

"If you're going to lecture me, I'll leave right now," he interrupted, feeling his face turn hot. Claudia seemed to be cheering him on, but she also looked interested in what her mother had to say, as if she were revealing some new side to her blue-blooded persona.

"No. I have strong feelings, obviously, and I'll try not to lecture. But there is much that neither of you understands—that most people don't know. You know the history of this city, don't you, how it was founded? By ancient people fleeing persecution, *assassini.* They hid on these swampy islands, withdrawn and isolated from the rest of the world. And in the Dark Ages, things were very dark in Venice indeed. The plague struck here remarkably hard. Religious zealots fought with pagans and hedonists. And if you didn't lose a family member from the plague, you lost them to the street battles."

The woman paused a moment, reached for her water and took a sip, beckoning both of them to wait. She cleared her throat.

"And some of Claudia's family has ties to Venetians—or Romans who settled temporarily in Venice. That's what we believe, anyway. Because Venetians are unlucky, you know? Venice is an unlucky city—it has always lived precariously on the edge of death and despair," she said with a shrug.

"I don't get that feeling at all," Louis protested. "If the city were so sad, so cursed, why would it have such an impressive history, and why would so many people come to visit?"

He looked at the contessa differently, noticing that her eyes seemed suddenly sad. Was she afraid of losing her daughter, or was there something more? Why would she be afraid of her daughter living in Venice, a city that was a mere hour's flight from Rome, when she'd pushed her to move to New York, a day's travel away?

"You must stay awhile," said the contessa. "Stay and soak it up to understand. And by the time that happens, you are drawn into it, and you can't leave, despite knowing you should. If you do leave, you escape as a refugee. Venice stays with you always, in some way."

"This doesn't make sense, Mother. I disagree, and it's not at all what I've learned at school," Claudia said leaning in to join the conversation. "I knew people from Venice and they never struck me as refugees."

"Well, of course they don't teach these things in class. These are all the unspoken, the things about life you will never find written in a book, or discussed on TV. Is that so surprising? Do you think that every aspect of life has been covered in a university class, or in some book? No, there's much about life that neither of you know—that I don't know either. But this thing I do know—and that is that Venice is not what it appears. It's a sinking city, and during a particularly high tide, maybe you can sense this. Or perhaps you attribute it to the natural ebb and flow of life and the sea. But ignoring the reality, the deeper understanding of what's going on doesn't make it false—just misunderstood. Venice has always been sinking."

"But there are plenty of people who live here, and they seem happy to me." Louis thought of his landlord, the neighbors, and the family who operated the café. Of course, he'd always heard that Venice was sinking. But wasn't every city threatened with something—falling into the ocean, being smothered by a landslide, or shaken to rubble? Nobody thought of Los Angeles as a dying city, but one day an earthquake could shake it right into the Pacific.

"Maybe they make the best of it," said the contessa. "You know the city continues to lose population. The only people who want to move here are Americans and Germans, romantics. And most of them are hiding from something or vainly attempting to create a life they've been denied at home. They are living in the past—or playing some ridiculous role."

Again, when she said *Americans*, it was with disdain. So why had she sent her daughter to New York if she was truly anti-American?

"And the city once had a number of opera houses—and now there is but one. Better known for what it *was* than what it is. That fact should tell you something about the fate of this place. The Bridge of Sighs is not named for lovers, but for the sadness that visits Venetians and the people who settle here—starting with the prisoners who first walked over that bridge. It's an unnatural place for a city—built half in the sea, floating on marshland and sinking slowly, gradually into the mud and water. It is for these reasons that Venetians sigh, because sadness and death are ever-present."

"Mother, that's absurd, really. You've never liked Venice—for whatever reason. It doesn't have enough class—it has *too* much snobbery. The food is bad, the people are cretins. The people aren't Christian enough. Why don't you just say you don't like the place? But you needn't condemn it for everyone. Or prohibit me from forming my own impressions or having my own experiences. You know, a lot of people like Venice, a lot of people come from around the world to see it."

"They come to see it, not live in it," she said, waving her hand through the air. The contessa sighed, shaking her head slowly. "Babba warned that I would one day have a daughter as headstrong as I was in punishment for what I put her through. Now I see that she was right. But she didn't fight me hard enough, and so I made mistakes. She didn't disown me, didn't cut me off. She funded the stupid decisions I made—actually funded them. Babba was far too indulgent."

"So why can't I get the same treatment as you did?" Claudia pleaded, leaning across the table.

"Because it was a mistake. Babba made a mistake—forgive me, Mamma." The contessa looked toward the ceiling and started crossing herself, but then stopped halfway and shook her head in disgust. "I won't contribute to your undoing the same way—well; I don't mean undoing—but bad decisions, the same way as Babba. Now you are making me say—and talk about—things I'd rather not discuss. Can't you simply obey your mother, consider her advice?"

Claudia's face clouded as if she were hearing some things for the first time, seeing her mother differently. Louis felt awkward again, hovering over the table like a scavenging bird at a picnic, as if he didn't belong there. The woman had wanted to say something to him, but now she was talking just to her daughter.

"But so far it is your decisions that have governed my life, Mamma. And they haven't made me happy. I went to the schools you chose, I dated the boys you chose, I even married the man you chose and moved to New York City. And look where it got me?"

"If every decision wasn't perfect, I'm willing to take the responsibility, but you must also accept responsibility for not trying—"

"Not trying?" Claudia's small fist struck the table, sending the wine and water trembling in the glasses. "That shows how little you understand."

The contessa shook her head slowly again, glancing harshly at Louis.

"It's nothing I did," he said. "Or am I to blame because I'm American and befriended your daughter?"

"If I've insulted you, I'm sorry. That was not my intention. I'm here to look after the interests of my daughter. I wish you no ill will, but by the same token, I have little interest in you. Maybe it would be best if you left now—I shouldn't have called you back, but I thought you might be persuaded with some additional information. I see now that I was mistaken."

Everything Claudia's mother said sounded vaguely insulting, as if he were too stupid to have understood.

"I think that's best, too," he said, leaning over her. "There's really little value in me hearing anything you have to say, and my time's probably better spent on educating myself in other, more useful ways. There are plenty of meddlesome mothers who make their daughters miserable. I can find plenty of similar advice elsewhere. It's hardly rare."

The contessa blinked.

Well, she was not the only one who could deliver insults. Was she so surprised that he would fight back? He glanced at Claudia. Would she forgive him for insulting her mother? It was one thing to hurl insults at your own family, but another entirely to have a friend do the same. But Claudia didn't seem to hear him. She continued staring at her mother, kneading her dinner napkin in her lap, seemingly pleading for him to leave, too.

Louis felt entirely self-conscious as he walked across the creaking floor of the restaurant, sensing all eyes on him. As if every diner in the place knew he was a finocchio, and a contessa just insulted and dismissed him. He was brilliant at wearing his shame. Funny how things like that followed you, no matter how far you went. He thought that such feelings would've been left behind him in Chicago. But the shame had simply followed him.

"Ay, Americano!" a familiar voice chirped. "If they won't have you, we'll take you."

In a blur of emotion, Louis hadn't even noticed he was walking right by the large table of Americans, including Irene and Tad. Couldn't they leave him alone?

"Gotta go. Sorry," he said, glancing in their direction, but not slowing.

Irene sidled up to his elbow, clasping it timidly. "Aw, come on. I saw it didn't go so well over there—we were watching. Maybe it helped for us to stop by and break up the tension a little. That old lady's face makes me pucker just looking at it. What's her deal?"

He suddenly wanted to explain, yearning to tell even someone as annoying as a stranger that Claudia's mother was cruel, controlling, and rude, but Irene wouldn't understand.

"Would like to, but I can't. Really," he smiled falsely, turning to her slightly.

"Maybe she'd be happier if you slipped her the giftie I put in your coat pocket last night," she giggled.

Louis snorted.

"There's no sense in it Renie," Tad called from the table. "Just let 'im go."

For an instant, Louis thought to stay and sit with them. Wouldn't that prove Tad, his old neighbor, wrong? The guy thought he knew everything about him, but maybe he didn't. In the end, though, sitting in the same room with Claudia's mother. What he needed was a stop at the café for a drink. By himself. And then an afternoon of writing. Things hadn't gone as planned, but it looked like Claudia would be staying in Venice. And that called for celebrating.

Then he'd need to think about what Claudia should do, help in some way. Saying she could live without her trust fund took only words. Actually living without money took courage and who-knew-what? He'd never had the luxury of living off someone else's money; he'd always worked. So he couldn't imagine what it must be like to walk away from money like that. What if he'd been wrong to encourage her to spurn her mother when she didn't really have anything to do?

"Just one drink. What'll that hurt you? You seem like you need the company," Irene said, trying to steer him toward their table. "The old lady upset you, eh?"

Irene seemed to be one of those people who always tried to fix things, that had limitless optimism that they had the power to make things right.

"Thanks, anyway," he said, gently unclasping her hand from his elbow. "But I have to go."

"Tad was dead right about you." She looked expectantly at his face, awaiting a reaction.

Louis shrugged. "You'll never know. And he doesn't either. Ciao, Irene," he said dismissively.

"Okay, bye then, if that's how you prefer it," she warbled in a mocking tone, her voice rising. She snorted a little, looking exasperated.

"Enjoy the rest of your trip," he said, knowing he didn't really care. Maybe he judged her harshly, but he never did like busybodies, and especially ones who were always trying to fix everyone's lives and insert themselves and their guidance where it wasn't welcome.

The truth was, he preferred drinking a glass of prosecco by himself to spending a lunch hour with Irene and Tad—or anyone remotely like them. No, if those were his choices, he'd remain alone. He'd gone halfway around the world with the precise aim of avoiding people like these—especially anyone from his life in Chicago. Not that anything terrible happened there, but he wasn't any longer the same person he'd been when he lived there, and he didn't want to be that person anymore, didn't want to still be a dumb kid living in his parents' squat old graystone in a neighborhood where everyone knew him. At least here, he could figure out who he was and what he wanted, without smothering under the heavy cloak of expectation.

As he walked back down the posh hall of the hotel, he glanced over his shoulder half expecting them to rush after him, Irene's new

Armani coat billowing behind her. But no one entered the hallway as he walked briskly through it and into the lobby. Within minutes, he was out of the quiet, dark, and somber atmosphere of the hotel and into the bright light of daytime.

In a way, though, he didn't feel like he'd completely left the Americans behind, or Claudia's mother, for that matter. Thoughts of them followed him as he prowled the back streets, the smallest ones he knew, or half remembered, avoiding tourist routes and haunts, and hoping to find the Venice of yesterday that didn't seem discovered, spoiled, or within reach of everyone he knew in Chicago.

He saw a toy wooden boat drifting in the green waters of the canal heading for the lagoon. He wondered if he could ever get so lost again in Venice. Standing atop a square bridge cut from blunt and mossy stone, he watched as a child spied the abandoned boat, quickly slipping from the grip of his mother's hand and rushing to the edge of the canal, leaning forward and grasping for the foot-long mast bobbing just out of reach of his chubby fingers in the dark green water.

"Dio, Dio!" the mother screamed, chasing after her son. She pulled the boy back from the canal's edge, slapping the side of his face with surprising force. The child started to cry and then held the back of his hand over his face.

"Never, never!" she said sternly, grasping his shoulders and shaking him slightly. She then pulled his face into her chest, wrapped her slender arms around his torso and hugged him, looking relieved.

The woman suddenly looked up to where Louis stood watching. She didn't look angry, though, but seemed self-conscious. "They must learn," she said apologetically.

Louis smiled faintly; embarrassed that he'd been caught observing them. Of course, what she said made sense, but her trembling fear surprised him. After all, it wasn't as if serpents or monsters lurked in the canals that would suck or hold a person under. Falling in could hardly be the end of anyone. Only if no one saw a child fall in could something tragic happen. But Louis thought this woman overreacted, as if her child's falling in meant certain death, though she'd been right next to her son.

The toy boat bobbed to the other side of the canal, just below Louis, lodging itself against the stone bank at the foot of the bridge. He walked down the few steps, leaned over, and plucked the boat from the jade water. Walking back up across the cold stones of the bridge, he strode briskly to catch up to the mother and son who had already moved down the street. They turned a corner, and when Louis rounded the thick-walled, ochre-colored corner of a tall building, they'd disappeared behind a heavy iron gate. Racing to peer through the locked gate, he saw a sunny garden full of budding magnolias and honeysuckle with a whisper of green buds on the vines.

"I've brought your son's boat," he called to the woman's back, her son just ahead of her and barely visible.

Turning, she shook her head.

"*Vada*!" she called, shooing him with her hand. "Go!"

"I'll leave it here by the gate," he explained, perplexed. "The boat, I'll leave it here."

"No, take it with you," she countered, sounding exasperated.

Turning, she disappeared into a hallway, her shoe strike echoing in the courtyard and out to the passage where Louis stood, the boat hanging limply from his hand. He walked to the nearby canal, dropping the boat into the opaque water with a splash, and watching the current right the boat and carry it slowly but deliberately away.

Chapter Five

Anna could hear hushed, somber voices, laced with undertones of concern and disapproval.

"She's on the balcony doing nothing. I don't think she wants to come in. I asked if I could bring her anything, too, and she said she wanted nothing."

A muffled voice responded, Contessa Lunardini's. She couldn't hear what the woman said, but the tone seemed exasperated, annoyed. The slippery sounding Venetian dialect, which had once struck her as melodic, sophisticated even, now sounded malformed, muddy. The maid asked what she should do.

"Should I ask signora when she expects to leave?" the maid asked sotto voce.

The contessa didn't answer immediately, not that Anna could hear her response anyway. A boat passed on the canal below, splashing its dirty wake against the empty pier and palace walls below, drowning out the old woman's response. When the whining engine of the boat had faded, and the water in the canal had gone still once more, she strained to hear the conversation, but there were no longer any voices.

Maybe the maid would announce herself again, walking tentatively onto the balcony, shielding her eyes from the sun, but avoiding Anna's gaze. Perhaps the diminutive woman would ask her to leave, tell her it was time to be going without ever saying so.

No one approached the open doors, though, walking across the wide, creaky floorboards. Anna cocked her ear toward the doors, seeking the sound of a whisper or an approaching footfall. There were no sounds, only sparrows chirping in a nearby tree.

The women intended to leave her alone, that must have been it.

It was clear that Anna needed to leave Venice. She had cried enough, mourned enough to make her physically ill. She hadn't eaten in days and had begun losing weight, her once tailored dresses hanging limply on her. Still she had no appetite.

She chided herself for having been foolish enough to hope and dream, to begin to fall in love. Hadn't her mother warned that the young placed too much emphasis on romantic love? When she pursued marriage again, she vowed it would be for different reasons.

She had loved. And that thought consoled her. Her dreams and plans had evaporated, disappearing like the charm the city had once held. Her life had been flipped to its ugly side, with all life's potential horrors and brutality revealed. She knew the truth then, albeit at a younger age than most people did. And some people never drank from this cup. She saw herself becoming one of those wise, vaguely cold women defined by the tragedy that had shaped their lives.

She could—would—accept her fate. Life certainly wasn't over, and she could still fulfill her grandfather's dream, which had become her own. He'd been right after all, had tried to warn her, but she hadn't listened.

A songbird landed on the balcony rail, singing a few notes and casting what seemed a sidelong glance at her. Was it tired from a flight across the sea, heading toward the sanctuary of the cool forests of the Alps or Sweden? She would like to fly with the bird, to be so light, leaving everything behind as if it were last year's nest. She yearned to find herself in a strange place where she knew no one, would be able to even speak the language. That would be the way to start life again, not to return to Rome, tail between her legs, always branded a tragic character. That *would* be her life, though, as much as she might fantasize otherwise.

Silly to be envious of a bird, she realized, shaking her head gloomily. At least she recognized the absurdity of the thought.

So she would leave Venice, which suddenly struck her as dirty and provincial. The brackish, brown water, which floated down the canals, softly lapping at the palazzi and houses like a well-behaved fountain, hid death. The whole city, every crumbling facade, and faded, cracked, and peeling corner fresco of the Madonna, reeked of decay. She longed to see automobiles, to hear the modern whine of Vespas thirty-strong racing down the curving streets of Rome, driving thoughts of death from her head.

A woman walked onto the little stone footbridge crossing the canal below, the same woman—she was certain of it—that had struck up a conversation with her in the corner café when she'd first arrived.

"You are new to Venice, no?" she'd asked.

The woman was middle-aged, maybe forty? She dressed like a much older woman, though, draped in black and gray with a few pieces of simple jewelry and a dull silk scarf tied around her neck. She looked like a widow, Anna thought.

"I am," she had admitted.

Something about the woman didn't seem right, as if she were carrying around some anger or disappointment that had poisoned her. She supposed being a widow might do that. They conversed about basic things, what quarter she lived in, where the best cafés were, and which were the best stalls in the fish market.

They'd enjoyed a friendly conversation until the woman asked where she lived.

"At Palazzo Lunardini," she'd answered reluctantly, knowing the woman would realize that Anna would not be doing any shopping at the fish market herself.

The woman's lips pursed as she quickly gathered her bags, telling Anna she would see her again. Maybe at one of the cafés she'd recommended. "*Il Principe* is my favorite," she'd said, but she sensed the woman didn't want to talk to her again.

As the woman had walked away, she noticed her stooped shoulders, her slow and methodical walk. She decided the woman looked sad, not angry. Maybe she'd been wrong about her.

And suddenly after so many months, there was the same woman on the bridge just below the balcony. Anna leaned forward to see where she was going, and at that exact moment, the woman looked up at her, as if she'd been coming to visit and expected her to be on the balcony in that very spot.

The woman, dressed in gray and blue, issued a half wave, wearing a wan smile.

"I was looking for you," she called to her. "Can I come up and speak with you?"

She found it strange that the woman remembered where she lived—rather, where she was staying. Their conversation had been so short, yet for some reason she had remembered it, too.

"It's not a good time," Anna called down, softly as she could. Could they hear her inside?

She signaled for the woman to wait, and then ran over to the open balcony doors and closed them quietly. She then returned to the balustrade and leaned over toward the strange woman.

"I'm a guest here, and it's not possible for me to have anyone visit." She wasn't so certain she wanted to talk to the woman, anyway. Why was she there?

"Would you like to meet me at *Il Principe*? To talk? That's the café I recommended. Do you remember?"

"Yes, I remember," Anna answered reluctantly, wondering what she wanted.

"If not now maybe another time?" the woman asked in an almost familiar tone, though she continued to use the formal tense.

"I'm sorry," she said awkwardly. "But it's not a good time for me. There's been an accident." Accident seemed such a silly word to use, so inadequate to describe what had happened.

"I know," the woman said, nodding her head slowly, thoughtfully. "I didn't think that you had much to say when I met you, if you'll forgive me for saying so, but now I realize I was wrong." The woman gazed up at her, her face consoling and inquisitive.

"What do you mean?" She found the woman offensive somehow. And how had she connected Anna with the story about Vittorio?—ah, silly how she could forget that Venice was a city of eavesdroppers and gossipers! Still, it was strange that she had remembered her and their odd little conversation. And remembered where she had said she lived. Palazzo Lunardini. The rest the woman must have surmised.

"I think you know," the woman said, rubbing her arm. "Just to talk some more. Would you like that?"

The woman pulled at the scarf around her neck, another drab, silk one tied sloppily. She looked nervous, sad.

"I would like to, but I'm leaving. Did you know I was leaving?" Now that she'd said the words, she couldn't wait to leave the city. It was as if the woman had been sent there to drive her away. She was haunting.

"No, I didn't. But I wondered if you might." The woman smiled wanly, raising her forearm above her head to block the bright sun that made her squint. "Are you sure you wouldn't like to talk?"

Anna suddenly felt like she might cry. Why did she want to talk about the accident? Was she some sort of angel of darkness, one of those ghoulish characters who seemed to enjoy death? And why did the woman think she would want to talk to a total stranger about something so personal?

Oh, my Vittorio, she thought, nearly crying.

She shook her head slowly, afraid that if she spoke, she might sob, sinking onto the worn surface of the terrace and never getting up again. The presence of the woman was unsettling, reminding her anew of what had happened, of all that she had lost.

"You're not alone, you know," the woman said, her voice shaking.

What a pithy, inane thing to say. She looked at the woman disdainfully.

"You don't know, do you? No one bothered to tell you, did they?" The woman looked genuinely sad, consoling.

"What?" she mouthed, her voice barely audible. "Tell me what?"

"Venice is a city of death," she said quietly. "It's always been that way." Her voice was melodic and mysterious, laced with sympathy.

"Why would you say such a horrible thing?" She should have left the balcony, gone inside to her room and closed the door and curtains. What crazy talk it was.

"I lost a child—*my* child," the woman said, looking around and then returning her pleading eyes upward to Anna. "She drowned in the canal. She wasn't watched, you know. And everyone knows that you must keep watch over children in Venice. It's not a city for children. The canals will take them if you're not careful."

"I'm sorry," Anna said. So this is why she had sought her, to have someone to share her sorrow.

"You know, there are many old stories and traditions about Venice," she said quietly, but just loud enough for Anna to hear. "People won't tell you about them—and I bet he didn't tell you about them did he?"

She despised hearing the woman refer to Vittorio at all—who was she?

"The first Venetians made a pact with the sea, with Neptune. They weren't Christians then, so they had the Greek and Roman gods. And Venice is built on little swampy islands, as much a part of the sea as land—maybe belonging more to the sea. During storms and high tides, these islands returned to the sea, to Neptune. And so, if the first people to come here intended to take the islands from the sea, to give them to Ceres and Athena, then they had to give something back to Neptune. So they give a child every so often—the offering that pleases Neptune the most because it's the greatest sacrifice. And temperamental Neptune sometimes just takes, and that is what happened with you. You see—"

"That's ridiculous," Anna shouted, her voice rising. "I don't believe any of that—that's absurd. I'm a Christian."

When was the last time she'd uttered such a statement, thought so ardently about religion, or believed so strongly? The woman's talk frightened her, made her think of the devil. The woman was crazy, had somehow dealt with the death of her child by turning to old mythology, to old pagan myths.

"I'm sorry," the stranger said, disappointment etched on her face. "Whether you believe or not, you're Venetian now. You see, you're part of a long, unhappy tradition that's as old as Venice itself. We like to think we're the city of lions, of trade, and love, but we owe a great debt to the sea—whether you call it Neptune or nature."

The woman shook her head sadly, before her face brightened as she sought Anna's eyes. "Please, come down and we can talk. That's the best way, no?"

"I don't think so," Anna said slowly, backing away from the balustrade. "I don't want to do that." The woman was obviously crazy, maybe made so by the grief of her lost child. When had she lost her child, she wondered, and how? She would like to know, but she would never talk to the woman again. And who could say whether the woman was even telling the truth?

The woman gazed at Anna as if she was an apparition, and she moved back a little toward the bridge so she could still see her. She looked sad again, her face frowning. "You are going?" she called, but it didn't sound like a question.

"Piacere," Anna answered, nodding, but feeling foolish. There was no pleasure in meeting her, and she wished there was something more fitting that she could say to let her know there were no hard feelings. She just wanted her gone, away from the street below and out of her mind. And if the stranger wouldn't leave, then she must.

"*Sarrebbe fosse piacere*," the woman answered. *It would have been a pleasure.*

Anna shook her head. She wouldn't be part of whatever the woman wanted her to share—even if she'd lost a child. She gave a little wave, nodding politely before backing away from the balustrade. When she could no longer see the woman, she turned quickly and went inside.

What was she frightened of—that the woman would rise and fly up to her on the balcony like some witch, to ask her one more time to talk, to force on her whatever tragedies and pain—as well as myths and tales—she'd been clinging to all these years?

Anna closed the doors behind her, turning the key to lock herself in. She then slowly, but deliberately closed the curtains.

She shouldn't look, but felt driven to peek out the window on the other side of the room that looked out over the canal and bridge. The window was ajar, and she peered out the gap and onto the bridge. The woman stood at the top of the bridge's arc, staring down the canal. What if she looked up and saw Anna standing there? It was best to get away from the window, leave the stranger as she was before she found her. As she stepped away, though, a figure caught her eye.

It was a desperate-looking man, about the same age as the woman. And he appeared to be headed directly toward her, as if they knew each other.

The man stopped just short of the woman, hovering at her elbow.

Anna leaned forward, cocking her ear toward the bridge. The man was speaking to the woman, but she didn't turn to acknowledge him. They both spoke quietly, maybe in a whisper. The woman looked unhappy, even angry. He stood behind her, looking contrite, sad. She could hear the soft hum of their voices rising from the bridge, carrying across the canal like the burble of a brook. She tried to hear, leaning farther out the window. The woman must have known him, though she wouldn't even turn to acknowledge him.

Then Anna caught pieces of their conversation.

"Unforgivable," the woman said, her voice rising.

The man apologized, kept saying, "*Ma sono passati tanti anni.*"

But so many years have passed.

The woman stood resolute, her eyes fixed on some distant point down the canal.

Had they been lovers? Was it her brother? Was the man responsible for the death of her child?

"*Mai, mai,*" the woman said.

Never forgive him?

The man swung his head mournfully, kicking his foot against the unyielding wall of the bridge.

"Leave me alone," the woman said loudly.

"Please," the man pleaded, tentatively grabbing her sleeve. She spun around, pushing his hand away.

"Leave me or I'll jump in the canal. The sight of you makes me ill."

With the voices of the two raised, Anna could hear nearly every word.

"What do you want from me? I'll do anything. I've said I'm sorry."

"I want you to leave me alone. Don't seek me out, avoid my sight. Can't you do that? Give me some peace?"

The woman shouted the last plea as a window on the other side of the canal creaked open. More eavesdroppers, Anna realized, as she knew that she herself had become one. Well, even more reason she needed to leave the city. But she couldn't keep her eyes from the couple on the bridge, wondering what had happened between them.

The man was handsome enough, but looked simple, working class. Standing idly behind her, he often shrugged his shoulders that were already drooped. He would move forward, then back, restless and fidgeting. His mouth would start to form a word, then stop. He looked defeated, resigned.

"I'll light twenty candles," he said, leaning toward her.

"What will that do? *Niente.*"

The woman was angry, her voice shaking and shrill. There were sides of people you might never see, and Anna would never have guessed the world-weary stranger who had spoken with such compassion to her, harbored such anger.

He must have been a lover, or husband maybe.

"Still, I'll light them. You have your ways, and I have mine. You used to light candles, you used to pray. Why suffer apart?"

"Niente!" she yelled again, raising her hand as if to strike the man. She turned away from him, staring with steely, bitter eyes down the canal.

Anna could see the man's pain, how he tucked his chin into his chest, how his shoulders drooped even farther. Only a parent or a lover could hurt you that much. And he was too young to be her father.

He drew near her back, whispering something. She stood stone-faced, looking at what on the empty, narrow canal? Was she thinking of jumping in, or thinking of how that canal might take her away forever?

She seemed to listen, and maybe even softened for a moment. But then Anna could see the hardness rush across her face again, like a shadow. She raised her hand as if to say *basta*.

Anna couldn't be certain, but she thought there was a glint of tears in the man's eyes. She felt sorry for him, longed to know what he'd done that was so unforgivable. But whom could she have asked? The maids were the only ones that might be friendly to her, and it would be awkward to ask them such questions. The only other person she could ask would be Vittorio's mother, but she knew that the woman simply wished for Anna to leave.

And she may as well, for there was nothing for her in Venice.

Did she feel a bond with the man because he was in pain, too? But why then hadn't she felt this bond with the woman?

The man stared at the woman's back for another moment, standing silent, but continuing to fidget. When he left, he walked away quickly, looking over his shoulder before he turned off the canal onto a tiny, shadowy via.

The woman never looked up to watch the man leave, but her shoulders also drooped after he left. She turned her face and looked directly up at Anna who gasped and pulled back from the window. Anna felt as if the woman had known she'd been there all along.

"Of course it's not a mystery what she wants, is it?" a voice behind her—*in* the room—asked.

Anna jumped, spinning to find Contessa Lunardini standing

on the other side of the room. She hadn't even heard her come in or perhaps she'd been watching her eavesdrop the whole time.

"You're now a part of them, you know," she said with a chuckle. "That's the oldest informal society in Venice."

The woman's eyes had grim gray circles beneath them, and she seemed to have aged in the six days since the fire department had flipped over the motorboat and found her son's body floating beneath it.

"What do you mean?" Anna was taken aback that the contessa had entered the room, let alone that she was speaking to her. Did she come to apologize, to extract some comfort for herself from what would have been her daughter-in-law?

"This is the introduction few visitors to Venice receive. In case you're thinking of staying …"

The woman's face betrayed her feelings, forming a vague frown while her lip curled.

That was why she'd come to her room—she wanted Anna to leave Venice.

"I'm not staying—I'll return to Rome," Anna announced matter-of-factly. Staying in the city would be unbearable, where every view reminded her of her dead Vittorio, and the canals now made her feel uneasy. It was as if the lagoon and waters of the city had conspired to kill what was very nearly her fiancé. She would return to Rome where the suffering would at least be less and where the omnipresent, ever-shifting water that now reminded her of death wouldn't surround her.

The contessa nodded, as if pleased. Did she blame Anna for her son's death or did Anna simply remind her of her lost son? Whatever the reason, Anna grew increasingly uneasy. And now, with that strange woman seeking her on the streets, she felt that it was surely time for her to take a boat to the train station and depart for Rome.

"You must have missed it. Did you?" the contessa asked. She seemed genuinely interested, friendly, but still with that reserved, observing manner that Anna had noticed immediately upon meeting her.

"I was getting used to Venice, actually, so I didn't miss Rome so much," she explained, as if her coming to like Venice, of having been persuaded and having come to love the city, would be some comfort to the woman, a comfort to herself.

"You would have brought my son back there, wouldn't you? Eventually? You'd have been content in Venice for a few years, but then you would do what everyone else does: leave."

It almost felt like the woman wished to argue, as if they were going to carry on with battles that might have occurred had Vittorio lived. Anna, fooled for a moment into thinking that the woman was congenial, now knew better. Maybe this woman did blame Anna for her son's death.

"Actually, that wasn't my thought at all," she said, trying not to sound angry. "At first, Venice seemed slow, quiet—an out of the way place where nothing ever really happened. A city that had used up its future and lived on its history."

Anna glanced at the contessa who seemed to be frowning. She was certain that the old Venetians who remained loyal to their city, and still loved it, must have been constantly offended by Milanese, Romans—and even New Yorkers—talking about the place in such terms. The woman seemed to want her to continue.

"After spending time here, though, I realized it's still very much alive. From the glassblowers and artists in Murano, to the fish market and the artists. And then there are so many movie stars that come here. Sure, it's not as lively as Rome, but it has its own allure, and I fell for it. I really came to imagine myself living here."

She thought this last confession would please the contessa, but the woman looked even more distressed, nervously clenching her small fists.

"And that was the attraction? The city?" the woman asked, not bothering to hide her irritation.

So she doubted that she had loved her son, was that it? Anna could feel the woman's displeasure floating in the thick, jasmine-scented air. She sensed that the contessa was on the verge of telling her unpleasant things, of saying cruel things. Maybe it was best that she left immediately.

"Of course not. You misunderstand," Anna said, moving away from the woman and toward a towering old armoire standing between the two sets of French doors leading onto the balcony. "Vittorio was the only reason I came here. He made me love the place, though I was already growing fond of it on my own. I'd decided that I could be happy living here."

"You were planning to move here then?" she challenged, cocking her head as if the idea might be new to her.

Anna didn't like the direction of the conversation, but she answered reluctantly. "I was. Vittorio had asked me to."

"And then did he ask you to marry him?" she said, following Anna to the armoire.

The contessa's lips were pursed as if it were a question she couldn't help asking, and one to which she wasn't certain she wanted to hear the answer.

Anna opened the creaking doors of the armoire with trembling hands, pulling out her suitcase and shoulder bag. She would run as if she were a bird sprung from the brush. Why had she waited so long to leave? Why hadn't she left the moment the funeral had ended? She trembled slightly, wondering if her sudden packing would anger the temperamental woman. Ever since the contessa had received the news of her son's death, Anna had worried that the words, which seemed framed and poised on the tip of the woman's tongue, would come rushing out of her small, frowning mouth in a torrent. The wiry, reserved woman had never seemed approachable or likable, but now that her son was dead, Anna found her unpredictable, caustic even. And the few times in a day when she saw her, she always looked like there was something she wanted to say. And perhaps that's why Anna had waited, to see what she had to say, and to comfort the mother of the man she'd loved. But now she could see that neither was reason enough for staying.

"I'd rather not say," she answered, leaning over her suitcase, her back to the woman. For some reason, it was important not to tell her. Hadn't she known or guessed that her son planned to ask Anna to marry him? Maybe she hadn't approved. For while Anna did have a name in her family, it didn't belong to her, as Vittorio had reminded. And if he'd known about her background, then certainly his mother did as well. And then hadn't Venetians always been insular, the type to marry their own? Who knew what Vittorio had planned to do? The answer was buried in the lagoon, or flowing out to sea, or maybe sifting through one of the reedy marshes on the nearby islands. She would never know for certain. The Venetian waters had taken her happiness, left her instead with questions, doubts, and a disapproving, petulant contessa.

Oddly, she experienced a sudden longing to attend Mass, but not at one of the local churches that smelled of damp and mildew, that reeked of death as certainly as a cemetery.

When she returned home, she would visit the Vatican, get lost wandering its wide halls, and get swept up in the steady stream of tourists and pilgrims. Then she would go to her local church, Sant'Agnese in Agone, which she hadn't visited for years, and talk to Father d'Abruzzo and whisper to him in the creaky confessional that smelled of incense and holy water. Of course, there was some reason this had happened, an explanation as to why God had punished her. Maybe for leaving her parents, ignoring their pleas for her to remain in Rome and marry a Roman, and not by any means date a Venetian, let alone follow him to his faraway city.

Venetians were rumored to be Christians of a different sort. Like that woman on the bridge, there were Venetians who were said to hold to the pagan gods of Rome, while worshiping Christ, too. And maybe Vittorio had been one of those. She thought again of the design on the boat, realizing she'd seen it before. Was it Neptune's symbol, or the Greek's more popular, earlier version of the god, Poseidon?

The contessa frowned, studying a dark oil painting next to the armoire. "My son had an independent streak in him."

"That's one of the things I liked about him. He wasn't so much like the average Italian," Anna explained, wondering what she might say that would further upset the woman. She could see the woman's distaste for her, the look of condemnation radiating from her small, colorless eyes.

"But sometimes he did things his parents—his mother, in particular—didn't approve of," she said, folding her arms across her chest.

The woman looked at Anna before turning her gaze to the suitcase lying open on the low bureau.

What did she want to tell her? Couldn't she just allow Anna to pack, leaving her to make a quiet and hasty exit from this city of death? The contessa had wanted her to depart, and now that Anna was obviously leaving, she seemed to want to talk to her, to delay her departure. She regretted again that she'd stayed, remembering the absurd, irrational thoughts she'd had that Vittorio might turn up somewhere, that she would round one of the ancient, tiny corners of the quarter to find him. Unconsciously, she'd caught herself looking for his face in cafés and on the vaporetti that steamed along the Grand Canal. But that was nonsense, she realized.

Maybe she was no better than the Venetians who believed in an angry, demanding god of the sea. Was her weakness part of the reason she'd been so harshly punished by her own God? Father d'Abruzzo, her parish priest who had approached her so many times, speaking to her in tones of dismay, might be able to help her figure it out. Would he tell her that he'd tried to warn her and that her grandfather had told her the same? Perhaps her appearance in his confessional or in one of the rickety, wooden pews of the small church would come as no surprise. Maybe he would say he'd been expecting her. She'd been so foolish.

"I should go," Anna said, feeling awkward stating the obvious.

"I see," the contessa said. "You don't care to talk to me—I see that, too."

Anna looked up from her suitcase lying open, yawning on the low bureau. The contessa looked challenging, bitter.

"I just don't know what the point is. My presence seems to bother you, so I thought it best to just leave." She could have told her that Venice seemed an unhappy place, recently haunted by strange characters and death. The frivolity and carefree spirit of Carnivale seemed very distant. Maybe the *joie de vivre* she'd sensed coursing through the crowds around the city just months earlier had been imagined. Or, she just hadn't noticed that beneath the facade simmered something different. Venice was haunted, its murmuring waterways and crumbling palazzi the lair of ghosts and sorrows.

"I find it interesting that you figured you would become my daughter, and yet you have nothing to say to me. You seem to want to flee. Is it that you fear me?" she asked, moving closer to Anna.

Anna pushed a dress into the suitcase, no longer caring whether her clothes were carefully folded. She could sense the contessa observing her, noting her lack of care, her sense of urgency. Rome! Rome! If only she were in Rome at that moment! In a quiet corner of her parents' house, listening to the splashing of the old fountain in the courtyard and watching the wheeling and diving swifts and swallows of the evening. Maybe she could deal with Vittorio's death there, coming to understand why it had happened. Here, though, none of it made sense. Venetians suddenly appeared cruel and barbaric. She would catch the first train out of the city—even if it meant changing trains ten times before she reached Rome.

"No," Anna lied. "I don't fear you. I think my presence here distresses you, causes you grief when you're already devastated by the death of your son. Given the circumstances, I think it's better that I leave."

She moved more frantically, taking the small stacks of her underclothes and socks from the dresser drawer and pressing them into the suitcase with trembling hands. She didn't look up from the clothes or suitcase, but could feel the contessa's eyes on her.

"Did you love him?" the woman suddenly asked.

So that *was* it: the woman didn't believe that Anna had ever loved her son, she'd been marrying for Vittorio's name and money. Maybe Venetians were like others after all, just as suspicious and cynical.

"Of course I did," Anna answered, trying not to sound annoyed. She stopped packing and turned to meet the woman's piercing gaze. The contessa reminded her of an old portrait of the nobility, fair skin, delicate features, and a faint expression of privilege. Perhaps that's what bothered her now: Anna was no longer vying to win her affections, to become her daughter-in-law.

"I wondered about that, I must confess," the contessa said, holding her gaze. "Because I've heard some things. Even here in sleepy, faraway Venice, we hear things, you know."

Had she acted as if Venice was inferior? Sure, the little city was no Rome, no Milan, but she'd never criticized the city and offered only compliments. And what had the woman heard? What could she be referring to? So the gossips of Rome had their connections even on the other side of the peninsula. Well, she should have known. The Italian nobility hadn't held onto their titles and wealth through two world wars and revolutions without the benefit of privileged information. She'd been a fool to think otherwise.

"I'm not sure what you're referring to," she lied. "I loved your son, and I was led to believe that he felt similarly," she said sincerely, removing the last of her clothing from the antique chest of drawers.

"I met your grandfather, you know," the contessa announced, stepping forward, feline-like, her eyes full of cunning. "Yes, it was many years ago to be sure, but I remember it still. And then I've heard much about him, too—we're actually distant relations."

What sort of news was that? Of course, nearly all the Italian nobility were distantly related. Centuries—and sometimes millennia—of intermarrying had guaranteed that.

"So what did he tell you? Or what did you hear about him?" Anna asked, not certain she wanted to hear. She looked away, returning her gaze to the clothes in her suitcase.

"He's a Pucci, but you are *not*." Now the tone of her voice was nearly condescending. "You're a *Maledetto*."

Why did she attack her when Anna was grieving for Vittorio as much as she was? She longed to fight back, to tell the old woman that she thought she was horrid, a bitter, dry-boned misanthrope. But she couldn't bring herself to confront the woman that might have been her mother-in-law. And she couldn't stop herself from imagining Vittorio watching and listening somewhere, eavesdropping on their horrid conversation. Would he forgive her or would he side with his mother, blood over love? The traditions and bindings of centuries of Lunardinis' would doubtless trump the love for a woman he'd met not even six months earlier. He would know that she had loved him, though she'd never said it. But, that was little comfort for her now.

"I'm well aware of who I am," Anna answered, her voice remaining steady despite her burning cheeks and quickening heartbeat.

"But it always irked your grandfather that your mother married a Maledetto—the *cursed*!" She laughed when she emphasized the literal meaning of her last name. "It's no secret that your grandfather's *raison d'être* was to have his granddaughter regain a proper name and restore the Pucci name to respectability."

The woman talked like a medieval baroness, instead of a powerless patrician with merely a surfeit of pedigree in an Italy that was quickly modernizing. The way things were going, with the Communists gaining more seats and more power in regions across the country, the nobility were apt to lose, not gain what little power they possessed. Still, she was shocked that the woman knew about her grandfather's wish. How many others knew of this wish? Whether the drive was born of her grandfather's constant and measured urgings, or a byproduct of her blood, she, too, longed to regain the right to be called noble—even if Europe was headed in the opposite direction. She would be much more modern, though, than the contessa standing before her.

What else did she have but possibility, especially at that moment? There were only so many nobles, so many Europeans with names, and a shared history. Getting a name back would reconnect her with her grandfather. She knew she would sound shallow, superficial, but it was the one small thing her grandfather had wanted his whole life. And she had come to want it, too.

"If you know my grandfather—then you must know the history

of my current name. Even if it's not noble, the name is respectable and can be traced back to the Middle Ages."

"Ha! I wondered if you would bring that up. I've heard that story, because you see, when Vittorio ..." she faltered, hesitating a moment. Her face softened momentarily, before she pressed on. "When Vittorio first mentioned you, I took the liberty of informing myself about you and your family. I went to the Doges' library, and then talked to some friends here who know a thing or two about you Romans."

"So you already know that the Maledetti were once the Benedetti, but sided with the holy and righteous pope—the true Christians—instead of the descendants of the Roman Empire, the pretender popes who were more interested in power and politics than the church." She recalled her father's lectures when she came home from school crying after classmates teased her about her strange last name.

The contessa laughed. "But the pretender popes were descended from the caesars, from the Roman emperors, so who really were the rightful heirs?"

So Vittorio's mother, anyway, was one of these Venetians who worshipped two sets of gods—the Christian and the pagan. She shuddered. So maybe Vittorio had been like his mother.

"Don't be ridiculous," the woman said, smirking. "I can see what you're thinking—that I'm one of those fabled Venetians who worships the gods of old—Jano, Mercurio, Nettuno. No!" she laughed. "You have a fundamental misunderstanding of the old gods—just like your literalists ancestors. I see you rely on the church for education, instead of an objective teacher."

Anna zipped up her bag, pulling it off the low bureau and setting it gently on the floor. "If you can read my mind, and profess to support the pagans who infiltrated the church, mixing the gods of old with Christ, then how precisely am I mistaken?"

"You take things too literally, like the followers of Savonarola or the Puritans. There are two sides to everything—the surface, what you see, and what is apparent—and what rests below the surface."

Anna shook her head slowly. Did the contessa intend to confuse her, compare her to silly characters like Savonarola and the extremist Puritans? She would consider herself a modern Catholic, neither prone to superstition nor afraid of science. "But what does that have to do with *Nettuno, Adone?*"

It was the contessa's turn to shake her head. "Of course you don't understand. Maybe ask a Jesuit, they are the one sect that respects mythology, one that respects the complexity of life." She sighed then, turned her gaze from Anna to her hands, then out the window. Was she thinking of her dead son?

"I don't see what this all has to do with me—or your son," Anna murmured. She felt weary, ready to be home in Rome—far from Venice. She didn't care if she never saw Contessa Lunardini again.

The woman shook her head, gazing at Anna sympathetically. "You probably think that Christ punished you by killing my son, don't you? Killed him because of something you did? Or because it wasn't the right match for you? Or maybe you didn't attend Mass that much—or from what Vittorio told me, not at all."

"That's offensive," Anna said, pushing her books, toiletries, and brush from the dressing table into a small bag, but she felt her cheeks burning again. "It's neither your place nor mine to question—"

"But you do think that, don't you? I've guessed right, haven't I?" she interrupted, shaking her head and approaching Anna.

Thoughts were coming into Anna's head, teachings from her mother and from the nuns and priests. They all flooded back, as if they'd lay stubbornly dormant within her for the past few years while she'd tried to push them away.

"I need to leave now. Can you call for a taxi boat to take me to the station?" Anna asked, her lip quivering.

She had strayed too far, she realized. How had she come to be so far from her parents, alone in the world without her nonno Pucci?

"Of course you'd rather not discuss this. But that's the only way you'll learn about life, isn't it?" the contessa asked. "To be honest about what brought you here? And what happened. You're eager to run back to Rome and learning nothing at all," the woman lectured, walking over to the windows and turning her back to Anna. She pulled the curtain aside, gazing onto the canal and bridge where the widowed baker stood cloaked in gray, staring back.

Anna didn't want to hear anything more. Could she really have been the same reserved woman that she'd encountered at dinner and while Vittorio was still alive? The contessa spoke nonsense, no doubt upset by the death of her son. Well, Anna was upset, too. If a mother can be distraught over the loss of a child, then can't a lover be distraught for love never unfolded?

The contessa sighed, her thin hand letting the curtain drop. When she turned to face Anna, she no longer looked bitter or angry. It was as if she were no longer in mourning. Anna shivered, as if a draft had swept through the cracks in the doorway and brushed her shoulder.

"I'll have Marco take you to the station. It would be silly for you to take a taxi," she said soberly. "I imagine I won't see you again, and I won't have you telling your Roman friends that I turned you out of my house or that the Venetians have no hospitality."

"I'd appreciate that," Anna answered. "I'm sorry. I hope I haven't insulted you on top of everything else you've experienced," she added, no longer certain of anything but her rediscovered faith in God. It seemed that nothing and no one was predictable. So this was why religion could be such comfort. She suddenly understood.

"Not at all," the woman said, almost smiling.

The straight-backed contessa, Vittorio's mother, was right—Anna would never return to Venice. She understood neither the seemingly cursed city nor its people and no longer cared to. The spell had been broken, and she viewed the place in a different light. She realized that she'd felt the uneasiness from her first encounter with the city, from that first enchanted visit during the gray, now bittersweet days of Carnivale. If only she'd persuaded Vittorio to go with her to Rome, they might have cheated the city of another death.

Ah, if only she had never gone to Venice at all, never came to know it. If she had been so fortunate, death would still be a stranger.

Chapter Six

The streets were unusually full of tourists for a late March day. Louis had taken the back streets to his little rented office, wanting to avoid going home. He felt it better to work when he had so much energy—even if it wasn't necessarily of a positive sort. He was still shaking from his encounter with the contessa, but he could feel some hope that Claudia might stay in Venice. In some ways, he wished he'd stayed to help his friend stand up to her mother, to ensure that she didn't back down as it seemed she had done nearly her entire life.

If he worked a little, it would get his mind off the lunch and help calm him. He'd mounted the stairs, with the sloshing of the nearby canal audible even after he'd shut the door to the building. But the agitated water—no doubt from gondolas—didn't overpower the faint crying he heard again in the stair hall. He stopped where he had previously, pressing his ear against the damp, thickly plastered wall. There'd been a momentary break in the crying, but then he heard a few sniffles before the man—at least it sounded like a man—wept again.

He felt drawn to the weeping, as if it were muse-like. Who was crying, where was he, and why was he crying?

And why was he so drawn to listen to another person cry? He wanted to comfort the person. But more than that, the crying presented him with a mystery he couldn't resolve. He sat on the cold stone step, leaning against the wall to listen. The timed hallway light would turn off in a minute or two, and then he'd be sitting in the half-dark.

The man sniffled again, blew his nose, and then launched into another fit of weeping. Faint strands of music came through the damp wall, along with a voice—was it the voice of Louis Prima?

An ominous click echoed in the hallway before the lights flickered off, plunging the space into near darkness. Surprisingly, as his eyes adjusted, there was enough light trickling in from the dust-covered skylights far above to illuminate the stairs.

The doorway on the first landing swung open and Signora Crespi, a squat, plainly dressed widow, waddled onto the landing above the stairs. The lights flickered back on, and he jumped up, but not before the old woman spotted him on the stairs.

"Giorno," she called, nodding, her voice unfazed by his presence ıs if she always opened her door to find him sitting there in the dark ›n the steps.

"Giorno," he echoed sheepishly.

"Dark stairs are a good place to collect your thoughts, aren't they? specially for a writer."

"I'm not a writer," Louis corrected. "I'm a translator."

She shrugged.

"You know, stairways are forgotten places, you take them up, you :e them down, but no one really thinks of them as places of and to mselves, do they?" She took the first step down purposefully, as if cending a ladder and not a wide, enormous stairway.

"Yes," he nodded, though he'd never thought of it before.

"It's quiet in a stairway, but not. You can eavesdrop on life—on ;, can't you?"

Louis blushed.

"No need to be ashamed," she said. "Everyone does—especially ıis city. You can't live so close and not eavesdrop. You can learn listening. What have you heard lately?" she inquired, slowly ›aching the step on which he awkwardly stood.

Did she think he was always here?

"Nothing, really. This is my first time sitting here. I've never done it before."

She gazed at him suspiciously, nodding, but not in agreement.

"There's nothing wrong with it. No shame in it," she said, passing him on her way down. He didn't know how she took more than one trip up or down the stair; she took it so slowly and painfully, favoring her stronger leg as she clutched her left knee.

"No, I guess not," he answered, but felt guilty. It didn't seem right to him, even if an old church-going Venetian assured him it was.

Another cry sounded, this time plaintive and more of a wail, as if the crier had mined some fresh source of pain.

The woman stopped on the stair, seeming to listen, though she didn't crane her neck or cock her head. Facing forward, she paused as the crying continued. There were a few more sobs, some whimpering and then silence.

"Venice is a city of eavesdroppers," she announced, staring vacantly.

Why didn't she acknowledge the crying, he wondered? Did she think him shameful, a lowlife for sitting in a darkened stair hall, eavesdropping on someone's torment and pain? He felt especially low being a foreigner, as if he were prying into a secret pain of Venice itself, a side that foreigners were not meant to see or share.

The woman nodded when the crying stopped, as if in agreement, and then continued plodding down the wide, cold stone steps. "Giorno," she called abruptly, not turning around.

"Giorno," he echoed.

Louis stood motionless, unsure whether to continue up to his office or to exit onto the street. He listened to the deliberate footfall of the old woman on the steps, shuffling gradually downward to the street. Then the opening of the door, its muffled creak, and the solid finality of it thudding shut.

The stair hall lapsed into silence again, a strange, ponderous quiet. Louis waited for the crying to begin again, but there was nothing. The lights flickered, blinking off again, but he remained on the stairs, waiting. The buzz of a boat motor on the canal sneaked under the door, bleating like a goat. A moment later, there was the water splashing over the edge of the canal into the little via the front door faced. He'd never imagined that the waves lapping onto the street could be heard from so high up the stairs, but there they were, caressing the buildings, smoothing the old stones.

Louis Prima, tinny and muffled, sang a different song, reminding him of some old movie. There were crackles and a little feedback, as if the record were being played on an ancient player. He imagined himself in an old cliché movie, as if he had jumped out of life's current for a moment. Standing in the darkened stair hall, motionless and silent, he felt like he was in a sort of hibernation. The sounds from the nearby canal, a hum—a jet overhead?—little sounds from the apartments, banging pans, melodious conversations, and maybe the sound of footsteps and wheelbarrows creaking down the street.

He stood a moment more, straining for the sound of crying, but he sensed it was over. Still, he was surprised at all he'd been able to hear by simply standing still in a dark hall. He thought of Signora Crespi catching him eavesdropping and he cringed.

He turned, following the old woman's route back down the stairs, deciding, after all, to get a prosecco. The afternoon's events had distracted him, and he wouldn't be able to concentrate at work. He dreaded the news from Claudia, wondering whether she would return to Rome, leaving him behind in the mysterious, but alluring city.

Not wanting to see anyone he knew, he headed toward the fish market. He knew he could get a drink there without running into anyone—not Claudia or her mother, not a neighbor or friends from Chicago. The utilitarian character of the centuries-old market bar attracted fishmongers and restaurant owners, cooks, and housewives shopping for dinner. Sure, there would be a few tourists—some even American—in the market, but only the sort who wouldn't frown at the overpowering smell of seafood, brine, blood, and the ancient, musty odor of the market itself. Mostly, there would be Venetians, fishermen, and fishmongers.

Irene would claim he was merely a snob. Maybe, but hadn't he seen dozens of tourists, guidebooks in hand, turn back toward the exit upon entering more than a few feet into the market and experiencing the full-on, pungent smells of the chaotic market?

Who was really the snob?

A thin veneer of dull gray clouds more typical of spring had overtaken the sky of robin's egg blue. The wind had shifted, carrying the scent of the sea mixed with rain, and the warmth of places to the south. Some days he could feel Greece, smell Africa in the warm air currents blowing off the Adriatic. The months or weeks between winter and spring sometimes struck him as depressing, not belonging to one season or another. Things remained predominantly gray and brown, despite the fuzzy hints of green on bushes and trees. Distant Greece would already be warm, and Africa, even more remote, would be hot. Venice could be hot and hazy, as steamy as a subcontinent jungle, or as bone chilling and damp as Oslo. Today it was somewhere between.

Following another circuitous route, he strolled along small, impossibly winding streets, avoiding the more major lanes frequented by tourists. He preferred taking the smaller streets, having to pay attention to where he was or risk losing his way, for Venice was a jumble of Renaissance palazzi and buildings that bled and blended with thousands of streets and mini-intersections resembling one another. No matter how many years he lived there, he would never know every street or recognize all the buildings. But after countless, aimless ambles, he was confident he could never be completely lost. Maze-like as the city was, eventually, a person arrived at the Grand Canal, the harbor, the bay, or the sea. On islands, no one was ever truly lost. Provided he didn't go in circles, but struck out in different directions, trusting the streets and his intuition, he would eventually figure out where he was.

The smells of the market greeted him long before its grand, decaying entrance rose before him. The market held vestiges of the Venice of earlier generations. Thick-ankled women ambled toward the market toting canvas bags and deep baskets. Like bees circling flowers, or planes congregating in the congested skies above airports, they collected in the streets and *piazette* near the ancient food hall. Singly and in pairs, they strode resolutely toward the stalls that teemed with mollusks both tiny and the size of fists, glimmering fish piled high, sometimes still crawling and twitching shellfish, and stacks of brightly-hued produce. The fetid, vaguely sweet smells of fresh and old fish melded with the odors of the sea and rotten vegetables, growing stronger as he neared the imposing entrance portico.

The hurly-burly of vendors singing and calling out mixed with the slap of leather soles on the worn cobblestone streets, rising to a near crescendo as he passed into the shadowy interior of the market.

I belong here, Louis thought to himself, feeling as if he were participating in a ritual as old as the city itself.

Like an animal in its burrow, he took familiar twists and turns around stalls, arriving at a crowded bar inside the chaotic market. He made for a narrow opening at the scratched zinc counter and sidled up to a squat, muscle-bound, white-smocked fishmonger and a widow dressed in black, her half-full market bag nestled between her feet and the counter. The woman sipped a glass of bubbling prosecco. One of the bartenders, a young, dark-haired girl whose mother owned the place and worked beside her, hurriedly poured a glass of vin santo, setting it on the scratched bar in front of the fishmonger. The man tossed back the drink and pushed two coins toward the bartender.

"*Grazie*," he sang.

"Grazie," the bartender answered.

The man hurried away, heading toward his stall. The widow eyed him, moving away away slightly.

The bartenders pulled late afternoon shots of espresso and *macchiati*, pouring beer, wine, vin santo, grappa, and prosecco. When the older bartender approached, nodding to say she recognized him, Louis ordered a prosecco. She smiled and quickly poured him a glass, fuller than normal.

Vendors, some with bloodstained smocks, jostled with market-shoppers for spots at the counter. Most drank their orders like shots, quaffing them with a flourish, and pushing coins across the counter. Louis and the widow lingered, sipping their prosecco methodically.

The smell of fish mixed with the damp air of the market was overridden by strong clouds of coffee-scented steam escaping from the bar's two enormous, shiny machines.

He caught the old widow stealing a glance at him. He nodded, but she quickly looked away. Hadn't he seen her before, waiting for someone, always at the same time, or at odd times? He didn't visit the bar regularly, but of course he'd seen her there before, the oversize canvas tote at her feet.

For a moment, they were the only two customers at the counter, and the owner and daughter hurriedly washed glasses and plates in preparation for the next rush. They joked about the extra strong odor of fish permeating the market. "Today the fish is saying it's not so fresh, don't eat me. But no one pays attention," the older one said. Her daughter laughed and continued to wash the glasses in silence.

The old woman became agitated, rocking from one foot to the other, opening her change purse in search of coins.

Had he unnerved her with his nod?

Walking slowly, but deliberately, an old man approached the bar. "*Bo' giorn, donne*," he called.

The bartenders smiled at the old man, glancing nervously at the old woman. They busied themselves cleaning the bar and washing glasses, staring at their hands or the glasses they washed.

The old woman looked in the approaching man's direction, as if to see if he had included her in his greeting. He studied her with uncertainty.

"Giorno," she mumbled, before returning her gaze to the change purse. Finding some lire, she carefully placed coins on the counter and pushed them slowly toward the barista.

"*Gia*?" the young barista asked.

"*Si. Parto.* I've got to do some shopping," she said impatiently, her voice a low growl.

A few more workers joined them at the counter, smiling at the owner or her daughter who began pulling shots of espresso or pouring vin santo before they'd even ordered.

The old man frowned, glancing nervously again at the woman who ignored him. The bartender and her daughter were suddenly quiet, somber.

"*Un corretto*, Piero?" the older bartender asked.

"Sì," he mumbled, glancing at the empty counter in front of him.

The old woman caught Louis' eye. He did a double take, but she fixed her gaze on him as if they knew each other.

"*Non si puo fiduciarsi nessun ma Dio*," she said to him, loudly.

You can trust no one but God.

The old man pounded his fist on the counter. "Is my corretto ready yet?"

"And God doesn't even exist!" the woman laughed, spittle flying toward Louis. Laughing, she wandered away, turning a shadowy corner and disappearing behind mounds of fish.

Louis would have liked to tell her that he didn't believe in God either, to let her know he was in on the joke, but he didn't want everyone else in the bar to hear. Though the other customers pretended they weren't listening—the bartenders included—he knew that wasn't the case.

The bartender blushed, biting her lip. Finishing off an espresso pull, she quickly set the foam-topped cup in front of the old man whose hands shook as he reached for it.

The man greedily slurped the drink, relishing it without the customary dousing of sugar or lemon peel. Finishing it in one noisy gulp, he glanced at the bartenders who busied themselves quietly at the other end of the bar, as if avoiding him.

"Another," he said timidly, glancing in the direction the woman had gone. Though the mother and daughter appeared engrossed in conversation, the younger nodded and stepped over to the giant machine.

There was something sad about the old man, his eyes a dim red, but not with the haze of alcohol.

Louis left some coins on the counter, catching the older bartender's eyes. As he stepped away, the old man touched his elbow.

"*Scuzi*," he said. "Do you live near Santo Gregorio? You look familiar."

"Exactly, well I have an office there," Louis answered, studying the man's face, but he didn't recognize him. "Do you live near there?"

"Nearby," the man said vaguely.

"In what building?"

"Close to there, it's a small building, just a small building," he shrugged.

The older bartender glanced quickly but significantly at the two of them. Why did Louis feel like he was being watched, studied? The bartenders continued working, cleaning glasses, wiping counters and serving drinks, but he could tell they were watching him.

"Oh, I must know it," Louis said. "I've been working there for a year now."

But the old man shook his head. "Just a humble old building. You wouldn't know it."

Why was the man so mysterious? Could it be that he was the crier? After all, the old man had started their conversation.

"I guess not," he said, not certain how to respond. "So we're neighbors then."

"Sì," Louis nodded, smiling. "Neighbors."

Louis looked at the old man and wondered what else to say. The bar turned quiet, with only the distant sound of footsteps in the market and fishmongers talking. Deciding to wander the aisles, he pushed the lire he'd left farther across the counter and turned to the old man.

"Piacere," he said, stepping away.

"Nice to meet you, too," the old man answered, smiling more broadly.

Louis hesitated, wanting to figure out somehow if the man was the one who poured his grief into the thick walls of his ancient apartment building. But could he be the one? And that woman, who was she?

“The lady that was here,” he decided to ask. “You know her?”

The man scrutinized him, narrowing his eyes. “You know the signora? You’ve met her?”

“I’m not certain. I don’t think so,” Louis said.

“I’d be surprised if you did,” the man said, looking down at the counter at his empty cup.

The older bartender, matronly with a few stray whiskers above her upper lip, coughed loudly.

The old man touched his empty espresso cup, revolving it slowly in its saucer and then he shrugged, almost imperceptibly. “I don’t know her,” he said quietly, almost inaudibly, obviously lying.

Louis guessed that the man’s old tweed jacket, faded but not frayed or moth-eaten, looked to be at least thirty years old. He remembered seeing such jackets in the back of his dad’s closet, unworn for years but hanging lifeless, seemingly in wait of the right occasion or simply to be remembered.

The old man must have known the woman, but why would he lie?

The bartender edged closer, wiping the zinc counter slowly, working out coffee rings, and catching a few cornetto crumbs. Was she moving slower than usual?

“I have to go,” Louis stammered. “Good to meet you and I’ll see you around the Dorsoduro, okay?”

The man shrugged, allowing a wan smile. Nodding, he turned to the bartender. “*Un altro.*”

The barista hurried to the bar to begin preparing another espresso.

Louis waved at the bartenders. The younger one at the bar must have sensed his leaving because she turned and gave him a quick wave, despite being in the middle of making the old man’s drink.

He felt as if the old man had dismissed him, as he didn’t turn or acknowledge Louis’ leaving. In a way, it seemed like the man had thought Louis had done something to insult him, but what could he have done? Louis started to walk into the heart of the market. He'd headed for the market for distraction, but now he found himself confronted again by an unsettling feeling.

"I've got to get back to work," he overheard the man say to the bartenders. "I left the shop open."

"You don't worry about anyone stealing things?" Louis heard one of the bartenders ask.

"I don't care," the old man said. "They do me a favor when they do."

Louis, too far away by the sounds of the shoppers and the market, did not hear what the man said after that.

It seemed the city was full of mysteries—people with histories, stories, and secrets. It would take years of living here to learn a fraction of the mysteries, to ever feel like he really belonged in a place that harbored so much behind the facades of its palaces and old apartment buildings, and the faces of the *Veneziani* themselves. But he would like to try, to see what it would feel like to make the place his own. And if Claudia could stay, too, that would be just enough to give him a good chance, enough of a platform from which to carry on building a life.

So the old man still worked? Louis would never have guessed it.

Relieved to have escaped their awkward conversation, Louis edged his way into the center of the market, confronted by the strong smell of mussels, crabs, and langoustines, clams of seemingly infinite variety, opalescent squid, and shiny, silvery-sided fish. The market's ageless smells and dingy, shadowy stalls left him with the feeling that little had changed for five or six hundred years, maybe since Venice first rose from the swampy, marshy islands of the northern Adriatic.

He decided to buy some tiny mussels, white anchovies, and a loaf of bread, in hopes that Claudia would be in the mood for dinner. Certainly, she wouldn't be having dinner with her mother that night. He decided to buy the seafood at his favorite stall, one where the gruff vendor dispensed smiles only on rare occasions. She was prompt, no-nonsense, and eager to wait on customers and he'd never heard her chat with anyone. The hand-painted sign over her stall done in old style lettering claimed hers was the oldest stall in the market and its seafood the finest.

Heading out of the market, clutching a small bag heavy with the weight of the mussels and anchovies, he opted for an unfamiliar route home, a tiny, shadowy passage that zigzagged away from the square.

He marveled at the number of ways he could get temporarily lost in the city. There were still so many streets he's never wandered down, via's that enticed with their crooked, seemingly haphazard routes and shadowy corners. It reminded him of his first encounter with the city—that of his imagination, anyway—at the Art Institute of Chicago when he'd been in high school. His Humanities teacher had taken the entire class to the museum for a day and told them to get lost, to wander, and see what they would find, and then to discuss what they'd experienced in class the next day.

Louis and a classmate had walked up the enormous, polished atrium stairs which were . bathed in soft light that made the gray winter day seem spring-like. They distanced themselves from the others who bounded toward the rooms filled with Impressionists and walked through the medieval rooms, the Fra Lippi and Fra Angelico's, until they found themselves in a large, quiet room with no one in it, not even a guard. Lining the walls were views of European cities, the countryside, and vast views of Roman ruins.

In the corner hung a Romanticist's view of a Venice already falling into ruin. The oil painting seemed enormous, as wide as Louis was tall. At the margins of the picture stood decomposing buildings, relics of their former grand selves. Fragments of elaborate cornices hung from the tops of palazzi, weeds and flowers growing from their ragged tops. Across the canal, the dome of an enormous church—which he later recognized as Santa Maria della Salute—rose from a jumble of fading buildings clustered on the distant shore. A few men, tourists maybe with their long coats, stockings, and canes, admired the view.

What were they looking at, he'd wondered? And what did they see? Was Venice the same then as it was now? Certainly, it looked the same, the identical grand palazzi, the domes of the churches, and the gently curving bridges arcing across the canals. Boats and people still swarmed the *piazze*, bridges, and waterfront.

Louis was first intrigued by Venice during that museum visit. He vowed right there in the bright midday winter light of that silent gallery that he would see the city for himself, breathe in its air, and listen to its sloshing canals and birdsong. There had been something in that painting that he couldn't describe in class the following day, a sense of the eternal and mortal at the same time. He'd never imagined such a place might exist that could provoke such feelings. He wondered even then, did it feel the same when you were there, or had the painter created something that didn't exist?

In class the next day, the teacher had asked the students what they'd seen. Most of his classmates had talked about the Impressionists, Monet's *Haystacks,* or *A Sunday Afternoon on the Island at La Grande Jatte*, and the artier ones mentioned Hopper's *Nighthawks* or Picasso. When it was his turn, he talked about the Venetian view.

"What do you think the painter was trying to say?" the teacher asked. "What did it say to you?"

"The city seemed like a mystical place, unreal and maybe even a little mythological, like the remnants of one of the great old cities of ancient times," he'd said, noticing the teacher appeared to be frowning. "I could see Marco Polo having sailed from this place, but hundreds of years earlier."

The teacher had seemed to want a particular answer, but Louis had been unable to provide it. At least that's how it had seemed. He talked more about the men in the view, who they might be, and about the feeling of the painting. To him, that painting had been laden with emotion, imbued with an otherworldly sense familiar and unfamiliar, ultimately inscrutable.

He hadn't realized it at the time, but maybe the painter of the giant view had been among the first of the city's tourists. Like a vulture, the painter came lured by the scent of death. Had that been what he'd recognized so long ago? Venice was already a half-ruin when that painter had captured it in the 1700s. How many years had it been dying? Was there a day, a year maybe when it began its slow descent, when its citizens no longer grew richer, when more people and ships departed than arrived?

When Louis had disembarked the crowded train at the cacophonous *stazione*, catching his first glimpse of the legendary city more than a year earlier, he found that the place was like in the painting, but even more compelling. In so many ways, Venice seemed anchored in a past he could scarcely imagine, but sensed in the lapping of the canal waters or the soft scuffle of shoes on the worn, ancient cobblestones. How could he feel a past that no longer existed?

Instead of hurrying back to the flat, he took the first small, unworn path that beckoned. Turning down a narrow passage that he'd stopped noticing months ago, he planned to head deep into the quiet old Jewish ghetto where tourists scarcely ventured.

The narrow street passed under a worn timbered passageway, then turned left. The cobblestones here, which had probably never felt the warmth of the sun's rays, were covered in dull green moss—except in the worn center. The passage jogged back to the right, under a faded Madonna shrine set into the thick walls of a faded ochre building. An old streetlight, rusted and cobweb-covered, jutted out above the old fresco. On a small shelf just under the image were plastic flowers and candles.

Just past the Madonna, the street forked, and Louis took the route heading farther into the quarter. Here there were no shops for tourists, only an occasional espresso bar, and a few darkened trattorias. Peeking in the window of one, he could see small wooden tables, a tiny kitchen visible in the back of the small room. He made a note of the address, hoping he would remember how to find it. No one shared the narrow via with him, as if this part of the city had for the most part, been abandoned.

Farther down, there was another fork, and he headed deeper into the unfamiliar area. The neighborhood changed from residential to commercial, with little manufacturing shops and studios. Some of the buildings had weeds growing from the rooftops—just like in the painting at the Art Institute, though they were hardly palazzi. Larger, plainer-looking buildings lined the walkway, the facades lined with huge barred and shuttered windows. Inside some of the open doorways and shutters, he saw giant machines, furnaces, and even a bellows, most covered in cobwebs and rust. Occasionally, a shop door stood ajar, allowing the sounds of the little studio, occupied by maybe two or three workers, to escape into the street.

One studio had its giant wooden double-doors open, the sound of hammering and the glow and heat of burning coals radiating into the street. Louis spied an old man inside hunched over an anvil pounding a flat object with an oversize hammer, the scene illuminated by the orange glow of hot coals. A carefully lettered, handwritten sign on the door outside read:

Welding
Tool Manufacture & Repair

Just beyond, another studio with a rotting wooden door stood open. There was no sign on the workshop, but the owner couldn't have gone far because the remnants of coals burned there, too. The light from the fire caught shiny glass objects lining shelves around the shadowy studio. There was no sign on the door or beside it, but two hooks and a dark patch on the doorway showed where one had once been. Just above where the sign had been affixed to the thick, crumbling wall, hung a rusticated black bell. The crude, aged metal object had lost its pull cord, though Louis could see an eyelet and the jagged remains of a small chain.

Louis peered in the doorway. He could see glass bowls, pitchers, and platters crowding the shelves, capturing and reflecting small bits of light from the bright sky and the glowing orange coals. Some of the pieces were dust covered, but despite the shadows, others glimmered with hints of rich color. Hundreds of pieces of glassware, ranging from little coasters and dessert plates to bowls and platters lined the deep shelves, piled on top of each other and extending back into shadowy spaces. Except for the tools and the glowing furnace, it looked like a storage warehouse—hardly a functioning studio, and certainly not a retail shop.

Why make so many pieces and not sell them? Were the pieces flawed, defective in some way? Louis glanced around to see if anyone was approaching and then stepped across the threshold. He felt the heat of the embers in the furnace as his eyes adjusted to the dimness of the interior. More pieces took shape on the shelves—each one perfectly formed, colorful, and sinuous. In the middle of the closest shelves, were a few dust-free circles where pieces had recently been removed. Whoever worked here apparently did sell his creations.

"You can't buy any of it," a voice over his shoulder explained, making Louis jump.

A middle-aged man in a baggy, stained set of coveralls stood in the doorway, the same one Louis had seen bent over the anvil at the workshop down the street. The man still gripped the flat-headed hammer with an oversize head. Slipping the hammer through a loop on a thick leather belt cinched tightly at his waist, he glanced around the studio.

"He doesn't sell anything. Just makes it and then it disappears. Maybe he sells it out of town. Maybe he dumps it in the canal. Nobody knows. *Il vecchio* works often, usually in the mornings, and makes a lot of things, but no one knows where he sells it."

The man drew back, as if realizing he'd told a complete stranger a secret. He examined Louis' face.

"Were you looking to buy some Venetian glass?"

"No, I was just curious," Louis said, stepping back toward the doorway. "The door was open and I thought it might be a shop. I've never seen so much glass, but the place looks half-abandoned. If I didn't see the coal burning, I'd think no one worked here."

"It's no shop," the stranger explained. "The man who owns this studio, il vecchio, makes pieces that are absolutely perfect—you can tell by looking at any of the finished pieces on these shelves. And if it's not perfect, he starts over, melting the glass again or breaking the piece and giving the shards to mosaic makers. Once he makes a perfect piece, it either sits neglected on these shelves or disappears, especially the grandest pieces. They might sit on one of those shelves for a day or months, but eventually they disappear. Maybe he sells them to an exporter, or to some unknown shop on the mainland. No one knows, but you won't see his stuff anywhere in Venice or Murano."

Louis didn't know how to respond. He shouldn't have let himself into the shop. But the man didn't seem surprised or bothered that he was there, as if he could understand what might draw a person into the place.

"I took one piece once, a perfect shallow bowl the color of the Aegean—at least the same color I've seen in photos, I've never been there myself," he confessed. "I figured that he'd either let that bowl sit there, or do something else with it, maybe break it because it didn't seem perfect and start over. So I took it. It was too beautiful to be destroyed."

Now the man was telling him that he'd stolen?

"I won't tell him," Louis chuckled nervously, glancing at the doorway.

"Oh, il vecchio knows, I'm certain of that. Eventually, if you spend enough time in this city, nothing much remains a secret. If someone doesn't happen to see you doing something, then they overhear you talking about it on a street corner or in a café," he said with a laugh.

"Did the old man say anything to you about the bowl? Will he be angry if he returns and finds both of us here?" Louis asked, worrying that the owner of the studio would be angry to find a thief returned to the place.

"Buon giorno. That's all he ever says to me. And he just leaves the door open as if inviting people to take things. He doesn't seem to care. The day after I took the bowl, he poked his head in the doorway of my studio."

"What did he say?"

"Buon giorno. Like I said, that's all he ever says. And he didn't say it with spite or suspicion. He seemed genuinely pleased that I took something. I tried to pay him for it, left him an envelope with some lire in it—unmarked. Strangely, the envelope was slipped back under my door—he knew it was from me. Just like I told you."

Louis admired the pieces at the front of the shelves. Even in the gloomy studio, he saw the vivid colors, the perfect shapes of the bowls, platters, and plates. He ran a finger along the smooth rim of a deep bowl, wiping a fuzzy layer of dust from the thick glass.

"The things he makes have more soul than some people," the man said. "There's something to the glass here. It's unlike any glass you'll find anywhere else in Venice. The blues and greens are medieval, like the stained glass of Chartres, they say."

"There is something about them," Louis agreed, thinking again of the inexplicable emotion elicited by the Venetian view at the museum.

"You American?" the man asked. "You speak Italian well, but you have a little bit of an accent."

Louis nodded, disappointed that his accent had given him away.

"You should take one, you know. They're a thing of beauty and it's a waste to leave them here. And I really don't think he minds. Maybe it's a relief to him, in fact. Some people say that the finest ones are thrown into the canal in the dead of night. They say they've seen him throw things that look suspiciously like glass bowls and platters into the canal."

The man gazed at Louis expectantly, as if he might be able to tell him why a man might do such a thing.

"I couldn't and have no need for one, anyway," he protested, wondering if the man was baiting him.

The man shrugged. "You'll find no better in all of Italy. And the colors reflect the sea perfectly, the azure blues and celadon greens of the lagoon and the Adriatic on a sunny day. It's as if he captures the sea and freezes it in glass. A tribute to the gods of the sea, you could say."

The well-formed shapes and radiant colors of the pieces, at least the ones not covered in a thick layer of dust, exuded perfection. Louis eyed a large bowl sitting on a bottom shelf, big enough to hold a dozen apples. What would a person use it for, such a large glass bowl?

"But I don't recommend taking a bowl," the man suddenly advised. "It's said that these bowls hold sorrow, are meant to hold it. You're better off with a platter."

"I'm not taking one, thank you," Louis said, growing irritated. It was as if the man was pushing him to steal. Did he want another one himself or was he trying to set him up? He suddenly felt fearful, alone on a deserted street with a total stranger, the two of them standing inside a dilapidated, haunted studio, a workplace that lay open to the street, but whose owner was nowhere to be seen.

"I have to go—piacere," he announced to the man and nervously moved toward the door.

The man studied Louis' face momentarily. "Piacere," he responded with more emphasis than Louis had.

He set off down the street, glancing back toward the studio as he issued a feeble wave to the stranger. Venice was full of such people. The thing was, it could be difficult to tell the crazy ones from the sane ones and the harmless from the criminal.

The quarter he had set about exploring, quiet and half-abandoned, was no longer of interest. In fact, he preferred to return to familiar streets that had some life. The meeting with the man and the studio, which seemed haunted along with the street, left him feeling unsettled. He worried again that Claudia's mother had talked her into leaving, that their plans wouldn't turn out and that everything would change.

Turning abruptly on a slightly wider street, he began to head out of the area, making an arc toward his apartment. The street, like most in the city, cut back and forth, zigzagging as it made its way across the maze of bricked-up islands and canals. He began to see others making their way down the street, carrying shopping bags or umbrellas, though the skies didn't seem to promise any rain.

He turned another corner and found the street blocked with a crowd. A tight cluster of people stood a safe distance from a three-story building that pitched forward. Was it one of the sinking houses he'd heard about but had never seen?

"Signora," he said to a woman clutching two canvas market bags in front of him, "What's happening?"

"This morning the house began to sink, they say it's leaning so far forward that it'll collapse any minute now."

"*Che vergogna*," he said sullenly.

"Especially for the Balena family who live there. You know them?" she asked, carefully setting down her bags, settling into watch the spectacle.

"No." He shook his head, happy that the woman hadn't noticed his accent.

Police had cordoned off the street, mechanically motioning the crowd back, though no one attempted to cross the lines on either side of the house. Building inspectors arrived, clutching clipboards, flashlights, and measuring tapes.

The inspectors, clad in hard hats, measured the pitch of the house, and interviewed the family. The men in the crowd pointed at the building, predicting how and when it would fall, as if the event were a regular occurrence. And the women were paired off, probably talking about the family and what it would do, silently thanking God that it was the Balena family and not their own.

Louis felt guilty joining them, playing witness to an event that ought to have been private. The family stood alone on the other side of the rope, but just on the other side and well away from their house. The wife cried, motioning toward the house, imploring the inspectors to—what?—let her in to get her jewelry, the china? Two children clutched her hands, staring wide-eyed at the house, probably the only one they'd ever known. The husband stood apart from his wife and children, shaking his head morosely, his arms loosely crossing his chest in resignation.

The building must have been sinking for years, maybe since it was built, and then suddenly one day, one minute, the structure gave up and began to crumble. Had there been signs, could they have guessed that it would happen that day?

The inspectors shook their heads, their faces grim, and apologetic. "Any minute," he overheard them say. "It could happen at any minute."

He glanced at the building again, which hadn't seemed to move. How could they possibly know? The inspectors moved back, nearly touching the cord.

There was a noise, a faint, shrill hissing, like a teakettle on low boil. A groaning and creaking started. Still, the building didn't appear to move, but continued looming over the street, its thick, brick and stucco walls revealing only a crack or two. On the second floor, flower boxes full of geraniums preternaturally vivid and lush, clung to windows. One of the giant, old shutters suddenly came loose, swinging on a squealing, rusted pin and hanging half open above the street.

With the squeaking of the shutter, the crowd became silent; so much so that Signora Balena's crying could be heard plainly. Her sob sounded low and animal-like, solitary, and hopeless.

The air hung thick with anticipation, but no one would admit what made everyone so tense, what kept mouths closed, and eyes fixed.

The building began groaning, pitching forward a little farther before easing to a stop. A sucking sound began, the same sound Louis remembered from childhood when a particularly deep and thick patch of mud took firm hold of one of his boots, refusing to release it and eventually pulling it down into the mud (one of the devil's slaves trying to pull him into the underworld, he'd believed at the time).

The walls shuddered, as if something was devouring the structure from within. A few windows shattered and panes popped outward, showering the street with glass. The crowd murmured as the building began sinking, slowly but steadily, as if being lowered on a winch. At first, the sinking occurred so slowly that it was hardly noticeable, but then the second story windows approached street level. A few cobblestones abutting the house tumbled, creating a narrow channel running in front of the house.

There was a whistling noise, almost a heavy sighing. The mud seemed to be sucking the house down. Timbers snapped and roof tiles tumbled onto the cobblestones skidding toward the crowd. Streetlamps attached to the sides of the doorway snapped off, pulled down with the building.

Louis saw cracks lining the walls now, and the burnt orange paint and plaster shedding like skin.

The firefighters, who had hoses trained on the building, began spraying its crumbling roof. What was the point, Louis wondered. The building was being sucked into the rising sea. Suffering a final indignity, the ancient structure was both pulled and pummeled by water.

The house twisted as if trying to fit through a small opening. The front of the building, which had hung threateningly over the street, gradually fell back, folding upon itself. Old bricks and timbers cracked and crumbled, most falling backward into the building, but some tumbling onto the street.

Signora Balena sobbed, wailing as if at a funeral. The crowd pretended not to see her, avoiding her accusing gaze. They must have felt as guilty as he did watching her house implode, witnessing the sea, the ancient mud of Venice and the unknown islands beneath the city take the house as their own.

Within a few minutes, there stood only a jumble of bricks and upended timbers, some broken and splintered. A mattress was visible, and a few pictures and chairs, but the rest of the family's belongings had disappeared. A cloud of fine dust hung in the air, but the fire hoses sprinkling the ruin pushed it away, out toward the sea.

The street was bathed in late afternoon, amber sunlight as Signora Balena sank to the ground, sitting on the cobblestones, her face buried in another woman's shoulder. She cried without shame and loudly, as if to make certain that all would see her sorrow.

So now, Louis had seen a house sink and wondered whether this was the fate of the entire city. He'd read that the rising waters ate at foundations, sucking the earth out to sea and eventually leaving the massive old brick, stone and mortar buildings sitting upon a bed of seawater and brackish mud.

If the founders of Venice had made a deal with the gods then something had gone terribly wrong.

Louis turned and picked his way through the dissipating crowd. The neighbors would go to church, shake their heads, discuss the event at the local bar, converse through second-story windows across narrow alleyways, and sip cappuccino early the next morning and discuss it some more.

The old ones would wonder what sin Signora Balena—or her husband—had committed to bring about such punishment. Others who knew their innocence would question, and still others would curse the gods of Venice that took as easily as they gave.

Since the street was blocked, Louis doubled back along the narrow passage and on to the street that he'd visited earlier, hurrying past the open studio. The door was shut now. The owner had probably come and gone during the hour or so that Louis had watched the house sink.

He peeked in the shuttered window, but could see only the shelves lining the walls. The bowl he'd seen was gone, a circle of dust marking its place. That was the very bowl the neighbor had pointed at, the one he said carried sorrow. Venetians had so many superstitions, and a saying for any of life's coincidences or troubles. In some ways, they seemed to have it all figured out, like the wise men of some ancient civilization. But were they any different from the fortunetellers, the palm readers, and tarot readers that inhabited Clark Street near where he'd grown up in Chicago?

He felt relieved not to see the shuffling neighbor around and hurried past the studio, crossing the bridge nearly in front of it. As he reached the top of the bridge, a faint glimmer shone from below. He stopped momentarily to study the gray-green water, but there was nothing, not even the wake from a passing boat. Cocking his head in order to see the sun reflecting on the water's surface, he thought maybe the bright sunshine would penetrate the murky, jade-green water. Nothing was revealed, though, so he hurried the rest of the way across the bridge, stealing one more glance over his shoulder in hopes of catching a glimpse of the colorful sparkle he felt certain he'd detected.

Getting back to familiar streets felt comforting. Did he feel lost, the solitude of the unfamiliar quarter infecting his mood? Even eternal Venice, which seemed permanent to him, so much more permanent and fixed than anything in the states, could crumble and sink, too. Was nothing certain?

When he got back to his apartment, he wouldn't take a nap, after all. No, the thing to do would be to go back to Harry's for a drink to exorcise the demons from his recent visit there. At that hour, it would be mostly regulars and maybe a few tourists—but only the most interesting ones, those to whom a late afternoon cocktail appealed. Irene and Tad would never sip a drink before five o'clock. Besides, they would be making the most of their few hours in the city by visiting St. Mark's Square, touring one of the art museums, or taking a gondola ride.

To be on the safe side, though, he would peek through the doorway before entering the bar. Given his gloomy frame of mind, having another encounter with his old neighbor and friend could make a complete disaster of the day.

If the city did sink, he hoped Harry's was the last place to go. Cliché it might be, but there was something about the old bar that enchanted and calmed him, as if the benign spirits of a previous generation still inhabited it.

Even a boatload of tourists and an obnoxious neighbor couldn't ruin the place for him.

Chapter Seven

Rome felt oppressive—structured days, Mass, and aged Father Angelo with his foul breath that reminded her of sour milk. Had there ever been a day that she'd been allowed to do just what she wanted? In those days, she must have been the only twelve-year-old in the entire city who felt so glum.

Her mother had chosen the most rigid and conservative school in the city for her daughter, the one to which Catholics sent their kids when they moved to Rome to work for the Vatican. As if they still lived in the Middle Ages or in a convent, students at Santa Cuore attended Mass at the start of every day.

In the few moments when Claudia wasn't answering to nuns, studying or attending piano or etiquette lessons, she daydreamed of escaping. She sneaked her father's magazines, *National Geographic, Arte,* and *Viaggi*, into her bedroom at night and read them under the covers with a flashlight, brushing her fingertips across the vivid photos of exquisite paintings and London, Paris, and Venice, a city that inexplicably captivated her. Her mother didn't want her reading anything other than what the nuns assigned, but she felt drawn to read exactly those things that had been forbidden.

"You'll have time to read other things when you're out of school," her mother had advised. "And by that time you'll lose interest in such superficial things."

She couldn't imagine ever losing interest in "superficial things." History and art fascinated her, and she fantasized about becoming an art historian, architect, or fashion designer. She longed to create something, but always struggled trying to force her hands to yield what had been framed by her mind's eye, whether it was watercolors, oil paintings, or the simple sculptures she executed in art class.

Her mother dismissed her paintings and watercolors with a wave of her jeweled hand. "Enjoy it as a hobby," she lectured. "But don't spend too much time and energy on it. Art is a pastime, a diversion, not the makings of a life."

Instead, her mother, Contessa Baggi, wanted her to focus her energies on working with the nuns and Father Angelo to establish a proper foundation for her life, presumably one that involved attending Mass on a daily basis and making appearances with other Roman blue bloods. Her classmates sniggered when the nuns were out of earshot, calling her a Maledetto, one of the *cursed*.

"I'm a Baggi," she would counter, unsure what they were talking about, but sensing that they shared some secret about her own family to which she wasn't privy.

Her cheeks turning hot and flushed, she would quickly lower her head before one of the nuns saw, and nervously run her fingernails across her throat as if to draw the heat and blood from her face to her neck where it would be less visible. When she was seen with her cheeks pink and blazing, the nuns would rap her desk, accuse her of some shameful thought, and shake their heads condescendingly.

"God can see inside your pretty head, and see the ugly thoughts you entertain," Sister Porgia once told her. What it was they thought she was thinking she wasn't certain, but wondered if it had to do with sex, a concept of which she knew little.

She once tried to ask her mother what her classmates meant by calling her a Maledetto, but her mother cut her off.

"You are Baggi, and descended from the Pucci's. Let them say what they like, if you read in the papers, you are Baggi because I am Baggi."

Opening one of the tabloids and pointing at a grainy photograph that was unmistakably herself, she noisily rapped her finger against the paper. "What does it say here, eh?" she asked, resting a manicured finger under the photo's caption.

"Baggi, Contessa Baggi," Claudia said in a whisper.

"That's right," her mother said, closing the paper as if to end the conversation. "Get your information from me, your papà, or the papers. Don't waste your time on kids at school."

Her mother suddenly smiled, as if realizing that her stern face and raised voice had frightened her daughter. "You are so pretty, *cara*. You should smile more, eh?"

Claudia produced a wan smile, knowing she would be cajoled into providing one before she would be released.

"That's better," her mother clucked, patting the top of her hand. "A fake smile is good, but a genuine smile is better still."

Claudia smiled more broadly, hoping she could please her mother.

Her mother nodded, releasing a sigh. Turning back to her letter writing, she started humming softly.

Days at Santa Cuore were long and tedious and sometimes Claudia wondered if she would survive them. Father Angelo sometimes entered her classroom, checking with her instructors to see how she was progressing and whether she was misbehaving. By the time she was twelve, any thoughts of misbehaving, of sassing a nun, or allowing a homework assignment due date to lapse unobserved, were easily overridden. Life was much easier for Claudia if nuns didn't send letters to her mother or inform Father Angelo, her mother's priest and confidante that she wasn't striving to behave and form herself into a proper and well-schooled girl.

"You should be so lucky to be half the lady your mother is," Father Angelo often told her, forgetting he'd told her this many times before. "You were lucky to be born into such a family, with such a mother, and so you have certain obligations, expectations from the church and from *Gesù Cristo*, no?"

As with the nuns and her mother, Claudia had long ago discovered life was easier if she agreed completely and enthusiastically, nodding her head vigorously and trying to exhibit even-keeled, but sincere passion, forgetting momentarily her love of books and art, the way her eyes were drawn to the rougher quarters of Rome that the car drove by on her way to school each morning. One morning she'd seen a young woman with immense sunglasses and tight pants walking languorously down a sidewalk in Trastevere. The woman's carefree manner, the vague smile on her face as if she were amused, made Claudia sad. Was it such a sin to want so desperately to trade places with this complete stranger, one who didn't live in an enormous old palazzo on a shady street with a view of the Borghese gardens?

If she could have changed places with the woman, she would have done so. To live in one of the small, humble apartment buildings along the narrow, winding streets of the working-class neighborhood turned bohemian seemed a fairy tale, an impossible-to-have life. More than that, though, she longed to leave the city completely, wondering how life would be without her mother's long, hovering shadow.

She'd read novels about unhappy girls whose overbearing mothers were balanced by loving fathers who compensated for their wives' rigidity. In her case, though, her father, while kinder and less severe than her mother, was mostly absent. Preferring his country estate, Villa Cipressi to living in the city and traveling often to New York and Geneva for his work with the United Nations, he seemed to be at home rarely. And when he was, Claudia learned early on that he typically deferred to her mother.

At least she learned from him that love could be gentle and unrestrained, more like a moving, nurturing force than a business transaction burdened with rules and expectations. In the end, though, she couldn't go to him for anything more than comfort. When her mother had first announced that Claudia would be attending school at

Santa Cuore for girls, she'd run to her father's solarium where he'd been reading a stack of bound reports full of small print and no pictures.

"Papà," she'd wept. "I want to go to art school, or to a regular school. I'll have no life at Santa Cuore. I don't want to be a nun, don't want to live such a dreary life. Can't you please convince Mamma? Can't I go to art school or take lessons?"

But he'd only hugged her, gazing at her with sympathetic eyes, and telling her she was right to want to go elsewhere, that whatever it was that urged her to paint, to wander, and to escape, was noble and natural. Only, she had to mind her mother.

"Do what she tells you," he advised, sounding unsure. "And sooner or later everything else will work out. Have faith," he added, kneading her shoulder. "Things will change—they always do. Before you know it, you'll be grown and making your own decisions."

That such a time in her life would ever happen seemed unreal as she stood awkwardly at her father's side in the quiet solarium.

"Won't Mamma always make me do as she wishes?" she asked, hanging her head. "It's no good to have my own thoughts about anything. It doesn't matter what I think."

Her father pulled her head up and stroked her chin. "You'll find your own way, trust me, eh? And one day, she'll figure out that you know what's best for you. Then she'll let you be."

"I can't imagine such a day," Claudia moaned, sitting on the corner of the iron table next to his chair. "She wants to control my every move."

"Trust me, the day will come, cara," he promised.

"And if you're right, then what do I do in the meantime?" she asked, hoping he was right.

Shrugging, he looked at her with apologetic eyes. "You'll have to be patient, that's all."

"You can't speak up for me, help convince her?"

The sun came out from behind the cloudiness of a spring day, washing the room in blinding midday light.

Her father clucked his tongue, shaking his head as he examined her with squinting eyes. "You don't believe I already do? Just because I don't do it in front of you, doesn't mean I don't advocate for you. No, I want what you want."

"Then why can't you make her, why can't you persuade her?" she begged, squinting in the bright light that seemed to mock the hopelessness of her situation.

How could her father, a man with a name, a *count*, be so docile? She couldn't imagine him acting the same way when he did his work at the United Nations. No, he didn't seem timid there at all, not with his work to broker resolutions to stop wars in Africa or Southeast Asia. Why couldn't he employ some of the same approaches with her mother?

"There are things you don't understand, carina," he started to explain. "Your mother's traditional about some things, and child rearing is one of them."

"So you have no say about what happens to me, it's all Mamma?"

The sun disappeared behind another cloud, turning the room gray once again.

"It's not that I have no say," he countered, his mouth twisting. "It's more that we've both agreed that your mother makes better decisions, she's more thoughtful and rational about things. And she has stronger opinions. You see, I've never been certain about most of life's *certainties*. On the other hand, your mother is quite certain about most things."

"She's opinionated?" Claudia asked, remembering a word Sister Porgia had used to describe one of her classmates.

"That's one way to describe her. Another is that she has ideas, thoughts, opinions, yes, opinions, too. And these guide her decisions. She's had experiences that have led her to conclusions about life. I haven't had these same experiences, so I can't say whether she's right or wrong. In these things, I'm just not certain."

"And you don't have opinions about what I should do, where I should attend school or whether I can paint or sculpt?" she asked, looking at him perplexed.

"Not as much as your mother. I'm a doubter; I don't really know what to believe in. So, I'm not the ideal one to raise a child. I qualify everything and claim to know little about these things."

"But you know so much about so many things," she protested. "You grow orchids, you know about architecture, and what about the work you do for the United Nations?"

"These are different things. Sure, I know about these things—and others, too. But your mother's happiness depends on her raising you and making the decisions. I make decisions about other things—"

"But what if she's wrong about decisions about me?" she interrupted, sliding off the table to stand before him.

"I'm sorry," he sighed, smiling wanly. "You can't know for certain whether your mother is wrong about everything. You have to trust her. Maybe not everything is immediately apparent right now. You're only twelve, you might change your mind when you're older and appreciate different things. And if she was wrong, well, then you'll have plenty of time to do those things that you want to do."

And so, Claudia's fate was determined. With a strong-willed mother and a father who wouldn't defy her mother, she had few options. So it was to be her mother's wishes, but some day she would do what she wanted.

With his slender face, thin frame, and small glasses, her father appeared almost fragile next to the contessa. While he shied from the title and expectations of being a count, avoiding the parties, social events, and charity balls doggedly planned and attended by his wife, her mother made a point of insisting that people, including the nuns at the school and Claudia's classmates address her formally.

Still, sometimes her mother's eyes would betray something deeper, a luminous quality that Claudia couldn't explain. She would turn a corner and catch her mother gazing out a window with a vacant expression, her eyes with a faraway look. Or, she might charge into the solarium or *sala* to startle the woman who'd been lying or sitting so still that Claudia hadn't realized she'd been in the room (or she would have avoided entering). And she knew better to ask. Despite her mother's stern looks and firmness, Claudia felt sorry for her, though she couldn't explain exactly why.

Her mother seemed to have secrets locked away, things that she never referred to or discussed. If her mother had had a life before meeting her father, she never referred to it. Maybe these were the same things her classmates whispered about and slyly referenced, things having to do with her being a Maledetto. And were these the things that made her mother occasionally pensive, or that drove her to attend church so often and to confide in Father Angelo? She couldn't imagine her mother committing any sins, though she sometimes wondered if her forcing her daughter to bend so uniformly to her will might in some way qualify, if even a lesser one.

For Claudia's church confirmation, her mother planned a big party in the garden. There was to be a quartet and tables full of food, but most noticeable were the orange and lemons hollowed out and filled with gelato that Claudia had chosen herself as a dessert. When discussing the party, her mother had asked Claudia what she would like, and she'd timidly asked for the treats that felt refreshingly cold in her hand and that were popular with all the girls at Santa Cuore. She hadn't been surprised when her mother had agreed, remarking that these were some of the most beautiful—albeit simple—sweets known to Italy. Her mother had moments of generosity and indulgence, but Claudia simply had to learn which requests were more likely to be approved, and which resulted in raised eyebrows and pursed lips. Sometimes, Claudia felt as though she were traversing a minefield, wondering what requests, names, or ideas might provoke her mother.

As they sat at the breakfast table in the solarium, her father misting his orchids along the perimeter of the room and her mother scanning the day's giornale, she thought carefully about asking for the two things she most desired for the party: to invite one of her visiting instructors, Signora Avanza who worked as a curator at the *Museo Vaticano*, and Antonio DiCastello who lived in the palazzo down the street.

During the previous months, Claudia's days had become markedly more interesting and enjoyable with the arrival of these two people in her life. The former had long, shiny hair that fell down her shoulders and could speak for hours; it seemed, about the creation and significance of the Boeotian Master's *Boy with a Goose*, the Acropolis, Michelangelo's sculptures, or the frescoes lining the walls of churches across Italy. Claudia sat mesmerized, taking notes, asking questions and longing for the woman's lectures to take up entire days instead of a mere hour three days a week. And interestingly, the woman looked remarkably similar to the one she'd seen walking through the Trastevere quarter months before, but that woman had worn tight pants and oversize sunglasses, not a long dress covering her arms and legs. Could Signora Avanza have been the same person, the type who would flaunt the rules of the Vatican, church, and school and dress that way? While she would never appear at the museum or school in anything but clothing that more closely resembled draperies, might she have another life outside the one of which Claudia had glimpsed?

After the first lecture from the woman, she longed for nothing more than to walk home, wandering the tiny, crooked streets between the school at the edge of the Vatican and her home, but Orzino, her mother's driver, waited dutifully at the tired, somber school gate and would never permit her walking. As they drove home, she could see the tiled roof of the Vatican rising in the distance, becoming smaller and then disappearing as they rounded a corner. As they passed through Trastevere, she wondered if she would see her instructor walking past one of the small galleries or sitting in one of the ramshackle cafés, but she caught no glimpse of her.

If she could invite the woman to her confirmation party, then perhaps Claudia could discover where she lived, what she did when she wasn't teaching at Santa Cuore or caring for the masterpieces at the Vatican. Signora Avanza fascinated her, giving her the idea that maybe there could be a different life for her after school, after she escaped her mother.

When it came to Antonio DiCastello, she had an interest of a different sort. As she'd grown older, she'd been permitted to walk to the nearby gardens on her own, or to wander the nearby streets peppered with marble-fronted boutiques and manicured planters and parkways. During the previous year, she'd encountered Antonio in front of his gated house, and then at the *gelateria* on via Galleta.

He smiled mischievously and had a cowlick that rose cockeyed from the side of his forehead. His tousled, unruly hair matched a personality that intrigued Claudia. During their first meetings, she learned that he attended L'Accademia Brunelleschi, one of the oldest schools in Rome, but one with no ties to the church. Only the children of Jews, scientists, artists, and eccentric old families attended the school, which made it even more appealing to Claudia. Santa Cuore felt claustrophobic, oppressive, but from what Antonio told her, L'Accademia encouraged students to pursue interests in painting, poetry, science, and architecture, exactly the subjects that interested Claudia. If Galileo were suddenly reincarnated as a girl enrolled at Santa Cuore, she felt certain that the nuns and Father Angelo, along with her mother and the school's administrators, would all refute anew his theory that the earth revolved around the sun. In ways, it was as if the Enlightenment had never pierced the school's thick walls on which no ivy grew.

She grew so smitten with the two new people that had suddenly entered her life that she sometimes fantasized about what life would be like to change places with either of them. And sometimes, as she drifted off to sleep with distant, watery street light bleeding through the enormous, curtained windows of her bedroom, she wondered what it might be like to one day be married to Antonio.

The moment she'd uttered the boy's name to her mother, though, she realized with a pang of regret that she'd made a mistake.

Jerking her head from her giornale, like a long, thin-necked bird that has caught a whiff of sudden danger, her mother arched her eyebrows.

"How do you know that boy?" she asked, alarmed.

If she told her mother, she'd met him in the neighborhood, her newfound freedom to wander would be curtailed, and she felt certain of that. Knowing she was about to commit a sin, she lied, her fingertips nervously grazing her neck.

"I've seen him outside the window, and the girls at school talk about him. I didn't even know he lived on our very street, and my classmates say he must be interesting, a good boy to know."

Her mother laughed, clucking her tongue.

"Which of your classmates told you *this*?" Not waiting for an answer, she continued. "The DiCastellos are an old family, that's true, and you could say with certainty that they are interesting, but such observations and assignations should be qualified, eh?"

Claudia gazed at her mother in confusion, pushing her fingernails into the palms of her hands, regretting that she'd mentioned the boy's name at all. She should have known.

"They are atheists and their pursuits are far too superficial, sinful even, for a mingling of our families—even if on a *shallow level.* No, we could never have that boy in our home, let alone to a confirmation party," she shook her head, turning toward Claudia's father.

"Can you imagine, Marco?" she mused. "They would rebuff such an invitation, anyway, wouldn't they?" Turning back to Claudia, she smiled sympathetically. "No, cara, we won't be inviting a DiCastello. You'd be hurt, anyway, as the boy would never attend such an occasion, and likely wouldn't even respond."

Claudia knew her mother was mistaken, wrong that Antonio would not attend and misinformed, too, about his family. While it was true that they didn't belong to the church, that they found it antiquated and repressive, they believed they were more Christian than most of the people calling themselves such, and particularly the ones residing in the Vatican. That's what the boy had told her during their many conversations at Athena's Fountain in the gardens. He'd also told her many things about the church that she hadn't been taught, and that started her wondering whether everything she'd been told by the nuns, priests, and her mother were completely true. But she dared not respond or she might lose any chance of seeing Antonio again, of having the freedom to meet him at the *gelateria* or in the Borghese gardens. And she dare not ever question the church or its teachings, not to her mother, the priests, or the nuns. She could only discuss such things with Antonio, who seemed to encourage her with all the questions he asked.

Her mother glanced up at her briefly, smiling more genuinely.

"The teacher we'll invite, yes, that's fine," she assented. "But not the boy."

Smiling, but not too broadly, Claudia relaxed her fingers that had been pressing painfully into her hands. At least her teacher could come, and that was something. Afraid her mother might understand how happy she had made her, she placed her napkin on the table with feigned carelessness, asking, "May I be excused? I'm finished."

Without looking up, her mother nodded. "Certainly. I hope you'll be studying, eh? Not many more school days left before the end of the term."

"No, not too many," she agreed, eager to leave. "I'll go study and get it out of the way."

Glancing at her father just before she stepped out of the room, she saw a vague, fleeting smile appear on his lips, leaving her to wonder if she'd imagined it.

If Antonio had begun opening doors that Claudia had never suspected existed, Father Franco, one of the school's administrators, closed others. While early on she'd accepted her mother's teachings that Jesus and God were full of wrath, ready—and to her, seemingly eager—to pounce upon sinners, something about the stories, the all-powerful and all-knowing being, revealed a god who acted unkindly, harshly and sometimes even unfairly.

If she was expected to act timidly, with justice and kindness, then why were Jesus and God given a pass on these same expectations and the cardinal rules that the priests, the nuns, and the pope stressed above all others?

Only after so many Saturday afternoon meetings with Antonio did she begin to see a different way, one that still encouraged her to strive to exhibit love, kindness, and charity, but didn't appear to possess equal amounts of rigidity, cruelty, and hypocrisy. And after she learned that Christianity was hardly the sole religion that valued kindness and justice, fractures appeared, which would later widen and become the undoing of her religion.

But Father Franco gave her a completely different view of the church, one that Antonio had been urging her to see from their earliest conversations.

Just prior to Easter break and weeks before her confirmation party, Father Franco, a friend of Father Angelo's, sent a notice to Claudia's geometry instructor that he wanted to see her in his office. Why did he need to pull her out of class? Couldn't he have asked her to come by during lunch or after school? While she had little interest in geometry and struggled to maintain good grades in any math class, she didn't want to miss a minute of lecture or an opportunity for assistance. With the end of the term approaching, she needed every bit of help she could get. However, there was no denying Father Franco, who also served as an advisor to the school. And no one in the school—from the students to the highest-ranking nuns—defied a priest, no matter the request.

Sighing quietly so that the nun teaching the class didn't hear, Claudia picked up her books and slipped out of the classroom. Heading down the high-ceilinged, empty corridor, she felt her throat constrict, making her breath shallow and labored. What could he possibly have wanted to see her about? Did he somehow suspect the conversations she had with Antonio or surmise that she questioned both the New Testament and Old Testaments and lately nearly anything the nuns taught her? But how could he possibly have suspected, she'd been tight-lipped, asking no questions in her religion classes and speaking to no one about it except Antonio. Had someone seen them in the gardens or wandering along the quarter's avenues?

She arrived in Father Franco's dark-paneled reception room, a beak-nosed nun pointing her toward one of the oversize, straight-backed, carved chairs. The upholstery was threadbare at the seat's edge, making the backs of her legs itch. Fidgeting in the chair, she found herself growing more uncomfortable the longer she waited.

The door to the reception room opened, revealing Signora Avanza, who smiled despite a crinkled brow.

"Is something the matter?" she asked. "How come you're not in class?"

Claudia shrugged and before she could be scolded for being rude, added, "I don't know; I was just called in to see Father Franco."

"Should I tell Father you're here to see him?" the nun interrupted, frowning at Signora Avanza. "I'm not sure he's expecting you."

"No," the woman answered, sitting beside Claudia. "I'll wait to see him after his appointment with *Signorina* Baggi, eh? That can't last long and I'm off this afternoon."

She smiled, pushing her dark-colored hair over her shoulder.

"You're not in trouble, eh?" the woman asked, whispering.

"I don't think so," Claudia said, wondering if she was. Did her teacher know something she didn't?

"I can't imagine you would be. Listen, I want to bring the class over to the Vatican one afternoon for a special visit. You seem so interested in art; I think it would be good for you to go. It's a class of older girls, but I think you'd do just fine. I think it would be good for you," she said, patting Claudia's arm.

Claudia smiled. "I'd like to go with you. That would be wonderful. I'll just have to ask my mother."

"I'm sure she'll say yes," Signora Avanza said.

For a moment, Claudia believed she must be right. Rocking forward, so happy with her luck at having a chance to talk to the woman, she was suddenly struck by a thought.

"Signora, may I ask you a personal question?" she said timidly.

The woman nodded, patting Claudia's arm again.

Unconsciously grinning, she asked if the woman lived in Trastevere in the bohemian quarter and if perhaps she owned a pair of oversize sunglasses.

Her instructor smiled, leaning forward, and placing her face close to Claudia's.

"I think you've seen me," she laughed quietly. "But listen, carina," she whispered, glancing at the nun who sat hunched over her desk. "Don't tell anyone I asked, but why do you attend school here? You seem like you belong somewhere else, somewhere *different*, eh?"

"My mother—" she started to respond, but a bell sounded from the nun's desk.

"Okay, *ragazza*," she called, nodding at Claudia. "The signore will see you now."

Signora Avanza squeezed Claudia's knee, winking.

Claudia grinned. "Will you come to my confirmation party, please?" she asked suddenly, wondering if her mother had already sent out the invitations.

"Sure, sure, send me an invitation," she said, nodding.

"Ragazza, please," the nun said, waving her toward the heavy, polished wooden door.

Claudia waved at Signora Avanza as she followed the nun. The thin, tall woman ushered her into Father Franco's office, which was darker than usual, the blinds having been drawn and angled upward to emit feeble shafts of light from a rainy April day outside.

Walking to an upholstered bench, which the nun motioned her toward, Claudia sat in the middle of the long piece of furniture. Giving her a quick glance and smile, Father Franco waved away the nun; a half-thankful, half-dismissive gesture that made him looked hurried. Looking back down at some papers, he issued a sigh, signing one of the pieces of paper and placing it in a folder. The whole while, it seemed to Claudia that he was aware of her presence, though he appeared preoccupied with the papers on his desk. Pushing a button and hunching over his desk, he spoke into an intercom box.

"Sister Parva," he called.

"Signore," a tinny voice responded.

"Will you please run over to the Vatican to pick up some papers for me? They're waiting for me at Cardinal Bernadino's office."

"*Certo, signore*," the voice responded.

After straightening the papers, he cleared his throat and stood. Turning to look out the windows behind his desk, he made a small grunting noise.

Walking around to the front of his desk, he scanned the large hanging oil portraits of past school administrators, scenes of churches, the Vatican, and St. Peter's dome viewed from the hills above the city. Finally, approaching the high-backed bench on which Claudia sat, he cleared his throat and sat next to her, his black-trousered leg pushing into her knee. Reflexively pulling her leg away and repositioning herself farther from the priest, she realized she'd been rude by sitting in the very center of the bench. This was just the sort of lesson a priest or nun would teach a student, that there were consequences for thoughtless, inconsiderate behavior.

Smiling, as if pleased that she'd understood the lesson, he cleared his throat again.

"Thank you for coming to see me," he said evenly and in an earnest tone.

As if she had a choice! She resented the way he'd recently taken an interest in her, first as a Baggi no doubt because of Father Angelo's urging, and for the past trimester as a concerned priest. Why was he always asking how she was doing, whether she had any questions about classes, or needed assistance with any of her course work? Even Father Angelo was not so persistent.

"Thank you for asking to see me, signore," she said timidly, aware of how close to a whisper her voice sounded.

"You needn't fear me," the priest smiled, patting her on the knee as he slid closer. "I just thought with your confirmation approaching that we should talk about where you are with your faith and with the church, eh?"

"But … I have geometry class … right now," she stuttered, trying to sound as if she were asking a question instead of protesting.

"It will hardly hurt a student as good as you to miss one class, don't you think?"

She shrugged, wondering if she should lie.

"That's not the way you're taught to answer a priest, is it?" he asked, smiling, as if joking.

"No, signore. I'm sorry," she said, sitting straighter and moving her spine from the upholstered seat back. "Missing one class won't hurt. I can stay late tonight and find out what I missed or review the chapter on my own."

"Exactly," he said enthusiastically, his voice elevated.

Why did he seem as nervous as she did, his voice jerky and uneven as if he, too, had a dry throat?

His knee suddenly pressed against hers again and she tried scooting farther down the bench, but realized she was already up against the heavy wooden arm, the end of which formed an enormous lion's paw.

"Do you doubt, eh, Claudia?" he said, looking concerned, but with his eyes on her knee.

"What do you mean, signore?" she asked, thinking of her many conversations with Antonio.

"You know, doubt the church, God's existence. You can tell me if you do. Many do and it's better to address these issues while you're young, instead of allowing them to fester," he explained, his voice sounding increasingly strained. "If you don't talk about them now, these sorts of doubts and questions tend to make for an unhappy life as we grow older."

Patting her knee with a shaky hand, he leaned his shoulder into hers.

"Now maybe you've been having conversations with certain people, hearing different things, other views of God and the church, eh?" he suggested.

How could he possibly have known? Had he somehow seen one of their meetings? Would he tell her mother? Scratching her throat with her shaking fingers, she could feel her cheeks turning hot.

"Sì," he said, his voice rising again. "I'm right, am I not?"

Claudia shrugged, uncertain whether she should lie to a priest, though she'd recently decided that lying to her mother about certain things was okay.

Shaking his head as if to scold, he clucked his tongue at her silence. "Not that again, is it?" he asked.

"Dispiace, signore," she murmured reflexively, deciding she would lie. "No, I've not been having such conversations. My mother won't allow me to see nonbelievers."

"So we keep secrets, do we?" he said, his eyebrows forming dark brown arches.

He sounded conspiratorial, as if they now shared something. It was almost as if he'd been pleased that she'd lied, as if he knew her secret and yet was somehow hopeful that she would lie about it. Did priests act this way, not wanting to hear if people had doubts? Or was this the way they thought doubts should be addressed, by deciding they didn't exist in hopes that eventually they might simply evaporate?

Her eyes on a corner of the deep red velvet of the bench, she weighed whether she should continue to lie to the priest. For a moment, her fingers trembling and her heart racing, she thought she might tell the truth, just tell him everything about Antonio and her doubts, how she didn't believe any longer. It was as if a voice somewhere were shouting for her to confess, but not to avoid sinning.

If she admitted everything to the priest, her mother would be sure to find out and then she would never see Antonio again. And who knew what else her mother might do, how she might react if she learned that her only daughter was no longer Catholic? Sometimes it seemed as if the most important thing to her mother was the church.

"No, I keep no secrets," she whispered, her voice trembling, seemingly giving her away as a liar, even as she denied his accusation.

"That's right," Father Franco whispered, his voice scratchy.

Leaning over, his chest pushing into her face and trapping her head against the bench back, he clamped one of his cold, trembling hands on her knee and began pushing it up her skirt. He smelled of mothballs and anise, and his jacket felt scratchy against her hot face.

Screaming, she bit the priest's chest, though her teeth seemed to clamp down mostly on the smelly, thick black jacket he wore. Wriggling, she squeezed out from under him, falling with a thud to the polished parquet floor.

Scrambling to her feet, she raced toward the heavy wooden door, expecting Father Franco's hand on her shoulder or waist, pulling her back violently. But she reached the door without hearing his footstep behind her. Glancing back, she turned the giant, carved brass doorknob.

Straightening himself as he brushed the front of his jacket where she'd bitten him, the priest had an expression of confusion more than shock or anger. For a moment, she wondered whether the incident had occurred. Blinking, she gazed at the man, wondering if she was thinking clearly. Father Franco appeared as unfazed by what had happened, or by her peering face, as he might if a student posed a difficult question.

Her heart racing, she pulled the door open and ran out of the office, slamming the door behind her. Uncertain where to go, she dashed forward, thinking that she needed to escape the school and catch a glimpse of the sky, breathe fresh air.

She ran directly into a chest and two arms that grabbed her and pulled her into a tight embrace. For a moment, she thought that Father Franco had somehow tricked her, inexplicably getting in front of her, or that another priest had been waiting outside the office in case she escaped. But the soft voice and a strong scent of perfume were pleasantly familiar.

"Why on earth are you running, Claudia?" the soft voice asked.

Pulling her way out of the firm embrace, she looked up into Signora Avanza's face.

"Ah … I … um," she stammered, uncertain what she should say, whether she should tell yet another lie. Start telling lies and you'll never stop, one of the nuns had told her. Maybe the nuns were right about some things.

What had just happened, anyway? How could she tell anyone, most of all an instructor who worked for Father Franco?

"Claudia, sit down, *here*," the woman said, leading her toward the same prickly chair she'd sat in minutes earlier. "Dio," she cursed, looking around hurriedly to see if anyone had heard. "You look like you're about to faint. What happened?"

The woman gripped Claudia's shoulders, sinking to rest on her haunches. "Take a moment, *breathe*," she commanded, rubbing Claudia's back.

When she no longer gasped and her mind stopped racing, she nervously eyed the door to Father Franco's office.

"Let's get out of here, okay? I want to go outside," she whispered, her voice trembling.

"Tell me first what happened? Tell me, Claudia," she whispered tersely, squeezing her arm. "You are safe here—safe with me."

Claudia shivered, her lips trembling and her hands shaking. Should she tell the woman? And if she did, what would happen then?

"Claudia," Signore Avanza said calmly, gently pulling up Claudia's chin to study her face. "Did Father Franco do something to you? Did he do something that frightened you?"

Claudia cast her eyes to the floor to avoid her instructor's penetrating gaze. Her face burned, even as her fingers and lips trembled from an icy coldness.

"He did, didn't he?" she whispered tersely, her voice rising barely above a whisper.

"Claudia, you must say, eh? If I'm right about this, will you nod your head? Just nod your head for me, okay?"

Claudia didn't know how to respond, her head spinning. What would her mother do if she found out? She would never take her daughter's word over that of a priest, let alone the school administrator. And what chance was there for her at a school where such a thing had happened?

She'd lied to the priest and that had backfired, so maybe she should tell the truth. More than anyone, she could trust Signora Avanza, she realized, slowly opening her mouth to speak.

"Sì," she whispered so quietly she wasn't certain she'd spoken.

Signora Avanza hugged her, enveloping her in soft arms and sweet perfume.

"That's wrong, terrible, carina," she whispered, stroking Claudia's cheeks with her fingers. "I'm so sorry."

Claudia stopped shivering, suddenly assured that Signora Avanza would protect her. What had happened, after all? If the priests were right, then what Father Franco had intended was as good as done, and he'd committed a grievous sin.

"Come with me, okay?" Signora Avanza said more loudly, extending her hand. "Are you okay to go back in there with me?"

While Claudia didn't like Father Franco, she didn't fear him, especially after seeing him looking so feeble and timid before she'd hurried out of his office. And if she could confront him with Signora Avanza, that would be okay. Nodding, she clasped the woman's hand, her bracelets tinkling.

The door swung into the office with an ominous creak. Signora Avanza, with Claudia in tow, entered the room, finding the priest in the same spot on the bench, his expression clouded as he studied the nearby paintings.

"What the hell?" Signora Avanza asked, her voice shrill. "What do you mean by this?"

Claudia had never heard anyone speak to a priest in such a way, let alone a teacher or a woman.

His face turning white, rigid, Father Franco stood and walked slowly, deliberately toward the two of them and then turned and approached his desk. Sitting, his hands still shaking slightly, he grabbed a folder of correspondence. Opening the manila folder, he glanced up at Claudia and Signora Avanza who stood with her hands on her hips. Peeking around the woman's hip, Claudia's ear pressed against her ribcage, she thought she could hear the woman's heart beating furiously, much like her own.

"You can leave now," Father Franco said, waving a trembling hand as he glared at Claudia. "I'll not tell your mother about your behavior today and your frequent meetings with that heathen neighbor boy if you leave now. And *you*," he said harshly, pointing at Signora Avanza.

"You, I no longer want instructing the girls here. This is none of your business."

"I'll report you," the woman threatened, her voice trembling.

"To whom?" the priest asked, glancing up at her. "You've seen nothing and have no one to report to."

"You're an animal, the exact reason why the church is a farce," she hissed. "Preying on little girls, *gli innocenti,* while proclaiming your holiness and everyone else's sinfulness. A wolf in sheep's clothing—you disgust me."

The priest shrugged. "Who cares what you think?" he muttered. "I suggest you leave. Both of you," he added, glaring at Claudia.

"Let's see what your mother has to say about this," Signora Avanza said, grabbing Claudia's hand and staring defiantly at the priest.

"Yes, let's do indeed," Father Franco muttered, reaching for a leather-bound book at the corner of his desk.

"*Sporco cretino*!" Signora Avanza cried, gesturing wildly. Leading Claudia out of the darkened office, she slammed the door so hard Claudia thought she heard a painting crash to the floor.

"Someone must tell your mother," she said in disgust, pulling Claudia through the outer office. "You can't return to school here. You mustn't."

"Can you do anything to him; can't he be forced to leave?" Claudia asked, sinking down into the seat of a taxi they'd flagged just outside the school, but she sensed deep down the answer to her own question.

Pulling Claudia into her arms, Signora Avanza brushed the girl's hair with her fingers, and rubbed her arms. "I'm so sorry, *cara*, so very sorry. But there's nothing to be done about him."

"But I heard you tell him—"

"He was right. I meant it, but that depraved priest is right: there's nothing we can do. Not unless your mother wants to take up the issue."

"My mother?"

"Yes, your mother. When we tell your mother, maybe she'll want to defend you, make sure that priest is removed. She's the only sort of person who can do something. I don't have the power to do anything and by the look of things neither do you. But your mother ..."

Claudia wasn't certain what the woman meant. Did she think Claudia didn't have the strength to say something, or that she knew that once told, her mother might not do anything?

When the taxi pulled in front of her house, Claudia could see her mother standing inside the open French doors of her second floor bedroom. Stepping onto the sidewalk and closer to the palazzo, she saw her mother talking on the telephone, watching her and Signora Avanza approach the front gate.

They hadn't even reached the heavy, towering iron gate when a buzzer sounded. The gate released, popping open a few inches. As they slowly walked up the sidewalk, Claudia's heart racing and her knees wobbling, the front door flew open.

"Claudia, what have you done?" her mother asked, her voice shrill. "What are you doing home from school? Come in quickly!" she barked, opening the door widely and disappearing into the shadows of the front hall.

"We've no chance," Claudia said dejectedly.

"When your mother finds out, there's no question she'll do something—at the very least pull you out of the school," Signora Avanza chided, pulling Claudia to her side. "Don't worry. I'll explain everything. Let me talk."

They entered the long hall leading from the front door, the thick carpet muffling their footsteps. Claudia had never noticed how quiet the palazzo was, seemingly covered with a thick quilt that drowned out all sound.

"Who is this?" her mother asked, waving them down the hallway.

"I'm Signora Avanza—"

"Ah, one of Claudia's instructors at Cuore. I was just addressing an invitation to you for my daughter's confirmation party," she said, sounding irritated. "I didn't realize you were an *art* instructor."

Who had told her mother that, Claudia wondered? She had

intentionally avoided including that bit of information, knowing her mother might not invite her if she knew.

"We should go somewhere private," Signora Avanza suggested soberly.

"I'm Contessa Baggi," she said with irritation, her brow furrowed. "You can follow me."

Claudia looked at the floor, her eyes on her mother and Signora Avanza's slender feet as they strode through the first floor corridor, then through the high doorway of the study.

"Close the door, *cara*," the contessa said to Claudia.

As she pushed it closed, the heavy door clicked solidly. Even more than the corridor, the study felt heavy with silence, not even the muffled sounds from the street or nearby city bleeding in through the thick walls and windows, the drawn drapes and blinds.

Signora Avanza took a seat in one of a pair of high wingback chairs that the contessa had pointed to. She caught Claudia's downcast eyes and smiled with encouragement.

"What has happened?" the contessa asked impatiently, sitting on the settee across from Claudia's instructor.

"It's difficult to explain, it's very sensitive," Signora Avanza said uncertainly.

Did her mother make her nervous, too, Claudia wondered.

"Perhaps Claudia can explain," she suggested.

"No, I'm not suggesting that," her teacher said. "It will likely be difficult enough for her to hear, let alone be forced to explain it herself."

The contessa shook her head, reaching for a cigarette from the low table in front of her. Lighting the cigarette, she gazed worriedly at Claudia's instructor. "I regret to say I'm unpleasantly intrigued, and quite frankly, anxious to have it over with. So, if you can please tell me quickly, we can finish this up and you can be on your way."

Claudia couldn't bear to watch her mother as Signora Avanza recounted what had happened, or what Claudia had admitted had happened, including Father Franco's response to their accusations when they'd reentered his office. Digging her nails into the palms of her hands, she wondered how her mother would react.

She couldn't have had a better champion. If she'd been somehow cursed by attending an unhappy school and having a rigid mother, and then by having a priest push himself on her, at least she'd been fortunate to have someone like Signora Avanza rescue her. What if the woman hadn't paid the office a surprise visit that afternoon or had arrived minutes earlier and then left before Claudia even arrived? Even if her mother blamed her, insisting that she return to school there, well, at least there was one person who knew better—two, actually. But she resolved not to think about Father Franco again, to focus on forgetting his narrow face, dark hair, and piercing eyes.

"Claudia," her mother said, interrupting her thoughts. "Look at me, daughter."

Reluctantly, she gazed at her mother. And etched across her face were lines of worry, a hollow, defeated expression punctuated by glassy, pink eyes that bore pain. Just as quickly, her mother inhaled from her cigarette, blowing the smoke indignantly toward the French doors that stood open to the patio and setting her jaw so that Claudia could almost see the muscles in her cheeks.

"Is this true, can this be true what *Maestra* Avanza has told me?" she asked doubtfully, biting her lip nervously, sounding unsympathetic.

Claudia nodded.

"And is it also true that you've been meeting that neighborhood boy, Antonio DiCastello?"

Signora Avanza stared at the contessa, her brow furrowed.

"*Mi scusi*," Signora Avanza interrupted. "But I hardly see what that has to do with what happened at the school today."

The contessa frowned, waving the cigarette at her guest. "Allow me, for just a moment," she explained. Turning to her daughter, she said, "You've been meeting that boy."

Claudia, pushing her nails so tightly into her palms that she thought she might scream, nodded her head slowly. She'd lied so many times the past few days, about seemingly inconsequential things that turned out to be very consequential, she no longer knew whether lying or telling the truth was desirable. If the priest had wanted her to lie, and she'd played along, did that mean she should tell her mother the truth or a lie?

"And what sorts of things did you and Antonio talk about? What sorts of things did he tell you?" she asked, inhaling her cigarette so vigorously that the tip glowed a fierce orange in the murky room.

"But, Contessa—" Signora Avanza interrupted.

The contessa waved her off again.

"I understand what you'll want to say," she said, jerking her head. "But you must realize that this boy from down the street, the whole family, in fact, is rabidly antichurch. And the boy has been putting all sorts of wild ideas into my daughter's head. I'm sure of it."

"What does this have to do with what happened today, though?" Signora Avanza asked, her eyes looking wild.

Claudia, watching her instructor, noticed that when the woman's long skirt rode up her calf as she leaned forward, a small tattoo on the side of her thigh revealed itself. Nearly gasping, she craned her neck to see the form of the tattoo, but as if she sensed Claudia's gaze, Signora Avanza pushed her skirt down.

The contessa shook her head as if it were obvious. "Father Franco knew about these meetings and tried to talk to Claudia about them, that's all. He called her into his office today, just prior to her confirmation, to find out what she thought of these conversations. I think he was very dutiful, the perfect priest to make certain Claudia was doing okay, that she hadn't been misled just before this important occasion."

Claudia's instructor gasped.

"But he tried to abuse her," she cried.

The contessa bit her lip, turning pale. Her eyes narrowing, she seemed to swallow, passing a few measured breaths.

"Signora *Avanza*," she said, emphasizing the woman's name. "I appreciate your view and I know you believe you are helping my daughter—and for that I'm grateful. But I must ask that you not insult the church in my company, regardless of your opinions. The church has salvaged many lives, including my own, and I owe it and God a great deal, well, *every*thing."

"And that's worth sacrificing your daughter?" she asked, leaning so far forward out of the wingback chair that she nearly teetered onto the floor.

"Ha!" the contessa cried. "I'm not sacrificing my daughter—I would never do such a thing! Can't you see," she explained, tapping the ashes from her cigarette into a large silver ashtray on the side table. "I'm *saving* my daughter! She has an active imagination; she simply misconstrued pastoral guidance as something base. And in her defense, I would submit that she's hardly the first, and unlikely to be the last."

Glancing at her daughter, she gazed at her sadly.

Gripping the armrest, Signora Avanza looked at Claudia who stared at her lap, then glared at the contessa.

"That's absurd, you really can't believe that, can you?" she asked, her voice rising. "That your daughter would make that up, imagine what happened?"

"And I'm to believe that a longtime friend, a church leader who has no history of such behavior has misled me? This is the behavior you expect of a man of God?" she asked in an equally shrill tone.

"Did he call you?" Signora Avanza asked, slapping her knee. "Did that *sporco* telephone you already?"

"Signora, as I asked you, *please*," the contessa said, grimacing.

"*Mi, spiace, signora*, but are you taking the word of the church over that of your daughter?"

"Of course I am," the contessa laughed. "Children lie, and we've already determined that my daughter lies. Is that a grievous sin? No, and certainly not for the young. But taking the word of a child over that of a priest, over that of the church—that makes no sense to me."

"But what of my word?" she asked, slapping her knee. "Does what I've told you mean nothing? I have nothing to gain from coming here."

The contessa shrugged.

"But you were not in that room either, were you? And furthermore, you have your own, shall we say, *critical* views of the church, too, don't you?"

Signora Avanza's face turned white, her fingers gripping the arm of the chair. She stared at the contessa, shaking her head solemnly as she silently exhaled. Turning to Claudia, she stood, leaning to embrace her.

"I'm so sorry, cara," she said quietly. "I must go."

"Will I see you back at school, will you come to my party?" Claudia asked desperately, suddenly fearful again.

"We'll have to cancel the party," the contessa interrupted, frowning. "And from what Signore Franco has told me, I don't think the signora will be teaching at Cuore any longer."

So this was how it went when you found a few mere people who you liked, Claudia realized, her heart sinking. Remembering her father's advice, she wondered how many years she would need to wait before she could be happy, before she could start living her own life instead of the one crafted by her mother or the nuns or priests at Cuore.

"Look for me in Trastevere or at the Vatican," Signora Avanza whispered. "And don't despair. Just be careful, okay? A day will come, eh?"

Claudia hugged the woman, wondering if she would ever see her again.

"You work at the Vatican museum?" the contessa asked, looking surprised.

"I do," Signora Avanza answered hesitantly.

Giving Claudia another quick hug, she nodded at the girl's mother.

"Piacere," she said dryly.

"Piacere," the contessa answered with more enthusiasm. "Thank you for taking an interest in my daughter."

"She's been my pleasure to teach," the woman said. "I hope she's permitted to blossom."

The contessa smiled, standing. "Of course, I could hardly stop her, could I?"

Claudia felt that in a way, Signora Avanza had been wrong. If the signora thought that the priests had fooled Claudia, and had the entire structure of her life rendered topsy-turvy, she'd been mistaken. Instead, Claudia felt like this was the sign she'd been seeking, the event that Antonio had promised would one day open her eyes. She vowed that the next time she saw Antonio she would kiss him. He'd been pressuring her for months, and now she felt certain that he'd been right about so many things.

But how would she ever meet him again? Her mother would certainly limit her free time and her ability to meet with Antonio. How could she have been so silly as to have believed just a few short months earlier that she could finally be happy, that between her art classes and Antonio, she had found a part of a life that made sense?

In the months that followed, she made furtive trips through Trastevere to find Signora Avanza, but never caught a glimpse of the woman again. Orzino became suspicious of her requests to drive down different streets in Trastevere in search of different stores or monuments she'd claimed she'd read about in history class. And when she finally made it to the Vatican Museum, the woman at the information window informed her that Signora Avanza was no longer employed there.

Years later, Claudia would remember that her art instructor was the first person she cared about that the world had seemingly swallowed up, leaving no trace. If there was such a thing as fate, it was certainly fickle. Why bring someone so interesting, a person whom Claudia felt certain could teach her things about life that no one else could, only to have her disappear?

But the incident and Signora Avanza made Claudia vow all the more ardently that one day she would do something different, something creative. She would live where she wanted and do something that excited her. She would have friends—and a husband—who were like-minded. And once she left the city, she knew she would never return to Rome, not with the depressing Vatican casting its shadow across the entire city. No, she would live somewhere full of art, somewhere unique.

By the time she returned to Cuore in September, Claudia had successfully pushed the memory of Father Franco to the far perimeters of her mind, so that on the rare occasion that she recalled the incident, she shrugged, feeling somehow resolved. At least Signora Avanza had seen things as they really were, verbalizing the names and accusations that Claudia only thought of in later years. The fact that her art instructor had stood up for her, and because Father Franco's cold, pasty hands had gone no farther than her knees, she suffered no bad dreams and had few fears that the man would call her into his office again.

And the following year, the priest left the school having been transferred to the Vatican, so she had only to deal with the stern-faced nuns and daily Mass.

At dinner just before the advent of Lent when Claudia was sixteen, she announced to her parents that there would be a school trip to Venice for the spring holiday. In her art class, they'd studied the unique style of the floating city, the East-meets-West melding of trade, wealth, and intellectual awakening reflected in its palaces, churches, and art and she'd been mesmerized. She'd gazed repeatedly at photographs of the vividly colored frescoes and giant oil paintings created by the city's artists, anxious to see them.

To Claudia, Venice was a city that was truly ancient, maintaining but a tenuous grip in the modern world. It seemed as odd and mixed up as her life.

"I don't want you going to that horrid city," her mother had blurted out. "There's nothing there that's unique. Yes, there are canals, but Milan has canals, too, and it's much more interesting. Venetians are world weary, provincial. Theirs is a culture of the past, not of the future."

"But the art and architecture, the bridges and museums," Claudia had countered, the words spilling out of her mouth before she could stop herself.

Frowning, her mother shook her head, ceremoniously picking up her knife and fork to cut a pale piece of veal resting on her plate.

"I've told you before not to spend too much time on those things," she scolded. "They'll only lead you astray."

"But certainly there's no harm in her taking a sanctioned class trip there," her father suggested, appearing timid behind his small eyeglasses. "I myself took a school trip there and my family visited a number of times. Don't you think it's worth seeing?"

Her mother's eyes flashing, Claudia realized she would never get permission to go. Her eyes small and hard, the contessa resumed slicing the cutlet methodically, glancing at her husband.

How she would never miss those looks when she moved away!

"I'm sure the school administration made a mistake by offering such a trip, one that I'm sure they'll correct. No, I'm certain schoolchildren have no need of trips to Venice, as they're more likely to be sojourns designed to stimulate the senses, and not the intellect. I'll call the school tomorrow. In fact, given that you're sixteen, we need to start discussing where we want you to be the next few years, and whom you might marry. It's never too early to start thinking about it," she said brightly, glancing up from her plate to meet Claudia's eye. Dropping her knife on her plate, she took a bite of the veal, chewing it slowly, deliberately.

Claudia's eyes had moved to her father, hoping to inspire him to insist that she be allowed to go, that he persuade her mother that the plans she'd revealed to him about hopes for art school and eventually living in Venice should be considered, but his eyes had fallen to his plate.

"Papà, you've been to Venice and you liked it, didn't you?" she asked, rocking in her seat, hopeful he would take up her plea despite a sinking, familiar feeling.

"I did, and it's a wonderful city, one that everyone should see before he dies," he remarked weakly, smiling at her and then casting a questioning look at his wife.

"Bad things often happen in Venice," her mother said, shaking her head dismissively. "It's not a place for schoolchildren."

"Bad things happen everywhere," her husband said, clucking his tongue as he reached for his wine.

"If Claudia must go to that dying city, then let her go when she's older and wiser, eh? What's the rush after all? If she feels she must go at sixteen, then she'll certainly have the same urge when she's twenty or thirty."

Taking a sip of her wine and cooing with delight at the rare vintage that her husband had opened to celebrate the coming holiday, she lifted her glass to Claudia and then pointed it to her husband, as if to close the conversation.

"One day you'll go, carina," her father said softly, nodding his head while looking at her intently. "Don't worry."

That was the last time Claudia mentioned Venice while she lived at Palazzo Baggi.

Chapter Eight

It was nearly dark, the remnants of the spring day holding to the northwest sky, a comforting harbinger of longer, warmer days to come, thought Louis. Venice would slow down with the warmer weather (if it ever really hurried), sit in sidewalk cafés, and linger on its old stone bridges. Boat operators would open the windows on the vaporetti, and passengers would lean out, pivoting their faces to capture the caresses of the warm sea breezes.

But what the hell happened to Claudia?

Louis was forever wary of rich parents because they often seemed to hold more sway over their children than even churchy ones carrying the fattest of bibles. Money offered independence, but only of a certain sort and rarely did it offer independence from parents.

Had her mother talked her out of staying? He felt that Claudia didn't have a lot of money—just the allowance and some relatively small inheritance from her grandmother. So she couldn't disobey her parents without suffering a change in her lifestyle. Yet at lunch just that afternoon, she'd seemed so ready to walk away from it. Maybe that had all changed now.

He dialed her phone again, listening to the voice mail but then hanging up instead of leaving another message. He'd gone to Harry's for his cocktail, but then grew nervous again so he returned to his apartment where he paced and stared out the windows. Every half-hour or so he dialed her number.

Was she avoiding him, not answering his calls because she'd decided to leave with her mother? Had she chosen the comforts of money and her parents' approval? Could he blame her if she had?

His door buzzer rang, a dated, jangling bell that seemed more fire alarm than bell.

He ran to the window overlooking the little via below. Claudia peered up, waving.

So she hadn't left!

"It's about time!" he called, racing to the hallway buzzer that released the door, humming spontaneously.

He opened the door, listening to the tap of her shoes on the heavy stone steps. When she arrived at his door, she looked like she'd been crying, her face puffy, and eyes bloodshot.

"Don't say a thing," she said wearily. "I know I look awful."

"No, no, you don't at all," he lied for the second time that day.

Had it really been only that morning they'd met at Tramonta and then gone to lunch with the contessa? So much had happened between then and now that it felt like a week, not a mere day.

She leveled her eyes at him, wordlessly pleading with him to stop lying.

"What happened? What else did your mother say after I left?" he asked. "I was worried."

"Nothing more really. She made more threats, hinted that maybe there would be no coming back if I didn't agree and leave with her today. Something about prodigal daughters being different from prodigal sons."

"Why is she so set against you being here?"

Claudia avoided his gaze and moved through the doorway and into his apartment. "Now she has even more reason. My mother's always concerned with what people think, of course, and so for that reason she doesn't like me being here *doing nothing*, as she describes it. She thinks I'll eat gelato and seafood and swell up like some fat fisherman's wife."

He chuckled. "She doesn't know you very well."

"Maybe she does—I don't know," she said, twisting her mouth uncertainly.

Louis looked at her frowning. Of course, he'd been right—her mother had talked some doubt into her.

"And then you know she's very controlling, wants to have things her own way. Of course, that's really what this is about. She really believes that she's saving me, doing the right thing. And that stupid priest she confides in is no doubt advising her on this, just as he has my whole life."

"It just seems like she's totally unreasonable. And what's wrong with Venice? I mean, couldn't she pull some strings and make something work out for you here? I don't understand."

"I don't either. In some ways, it doesn't surprise me, but then seeing her so strongly and irrationally against it makes me wonder. You know she despises Venice?"

"Really? What person despises Venice?"

"No one. People don't care for it, say it's smelly and bug-filled in the summer, call it a dead city, but I've never met anyone who despises it."

Louis led her into the high-ceilinged living room that felt chilly from having had the enormous windows open earlier. That was when he was desperate for some fresh air to invade the stale air of the place after he'd returned from Harry's, which had been smoke-filled and crowded. Now it seemed too cold and Claudia rubbed the tops of her arms.

"Do you want a coffee or tea?"

"Sure. An espresso. I'm tired, and could use the pick-me-up."

She shuffled down the hallway after him and into the cavernous kitchen where he began preparing the espresso. Her footfall on the wooden floor sounded tired, defeated.

"I don't get it," he said again, switching on the espresso maker.

"She says the Baggi, have never gotten along with the Venetians. Not since before the Renaissance. How absurd is that? A five hundred-year-old grudge?"

"There must be something more to it than that. Maybe there's someone here she doesn't like."

"Who knows, my mother's shrouded in secrets. Sometimes I wonder if I shouldn't believe some of the crap they print about her in the *giornali*. Maybe I'm the one who's got her wrong."

"Yeah, that whole bit about this being a cursed city was strange. I've never heard that before, have you?" he asked, pulling two shots of steaming espresso from the machine.

He pushed the shot of espresso in its tiny cup across the counter toward Claudia, setting another beside it for himself.

"I've never heard such a thing. But I think—again—there's something she's not saying. She was so mysterious about being strong headed toward her mother, and yet wouldn't say what it was that she herself had done to anger my grandmother."

"She didn't say anything more after I left?" he asked again, wondering what they'd talked about all afternoon.

"Not really." She sipped the coffee, slowly pulling the hot liquid into her mouth and sighing. "We talked for another hour and then I walked around the city, took a vaporetti out to Murano, and back and just thought. And here I am."

Sitting down next to her, Louis took a sip of the dark, caramel espresso.

"I thought she might tell you something after I left, maybe explain things a little more," he said.

"Well, she did hint again that there's some sort of secret—that she's justified in not liking Venice, and that I should accept this, too, without proof. I should trust her, she says." She cast Louis a sarcastic look.

"Strange. Do you think she had a bad boyfriend here who burned her?" he laughed. "It can't be the five hundred-year-old grudge, can it? Do Italians really buy into that?"

Claudia pushed her small frame onto the kitchen counter, sitting with her thin legs dangling off the side. "I don't know what to think. Of course, there are still family and town grudges—that's what *Il Palio* in Siena is all about. So for me to say Italians don't buy into it wouldn't be exactly true. But in this case I don't know."

"So you wouldn't say definitively that it's not true?"

"I wouldn't," she answered, shaking her head and taking a last sip of espresso. "But it seems a little far-fetched."

"Now we have a mystery, eh?" he announced, mimicking her.

"One that'll be hard to solve." She shrugged, ignoring his teasing and casting him a hopeless look. "She didn't give me much information to go on."

"Seems like such mysteries should be easy to solve if they're about Venice. Doesn't everyone gossip here?" he asked smugly. "There's got to be someone around who knows about your mother—if something really did happen to her here. I think that maybe she's making it up because she can't control you here. Maybe it's as simple as that."

"That may be," she mused. "And that sounds like a great idea to find out if there's something to what she says, but how does that solve my current dilemma?" she asked, setting down the cup.

"What's that?"

"I'm cut-off and have no job," she sighed.

Louis sipped his espresso to make it seem as if he was responding casually, as if her being cut-off and without a job was nothing to get upset over. He nodded slowly, pensively. "There's that, I suppose. But that can easily be remedied, right?"

"Easily remedied?" Claudia's eyes flashed. "You're joking right?"

"No, I don't mean to. I just think that you have enough talents and interests, and that Venice is full of opportunity, for something *not* to work out."

Was he telling his third lie of the day? Or was he responding to a feeling in his gut?

"Maybe that's the problem—there are too many options. And not enough money. How do I start something with so little money? And if I spend all of the money my grandmother left me, then that's it—there'll be no more. And where do I work if I can't start something? If I have to, I suppose I can work at some firm or do special events—maybe even at a hotel. But I just can't picture it."

She shook her head slowly, staring out the window at the sky, which held only a trace of color from the sunset.

"I think there's got to be something else. Think about what it is that gets you excited, what you would want to do more than anything else," he suggested. A pang of desperation surged in his chest. She hadn't left, but how could he help her to stay?

Louis pushed his stool from the counter and searched a stack of magazines and books on the shelves. He grabbed a pad of paper from a shelf.

"Here," he said, handing the notepad to Claudia. "Write down whatever comes to mind—nothing's too silly."

"I can't think of anything—I'm too exhausted. And I haven't had the chance to think about what I want to do. That's always been taken care of for me." She rubbed her forehead, looking tired.

"Do you want something to drink instead of coffee? A Campari?"

If he joined her, he wondered if he would suffer a heart attack, given the quantity of coffee and drinks he'd downed that day.

"That would be good. Makes me think of summer. And maybe that will calm me down. I feel like I'm going to lose control, completely fall apart." Her eyes moved along the uneven plaster of the kitchen walls to the enormous windows facing the sky. Oddly, there was nothing in the sky—no glowing clouds, stars, or jets, just a blanket of cobalt blue.

Louis leaned over and rubbed the base of her neck lightly, reassuringly. He'd never touched her like that and it made him feel a little awkward. She seemed to appreciate the gesture, though, and he could feel the muscles in her back relax.

"There's no reason to think that," he said. "You just had a fight with your mother, and you stood up for yourself, that's all. You're simply cutting the strings to her and that's why you're scared. She's made all the decisions for you and now you're making them yourself."

Claudia nodded. "It felt strange to stand up to her like that. And that felt good, but what do I do now? It's easy to say you're old enough and smart and talented enough to make your own decisions, but how do you do that? I don't even know."

Louis poured two glasses of Campari, splashing a little soda in the highballs, and cutting and placing a slice of lemon in each. He set the glass in front of Claudia who picked it up immediately and took a big gulp. Already he felt the rush from the espresso, which would soon dissipate after a drink. When he was older he would show more restraint, but for the moment, he would drink whatever he wanted, whenever he wanted.

"That's awfully bitter to gulp like that," Louis said.

"It tastes good. Maybe it'll clear my head, too. Between the espresso and the Campari, something should make me feel better. I feel awful."

"Okay, well why don't you try again, think of anything you'd want to do." Louis felt anxious. He'd always believed she could do a million things; she possessed a million talents, but how to help her find the right one? The hopeless feeling felt washed away by a wave of optimism, a certainty that she would find or stumble upon a perfect fit. But what? Was it the espresso talking, or something else?

"I like film, filmmaking. Acting. I like that, too," she timidly offered.

Was she crazy? There was hardly a theatrical scene in Venice—she'd need to go to Rome for that.

He needed to stay positive, though. Maybe the ideas started with the absurd and undoable and ended with something practical. "Okay, write them down," he said, hoping she came up with something better.

She scribbled them one-by-one on the notepad, then went back to number them.

"Painting, too. I've always wanted to paint." She brought the glass of Campari to her lips, taking a sip and smiling faintly.

"Write it," he said again, nodding. Another one that was impossible, but at least she was getting more confident. She could paint and join the legions of Venetian artists, only a few of which made a living off it—unless she wanted to do assembly line paintings of Venice for the tourists. Those were a sure bet, but he could hardly imagine her doing that.

Then there was a knocking, a soft but steady rapping on the big wooden door to his apartment.

"Who's that?" Claudia asked, scowling. "And how did they get in? I never heard the doorbell."

"I don't know," Louis said, slipping off the barstool and heading out the doorway and into the hallway.

He unlocked and opened the door slowly, finding Sacci grinning sheepishly. He was dressed up and shaven, wearing what looked like new clothes—or at least a sweater and khakis that Louis has never seen before. The pugs panted at the man's feet, their stub tails wagging, and eyes bulging.

"Stay," Sacci commanded, but the dogs rushed across the threshold, gathering at Louis' feet before spinning and jumping on his shins. He leaned down to pet them, remembering why his landlord was stopping by.

"I saw Signora Baggi come in and figured you were here," Sacci explained.

"Oh, I looked at my calendar," Louis lied, looking up from the dogs. He'd forgotten about their earlier, rushed conversation and hadn't even located his planner. Still, what could he have scheduled that would stop him from watching the dogs?

"I can watch them," he said, noticing, as he looked at Sacci's pants there was a price tag still affixed to the back of the waist.

"Perfetto—what a relief. I don't like to have just anyone watch them, you know?" he smiled.

"Sure. They're like your kids, right?" Louis said, feeling his cheeks grow warm.

"*Si, si, si. Exacto*. And they're not comfortable around everyone. They like you, though."

Sacci smiled again, his eyes moving between the three dogs and Louis hunched down petting them. They licked his hand excitedly, pawing him.

"*Grazie tante*," Sacci awkwardly gushed. "When I return I'll have you to dinner if you'd like—to thank you properly."

Louis looked up at the man, wondering if he should read something into the invitation.

Was he right about his hunch, could the man be gay?

"Who is it, Louis?" Claudia called, peeking into the hallway from the kitchen.

"*Cani! Che cani bellissimi*!"

She hurried down the hall, clapping her hands to beckon the dogs. Two of the dogs snapped to attention and raced down the hall toward her, but one of the black ones—Louis could never remember their names—raced away from Claudia and into the bedroom.

Sacci bolted after his dog. "Sorry, sorry. This one likes your room for some reason." He started into Louis' bedroom, but then abruptly turned toward Louis who followed. "It's okay if I go in?"

The man was suddenly strangely polite. Louis blushed. Was he embarrassed by what happened the last time? Louis nodded, rubbing his sticky hands on his jeans. "Sure."

Sacci disappeared into the bedroom with Louis, Claudia, and the snorting dogs trailing.

"Tonto!" Sacci called.

But the dog had disappeared—probably under the bed. Sacci dropped to his knees, peeking under the bed. "Tonto?" he called, moving his head closer to the bed's underside, breathing unevenly. "Tonto? Where are you?" But no dog emerged.

Claudia dropped to her knees, too, and then onto her stomach. "Tonto?" she echoed. "Tonto?"

He felt awkward standing, so Louis lowered himself to the floor, too, his heart beating frantically. "Tonto," he called. They pushed farther under the bed, each from a different side. The other two dogs rushed around them, spinning and butting their heads against stomachs and thighs, thinking they were playing some sort of game.

Sacci laughed the same almost child-like giggle he'd made last time. Louis was surprised again, finding it so out of character, so unlike the dull, lifeless persona his landlord had exhibited since he'd first rented the place.

Louis spotted a dark form, Tonto, crouching behind a box of shoes. "I've got him," he whispered, reaching forward to grab the dog gently. But his hand sunk into hair, not fur, as he realized he'd grabbed the back of Sacci's head.

"Sorry," he bleated, pulling away his hand so quickly he rapped it against the bottom of the bed. "Ow."

Louis felt equal parts foolish and excited, having touched the man, actually putting his hand into Sacci's thick head of hair. Sacci laughed harder, suddenly grabbing Louis.

"I'm not dog," he said slowly in English. "I'm not dog." And then he started mimicking how Louis had grabbed his head. "*Tonto*?" he mocked. "*Tonto*?"

"What just happened?" Claudia asked from nearby. "I can't see—do you have him?"

"He grabbed *me*," Sacci laughed. "He thought I was il cane. Can you imagine?"

Well, it was dark under the bed. How was he supposed to have seen what he was grabbing? And if Sacci thought it was so funny, not thinking it better to keep quiet, then maybe Louis was mistaken about him. Suddenly it didn't feel like they were flirting and he thought again about how many times he'd misjudged a guy's intentions.

"I couldn't see," Louis said, annoyed.

"Don't be angry. I only tease you," Sacci reassured him in English.

"I'm not angry," he protested, but the tone of his voice gave him away.

Sacci giggled, further frustrating Louis who wished he could see his face, figure out what he found so goddamn funny, and see if there was anything in his eye that gave him away. Was Sacci merely laughing at him, or was it the idea of three adults groping around in the dark under a bed for a pug—a dog that happened to be small and black.

"I've never heard you laugh so much before," Louis said, making an effort not to sound irritated.

"I'm in a laughing mood," Sacci said. "Maybe it's the warm weather. Or something in the air. But I feel better, so I'm laughing all the time, it's true."

Louis lay there quietly. How strange it was that they were having a conversation lying under his bed.

"You've always seemed so quiet," he added.

"Sì, sì, sì. I have been like that, too. But this is also me. I am sometimes happy, too."

Louis remembered Claudia was there, also lying with them in the darkness under the bed. Why was she so quiet? Was she thinking about what she would do, or was she noticing the strange behavior of her friend? She knew him well enough to figure out something was going on, he figured. And she would probably ask him about it. Would he admit that he had a crush on the man, that the feelings arrived from nowhere, as they always had, to make him feel hopeful, alive?

"Are you still here, Claudia?" he asked tentatively.

"Sì. I'm still here."

The dogs had settled down, one nestling against his hip. He heard the other panting quietly, probably leaning against Sacci, or maybe Claudia.

"Dio. We should be figuring out what to do for work for you, not chasing dogs," he said, his voice shaky.

"Sorry, it's my fault. You're out of work?" Sacci asked meekly.

His voice sounded different under the bed, mellower.

"I've just been disowned," Claudia laughed. "And I have no work.

The truth is, I've hardly ever even worked, so prospects aren't that good."

"How do you know Signore Howard?"

"Sacci, you can call me Louis," he interrupted. "We're lying on the floor under my bed. And I'm going to watch your dogs. You can call me Louis."

"*Louis*—that's right, I forgot. So, how do you know Louis?"

"We've been friends for about a year now. We met here. We'd both arrived on the same train and didn't know anyone. Well, we were both pretty lonely and so we became friends."

"That's good," Sacci mused. "No one should be alone."

"Oh, we're not dating," Claudia said quickly. "We're friends."

"That's still good. Good to have friends."

They should have moved out from under the bed, Louis thought, but no one made a start, not even the dogs. It was as if they'd forgotten completely about retrieving the dog, and had started conversing in the half-light and close quarters under the bed. The thought of making the first move seemed awkward, so Louis remained with his back and shoulders pressed against the cool wooden floor, staring at the shadowy, dark bottom of the bed.

"What do you like to do?" Sacci asked.

"We were just discussing that when you knocked. There are some things I like, but I just haven't done that much," Claudia answered, her voice muffled.

"I have lots of friends in Venice. I grew up here, my family is from here, so maybe I can help," Sacci said enthusiastically. "There might even be something that *I* could offer you."

There was silence long enough that Louis began to hear his heartbeat.

Say something, Claudia, Louis silently urged. What an offer! What luck!

Finally, she spoke, but tentatively.

"*Grazie tante*, but I couldn't. I don't even know you, and you don't even know me, so I couldn't."

"Okay, but maybe you can help me. My family has an old palazzo—just blocks from La Fenice. We've wanted to do something with it, to convert it into a hotel, but I haven't met anyone I can trust to do it."

"You're thinking that I can renovate an old palazzo?" Claudia chuckled.

"It just takes someone with intelligence and some enthusiasm," Sacci said flatly, sounding offended. "You don't have to do the work yourself—you just organize it. And then maybe run the place."

"Run a hotel?" she asked uncertainly.

"Sure," he countered, clucking his tongue. "It's not so difficult. You just need to be a detail person and be good with people and love art and architecture, and from what I've heard you seem perfect."

"What have you heard?" she asked, sounding annoyed.

It was silent for a moment more before Sacci chuckled.

"Well, you know how Venice is," he said sheepishly.

"I guess I shouldn't be surprised," she replied, sighing, but sounding vaguely relieved.

Why couldn't she at least say she was interested, tell him that she'd like to talk about it?

One of the dogs started whining, pawing the floor.

"Tonto, is that you?" Sacci asked. The dog whined again, walking under the bed to lie beside him. "Ah, the dog has been found—or has found me," he announced.

Still no one moved to get up off the floor. Louis knew what was keeping him in the cramped, dark space, but what about the other two? Staring into the darkness of the bed's underside, he barely made out the slats supporting the box spring. The thick dust ruffle that had come with the bed blocked out most of the light, making it seem as if they were in a tent. He could hear Sacci and Claudia breathing, one of them dragging an arm or leg across the floor.

"Do you know of anyone else who's looking for someone, who has an available position?" Claudia asked.

"I can ask around, see what might be available," Sacci said wearily. "But there'll be nothing as good as what I'm offering."

"You just need someone to manage the place?" she asked, sounding doubtful.

"Best of all would be someone to invest in it, too," he said timidly. "A partner."

"Ha!" Claudia laughed. "And how do you even know I have any money to invest?"

"Well—" he started to say, but she interrupted him.

"No, don't tell me," she said. "You probably know exactly how much I have."

"I haven't heard that," he said softly. "But from what I know, it should be enough for what we need."

"So you're not just offering me this because you want me to work for you, but because you need my money, right?" she asked warily.

Louis had never heard her sound so cautious.

"We could do it without your money," he said defensively. "But what we really need is someone who can manage everything, and then run the place. And having a partner would enable us to do a better job. This place deserves to be a special hotel, managed by someone who can appreciate the history of the place. It needs someone who can make it come alive. And then it wouldn't hurt to have your name attached to the place."

"And what makes you think I can do that?" she said soberly.

"I think you can," Louis interjected.

He imagined Sacci shrugging. How did he know, or was he simply guessing, relying on gossip? Did Sacci notice the same feeling that he got from Claudia—that she was merely waiting for the right opportunity to come along?

The dog whined again and Sacci shifted his weight on a creaky floorboard. "I should go," he said. "Why don't you think about it, eh? Or at least come by and take a look at the place, okay?"

"I guess," she answered uncertainly. "I guess it couldn't hurt to look at the place."

"*Brava*," Sacci said. "I think when you see it you'll realize it's a perfect fit."

"But I don't even know you—and you don't even know me," she protested.

Why didn't she just agree to look at the place? What would it hurt?

"I know it sounds silly, but I just have this feeling," Sacci announced, loudly slapping the floor.

"And I do, too," Louis added, moving restlessly beneath the bed.

Silence again filled the dark space until one of the dogs whimpered impatiently.

"Come on—just think about it," Sacci pleaded. "Can it hurt so much to merely think about it for some days, to take a look at the palazzo? Why don't we set up a day for you to visit?"

"Okay," she agreed, sighing. "It can't hurt, right?"

"No, it can't," Louis barked.

"It can't," Sacci echoed.

"I will then," she said, her voice sounding more confident. "Just let me know when. My schedule's pretty open. Completely open, actually."

"Great," Sacci said. "That's decided then."

It almost sounded as if he was referring to more than just an agreement for Claudia to look at the palazzo.

"Hey, why don't you have a coffee with us?" she asked suddenly.

Did she remember that they had unfinished, waterlogged Campari sitting in the kitchen? Or that they'd just had coffee before switching to cocktails?

There was silence again, uncomfortable for Louis who was hoping that Sacci would stay. He heard the man stirring so close to him he could have touched him with the slightest motion of his arm, so near he could smell his cologne.

"Grazie, but I should leave. I brought my dogs and myself in uninvited and now I somehow find myself under Signore Howard's bed—again," he giggled.

"*Louis*," he corrected.

"Yes, *Louis.* Sorry! I intrude like this and then you treat me so nicely. I think most tenants don't like landlords hanging around, let alone diving under their beds. Or bringing their dogs around."

"No, it's fine," Louis insisted, regretting that he hadn't shown more enthusiasm when Sacci had arrived. Still, he didn't want to show too much enthusiasm. What if he was wrong again?

"Okay, I go now," Sacci announced. The dogs hopped up at the sound of his voice, their nails clipping the floor. They spun—Louis could hear it—and began yipping again.

"I suppose we can't hide under the bed anymore either, Claudia," Louis said, rolling onto his side.

"Lying here in the dark has made me sleepy," she yawned. "I think I need another coffee. Will you fix me another?"

"Sure," he agreed, wondering if he should ask Sacci again if he wanted one—but hadn't Claudia already asked him? And he didn't want to sound pushy, didn't want to seem obvious. If he were, maybe Sacci would grow suspicious and Louis would look like a fool. No, this time he would go slower and not make it so obvious that he had a crush.

The three of them slid across the floor, standing up awkwardly and squinting in the bright lamplight.

"Well, sorry again for the dogs. Maybe I need to put Tonto on a leash when we visit." Sacci shrugged.

Louis brushed off his pants, noticing dust bunnies on the back of Sacci's sweater. He thought to brush them off, but decided against it. And he would have felt self-conscious touching him, anyway. At least there had been no pairs of dirty underwear under the bed. And no large purple dildo, so maybe a little dust wasn't the worst thing. Still, he vowed to clean under his bed regularly.

"You sure you won't stay for a coffee?" Claudia asked again. "Louis makes a very good one."

Louis glanced nervously at Claudia who had either figured things out or wanted to talk more about the palazzo. He couldn't determine which.

"No thanks. I have things to get to. I'll be late." Sacci looked around the room, snapping his fingers for the dogs, though they'd already gathered at his feet.

"You should have a coffee with us," Louis blurted out, hearing the words tumble out of his mouth before he could think.

"Oh, come on, you should stay," Claudia gushed. "Just for a few minutes, maybe we could talk some more about your idea."

Sacci smiled, glancing at Louis nervously and then shaking his head slowly. "No, thanks, but I should leave now. I'll call you to set up the tour, okay? Maybe tomorrow?"

He walked out of the bedroom, moving slowly down the hallway with Louis and Claudia following. As he hurried out the front door, he waved, leaning down to scoop up one of the dogs that had lingered in the hallway. He suddenly seemed in a hurry to leave. Did he sense that Louis was gay? Why was he suddenly so nervous? Italians were hard to figure out, sometimes so laidback, and other times mysterious and emotional. When the door shut, Claudia stared at him.

"What?" he asked.

"Nothing. I'm just thinking." She moved toward the kitchen, motioning for Louis to follow.

"You want me to make you that coffee?"

"No, I don't care," she shrugged, plopping down onto one of the stools.

"I thought you wanted a coffee," he said. "Isn't that what you said under the bed?"

"I changed my mind. I don't want one now," she said casually, opening a magazine.

Louis shook his head. "You're hard to figure out. Well, if you change your mind, you have a few minutes because I'm making one for myself."

He took out the coffee and prepared the machine. When he looked up, Claudia was studying him again.

"Why do you keep looking at me?" he asked, annoyed.

He felt like he was hiding something, his little crush. For some reason she irritated him, as if she were prying. He grabbed the watery Campari cocktails he'd fixed earlier and emptied them into the sink, glad to have a reason to hide his face, but wondering if she could tell that he was hiding something.

"Sorry, I don't know why," she said blankly, frowning.

She shrugged, looking down at the counter.

The water in the machine began to steam, gurgling pleasantly. Louis placed the coffee in the cup and twisted the handle. Hot water noisily coursed through the ground coffee, filling the room with its fragrance.

"Sacci's interesting, and he seems kind—not at all how you described him," she said, turning a page in the magazine sitting on the counter. "And that was really something, dropping a bomb about that offer."

"He's not at all what he *was*," Louis protested. "Really. I swear he's suddenly been a different person just the past few days. He used to be so quiet and I never gave him a second thought. And I was just as surprised as you by the offer—which, by the way, you'd be a fool not to look into—"

Louis realized he'd nearly admitted something. But why should he say anything to her when there really was nothing, nothing but a schoolboy crush?

Claudia glanced at him, her eyes nervously darting away when he looked up to see if she noticed how he'd stammered.

"I'd pictured a sort of recluse or nerd. But he's actually handsome. His clothes are a little plain, but he's *bello*, eh?" she asked, smiling again.

"I don't know. I guess," he admitted, trying to sound casual. Why did it irritate him so much that she asked so many questions about Sacci? Was it because she found him handsome, too, and he had the screwed-up view of her as some sort of competition? Or did she sense that he was fond of Sacci? Even if she asked outright, it would be too embarrassing to admit. The thing would never go anywhere, so what would be the point?

And why did he develop crushes on the most improbable guys?

Claudia sat silently a few minutes, listlessly turning pages in the magazine. He imagined that she wasn't even reading—and was hardly looking at the pages.

He pulled his cream-topped espresso from the machine, setting the plain little cup on its saucer and carrying it to the counter next to Claudia.

"I think he was married, you know," she said meaningfully, her thin face still pointed toward the magazine. Were her cheeks slightly pink?

Louis shrugged. Was she trying to play matchmaker or trying to get him to confess? He didn't want to talk about his silly crush, for if he did it seemed even more unlikely that anything would come of it. Then he'd look like a fool, and though he knew not admitting his crush was perhaps even more ridiculous than entertaining it, he felt too much shame to confess.

Wanting to change the subject before she asked him a more pointed question, he sat down next to her. "Have you thought more about Sacci's offer, or another job?"

She closed the magazine, tossing it carelessly aside. Sighing, she raised her hands to her face, shaking her head slowly.

"Right now, I don't want to think about it—just for an hour or two. My head's spinning and I can't think straight, so it's better if I just shove it out of my mind for a while."

"And when your head clears, *voila*, the answer will come."

"Exactly," she nodded, playing with a strand of her dark hair.

Louis shook his head slowly, drinking the last of the espresso. He spooned out the last of the crema at the bottom of the cup. For some reason he had a good feeling, though he couldn't say why. Was this sense that things would turn out, that the universe was conspiring to keep them both in Venice as misplaced as his childhood belief in Jesus?

"My mother said to beware of Venetian men," she said suddenly, her eyes fixed on the espresso cup. "'They'll betray you,' she told me.

'And worse.' I asked what she meant by that, but she wouldn't say. I've never seen her so tight-lipped."

"Another part of the mystery," he said, nodding vigorously. "So it must have had to do with a man, eh?"

"I can't imagine her doing anything inappropriate, getting pregnant or anything like that. She's so *Catholic*."

Louis shrugged. "Sometimes the ones who preach the loudest, who go to church all the time, and seem the holiest are actually compensating for their own sins."

Playing with her hair again, she glanced at him. "Could be, but I think it's something else. My mother seems sad sometimes, as if there's something unresolved in her, and she actually seems angry when even the word 'Venice' is spoken—which makes me wonder how it was that she actually traveled here. But, I don't think a man jilted her, or that she got pregnant or anything like that."

"Strange," Louis said, wondering why there'd never been anything in the papers about the contessa's past. Maybe if he brought up the topic at the fish market bar the old man or the bar owner might have heard something.

"You know, when we parted, and it seemed that she would almost cry from anger, she squeezed me tighter than she ever had. I didn't know what to say, so I asked how long she was staying and she shook her head. Do you know what she was doing?" Claudia asked, looking at Louis with wide eyes. "She was taking a taxi boat directly to the train station, and not walking down even one via. 'I don't want to see any of the city.' she told me. Odd, isn't it?"

"She must have hated leaving you here," he suggested, poking his pinky finger through the tiny handle of the demitasse.

"As I was leaving, actually saying good-bye, I thought she might give in and decide not to cut me off."

Louis shook his head. "When I watched and listened to her this afternoon I never thought that was possible."

Claudia sighed, picking at a cuticle. "You were right. It was silly of me to think so. After all, I've known her my whole life."

"And that was it, no final promises or potential compromises?" he asked.

"She asked how much money I had left from Nonna, biting her lip the whole time."

"Not much, eh?" he asked, realizing he'd never known for certain how much money she'd left her. But based on what Sacci had said, maybe it was more than he'd imagined.

Smiling sheepishly, she looked up at him, her face brightening. "Actually, I have over a million lire. So I have a little more time, but I can't blow through all that money without doing *some*thing with it. Once that's gone, that's it."

"A million lire—that's nearly a hundred thousand dollars!" he gushed, amazed that she'd never hinted that she had so much money, especially now that she'd realized she might be cut off. "Well, that should make things a lot easier, I mean, give you a lot more options—if you don't take up Sacci on his offer."

God, she could be secretive about things. He really thought she had just a little money left to her by her grandmother, and now she suddenly announced she had a hundred thousand dollars. He always forgot who she was, after all. For him, broke meant he didn't know how he was going to pay the rent. For her, it meant having only a hundred thousand dollars and no monthly check from her parents.

"I shouldn't spend one lira of it until I have a plan," she said, soberly, her mouth turning into a frown. "This can buy me a life—it's got to because there'll be nothing more to buy it with. If I know my mother, she won't be showing up here again. I've been written off."

"I wish I had your troubles," he joked, trying to get her to smile.

Claudia looked hurt, like she might cry again. "Okay, I know I have a lot of money that I never even earned—you may as well have pointed that out—and that that gives me opportunities most people don't ever have. But I don't have the talents they do—or skills like you. I can't write or translate, I don't know how to manage, and I sometimes think my mother raised me to marry and that that should be my career. I don't know what the hell I should do—at least you do. And I've been used to having someone take care of me, and I no longer have that. So while it might look great to you, my situation is hopeless."

"Sorry," Louis said, his shoulders dropping sheepishly. "I forget that things always look different when you're in it."

"Why does my mother have to be this way?" she asked, gazing forlornly out the giant window.

Louis nervously chewed his bottom lip, unsure what to say.

Claudia eyed him. "Why don't you say something?"

He shrugged. "I'm not sure if I should say anything—I seem to make things worse if I do."

Claudia turned back to the window. "No. Even if I seem pissed, at least I can talk to someone and I know you're on my side."

"Well, then my advice is that you find something to invest in, to become a partner in some sort of business. Like the one Sacci is proposing."

"But I don't even know him—*you* don't even really know him," she said, leveling her gaze at him.

Looking away, he shrugged. "But he's from Venice and if he weren't an honest person, we'd certainly have heard about it by now. I've never heard anything but good things about him."

"That's true," she said, staring out the window again. "The whole thing just makes me nervous. Even if it sounds interesting."

"And appealing? Exciting?" he asked.

"Sì," she admitted, offering a desultory nod. "I have some silly, irrational good feeling about it, but I don't trust it."

"Why not?" he asked, wondering why he was suddenly so certain that Sacci's offer was the perfect solution. Had his crush carried away his common sense?

"I don't trust myself," she admitted, drumming her fingers on the counter. "And so if I have this good feeling about this, in fact, *because* I have a good feeling about this, I don't trust it."

"What else is there?" he asked hesitantly, hoping he didn't make her angry. "We can ask around, see what people say about Sacci. And then take a look at the palazzo, see what he's proposing."

He felt a wave of pleasure just saying the guy's name, knowing that his crush was becoming full-blown. Claudia eyed him, and he wondered if it was with suspicion.

"You're right," she said, grinning. "Fear's my greatest enemy."

Louis nodded, hoping his gut was right. "I've just got this feeling that this is all meant to be. That Venice is where we were supposed to end up."

"You think God, or some being predetermined all of this, down to my mother cutting me off?"

"Not quite like that," he said, trying to explain what seemed only an inchoate idea. How could he explain? "Let's just say that it's intuition, that I have a good feeling about all of this, okay?"

She rolled her eyes, popping up from the counter. "I won't question then, and will just try to go with it." She smiled, nodding. "And speaking of going, I need something to distract me for the rest of the night. I can't think about it anymore. And I need to get outside, so let's go to that little neighborhood trattoria you found a few weeks ago near the old Jewish Quarter."

"But I bought seafood at the market, I thought we'd make dinner here," he protested, pointing at the bread and greens sticking out of a basket at the end of the counter.

"If we stay here we'll talk more, and I just need a little escape, to get out and be around people. If we go to that little trattoria, we'll have to share one of those tiny tables with complete strangers and so we can't talk about *any* of this. We can eat some sweet miniature crabs with garlic and parsley, smoke some cigarettes after dinner, drink some grappa or moscato and then maybe I'll share your sense of optimism, eh?"

Louis grinned broadly at her and grabbed his jacket. "And maybe a little corner bar after?"

"Perfetto," she said, pushing her hair behind her ears.

When they got into the street, a stinging wind from the north blew, making it feel like winter again. The next day would probably be cloudy, more like a typical late March day on the northern Adriatic.

Louis swore he could feel the chill from the distant snowfields and glaciers in the Alps. Claudia shivered, leaning into him.

"I'm ready for spring," she said wistfully, ducking her head to escape the full brunt of the wind.

"It'll be here before long," Louis assured her. At any rate, they'd soon be in the tightly packed restaurant with flames from the stoves of the tiny, open kitchen to heat them, and the aroma of garlic, langoustines, fresh herbs, and saffron filling the air.

Chapter Nine

Before the tourists came, it wasn't such a smelly city. No, it was the tourist boats, the big hotels, the crowds, and all that that made the city stink.

It was her favorite time of day, the quiet hours of dawn when the city was still waking up. When she was a child living out on Murano, her family had chickens, and their soft clucking always marked the mornings. She would lie in bed while the broad sky outside the window slowly took shape, glowing purple, pink, orange, and red. Her bedroom sat above the kitchen, and she could always smell coffee wafting through the floorboards and heating grate. So it was only natural that she came to love the beverage at an early age, long before her mother thought it natural or proper.

"It will stunt your growth," she chided. "It's not right for a little girl to drink coffee."

Her father would laugh. "Better she drinks coffee than grappa, no?"

Her mother clucked her tongue like one of the chickens, frowning with resignation. And whether it was coffee or moving to the larger quarter of Cannaregio in Venice proper, Constanza always seemed to get her way.

Her mother never approved, always wanting to drag her to church to see a priest.

"I pray for you," her mother used to say.

And she did. But then, she prayed for everyone.

Constanza learned the art of praying from her mother, praying constantly and in earnest, like a nun or an old woman. She prayed about little things and big things, and she prayed that her life would turn out the way she wanted, not the way her mother wished it to.

And up to a point, she had gotten her way—except for those few, unforeseeable happenings that would transform her life completely. And in ways, neither she nor her mother could ever have guessed.

In those days, Constanza believed, too, that prayer made a difference, that it could help determine fate, tip the scales in a person's favor. So she would pray even harder against her mother, praying that she would find a job using her hands, that she would move to Cannaregio, and that she would fall in love. And she prayed, too, that she would be forgiven for disrespecting her mother, for praying that her mother's wishes wouldn't be realized.

But there were too many prayers to be said; life was too complicated. She thought if you missed one little overlooked aspect of your life, maybe something unanticipated looming on the horizon, you suffered the consequences. It was as if this God of Prayers expected you to know the future, guess what was around the corner or in someone's heart, so that you could gauge your prayers accordingly.

She came by this attitude through her mother, who used to say, "God will reveal all to you, if you only ask the right questions." In her opinion, a tragedy or dilemma was the simple result of a lack of or heartless prayers. The way her mother taught it, a person was responsible for the bad that happened in life; God brought the good. And constant, fervent prayer made the latter a possibility and the former less likely.

So, Constanza used to try to think of the right questions, and then pray in earnest for good grades, honor, a kiss from Giacomo Puglia, and later a date to see a movie with Piero Agostino. And that's when things changed for her, when her life opened up. And eventually swallowed her.

"Be careful what you pray for," her mother had also warned.

She should have remembered her own advice. In those days, Cannaregio still had Jews living there, though only a few. Their bizarre, Byzantine temple stood in a small piazza, looking somehow abandoned and forlorn.

"You shouldn't live so close to the Jews," her mother complained.

"There aren't so many there. And they don't seem evil to me," she'd countered, not knowing that eventually they would all be gone.

"I'll pray for you. Pray for them," her mother had said, nodding vigorously. "They're not saved," she muttered.

"I know, Mamma," she said dispassionately.

They seemed nice enough, good enough to her. Why should they go to hell for not believing Christ was the Messiah?

Did her mother come to believe that her prayers were answered because eventually the Jews left? By the time they'd disappeared from the neighborhood, though, her mother had greater things to pray for than the salvation of Jews, or her daughter's move to another quarter.

Piero Agostino had grown up in Murano, too, where his father ran one of the oldest glassmaking shops, a small medieval-looking store with a workshop in back. In those days, few tourists ever bothered to visit the island, so except for the heavy smell of molten glass and the coals that fired the furnaces, there wasn't much of anything on the islet.

While as a young girl Constanza had liked the feel of living on a sleepy island that felt almost country-like in some ways, when secondary school started, she and her friends began taking the vaporetti to Venice. They would hang out of the sides of the boats, staring at the tourists, and particularly at the glamorous women from Paris or London who wore sophisticated clothes. The tourists stared back, and sometimes even took their photographs, a bunch of schoolgirls in dark blue uniforms and hats. Did she look as exotic and unusual as they did?

Her mother didn't like her constant trips to the city, but her father encouraged her.

"Be careful," her mother warned. "And if you must go, never go alone. Every time you go, I say a prayer for you, for your safe return. And that you don't do anything to shame me or your father."

Constanza shook her head, but not too hard or her mother would accuse her of showing disrespect. She would kiss her mother and head for the door. If Constanza turned to steal one more look, she would see her mother already whispering prayers under her breath, massaging her crucifix between her thumb and fingers, bent over them as if in study.

"I'm too old to fall into a canal and drown," she reassured her once, knowing that was her mother's worry, the unspoken fear of every Muranese and Venetian mother.

Some days she thought of moving back, to live in the small house she'd grown up in. She liked seeing her friends and acquaintances, though, and liked her role in the city as its conscience, a constant reminder of how praying got you nowhere and the god of Venice was a farce. She enjoyed seeing people whisper, casting their sad gazes in her direction. Maybe they would realize that they, too, could fall prey to the vicissitudes of life, and when that happened, not all the prayer or religion in the world would help a whit.

The small bakery she worked in, one she would eventually purchase, had a reputation for making the best breads in the neighborhood. She'd been fortunate to have a mother who baked bread as well as she prayed. Constanza liked to think her mother became such a good baker because she needed to do something with her nervous hands. And kneading dough, a tiresome task, could take the energy right out of your hands and even distract you.

Was the yeast good? Did it smell right? Was there enough heat to make the dough rise properly? Her mother hovered over the loaves, peeking under the thin cotton cloths she draped over them, and moving the fragrant pillows of dough closer to the oven if they weren't rising. She tended the bowls as if they were a row of newborn babies.

When Constanza thought of that house and Murano, she

remembered the smells of coffee—and fresh bread—wafting from the kitchen below. When the aging bakery owners had asked her how she started baking bread, she told them she didn't have a choice. Her bedroom sat above the kitchen and her mother was an avid bread baker. She left out the part about her mother being an avid prayer, too, but the two had become intertwined in her mind.

Living in the Cannaregio quarter seemed like a dream. Constanza would rise at 4:00 AM so that the first loaves of bread came out of the oven by 7:00 AM. While the dough rose for the breakfast bread, she would start making *cornetti*, sprinkled with almonds and sugar and then make heavier, German-style breads. She worked alone, and liked it. The dough kept her company, constituting a living, breathing thing that she helped form. Those loaves of bread were the first thing to which she gave birth.

Breva was the second and best thing, of course, but she came later.

Constanza would leave the bakery kitchen at noon and walk around the neighborhood or sometimes all the way to Piazza San Marco. She thrilled at seeing the tourists, many from America, but a lot, too, from England, France, and Germany. Then there were the scholars and artists, always immediately recognizable by their clothing. While the tourists were always rich and dressed in cashmere, linen, or thin wool, the scholars and artists were dressed plainly, if not sloppily—especially the artists.

At times like these, she felt as if Venice was a powerful place, pulling people—important people—from all over the world. What were they coming to see and do? What did they do here?

She wished sometimes that she could talk to one of these important people, but she was a baker who spoke no English, and they were tourists who spoke no Italian, so there was no hope for conversation.

She felt content to have escaped somnolent Murano, which felt more like a sleepy island or a small country town, even if she couldn't talk to the tide of tourists and foreigners that swept in and out of the city.

Piero never wanted to live in Venice, preferring the sleepiness of Murano. But from his first glimpse of her during an Easter procession, he was smitten. They had both finished school, and he began working every day at his father's glassblowing shop while she learned baking from her mother.

He thought she was strong-willed and different from the other girls in Murano. She had the coal-black hair of a southern Italian and smallish, penetrating eyes that seemed to see everything. Sometimes he thought she could read his mind, his simple romantic thoughts, and plans for the future. He believed in love at first sight, so it didn't surprise him that at first glance he wanted to marry her. She'd been interested at first, but her manner cooled when he started talking about marriage after a few weeks. What did her piercing gaze see that he didn't? He felt certain that they were meant to be together.

The fact that she baked, seemed to enjoy baking, surprised him. He liked to watch her at work, though he never arrived at her parents' house early enough to see her make the first batch of bread. By the time he arrived, the first long loaves were cooling on racks, and her mother would serve him a bowl of milk coffee beside a steaming half-loaf of the bread.

After Constanza had perfected coarse, crusty, soft, and sweet loaves, apple *crostata*, biscotti, and *mille foglie*, she grew bored. Everyone knew her on the island, and all she could expect to do was marry Piero. She began to fantasize about living in Venice and owning a bakery or opening a restaurant instead of taking the vaporetto there and back for the afternoon.

It struck her as amazing that the quiet and isolation of Murano that had charmed her as a child, now suffocated. While at first she thought she had fallen in love with Piero, she figured after a short amount of time that she could do better.

Her mother never liked Piero, finding him suspect for a few reasons.

"He'll make nothing of himself—you watch," she warned.

"I'm the one encouraging *him* to leave, Mamma."

But to marry Piero, as much as she loved him, would be a death sentence of sorts. She would bake, cook, and clean, and her life would consist of Murano and its half-deserted streets, the fetid smell of the lagoons on hot August days, and the cool, gray days of winter when the streets lay mostly deserted. There would be children to keep from falling into a canal in their early years, her parents nearby, familiar neighbors, and what else? Nothing. She already knew now of what her life would consist, void of any mystery or surprise.

And so she surprised everyone with her idea of moving to Venice.

"It's not proper for a girl your age—for any woman to move by herself—anywhere. And what will you do? How will you live where you don't know anyone?" her mother asked.

"Women go to Paris and London all the time. I'm just doing the same thing, but going to Venice."

"What's in Venice?" her mother used to ask. "It's a sinking city, a dying city, and there's nothing there."

She wanted to remind her mother that if Venice died, Murano would die, too, but she didn't want to argue. And Venice held some opportunity, at least to meet some new people, instead of always seeing the same neighbors, schoolmates, and relatives. Even then, Venice was losing its younger people to Milan and Rome, but it was still a buzzing, active city, not like the sleepy backwater of Murano.

Her father encouraged her to go, but no farther than Venice. "There'll be enough in Venice to keep you happy," he assured her.

Right after she moved, Piero followed, opening a glassblowing studio on a loud street in an industrial quarter. He too rose early, joining her while she baked bread. He would sit at the table, dipping a piece of fresh bread into the *caffè latte* she had made for him. After half an hour, he would hurry out the door to his studio. At first, she resented his visits, hardly speaking to him as she mixed the dough or kneaded the batches that she'd made before he arrived. But after living in Venice a few months, she called no one else friend, only the Veranos who owned the bakery, and a quiet family living in her building.

Hungry for company, Constanza started to enjoy her mornings with Piero and even looked forward to them. They talked about news from Murano, which while only a short boat ride away, seemed a day's journey. And after Piero moved into the same neighborhood, they started discussing the different people with whom they shared the neighborhood.

While she hadn't intended to fall in love with Piero, who seemed slow and plodding, overly devoted to the memory of his deceased parents and to her, she realized one day that in a way, she did love him. But she didn't like the way he wanted to take care of her, or the way he took care of anyone he became acquainted with. He fed the feral cats, even going so far as to save scraps from dinner to bring down to the street the following morning. He was sentimental, like one of those boys who loves his mamma too much. And she was not. She had too many things on her mind to be sentimental.

For so many years, she had prayed for a passionate, life-changing love. One so strong it made her hurt. She did not love Piero in this way, so he couldn't be the one. Still, she could do worse, she decided, and he'd proven himself a good companion, someone whom she felt relaxed around, as if the two of them had grown up in the same family.

The first morning he'd asked her to marry him was memorable for its darkness. There were rarely thunderstorms in Venice, but strong southern winds were bringing moisture from the sea along with the warm air of Greece and more distant Egypt. She could smell the sea air seeping through the drafty windows of the old bakery and was thinking of where the air had been, what it had seen, and the different treetops and cornices it had raked.

Maria, the bakery owner, had told her not to bake as much as usual because business would be slow due to the coming rain.

"My joints ache terribly," Maria had said. Then she matter-of-factly predicted, "It will storm all day. So make half the bread as usual."

Constanza was suspicious of the woman, doubtful of her

pronouncements, but then she always seemed to be right—especially about things like the weather. Or fate.

At that point, she hadn't realized how right the woman would be. She set about making the first batch of bread as the lights flickered after a particularly loud grumble of thunder.

"Poseidon's angry, eh?" Maria said, shuffling out the door. "Sending a storm from the sea to drown us!"

Why would she say such things? *Bless us Dio, and save us. Forgive Maria, she doesn't know better.*

The sea had never taken Venice, why would it now?

Constanza worked steadily, preparing the pans for the rolls and lighting the oven. She wiped out the giant metal bowls in which she mixed the dough, and began dusting the massive wooden table, scarred, and discolored from years of use.

She whistled—something inspired by Mozart that she had made up. The tune was half *le nozze di Figaro*, half *Don Giovanni*. Ah, she should have been a composer!

The sky outside the yawning casement windows lightened a little, but remained an inky blue that was atypical for that hour in May. By now, the sun should be streaming in through the windows.

Crackles of lightning continued to illuminate the sky, making her jump at her work. She would never get used to such storms. To her, the world did seem angry—otherwise, why such tumult, such noise?

The oven heated the room, chasing the damp she felt from the rain that pelted the windows and gathered in glowing puddles on the street. The whistling wind pushed the door against the jamb, rattling loudly.

She'd just pulled out the first batch of cornetti, redolent of yeast, butter, and eggs, when a knock sounded against the door. She wondered who it might be. She wasn't expecting to see Piero since he could choose not to work. Who would choose to work on such a day if they didn't have to? With such a storm, few stores would open and the leaky roof of his studio would make working uncomfortable if not impossible.

"*Prego, prego!*" she called, her hands full with the baking sheet lined with cornetti. The door was always unlocked, why did he have to knock every morning?

Piero stepped into the room and called cheerfully, "Buon giorno."

"Giorno," she responded, glancing over her shoulder. "*Il caffè prontissimo.*"

Removing the pastries from the sheets and placing them on racks on the worktable, she listened to the soft rustle of clothing as Piero carefully removed his raincoat, and placed his umbrella in the stand.

When she'd finished with the pastries, she moved quickly to the espresso maker, pushing the lever to begin heating the water. She'd already placed the coffee cups on the counter, each with its two teaspoons of sugar at the bottom.

Gray, dissipated light came through the big windows. She would need to leave the lights on, as if it were still very early morning.

"No fish today," Piero said matter-of-factly, placing a newspaper on the counter and sliding onto his usual stool next to the counter.

"No *nothing*," she said, kneading the dough for a *rustico*. "Crazy weather, eh?"

He agreed, drumming his fingers on the old zinc counter.

"Will you work today?" she asked.

"Maybe," he said, but his faced looked odd and he avoided her gaze.

She noticed his fingers trembling slightly.

"I'll be finished early," she said, returning her gaze to the ball of dough. "Signora Verano told me to bake only half what I usually do. She says it'll storm like this all day and that we'll have half the customers."

"She's smart about these things," Piero said, opening and then closing the newspaper.

"Not so smart," she answered. Constanza didn't like him thinking the old woman's superstitions made her smart. There was nothing to admire about the woman except that she had a talent for making breads and pastries and for running a successful *pasticceria*. There was nothing else remarkable about her.

When Constanza brought their coffees and steaming bread to the counter, she went back for two cornetti.

"These are special today—with cream. I had more time," she said modestly. "I figured you wouldn't come in today because of the storm."

He smiled, moving the small plate with the light brown pastry closer to his other plate filled with a half loaf of bread.

"What did you hear from Murano yesterday?" she asked.

"Niente," he answered. "Nothing happens in Murano, you know that."

She nodded wistfully, wishing he liked to talk more. Still, it felt good to have someone from the place she grew up. At least he knew whom she was talking about when she gossiped. She liked their quiet mornings together, her baking bread and pastries while he read the paper, or talked about his projects at the studio. She found herself strangely fascinated when he talked about getting the temperature of the molten glass just right, and then how he mixed the colors and blew and shaped the glass based on the specifications of an order, or occasionally, following a vision he had in his mind's eye. It reminded her of baking bread.

"You're an unlikely artist," she'd told him that day.

He looked hurt, his eyes uncertain and dim.

"I mean nothing bad by it," she said brightly, wondering if there had ever been an Italian man with skin as thin as Piero's.

If it hadn't all ended so terribly, she might laugh now at how forthright she'd been, practically pulling the proposal out of him.

She hadn't meant to watch him, but she'd sensed that there was something odd about the way he was acting that morning, how he'd finished his coffee so quickly, and nibbled his pastry and bread rabbit-quick. Without even being aware of it, she'd been studying him when he looked up.

He blushed. She realized it was the first time she had ever seen his face color.

"What?" she asked. "What's the matter?"

He stammered, moving the plate away from and then back toward him. He picked up a few crumbs by pressing his thumb into the zinc counter and releasing them over the plate.

"Niente," he answered evasively, glancing at the oven.

She saw immediately that he wanted to talk, wanted to divulge something.

"You can tell me," she'd reassured. "Really."

He didn't look so certain—the most timid she'd ever seen him.

"Can I have another coffee," he asked suddenly, pushing the empty, foam-lined cup toward her. He gazed out the rain-streaked windows and drummed his fingers against the table, a habit she'd never noticed.

"I'll fix you another and then you must tell me what's weighing so on your mind, okay?" she said, mopping up some crumbs with a linen cloth.

She carried his empty cup toward the brightly polished coffee machine, not waiting for his response. When she returned with his cup a few minutes later, crowned with a creamy white and toast-colored head of foam, he appeared even more nervous. The ominous clouds growled with thunder, dimming the skies again, and casting a greenish-gray light through the windows into the heavy silence of the room. Lightning flashed, followed by a flickering of the lights and a sighing of the glowing fire in the bread oven.

"What, what?" she boomed, growing impatient. "Just out with it, okay? You'll make me angry."

She turned back to the remaining bowls of rising dough, hoping he could talk to her back or hands easier than her face.

He proposed to her, of course and then his behavior made sense.

"We should get married," he'd said.

She'd continued punching and then kneading the dough, as if she hadn't heard him. Why hadn't she guessed?

So this is where it ends up. In a way, it did seem a natural progression. She'd grown fond of his company, their early morning meetings, and Sunday afternoons and evenings. They'd even taken to returning to Murano together, usually leaving on Saturday afternoon when she'd finished baking bread.

How to answer him? He made it sound like it was the logical thing to do, but certainly he wanted to marry her for more reasons than that?

"I mean, would you marry me?" he'd corrected himself, his voice unusually high and thin.

Turning her eyes briefly but fully toward him, she saw that he continued to look out the window. Was he so shy or afraid she would say no?

She went back to kneading the dough, wondering how to answer. She was fond of the man, even loved him a little, she supposed. And maybe her feelings would grow with time, or then maybe not. Did it matter anyway?

He was a glassblower, but didn't meet the stereotype, the wandering, fickle craftsman. She felt confident that he would always remain in Venice, the restlessness of the trade never having occupied him. He was an artist and alchemist; he was not itinerant.

So why not say yes? She could do no better; he loved her, would be a good provider and she'd grown to enjoy his company. Perhaps most of all, she sensed he would be a good father, thoughtful, generous, and loving with his children.

These things were enough on which to base a marriage, weren't they? Her mother would disapprove, but what alternative could *she* propose?

"Yes, I will marry you," she'd said, though it sounded to her ears as if she'd just completed a business transaction.

Piero's face lit up as he raced around the worktable to her side, slapping the tabletop.

"I'll make you happy, I promise!" he'd cried. "And you'll give me children?"

What other reason was there to get married?

"Of course," she laughed. "How many do you want?"

"As many as we're given," he said, glancing skyward.

She shrugged her shoulders, smiling feebly.

"It's okay?" he asked.

"Sure, it's okay." She took her hands out of the dough, turning to face him.

He leaned in to kiss her, and she leaned forward to meet his lips. He surprised her with a deep kiss, but not one of those hungry, sloppy kisses that the few other men she'd kissed had given her.

Maybe she would even fall in love with him. Turning to the bowls of dough and smiling, she felt it was possible.

"*T'amo*, Constanza," he said sheepishly, at long last dropping the formal tense.

"*T'amo*," she echoed, wondering where the feeling had come from.

They made plans to go to dinner that night to celebrate, and then he rushed from the bakery, grinning and buoyant. He forgot his umbrella, though, and within minutes, the skies darkened again, followed by a downpour that sounded like a drumbeat. He would be soaked.

Now she would have to start looking out for him, reminding him to take his umbrella, to dress warmly on days when she knew his workshop would be cold. And she would need to make him a lunch. These were all satisfying, pleasing thoughts.

Whether her mother's prayers against the marriage were responsible for what had happened, she couldn't figure, but she always wondered.

Be careful what you pray for.

She had wondered if she could marry someone as quiet as he was—someone so methodical in his work and life. Then there was the inherent restlessness of glassmakers, brought about by their wandering lifestyles centuries before. A glassblower spins fragile creations from the most mundane of materials. They were an unpredictable lot—but Piero seemed different. She was certain he was.

"Glassblowers can't be trusted," her mother had warned. "You'll never know him completely. Glass is a trick against nature, so nature will always have a score to settle with the glassmaker."

Too bad she hadn't listened.

The first year of marriage complemented her bread making perfectly. Her doubts about Piero had evaporated; he seemed steadfast, if a little slow. The tendencies of glassmakers, as elaborated by her mother, didn't exhibit themselves.

Her parents reluctantly bought them a small flat in the same neighborhood, a cozy place with two small bedrooms, a dining room, a sala, a big kitchen, and a shared bathroom in the hall.

"I suppose this means you'll never return to Murano, eh?" her mother said, her eyes wet with blossoming tears.

She still thought that Piero had led them to Venice, forgetting completely—and perhaps intentionally—that it was her daughter who had left Murano first.

"Why must the kitchen be so big?" Piero had asked, when she'd demanded that the flat they purchase be the one with the largest kitchen they'd seen. "You already have one kitchen—the bakery."

"But I'll be cooking, and I can't stand to be shut up in small places," she'd said, pleased that he seemed willing to allow her this small consideration.

Her mother couldn't understand either, since she'd always cooked in a cramped kitchen, and thought the massive kitchen was a waste of space.

"Better more space for the sala," she'd advised, shaking her head at her daughter's behavior. "You'll do yourself no favor by marrying a man who indulges you."

After a wedding in the parish church, and a celebratory gondola ride, there was a dinner for their families at Trattoria Tucca in Murano. The next day she'd gone to work as usual, though her legs and midsection were sore. She hadn't expected to hurt so much from the previous night's lovemaking, but her mother had given her little hints to expect that it might not always be pleasant.

Constanza drank an extra cappuccino, leaning carefully against the worktable so her weight rested on her hip. Things were falling into place: the Veranos were ready to sell the bakery and she would eventually buy them out, maybe even one day purchase the building that housed the shop, the kitchen, and some upstairs apartments. She'd already increased sales by adding different pastries, and baking big round loaves of bread coated with flecks of sea salt and bits of rosemary. She'd gotten the idea from reading a magazine article about Toscana, deciding to create bread that was coarser and completely round. The loaves soon sold nearly as fast as the traditional ones, and when she tracked the daily receipts, she could see that each month the shop was making more money.

The Veranos had to either pay her more money, or begin selling her the business, she figured. Signora Verano hardly baked anymore and nearly every item in the shop—especially the new breads and French-inspired pastries—was made by Constanza who had quickly developed a reputation as one of the city's best bakers. If she left the shop, a number of customers would follow her, hooked as they were on her breads and pastries. And for these reasons, the Veranos, who saw the writing on the wall, soon approached her about buying them out.

She hadn't been surprised, as she'd prayed for just such a development, and had been making the exact same plea almost since the day she set foot in the high-ceilinged, well-lit kitchen of the modest, squat medieval building.

Dio, she'd whispered on so many mornings as she lit the oven fires, *if you allow me to one day own this bakery, I'll create the finest breads and pastries in your name and will raise children in the tradition.*

Two months later, the smell of yeast and dough made her perspire and feel nauseated. And a month after that, she figured out she was pregnant.

Constanza knew immediately it was a boy because he drained her energy, remembering the advice her mother had given her. Before the pregnancy, she'd easily risen from bed without a clock or an alarm. She could sense the time, feeling as if the bakery determined her waking and sleeping as much as the sun and moon—and much better than any clock. She would be alert and eager to arrive at the cold, dark bakery and begin making the shop come alive with warmth from the ovens, bright puddles of light cast from the hanging, overhead canisters, and the sight and smells of dough and fresh bread.

But she now found she often overslept and had to set an alarm, which awakened Piero, too. In his plodding, routine-loving manner, he sighed loudly, rolling over with a loud rustle of the bedcovers as he turned away from the light cast from the small lamp that sat atop the simple bureau. After she had arrived at work late a few times, confronting customers who would show up at their usual times seeking her bread, cornetti, or pastries, only to have her beg them to return an hour or so later, she began winding and setting Piero's heavy metal alarm clock.

A few weeks later when Piero joined her at the bakery at the usual time for his cappuccino, he asked if she was feeling well.

"I imagine I'm pregnant," she confessed, pinching and folding dough into the shape of cornetti.

Her back turned to him, she could sense him smiling, hear him slyly and quietly laughing.

"*Brava, bella*!" he shouted, slapping the counter. "I knew, I knew it!"

She shrugged. After all, he'd been as responsible as she was.

"Grazie, Constanza," he said softly. "Grazie."

Filling a tray with cornetti, she turned to face him where he sat on a stool across her worktable. She couldn't resist smiling herself, feeling a warmth and affection for Piero rise in her chest.

Jumping off the stool, he approached her from behind, enfolding her shoulders and torso in his arms. For a moment, she forgot the blazing oven, cornetti, bread, and pastries and the aching and swelling of her knees and hips. For the first time, she felt deep and abiding affection for her husband, forgetting that she had once felt ambivalence toward him.

He will be the perfect father, a loving father to my child.

So this was the feeling that her mother had spoken of, the sense of being cared for, protected. She'd prayed to know what love is, to be consumed by it. And even though her love for her husband wasn't fiery or passionate, maybe that would come.

In the meantime, she would enjoy a stable and gentle love that seemed soft and warm as the seawater at the Lido in August.

For the first time in their marriage, she didn't break away from his embrace after only a moment, but lingered, keeping her eyes open to commit to memory the look of the bakery at that moment. Warm morning light spilled in through the open windows, and the flames and hot coals from the ovens glowed. Her cup of coffee and milk sat near his, across the flour-coated worktable. Bowls of rising dough covered with muslin, sat closest to the ovens capturing the heat. The casement windows stood ajar, releasing the fragrant aromas of slowly baking bread and pastries, while admitting fresh spring air into the kitchen.

She pushed back into his chest, allowing him to support her weight. Was this how it would be now? She had never been prone to great displays of affection or emotion, but here she was acting like her mother, soft and yielding.

The abrupt sound of the door being pushed open made her jump, and she turned from his embrace, delivering a quick, but firmly placed kiss on his cheek.

"*Mi scusa*!" the nearby coffee bar owner's wife barked, smiling broadly. She marched from the door to the counter, setting canvas bags on the countertop.

Constanza felt embarrassed. It was as if the woman had seen a vulnerable side to her that she'd shown no one. She walked over to the counter, leaving the tray of cornetti on the table.

The woman, who came in early every day to get rolls and loaves of bread for the *panini* and light breakfasts they served with coffee, looked surprised, and maybe even smug.

"It's spring," she announced. "*Un bel giorno*."

Constanza felt certain she meant something by the comment, but chose to ignore it.

"Sì, it's good to have the windows open all the way and to have so much fresh air."

She gathered the bread and rolls for the woman, allowing her to see the loaves, rolls, and cornetti she had selected. Carefully placing the rolls in the bottom of one bag, she stacked two dozen cornetti on top, and then filled the other bag with two dozen small baguettes, and four squat, crusty loaves for *panini*. She handed the bags to the woman, providing her with an order form to sign.

After the woman had signed the order and left, Constanza rushed over to the table and carefully pushed the tray of cornetti into the oven.

"I should go," Piero said, slurping the last sip of coffee from his cup.

He seemed embarrassed, too, as if he wanted to leave.

She knew it didn't make sense, but she was resentful that the customer had intruded, interrupting what? Why couldn't they go back to where they were before the woman had entered?

Constanza gazed at Piero expectantly. Would he hold her again? She stood where she'd been, but wasn't certain whether to face him or not. Sighing, she turned her back to him, placing one hand on the counter, and peering over her shoulder at him.

He smiled, folding up the giornale he'd been reading.

"Would you like another coffee?" she asked, hoping he would stay for another. She turned to face him, disappointed that he hadn't understood—or hadn't wanted—to hold her again.

Could she simply ask him to hold her again, to stay longer? But she couldn't utter the words, which seemed to hover in the middle of her throat, just short of coming out.

"I have to go," Piero said, putting on his hat and picking up the giornale. He picked up a cornetto, wrapped it in a napkin, and pushed it into the pocket of his worn jacket. "Tonight we'll celebrate, okay? And we should think of names, right?"

She gave him a small nod in response, placing both hands on the lip of her worktable, which felt cool to the touch. For the first time, she felt awkward, aware of her body, and unsure where to place her hands and long arms. She felt swollen already, as if her body were straining against her skin.

"I'll go to Mass first, before I come home," she explained, knowing she should attend more frequently to demonstrate gratitude for their good fortune.

He nodded, smiling, and hurried out the door.

Was she unattractive to him? How did she look to him—to anyone? She'd never much cared, but suddenly wondered. She never took much care about her appearance, just brushed her hair, and washed in the early mornings, thinking about little more than getting to her baking.

For the first time since she'd starting baking, she was bored. Looking around the bakery, she still had more batches of bread to bake and then she'd planned to make some apple *crostate*, too. What she wanted to do was to return to bed, sleep a little longer.

She remembered hearing her mother talk about how pregnancy made some women moody, angry, sad, or deliriously happy. Lonely was what she felt. Lonely and suddenly bored.

Turning on the steam of the espresso machine, she drew another shot of coffee and drank greedily. She leaned against the counter, resting her chin in her hands.

How could her life, which had until that moment seemed so busy, suddenly seem so empty, meaningless?

She sunk to the floor, sprinkled with flour and breadcrumbs, and leaned against a cabinet. Staring out the window, she watched an enormous cloud scuttle across the sky, carrying with it the rays of sun that had slanted through the windows. Glad for the temporary shadows, she closed her eyes for a moment, feeling her buttocks and backside of her thighs meld with the cool, crumb and flour covered floor. When the sun reappeared, striking her face brightly and prompting her to open her eyes, the ominous, unfamiliar feeling had gone.

Jumping to her feet, surprised at her sudden energy, Constanza wanted to get the bread finished, and maybe bake some crostate too. Racing to the door, she stepped outside into the now-balmy air, but looking down the street, she couldn't spot Piero who had disappeared around the corner.

Just as well for she would see him tonight and every night for the rest of her life. Smiling, she made her way back into the bakery, leaving the door ajar.

Chapter Ten

"I know it doesn't look like much," Sacci said, unlocking the immense wooden doors. "But it has a lot of potential."

Rusted bolts, the size of golf balls, rose from the dull, dried surface of the doors. The palazzo had a sullen, unkempt appearance, but there were still signs that it had once been a palace. Huge windows dominated the second floor, and there was even a terrace on one side of the building. There had been a garden on the second floor loggia at one time, but only some weeds and vines survived the neglect, sending spindly heads and tendrils over the terrace wall. Byzantine archways curved upward, partially obscuring what looked to be an incredible space with views down the street—and who knew of what else?

"Ah, the loggia," Sacci said, following their gaze. "That's possibly the best feature of the place. Great views of the neighborhood—just by luck, though, because it is only one floor above street level—and very airy, yet private. The perfect place for a café or restaurant. Not every hotel in Venice has a loggia like this. You could do fashion shows here, art openings, parties. Maybe weddings. You'll see when we get up there."

Claudia nodded vigorously, moving her fingers carefully across the stone doorway and onto the massive wooden doors. "It's a beautiful palazzo, really grand. And not ostentatious—I don't like ostentatious."

"This is the building for you then," Sacci said, smiling sheepishly. "The main entrance is on the canal, on the opposite side, of course, but you can see that this doorway will serve quite well as the entrance."

Claudia studied the doors, then turned to look up and down the via. Clumps of tourists plied the street, maps in hand, and shopping bags in tow.

"And what is that grand building there," she asked, pointing where the street curved and an imposing building pushed its way toward the sky.

"*Il teatro la Fenice*—the opera house. You know it, don't you?" Sacci asked Louis.

He felt ashamed, for though he'd lived in the city for more than a year, he'd never even walked by it. "I've meant to get there, but haven't yet." Did his response sound stupid, uncouth? Then, Claudia didn't know what it was either, so at least he had company. And she was Italian.

Ah, it was ridiculous that he cared at all. How stupid to have a crush on a straight man, on an Italian who sent mixed signals. He looked at Sacci, who seemed to be studying him before looking away. Why was he even thinking about him like that, entertaining a silly, schoolboy crush?

"And San Marco is not so far from here?" Claudia asked, interrupting his thoughts.

Sacci gestured in the direction of the street, up toward the towering La Fenice.

"Not far at all. I'm telling you, it's a fantastic neighborhood. We've had offers to buy the palace to make it into a hotel, but they see the inside and decide it will cost too much. It's either too big, or not big enough. Too ruined, or not gutted enough. We've got the resources, and the manpower—and now the project manager," he said, smiling at Claudia. "So we'll do it ourselves. Finally, eh?"

They all gathered at the entrance, eagerly awaiting Sacci's push of the door.

"I think it was meant to be that we never found another use for it or a seller. I always thought there should be something unique here because this building has quite a history." He pushed the door open, and an uneven, dusty mosaic floor caught the daylight.

"Incredible," Claudia sighed, rubbing the sole of her shoe across the tiles to clear the dust.

An intricate border appeared, rows and rows of checkerboard and vines, flowers and stylized suns. Though it was difficult to guess the colors, the tiny squares were different shades of gray and brown that hinted at a riot of color obscured by the dust.

"When was the last time anyone lived here?" Louis asked. "Or worked here?"

"Oh, it has electricity, plumbing, all of that, so maybe not as long ago as you're thinking. But it's all old stuff—old electricity, old telephone. Not much heat. My mother lived here as a child, then gave it up when she got married. She never liked Venice, couldn't live in a place that even the newspapers admitted was sinking. So, what she didn't move to Trieste, she sold, and the palazzo has only had a few temporary renters and housed an office once or twice."

Sacci searched along the hall, finding a button, which he pressed, turning on massive old glass-enclosed lighting fixtures hanging down the center of the hall. The light fixtures were coated with a thick layer of dust, too, as were the walls and a few scattered pieces of furniture.

"Incredible," Claudia sighed. "But how long will it take to get this cleaned up? I can't do this by myself—even if I agree to do this."

"I can help and my brothers and cousins can help, too," Sacci said quickly. "After all, they're co-owners of the palazzo, so it's in their best interest."

"Do they really want to help fix it up for a complete stranger?" Claudia walked down the hallway, staring at a huge staircase curving upward.

"They owe me and so they'll do it. And I don't think they'll mind, anyway. There's not *that* much work here—it looks worse than it is. Besides, nearly everyone I know has a little extra time—no one's rushing around like the Milanese. We can get a lot of people to help a little, eh?" He led them toward the stair, pointing at the intricately carved beams stretched across the ceiling. "Incredible, huh?"

Louis and Claudia nodded their heads, walking slowly across the dusty floor toward the heavy staircase at the other end of the wide, echoing hallway.

"Do we get to see the rooms down here before we go up?" Louis asked. There were four pairs of doors set into the thick walls and framed by old stone pillars flecked with faded, flaking paint. The original design painted on them was still visible—swirls and paisley-like forms interspersed with flowers and fish. Strange combinations, he thought.

"Let's see the most impressive thing first," Sacci said, urgently waving them up the steps. "Then we can see the rooms downstairs."

Climbing the steps slowly, they reached the second floor after two broad landings with pairs of shuttered windows overlooking what? Louis wanted to open everything up, throw the windows wide to let in some light and to see all the carvings, the intricate beams and painted walls and pillars that lurked in the shadows. When they reached the second floor, the *piano nobile*, it was nearly too dark to see.

"I can't recall where the light switch is around here," Sacci said, bumping into Louis who stood near a wall.

Louis could smell him, the faint scent of cologne, and something like leather. His heart skipped a beat and he couldn't help wishing that Claudia would agree with Sacci's proposition to convert the palazzo to a hotel just so he would see Sacci all the time, maybe every day. At first, the palazzo had made sense because it seemed the perfect occupation for his friend; now the opportunity appeared promising for him, too.

He could sense something happening already, this deepening of his crush. It felt as if he were falling, being unable to stop himself, though the situation seemed hopeless. He'd come so far since the baseless infatuations, and childish loves that had marked his life in America. Would he ever grow up?

Sacci pushed Louis by the shoulders, guiding him gently away from the wall. Louis could hear him tapping the walls, his hands scraping and exploring the dusty, cold surface looking for the light switch.

"Ah," he said, flicking the switch. A flash of light illuminated the hallway, followed by a pop and then darkness again. "Damn, the light's blown," he murmured.

"Now what?" Louis asked. "Did you bring a flashlight?"

"No problem," Sacci reassured, moving away. "Just help me open the shutters. We'll open the windows for light—it's better anyway and time for all of them to be opened. Let's start with the ones on the landing."

Louis followed Sacci back down the wide stairway to the first landing, where the light from the hallway below shone up feebly. Sacci stood before the pairs of closed and fastened shutters, grabbed the closest heavy metal latch and pulled it upward. Sliding the enormous interior shutter toward him, he stirred up a cloud of dust that swirled in the beams of light flooding the landing. A draft from the enormous mullioned windows carried the dust onto the landing, making Claudia sneeze.

Louis gazed out the window, while Sacci gently moved him aside, opening the rusted French doors, and waving them toward him. Below snaked a small canal, traversed by gently arcing bridges. A waxen, black gondola plied the jade-colored waters of the canal headed toward St. Mark's Square. Louis leaned on the balustrade of the narrow balcony, peering directly below at the worn stone step and giant doors of the palazzo's old canal entrance.

"What are you looking at?" Claudia asked, squinting as she pushed her way onto the sun-washed balcony.

"The canal doors and gate," he answered, pointing below.

Claudia studied the doors silently, leaning over the railing.

"What?" Louis asked, noticing that she seemed lost in thought.

"Just imagining a big event and people coming in from the canal. Maybe gondolas full of people."

She seemed to want to smile, the corners of her mouth twitching.

"I told you it had great potential, eh?" Sacci said. "Just needs some work."

He opened both of the doors, locking them into position behind large metal hooks secured to the thick walls. Light flooded through the tall, dusty glass doors.

"Now we can see where we're going," Sacci exclaimed, waving them back onto the landing and up the steps. At the top of the stairs, they continued to the end of the dimly lit hall where Sacci started opening more of the heavy wooden accordion shutters. Louis grabbed one and helped Sacci free the fasteners before opening the dust-caked windows. Warm air rushed in, bringing with it scents from the canal and the springtime air, and the faint, melodic sound of birdsong.

The upstairs hall was even more elaborate than the one downstairs, though the paint on the walls and curtains were faded and covered with cobwebs and dust. The floors were scratched and made of uneven, sometimes slightly warped parquet tiles, but some of the walls still had colorful, perfectly designed frescoes with designs of leaping fish, shellfish, and boats.

"The family who owned this in the 1600s owned a fish market," Sacci explained, sweeping his arm down the wall. "There are carvings, too."

He pointed above them at fish and seahorses carved into the capitals of the columns flanking the doors. Following the same floor plan as downstairs, there were four sets of double doors—two on each side. The doors opened out, and Sacci led them to the ones on the right, toward the loggia.

"We'll go directly to the most interesting, inspiring feature of the palazzo," he said excitedly, grabbing one of the thick, metal handles and opening the squeaking door.

Claudia and Louis backed up to allow the door to swing past before peering into the darkened room. A path of light fell onto the floor of the room, but shadows obscured all but the intricately carved floor directly in front of them. Sacci flipped a switch, bathing the room with warm light from the dozens of bulbs of an immense glass chandelier. At one time, the room had probably been a bedroom, but now contained just a few enormous wooden desks.

"I think there used to be lawyers up here," Sacci explained. "They were the last ones to rent the building."

"Why would they have their offices up here, off the ground floor?" Louis asked, wondering why clients or the lawyers themselves would want to mount the long, massive stairs multiple times in a day.

"Because of this," Sacci announced, strutting across the room toward two sets of tightly shuttered French doors. Hurriedly unlatching and pulling open one set of shutters; he revealed another giant set of paned doors, this set opening onto the loggia they'd seen from the street below. The first section of the loggia just outside the doors lay in shade, maybe twenty feet, and another ten feet lay exposed to the sky, its terracotta tile floor glowing orange in the bright sun. Carved, Byzantine columns and archways divided the two spaces, framing the view down the canal, and rising perhaps fifteen or twenty feet to vaulted ceilings marred by cobwebs and mud nests of swallows in the corners.

"This is where the opening party should be," Claudia sighed, quickly adding, "—if we were to do this."

She could imagine a runway down the middle of the loggia, maybe for a fashion show, or art scattered around the perimeter of the room and out on the section exposed to the sky. And a jazz quartet performing under the loggia near the doors would be perfect, silken music wafting down the stairs and out the archways into the air above the street. The view was amazing—the opera house rose monolithic a few buildings down and a jumble of tiled roofs and elaborate cornices surrounded them.

Claudia took in the view, rocking on the balls of her feet. A nervous look clouded her face and she began to look overwhelmed. "I don't know," she sighed, glancing up at the vaulted ceiling of the loggia and at the dry fountain in the corner, the rusted end of a pipe jutting from the parted mouth of a sculpted lion. "This is bigger than I thought it would be. I thought you said *un piccolo palazzo*, eh? And the building needs so much work."

Sacci nodded vigorously. "Sì, sì, sì. Of course, but we have the workers and lots of others who can help. We just need someone to lead the project, to organize everything. To bring it together." He looked at Claudia expectantly, nervously.

Louis felt a pang of jealousy. Was Sacci flirting with Claudia? He told himself to ignore the feeling, to stop the attraction, but he felt helpless.

"I don't know. It's so huge a project—"

"It's not that huge. It'll be maybe a twenty-room hotel. And you'll have plenty of help. It's not like you'll be doing this on your own. My family will be involved, and I bet Louis will help." He looked over at Louis, winking.

"I don't get it," Claudia whispered, shaking her head. "Why are you offering me this? Why don't you do it yourself?"

"Because I think you're perfect for it," Sacci said soberly. "And I am not. I loath details; can't keep track of things or organize anything."

"But you don't even know me. You've just met me!" she protested.

"True," he said, "but I have a feeling, a feeling in my gut that you're perfect for this. And my gut is never wrong." He glanced at Louis, winking again.

Louis wished he wouldn't wink at him, but the poor guy must have had no idea.

Claudia ran her hand across the worn stone balustrade of the loggia, gazing again down the canal and the jumble of pink, ochre, and russet buildings, shutters and windows alternately opened and closed, church towers, and the elaborate, carved tops of palazzi rising above the nearby rooftops. A black and white wagtail landed on the other side of the loggia, eyeing her and chirping as it moved its long tail up and down.

"I don't know," she moaned. "It is so very tempting. It sounds like such a fantastic opportunity, and you are so kind to offer me—a total stranger—such a wonderful chance. But I have to be realistic. And I hate to sound ungrateful or greedy, but I just have to know—would *have* to know—how much I would be paid and how much money you would expect me to invest. I don't have that much money."

Louis stared at her, shifting his gaze when she met his. Of course she had to ask the question, but he worried that somehow it would make her appear ungrateful or would somehow put the entire deal into jeopardy.

"I've already got estimates for how much it would cost," Sacci said quickly, tapping his leather briefcase and shrugging. "My brothers and I have been looking into it, just waiting for someone to come along that could run this thing. We're better at providing the funds, getting the workers. We're not so good at the ideas, or managing. That's where you come in, I think."

"Yes, but you don't even know me, I'm a total stranger!" she said again. "And you're going to trust me with your business, with your investment and your family's palazzo?"

Louis thought Claudia looked nearly angry or frustrated, as if she couldn't understand what he was offering or why he was offering it.

"Such as it is," Sacci laughed. "Sure it's a palazzo, but what good is it to us in this condition? No, I need someone who can do something with it or I may as well sell it, which no one in my family wants—"

"Still," Claudia interrupted, shaking her head. "You hardly even know me."

"It's not like you're unknown to me," Sacci grinned. "I see you visit Louis all the time. And you know how Venetians talk, much as it sometimes annoys me. I've heard things about you, and then I know about your family."

"But then you must know that I'm divorced or soon to be so." She hated bringing up these personal details, but she figured if she was really going to do this everything would have to be out in the open.

Sacci shrugged. "What do I care of that? I'm not hiring and taking a couple as partners—I'm approaching just you. And I'm not one of those old-style Italians who care about any of that stuff, anyway."

Claudia studied his face, looking for signs that she was being manipulated. Too many encounters with her mother had made her paranoid. With her mother, she could normally tell—especially after so many years—but with this guy, she wasn't certain what to think.

"Tell me again why I should do this?" She felt like she was staring him down, but he merely smiled back, still confident as if it were only a matter of time before she could be persuaded. God, she hated that. Couldn't he sound more desperate, more uncertain, more like she felt?

Louis groaned unintentionally, the two turning quickly to look at him in surprise.

"Why are you so worried?" he asked impatiently. "It's an opportunity of a lifetime—and if there's something better out there, I can't think what it might be."

Why was she being so obstinate? He hated to make her sound desperate in front of Sacci, but wasn't that the truth? Besides, he was certain Sacci had already heard about her predicament. The past few days she seemed to mistrust and second-guess everyone, including him. He wanted to shake her, make her realize that Sacci's offer was just the thing, as if it had been planned this way. And, if she didn't agree, then what else was there for her, he wondered? Yes, the thing just seemed meant to be—and for more reasons than his wanting to have an excuse to see Sacci regularly.

"Sorry if I sound hesitant, but this is the only money I've got and very likely the only money I'll be getting," she said sheepishly. "I need to feel good about doing this because the whole rest of my life will turn on whether this ends up working out. If this turns out to be a bad decision, if this doesn't meet with success, then that's it for me." She stared at Louis, willing him to understand. "You see, Louis? You've got talents to live on, and I don't."

She hadn't meant to sound so pathetic, so downtrodden, but then, wasn't that how things really were?

"You've got plenty of talent, trust me," Louis said, frowning. "You've just never been asked to use it."

"Even I can see it," Sacci said, his hands moving through the air imitating a conductor. "The way you dress and carry yourself, eh? And your enthusiasm, the way you get along with people, your knowledge of art and architecture, and I heard you did quite well at architecture school."

"Where did you hear that?" she asked, looking surprised.

Sacci blinked, suddenly embarrassed. Shooting a look of apology, he pointed at Louis. "From him," he confessed. He wasn't certain whether Claudia was pleased with the compliment.

She glanced at Louis, shrugging.

Was she angry, he wondered?

Turning to Sacci, her lips forming a faint smile, she nodded.

"I have a good feeling," she admitted slowly. "I mean, about you, and the hotel, and everything about the idea and the place. It's just ..." Her voice trailed off as she turned toward one of the imposing ochre buildings across the canal, the bright sun causing the building to glow. She squinted, bringing her hand up to her forehead, casting a shadow over her eyes.

"What is it?" Sacci asked timidly.

Maybe she had never had to plan, to budget, or to think about the direction her life might take. For Louis, it had been easy; he'd never had great expectations. There had never been anything grand waiting in the wings. He'd always had to make his own life; there was never anyone else making decisions for him, so he could only imagine what it must be like for her.

The previous few days, Louis thought Claudia had been looking more serious and a side to her had emerged that had only been hinted at previously. She read the newspaper at Tramonta and didn't order prosecco at breakfast, seeming to weigh the coming decision as if it were the most important one of her life. Though there was still a chance that she would fail and have to leave Venice, he began to think that her mother's cutting her off might have been the best thing that had happened to her.

Studying the endless view, he admired the way the warm sun struck the buildings, turning the structures vivid shades of orange, ochre, and rust. The sky, a robin's egg blue so delicate it looked like it could break, was cloudless, marred only by a small flock of swifts, which rose and fell in unison. After a moment, the flock darted downward, disappearing into a towering chimney.

Louis suddenly realized that what he wanted, perhaps most, was to have the same sort of relationship he had with Claudia, but with a man. Was it even possible? Was this the reason he'd become such close friends with her, only to realize that his friendship with her was how a relationship ought to be?

They all watched the swifts gazing at the vivid blue sky in momentary silence, waiting for Claudia to respond. She cleared her throat, running her hand across the thick top of the balustrade.

"I just don't have anything to base it on, that's all," she said uncertainly, twisting her mouth and grazing her fingers across her throat. "It feels right, looks like a good idea, but what if it doesn't work out? And how do I even know what a good opportunity is—I've never had to seize one?"

"I never have either," Sacci said with a half-smile. "I've been lying low my whole life, living quiet as a hermit. Now there's this, an idea and something bigger than I've ever encountered. So I'm no expert either. I don't know exactly how to approach this, but it feels right and the timing's right. And what else do I have? I could move to *Milano*, or to *Roma*, but what would I do there? No, my home is here in Venice, so what can I do other than be a landlord? There's not much opportunity here, not like in other cities, and I've never had a great drive to do anything, anyways. Not until now."

Claudia nodded, her eyes glued to the building across the canal. Sacci's appeal had to make sense to her; it made sense to Louis. After all, weren't they all in the same boat?

Sacci glanced nervously at Claudia, shaking his head.

"I think it's right," he repeated, clearing his throat. "And thinking it's the right thing makes it the right thing, doesn't it? I have a feeling, too, that you're the perfect person for this. Yeah, it's just a silly feeling, but a lot of my feelings and hunches have turned out to be right."

Louis glanced at Sacci who was frowning as he started across the loggia, out toward the path of the canal that wound through the densely packed jumble of earth-colored buildings. The three of them stood awkwardly on the sun-drenched terrace, Sacci and Louis waiting for Claudia to speak.

Claudia cleared her throat, biting her lip and looking as if she were going to remain obstinate and turn down Sacci's offer. Then her face brightened as she began slowly nodding her head.

"How much is it going to cost?" she asked, breaking the silence and turning to Sacci. "I mean, how much would you need me to invest?"

Sacci grinned, following her gaze toward the bird still perched at the end of the loggia. He pulled out his list of calculations and jabbed his forefinger at one of the neatly printed lines of numbers.

"We'd need that much," he said. "I've already had workers provide estimates for nearly everything. And, of course, we'd need a little extra to decorate, but here's the estimate for converting it."

Claudia glanced at the figure with a worried face.

"I don't know how I'd live," she said slowly, beginning to frown. "That would be most of the money I have, and I wouldn't have any income until the hotel opened, right? I mean, where and how would I live?"

Sacci looked puzzled, and then his face lit up.

"Here!" he gushed, sweeping his arms through the air to indicate the whole palazzo. "Why, you could live here!"

Claudia looked through the doorway at the dark and dusty palazzo, the bits of plaster on the floor and the vision of neglect on the terrace.

Sacci saw her frown, the way her eyes crinkled.

"It could be fun—to live here as it takes shape, and it would be good to have someone staying here while we're working on it. Think how you'd see it take shape, the quiet nights when you'd have the whole place to yourself. Then you'd be living for free, and if my family and I invested a little more and fed you, then what else would you need?"

Louis thought to say, "Money for prosecco and coffee," but he bit his tongue, avoiding even a joke if it might dissuade Claudia from saying yes.

"This building has a history, you know," Sacci said, slapping the balustrade for emphasis. "Lots of interesting and beautiful details. By living here, you'd become a part of it, eh? You want to find something to do—a task that matches your talents. And you love Venice, right? You're very social, and might even enjoy entertaining, I bet."

Claudia nodded thoughtfully, her eyes glued to the glowing buildings across the canal.

Where was this used car salesmanship coming from, Louis wondered. He never suspected Sacci of harboring such a talent for persuasion. He could see so clearly that the opportunity was ideal for his friend. Why couldn't she see it?

But Claudia avoided their imploring eyes, rubbing her hand across the stone balustrade as if seeking an answer from the palazzo itself. It reminded Louis of when a woman felt the material of a dress or linen before purchasing it.

He imagined the three of them having lunches on the terrace. There would be bright-blooming roses in front of the pillars, maybe some sweet-smelling jasmine, and honeysuckle vine climbing the thick columns of the loggia. Between projects, they could take a long lunch, drink some prosecco, and take the afternoon off occasionally.

Sacci leaned toward Claudia and gently grabbed her forearm. Tentatively, he said in a near-whisper, "Maybe not shopping or cutting back on dinners out you could make it, eh? Would it be enough if just while the construction is going on you lived with a smaller budget?"

Louis shuddered, staring at Claudia to see whether she'd bristled. He feared that Sacci had gone too far, but Claudia didn't react, her gaze fixed on the distant buildings. Maybe he could help her out, too, if she'd accept money from him. But he could be creative in helping her, by picking up drink tabs or having her over for dinner. That might help—a little, anyway.

"There must be some way to make it work," he said, glancing

at Sacci conspiratorially. "Can't we figure out some way to make it work?"

They both looked at him, and suddenly he felt self-conscious for having used "we" when the problem wasn't his at all. Sacci eyed him strangely.

"I suppose I could ask my brothers for some more money," Sacci said uncertainly, twisting his mouth while studying Claudia.

"No, you can't do that—I won't let you!" Claudia exclaimed, turning to face him. "Not for a total stranger; I'm not even sure I can do this. No, I wouldn't—*couldn't*—let you do it. You don't need me for this, really you don't. You've got it all figured out, and you and your family can do this without me."

"But …" Sacci began.

"No," she whispered. "I won't allow it. It's a big enough project as it is. I couldn't live knowing you and your family put in more money just because I don't have enough."

And what had she been taking from her parents all these years, Louis wondered?

"But we've got to have someone to do the organizing, to coordinate the workers, the schedule, and then to manage the hotel. I can't do that—I'm used to running my little apartment building and I can scarcely do that," Sacci argued. "Someone needs to be here all the time. Then when the hotel opens, we'll need someone who's good with guests, makes them feel at home. I'm shy, quiet, and my family members aren't even interested in *running* a hotel."

"How about if I help out on weekends or evenings, in my spare time from whatever job I find?" she asked.

"But you won't find a job here that pays more than this," Sacci said, shaking his head frantically. "At least once things get going. You can't be a waiter or front desk worker at a hotel and earn any more. This is Venice—there's not much more for you to do."

"There must be other jobs," she said, rubbing the palms of her hands on her thighs slowly, and then abruptly clasping her neck.

"A glassblower? Maybe a gondolier?" Sacci asked, grinning. "A baker?"

Suddenly, Sacci looked disappointed, hopeless. Was he concerned about the hotel, or Claudia? Louis couldn't tell. He sensed that Claudia wanted to say yes, even seemed excited about the prospect, but why wouldn't she allow herself to agree? Why was she so worried about the money when she obviously had enough? Besides, what else would she do with such a sum of money in Venice? And what else would she *do*? Sacci's proposition was ideal—it offered something to do, a reason to stay in Venice.

"He's right," Louis added, but Claudia, her shoulders drooping, had already started walking slowly across the loggia, heading toward the large French doors that remained ajar.

The two men shuffled behind her. Louis felt foolishly jealous—was Sacci interested in Claudia? Even if the man wasn't, he felt strangely conflicted, wanting Claudia to accept Sacci's offer and stay, but at the same time, was resentful that Sacci seemed eager, desperate even, to have Claudia become his partner. Well, he'd been disappointed plenty of other times, knew even now that the crush was likely unwise, juvenile. But if a little pain and disappointment resulted in Claudia staying there, in him staying there, too, then it was okay.

Sacci followed slowly behind Claudia, his face pointed toward the stone floor of the loggia. When they crossed the worn marble threshold and back into the shadowy, upper salon, Sacci suddenly came to life again.

"So beautiful, isn't it?" he cried, pointing at the stairway, the columns around the doors, and the view out the open doorway. "And there are incredible frescoes in this other room—just down this hallway."

He walked quickly across the cavernous room and down a shorter hall, waving for the two to follow. A giant oak door, simply carved but thick and lustrous, stood open. Sacci flipped a switch and an enormous dusty chandelier flickered to life, illuminating the oblong room.

"This is the best place of all—wait until you see the views," he called, hurrying across the floor, the leather soles of his shoes softly slapping the wooden planks.

He walked to the shuttered windows, which towered over the tallest of them by three or four feet, unfolding the interior shutter doors quickly, and then opening the honey-brown, mullioned doors. Finally, he threw the exterior shutters outward, allowing light to flood in while revealing a view that seemed to go forever. In the distance, the clustered domes of San Marco and more distant Santa Maria della Salute rose above the red-tiled roofs, graceful spires, and cappuccino-colored towers of the city.

"Bravo," Claudia sighed, rushing up to the window and leaning out to gaze at the sky.

"The palazzo is far enough back from the canal that you get a few views like this in some of the rooms—all on this side of the building, of course. Amazing, eh?" Sacci asked.

The man grinned slyly, watching them standing at the railing, smiling as they admired the view. Below, gondolas with tourists glided by. One gondolier moved his long, narrow boat effortlessly down the canal. The couple—American—was arguing, unaware that voices traveled upward, echoing off the old stone and mossy brick walls.

"You've been sullen since your mother died—you have," the woman said. "You're awful to be around, acting as if life were over."

"Ridiculous," the man responded. "Let me mourn a little, that's all, okay?"

"So this is how Venetians hear everything?" Claudia said.

Sacci nodded, moving his eyes toward the pale sky.

"And where's that fresco you were going to show us?" Louis asked.

As they backed out of the window, Sacci hurriedly closed the shutters and doors, waving them indoors. "And now, the best feature of all—perhaps in the whole palazzo."

He headed toward a corner of the room where cut into the wall, was a simple, shorter door. Before they reached it, though, Claudia gasped.

"There!" she exclaimed, pointing at a large fresco on the opposite wall, running above the doorway through which they'd entered and continuing nearly its entire length. "Dio!"

A serene woodland nymph frolicked in a grassy clearing while fauns and maidens looked on. Gardens full of blooming shrubs and clumps of flowers surrounded the nymph, punctuated by an occasional temple, petite and columned like miniature Acropolises. The fresco was remarkably intact, with only a few spots damaged by water or plaster flaking away.

Sacci smiled again, more subtly this time.

"Very unusual—maybe unique," he explained. "My great grandparents were fascinated by mythology, so that's Venus accompanied by the nymphs of the hills and woods of the Veneto."

"I thought they'd stopped making frescoes hundreds of years ago," Louis said, remembering an art class he'd had.

"There are actually schools that still teach it—mostly so artists can repair and restore the thousands of frescoes around here. But some still create new ones, and that's what this is—well, it's now sixty years old, so not exactly new."

"Incredible," Claudia cooed, her head moving slowly as her eyes drank in the mural. "It looks so old."

"My great grandparents wanted it to look that way to match the palazzo, and they commissioned the best Venetian artist of the time to complete it. In the mornings, when the sun shines through those windows, it illuminates this room and the mural. It's something to see."

Louis caught himself hanging onto each word of Sacci's, marveling at how many secrets he seemed to have.

"And now the best thing next to the mural and the terrace," Sacci said excitedly, beaming, his voice trembling. "Follow me."

He led them to a locked, intricately carved door in a shadowy corner. Drawing a key from his pocket, he grinned conspiratorially.

"When we were renting the palazzo for offices and such, we didn't want anyone coming up here—it's private and old, and besides, no one working in here would really have a need to come up here."

"What is it?" Claudia asked, wide-eyed.

"You'll see," Sacci smiled, waving her forward.

"Better than the fresco?" she asked, pushing a lock of hair behind her ear.

Louis realized that Sacci knew just what he was doing, marveling that he'd not given him enough credit.

Sacci inserted and turned the long skeleton key in the door, ceremoniously opening it inward to a small, paneled vestibule. He flipped a light switch that illuminated a small area and a simple, narrow wood stair heading up one floor.

"There's nothing here," Claudia said, looking perplexed.

"Up there," he prodded Claudia, pointing toward the stairway. "You go first," he instructed, grabbing Louis' elbow and steering him behind her.

They climbed the stairs, which looked virtually dust free and clean—maybe because the door hadn't been opened for years. At the top of the stairs, they discovered a small sitting area with a small, leaded glass window looking toward the canal.

"That's original—from the 1600s," Sacci said from behind them, pointing at the thick glass, which distorted the view of the buildings across the canal, but allowed in a vibrant beam of sunlight.

"Where now?" Claudia asked, eyeing two doors, one directly in front of them, the other to the side.

Sacci nodded toward the one before them and she stepped forward eagerly, pushing open a pair of tall, painted doors. She gasped, stopping at the threshold.

Claudia blocked Louis' view, but he could see over her shoulder that the floor, and the walls halfway to the ceiling, was covered with mosaic tiles. A row of casement windows set directly opposite admitted shimmering sunlight that illuminated the tiles and the entire room.

"The bathroom," Sacci announced excitedly, motioning them in.

"The bathroom?" Louis echoed, squinting.

As they moved farther into the room, Louis saw all sorts of designs in the mosaics—sea nymphs, Neptune, porpoises, octopuses, crabs, lobsters, waves, tridents, scallop shells, and stylized, blazing suns. Like the mural below, the mosaics, though appearing ancient, were in near perfect condition.

"Your great grandparents found an exceptional tile maker to create these," Claudia said. "There are so many and the colors and pictures seem alive!"

Sacci shook his head, his eyes twinkling. "These are not fake and they're not reproductions."

"What do you mean?" Louis asked, running his fingers across the nearly even, perfectly smooth surface of the tiny mosaics on the wall. His fingers brushed across a trio of blue-gray dolphins, arcing above a turquoise-blue sea. The tiles felt like smooth, cool-to-the-touch pearls.

"These came from a Roman bath found right under this palazzo," he explained, smiling broadly. "My great grandparents had to do some structural work on the foundation, and when the workers dug into the mud under the main floor, this is what they found."

"But the colors are so bright; the tiles look perfect, *new*," Claudia exclaimed. "It can't be possible."

"They'd been encased in mud for nearly two thousand years," Sacci explained. "They were cleaned up and moved up here. The mud preserved them, even kept the colors as if they'd been made just a few decades ago."

"Why keep them hidden like this?" Louis puzzled.

"They should be in a museum," Sacci answered. "There aren't many such Roman baths so well-preserved. And my great grandparents didn't want to give them up. They felt that they were as much a part of the spirit of this place as the stairway, gargoyles, and stone foundations."

"How did they keep it a secret?" Louis asked, continuing to run his hands across the tiny tiles that felt like small, polished gems.

"That's the amazing part—that they could keep such a secret in this city. But they did. The workers they brought in from Verona were sworn to secrecy, and besides, no one would have an interest in telling the government and having it come in and seize the tiles—well, the whole bathroom, really."

"Aren't you afraid someone will come in and steal the tiles?" Claudia asked, walking into the center of the room, her head moving back and forth, pendulum-like, as she studied the mosaics.

"I don't think there are many of those workers left—well, there would be none, really. So perhaps there are some rumors that there's something in this old palazzo. Or maybe there are some secrets that Venetians prefer to keep," he said, tracing his fingers across the arcing dolphins.

"I can't believe that no one talks about it, that no one's heard about them," Louis said.

"Venice is full of rumors," Sacci scoffed. "Maybe people think it's bad luck to remove them, or maybe they're no longer certain of what's in here. But who's going to steal them? The tiles are firmly affixed to the walls and it would take days to pry them loose without damaging them. So they've remained here, serving as the secret bathroom, a sanctuary of sorts for my great grandparents. Now if anyone asks, we just tell them they're a reproduction."

"Why didn't you pull them out and put them in your place? Or why didn't your mother take them with her to Trieste?" Louis asked.

Sacci shrugged. "If we took them out now, people would find out for certain, and probably the government, too. Someone might want a reward, or simply be jealous. And maybe we believe, too, that the tiles belong here—not in Trieste or in my apartment—and least of all, in a museum. So they stay here, waiting for this palazzo to come alive again."

His eyes moved slowly across the walls silently studying the mosaics before turning to Claudia.

"This could be your bathroom, you know," he said, nodding his head frenetically. "Even if everything else here is a mess, dirty, and in need of work, you'd have a bathroom at least—and one of which even the Agnellis or Rockefellers can't boast."

"It's beautiful, like being in a movie," Claudia said, a sly grin forming. "Every day I'd start and finish here. I can picture it."

She looked out the thick, leaded windows, which distorted a view similar to the one they'd seen from the bedroom below. But these windows were even taller, and this part of the palazzo stood slightly higher than the neighboring buildings. Like the top of a tower or aerie for a wizard, the bathroom rose subtly above the nearby rooftops. At some point, the room had probably served as a refuge or a strategic spot from which to defend the palazzo six or seven hundred years earlier.

"Do these open?" she asked, running her hands across the uneven glass of the casement windows, which felt cool to the touch.

"They used to," Sacci said, walking over to one of the windows to take a closer look. He unlatched the thick iron latch, pushing one of the big windows outward to reveal an expansive vista of rooftops, towers, and blue sky.

"I could take a bath in this enormous tub with the skyline of Venice framed in all of these windows," she sighed.

"You'd be the envy of the world with such a bathroom," Sacci said.

"And maybe I could come over on occasion, too, just to take a bath," Louis said, sounding more envious than he'd meant to sound.

"I'm sure she'd share," Sacci smiled. "If she was going to live here."

Once again, they stood silent, not facing each other, but each smiling vaguely, sensing possibility as tangible as the sea creatures frozen in motion on the floor and walls.

"What do you say, Claudia?" Sacci asked.

Please say the right thing, Louis pleaded silently, catching her eye, realizing it might be the last time Sacci would ask.

Sacci continued, no longer smiling. "It's perfect, I tell you. Your bedroom's down the stairs—and that other door? That leads to a study with views as good as these. We'd clean up your room first—and the hallways—so you could get to your rooms. We'll start with these, and then go room by room. You pay no rent, you live free. And then you work on your home and the hotel."

Claudia continued shaking her head, but Louis noticed she seemed to be suppressing a grin.

"Come on," Louis said, grabbing her arm. "What else have you got going? And what better situation are you going to find than this? It's the perfect revenge—no chance it won't be a success. We're a stone's throw from the opera house—the palazzo's a landmark. And you've got the vision to realize it, to make this ruin a hotel."

Sacci's masterful, he thought, but he didn't want to look at him, didn't want his eyes to betray the affection he felt for him.

Fool. It was exactly the way he'd gotten himself into previous messes, falling for guys who couldn't love him. Didn't he fall for the ones who were somehow ultimately unavailable? God, a shrink could have a field day with his life. But where would he start, and where would it end? He knew what to do—no shrink could tell him anything he didn't already know. He just needed to stop himself, for once.

He looked up and saw Sacci and Claudia studying him. He felt suddenly transparent. Did they see his wounds and his imperfections as well as he did?

"Well?" he said quickly, eyeing Claudia. "Are you going to walk away from the best offer you've got going? Walk away from this?" he asked, unable to suppress a grin as he ran his hand across the tile again, gently slapping the cool, solid wall as he pushed the thoughts he'd just had from his head.

"It sounds great—too great," she sighed, clutching her throat. "Where's the catch, though. I keep wondering what the catch is?"

"Now where's the less complex, more Pollyanna-like Claudia that I know?" Louis clucked, shaking his head. "The one who would assume that everything will go just right? The one who protests the cynicism of her mother and wants to anticipate only that good things will happen?"

Maybe he wasn't playing fair by dredging up things she'd said in past conversations at Harry's over cocktails, or during caffeine-fueled morning meetings at Tramonta. But she would eventually see what he—and obviously, Sacci, too—saw and felt so clearly. She just had to say yes.

Claudia's eyes searched the walls, following the ebb and flow of waves, Neptune's gaze, the arc of porpoises, the innocent grins of sea turtles. Then a look washed over her face and Louis sensed that she'd finally decided.

She continued gazing at the walls as her face broke into a smile. Nodding slowly, but gradually with more enthusiasm, she threw her arms in the air.

"Yes, yes. Of course, you're right," she shrieked, laughing. "You're both right. I'll do it!"

Louis pulled her to him and hugged her tightly. He felt like they were on the cusp of some wonderful adventure, as if he was turning to the first page of a wonderful new book.

"Bravo!" Sacci yelled, wrapping his arms around the two of them. "Perfetto!"

Louis glanced at him, enjoying the feel of his arm around his shoulder, and the faint smell of his cologne. Claudia looked at Louis, relief and excitement reflected in her eyes.

Now they can start, he thought to himself. Yes, now life could begin.

Chapter Eleven

The ringing of the phone filled the apartment with its old-fashioned sound of tinny, little bells. Louis sat with a coffee in hand, gazing out the window, while Claudia pored over the hotel project book, searching for overlooked details. He saw Claudia look up at him. She probably thought he didn't hear the ring, but at that point, he was merely tuning it out, pretending that there hadn't been nearly ten calls that day.

"That's your mother again," she said, drolly. "Why don't you pick up the phone?"

Louis scratched his head, a nervous tick.

"I just don't have the time to talk to her right now, to explain everything."

"When did you talk to her last?" she asked awkwardly, feeling uncomfortable trying to get him to talk to his mother when she no longer spoke to hers. But Louis' mother hadn't cut him off, she had sought him out. Claudia felt sorry for his mother, unable to figure out what she'd done to make Louis want to keep her so distant.

Realizing that Claudia sympathized with his mother, he reasoned that she simply didn't understand. She didn't know his mother. Claudia would just have to accept his being distant with his mother.

"I called her a few months ago. Not too long ago." He returned his gaze to the large window overlooking the canal.

"How did she find out where you were?"

"I don't know, but I'm guessing it was Tad—the guy from my neighborhood that I ran into at Harry's." That day was a low point for him—maybe the lowest since he'd been in Venice. Since running into Tad and his friend, he'd had his first thoughts of leaving Venice. His parents—anyone from his old life—could find him if they liked, a thought that made him uneasy.Claudia laughed. "Tad was with that awful woman who stopped by the table when we were at the restaurant with my mother? The day I was disowned?"

It was good that at last she could laugh about it, good that things were going so well that she didn't even seem to fret she no longer had a large deposit of money automatically placed in her bank account every month.

"Yes. Those were the two. They were asking questions about my love life."

Claudia's smile faded, her face contorted. "You know, that isn't the worst thing, really."

"What?" he asked, shifting his gaze from the window and sky outside to her.

"For someone to ask about your love life," she explained, shrugging. "It's just not the oddest thing, you know."

"I don't understand," he said. "That woman was a total stranger. And I don't like Tad."

"But he was a neighbor," she countered. "Someone you knew from all the way back to your childhood."

"Are you taking their side?" he asked, his voice sounding strained. Louis could feel his face getting warm.

"I'm not taking their side. It's just that maybe that's not so strange for someone you've known all your life to ask about your love life. That's all."

She was betraying him. That's how it felt, anyway. What was she trying to say—that he needed to talk to anyone who approached and asked him any old question about whatever it was they wanted to know?

"You're angry," she said, her eyes flashing.

That was the problem with Italians: arguing with them—having it out or whatever it was called—wasn't considered unpleasant or to be avoided. They considered it as much a part of life as eating. You couldn't just stew, or agree to disagree; you had to have it out.

"You seem to be on their side," he accused, his fingers trembling. "They're awful people but you take their side. *I'm* bad because I don't talk to them about my love life."

Claudia shook her head slowly, pushing a glass of prosecco away from her. "*You* don't talk to me about your love life either. I don't think you talk to anyone about it, do you?"

This was one of the reasons he didn't like to stay anywhere too long. At some point, acquaintances turned into friends and started asking too many questions, expecting too much. Was Claudia suddenly changing, wanting more from him than he felt comfortable providing?

"But that doesn't mean anything. I don't talk about it with you for different reasons. I mean, I'm just a private person. That's all."

How unfair, he thought. His mother was hounding him, and he had done everything he could to help Claudia get the palazzo converted into a hotel. Now, she was suddenly outlining his shortcomings. Taking the bottle of prosecco with a shaking hand, he grabbed an empty glass from a shelf and quickly filled it, the tiny bubbles shooting out of the glass.

"I should be easier on you because I don't think you even realize—"

"Realize what?" he felt annoyed, cornered.

"I don't know why you're so angry at me," she said soberly, trying to catch his eye. "I'm trying to talk to you about something that I've wondered about since we first became good friends—something that I think you aren't even aware of, but you make it almost impossible. The look you just gave me scared me, as if you might shut me out of your life, never speak to me again."

Her lip trembled as she pushed her hair back from her face. She looked down at the table briefly and then back up at him.

"I'm sorry," he said. "You're right. I don't know why I'm so angry. I guess I feel betrayed."

Why did he feel so trapped? Why was it such a big deal to talk about anything personal with him? "I'm not betraying you, okay?" she assured, clucking her tongue. "I didn't bring this up because I don't like you, or don't care about you, or give a—how do you say it, a flying fuck?—about that Tad or his dumb girlfriend. If what you want from a friend is someone who nods her head yes, and keeps out of your life, then that's something entirely different from what I thought of our friendship."

Hanging her head slightly above the glass of prosecco, she thought she might cry. "Just when I think things are looking up." She sighed.

How did the conversation get to be about him? He was so much more comfortable when they were discussing her problems.

"Things *are* looking up," he said, realizing that he had sounded like an ass. "You love your work on this hotel, and you're doing it—the hotel is going to open."

"It just seems like there's always something to bring me down. Nothing can go completely right." She sighed again.

"Sorry," he offered, feeling genuinely bad. Maybe it wouldn't be the toughest thing in the world to talk to her a little bit. Maybe even tell her about his stupid crush on Sacci.

"To tell you the truth, I don't know exactly why I don't want to see my mother," he said, tracing his finger along the counter. "I mean, don't get me wrong, I love my mother and I'm actually excited about talking to her. But I'm also nervous because I know she'll want to *talk* to me. Try to get at something she thinks is going on with me, or subtly analyze what I've done."

Claudia gave a wan smile. "Sounds easier than my situation. And not so unnatural for a mother to want to know what's going on with one of her children, eh?"

"She's not that bad, I guess," he admitted, drumming his fingers on the counter. "At times, though, she makes me uncomfortable because I feel like she's herding me like a sheep, pushing me toward something. Isn't that odd? I mean, here I am thousands of miles away and I have no daily contact with her. She doesn't want me here, in such a foreign, faraway place and yet I think she's pushing me toward something, directing me somehow."

"In that respect, she sounds like my mother," Claudia nodded. "Only the contessa isn't so subtle."

Claudia closed the hotel project book and leaned back in the stool.

"Now that she knows where you are, do you think she'd ever come here?—I know my mother would—well, she did!" She laughed at her own joke.

"Never," he said, shaking his head soberly. "My mom isn't like that. She's not so adventurous and wouldn't ever go somewhere uninvited, not without a very good plan."

He remembered their family summer vacations, the AAA books full of maps, and their route across at least half of the fifty states highlighted in bright yellow. They could never get lost, not with maps like those and every inch of the trip planned.

Claudia nodded her head. "Louis, do me a favor, will you?"

"Sure," he agreed, assuming she was switching the topic of conversation to the hotel.

"I know this sounds strange coming from me, but when your mother calls next, would you promise to pick up the phone, to talk to her? *Please*?"

He sighed, looking out the window. "Can I say maybe, can I promise that I'll seriously consider answering her call?"

"*Dai*, Louis," she scolded. "It's your mother. And it isn't as if she's cut you off, you know."

Louis continued gazing out the window, watching thin wisps of clouds scuttle across the pale blue sky.

"You know, when I first met you, I thought you were a lot of fun, but not too serious or thoughtful—"

"Oh, thanks," Claudia groaned. But she knew that that was the exact image she was trying to project—because she'd felt so lost and wounded after leaving New York. And who couldn't play the role of the fun, careless, mid-twenties trust fund baby? She hadn't had to dig too deep to play that role.

"Sorry," he said.

Claudia waved her hand before picking up her glass. "Don't worry about it—you were right to think it."

She looked at Louis with a vague smile, silently observing him. He gazed back, but after what seemed like a very long time, he averted his eyes. He had never been very good at maintaining eye contact.

They sat in silence for a few more minutes with only the distant sound of a boat's wake sloshing the side of the canal and swifts calling as they circled above the building. Venice was nearly silent, a city full of milling tourists, a few glassblowers, old, thick-legged women, and wide-shouldered, stoop-backed retired fishermen. Even the gulls wheedling high overhead seemed to move in slow motion, as if they, too, had been infected by the city. Louis sipped the prosecco, wondering if he'd been mistaken to think things were coming together, that things with Claudia would work out, and that he would at last feel content to stay in one spot. Listening to the fading slosh of the boat's wake, its whining engine weakening to a faint buzz, he sat up, and looked around the room before he fixed his eyes on his friend. She scowled.

"What can it hurt, right?"

Before he had time to think, he had promised to pick up the phone when his mother called again.

"Exactly," she said. "It wouldn't hurt to find out what she wants, eh?"

"No," he answered, feeling as if he wasn't quite telling the truth. "I suppose it wouldn't hurt."

Chapter Twelve

Louis opened his eyes to pinpricks of sunlight that had made it through the cracks of the accordion window shutters. He should have closed the shutters tight the night before, but he'd had one bourbon too many and felt fortunate to have made it home and into his bed at all. How long had his head been pounding?

He rolled over, adjusting his head on another pillow away from the mini-shafts of light. He heard something unfamiliar, like the wind or a draft, but it felt very close. He opened his eyes again, looking around his darkened room.

There it was again. A sort of panting noise.

What the hell was it?

Peering over the edge of the bed, his gaze met that of a pug's: Torta.

"What are you doing here?" Had he agreed to watch them again? Had he somehow forgotten? His mind raced back to the day before, seeking some memory of Sacci having dropped off the dogs. And the other dogs, where were they?

"Tonto?" he called, but no dog raced from the other room and no yip sounded from under the bed.

"Just you?"

Torta wagged her stubby tail and jumped halfway up the bed.

Louis reached down, pulling her compact, fawn-colored body onto the bed. The dog burrowed under the covers, leaned against his thigh, and began to snore loudly.

"That's what I should be doing, too," he thought, but the pain in his head was too intense.

Then he recalled that he'd promised Claudia at dinner last night that he would help at the hotel today—the dreaded hotel! How many times had he wished he'd never encouraged her, practically pushing her to work with Sacci converting that palazzo into a hotel? Had he known how much work it would be for him, he might have recommended that she do something else.

He would rest for a minute longer, he reasoned, to see if his head felt better. Then he remembered that the new "on-time" Claudia would be calling him, wondering why he wasn't there when he said he would be.

But where was Sacci and how had the dog gotten in?

The phone started ringing, clanging really. Was it Sacci, calling to explain that he'd left his dog there?

He decided to let the answering machine pick up. He was too tired to talk to anyone. Even to Sacci. Just a little more sleep and he'd be fine—if he could just get rid of his headache.

The phone rang again, followed by the efficient-sounding click of the answering machine.

He heard the tape running, knowing the caller was listening to the same message recorded in Italian. There was a beep, and then a breath, a hesitant voice.

"Louis? … Louis? … Um, this is … your mother again. Hi."

He bolted upright, recalling the promise he'd made to Claudia. He sat frozen, shocked, and sluggish, unable to run for the phone. Couldn't he call her back?

"I know you're probably wondering how I got your number, how I know where you are," she continued, as if reading his mind thousands of miles from where she sat in her small study on the second floor of an old row house in Chicago.

Well, he could probably guess the latter: Tad the moron, busybody neighbor had run into her on the street, or maybe he'd rung the bell outside the thick-wood door of her brick building as soon as he'd returned from the cruise. But he'd been wondering how she tracked down his phone number. He was nervous, drawing his legs up to his chest, leaning back against the headboard. The call sounded strangely clear, not like the previous ones.

"Tad told me," the voice went on to explain. "And then I called the Red Cross. Would you believe? They can track people down for you—if they're missing. I told them you were missing. I know it was kind of a lie, but then not really, right? I mean … I don't—didn't know where you were. Sorry I'm calling—that I've been calling so many times—but I need to talk to you."

Why was she telling him these things, as if to explain her numerous calls? True, he'd been wondering, but it was as if she knew exactly what he was thinking and even knew that he sat there listening. Her voice sounded pleading, apologetic. And strangely old. But his mother couldn't have aged so much in two years.

He'd call her back after he was up and had had a few coffees, he really would. And that wouldn't be breaking his promise to Claudia. After all, he really would have picked up the phone if he'd felt better. How could he even have a conversation with his mother when he felt so awful?

When his mother had first called, he felt found out, but also strangely childish. He felt betrayed and exposed. This time, though, her voice sounded different, but he couldn't put his finger on it.

"I'm, um … I'm at a hotel," she went on, her voice speeding up, maybe realizing that she couldn't speak forever on the tape. "Maybe you know it. It's a small, cute hotel. Lots of history, charm, you know … a place you would like."

Where the hell was she? And why was she calling him from a trip?

"It's a palace, ah … a former palace … the hotel I'm staying in.

And it's … well … um … you've probably already guessed … but it's in Venice. I mean, I'm in Venice."

The answering machine beeped, cutting her off, and leaving the apartment silent again except for the muffled sound of the dog's snore from beneath the covers.

She was here. In Venice. *What the hell was his mother doing in Venice?*

His head pounded harder. He could feel each pulse of blood course through the veins of his head, making it hurt even more. He sat completely still, as if he'd been dreaming, frozen into a pose of shock and denial. The dog whimpered under the covers, pawing his leg.

"Yeah, yeah, yeah, I'm still alive," he muttered, sliding under the covers and patting the dog as it re-settled against his legs.

Maybe Louis had just dreamed the past few minutes. He opened his eyes, studying the crudely carved ceiling beams. How had he never noticed them before, never wondered how long they'd supported the floor above, how many of them propped up the building preventing it from collapsing into a pile of rubble.

Then the phone rang again, making him jump.

So it hadn't been a dream and she was calling back. When the answering machine picked up again, he was still lying still in his bed. What the hell was she doing in Venice?

"It's me again. I talked too long. I'll try to keep it brief this time. I'm at the Palazzo Serenità. Are you there? Louis?"

He bolted upright, the dog jumped, too, and quickly made its way out from under the covers. His mother must have known he was here. Perhaps she could sense he was listening to her. How shameful. What kind of person lies in bed listening to his mother talk on his answering machine after he's hardly spoken to her for a year, and doesn't even leap up to take the call?

"… Okay … well … will you call me then? Call me at the Palazzo Serenità. Please?"

There was a click, then the thick silence of his apartment.

What an ass. He should have picked up. He had nothing against his mother, didn't hate her, *loved* her in fact. So why was he agonizing, why didn't he want to talk to her? He couldn't seriously think of not calling her back. No, she'd sniffed him out and traveled thousands of miles to see him, and he couldn't picture his mother traveling thousands of miles on her own, yet she hadn't even mentioned his dad. Where was he?

Torta stared at him, eyes bulging. Why did the dog look so damn sympathetic?

"Do you want to go outside?" Louis asked, still confused as to how she'd arrived in his bedroom.

The dog wagged her stubby tail and spun a few times, her small pink tongue hanging out of her mouth. He had no idea how long she'd been in the room.

Slowly, deliberately, he shoved aside the covers and carefully placed his feet on the floor. He stepped across the cold floor to the answering machine and pushed the play button. He listened to a few old messages and then heard his mother.

"*Call me. Please?*" her voice sounded plaintive.

She actually feared that he was shitty enough not to return her call. That she would travel across the world and sniff out her son's number, only to have him refuse to see her. She didn't think he was *that* hateful, did she? How had it come to this?

He'd been meaning to return her calls before, but that was different. Not to return a call home was one thing; not to return a call when a parent surprised you by traveling halfway around the world was something entirely different.

She was *here.*

No, he really would return her call, even if he didn't want to talk about things, didn't want to hear that he needed to move home, that he was wasting his life. He was too adult for such a conversation, but he knew how his mother could be. But then when he thought about it, the last few times he'd talked to her, she purposely seemed to avoid dispensing any advice. She would merely ask how he was doing, if he was happy, or if he was seeing anyone. She'd even learned not to ask where he was. After hearing "All over Europe" a half dozen times, she'd caught on. But what could she want now; jumping on his trail so soon after Tad had been there as if she'd been fearful that the scent would grow cold?

Maybe she merely longed to *see* him. Put her arms around him, size him up, and make a pronouncement as to whether he was doing okay.

If he didn't call, she would be crushed, and she would suffer a hurt that would be unforgivable. And he didn't want to hurt her.

He found the number for the palazzo in the phone book and dialed the number slowly, deliberately. Why was he so nervous, filled with dread? It was his mother. Did he despise her? No. What was it then? Maybe that she found him, followed him there? Was that the unforgivable sin: following him?

The world seemed very small. In the end, maybe he'd been foolhardy to think that a person could actually hide anywhere.

The hotel front desk patched him through to his mother's room. As soon as the phone in her room rang, she would know, of course, that he'd been there for her call, listening to her message.

"Hello, Louis?" a hopeful voice said.

"Hi, Mom." The words sounded so casual, as if he'd just talked to her last week.

"Thanks for calling me back," she said, sounding relieved.

"Well, of course, I would call you back. Did you think I wouldn't?"

"Sort of. I mean … not really," she stammered. "I just had this fear that maybe you wouldn't, since you didn't return my other calls. I know, those were from home, so I guess it's different. And I'm not meaning to lecture. I'd sneaked to get your number when I knew you wanted to be the one to call us, so I was asking for it, I guess."

"I was meaning to call soon, really I was. In fact, I just promised a friend the other day that I would," he said, aware that he was bending the truth a bit. He could never tell his mom that he'd merely promised to consider answering her call, and hadn't even—couldn't even—promise that he actually would.

There was a pause.

But his mother picked up where she'd left off, as if she were reciting rehearsed lines.

"I think I had an irrational fear that you might not see me. It was a long trip to come here, and I wasn't sure I should, and then I thought sometimes that after all this trouble and expense of getting here, that maybe in the end you wouldn't even see me." She laughed nervously.

"I wouldn't do that. Of course not." What an ass! He'd only moved to Europe, and he was busy creating a life for himself in another world. He hadn't intended to hurt her in the process.

"No, I should have known better. It was a silly thought." Her voice hesitated a moment, then proceeded tentatively. "So, how are you? What have you been doing?"

"Just enjoying life here. Doing my copy writing, my translating. Meeting people. Experiencing this incredible city."

"Oh, it's really beautiful," she gushed. "I should have come here with your father years ago."

"Is Dad okay? Why didn't he come with you?"

"Oh, he's fine. Just didn't want to come with me. He thought one of us was enough. Two might be too many."

"He let you come by yourself? That surprises me." He couldn't imagine his dad allowing her to travel so far alone.

"Well, he didn't have a choice. He didn't want to go, didn't think I should be going. He thinks it's a mistake. That I should leave you alone."

He heard that nervous laugh again.

"So he just let you come by yourself?" Louis asked, his headache seeming to lessen the longer he stood talking on the phone.

"No, he changed his mind, but by that time I'd already gotten used to the thought of coming here alone. And he thought it might be too overwhelming if both of us just popped up here—bad enough for just one, right?"

"It's not bad," he said, aware that he might not sound sincere.

There was a long pause, his mother seeming to want to say something.

"Yes? What is it?" he asked, figuring the least he could do was to help her out after he'd been such an ass.

"No, nothing big. I was just wondering if we could get together instead of talking on the phone."

"Well, of course," he said, feeling half excited, half filled with dread at the prospect. "Why don't I meet you at your hotel? You'll never find my apartment—it's difficult to find anything here."

They arranged to meet in an hour, which would provide Louis with just enough time to shower and drink an espresso that he hoped would conquer the remaining dull ache in his temples. In the shower, he couldn't stop wondering what their conversation would be like. Would they talk about Tad? What Tad had seen and might have assumed? Or would she want to know what was going on in his life? Was his mother sick? Would she try to persuade him to move back to Chicago? What had she come here for? Part of him found it completely natural, and the other part was completely suspicious.

When he stepped out of the shower, he heard a knock at the door. Torta started spinning, yipping at the door, and he could hear a voice outside.

Damn, he'd forgotten to take the dog for a walk.

"Torta, are you in there?" the voice called.

There was another knock, this time louder.

Louis called down the hall from the bathroom doorway, his voice shaky. "Just a minute—who is it?"

"Sacci."

He'd already guessed who it was. Of course, the guy was arriving just when he had to meet his mother—Sacci always seemed to stop by when Louis had somewhere to go. They would never go out for that coffee—or for a drink—the way things were going. The timing always seemed bad, and Louis was beginning to think it was meant to be this way, that maybe if they went out he would just start to imagine something happening that might never materialize. Was reality conspiring against the world of hopes inside his head?

Remember, he's *straight*. Louis wanted him to be gay, hoped he was, and even had silly, little daydreams and fantasies about him. Sacci would take him to hidden trattorias in neighborhoods and on islands he hadn't known existed, and then when he imagined kissing him, feeling the man's always razor-stubbled face against his, he felt lightheaded.

Louis threw on a robe and hurried down the hall. When he opened the door, Sacci jumped back in surprise.

"Oh, you're here," he smiled, stepping through the open door.

"Sorry, I left my dog here," he exclaimed, glancing at Louis' robe and gesticulating as if he were nervous. "I needed to check the pipes under your kitchen sink this morning because there was water leaking into the apartment below, into the Signorile's place. We weren't sure where the leak was coming from, so I came into your place—I'm sorry, but I had to. I knocked on your door, but you couldn't be awakened. I thought you must have been out already, and didn't even realize you were here until I'd already looked under the sink. Then I heard you … um … and then said hello and tried to wake you, but you looked to be sleeping so peacefully I just crept out."

Blushing, Louis asked, "So how did Torta get in here?"

"I didn't even realize she'd followed me up the stairs, and she must have gone under your bed. She likes you."

So he'd looked in on him while he was sleeping, passed out from too much bourbon and probably snoring with his mouth agape. Louis could feel his face turn hot with embarrassment, but part of him felt glad that Sacci had seen him sleeping, had maybe stolen an extra glance at his face. He leaned down to pet the dog so Sacci couldn't see him blush.

"That's okay," Louis said, looking at Sacci's feet while the dog spun around beneath his outstretched hand. "So that's how Torta got in. I was wondering."

He patted the dog's head and stood up slowly as he felt the color leave his face.

"I must've left the door open, or she raced in when I opened it," he said, shaking his head in apology.

"No worries," Louis said quickly. "I like the dogs."

"I go to my mother's soon," Sacci said. "Maybe you can watch them again?"

"Sure," he agreed. "But I may have to take them to the hotel with me. Claudia wants me over there working whenever I don't have an assignment."

Sacci grinned, rocking on his heels. Suddenly, he leaned forward, his fingers running back across his thighs.

"Can you go for a cappuccino?" he asked in a loud voice, leaning over and scooping up the dog. "Claudia told me you were headed to the palazzo this morning to work and I'm going to go help, too, so I thought we could go together, get a coffee first."

Didn't it figure?

The man seemed lonely, his eyes darting around the room, seemingly taking in every detail. And his mother's call had made him forget about meeting Claudia, painting, and plastering, cleaning and polishing for her at the palazzo! Well, that would have to wait. He could work for her after he met his mother first. Wait until he told her his mother was *here* and that he had a meeting with her!

"I wish I could," Louis said, shaking his head regretfully. "But I'm meeting my mother."

"Your mother's in town? And she's not staying here?" he said, frowning.

Was he frowning because he'd declined his invitation or because his mother wasn't staying at his flat? This was that peculiarly Italian thing. When family came to visit, it was an insult not to have them stay in your place—no matter how small or impractical.

"She prefers a hotel," Louis lied, knowing his mother would have preferred to stay with him. And what if Sacci discovered that his mother had tracked him down, hadn't even known that he was living in Venice? How could someone who visited his mother every week understand someone who just wanted some space, a little distance from everything familiar?

"You didn't mention she was coming into town. You never mentioned her, in fact. I don't know why, but I thought you didn't have a mother—I mean I thought that she'd died—of course you *had* a mother, you see." Sacci laughed at his joke.

"She's come into town at the last minute," Louis explained, wondering how much he should tell him. In Italy, you would never abandon your mother. That was like abandoning the Virgin Mary, committing the gravest sin possible. He would keep his story to himself—Sacci wouldn't understand, anyway.

"But I've really got to get going. I'll be late," he said regretfully, but without moving away from Sacci.

"And it's bad to keep your mother waiting. Disrespectful, eh? Sorry if I've made you late. The cappuccino another time then?" he asked, also remaining just inside the door.

"Sure," Louis answered, trying to sound casual. Should he try to set a date and time when they could get together? The words formed on his tongue, but his mouth froze. Stupid, stupid! Why would he ask him, pursue something as stupid as a relationship with a straight Italian man?

Sacci suddenly made an awkward, uneven step farther into the hallway, seeming hesitant to leave. Torta circled his legs, uncertain whether his master was going in or out. It seemed like he wanted to say something, so Louis looked at him expectantly. Sacci looked up, looked away, and finally shuffled slowly out the door.

"Thanks," Sacci said nervously, mumbling. "And sorry about the dog. You know how crazy they are."

Louis felt sorry for his landlord. His mother lived in another city, and besides, he thought that even if you were Italian and worshipped your mother, she couldn't be your whole life. It was strange, though, that the guy seemed to come from an old Venetian family—one who could own an old palazzo and shrug about it—and knew everyone in town. Yet, he didn't seem to have many friends, just acquaintances and old neighbors. He didn't get it—Sacci seemed normal, if a little low key and quiet, and was handsome in that classic Italian way that made you wish Italians still hung around naked in bath houses like the ancient Romans did. It was embarrassing to want to see the man naked, but he'd started thinking about it.

Well, the guy was straight, anyway, must be, and Louis would never act on it—he would simply admire Sacci's good looks and let his crush die.

Louis knew exactly where his mother's hotel was located, but wasn't sure of the best route there. He wandered the tiny, winding streets in the neighborhood of the hotel, and eventually circled in on it, turning a narrow corner, and finding it directly across a canal with a heavy, old mossy stone bridge leading straight to the hotel's heavy wooden door propped open to the street. He knew this building because it was one of the oldest in the city and one of the most unusual with its late Gothic gargoyles and faded stone carvings. He crossed the steeply arcing bridge and entered the small, dark hotel lobby. His eyes hadn't had time to adjust from the bright sun when he heard his mother's voice.

"There you are!" she exclaimed, sounding both excited and anxious.

His mother was sitting, her small frame nearly swallowed by the large wingback chair she occupied. She looked older, smaller. Hadn't he read or heard it somewhere that at a certain age, children inherited the vitality of their parents, and while they continued growing, their parents began waning, shrinking? It was as if the children literally sapped the life out of their parents, taking their vitality and energy as their own. She wore a gray wool turtleneck and jeans, which made her look younger than her sixty years. She popped up, hurrying over to hug her son.

Stepping back but keeping her arms around his waist, she studied his face. "You look older, more grown up," she said, smiling too broadly. "And you look happy."

"I'm okay," he said, nervous already about when the conversation would take a turn to the subject she'd come all this way to discuss.

She frowned a little, looking uncertain. "Should we go somewhere—for lunch or a coffee? Maybe a glass of wine? It's so good to see you."

She sounded like she wanted to say more, but smiled instead, squeezing his arm. She looked nervous, fidgeting with her fingers and shifting the weight of her small frame from foot to foot.

"Sure. How about the Veneto Wine Institute?" he suggested, remembering that he'd always thought his mother would like the place after Claudia first took him there. "They carry a lot of the wines of the Veneto—and mostly the best ones."

She'd always loved wine—long before anyone in the neighborhood had discovered it. In that way, she'd always been a mystery, knowing obscure wines and taking bits of money that she saved to the dusty, cramped wine store on Clark Street. She'd assembled a collection of about a hundred wines in a converted basement pantry that still had shelves from when it had been used to store preserves and bushels of apples. His dad had threatened to replace the seasoned wooden shelves, stained from a hundred years of leakage from bottles and cans and jars of preserves, but his mother had protested, preferring the old shelves and the worn feel of her improvised wine cellar.

She nodded, smiling again, this time not so nervously. "That sounds perfect. I'll follow you."

He suddenly felt old, his mother placing complete trust in him to get them somewhere. Had he ever been in such a position before?

Il Istituto was a former palazzo, rather small and insignificant and only a few minutes' walk from Piazza San Marco. The lower floor, covered with swirling mosaics and small stones, had a few heavy Turkish rugs that gave the place the feel of a serene, musty private club. Whatever his mother intended to talk about he would have to hear, but at least they could be somewhere with privacy.

The *maître d'* led them through a dim anteroom with ceilings that seemed twenty feet high. Oversize floor lamps with glass amber shades cast warm puddles of light onto a few groupings of armchairs and settees. The palazzo must have been formed by joining a few houses together because the floor plan was unusual, with irregularly spaced and odd-size small rooms spanning the building's front. The *maître d'* stopped at the doorway of the largest room—one Louis had never seen.

Since it was early afternoon, all the rooms they'd passed through were virtually empty. Louis noticed some wine buyers from Germany talking loudly on one side of the room, and a couple—probably honeymooners—sharing an overstuffed, brocade sofa and a bottle of wine.

The *maître d'* pointed them toward two wingback chairs angled toward each other, a small marble-topped table in between. While they looked over the wine menus, a waiter brought them a dish of hot nuts and wedges of pungent-smelling *taleggio* and *Parmigiano* . The *taleggio*'s strong scent nearly overpowered the swirling smells of wine and cigar smoke.

"What do you recommend?" his mother asked.

"I usually get what the waiter recommends," he admitted, not knowing that much about the wines of the Veneto, despite the time he'd spent in Venice and the number of times he'd visited *Il Istituto.* He always drank espresso, prosecco, bourbon, and wine, in that basic order in terms of quantity and frequency. And he knew next to nothing about wine, even if he often drank a glass with Claudia.

His mother eyed the menu, nodding her head a few times. "There are some I would recommend," she said timidly, not looking up from the menu.

Was she afraid he would be offended if she chose something? She was so funny about not appearing like one of those wine snobs. If anyone else at a table or party claimed to know something about wines, she always remained silent and deferred to that person. Most people didn't know she read about and tasted wines with the passion of a sommelier, or had her own small, but growing collection of wine.

"Go ahead and order what you like," he said. "I'm sure it'll be good."

She ordered a Teroldego. "One of the original Veneto wines that you can't get in the states," she explained. That was about as much as you ever got out of her about the reason for an order. But she rarely ordered wrong.

After the bottle arrived and was ceremoniously uncorked and poured, Louis began to believe that maybe the afternoon would be more about catching up and visiting rather than whatever it was his mother had come to discuss. Would she keep the real purpose of her visit as quiet as she did her knowledge of wine?

But a moment after they toasted and clinked glasses, she cleared her throat, a serious expression clouding her face. She took another sip of wine, a large one, looking distractedly over Louis' shoulder, as if she were concentrating on something beyond him. But it was clear the distraction came from somewhere else. Setting her glass down, she turned her gaze to Louis.

"Well, I suppose I should ..." she trailed off, seeming to lack the courage to speak.

Immediately, Louis understood that he hadn't been mistaken—she planned to confront him right away. This was okay by him. He preferred not to spend hours and maybe even days skirting the issue and building up to it. Better to get it over and done with.

He returned his mother's gaze, smiling and trying to look encouraging. He could at least do that for her.

She continued studying him, swallowing hard. Nodding, she cleared her throat, setting down her glass of wine.

And then she seemed to lose courage again.

She talked about the neighbors, about what his sisters were doing, and what changes there'd been to the neighborhood. She railed about the closing of corner groceries and some of the old small shops on Clark Street and Halsted. Owners had died or retired and large chain grocery stores were opening in the city. The line of row houses on Alta Vista were the same as ever—since they were a historic landmark, there was little chance that anything would ever change on the block. He nodded, asking a question occasionally, but otherwise listening to her talk, with only a slight warble a few times, or the tremble of her hand, to indicate that there was something else.

They were each on their second glass of wine when she abruptly sat up, squaring her small shoulders. Her face was still pretty, especially when she smiled nervously. He had an idea of how she must have looked as a timid young student dating his father.

She took a deep breath, blurting it out. "Why are you … well, why are you … *running*?" her voice tremulous, rising as if it hadn't occurred to exactly what she thought he'd been doing up to that point. "What did I do?"

She appeared relieved to have said it, to stop talking about things that while pleasing, were merely necessary to get to the reason she had come. And he could see that she was determined—despite her timidity—to have a certain discussion.

Running? Of course that's what she would think, probably what everyone figured.

"You didn't do anything. I just wanted to be somewhere else. I'm not running," he answered reflexively.

His mother leaned forward, moving her thin face toward his. She didn't look threatening, but more as if she might cry.

"Is that so? Then why don't you even want us to know where you are? Why do I need to find out from a jackass neighbor down the street whom I like even less than you like? How hurtful is that?" Her lips trembled as if she might cry. But at the same time, she looked angry. She picked up her wine, studying it thoughtfully before taking another big swallow. She didn't seem to taste the dark liquid, but instead, drank the wine greedily with barely a breath between gulps.

How did things he hadn't even thought about come back to haunt him? As his mother explained it, she made perfect sense. Of course, it must have been insulting to hear from Ted of his whereabouts, but he just hadn't thought it all the way through to the potential finish. That had been his problem.

"I didn't mean it," he protested, his voice plaintive. "Didn't mean it to happen or seem that way."

It really didn't mean anything personal that he hadn't told her—hadn't told anyone—exactly where he'd been these past two years. Why was she taking it so personally? He'd just needed some space.

"I don't know why I wanted to keep my whereabouts a secret," he mumbled.

"Maybe you could try to figure it out. Because your father and I aren't getting any younger you know, and maybe there's not that much time left," she said without a trace of sarcasm in her voice.

"What's that supposed to mean?" he asked, suddenly worried. Was one of them ill?

"Nothing. I mean, just what I'm saying. I'm not threatening, not trying to scare you. As far as I know, there's nothing wrong with either of us. But we're in our sixties now." She shrugged, her shoulders suddenly looking slightly drooped. Sighing, she ran a finger across the plain white tablecloth as if she were tracing a line.

"It's something I've been meaning to get to, that I will get to," he said uncertainly, avoiding her gaze. She looked tired, a little old. "I just have to be here now. I know I should call more, visit more, too. I will, really."

"When are you expecting to do this? To start establishing a relationship with your dad and me?" She stared at him, her expression half anger and half hurt, her lower lip trembling.

How could he answer that? He hadn't thought to create a timetable. His answer would only make him look more careless, thoughtless. He just figured that one day it would happen, naturally, like puberty or adulthood had. You didn't plan for it to happen, mark your calendar or set a date, it just happened. You woke up one day and there it was—you were in a different phase of life. At this moment, he was here, in Venice, but at some indistinct, unknown date, he would be somewhere else possibly, and part of his plans included seeing more of his parents.

"So why did you leave? Do you know why?" she asked, trying to sound patient. She asked her questions in a measured, soothing voice, as if she'd practiced asking them many times.

"I just left. I wanted to go somewhere else. Leave Chicago. It was too stifling."

He sipped from his wine with a shaking hand, rubbing a nub on the tablecloth with his other hand.

"The third largest city in America is too stifling? Do you really think that's what it was?"

He could see his mother's hands trembling slightly. She was clearly uncomfortable and so was he.

"I needed to get to another place to be happy, I think," he said uncertainly. He meant to take a sip of wine, but opened his mouth too wide and gulped instead.

His mother gazed absently at her glass of wine and then lifted her eyes. "Does it ever work to go somewhere else?" she mused. "I mean, people move all the time, from Chicago to New York, from Des Moines to Chicago, from everywhere to bespoiled California. But does life really change when you get to that next place? I don't know, I just don't see it happen for most people."

"Are you saying I shouldn't be here, that I shouldn't have come?" he asked, his voice beginning to sound shrill.

"Not that. This is a beautiful city, and what a great opportunity. I'm just wondering what drove you away, that's all. And what you're looking for here," she explained, brushing her fingers along an unseen line on the table. "Don't you see these people? Haven't you encountered the types who get to the next place and what bothered them about their life or the previous place simply follows them to the next?"

He nodded, wondering what it had to do with him. He hadn't ended up in Venice because it was a trendy place or because others raved about the opportunities there. No, he'd gone for different, inexplicable reasons.

His mother continued; a determined look on her face.

"Are people any happier in San Francisco, Paris, or Boston?" she asked, hesitating a moment before giving a desultory shake of her head. "I don't think so. There's no heaven on earth—not even in Hawaii. People hate life everywhere; they struggle and cry, curse and go on. No, I don't think place is the big constant, the guarantor of happiness. As there are unhappy people in every place, on every corner of the globe, so there are happy, content people."

"Then what is it?" he asked.

"I wonder if it's something completely different," she said.

"But what?" he asked, trying not to sound annoyed, wondering what she was getting at.

"I'm not certain; maybe it's a combination of things. I just don't think it matters where you are."

She looked at him uncertainly, as if things were not going as she'd planned, as if they weren't where she thought they'd be at that point in the conversation. She looked thoughtfully at Louis' hands lying idly on the table, her face brightening as if she'd tapped into a further reserve of determination.

"Your father and I gave you space, we never dropped by your apartment. We wanted you to figure out who you were, to grow up without us breathing down your neck," she said, her hand shaking a little as she reached for her wine.

Was this the conversation every gay man had with his mother sooner or later? Why hadn't he read about this, been told about this anywhere along the way?

He found himself swirling the wine in his glass, watching it aerate and create legs along the generous, perfect curve of the glass.

"I guess … I guess …" he stammered, realizing he was searching, digging for what it might really have been that had driven him from home, pushed him to hide thousands of miles from his family before stumbling on something, a tidy answer. "I figured you were ashamed of me somehow."

There, he said it without ever realizing he'd thought it. Once he'd verbalized it, his thoughts embraced the idea and he recognized its truthfulness. Why was he just realizing something so fundamental?

"*Ashamed*? I don't understand," she exclaimed, her eyes turning glassy, pinkish, and sad.

He hadn't wanted to hurt her, but why was she pressing him so? Couldn't they simply agree to patch things up? And he would be better about calling and visiting.

"Oh, maybe I don't know what I'm talking about," he whispered. "How about if I promise to be better, to visit and call more, would that be okay? Would that make things better?"

If they could just finish the painful conversation, an awkward dance to which he didn't know the moves, and talk about something else. He wished he hadn't told her what had popped into his head. He felt a knot in his chest, bound with threads of thought he'd never unraveled.

She shook her head slowly. "You started to tell me the truth. Don't back away from it now. You've got to be honest … tell me."

Did she really travel all this way for that, to hear painful words, accusations maybe, from her son? They'd never talked about such things—couldn't they simply carry on as they had before? What was the point in talking about such stuff? He glanced out the window, seeing a cluster of tourists with linked arms, insouciantly strolling down the street, pointing at the buildings, and looking untroubled, enchanted even. He wished he could trade places with them. His existence had always been so tortured, never the carefree sort of life that the average person lived. He could never see himself walking down the street with arms interlocked with a friend, mother, or boyfriend, though he'd always longed for it, longed to be *normal*.

He could feel her eyes on him, searching for clues, waiting for him to speak.

"You've got to talk about it, Louis, figure it out," she urged, nearly in a whisper. "That's the only way out."

"Out of where?" He sensed what she was talking about, but everything seemed so inchoate, malformed. How did he get so confused?

"I think you're stuck, aren't you? You can't go forward, and you don't want to go back." She reached across the table, one of her thin hands seizing a packet of sugar, which she began playing with.

"I feel like I'm making progress, doing what I want to do," he timidly offered.

She was right, though. He felt stuck, and in some ways, stuck in adolescence.

She watched him with imploring eyes, sitting patiently waiting for him to talk more. The only betrayal of her inner anxiety was the way she methodically fingered the sugar packet. Back and forth, she moved it between her thumb and forefinger. Back and forth, like the motion of a caged animal at a zoo.

He thought back to when the rift first formed. He'd figured out he was gay, but did he move away from his family or vice versa? Even before he'd come out, before they'd made it official, there was a heavy knowing that cloaked the house. And that was the beginning for him of the longing to run. Now it seemed too unclear. Who had rejected whom?

"If we made you feel ashamed, I'm sorry. We didn't mean to. And we're not … not ashamed." She nodded her head for emphasis. "We just didn't understand at the time, it just took us some time to come around. But we were never ashamed."

How do you define shame, anyway? Maybe she was right somehow, but maybe he was, too? He thought back to the conversations about how he should have a girlfriend and how someday he would marry, and he could feel the weight again of the pressure to do and be something he was not. That was what had pushed him away. Wherever he'd gone since leaving his parents, he could be himself without expectations.

"It just seemed like you were ashamed. You had plans for me," he said quietly.

"Every parent does. And I don't care if they say they don't—they do," she argued, her cheek quivering.

His mother's eyes flashed—she actually seemed angry. Defensive?

"But when you told us—well, even before that when we suspected—we began readjusting. I'm not saying we did that perfectly, but we always loved you," she said, emphasizing the last few words, pressing her hand firmly against the table. "And we were never ashamed. We just wanted to understand, and maybe just needed a little time. But before we knew it, you were gone. And there wasn't any more time to explain, to come to understand. And so here I am."

She shrugged and then smiling wanly, dropped the packet of sugar and reached out for his hand. He offered it, and she grabbed and squeezed it, then let it go, which was okay by him. He had spotted the waiter approaching the table.

"*Tutto a posto*?" the waiter asked. "Something else?"

They both nodded silently, hearing his question but lost in distant thoughts.

"Niente," Louis finally answered, relieving the troubled waiter.

"Should we get the check?" he asked, the simple question startling him.

She nodded, looking tired, uncertain.

And then things started to make some sort of sense to him. Was this what they called an epiphany, brought on by his mother's visit?

There was a surge of emotion, so much so that he thought he might cry. His youth was gone, but those uncertain days, full of energy and discovery felt as near as yesterday. When he'd first accepted that he was gay, and then started hanging out with a group of friends who were gay, he was amazed at how liberating it felt. Here was a group of people who understood his jokes, understood how painful it could be to be gay in America. Maybe anywhere, he was learning.

At any rate, he grew so comfortable with his friends, not having to think about how he might be perceived, make someone uncomfortable, or just feel so unlike anyone else, it was a new sensation. Though he must not have sensed it at the time, he no longer needed to expend energy on fitting in or worrying what anyone else was thinking. With that group of friends, he was accepted and understood. Sure, it sounded juvenile, like a run-of-the-mill, misunderstood coming-of-age teen story, but that was exactly how it had happened.

And shortly after, the moving started. Maybe he'd been wrong, but the way his family had treated his gayness was different from how his friends had treated him. If he went out and came home late, the questions in the morning—if they came at all—seemed vague, less strict than the queries directed at his sisters.

"We never said we didn't accept you, didn't accept who you were," she said, leaning forward again, as if reading his mind.

She would give it one more try.

He must have looked like he needed persuading, but he knew she was right, though it was all still confusing to him. Somehow, he thought that they would embrace him more fully, though he couldn't say exactly what they should have done, how they should have showed their love.

"I know," he admitted. "You never said you didn't accept gays or didn't want me to be that way, but you and Dad just didn't act like I thought you would. To me, you were being nice, acting like loving parents, like you thought you should, but maybe your heart wasn't really in it? Maybe you were playing a role."

His mother's eyes turned moist again. *God was he an asshole.*

"I don't know what I'm saying," he offered, wishing they were instead marveling about how the floor of ancient St. Mark's had come to be so jumbled and uneven, or how one building after another seemed to rise grandly from the serpentine canals. Just when the stalemate had started to get resolved, when he felt like they had put it behind them, he realized they weren't quite finished. "It's all confusing to me. And I don't want to hurt you. Can't we just leave this be? I don't know if I want to go back and talk it all out."

She shook her head slowly, defiantly. "No, it's best to talk about it, I think. And you seem just about there. Think about it just a little more," she prodded, looking once again like the mother of his childhood and youth, the woman who patiently taught him how to read and introduced him to the hidden corners of the Field Museum and the musty, light-infused galleries of the Art Institute. She had been the great revealer, but how did she intend to make sense of the clutter in his head? What was it she sensed, the knot in his chest that he'd only moments earlier become fully aware of?

"Okay, then," he begrudgingly agreed. He felt a little annoyed that even after all this time apart and his independence that she thought she could teach him something. Maybe she was right. He didn't know what he thought—the reason he was living in Venice. The city was far from everyone and everything he'd known the first few decades of his life. And if he couldn't explain the reason for it, maybe he couldn't explain anything at all.

"I just expected more, I guess. Thought you would act different," he repeated, as if returning to an earlier thought could help him retrace his steps.

Timidly, she asked, "How did you think we would act? I mean, how did you want us to act, or what didn't we do that you'd wished we had?"

He thought back, remembering one gay friend who had been thrown out of his house by church-going parents, and another whose parents didn't kick him out, but cried and hounded him incessantly. What had his parents done? Hugged him, asked if he was certain, and how long he'd known. And then said they were there for him. What was it that was missing, that he couldn't get his head around?

"I don't know. There was just something missing," he insisted, his voice shaking. "I told you and Dad and it was so uneventful, like it was no big deal—"

"In a way, it was no big deal," she interrupted. "We'd already figured it out. We'd just been waiting for you to tell us."

She looked awkward telling him, as if she shouldn't have figured it out on her own, before he told her.

"Couldn't you have reacted some way? I mean, not like some other friends' parents did—by kicking them out, or rejecting them. But, it was as if you really didn't care, I guess. Care about me—maybe because I was that way?"

He could see the three of them again, grouped around the long, cold fireplace on a late summer night, bathed in soft, humid heat that left little room in the air for words. His parents sat while he stood before them, confessing, as if they were holding court or he was testifying. He recognized feelings of terror and *shame*, still as fresh to him as that day. He'd wanted to hide, not stand there in front of them exposed, them thinking the whole time of him having sex with men. They *know* I have sex with *men*, as if when you got down to its essence that was what being gay meant. After firmly gripping and hiding his secret for so long, he'd felt nude without it.

She shook her head quickly this time. "No, no, no. That wasn't it at all."

She reached her seeking, opened-wide hands across the table for his again, grabbing and squeezing them firmly, as if imparting something. "We did accept it. Is that what we wanted for you? No. But we accepted it. It was good that we had two years to come to terms with it before we ever had that discussion—do you remember it?"

He nodded. It was as if she were reading his mind the whole time, watching him jump from stone to stone, crossing the stream behind his uncle's farmhouse.

"I recall exactly what you looked like. How you were," she said softly, running her fingers up the stem of her empty wine glass, shaking her head again as if trying to undo something.

"I remember," he said. "But how was I? What was it you saw?"

She hesitated, her eyes measuring his face, fixing on his eyes.

"I saw shame," she said slowly. "Shame. And I didn't know what to do, how to erase it."

"I was ashamed. That's exactly what I was saying," he said, frustrated at her lack of understanding. He felt on the cusp of getting it finally. They *had been* ashamed, but why didn't she understand?

"But don't you see, we weren't ashamed of you," she explained, shaking her head slowly, meaningfully, directing her misty, pink gaze toward his eyes. She clasped and unclasped her hands, as if juicing an orange. "Your father and I weren't ashamed of you. And we tried to make you see that. We treated you like your sisters, or paid even more attention to you at times so that you wouldn't feel that way. But it didn't work. And I still don't know what we could have done to convince you."

Her shaking hands smoothed the tablecloth, touching the base of the empty wine glass before returning to her lap.

So his parents really weren't ashamed of him? Then what had pushed him away, leading to the feeling of wanting escape, to be with people who were like him or understood him? He was certain that what he'd felt in front of his parents that night was shame. And he'd felt it after that, too. *They are ashamed of me*, he remembered thinking when he'd gotten back into his room, hiding under sheets and a blanket in his bed, shaking.

"You just admitted that you saw me as shamed, that you saw it in me," he said petulantly, beginning to sob.

He was crying, fighting back stinging tears that gathered in the corners of his eyes. His lungs conspired against him, tightening and constricting his breath. He felt awful, wrecked and inadequate, full of shame again. What didn't he understand? Why wouldn't it come together, allowing him to understand the mystery that seemed to define him?

"Don't you see it, Louis?" she said in the same tone that she'd taught him to read, shown him how to look at paintings. Her voice was as hushed and soft as the delicate Venetian spring air, the thick carpet muffling the sounds around them, enveloping him.

His eyesight, blurred by tears, he jerked his head back and forth, unable to understand, unwilling to talk. He felt stupid, frustrated, broken.

"It wasn't your father and I who were ashamed," she continued, seeming to carefully choose and measure each word. "We accepted you. We always loved you."

She looked at him with sorrow-laden eyes, the same way he'd looked at her earlier when he thought he was hurting her. But maybe it wasn't quite the same after all.

"Do you understand?" she said softly. "Do you see it yet?"

Then he understood, like a ton of bricks smashing his insides, turning his body inside out, he suddenly understood. He let out a stifled cry, pushing his face down to the table, feeling the cool, heavily starched cloth against his burning cheek. As warm tears rolled down his nose, dripping soft as rain onto the pressed white tablecloth, he understood for the first time his shame. And the knot in his chest began to unravel.

Chapter Thirteen

From the moment Breva could walk, she pointed out the window, spying on the sun, a bird, or a tree. If Piero didn't have the itinerant nature of his trade, his daughter did. If they were indoors and it wasn't dark out, she wanted to be outside. And when Constanza took her for walks in the perambulator, she rocked back and forth, urging her mother to push her faster, farther, or longer. Just a little more than three years old, Breva walked everywhere. She explored every inch of the flat, measuring out the floorboards with her tiny feet, and running her small, perfectly shaped hands and fingers along the polished and gleaming baseboards and chair rails.

Breva exhausted Constanza, but she delighted in her only child. Never had she believed that she would so easily trade the bakery for staying at home with her daughter, but from the start, she preferred to remain at home with her. Piero had enough orders and made enough money to keep them comfortable, though just barely.

As much as she had longed for another child and as hard as she prayed, another baby never came. She had become pregnant a second time, but lost the baby after only a few months when she had a stomachache marked by stabbing pains so severe she could hardly breathe. After she'd lost the baby, the doctor told her she would have no more children.

That was the first indication that according to her mother, Constanza had done something sinful, something to displease God. But what?

"Well, I already have a child," she told her mother, trying to sound pleased with her fate. In some way, though, Breva, who filled her with delight, *would be* enough—all that she would need.

Her mother had cried for her unborn grandchildren, clutching the sheets on Constanza's sickbed and refusing to comfort her daughter. She had come immediately upon receiving the call from Piero, arriving only a few hours after the doctor left.

"He was never right for you," she'd said shakily, after she'd finished sobbing. "He's to blame."

"I lost the baby, not him," she countered.

Why did her mother still despise Piero? And why did she blame him for anything bad that befell them?

"One is enough for us, Mamma. She is beautiful, a *vera regala,* no?" she'd said, hoping her mother would agree.

"*Certo,*" her mother sniffed. "But I was right all along. You should have listened to me."

Constanza longed to cry for the children she wouldn't have, the boy she had dreamed of having and watching over. She'd even promised Breva a baby brother one day. Now she would have to tell her there would be no brother, that she had been wrong.

But she couldn't feel the pain, didn't want to feel that she was somehow being punished, or that her mother might somehow be right that she should never come to Venice, and that Piero was not right for her.

As soon as her mother had arrived, Piero left for the workshop.

"I have to get some work done, some orders that are late," he had explained. But Constanza noticed that he wouldn't look her in the eye, not wanting to take in her ashen and weak figure lying in their bed.

Her mother shook her head, silent, but with eyes full of condemnation. They had both watched Piero shuffle awkwardly toward the door, his shoes scarcely making a soft scraping noise on the floor.

"Where's Breva?" Constanza asked him.

He turned. "Next door. I'll collect her when I return," he answered, closing the door softly, a slow click announcing his departure.

She had never seen her husband look as unsteady as when she first fell to the floor in pain. Constanza had always been strong, never experiencing so much as a cold since they'd been married. Now she could hardly walk. She couldn't blame him for not wanting to see her like this. The few glimpses she'd caught of herself in the bureau mirror frightened her. She had the color of a corpse, the look of dead, pasty white squid piled in the market.

Better that he was at work. As long as she had her mother, her husband could only get in the way and remind her of how sick she looked and felt. Piero's eyes always told the truth. She had seen that they were marked with pity and fear.

Out her window, the wisteria vines lay bare, clinging to the side of the building. It was difficult to believe that come spring the branches would be thick with leaves and flowers, and that she would need to duck down to get a clear view out the window.

With Carnivale only days away, there should have been parties and balls, but the city lay silent, as if under siege. Handfuls of soldiers wandered the streets, but what could ever happen in Venice? With no roads and only narrow canals, there was little to take and less to patrol. She'd heard there were many troops stationed at the port and some on nearby islands.

"There are a lot at home," her mother soberly announced.

"Why in Murano?"

"For the glassmakers. They need the glass for planes and other things, so Mussolini has practically taken them over."

"But what can they do with brightly colored Murano glass?" she laughed, suddenly feeling out of breath.

Her mother shook her head. "They're no longer making bowls and chandeliers," she explained.

Was that what Piero was doing in the studio? Certainly, they would have him make war items, too. If they hadn't already. Why hadn't he said anything?

Her mother sat staring out the window with her back to Constanza.

Constanza could just see buildings across the small piazza in front of their flat, but not anything that was happening in the streets below.

"That's one good thing," her mother remarked absently.

"What's that?"

"The Jews are leaving—you should see."

Her mother moved her face closer to the window, blocking the light and any view Constanza might have had.

"They're my neighbors and they don't bother me. I'll miss them," she announced defiantly.

She found it hard to believe that people suddenly thought their Jewish neighbors were a danger during wartime. And she knew her mother was one of these people; of course, her mother had never liked the Jews, had despised anyone who wasn't Christian.

"It's not good to talk like that," her mother said, pushing the curtain back for a better view. "You should just accept that people don't like them here and that they need to leave."

Constanza frowned, shifting her gaze from the window to the blanket on her bed. She wouldn't get to say good-bye, explain that she didn't want them to leave. But they would be back when the war was over—which would be soon enough—and then she could explain. She picked absently at the pills on the wool blanket.

"It'll be quiet without them around," Constanza said.

Her mother sighed. "It's quiet already."

After she recovered, life grew more normal, but it never returned to the life she had before her illness. Piero hardly spoke to her in the evenings. He worked long days, arriving home well after dark. The war needed glassworkers, well behind the lines thankfully, to make all sorts of glass components for planes, bombs, and vehicles. At least he wasn't fighting.

He was sullen and ate his dinner in silence. She started rising early again, making a little bread for the bakery and cornetti and a few small loaves for their own use. If she made too much bread and it went stale, she used it for a *pappa e pomodoro* or other soups. Piero gulped down the ever-weaker milk coffee she made for him, usually while standing above her where she sat at the table. Breva would sleep another hour, so Constanza would scrub the floors, clean, or start a stew for that night's dinner.

There was less flour, fewer eggs, and milk was increasingly expensive, but they managed to eat well enough. There were still plenty of fishermen, and plenty of fish, so they ate more seafood, but she rarely saw meat at the butcher's anymore. If she did, it cost at least a day's pay and it wasn't fresh. If the army wasn't demanding their food, then it was needed in Rome or Milan. But who could complain? She had heard it was worse in all the other cities. Venice seemed nearly forgotten, a fairy tale city barely touched by the war. Sure, sometimes there were squadrons of planes flying overhead, or the hum of giant transport planes, but most of the time the city was even quieter than usual, wrapped in a cloak of isolation. Tourists, who usually gave the city so much life, especially around Piazza San Marco, hadn't been coming for a few years. Off-duty soldiers from other parts of Italy climbed the tower, wandering through the *duomo*, or sipping coffee or wine in the remaining small cafés lining the square, but there were few of them. And most people took their coffee and wine at home these days. After all, who could afford to go out much anymore?

The mornings spent at the bakery, drinking coffee and casually nibbling warm, crusty bread with Piero, seemed like another lifetime ago. Had he really lingered so long in the bakery with her before they were married, before Breva had come? She couldn't even recall when those mornings had ceased to be, when they'd stopped sharing gossip from Murano or about the neighbors as their quarter became home.

Now with the Jews having left the neighborhood, and some of her few friends having left for the countryside, she knew a loneliness she'd never encountered before; the quarter sometimes felt deserted. If the piercing feeling of solitude persisted, despite baking, cleaning, or cooking, she would wake Breva early, and take her on walks through the neighborhood, and sometimes all the way to Piazza San Marco or to the Lido, with its shuttered hotels and empty beaches. Where would she be without Breva? She wondered where those strong feelings she'd had a few years ago had gone, when rising early and baking for hours had been enough, when she hadn't silently begged for scraps of conversation or company from her husband like a forsaken pet.

Breva never tired of being out. It seemed that she wanted to walk every corner of the subdued city. And the canals fascinated her; Constanza had to watch her closely or she would step right into one. Raising a child was difficult enough in Murano or Venice, what with all the canals and the myriad stories passed down through generations of toddlers and children who had fallen into a canal and drowned. Constanza never let her daughter out of her sight when they were outside and started each day with a long and heartfelt prayer that the girl be protected.

One day they rose early, and at Breva's urging, started on a short walk after Constanza had put the day's bread in the oven.

"Just a short one and only in front of the building because the bread's baking, and I don't want to be gone too long or go too far," she warned. When was it time, she suddenly wondered, to warn children about fire?

They'd walked outside to find the end of the street flooded from high tide the night before, so they could walk no farther than the end of the street, anyway.

"Mamma, *nonna* told me that Venice is sinking into the sea," the child said, her lower lip protruding. "Is that true?"

Why would a grandmother tell a child such things? Still, if Constanza lied to her daughter, she would learn soon enough.

"Sì, Breva," she admitted, trying to sound casual. "Venice is sinking."

"But shouldn't we leave then?" she asked, gripping her mother's hand.

"No. It won't happen right away," she explained, squeezing her daughter's hand. "We have time. But it just reminds you that when you're living your life, you have to enjoy it as much as possible because it could change. Venice—the city we live in—could be gone any day. Understand, *cara*?"

"No, Mamma."

Curse her mother for filling her daughter's head with such ideas. Maybe she could simply make light of it.

"If Venice sinks, then we simply swim," she laughed with false confidence, letting go of Breva's hand and racing toward the edge of the canal. "It's nothing to worry about, *capisci*?"

Breva nodded vaguely, seeming to lose interest after hearing the water make a slurping sound as it retreated from the sidewalk.

"The water smacks its lips just like I do, Mamma!" Breva shrieked, chasing the retreating water.

"Sì, sì, Breva," Constanza chuckled, grabbing Breva's shoulders before she reached the water's edge. "Let's go back to the house—Mamma needs to get the bread out of the oven."

"*Pane, pane*, the staff of life! Right, Mamma?" the girl warbled in a singsong voice, repeating an old nursery rhyme.

"That's right," Constanza smiled, smoothing the curls that had started springing from the sides of her daughter's head.

She enfolded Breva between her arms and hugged her quickly, which reminded her of when her own mother had hugged her with her baking apron when she'd been young. When Breva had a child of her own, would she remember the yeasty scent of her mother's apron, recalling fondly the smells of the bakery and these slow-moving days spent with her mother? Years from then, would those memories and a love of bread and baking serve as small, sweet-tasting tokens of those hours?

One day Piero came home late in the evening, long after Constanza had put Breva to bed. Constanza lay in bed with the blinds tightly closed, burning a bedside oil lamp that didn't rely on the tepid flow of electricity that seemed to falter in the evenings anyway. The government hardly needed to worry about Venetians disobeying the air raid, lights-off policy given the near lack of electricity most nights.

Let the Americans come if they would, she decided. She was tired of the war and had never liked Mussolini, so let the Allies come and rescue them from their cold, and dull gray existence. After all, what had they gotten for the war? Nothing. Life was harder, with Piero working more but bringing home less money. The markets were no longer full of food, except for the ancient fish market that still had piles of crustaceans and silver-scaled fish that shone even in the gloom of the old hall, which also had had its lights cut. At least the fish and creatures of the sea didn't rely on man to survive, and enough old fishermen who couldn't be called up to the front lines had remained on the islands to oversee the boats and deliver fish so the ever-smaller population of the city had food to eat.

Restless, Constanza turned onto her side just before hearing the click of the door lock. The door creaked softly, opening slowly and tentatively. He should have been embarrassed coming home so late, she thought, but then, maybe she was to blame, after all. What good was a woman who couldn't have children and whom had given her husband only a daughter?

Lately it had begun to seem as if they were being punished, but for what? She vowed to pray more often, something she'd been neglecting to do. With the war, the loss of the baby, the departure of the Jews, and the seeming bleakness of life, she felt hopeless.

Signore, let things be better, she pleaded. *Give me back my husband and let things go back to the way they were.*

If only there was no war, if she could bake again in the shop, which a cousin from the mainland was now running. Piero could come again to the bakery in the golden mornings while she kneaded dough that was cool to the touch and gently fold the crusts for crostata.

She expected to hear Piero's tired footfall in the hallway, heading for their bedroom, but the flat was enveloped in silence. What was he doing?

Pushing away the sheet, she planted her feet on the cool floorboards and made her way to the door. When she opened the door, she could see a soft yellow light cast from an oil lamp in the kitchen. Walking softly along the hall, she gasped when she reached the kitchen door.

Piero sat with his cheek pushed against the table, a bandaged, blood-soaked arm spread in front of him. An open bottle of grappa stood close to his head, an empty glass beside it.

"What happened?" she whispered hoarsely, trying to keep her voice low. She grasped his shoulders, kneading them lightly.

His eyes blinked open, looking upward toward her face. His eyes moved slowly, focused uncertainly. He was drunk.

"I hurt myself," he said in a labored voice.

"I see," she said, beginning to cry. Hot tears rolled down her cheeks, burning. What had he done to himself?

Signore, she prayed. *Why*?

"It was stupid," he said, lifting his head slightly from the table. "I'm just not used to the glassmaking machines. I'm a glassblower, not a glassmaker."

She had prayed for him—for *them*—too late. Maybe that was the lesson she should have thought to pray days, weeks, and months ago, not hours.

"They make you work too long," he muttered. "You're too tired to make work, that's why it happened."

To hell with Mussolini and Hitler both, she thought. She was bone-weary of the war, tired of the sacrifices they were making. And all of this for what? Oh, let the Americans come quickly and save them!

Not wanting to point, she gestured vaguely toward the lifeless arm splayed across the table. A soft, pink blush of blood seeped through the gauze bandages wrapped around his arm from his elbow to his fingertips.

"Is it your arm? Your hand?" she sniffed, dejectedly tugging a lock of hair that had danced across her cheek.

"Burned it," he said bluntly, his sullen, watery-pink eyes remaining fixed on the tabletop. "Stupid for a glassblower to do. Who doesn't know that molten glass burns?"

"How did it happen?"

Did it really matter, she wondered.

"I was thinking about something else. I wasn't paying attention to what I was doing," he shrugged, avoiding her gaze as he stared absently at the bottle of grappa.

"Want some?" he asked, nodding at the grappa as he met her gaze for a moment.

She shrugged. Were they cursed? If they were, mustn't the whole world be cursed then? For the first time, she wondered if it had been a mistake to move to Venice, to marry Piero. The parade of dreary thoughts marching through her mind invited too much misery.

"I'll take a glass," she answered, moving toward the cabinet and removing a small tumbler.

If she wouldn't sleep tonight, she may as well drink.

After they both had two small glasses of the grappa, which burned her throat but filled her insides with warm liquid nonchalance, Piero slowly pulled his arm off the table.

"I can't feel it now, but wait'll tomorrow," he mumbled, shaking his head while staring dumbly at his arm.

"What about tomorrow?" she couldn't stop herself from asking, her voice sounding nervous and strained despite the grappa. "How will you work?"

How would they buy groceries? They had enough money for food for a few days only, then what would they do? Should they move in with her parents, return to Murano?

"I can't work," he croaked, his voice receding. He shrugged his shoulders. "Probably not for weeks, maybe months."

"But what do we do? What *should* we do?" she asked, sighing heavily.

"I'm sorry," he said softly, his voice nearly a whisper. "I didn't mean to."

Continuing to avoid her eyes, he cocked his head away from his right arm, which he'd gingerly laid over his right thigh like an afterthought.

"Of course you didn't," she said, saddened that he felt he needed to tell her that.

Why would he say something so ridiculous? Had she given him reason to believe that she thought he'd injured himself on purpose?

"That's stupid to say," she thought to add, shaking her head.

He glanced at her, then away, his eyes resting on the shaded window behind her.

"Still, I'm sorry."

"Okay," she said, motioning as if to brush the disturbing thoughts from the air. "But what should we do? To eat? To live?"

"I don't know," he said. "Move back to Murano? Live with your parents?"

She studied him, wondering if they should go to bed and finish the conversation in the morning. Was he too drunk to understand how serious it was that he couldn't work and that during wartime every man was expected to fight—or to work?

"I could work again, you know," she surprised herself by saying. "I could go back to the bakery, relieve my cousin. That would be something."

The idea gave her a shot of excitement, of possibility. Maybe things would return to the way they were when they first moved to Venice. She would bake, her mornings once again quiet and structured, with the routines of making bread and running the bakery filling her days. He could spend his mornings at the bakery, this time with their daughter in tow, too.

As if reading her mind, he asked, "Who will watch Breva?"

It seemed obvious, but she tried not to sound irritated.

"You," she offered timidly.

He paused, seeming to ponder her answer.

"I don't know what I would do with her for so many hours," he admitted. "What would I do?"

He seemed genuinely puzzled, as if he had never given a thought to what their days had been like the past four plus years while he had been working.

"It's not so difficult," she said, rolling the empty glass between her palms. "You read to her, play a little, but mostly, she likes to take walks, to wander."

"And cooking? Would I cook then?" he asked.

She shook her head, setting the glass on the table.

"Come to the bakery for breakfast when she wakes up, and then I'll be home in the afternoon to make dinner—as it used to be," she said, growing more excited as she began to put the pieces together.

Dull-eyed, he glanced up at her, frowning.

"I don't know if I could do it," he murmured.

Why was he so obstinate, selfish? She felt her cheeks grow hot.

"Don't you care for your daughter?" she asked, her voice trembling.

Piero gave her a hard look. "Of course I care for her, I love her. I just don't know what it means to watch a four-year-old. That's all."

"Do we have a choice?" she asked. "What else can we do?"

"I was just thinking aloud," he said, his voice slurring. "Just talking about it. I've never watched Breva for more than a few hours. I wouldn't expect you to take to glassblowing without thinking about it a little."

Maybe she should have gone easier on him while he was still drunk, giving him some time to think about the idea. And who knew what pain he was in from his arm. Still, they would have to figure out something—and quickly. They had no savings and barely enough money to last a few days. She felt desperate to settle on a solution right away, especially since she was suddenly eager to begin baking again.

"But glassblowing's much harder. Watching Breva is easy," she tried again, this time trying to sound encouraging, less petulant. "She's easy. I'll be nearby, at the bakery. You can always come by, I can help you."

She felt somewhat deceptive because Breva demanded attention, mostly to be taken out in the quarter or to wander the city. While her demands were simple—to be mobile—the result was that Constanza had never had much time to read, to clean, or to do anything else. Based on what he did on the few days he was off, she figured that Piero would want to read, maybe sip wine in the afternoons, but Breva would fight it every minute. And what would he do with so much time? Since the war started, he'd worked five and sometimes six days a week, staying at the factory until dinner and occasionally even later. During the past year, he'd only been seeing Breva on Sundays or sometimes on Saturdays if he finished work early. It would be a change, a significant change. But what else could he do—what else could *they* do?

"It's not for long," she said, her voice softening. "And maybe you could leave her with me some mornings at the bakery—if you just needed some time to do your things."

She wondered what would those things would be. He hardly had any free hours since they'd been married, and she couldn't guess how he would spend all the hours of a day. Most of his friends had been drafted or working the same long hours. Her days were full of cooking, cleaning, and watching Breva. He would only have Breva to watch.

"Let's see," he said, sitting straighter in his chair, adjusting the position of his arm. "I'm tired and the pain is beginning and it all seems so confusing to me. I don't know what we should do."

"I'm sorry," she said, wishing she'd dropped the subject and urged him to go to bed. "I haven't been very sympathetic. Can I get you something? Change the bandage?"

He frowned, his eyes seeming to focus on nothing in particular. "I just want to go to bed. *Va bene*?"

They could finish the conversation tomorrow, of course. She feared she'd pressed him too hard, made him feel even worse than when he'd arrived. Glancing at his arm, she worried how long it would be until he could use it again. Would that it didn't last long and that he recovered quickly, then this whole thing would be over before they knew it. By then, maybe the war would be over, too.

"Va bene," she answered, gently placing her hand on her husband's shoulder and standing up. She removed the bottle and glasses from the table and she set them on the counter for washing in the morning.

"I'll help you to bed," she told him consolingly, vowing to avoid the topic until the morning.

As they walked down the dark hall, her arm guiding Piero's unsteady frame as the floorboards announced their passage, she made a fervent prayer.

Let this phase of our life end quickly, Signore, she begged. And let me return to the bakery so I can take care of my family.

After she carefully tucked Piero between the sheets and blankets, she blew out the oil lamp, and climbed into bed finding it had grown strangely cold and unwelcoming in the damp night air.

The first week of their new life went well. Piero seeming to enjoy the time with his daughter and resuming their simple, quiet mornings at the bakery. Constanza no longer fretted about the war, the empty streets, or the lack of tourists. She baked different kinds of breads now, especially since refined flour wasn't typically available. She made heavier, peasant-style breads, and dark-crusted, round wheat loaves. If there were refined flour, she would make a crude crostata or two, thinking wistfully of the days when she would have made five or six without giving it a thought.

She'd missed baking, and wondered at her seeming turn in luck, the answer to her prayer. Of course, Piero was still hurt and that was no sign of good fortune, but they were luckier than most since she was a skilled baker and was able to return to her shop. Not many would have anything to fall back on, though it was true that they were earning much less on the dribs and drabs of lira she received for her baking, instead of the regular, decent wages that Piero had collected from his glassmaking.

They wouldn't have much money to treat Breva to a gelato, but Constanza already found that they could get as much or more food by trading bread for tomatoes, fish, and potatoes—and these only in the first week.

Within a week or so, they'd already fallen into a comfortable routine, with Piero bringing Breva to the store just before 8:00 AM, much later than he'd come in when she'd last worked at the bakery. When she arrived each morning at the dark and cold bakery at 4:00 AM, she would make a quick espresso just after lighting the oil lamp and the oven, saving the grounds to make cappuccino or coffee mixed with thick, canned milk after Piero arrived a few hours later. She would begin her day activating the yeast just after starting the ovens. By the time the wood burned down to gleaming coals and the oven bricks had heated up, the first breads were ready to go in, followed by a lone batch of cornetti. Without much refined flour, she didn't make too many of the rolls anymore, one of the many concessions they had made to Mussolini and to the war.

Her customers complained about the coarse breads, the lack of cornetti and pastries, and mostly the scarcity of milk for their cappuccino and milk-coffees. But what was she to do? Not one woman she knew had been for the war or even for Mussolini. Now it was the men—the ones who had seemed in favor of the war and *Il Duce*'s biggest supporters—who complained the loudest about the sacrifices they had to make.

But things were going well for neither the Italians nor the Germans, so who knew what would happen next. She only prayed that things didn't get worse. Venice was a still a relatively good place to be, after all. For the glassworks were in Murano, and there was little in the sinking old city to interest the Allies. Even the soldiers and sailors on leave and the Nazi officers who had once seemed to prefer the city no longer visited.

While the quiet could sometimes be unnerving, at least the nights didn't hold more than an occasional air raid siren or the flicker of bombs lighting the inky-black sky over the distant mainland.

As long as she was baking, she didn't seem to mind the war as much—much less than when she tried to entertain Breva all day. For some reason, the city seemed a prison when she explored its piazze, bridges, canals and vie with her tireless daughter. At least here, she had something to make with her hands and a schedule to keep. And she was feeding her family, getting them through the day.

She could never tell Piero, but his accident had somehow brought her exactly what she had wanted. When her mother had called later that day, asking if she was needed to watch Breva, Constanza had nearly told her that the first few weeks had been wonderful. Her mornings were exactly as if she had dreamed them into existence: the quiet early hours of baking alone, followed by a few hours with her family, and then a few hours playing with Breva while Piero napped or sat at one of the quarter's bars.

Somehow, her prayers had been answered, though in a much different way than she'd imagined.

When she'd been tempted to tell her mother, though, she stopped herself just in time, remembering what her mother would say. But couldn't she allow herself a little happiness that despite Piero's accident, the war, and her barrenness, life might be budding again, showing promise of renewing itself? Constanza simply couldn't adopt her mother's bleak outlook on life; couldn't a person sometimes get just what they wanted?

After the third week of their new life, Piero's arm began to heal quickly and Constanza detected signs of a growing restlessness in her husband. Instead of smiling and sitting relaxed at the table in the bakery, Breva sitting beside him or exploring the kitchen, he drummed his fingers on the counter, finished his coffee quickly, and devoured the small loaf of steaming bread his wife had put before him.

One Tuesday, he asked if he could leave Breva at the bakery for a few hours, casually shrugging his shoulders. He would return to pick her up in just a few hours, providing Constanza a few hours to finish her baking.

What could Constanza have said? Breva had her doll and a picture book, and seemed not at all her usual restless self. She could certainly watch the child and still bake, though she hoped Piero didn't make a habit of leaving her at the bakery in the mornings. Maybe, she wondered, Breva would be interested in watching her at work, seeing her knead and handle the different dough, and transforming the sticky, viscous blobs of simple ingredients into solid loaves of bread. If her daughter did get anxious, she could have her make coarse sugar cookies topped with dried cherries and blood oranges, bags of which she'd bartered for at the market.

"Va bene," she told him, trying to hide her disappointment under a wan smile.

Already he seemed bored during their mornings together, having little to say and playing with the crumbs on his plate. Did he ever miss those carefree mornings they spent together before they'd been married, before Breva had come along? Maybe he was simply tired of her. But the first week he *had* seemed content to be with her again, to spend time with her and Breva, and sipping coffee and talking about everything they would do when the war ended.

Constanza blamed the war and Mussolini for his restlessness, worrying, too, that her mother had been right, that a long latent restlessness and desire to wander were asserting themselves. In the end, was he to be just the kind of glassblower portrayed since Roman times and through the Middle Ages?

He couldn't be, though. To her, he appeared more rigid and tied to a routine than was she. Then it must be the ridiculous war, the constant working, scraping, and joyless somnolence of the city that was wearing him down. And he hadn't been able to create works of art, bowls, platters, chandeliers, and glasses, for years. When he returned to work, he would once again be subjected to the mindless, boring, and uninspired craft of making common glass items.

Eyeing her daughter, she wondered again if the girl might have gotten her restlessness from her father. Was it just rubbish, the previous generation's out-dated tales that her mother had refused to give up?

Breva sat upright in a pool of sunshine, talking with her doll while rocking back and forth slightly. Unaware that her mother was watching, she observed her doll contentedly, pointing at the vines growing outside the casement windows and the way the bright sun illuminated the dust swirling through the air. She looked like she could be left alone for at least a few hours. Constanza turned from her and formed the dough into loaves so they could rise one final time before she placed them in the oven. She gingerly edged the previous batch of loaves into the oven with a large, thin wooden board, smiling at how smoothly the day was going.

Maybe the arrangement would work out just fine, she decided. If the rest of the time they spent alone went so well—and she had a feeling it would—then maybe she could continue working after Piero returned to the factory. She would never have to leave Breva with a neighbor or her mother, working every day and seeing her only when she arrived home in the late afternoons. But if they could spend most of the day together in the bakery, then Constanza could bake again regularly. She hadn't realized just how much she missed kneading the cool, sticky dough, creating loaves of bread and simple pastries from flour, water, and butter, and selling and bartering them around the quarter and even to some of the trattorias. Starting the ovens while nighttime shrouded the neighborhood and most Venetians slept made her feel like she was doing something important. Bread was the staff of life, the old saying went, and making it filled her with satisfaction.

She smiled, remembering Breva singing the nursery rhyme.

All she needed was Breva, Piero, and baking, it seemed. The rest of the world could go away, cease to exist. She could survive with just these three things, she determined. Well, and God, too. But he wasn't of this earth, anyway. When had she become so focused, so simple in her needs? She was like one of the provincial women who moved into the city from a Veneto hill town, unaccustomed to buying anything in the stores and baking, cooking, or making things herself, or doing without. While Constanza didn't live quite so simply, her suddenly simple life appeared very ascetic.

By the time she peered over the counter again, the sun's rays no longer struck Breva, and the child lay on the floor napping, her doll tucked beside her.

Certainly, it was meant to be, she thought.

The bells on the door sounded, and Piero was already walking into the store, smiling broadly.

"How was she?" he asked, but he'd already observed his daughter lying asleep on the floor.

Breva stirred at the tinkle of bells, her father's voice.

"Papà," she murmured, smiling with eyes only half-open.

Constanza wondered where he had been, but she wouldn't ask. She had always trusted him—she mustn't start questioning and suspecting. She'd been independent, too, and knew she had to allow him time to do what he wanted without her knowing where he was every minute. Still, she was curious. Had he gone to play cards or gone to a bar? Had he strolled through the city or spent time reading the giornali?

She scrutinized his face, but for what? Signs of physical exertion, or a flush from drinking? He'd never been the type to drink heavily. Might he have visited one of the prostitutes on the dingy, narrow viale dello Zucchero? She searched for some clue as to where he had been, but she might as well have consulted the newspaper. He seemed content, nothing more.

He walked over to Breva, awkwardly pulling her languid form against his hip, his arm hanging awkwardly in its sling. Guiding her to the counter, he carefully sat down, folding her into his lap.

"Is it too late for an espresso?" he asked.

"I'll pull you one," she said, putting aside a half-tray of cornetti.

She observed him out of the corner of her eye drinking the espresso, allowing Breva to pull the finger of his opposite hand, which stuck out of the sling. He drank the shot greedily, set the small cup down on the counter, and pushed it toward Constanza.

"Va bene," he announced, standing. "I'll take Breva now and you can finish up."

"It's okay if you'd like to stay while I finish up," she said.

"*Beh*, we'll get out of your way," he said. "Otherwise, it'll just take you longer."

Her mind was playing tricks on her—rather, her mother's way of thinking suddenly flickered. For a moment, she felt on the threshold of some massive disruption, as if standing on a precipice of an unpleasant change.

"Why don't you stay? You won't be in the way at all," she said, trying to sound calm despite the sudden, flickering fear in her heart. "I'll pull you another espresso."

Had she turned sentimental overnight, so reliant upon the company of her daughter and husband that she didn't want them to leave for even a few hours? She scarcely knew herself, so quickly did her moods change.

She wiped some crumbs into her damp palm, mindful of her husband observing her. No doubt, he sensed something different about her—just as she was aware herself. If she looked up, he might detect in her what it was that she didn't even recognize but could sense. Deciding it was better to keep her eyes downcast, she continued wiping the counter as if it didn't matter, just as she might have done in the years before she stopped working at the bakery.

"I want to go, Papà!" Breva chirped, pushing her face into his shoulder. "I want to go for a walk, to the piazza to watch the people. I've been sitting in the bakery all day and I want to go out."

"Maybe I should take her," Piero said, continuing to watch his wife.

"It's probably better as now she'll be acting as antsy as a crab when the tide comes in," she said carefully, trying to sound indifferent.

Hoisting Breva onto his back with his one good arm, Piero nodded.

"Okay, we'll see you at home then," he called, backing toward the doorway.

"I want to go to the big piazza," Breva said.

"San Marco?" Piero asked.

"The one with the tower and the soldiers."

"San Marco," Piero affirmed.

"San Marco!" Breva echoed, giggling with excitement.

Breva, still clinging to his back, Piero pushed open the door with his shoulder. "Say good-bye to Mamma."

"Ciao, Mamma," she called over her shoulder, digging her heels into her father's sides as if she were prodding a languid horse.

The bells on the door tinkled—always with a different sound when someone was leaving the shop than when entering. Even from the back room, Constanza knew when anyone was coming or going.

She longed to follow them out the door and to San Marco, wandering according to the whims of Breva. That she had ever been annoyed or tired from their excursions now seemed impossible. If only she could wander with her at that moment!

Hurrying to finish, she wrapped the loaves she would deliver on her way home before they had quite cooled. And if Breva and Piero hadn't arrived home yet, she could meet them coming back from the piazza.

Why was she so desperate to see them, to be with them, especially after the renewed sense of joy she'd experienced at being at the bakery again? Maybe it was the war, perhaps Piero's accident? But she sensed something, felt it in the air. What was she afraid of?

"*Signore, be with us ...*," she prayed in a whisper, making the sign of the cross.

Would she turn out to be just like her mother, whom she mocked for her constant and ardent prayers? Maybe prayer making, fear and superstition lay embedded in her bones, put there by her mother, and her mother's mother. What chance had she against what was bred in the bone?

She couldn't help herself. And what would it hurt, anyway?

Why had the change come upon her so suddenly and recently? She'd always prided herself on her practical view of things and considered herself satisfied—happy even—baking and living her simple life in Venice. She remembered when she first arrived in the city and had actually thought about remaining single, working by herself and with another hire or two at the bakery she hoped someday to own. Those and occasional trips home to somnolent Murano seemed like more than enough in which to construct a satisfying life.

How much she had changed! While she still enjoyed baking and could not imagine going without it, it was Breva—and Piero—whom she considered the foundation and center of her life.

When had this change taken place, seeping into her and making her a different person than when she'd arrived in the city? Strangely, she didn't desire to be independent and alone as she'd been then. Worried and longing for her family as she was, she preferred her current life to that of her youth.

Her youth! When had that drained from her? Twenty-four and with a child and a marriage of nearly five years, she had lost her youth without knowing it.

Having filled the rolling cart with loaves of bread, that day less carefully wrapped in brown paper than usual, Constanza left the bakery a full half hour earlier than normal. The following day she would do a more thorough cleaning of the bakery, but that day she would try to join her family at San Marco. She could even light a candle at the church and buy Breva a gelato, spending a few of the handful of coins she'd received that day for bread.

Turning the key to lock the door, she realized she'd forgotten to turn the sign in the window to show that the bakery was closed. OPEN, the sign read. Shrugging, she removed the key and headed down the street without turning it. No one who came so late in the day should expect to find any bread, or to find bakeries open. Already, the hush of the afternoon lunch hour had descended, giving the already quiet city a near-desolate air. That was good—Breva and Piero would be easy to find. But she must hurry to deliver the breads or she would never catch up to them.

At dinner, Piero fidgeted, fingering his knife and fork and running his thumb along the edge of his plate. She could see he was restless, probably tired of not working. Maybe her mother had been right: perhaps glassblowers were different, needing always to dance between the worlds of reality and fantasy, and never staying put or settling down. Glass was the product of two worlds, belonging to neither, her mother used to say. And those who brought the substance into being fell subject to the same rules.

Her mother had been wrong about that part—Piero hadn't had any problems settling and staying in Venice. But lately she'd observed some behavior that reminded her of some of the things her mother had told her. When she arrived home in the afternoons, he wandered from one room to the next, opening a book, and then closing it a few minutes later. He would ask for an espresso, but then leave it to grow cold. He opened books, but never finished any, eventually replacing the books on the shelves, and returning the borrowed ones to neighbors and friends.

Still his arm hadn't healed completely. She'd grown accustomed to looking at the raw limb that reminded her of meat—a lamb's leg or a piece of beef, though she hadn't seen either for nearly a year. The scalded-looking part grew smaller, contracting at its edges where it left bubbled white skin—a scar nearly as unsightly as the burn itself. She studied his lesion every day, wondering if life might return to normal when his wound healed.

One day she awoke before her alarm sounded, wondering what had awakened her. Piero lay breathing beside her, softly and deeply, far from the bleak war and the idleness of his days. Then she heard a call, the unmistakable hoot of an owl. Unusual right in the middle of Venice. Was that the sound that had awakened her? Wondering what her mother would say of it, she crept out of bed slowly, cautious not to wake Piero. Clicking the alarm lever, she turned it off and dressed quietly in the dark. She found herself outside the door, the cool, damp air of the night hugging her. She studied nearby treetops and chimneys, hoping to catch sight of the mythical creature, but she saw no sign of it. Had she imagined its call?

Walking quickly down the dark streets, she let herself into the bakery after glancing up and down the via, still hoping to spot the owl. The fire in the oven had just begun hissing, spreading its warmth into the chilled air of the room when a knock sounded at the door making her jump. Walking rapidly toward the door, she caught a glimpse of men in uniform.

"Signora," a voice called while a dim figure in a red coat saluted her. "Sorry to disturb you. We're from the Hotel Aubergino on the Lido and we need your help. We're one of the only hotels open, mostly serving the army and our allies."

"Yes, I know," she responded, surprised at the way her voice shook.

She laughed at herself, realizing that no one in the army wore long red jackets with epaulettes. Sighing deeply, she swung open the door to find a red-suited young boy, tall enough that he'd looked like a man at first glance, and a suit-clad, older man. She wondered who would be staying on the Lido at that stage of the war with the Allies marching up the peninsula, merely days away, they'd heard. No doubt, it was government leaders or their families, the occasional general looking for an escape from the frontlines, maybe meeting his family, but more likely bringing a lover.

"You've been recommended to us, signora," the older man said formally, bowing slightly as he crossed the threshold in an old-fashioned manner. "And we've had a problem—our baker left town yesterday, they say she's run away to the mountains, and we have a full house, lots of officers from the army, a general even, and within a few hours they'll all want bread."

Constanza knew she was popular in the neighborhood, but was surprised to find that any hotel on the Lido had ever heard her name.

Realizing that she'd have to work quickly, she nodded her head, but not without frowning.

"Signore," she started. "I would like very much to bake for your hotel, it would be an honor, but I have to admit that I haven't any more refined flour. And at this late notice, I could only do crude breads and pastries."

"Whatever you could do would be adequate, more than what we would otherwise be able to obtain," the man said, bringing his hands together as if in prayer, as if beseeching her. "*Per favore, signora,* you would be a great help and we would ensure that you're properly rewarded."

"I'll do what I can," she smiled, wondering at her good fortune, forgetting the owl. "But just so you're aware that the breads will be coarse as I haven't any refined flour as I mentioned."

"I've got refined flour just outside with the bellman—a twenty-pound bag," the man said, waving at the red-suited figure hovering near the doorway. "I realized that most bakeries still operating haven't any refined flour, so we've brought our own for your use. And you can keep whatever remains."

Constanza and Piero had already gone through their meager savings and just the evening before she'd thought about taking a vaporetto to visit her parents to see if they had any money they could borrow. Now this, falling into her lap!

"Grazie, Signore," she whispered earnestly. "I'll be able to create wonderful things for you."

She could work late and Piero would simply have to watch Breva for a few hours longer. He was certain to understand.

"And tomorrow?" she asked the hotel manager.

"If we like what you make—you come highly recommended, you know—we'll place a regular order—*and* provide refined flour, of course. You'd become our regular baker." Then he grimaced, glancing skyward. "For as long as we're able to remain open."

She nodded enthusiastically, rubbing her arms. "If you can have someone come by at eight o'clock, I'll have your baguettes," she promised.

"I'll send the doorman," the man said, waving at his companion.

The manager touched his hat in and walked out of the shop. After he opened the door, he held it for the doorman outside.

"Bring it in," he called.

A young man—a boy really—with pinkish pimples resembling mosquito bites and a beak-like nose carried in the bag of flour and deposited it on the counter.

"There you are," the manager smiled.

The bellhop nodded his head and bowed slightly. Was this how they treated the guests at the hotel? They made her feel awkward, though she sensed that they felt just as uncomfortable. When they left, gently closing the door behind them causing the bells to gently ring, she felt relieved.

Now she could bake, she could really bake in a manner she'd been unable to enjoy for years.

Constanza lost track of time. She had prepared twenty-four baguettes and had dough rising for more bread and rolls. The hotel doorman had arrived early, pacing outside the bakery at 7:30 AM before picking up the baguettes, which scarcely had time to cool. She hoped she would have time to do a peach crostata—she had the refined flour, after all. And peaches were flowing into the city like the tide. She would accomplish much that day.

She had just taken a round peasant loaf out of the ashes and placed it on a cooling rack when a slight, sharp pain coursed through her midsection.

She was hungry, she realized. Hard to believe, but then what time was it? She noted the kitchen was brighter than usual, scarcely seeing how the light olive green walls had taken on a fuller color with the rising sun. Her head ached a little, like she had forgotten to drink coffee—and she remembered then that she'd completely forgotten to have any. Glancing at the clock, she realized that Piero was late and so she hadn't even had the second coffee that she normally shared with him.

But Piero and Breva weren't outside the bakery, nor down the via. They were very late and having baked so much, so quickly, she'd lost track of time.

Walking to the espresso machine, she stuck a fork into the coal-black grounds left from her coffee the day before and prepared to make another using the same grounds. If Piero weren't coming, she would need to have a quick shot or two by herself. If only she didn't have to stop. There was so much left to bake and so little time. The coffee would ease her headache, she reasoned, helping her work faster, so stopping for even a little bit would be an advantage in the end.

As the temperature gauge on the steamer rose and liquid coffee began falling into her cup in a silky black stream, she heard the tinkle of the bells on the door.

"Mamma!" Breva shouted happily. "We are late!"

Turning toward them, she saw her daughter, beaming while rushing around the counter to hug her. Behind her, Piero stood smiling, though he appeared uncomfortable, his arm out of the sling and hanging limply behind him.

Glancing at the clock on the wall, she saw it was nearly ten o'clock.

"What is it?" she asked. "Why are you so late?"

Neither one looked troubled, though Piero possessed the strange expression he'd been wearing the past few days.

"Papà wanted you to have more time to work because I'm to stay with you today," her daughter said, smiling bashfully.

Constanza stood up from hugging Breva and turned to face Piero. "What's this?"

Sheepish, he answered, "I need to stop at the factory. They need to ask me some questions and have the doctor there look at my arm. They think I should be ready to go back to work."

He avoided her eyes, glancing instead at the bread and cornetti on the counter. Was he ashamed of having to leave Breva with her, knowing it could make for a difficult workday for her—and on that day of all days? Or was there something else?

"Piero, this is a terrible day—the worst day to ask me to do this," she said, wiping her hands on her apron more from frustration than necessity.

"But I must go, I have to go," he said tersely. "You can bake with her here, you've already tried it just a few days ago, and it went well."

"Maybe today it won't go so well—who knows?" she muttered, shaking her head. "But it's impossible today because I can hardly even afford the few minutes we are taking discussing this."

As if to emphasize her point, she punched down a bowl of rising dough.

"I don't understand," he said. "That's why we came late to give you more time by yourself so that it wouldn't be a problem. And then I can come and pick her up early again so you'll have a few more hours at the end of the day."

"That's what Papà told me, too, Mamma," Breva affirmed, nodding her head soberly. "That's why we came late."

Constanza folded her arms across her chest, leaning on one hip.

"I'm sorry, but today is a terrible day for this. The Hotel Aubergino from the Lido, that big one that looks like a palace, lost its baker and wants me to do their baking for today—maybe forever if they like it."

"A Lido hotel?" Piero asked, smiling. "*Brava.*"

"They placed an enormous order, and I've still got the lunch and dinner items to finish. I can't look after Breva—I won't have even a minute," she said, scurrying toward the oven to check on the breads.

"Mamma, I'll be good, I promise!" Breva pleaded, her voice rising as if she might cry. "I want to stay with you, *please.*"

Constanza steamed a carafe of milk, poured a bit in the cup with the coffee, and spooned some foam on top. She pushed the coffee across the counter to Piero.

"Drink it—I'll make another for myself."

Piero looked embarrassed, but began sipping the cappuccino. He shifted his weight from foot to foot, looking unsure whether he should sit down.

Just what was he up to? Well, she would be certain that he didn't get his way, whatever it was. No, she would insist that he take Breva. There was just no way she could watch her daughter that day.

"*Bella,*" Constanza cooed, leaning over to put her arm over Breva's shoulder. "Mamma would like to have you here all day, too, but I've got too much work. It's better if you go with Papà."

"If I stay quiet and play in the corner or by the door—"

"But you always wander somewhere after awhile and I can't look for you—I can't watch you."

"I won't, I won't," Breva promised, her little voice rising.

Constanza smiled reassuringly, but Breva's eyes turned pink and watery. She looked like she might cry again.

"Why don't you want to stay with your papà?" Constanza asked.

"I do, but I like to be in the bakery more. It's more fun," she pouted, dropping to the floor resolutely, looking as if she might not move.

"Today is no good, Breva," she explained impatiently. "Today's a really bad day for Mamma, so how about tomorrow—you can stay with me then."

"If she's good she can't stay with you? She's promised to be good," Piero said, sipping his coffee.

Constanza looked at him in disbelief. "Tomorrow, fine. Today, no."

Pacing, she turned back to the espresso machine, watching as the coffee streamed out of the machine. She could feel Piero's eyes on her back. Why was he so stubborn about leaving Breva with her? She couldn't put her finger on what it was that seemed odd about him, his eyes stealing glances, but never meeting hers. Was he hiding something?

She felt a stab of pain in her gut. Was he having an affair? When would he have started it and with whom, she wondered, keeping her back to him so he couldn't see the way her fingers shook as she steamed the milk. But it couldn't be. Who could have an affair without someone finding out in such a city? But that didn't make sense either—that wasn't Piero, she felt certain. No, it had to be something else.

"Piero, why can't you take her with you? Why? You won't have to work—your arm is still healing. So please take her with you," she said, her voice rising. "I don't know that I'll ever have another chance like this. I have twice the number of things to make and I scarcely have time to drink even a cappuccino let alone watch Breva."

They rarely argued and it surprised Constanza how forceful her voice sounded. Looking frightened, awkward even, Piero leaned forward on the counter, as if he might say something. Maybe he would come out with whatever it was that was bothering him or what he was really doing—if he knew it himself. Could he be acting odd simply because he hadn't worked for so long? And with the war raging nearby and squadrons of planes flying over every day, it was a wonder they all weren't crazy.

"I guess I can take her with me," he said finally, scooping foam out of his cup with his forefinger and licking it thoughtfully. "And just hope she won't be in the way."

In some ways, he seemed so casual, but he was hiding something, she felt certain. But how much could he do, what could he do with his daughter at his side?

"You'll go to the factory?" she asked, studying his face for a reaction. "And she'll be in the way while they look at your arm?"

"Exactly," he said. "But I can see that maybe it'll be hard for you to have her here. And you're right—with all that you have to do, maybe it's not the best thing for her to be underfoot."

"She'll definitely be in the way here," Constanza said. "I'm sorry—I just have too much work. Now you know—any other day I could do it, but just not until I see how this goes. And we need the money."

"I know," he sighed, shaking his head apologetically. He looked at his arm with a puzzled expression, as if he were wondering how this damaged arm had come to be attached to his body.

Why did she push so hard, as if to prove something? She felt that—what did they call it in the French?—déjà vu? As if everything she said and the events unfolding had been predetermined. She was merely an actor, reciting already familiar lines.

Events felt as if they were headed somewhere, though she couldn't sense where. Was this the answer to her prayers, the eventual return to normalcy for them all? She'd heard that the Americans were sure to win the war, and maybe within weeks or a month Venice would be taken. When that day arrived, they could breathe a sigh of relief.

Maybe she could watch Breva, but this opportunity from the hotel had come on that particular day, and by chance, Piero had something else he wanted to do. Whatever it was. What could it hurt to have her way? After all, she was working. As much as she would like to have Breva around, she wouldn't have time to watch her napping in the sunshine, let alone wandering out the door. No, Piero would have to take her.

"Okay," Piero sighed, pushing away the empty coffee cup, his face brightening. "You're right—it doesn't make sense for her to stay."

"But I want to stay," Breva interrupted. "What about what I want to do? I want to stay with Mamma!"

Frowning, Constanza had already begun measuring out flour and water to mix another batch of dough. Strange how the other day she had wanted nothing more than her daughter and husband and now she was choosing work over them. What choice did she have, though? If she baked for the hotel, her family wouldn't have to worry so much about money. And she wouldn't need to borrow money from her parents—if they even had any to borrow.

"Don't argue, Breva," Constanza said impatiently. "Can't you see Mamma is busy working, eh?"

"But I don't want—"

"Piero, take her for a gelato on the way, okay?"

Piero nodded, extending his good hand. "Come on, *bellina*, let's go, okay?"

Constanza's idea worked, and her daughter popped up, her face already brightening at the prospect of gelato. She would forget about her mother within moments.

"Grazie, Piero," she said with significance, smiling warmly. "I'll make you a special dinner tonight with the money I get from the hotel—I'll see if there's meat at the *mercato*, okay?"

Piero waved, the door with its tinkling bells closing behind them. Breva didn't even wave, her inconstant nature having already turned its attention to a walk to the piazza and the ice cream she would soon eat.

For some reason, Constanza craved a wave, a blown kiss or even a "ciao." But the last view she had was Breva pulling her father forward down the street, sidling right up the side of the canal as she always did.

She never turned back, as she sometimes did, to wave to her mother or catch a glimpse of her working through the casement windows standing open to pull any wandering breeze into the bakery, while releasing the scents of fresh-baked breads upward into the hazy, somnolent Venetian sky.

He would tell her, of course. Tell her as soon as she finished her ice cream. And when he arrived home that night, he would confess to Constanza, too. There had been no real sense in keeping it a secret, as if he were having an affair or gambling the little money they had on *bocce*. Though they had been married just under six years, Constanza could read him. Of course, she'd sensed something was wrong with him, that he was hiding something. He saw the suspicion in her face, the way she'd turned from him at the espresso machine.

What would have been the harm in telling her?

But maybe she would have objected, and then he wouldn't have been able to go. If she'd grown angry and convinced him not to and the yearning returned when he'd left the bakery, then she'd have every right to curse him for ignoring her. As it was, she could only be a little angry with him, as he never asked her for permission.

And who could really find fault with the one simple desire of his, to blow glass again for just an afternoon? Constanza, even when she hadn't been working at the bakery, had been baking bread every day. She could certainly understand what drove her to bake, or him to blow glass, or others to paint, or sew. And that if a person didn't, life felt dried up and dull.

He hadn't blown glass in years, not since shortly after the war began. And the desire to return to his studio had grown steadily until he knew that he would have to blow glass again, even if it was after he had finished for the day at the factory or on a Sunday when the rest of the neighbors were holed up in their homes eating dinner together or chatting in their now threadbare, finest clothes in the piazza.

Others might be content to work, eat, and sleep, but he needed something more. And not by choice either—he felt driven, as if he might burst if his hands and eye weren't playing with the forms and colors involved with glassblowing.

Constanza should understand because she was like him in that way, in this most fundamental, but mysterious of way. She worked with her hands, too, and only those who worked with their hands, who coaxed something transcendent out of ingredients, which on their own amounted to nothing, could understand.

Since he'd been a child, people had always looked at glassblowers askance, wondering at their ability to create beautiful objects from the most mundane of materials—sand, seaweed, and fire. When he'd first worked as an apprentice in his father's studio on Murano, he'd been told the stories of the first glassblowers, the itinerant artists indispensable to cities and towns, loved by emperors, the nobility, and caesars alike. Superstitious people had feared the wrath of the gods who they believed would be angered by men who should act more humble, who shouldn't use fire to forge something hard yet transparent from sand and seaweed. It was okay if the gods played tricks, if they and the demigods played their magic or performed a sleight of hand, but man shouldn't do the same.

And what was glass, after all? Created from molten red liquid and reminiscent of lava thrown from volcanoes, the otherworldly substance remained a mystery. Perhaps the drive to work with the molten material, giving form to the shapes and figures of his imagination, was just as much a mystery.

"Papà, why did we stop by that building on the way here?" Breva asked, interrupting his thoughts as she reached the bottom of her ice cream cone.

"You'll see, *bellina*," he said, patting her head.

Pushing her dark brown curls from her cheek, which was dabbed with melted bits of ice cream, he smiled.

"Today you get to watch Papà work," he said, stretching his arms, the fingers and hand of his withered arm shaking.

"Okay," she said, nodding with conviction. "I've never seen Papà work."

He could tell she didn't understand what he did, that she was simply interested because they would be doing something new. That was enough to satisfy her.

"When do we go?" she asked, crunching on the cone.

"We can go *now*," he answered, looking at her expectantly.

Popping up from the bench, she tossed the cone to a cluster of strutting pigeons, clapping her hands excitedly.

"I'm ready, Papà. *Andiamo*!"

Charging from the benches alongside the fountain, Breva headed toward the duomo.

"Wrong direction," Piero yelled after her. "This way, okay?"

Extending his hand, he watched as she studied it before grasping it tentatively. Was she still so uncertain of him even after nearly a month of mornings and early afternoons spent with him? He felt a pain of regret, wondering if she preferred to be with her mother. Walking quickly, he headed down the winding streets toward the studio, as if he'd walked the same route hundreds of times.

When they arrived at the worn door to his workshop, his heart raced. He'd stopped by earlier, leaving Breva for half an hour or so with Signora Testa who lived across the street so that he could quickly get a fire going in the furnace. Now, a few hours later, the dry wood in the furnace had been reduced to glowing hot embers which would provide steady heat. Opening the rusted metal door, he was confronted by all the old smells he'd never realized he would miss so acutely. Though he hadn't blown glass in the studio since a year after the war began, he could still smell the wood smoke and molten glass, the sharp, acidic scents lingering in the rafters, the wood shelves, and the musty, gossamer-strewn corners that had not seen sunlight for years.

A studio smacked of work, craftsmanship, and artistry, and he'd forgotten how completely different it was from a factory. Now that he was back in the familiar space, with the furnace heating the room and bringing out all the old smells, causing shadows to recede and cobwebs to blow away or evaporate, he resented that he'd ever had to give up his work.

What had the war done for him?

That swine Mussolini and the rest had swindled the common Italians, leading them to believe they'd be better if they were stronger. They had done their fighting for years now and had gained what? News of what Hitler had done to the Jews and anyone who opposed him had blown across the Alps like a chill winter wind off the glaciers. His neighbors and some friends had been slow to accept the stories, but he'd never doubted, having seen the world as an outsider, a glassblower. From the beginning, the bluster and promises of Mussolini had appeared hollow, malformed. Now that his suspicions had been confirmed and the rest of the country was arriving at the same conclusion, what would they do?

For three years, he'd mindlessly worked in a factory making glass for a hundred different armament and airplanes that he couldn't even recall. Were the artisans of Germany as shamed and humiliated to have had the crafts and traditions practiced by their forbearers and theirs before them trailing directly back to the Renaissance and Middle Ages replaced in one fell swoop with factory work? That his work at the factory helped the war continue, while at the same time keeping him away from his real work, left him feeling disturbed.

"Papà, what's wrong?" Breva asked, playfully poking him.

"*Niente e tutto*," he replied, blowing the bellows on the embers.

Why should someone so young pay with her childhood what adults had surrendered so readily?

"I'm happy," he said, feeling the words rise out of him as if water from a spring. "I can work again—just wait and see."

"What will you do?" she exclaimed, spinning. "I want to see!"

"I'll make glass—I'll make whatever you want in whatever color you want, carina. What do you want me to make?"

Grabbing her shoulders, he pulled her into him. He leaned down, allowing her to bury her face into his neck. She wrapped her little arms around his neck, hugging him back.

"Papà, I don't know," she said, looking confused. "What do I want?"

He should have showed her what he made long ago. Why had he never thought to show her the things he had made—bowls, plates, and vases that they used in their own house—that he had made with his own hands?

"Do you want something that captures the night sky, the stars, and the moon, or maybe something that reminds you of the sun and flowers? Does that make it easier?" he asked.

Her face brightening, she chose the stars and moon. "I want something with those in it, with things from the nighttime."

"You'll have it," he promised. "By tonight, you'll have a bowl that captures the night sky, the stars, and the moon. And it'll belong to you, *principessa*."

Beaming, Breva jumped up and down, breaking from her father's embrace. "Sì, sì, sì!" she called. "Grazie, Papà, grazie."

Before standing, he drew her to him once more. She'd been infected with the spirit of motion that rose in her ever more frequently, though, and she quickly pulled away.

"Start working, Papà, per favore," she cried. "I want to see you work, I want to see you make the glass."

"Va bene," he said, standing quickly. "Watch me then."

Motioning her to follow, he walked to the furnace, checking the coals, which had formed from the burned wood. The pieces he'd thrown in earlier glowed orange-red, nearly ready to create glass. He would have just enough time to prepare his tools.

"Watch from over there, *bellina*, okay?" he said, motioning for Breva to take a seat on a bench safely out of range of flying sparks.

"But it's so far from you, Papà," she complained. "What will I do?"

Cleaning his blowing tube and donning an apron, he waved her off. "You can walk around the studio, but just don't come too close to the furnace okay? Stay close enough to Papà that you can see what he's doing, but far enough away that you aren't burned, okay? The fire's hot, you see, and the glass I'll be working with is even hotter. When you see the glass when it's melted by the fire, it'll look very pretty, like fiery taffy, but you must stay away, okay?"

"I'll try, Papà," she promised, shifting restlessly on the bench. "But can't I just take a little closer look?"

"No, I'll come to you with the glass and you can look at it—but never touch it, okay?"

"I won't touch it, *ne prometto*."

"Va bene," he smiled. "Then I'll begin."

At first, the tube felt unwieldy and unfamiliar in his hands. He was surprised that a tool he'd held for so many years suddenly seem so foreign, especially with his still stiff, emaciated arm?

"Have you started yet, Papà?" Breva asked impatiently.

"I'm just getting prepared, that's all," he explained.

"Is your arm okay to work, to hold that pipe?" she asked, her mouth contorted in concern.

"If I move slow and am careful, it's fine," he said, wondering if she'd noticed how tenderly he treated the arm, how slow and deliberate he moved.

Did she sense his hesitation, his inability to jump back into his work? Pumping the coals with the well-worn bellows, he watched the studio turn fiery orange. The heat and burst of flame brought Breva running over.

"Stay back—sit on the bench," he cautioned, waving her away with his free hand, the one that no longer moved so easily. Out of the corner of his eye, he could see her trudge back to the bench, sitting down with resignation. He'd raised his voice more than he'd intended, but she could easily burn herself. Better to be firm than have her end up burned.

"It'll be interesting in just a few minutes," he promised, smiling reassuringly as he looked over his shoulder. "Just give Papà a few more minutes."

Breva didn't look too convinced, taking his promise as an invitation to leave the bench for a few minutes and return to exploring. Walking through the studio, she touched the equipment and shelves and picked up rejected pieces of glasswork. Most of the pieces looked fine to her. Why had they been left to gather dust? She liked the smoky scent of the studio, but it was so dark inside—even with the light from the glowing fire and the windows on the ceiling.

"Can I have this, Papà?" she asked, showing a multi-colored orb she'd picked up and held up to the window. She liked the way the rays of sun caught the glass, sending glowing dots of color onto the floor and wall behind the orb.

"Sure—put it in your pocket, *bellina*," Piero smiled.

She wiped the dust covering the piece of glass onto her dress, marveling at the colors.

Settling the iron pot of molten glass back into the coals, Piero walked over to Breva and helped her tuck the orb into a pocket of her dress and then turned back to his glassblowing.

"I want to look at it, Papà," she protested, her small hand rubbing the orb through her dress. "Can't I play with it?"

"Fine, then, you can take it back out of your pocket," he shrugged, turning again to prepare the glass.

Why did he need to think carefully about every step? All the things he'd done without thinking for so many years suddenly seemed foreign. Still, it was comforting to be back in the studio, to smell the hot furnace and the molten glass, the smoke and the dust. He liked the way rays of sun slanted through the skylights, setting dust motes aflame. Wasn't he doing the same thing he'd first learned as a mere child?

The light cascading through the rows of skylights was friendly, even warm. Who needed electrical lamps, like the ones strung along the ceilings of the factory, making everything under them—including the workers—appear ugly, harsh? Even the light from the grayest Venetian winter day possessed qualities that made the whole studio glow pleasantly. A person could walk into the street and find everything gray and depressing, but in the studio, the angled skylights captured the light and transformed it, filtering out the colder colors. The magical light had inspired Piero to work since he'd first opened the studio after following Constanza to Venice, challenging him to create pieces that captured the generous light spilling through the windows—whether gray and tepid, or golden and fiery.

Grabbing his tools, he approached the fire tentatively, wondering if his hands and eye would remember. His first effort came out lopsided from uneven blowing, leaving him saddened, but not disconsolate. He knew how to do this, so how could he be so clumsy after only a few years?

His next attempt turned out better than the first, though it, too, was not a perfect sphere. Tossing the cooling glass back into the iron molting pot, he looked around the studio for Breva. Still playing, she held her newfound orb up into steeply slanting rays of sunshine falling through the paned glass door, mesmerized by the spectrum.

Maybe she would be a glassblower, too, he thought. He'd never heard of such a thing, a woman making glass, but why not? With the war, women were working in factories alongside men and oftentimes kept up with them, so why couldn't his Breva be the first? She had the faraway, wandering look of the glassblower—a look his father said he lacked. Still, Piero had become a decent blower who could create both inspired and reliable pieces. If a customer wanted a set of matching goblets or a light fixture with symmetry, he could make each goblet or arm of the chandelier so near the other that only the sharpest of eyes could detect the differences.

His life seemed a simple refutation of all the old tales and superstitions—he wouldn't grow weary of his life in Venice, nor of Constanza and Breva. In this way, he seemed verily different from other glassblowers, even from his father who had done a poor job of hiding the women with whom he had affairs. And his father had certainly been infected with the itinerant nature of the glassblower, having always talked about moving to Milano or Roma, Verona or Bologna. In the end, he'd only traveled to the cities and any others in which he could find work, tiring of sleepy Murano where he complained that the only thing that moved was the tide.

But this one thing, glassblowing, he must have. He would never give it up again.

Breva, though, had a faraway look in her eye that reminded Piero of his father. Could such things skip generations, leaving him content to remain in Venice while his daughter was destined to travel to other places?

Having stirred the molten glass, he scooped out a blob and placed it at the end of the metal blowpipe. He would recall how to work the pipe and material, at least get to the point that the spin of the pipe and the feel of his breath pushing the molten glass outward felt like second nature, as if catching his stride while running. He could become as talented as he'd been if he'd just push a little harder; try more desperately to remember how the tools should feel in his hands, and how he should move them.

Yet another reason to curse the war, the endless, grim conflict that seemed to have altered the course of his life, bringing an abrupt end to what had been a blissful beginning to his years in Venice and his marriage to Constanza, right up to the birth of their daughter. Now nothing seemed to go right, but perhaps with the hope that the war would end was also the hope that they could recapture some of the life they'd had before the fascists had risen to power, taking Venice with them.

By the time he dabbed the sixth drooping bit of molten glass on the pipe, he could sense what he'd done wrong the previous times, spinning the pipe a little faster and with a steadier motion, despite the stiffness and lack of range of his injured arm. He sensed that the piece would be worth keeping, one that would restore his confidence.

Spinning frantically again and again, and pushing measured bursts of air through the pipe, he watched as a glowing sphere emerged—one that was perfectly shaped, seeming to magically inflate from the end of the pipe. Resisting the urge to smile, Piero spun and blew, deftly scraping the few deposits and bumps that formed on the walls of the cooling glass.

A glassblower raced against time, trying to create the desired shape before the molten material hardened, spotting and correcting blemishes before they became fixed. And if the glass didn't harden quickly enough, he had to work just as diligently to prevent the perfect shape he'd created from collapsing or warping. Spinning and blowing, and sometimes using bellows to cool the glass were important, but a feel for the material was the most critical ingredient. If a glassblower didn't sense when to spin or blow, and how much to spin or blow, he could never create anything worthwhile.

Of course, there were plenty of average glassblowers in the city; those who once sold their wares to tourists and now sold them to soldiers. But Piero had never been such a blower. He never showed or kept an object that didn't boast a perfect shape, an inspiring color, and a luminescent quality that seemed indescribable, but that he could detect the moment the glass had hardened.

If the object lacked any of those qualities, he broke it, selling some of the colorful shards to mosaic and tile makers who prized the colorful bits. In this way, he wasn't wasting precious materials that he could scarcely afford to waste—even before the war. But there were no longer any tile or mosaic makers to purchase the shards, even if they had any money.

This time, he would have to reuse the molten glass before it hardened if it looked like there was an imperfection. Or try to sell the item even if it wasn't perfect. Times had changed; he no longer had the luxury of being a perfectionist.

With the piece forming at the end of pipe, he would have to trust by the fading molten red and the liquid essence of the glass that the color and luminescence would be present—he couldn't break or throw away this piece. Throwing away anything—even an imperfect bowl or vase—was like throwing away money.

If he got the piece right, it would be a gift for Breva, to be certain, but perhaps it would be an even greater gift for himself. Had he captured the night sky, the pinpricks of stars, and the soft glow of the moon? Would his daughter recognize these things in the bowl he'd created? While the orb was moon-shaped, he wouldn't know how the colors had turned out until it dried and hardened.

His arm started aching, a dull throb emanating from the stretch of his burned forearm. He could rest now, knowing that he was a glassblower again, that the war hadn't taken everything.

"*Bella, bella*!" he sighed. "*É ritornato. Grazie a Dio.*"

He felt lucky. It could have taken much longer for the feeling to return, this synchronicity with the glass, the feeling that the form lay hidden in the molten material, waiting to be shaped.

The earliest glassblowers had suffered both resentment and adoration. Resentment because they made something from unremarkable ingredients, a sort of magic that was a trademark of the gods—not mortals. Adoration for being creative and ingenious, traits that also pleased the gods.

While Piero didn't believe any of that rubbish, he understood what they meant.

What god shouldn't take delight in seeing one of his creations craft an object of beauty from sand and seaweed? In some ways, Piero was a creator, too—just like the gods. Like Icarus, he could fly high enough to feel them, even if he couldn't see them. That's what glassblowing felt like.

Snipping the neck of the vessel, he removed the pipe, placing it on a table behind him. The glass was already cooling, beginning to shine and reflect the soft light of the studio. The piece looked perfectly shaped, pleasing to the eye, and just as he'd pictured it. When it cooled, it would be pleasing to the hand, too, delightful to the touch. Liquid-smooth walls would invite fingertips to explore, to feel the otherworldly perfection of the glass.

Everyone took the material for granted, finding it as natural as rock or wood. But glass was a mystery, straddling the worlds of reality, nature, and myth. How else could you explain a material that only man's hands rendered, and that seemed as liquid as it did solid. If he'd been one of the first glassblowers, practicing his craft in ancient Persia or Rome, he would have been considered a magician or sorcerer who dealt with the other worlds. But he realized he was considered quaint, a tourist attraction, or an artist before the war, and a common factory worker during.

The pipe in his hands had felt good, fitting naturally like the suit Constanza had insisted he have made for Sundays. Gazing at the bowl, he realized there were three things that gave his life substance: glassblowing, Constanza, and Breva. The rest he could survive without.

But how to continue blowing when he would need to return to work? If anyone discovered he was blowing glass, the government would revoke his temporary discharge. Could he blow glass secretly, stocking up his creations until the war was over, until some future day when no one remembered that he'd had a burned arm and was supposed to have worked in the factory?

The glass had cooled, taking on the characteristics that defined it—transparence, an aspect of frozen water, liquid light, and facets of the night sky. He had successfully worked magic, remastering the ancient craft he'd known since childhood.

"You can see the glass now, Breva," he called, excitedly. "Come here and take a look, see the night sky forming."

Piero smiled with satisfaction, as if he'd solved a puzzle, marveling at how completely lost and disconnected he'd become in the years since the war had begun. Looking up, he glanced around the studio casually, noticing the dim corners, which contrasted with the rich amber light. But Breva must have grown tired of watching, disappearing into one of the deep recesses. Or perhaps she had lain down somewhere, bored with watching his repeated efforts at creating her gift.

"Breva?" he called again, the uncertainty in his voice surprising him.

Where had she gone?

Moving away from the pool of light created by the hot coals, Piero moved deliberately along the walls, scanning the shadows and gossamer-filled spaces behind the shelves and worktables.

"Breva!" he called, feeling his irritation grow.

That was why she shouldn't have come with him, exactly why she would have been better off with her mother in the bakery. Why did she never sit still, but always had to be moving? He'd been worried that she would touch the hot glass, disturb him while he was blowing, but he hadn't worried about her wandering away. Where would she have gone? The studio was large enough to provide tucked away hiding spots under tables and behind cabinets, but it was only a large one-story room with dust and cobweb-covered rafters and the dirty windows of the skylights cut into the ceiling. She couldn't hide for long.

Piero continued his lap around the perimeter of the studio deciding that she must have fallen asleep in some corner.

"Breva," he said, his voice petulant. "Where are you? Come to Papà now."

His voice sounded unfamiliar, tinged with anger.

As he neared completion of a lap around the studio, his eye caught the open door. He'd shut it, hadn't he? The massive old door, medieval in appearance with its hammered, rust-tinged metal bandages marred from years of use, emitted a shaft of bright light into the shadowy interior of the studio, as if to lead him outside.

Certainly, she wouldn't have squeezed through the door—he would have heard the immense, squeaking hinges. She had to be in the studio.

Tentatively, he called her name again, lightly resting his hand on the cold, metal doorknob. Turning to cast his eyes quickly across the room again, he expected to see her head bobbing above the worktable or to take in some movement prompted by the calling of her name. But there was no movement in the studio.

Why had he ever agreed to bring her here? He cursed himself—if only he'd explained to Constanza where he was going and why he needed to go alone, she might have agreed to keep Breva. Why a feeling of panic when he would most likely pull open the door and find his daughter playing on the street outside or down the street? Maybe she'd wandered somewhere close by, to a neighbor's or back toward piazza San Marco. Anyone who spotted her would have taken her in or brought her back to the studio, if they recognized her and knew of his studio. No one permitted a small child to wander the streets in Venice. Yes, someone would have picked her up.

Roughly clasping the knob, Piero pulled open the huge door, revealing a sun-dappled street, empty of pedestrians, devoid of even a circling bird or a passing gondolier.

"Breva," he called in a scratchy voice, at first timidly, but gradually louder. She wasn't just outside as he'd hoped, and there was no sign of her, as if she'd evaporated. He quickly looked up and down the street, seeing nothing but shuttered windows, closed studios and shops. Had he missed her inside somehow, had she crawled into some corner out of his view? Glancing back indoors, he shook his head at the futility of searching where he'd already searched. No, the studio wasn't that large that she could have hidden herself so well; she must have wandered outside.

Since he'd opened the studio in an out-of-the-way neighborhood, he'd liked that it was mostly a quarter frequented by workers like him. With the war, though, the area was quiet, void of its usual street life. If it had been before the war, Breva wouldn't have gone fifteen feet without someone stopping her. Why couldn't someone have passed by chance, have returned her to his studio, the only shop with an open door within view?

He would start walking every street nearby, every twist and turn, knowing that she could have wandered anywhere. Why did she have to be such a wanderer and so ill content to stay near one of her parents?

Fifteen feet in front of the door were the placid, murky waters of the canal, mocking him. He would not search the waters, though he reluctantly glanced toward the edge of the stone via, its mossy lip only a few feet higher than the water. What was he looking for? Breva's floppy hat? Her drooping doll? No, he remembered seeing the doll sitting in a corner of the studio.

Was he looking because that's what you expected in Venice, for a missing child to turn up in the canal?

Slapping his forehead, as if to banish such thoughts, he glanced helplessly up and down the via.

"Breva, Breva," he called, resenting the trembling, strident sound of his voice.

Why would she have gone toward the canal, knowing after so many scoldings that she was to avoid the water, to remain far from the steep and slippery canal edges? Stupid thoughts! Of course, she'd wandered down one of the streets and engaged at play in some corner, or on some bridge, he told himself, while beginning to drive him mad with unbearable whispers of thoughts he couldn't even permit himself to hear.

What would entice a child to jump into the canal, to leave the safe, firm stone and brick underfoot for the slurping, cloudy waters of the canals? No, nothing would entice a child to do such a thing. She liked to explore, to wander, but to explore the streets and the city, not the water. He'd never even noticed her take an interest in the canals, to grab his hand and lead him to the water's edge.

But how did a person decide which street to take, which way to go when each route presented itself as promisingly as the next? If he hadn't been an impractical glassblower, he could have been sensible by determining the most logical route. But each way seemed sensible to him. He could have set out across the bridge, crossing it and then turning to the left or right. To the right, the street veered away from the canal along a crooked path between buildings. To the left, the street shouldered the waters of the canal, until the canal took a turn to the left a hundred feet down. Or should he have stayed on the side of the canal that he was on?

He was wasting time! Just go in any direction—start somewhere, he chided himself, aware he was losing precious time. Rushing to the left, he broke into a desperate run, fighting the nauseating panic in his chest.

She was around, somewhere nearby, he assured himself. She couldn't have fallen into the canal unnoticed, he would have heard her shout, *and someone* would have heard her. The waters of the canals didn't rise up and take anyone—no—he didn't believe in the childhood tales *Stay away from the murdering, treacherous waters of the canals!* Adults told those stories to scare children, but he knew better; water just didn't rise up and snatch anyone.

The quarter suddenly felt immense, each intersection presenting myriad options. Why did he panic so? Had he so little faith, as if he expected punishment for something that a simplistic, jealous-ridden god would steal his baby girl because he hadn't been religious enough or worse, because he'd done something as stupid as lying to his wife and going to blow glass? By practicing his art, had he stolen fire from the gods? Such a world would be unbearable, ridiculous.

Where could she have gone? Racing up and down the streets, he systematically covered each via leading from the studio, running for a few blocks before retracing his steps and taking another twisting, turning street threading its way through the quarter. He wished he could walk calmly; assuring himself there was no reason to hurry, that she would turn up in some courtyard or on some bridge, but he felt unable to quell the urge to run. If he had faith that she was in some corner, sitting on some doorstep, or playing with a cat on a bridge, why did he need to run?

Finally, he saw a signora, walking stiff and bowlegged, her market basket overloaded with wilting, immature leeks, and flour-dusted bread.

"Have you seen a little girl?" Piero asked, trying to catch his breath.

The woman gazed at him solemnly, her eyes slowly widening. She took in his disheveled hair, the panic on his face, his flushed, sweat-soaked cheeks.

"No, Dio caro," she said, shaking her head. Then she crossed herself, still shaking her head. "I'll tell my neighbors to look—where?"

"Near via Bernice and calle Colombo, just by the bridge there."

"My husband and I will head there *prontissimo*," she said. "We'll search the streets. And my neighbors are home—I'll get them, too."

"Grazie, signora," he called, spinning on his heel and continuing his race down the street.

At least he wouldn't have to search alone! Soon there would be enough people to comb the area and then Breva would be found—or if someone took her in, they would soon hear that her father was coming to claim her. If only that woman hadn't crossed herself. It felt like bad luck, though he shouldn't have been surprised. No doubt she was superstitious, too, like most Venetians. They'd all been raised on stories of children falling into canals and being swept out to sea, never to be found again as punishment for not minding their parents. Before those tales, the story was it was Poseidon's way of exacting a toll from the city's founders who'd brazenly built their city on the sea.

Silly superstitions—he was too old and too wise for those.

Still, it was a relief to have others looking for his daughter, too. He couldn't search even that neighborhood's labyrinthine alleyways and vie solo, let alone comb the neighboring quarters.

Like wildfire, he knew that word would spread that a child was lost in the old manufacturing quarter. More old women would cross themselves, shake their heads superstitiously, and purse their lips as they silently recalled the old tales. Some might even remember the old superstitions about Poseidon. For beneath its veneer, Venice was an ancient, backward-looking place. Modern signs of the outside world such as electricity, motorized boats, and the telephone might hide it, but he guessed that most people weren't so different in their beliefs than their ancestors had been. Maybe they weren't even that different from the first refugees who built homes on the marshy islands.

"Breva! Where are you!" he shrieked, turning another narrow corner.

Sweeping through another crooked street, he slowed only enough to glance down smaller passageways immersed in shadows, or into courtyards with entry gates ajar.

It was good that the word was out, much as he wished it were his own secret, a secret to be dismembered and disproved after only a few minutes or hours more of searching. When she was found, he would have to explain how he had allowed her to wander away from him and hang his head shamefully. Who cared, as long as he had his smiling, mischievous Breva in his lap again?

Constanza! Of course, she would hear about a missing girl as word swept through the neighborhoods. All the better that there would be more people searching for her shortly—probably already *were*! If enough people were looking, she would be found before Constanza ever realized her daughter had gone missing. But why was he thinking that his wife would so quickly assume it was her daughter anyway?

He must find Breva before Constanza heard.

The harder Constanza worked, the more troubled she felt. She'd surprised herself at how quickly her skills returned, putting together the order for the hotel, and baking the usual small orders that she had enough flour to fill. A few times she'd caught herself humming, a habit her mother had practiced whenever she baked.

Mechanically, she executed each of her tasks, enjoying the cool, familiar feel of the different dough, and sensing by sight, smell, and touch when each batch was ready for the oven, and then by aroma and appearance when the rolls and breads were done.

She hadn't worked with refined flour for a few years, nor baked so much since the war had started and Breva had arrived. But the feel of the dough and her little tricks and habits returned in the same way that the disparate ingredients came together to create yeasty, sweet-smelling dough. Such things were bred in the bone and couldn't be removed, she figured. Did people who worked in factories, in offices, or in fishing boats have similar feelings? It didn't seem that they could, though maybe fishermen sensed some interplay, some larger game being played with the forces of nature. But people who worked in offices or factories—like Piero lately—did they have a sense, a calling, and a drive for what they were doing?

Baking came naturally to her, even the way she created light, flaky crostata and cornetti. Some labored to learn her secret and then wondered if she'd held back the vital step of her baking routine that resulted in her perfect pastries. But she told them everything she knew. What she didn't know, but merely felt and did with her hands, she couldn't explain. And perhaps what was unsaid, what couldn't be put into words made the difference. The ingredients and steps might all be the same, but the handling of everything was somehow different, and perhaps it was these things that couldn't be copied or duplicated. If they didn't reveal themselves from within, asserting themselves as a baker became familiar with handling the dough, then the baker was likely destined to always be merely average.

That was her hunch, anyway. Just another of her countless beliefs and superstitions about how and why the world was ordered and unfolded the way it did.

She had sat down for only a moment, sighing contentedly at how welcome the stool felt to her tired limbs, when the bakery door opened. A younger woman she'd seen around the neighborhood entered tentatively, leaving the door open behind her. Constanza was struck by the absence of the tinkle of bells—upon the door opening and upon the door closing—and so the customer's entrance was bothersome. She'd intended to rest for mere minutes—why did the woman need to enter at that moment?

It was no time to be lazy, she chastised herself, pushing herself onto her sore feet. She and Piero needed every *lira* they could earn.

"Buonasera," Constanza called, trying to sound cheerful, but avoiding the woman's eye.

"*Sera*," the woman responded, setting her shopping basket on the counter.

Constanza approached from the opposite side of the counter.

"*Si?*" she asked, deciding to be parsimonious with words.

The woman had a wild-eyed look about her, a self-satisfied air that annoyed Constanza. She would have liked to snub her, to pretend to be busy checking the rising dough or glancing again at the breads baking in the oven.

"I've been meaning to come over for hours now, but another

chore called out before I had a chance to head down the stairs. I hope you have some things left so late in the day?" she asked, opening her bag expectantly.

Constanza nodded. She longed to rest for a moment, to watch the last golden shafts of sunlight shoot through the casement windows before they disappeared behind the hulking form of the building across the street. Those were her favorite moments in the bakery—alone and immersed in her work, the shop redolent with sweet, fragrant scents. She knew she would return to baking when the woman left. As it was, the moments she'd planned to spend in idleness were gone.

"I have some bread, even some loaves made with white flour," she bragged, recalling how fortunate she'd been. "And some cornetti still," she added, motioning to the baskets on the shelves behind her. At one time, every basket on the shelf would have been full. Still, there was more than there had been for years. "Not bad for the middle of the war, no?"

The woman nodded solemnly, gazing out the window. Constanza could see her eyes follow someone moving by quickly. She turned to see a man disappear from view down the street.

Clucking her tongue, the woman frowned. "They're searching, but they know they'll never find her," she scolded, turning her gaze back to Constanza.

"What was that?" Constanza asked, stepping back as if she'd been struck. Her breath got caught in her insides, like the time the water taxi almost tipped while crossing the lagoon.

"You haven't heard? A missing girl—young, very young child. Left alone for a few minutes, and well, I don't have to tell you," she said, looking knowingly at Constanza.

The blood drained from her face, leaving her body numb, nearly lifeless.

Dio, no. No, no, no.

It was a familiar moment, accompanied by the realization that somewhere in her core she had known it would happen. But how could she have known—no, it couldn't be!

"*Sta bene, signora*?" the woman asked, extending her arm as if to steady her.

Constanza stared absently at the outstretched arm. It was crazy, her imagination gone wild.

"Tell me—where? Where did she go missing?" she asked hoarsely, her voice not her own.

"In the manufacturing district—on a quiet street," she answered, shaking her head.

"Oh, grazie, Signore, grazie!" she gasped, relief washing over her as she made the sign of the cross. They would have been near Piazza San Marco, she knew. Laughing, a bird-like, cackle, she rested the palms of her hands on the counter, leaning forward.

The woman drew back, screwing up her face.

"I don't mean to laugh ... no ... I'm sorry," she stammered, realizing how strange it must have sounded. "I'm merely relieved, that's all. You say she was lost in the workshop district, and now I'm relieved because it can't be—"

"Someone you know?" the woman said finishing her sentence as she softly beat her chest. "Then I'm so relieved that I'm not the bearer of such horrid news. I would never have—"

"I felt for an instant—felt certain—that it was my daughter," Constanza interrupted, scarcely interested in what the woman had to say now, feeling faint.

"But thank God it can't be," the woman said. "I've seen her playing at the door when I come by, or coming in with her papà. She's a delight, always smiling."

The woman scrutinized Constanza, perplexed. "If I may, why did you think it was your daughter?"

Constanza turned and looked out the window at the nearby canal that had begun rising with the approaching tide. How could she answer when she wasn't certain herself?

"I don't know," she shrugged, feeling chilled despite the sunshine and heat from the oven.

The woman drew back from the counter, a shadow crossing her face.

"Thank, God," she repeated. "I can see now why you were so relieved."

Constanza nodded, longing to return to her stool for just a moment, to sit and rest. She wished the woman would leave.

"I'll just get a few things and be off then," the woman announced, nervously touching her bag on the counter.

Constanza stared at her blankly, a feeble, polite smile forming on her lips.

"If I can just have a few things?" the woman asked, picking up the handles of her bag, pushing open its sides, and turning to gaze at the loaves of bread on the shelves.

"Of course, then, what would you like?" Constanza said distractedly, moving to the side so the woman could see what remained on the shelves. The question sounded silly when there were so few items to choose from. Still, there were more baked goods than usual. Never had she thought there would be so much bread available until after the war was over.

The woman pointed at one of the white loaves, cooing when Constanza methodically wrapped it in brown paper and placed it carefully in her bag along with two cornetti and a round brown loaf.

When the woman backed out of the doorway, sneaking glances at her, Constanza started crying, the tears rolling quickly down her cheeks flecked with flour. She knew odd-looking, zigzagging trails would form along the sides of her face, but she couldn't stop. How close had death come? She felt certain that it had come very near—and how had she not sensed it that morning, or even the evening before? When she thought about it, there had been a vague uneasiness, and she'd felt more protective of Breva, hadn't she? And when the woman had told her about the child, she'd felt an icy wave roll through her, making her shiver. And then there was the owl, too.

Why had she pushed Breva on Piero despite the sense of foreboding she'd experienced earlier? She'd been wrong—that was why. If it had come close, death had provided her with a warning, for whatever reason. She wouldn't ask—didn't want to ask why or what it meant.

To be thankful would be enough.

"Grazie, Dio," she whispered, glancing skyward. "I'll pray more—I promise," she added, dwelling on the fact that she prayed less than in the past.

She experienced a flash that felt incomprehensible, realizing that the lost girl's parents had to be reeling. The cursed parents—their lives ruined, transformed into wretched minutes and hours that would eventually form into weeks, months, and then years, but always with the knowledge that a few moments of carelessness had cost them their child. And who in Venice could say they hadn't been warned, that they hadn't been raised with the stories of children who wandered out their doors, down from the *piani nobili,* and found their fate awaiting them at the bottom of one of the murky canals? That was the curse of living in Venice.

And everyone knew it.

Constanza shook her head, wiping her eyes as she leaned on the stool for a moment peering out the window.

Another woman from the neighborhood hurried past, glancing into the bakery with a ghastly expression. Upon catching sight of Constanza, the woman averted her eyes—as if she hadn't seen her! Looking as if she might burst into tears, the neighbor cast her eyes downward, away from the bakery. Clutching the collar of her dress, the woman hurried down the street, overtaking the woman who had just left the shop.

The two women spoke with arms flailing, directing nervous glances at the bakery.

Did the second woman think it was Breva, too? Then she saw both women shake their heads, staring gravely at the shop.

"No, no, it cannot be, cannot be," Constanza moaned. She turned away from the window, moving her trembling hands toward the last of the rising loaves of bread. She should punch them down, put them in the oven, but her hands were shaking.

Of course, that was it. How naive she'd been.

"Signore, please let her be found," she begged, wondering why she was to be so severely tested.

How had he lost track of her? How could it have happened? Certainly, the girl had wandered somewhere, had gone off as Constanza had always feared she would. Why did she have to wander so? Couldn't she be satisfied to be near one of her parents, to allow them to set the pace for her to discover the world? Why had she inherited the fate of the glassblower, the curse of the wanderer?

If *that* were it, if her worse, numbing fears were true, then she would die, unable to go on living.

"If you take her, you kill me," she whispered, crossing herself. Did they do any good, these impassioned prayers? She'd sent enough petitions heavenward during the years and had begun to wonder whether anyone was listening. Now it seemed punishment had come. Why punish someone who prayed, even if it wasn't as often as it should have been?

"What have I done to deserve such sorrow," she whined, her vision blurred by tears. Should she have stayed home with Breva that day, never having thought to bake again? They could have moved back home with her parents until Piero recovered, and if they'd done so, if she hadn't forced Piero to allow her to bake again, she wouldn't be standing in the middle of a bakery she couldn't even see, smell, or hear, feeling the world spinning recklessly.

A sudden thought occurred. Breva was not dead yet, *no*, and hadn't there been false scares when the children had been eventually found? With Breva, it was certainly possible. She wandered so, possessing an unflagging energy and a curiosity to explore, and why would she go near the canals after so many stern warnings from both of her parents and her grandmother? No doubt, she could wander for hours even, and was probably doing so at that moment. Or perhaps she'd curled up to take a nap under a café table somewhere or maybe in some doorway. She could be anywhere, but she wasn't necessarily dead.

Constanza's chest hurt, as if someone were sitting on her. The air in the bakery was suffocating, hot. She would explode or collapse. Laugh or cry.

"My Breva, where have you gone?" she whispered, her shoulders drooping. "What have you gone and done?"

Maybe she should have been stricter, disciplined the girl more, and kept her close by her side. She could have scared her as her parents had done, made her believe that sea snakes or mischievous mermaids might rise up out of a canal and snatch her. Even as a teenager, she feared and mistrusted the canals because of those silly old stories and never wanted to be alone by one. If only she'd taught fear to her daughter.

She shoved the bowls of rising bread from the counter onto the brick floor, shattering the heavy ceramic containers.

"*Breva*!" she wailed, stomping her aching feet.

The two women in the street heard the crashing of the bowls and ran toward the shop, clutching their plain print dresses at their knees to keep them from blowing up. They would try to comfort her—but she didn't want it, didn't want them there. Breva wasn't found yet, and they didn't know how she wandered, so what did they know? She wouldn't be like the other children who went missing, who turned up floating in the lagoon or surfaced in a small, out-of-the-way canal, or worse yet, never appeared again, remaining a heart-wrenching mystery. Her story would be different, not ending tragically. She must be alive or Constanza couldn't bear it, wouldn't bear it.

The women rushed through the doorway; the little bells tinkling maniacally as they quickly pushed open the door.

The bells had never sounded like that, frantic and irregular, distressed.

"*Signora, mi dispiace, dispiace*!"

The thin, bird-like woman from across the street tentatively clutched Constanza's arm, squeezing it uncertainly. The other woman extended her arms, offering to embrace her. They stole quick glances at the shards of ceramic bowl on the floor, the deflated blobs of dough, which looked like they'd been violently flung to the floor.

"No, she's not dead yet," she moaned, pushing them away. "You don't know her, my Breva—she loves to wander, she's the wandering type. She could be anywhere."

"Sì, sì," the neighbor said in a consoling voice. "She could be anywhere."

"You don't know, do you? Tell me you don't know!"

The women shook their heads, grimacing. "No, we haven't heard anything but that your daughter is missing."

Constanza noticed the women glanced at each other and then turned their faces toward her mournfully.

They were thinking of all the old superstitions, of course. She saw it on their faces. Let them think what they like, she decided. They didn't realize that with Breva it *must* be different. And she'd prayed with increasing frequency the previous few years, even if it wasn't as often before the war started or as much as her mother did. Certainly, she would be spared such a fate. And poor, innocent Breva. Why should see die for her mother's sins?

"Signora, please. We'll help you look, okay?" the thin woman suggested.

Why would God do such a thing, scaring her senseless and making her heart feel small and frail as it pounded frantically like that of a hunted rabbit about to be devoured. How would she walk, talk, or ever eat again if she didn't find her baby girl? Who would do such a thing, tormenting her so?

"But you said the girl went missing by the workshops—that couldn't be my Breva," she remembered, hoping again that they'd been mistaken.

But Venice was too small, she knew, they wouldn't make a mistake about whose daughter had gone missing. Such things caused mothers to jump in the canals themselves, or take poison. But couldn't this time be different, couldn't they have made a mistake *just once*?

"Yes, your husband was at his studio—" the neighbor started to explain.

"At his *studio*?" she interrupted defiantly. "But no, he was going to the *factory*—why would he go to his studio? There's nothing there for him—he hasn't blown glass for years now."

She shook her head morosely, as if they'd gotten all of it wrong.

"Signora, I'm sorry, but my sister lives on via Pescatore, and she told me it was a Signore Agostino whose wife owns a bakery on via Santucci. I don't like telling you, but it must be your daughter," she said softly. "They said her name must be Breva."

"But why was he at the studio, how did she wander away from him?" she cried, slapping the thick counter, kicking a piece of the shattered ceramic bowl.

The women stroked her arm, whispering.

"We'll find her. If she's playing on some little via somewhere, we'll find her soon enough and the nightmare will be over, eh?" the neighbor said, trying to smile while nervously caressing Constanza's arm.

Of course, they didn't realize that Breva was different. She was just a wanderer, the daughter of a glassblower.

She had just one Breva, just one daughter, just one child. Who would take her—no, it could not be. Life could not be so cruel.

"*Signora*, you're shaking," her neighbor said, gesturing toward her trembling arms. "You should have a drink of something—then we go look, no?"

Constanza nodded her head slowly, like the crazy women she'd seen in front of the train station.

"*Signore*," she whispered.

The women made the sign of the cross.

"We'll pray with you if you like," one of them suggested, grabbing her shaking hand. "*Serenità*?"

"I don't like," she said, surprising herself. "It's too late for prayers now. If she's gone, she's gone and no prayer will help."

"You shouldn't speak so," the taller woman said, her face looking alternately scolding and sympathetic. "I know you're troubled, but these are the times to have faith. To believe in him."

"I'll believe if my Breva is alive somewhere. Otherwise, I've stopped believing."

Was she cursing herself and damning Breva at the same time? But it just didn't make sense to her. If she prayed at that moment, would God pull her daughter out of whatever canal she was in, if she was even in one? Would he breathe life back into her cold, watery lungs because three women, three devout mothers were praying in a sweet-smelling bakery on a quiet street? And if Breva wasn't in a canal, but was playing somewhere, biding her time until her parents found her, then would God direct her to a canal because her mother had refused to pray for her, and had cursed a God that would play such a game?

Constanza's life felt at a turning point, as if something lifted and revealed the unthinkable. The moments seemed crystalline and raw, and she felt as if she could feel and hear the blood coursing through her veins, and detect the heartbeat in her ears. It was as if she were seeing the ugliness that lay beneath a veneer the whole time, but that she'd never noticed.

"I'm alone," she whispered, feeling certain that Breva must have been dead, her fingers tracing a crooked line across the cool, hard countertop.

"Don't say such things," her neighbor whispered hoarsely, biting her trembling lip and fastening her eyes to the floor. "We're here and soon you'll be with your husband."

"Where is my husband—why didn't he come?" she asked, glancing out the window at the empty street.

The women looked at each other blankly, shifting their weight from one leg to the other. Turning to Constanza, the neighbor gave a wan smile of encouragement.

"He's looking for your daughter—I'm sure of it. I guess he wanted to find her first before coming to bother you."

Constanza looked at the breads baking in the oven that would be the last of the day, maybe the last ever. If she could just have gone back in time to when the dough for those very loaves had been rising—how easy things would be! If they could return to that sunny, quiet morning with the air in the kitchen thick with the aroma of espresso and the building warmth of the oven, she would never have allowed Breva to leave. She would not have known emptiness, the yawning chasm of despair.

Tears burned her eyes, blurring the kitchen and the images of the two women standing wordlessly, breathing heavily. She didn't care a whit about the bread, about the bakery. The bread could burn, the bakery could burn. The whole of Venice could sink, for all she cared.

"I want my daughter!" she moaned, closing her eyes.

I can have all of this, even white flour, but I can't have my daughter, she thought. Cruel god—cruel *gods*. What had happened sounded like the sort of thing the gods of the ancients would do—not Jesus or the God she'd grown up knowing.

"Should we look for her, or do you want to stay here until she's found?" the older woman softly asked. "I mean, until they find her."

Constanza knew what she'd meant.

"I want to go find her," she said, her voice trembling as she watched her fingers twitching as they clutched the sides of her arms. "If they haven't found her yet, I'll find her. A mother is better at these things."

"Where should we look?" the bird-like woman asked.

"Near the studio—I want to search the streets around the studio."

That's the place Constanza felt drawn to search. If the gods would play with her, she should listen to what she was being told. She would have to go along with it, play whatever tragic game they were playing.

"Why toy with me?" she said aloud.

The women glanced at her quizzically. She waved away their concerned frowns. "Let's go then, to the studio."

Constanza stepped toward the doorway, herding them toward the calle.

"I'll just pick up these things before we leave—it'll take just a minute," the neighbor said, leaning toward the shrinking balls of dough, grabbing a large chunk of the ceramic bowl.

"I don't care—just leave it. I want to find my Breva," she said with finality, walking toward the open door and leaving the woman standing slack jawed behind her.

"You've forgotten your bread," the thin woman said, pointing at the oven. "I'll take it out for you."

"Let's just leave it—I don't care," she scoffed, motioning them from where they'd stalled in front of the door.

"They'll burn—the bread will burn," the skinny woman said incredulously.

"I don't care. Let it burn," she insisted, motioning them again to step outside of the bakery.

"But the coals—" she started to say.

"I don't care about the coals," Constanza said, her voice rising. "They can burn out or flare up. They won't burn down the building, if that's what you're worried about."

The bird-like woman stood her ground, refusing to exit the doors.

"I'll put them out for you," she said.

"Signora, kindly don't touch them," Constanza said. "I want them to burn."

Both of the women shook their heads, brows furrowed.

"I know it's a sin to burn bread, but I don't care."

The women avoided her gaze, their heads undoubtedly filled with thoughts of what punishment might still await her. Why would she provoke God so?

Constanza began closing the doors, and the two women hopped onto the cobblestone street likely realizing they had no option but to follow.

"You'll have to keep up with me—I want to get there quickly," Constanza gasped, pinning her flour-specked dress to her knees with a hand and breaking into an awkward, unsteady run.

"We'll be right behind you, signora," they called, running even more haphazardly. "But, don't go too far ahead of us, we can't run so fast."

She would run as fast and as far as she wanted, until she found her baby. And they could keep up with her or not.

"Signora, signora!" she could hear them calling from behind.

Out of breath, she thought her chest might explode, that she would stumble from exhaustion. Her legs felt leaden, stuck to the uneven cobblestones, and unwilling to move as she wanted. Running suddenly seemed so difficult, as if she were towing a wheelbarrow full of bricks.

Turning a corner, she passed some soldiers on a bridge overlooking the canal.

"Signora," they called, flirtatiously. "What's your hurry?"

What was she to say? Tell the truth? Shame them for their impertinence? Best that she ignore them—why should she care about them at all? Heading down the via, she realized she'd started scanning the murky waters of the canal. The studio was nearby, and Breva could be anywhere.

"Signora!" she heard the women's voices calling, echoing down the narrow street, mocking her. Passersby stood back, allowing her to pass, observing her flushed face and heaving chest. Could they tell by the desperate, crazed look on her face, did they sense immediately that her daughter was missing? Pedestrians in her path seemed to melt away, to duck into doorways or climb onto bridges.

The farther she got from the bakery, the faster she ran. And thoughts like stabs of pain pierced her. She was gone, her only daughter. She was dead already. Out to sea. Taken. Gone. Dead. Children don't disappear and then turn up. They've surrendered to the canals, to the sea, to God, to Poseidon, to whoever took babies and the young. Did it matter who they were? They were all the same to her.

That was the way of the city, the price that Venetians had been paying since they first erected their improbable houses on shaky foundations built upon swampy islands, carving a city out of the land and sea. Didn't the earth exact a price no matter where people built or how they lived their lives?

Crying, her breath hot against her cheeks, Constanza slowed to a walk, hanging her head, gasping for air. What was the point in running so fast? Why was she in such a hurry? She couldn't run anymore. If only she could breathe, maybe things would make sense, she could believe that the irrational thoughts flying through her head were rubbish. Her lungs expanded and collapsed, rose and fell, but still she couldn't breathe, couldn't pull in enough air to calm her frantically beating heart, which tapped furiously against her chest.

The women caught up with her, clutching her arms, their faces flushed and flecked with perspiration.

"Don't worry, don't worry," they said consolingly. The women wouldn't look at her face, but gazed sadly at her arms, which they stroked. "You shouldn't go so fast," the thin woman panted. "You'll make yourself sick."

They each gently dabbed their dress sleeves against Constanza's temples and forehead.

Why shouldn't she worry and what shouldn't she worry about?

Stupid women. Didn't they know? When your child is lost, you haven't lost your mind as well, though she knew it could happen.

After. After you knew.

Maybe they knew, sensing it in the air, as she did, but how could they have the same feeling when Breva had no connection to them, hadn't sprung from their loins, and didn't share the same blood?

But I can't give up hope, she told herself, her thoughts like a wildly swinging pendulum. One moment she felt convinced Breva was gone forever, that the sky and air felt heavy with loss, the bitter unfairness of life. Then she turned, thinking her daughter lived, could not have drowned somewhere alone, struggling against the waters that had always poured through these canals, lapping the edges of the city like a hungry tongue.

Despite her labored breath, she no longer ran, but walked quickly toward her husband's studio. Why did the city look so different, dirty, and shopworn? Familiar streets, which had once felt like home and had looked so appealing with their stone foundations, tile roofs, ochre, and orange-red walls, and gargoyles and shutters, now appeared sinister, capable of profound disappointment, searing loss. Had they always had this air about them?

Mounting a bridge, she stopped at the highest point, searching both sides of the canal, unable to take her eyes off the water.

"Breva," she called, peering down, her hand sheltering her eyes from the bright sky. "Breva!"

She didn't call into the water, but into the air, down the passageway lined with sidewalks created by the meandering canal. Such a maze!

The women hurried to her side, taking her arms and leading her down the other side of the bridge.

"Let's look down the canals—er, streets—closer to the studio," the bird-like woman suggested.

Stupid women. She would follow them, though, feeling as if she was losing any will of her own. What was the purpose in fighting, in asserting her will when the die had been cast? Like the waters that slipped and pushed through the city, she would allow the currents to carry her, cease pushing against them, and stop struggling.

I'm dying right here, she thought, gazing at the bleached sky.

"God doesn't want to show his face," she scoffed, gesturing upward. "He's hiding."

"Signora," the skinny one scolded, grimacing but avoiding Constanza's eyes. "You shouldn't say such things."

That must be how it felt, a letting go, a surrender.

"Have your way with me," she whispered.

The women exchanged looks as they guided her down the street. The younger of the two tripped on a cobblestone, nearly pulling Constanza down. But the two regained their balance, continuing their sloppy, hurried walk toward the studio.

As they rounded a corner, a faded fresco of the Virgin nestled in an alcove above them, and they could see a small cluster of people farther down the street. Mostly women, with the few men remaining in the city at work in the factories, the crowd swayed and undulated, moving like seaweed in the current.

Constanza's heart beat faster. Oh, no, why that crowd of people? What was happening?

Wordless, the three walked faster, heading directly for the group of people. When they were closer, they could make out a figure on the ground among the women standing in a malformed circle.

Constanza felt the two women gripping her arms tighter. *Leave me alone*, she longed to say, but couldn't speak, her tongue leaden. If she could have pushed them away, imploring them to leave, she would have, but she had scarcely enough will to move forward steadily, gradually. Clinging like barnacles, the women suffocated her, pulling the oxygen from the air, making it hard to breathe. She longed to be free of them, to charge the group of people and see what she would see, but her legs and voice seemed hardly her own.

It couldn't be! She told herself. She was mistaken.

The busybody women shouldn't worry; they should return to their homes and make dinner for their families, for their husbands. It was a man on the ground, not a little girl. There was no sobbing, no wailing, just a thick, ponderous quiet that haunted.

Between two women, she caught a glimpse of a jacket on the ground, a familiar gray jacket.

Piero's.

What was he doing on the ground, though? Had he been hurt, was it his arm? Then she realized the jacket contained a form that lay beside him, tucked into the curve of his body.

Pushing people away, clawing her way into the crowd, she knew in an instant that her daughter was dead.

"What have I done," she moaned. "Dio, what on earth have I done?"

Breva's fine straw-colored curls stuck to her apple cheeks and thin neck. Her baby looked like a street urchin, or something washed up by the sea. As if sleeping, her innocent face lay turned toward the sky with a blank expression.

Yes, it was her sweet daughter, but how transformed she was!

Lifeless, her sparkling eyes closed to the blue sky, her daughter resembled a rag doll.

How had this happened! How could she be dead!

No, no. She would squeeze her back to life, give her the will to return from wherever she'd gone, to occupy her little body once more and never wander the streets alone again.

"Dio, Dio!" she screeched, eyes cast upward to the pale sky.

"Constanza!" Piero cried, his face a muddle of tears. He tried to push more words from his mouth, but could only gasp and weep.

Constanza scarcely recognized him, his face bright red and contorted; his eyes small and full of terror. Lying on the ground, he clutched their daughter, slowly rocking back and forth as if he were about to put her to bed.

She would hug Breva, get down on the ground, too, and wallow, pushing her loins into the cold, hard cobblestones, begging for the earth to swallow her whole.

Every minute of the day seemed to have led to this one, and the days leading up to this day held shades of Breva's death. How could she not have seen? But, why was she being punished? And Breva, poor, innocent Breva, what had she done?

Her heart would break and she would collapse. Her knees felt weak, her throat dry, and choking. She grew aware of the women clutching her again, others pressing their hands against her back and shoulders.

"Leave!" she bellowed, beginning to sob. "Go, go!"

Falling, she felt the rough surface of the cobblestones rise up to meet her body, bruising the softness of her flesh. Rolling to the other side of Piero, she grasped Breva, pulling her from his arms and onto her chest. She fit so neatly, so easily there, as she never had when the girl's restless limbs had struggled against her mother's restraining embrace.

So cold, she was. Bitter cold, like the bottom of the lagoon or the chill winter ocean current. How long had she been in the water? How quickly had she died?

Did my baby suffer? Was it quick and painless, or full of pain?

Had she been frightened, or did it come so quickly that she didn't even know?

Curse Christ! Curse the gods. Curse the world and Venice. Why such a city, why a city of canals that takes children!

"Oh, let me die, too, cursed earth," she sobbed. "You may as well take me, too."

Moaning, Constanza clutched Breva to her chest. Rocking the child as if she were alive, she sobbed, seeing nothing but bright red and maroon. Were her eyes open or closed? She couldn't even say and wouldn't remember.

Piero rolled alongside her, nestling her head under his arm. "*Dispiace, mi dispiace*," he sobbed. "Forgive me, please."

"Get away!" she screamed, pushing him as she pulled Breva's small body more firmly to her bosom.

A mother should be alone with her dead child.

"Constanza, Constanza," Piero moaned. "Don't, per favore no," he begged.

"Leave me, leave me," she gasped, her lungs still denying her air, making her feel as if she'd drunk bottles of wine and needed to become sick.

She rolled away from her husband, curling Breva into her body, which from above looked like a question mark. Only there would be no one to see as the crowd had melted away, creeping back into their homes or to the nearby cafés to have a vin santo or grappa to help them calm their nerves, forget what they'd seen. Some peeked onto the street from behind curtains and closed shutters, simultaneously repulsed and intrigued by the drama unfolding in full daylight in front of their homes and shops. Helpless to pull themselves away, they watched, as the stories they'd heard from childhood now became reality. Some would go to church to pray, others would vow never to attend church again. And some would sail out past the lagoon, into the sea, allowing the waves to work with or against their boats, taking them where they might.

As for Constanza, she would never board a boat again, not even the cigar-shaped vaporetti that tracked between Venice and her home in Murano, leaving the churning and jade-colored lagoon waters in their wakes. As much as she would despise Venice, she would stay, refusing to leave the city that had taken her Breva, and wondering always if her wandering daughter might turn up somewhere, in some courtyard, or perhaps in a forgotten, crumbling doorway.

She never prayed again.

Chapter Fourteen

Whoever said Venetians exhibited the tendencies of a sloth had been mistaken, or at least they'd experienced a city radically different from that inhabited by Claudia, Louis concluded. Since that auspicious day when they'd signed the legal papers, enjoying an enormous, prosecco-drenched lunch in one of the private, upstairs dining rooms at Harry's, the normally languorous, stifling days of summer, thick with humidity and tourists, had been marked by perpetual, feverish activity.

Sacci had produced long-held sketches drafted by an architect friend, which were quickly finalized and submitted to the city. In the meantime, cleaning crews comprised of Sacci's family cousins and nieces and illegal, immigrant Czech girls showed up early before the heat of the day and took over the palazzo. As promised, Claudia's room was the first to receive attention, and she eagerly pitched in, getting on her knees to revive the parquet floors and lightly dusting the frescoes until their vibrant colors once again shined.

Plans for each day that fell between the signing of the partnership documents and the opening scheduled for late September were laid out by Sacci. He had drawn up a calendar that included major work, such as the construction or remodeling of bathrooms and the kitchen, as well as delivery dates for beds, silverware, lamps, armoires, and even bed linens. With the limited amount of money they possessed, Sacci and Claudia had little financial wiggle room and had to track carefully each expense. Early on, they'd decided Claudia should move into the palazzo as soon as the bathroom's plumbing was cleaned, tightened, and operational, which would save her six hundred thousand lire a month—a not inconsiderable sum that was diverted toward paying for the transformation of the palazzo.

"I can't believe I ever paid that much simply for a place to live," she confided to Louis. "If only I'd rented a smaller place like you have for half the amount I'm currently paying, I'd have a little more money to live on."

"Enough to keep you from growing thirsty for prosecco," he'd joked, but she scowled, her cheeks turning pink.

"I'm not thinking that way, anymore," she protested. "I'm trying to be serious about this and am really beginning to think I can do this, that Sacci's crazy notion isn't so far-fetched."

He blushed, feeling genuinely bad about having teased her. She'd become so sensitive, fragile even. But could he blame her? Since her mother had cut her off and she'd begun working on the palazzo, her life had changed completely. If he'd doubted her commitment to the hotel during the celebration luncheon when she'd insisted on pink, buttery orbs of foie gras and bottles of dark red Barbaresco, drinking so much she slurred, his mind was quickly changed in subsequent weeks—starting with how quickly she packed her belongings to be moved into the palazzo.

Claudia's bedroom was being quickly transformed, the cobwebs and dust having been cleared from the corners. She'd begged Louis to show up early on the day she'd planned to finish cleaning her bedroom and have her things moved from her apartment.

"Drink as much coffee as you need before coming," she'd warned. "There's no espresso machine—*yet*. That'll be the first thing we get."

He assumed that he would arrive at the worn marble front steps of the palazzo before his habitually late friend, but when he arrived at 8:00 AM, an hour later than he'd promised, the enormous wooden door stood ajar, a small note taped to the rusty bell chain.

Louis,
I'm upstairs.
Claudia
(You're late.)

Sheepishly, he pushed open the creaking door and peeked inside as light from the bright sky dispersed the shadows. The entry hall looked nearly as it had during his last visit—dust-covered pieces of furniture, stray pieces of paper, and bits of dirt in the corners. The walls of the palazzo were so thick he couldn't hear anyone. Creeping up the wide, marble stairs, he was surprised at how bright the upper floor became with many of the shutters opened. Sunlight blazed through the open windows and slats, illuminating the high-ceilinged space and catching the still-dusty glass pendants of the giant chandeliers. Though he'd only been in the building a few times, he instinctively walked into the upper salon and down the small passage toward Claudia's room.

He could hear her talking and other voices engaged in singsong conversation, and could hear the swish-swish of scrubbing. When he reached the threshold of Claudia's space, he saw a room already transformed.

Two teenagers, a boy and girl—probably Sacci's niece and nephew—sat on their haunches, chatting as they scrubbed the parquet floor with brushes. Claudia stood before the open windows, furiously cleaning the panels, a pile of white rags at her feet.

"Ah, Louis!" she cried, waving a rag. "Just in time. We have to get all this clean before the painters come. They're due any minute."

"In time for what?" he asked, as it looked like the two projects were only midway toward completion.

"Can you clean windows?" she asked.

"Sure. I cleaned windows for years—that was one of my chores when I was a kid."

"Without making streaks?—I can't stand streaks!" She pushed

the door half closed, pointing at the sunlight pouring through the panels—some of them streaked.

Louis stared at her in disbelief. That she might even notice a streaked window had never occurred to him. When the centuries-old palazzo was finally transformed, would anything or anyone remain familiar, Claudia included?

"I'll give it a try," he promised, wondering whether he would work any better or faster than she would.

But he was able to clean the windows, polishing them until they sparkled. By mid-afternoon, the room, as well as the stair, bathroom, and study on the level above, had been scrubbed, painted, polished, and waxed. The workers had arrived and had begun painting the walls of her room and the trim that didn't contain *trompe l'oeil* or frescoes.

"It's ready for me now," Claudia sighed, as the two of them sat on a sofa from her apartment watching the painters packing up their equipment for the day.

Louis walked on his aching legs to the hallway where he'd hidden a bucket of ice and a bottle of prosecco.

"Where are you going?" she called after him. "Let's rest a minute, okay?"

When he stepped back into the room with the bucket and sparkling wine, Claudia smiled.

"What a friend," she gushed. "I think I've very nearly forgotten what prosecco tastes like."

"Maybe it's premature," said Louis. "Maybe I should have saved it for tomorrow night when the painters are finished in here—"

"I'll need it to help me sleep here alone!" she interrupted, frowning slightly. "Tonight's the perfect night to have some bubbly. I haven't rested for the past two days, let alone sipped any prosecco, so pop it open."

Louis forced the cork, a deafening pop echoing through the half empty, but freshly painted and scrubbed room. He poured the light, honey-colored, bubbling liquid into the two glasses he'd brought from his apartment and handed Claudia the first one.

They toasted and Claudia drank until she drained the glass. Using her finger to catch a dribble that had escaped her mouth and run down her chin, she sighed heavily. "Oh," she said softly. "Delicious."

Louis poured her another glass as she leaned back into the sofa.

"I didn't realize how thirsty I was," she explained.

He smiled. Had she ever enjoyed a more deserved glass of prosecco?

Slouching farther into the sofa, she nestled the glass between her lower thighs, smiling contentedly. Within moments, she was gently snoring.

"Claudia?" Louis said, softly shaking her shoulder. "You should go to bed … er … I should help make your bed."

He glanced at the immense, unmade canopy bed that Sacci had taken from an unused room of his mother's house in Trieste and the pile of linens surrounding it.

But she continued snoring, her arms falling to her sides and her head dropping onto the arm of the sofa. One of her legs drooped to the side, releasing the nearly full glass of prosecco, which Louis barely caught before it fell to the floor.

He studied Claudia, having never seen her sleeping. Wisps of her dark hair and beads of perspiration clung to her forehead. Her nose was beyond shiny; actually, it looked oily. Bits of dirt showed beneath her fingernails, and her jeans and T-shirt were wrinkled and slightly dirty. If he hadn't known it was his good friend, he might not have recognized her.

Should he force her awake or let her sleep? As if she'd heard him pondering, her other leg shot forward as her torso fell completely into the sofa.

Perhaps it was right, after all, that they'd had the prosecco on that night. He closed the shutters tightly, leaving the slats open to admit the little bit of air circulating on the warm Venetian night. Soon the heady scent of gardenia and honeysuckle would waft through the air, perfuming the air of the palazzo as it would the terrace. Too bad the terrace wasn't more comfortable—it would be ideal to sleep out there on such a warm night. He turned up the ceiling fan to its highest speed, and flicked off the floor and mantle lamps, plunging the room into darkness. He stood by the fireplace, waiting for his eyes to adjust to the dark. When he could see again, thanks to the small bits of light filtering through the shutters, he made his way across the room to an armchair next to the sofa where Claudia slept. Feeling as exhausted as Claudia looked; he slouched down into the chair and quickly fell asleep.

What amazed him the most was the way she took to the worn building, caring for it as she might her own grandfather's revered palazzo. When she mentioned that she needed to buy books on caring for ancient mosaics, frescoes, and wood and he'd agreed to accompany her to Rizzoli, she sighed with disgust.

"Too expensive!" she'd exclaimed. "I'll pay a fortune for books that I could buy for a fraction of the cost at Il Turco. I don't need coffee-table books—I don't need photos at all," she'd declared. "I just need to know what to do."

Within a few days time, she'd become knowledgeable on what detergents to use, and what products to buy to treat everything in the palazzo worth saving or restoring. He wondered how she had even known about Il Turco, a small discount bookseller near the train station. And that she even gave a thought to cleaning and caring for the mosaics, frescoes, and wood surprised him. Had such thoughts, ideas, and tendencies lurked within her for years, patiently awaiting the right opportunity to bring them to the surface? Or were these thoughts and drive born of necessity?

Whatever, his Roman friend was quickly evolving into a transformed person. They would have some memorable lunches, first on the dirty terrace, which would be the last part of the palazzo to receive attention, but eventually on a terrace studded with market umbrellas that warded off the blinding, broiling summer sun. The smell of the lifeless, tepid waters of the canal, the distant sea, espresso machines, and simmering tomatoes and basil filled the air, especially during the hottest parts of the day. In the evenings, a breeze often sprang up, carrying fresher air from the Adriatic.

When Louis complimented Claudia on the oversize umbrellas she'd purchased, which dressed up the still neglected terrace, she waved her hand excitedly.

"We paid next to nothing for them—just for the materials. Sacci's mother has friends who make them for a company in America, and they agreed to make these all for free. They'd just like to be invited to the opening party."

Almost from the start, such luck seemed to mark the venture, and Louis grew confident that everything was falling into place. As if it were meant to be, exactly as it had felt from the moment Sacci had made his proposal to Claudia. And to think that he'd nearly gone to Crete instead of Venice—but then, maybe there'd never been any real chance that he would end up anywhere else. He wasn't a fatalist exactly, but didn't some things seem destined to turn out a certain way?

During one lunch on the terrace, Claudia sighed, looking around her at the still neglected surroundings. "If only there were some life out here," she lamented. "Anything at all to complement the umbrellas would give it some cheer. And I'm just tired of there being all this sun and sky, but nothing green."

And so Louis found himself infected, too, driven to help in a small way while his friend concentrated on bigger projects—the long list that Sacci had created. Noticing his friend's shorn fingernails and hands already calloused and discolored from wood stain and dirt, he headed to a garden store near the train station one afternoon when he'd finished another translation assignment for *Il Corriere della Sera*.

"What can I get that's fragrant, grows fast, and is colorful?" he'd asked the owner of the little shop. The little bent man pointed at terra-cotta pots of jasmine, honeysuckle, ivy, gardenias, petunias, and geraniums. The shuffling owner then led him to bigger pots containing sweet-smelling, shiny-leaved lemon trees and stately palms, but as it was, Louis would be withdrawing funds from the meager savings he'd put aside in his bank account, so he chose the less expensive, smaller plants. Any day another check would arrive for translating work, so he rationalized spending the money. Claudia needed the boost now—what good would it do to wait until summer was nearly over? The vines would need to start growing, and the flowers would bloom by the time of the hotel opening in September.

He knew that Claudia would be visiting furniture stores and a flea market on the mainland a few days later, so he arranged to have his secret purchases, enormous bags of soil, terra-cotta planters, and a variety of plants and flowers, delivered to the palazzo. Everything would arrive by boat, of course, and delivered through the once-neglected, already heavily trafficked main canal door of the palazzo. And Sacci would know about it, too, which gave Louis twice the pleasure when he thought about it.

Before she left on her shopping trip, he'd asked for the keys to the canal door.

"I've got a friend who's coming to help clean," he lied, hoping she wouldn't ask whom.

"That's wonderful," she answered, pressing two large keys into his palm. "We're still trying to get the kitchen cleaned up before the ovens and refrigerator are delivered."

"What about an espresso machine?" he asked hopefully, realizing he would easily surprise her. She appeared to have no idea what he was up to.

"Still haven't found one," she groaned. "We can't afford one that's grand—like the ones that you're always pointing out or the huge one at Tramonta. I know I promised one week ago that we'd have one, but I just haven't found the right one."

"But an espresso machine makes the place," he argued. "What self-respecting institution in this country doesn't have a big, shiny espresso machine?"

Claudia frowned. "I'd like to have one as much as you, believe me, but there's just no money for it. I'll keep looking for a used one that we can afford. It might not be so pretty, though."

She gathered her bags and glanced at her watch. "I've got to go—sorry, I'll be late."

Hurrying out the door to meet Sacci at the train station, she waved at Louis without turning around. The moment she was out the door, Louis raced to the newly connected phone—an old, clunky black one he'd insisted upon—and dialed the number for the plant shop.

Two hours later, a long, narrow boat pulled up at the canal doorway, sending waves up and over the giant stone doorstep to the palazzo. A muscled, middle-aged man unloaded the pots, dirt, and finally the plants.

"Where do they go?" he asked.

"I'll carry them up," Louis said. "I can't pay any more for delivery than I already have."

"*Con piacere*," the man explained, waving Louis aside. "I'm a childhood friend of Sacci, so this I do for free."

Louis shrugged and pointed at the terrace walls above them. "That's where I need them."

One by one, the man carefully raised each enormous terra-cotta pot and hauled it up the stairs. He gingerly deposited the pots and bags of soil in the shaded loggia. Sheepishly, Louis followed him each time, carrying the lighter flowers and plants. When everything sat grouped around a dirty metal table, he followed the man back down the stairs one final time, offering him a small tip, but the man refused.

"Please," he repeated, waving away the lire. "I'm a friend of Sacci."

Louis watched him untie the boat, start the outboard, and motor off down the canal. Quickly securing the iron courtyard gate and then latching and bolting the thick door behind him, he bounded up the stairs to the loggia. Filling the pots with the soil, he planted the flowers and vines, deciding to set the pots with the vines at the base of columns. The jasmine, he placed at the ends of the terrace, recalling that the storeowner had said they liked lots of sun. The small plants, which were already beginning to bloom, would spread their subtle fragrance across the terrace, maybe even through the large doors opening into the hallway.

When Claudia returned late in the afternoon, her arms full of packages, she found Louis waiting at the front door.

"How did you know I'd be home now?" she asked.

"Just had a feeling," he smirked.

He took her arm and led her up the stairs. "Let's have a prosecco," he suggested, having placed a bottle in a bucket of ice in the shade of the loggia a half an hour before she arrived.

"No way," she protested. "I've wasted nearly a whole day shopping and I've got too much to do."

"Just one, just a sip," he insisted, still unaccustomed to having to use any sort of persuasion to get Claudia to share a drink. "Come on."

Reluctantly, she agreed, following him up the stairs. The stairs had been cleaned and polished, the worn centers of the marble steps gleaming. Above her, an electrician balanced on a ladder, rewiring one of the immense chandeliers and changing worn-out bulbs. She wondered what all had been done while she'd been gone; feeling a nervous flutter in her chest at the wasted hours she'd spent shopping.

"What all did you find?" Louis asked, as they neared the top of the staircase.

"Headboards for nearly every room, three armoires, dressers, nightstands—and so many other things."

Listing all the items they'd found made her feel better, knowing she could mark the items off the list, which still seemed far too long.

"Did you get an espresso machine?" he asked timidly, annoyed that he still couldn't fix himself any coffee while he was there working, but had to run a few doors down to a coffee bar.

"Sacci wouldn't allow it—the strangest thing, really," she answered mysteriously. "He told me he had an old one that we could use, but he'd never mentioned it before. In fact, he said he's bringing it over this afternoon."

"That'll make the early mornings much easier for me," Louis sighed, disappointed that it would likely be a small, utilitarian espresso machine and not one of the grand, shiny machines that were the centerpiece of Italian cafés and restaurants. Well, at the start, maybe the place couldn't be perfect.

They hadn't even reached the doors to the loggia when Claudia spotted the greenery and pots outside.

"Oh, Louis! Who did this! Did you do this?" she cried, rushing through the doors and loggia and onto the terrace. She raced from planter to planter, tenderly feeling the different plants and flowers, almost as if petting them. "*Bellissima*! You've been busy this afternoon!"

"I just wish I'd had time to clean," he said with dismay, eyeing the dirty parapet wall, ledges, and tile floor.

"But it already looks so much better with some greenery, some life up here," she smiled. "Now I'll have to get someone to get the water working out here right away." She pointed to the rusted spigot, eyeing the few dozen planters that would need to be watered.

"You bought so many," she said, shaking her head. "I should pay you back—I *will* pay you back. But someday, not today."

"It was a gift," he said, shrugging. "I don't want to be paid for them. And besides, Sacci's friend worked at the nursery and gave me a deal."

Well, it wasn't a complete lie.

"That Sacci has Venice in the palm of his hand," she smiled. "He knows everyone."

Suddenly, Sacci's pugs raced onto the terrace, snorting and yipping. They eyed Louis and Claudia, speeding over on their tiny legs and running tight circles around them. Louis reached down snatching Tonto and pressing him against his chest.

"Sacci's back—he said he'd be bringing a surprise!" Claudia said, motioning for him to follow.

"But the prosecco—"

"Later, we'll drink it later," she interrupted. "I want to see Sacci's surprise. It's his first, you know. I don't think he's the type who's accustomed to engineering surprises. It's very intriguing."

Claudia walked quickly toward the doors and the hallway with

Louis directly behind, Tonto tucked under his arm. Tito and Torta noisily followed practically underfoot, occasionally pawing a calf or foot, still begging for attention. They hurried down the broad stairs, but the front door wasn't even open. Where was Sacci?

"Back here!" his voice called.

Louis heard a murmur of voices from the direction of the canal door. Whom was he talking to?

When they reached the end of the hall next to the oak paneled and marble clad vestibule of the canal entrance, the massive double doors stood open to the courtyard. Sacci stood in the small room, motioning and talking to someone just outside. Crowding behind him, Louis and Claudia peered over his shoulder, the dogs continuing to circle and bark.

A large boat was tied to the posts on the doorstep, and three men struggled with a burlap-wrapped pyramid-shaped object that was easily five feet wide at the base and perhaps just as tall.

"Careful, careful, per favore!" Sacci urged.

"What could it be!" Claudia exclaimed, trying to push Sacci aside to let her pass into the courtyard.

"It's coming in—better to stay out of the way," he said, gently pushing her behind him. "This way, this way!" he called to the men who struggled with the hulking object.

Sacci herded them away from the doorway, out of the vestibule. "*Cani*—out!" he barked, snapping his fingers at the dogs and directing them up the stairs. Whimpering and wide-eyed, the dogs raced halfway up the stairs watching the commotion below from the gaps between the twisting, marble balustrade posts.

The deliverymen, using small, strained steps, eased the package into the vestibule. Breathing heavily, they kept their eyes on the hulking object while following the sound of Sacci's voice.

"This way, this way," he called, inching down the corridor and toward the front of the palazzo.

"Where's it going?' Claudia asked. "What is it?"

"You'll see," he said, looking at Louis and winking.

Louis blushed and looked away. That was nothing, he told himself, annoyed at the way his heart lurched. Why did he continue to dissect the man's every word and gesture?

"Is it a piano, a harpsichord?" Claudia guessed.

Sacci shook his head slowly, keeping his eyes on the deliverymen and the package. He turned into the doorway of the dining room, standing there until the men caught up with him. At the end of the room, just outside the kitchen stood a large marble counter that hadn't been there the day before.

"Up here, up here," he directed, patting the counter.

"When did that get put in?" Louis asked.

"Beats me," Claudia answered. "Must've been this morning or yesterday afternoon."

Sacci smiled mischievously, rubbing his hands together.

The men slowly lifted the bulky item, sliding it carefully across the smooth white marble surface.

"Stop!" Sacci barked excitedly, motioning for them to stop moving it. "Perfetto. Now, the unveiling."

Smiling self-consciously and reaching for the burlap covering, he found a seam and began tearing upward with small, precise movements. When he'd torn the seam as far up as he could reach, he waved the workers to the other side of the counter. "Now pull it away—carefully, though—you don't want to damage the top!"

As the workers pulled away the burlap, shiny gold and silver sculptures, canisters, and pipes appeared. The pugs that had crept into the room, barked as the machine was unveiled, jumping on their hind legs, but cowering in the back of the room.

"It's the most incredible, beautiful espresso machine I've ever seen!" Claudia gasped.

It must have been twice the size of the one at Tramonta. At its top, an angel flew, its massive gold wings spreading outward above the domes and wisps of clouds fashioned from forged bits of metal below it. At the angel's feet, doves flew, surrounding a small group of old Roman letters which read SPIRITO.

"Where did you get it?" Louis asked. "I've never seen one so big or with so much detail." It was true—even the old cafés in Rome and Milan didn't boast such a unique machine. "And I've never seen one with an angel atop it."

Sacci beamed. "It was sheer luck," he explained. "Last week there was a flyer in my mailbox announcing that someone possessed an old, retooled espresso machine, originally used in an old hotel on the Lido."

"But it must have cost a fortune!" Claudia scolded, circling the machine in an attempt to see every feature. "It's so shiny and clean it looks new. And that angel!"

Sacci laughed, shaking his head. "No, that's the thing that's even stranger. The sellers were asking for the best offer—can you believe? I can't imagine what it's worth, but they just wanted to get rid of it, they were moving or something and wanted it out of their palazzo."

"But why did they have it refurbished and cleaned just to sell it?" Louis asked.

Sacci shrugged. "I hadn't thought to ask."

"So how much did you pay for it?" Claudia asked, her eyebrows crinkling.

"A hundred thousand lire," he answered proudly.

"That's not even a hundred dollars," Louis said. "That can't be. You can't even buy a little countertop DeLonghi for that price."

"No, no, that was the price. The owner really just wanted to give it to someone who would use it and not a collector."

"But there must have been many others interested in it. How did they decide to sell it to you?" Louis asked.

Sacci nodded, as if equally surprised. "I guess I—*we*—just got lucky. I was amazed, too, that I was the one who ended up with it. But then, like so many other things that are falling together, it felt like it was meant to be."

"That the seller meant for you to have it?" Louis asked. "That's crazy."

"Exactly," Sacci said.

Running her fingers across one of the gleaming domes, Claudia pursed her lips. "So who were the owners?"

"I don't know," Sacci answered. "There was a middleman, some number that I called and I did everything over the phone. I'm not even sure where it came from, which palazzo or hotel. And stranger than that, when I offered a million lire if I liked it upon seeing it, the man I spoke with said the owner just wanted to get rid of it so he'd take a thousand. *And* they'd have it delivered. He said it was used and that they'd have their workers clean it up for us."

"Sounds suspicious," Louis suggested. "Do you think it's stolen?"

"I don't know, but why question good fortune, eh?" He turned toward Louis. "I thought about how often you said that a big, beautiful machine would be essential, and I couldn't believe our luck. So why be suspicious? If the gods smile on you, smile back."

Claudia shook her head. "It just sounds too good to be true, and when I was in America, they always warned about accepting offers that sounded too good to be true."

"But what can possibly go wrong with this?" Sacci asked, tapping one of the shiny pipes of the machine.

"Does it work? Did you try it?" Louis asked.

"No, but for a hundred dollars, even if it doesn't work, it'll look good in this room, right?" Sacci smirked.

"Why didn't anyone else want it? I still can't believe that no one got to it before you did, that there wasn't a bidding war," Claudia said, perplexed.

"That was the other odd thing—I asked the neighbors if anyone else received the flyer, but it appears that I might have been the only to receive it," he said, shrugging again. "But maybe they didn't look closely at their mail. Maybe the other flyers got lost. Or possibly the previous owners heard I was opening a hotel and thought I could use it."

"It really does sound like someone wanted you to have it," Louis suggested. But who would just give away an antique espresso machine worth thousands, if not tens of thousands of dollars?

Claudia continued puzzling, shaking her head while gazing at the machine. "It's beautiful, and we needed just such a machine, and you were right, Louis that it would be outstanding in the dining room, but there's something suspicious about it."

"Do you think someone in your family, your mother maybe, arranged for you to get this?" Louis asked.

Frowning, Claudia shook her head. "It doesn't make sense to me that this seemingly fell from the sky, but on the other hand, my mother couldn't possibly be behind it. She's not the sort to kiss and make up or to do kind things behind the scenes. And my papà would never do such a thing behind her back. Still, someone wanted this to be in the hotel."

"Tsk-tsk," Sacci scolded. "This is no Trojan horse—if you want, peek inside the water and steam drums, tap your knuckles on the sides."

To demonstrate, he rapped his hand against one of the copper drums. "See, *hollow*—that is, until we put some water in it and get it going. The gods won't like such doubt, the way you question their generosity," he snickered.

"Signore, can you pay us so we can be on our way?" one of the deliverymen interrupted.

"Scusi!" Sacci apologized, reaching for an envelope sticking out of his back pocket. Handing the envelope to the man, he thanked him and the other men and herded them out of the room and back toward the canal door.

"Just a minute!" Claudia shouted, following them into the hall. "May I ask where you picked up this machine? Who delivered it to you? Where did you get it?"

The deliveryman who had taken the envelope turned to Claudia.

"Sure, but it's a mystery to us, as well. A very unusual pick-up, to be sure."

"So tell us," she urged.

"The train station, signori," he said, twisting his lip as if confused.

"It was in the freight room, but it had no shipping papers, no tags whatsoever."

"What did they say at the station? How did they know then that it was for you?" she asked, tugging at one of her small earlobes.

"We had special instructions, ask for the large item for delivery to this palazzo, and the clerk showed us this," the man said. He shrugged, turning back toward the door. "And that's all I know. But I agree with your friend here," he said, nodding at Sacci. "No sense questioning—someone wants you to have this, and so you should have it."

He and the other men hurried back through the gate, untying the now-empty boat and jumping into it. Sacci waved, closing and locking the iron gate behind them while the flat-bottomed boat puttered down the canal, leaving in its wake small waves lapping at the oversize, moss-encrusted doorstep.

"I'll leave the door open for the evening to let in some fresh air," he said, waving Louis and Claudia back into the hallway. "Now, let's try this machine, okay?" he urged, steering Louis toward the dining room.

For the remainder of the summer, Claudia's days fell into a routine of sorts. She rose early because she went to bed early. And she went to bed early for a few reasons, the most notable being that she was exhausted, a bone-weary fatigue such as she'd never experienced.

Her world had shrunk, consisting of the palazzo, terrace, and the immediate neighborhood. Occasionally, Louis or Sacci would force her to go for lunch or dinner or just cocktails. If she drank two Negroni—or even a few glasses of wine—her body would ache for the comforting embrace of her bed. In the course of a few months, she'd lost all desire to stay out late and to haunt the few nightclubs and cafés around San Marco as she'd used to. What she longed for most as the day faded to night was to take a quick bath in the old marble tub, watching as the sky turned from turquoise to cobalt and finally to midnight blue. By the time the stars hung heavy over the city and nearby Adriatic, her eyelids would droop and then she would drain the tub, and stumble down the stairs to the enormous, canopy bed.

She had hung a large chalkboard in the kitchen, which contained the schedule for all the remaining major tasks. She studied the list only once, in the morning, because seeing it before she went to bed made her anxious. New baths and plumbing had been installed in each guest room, but the workers couldn't install the wall tile until the plasterers had redone the walls. And the electricians were running behind schedule, which she began to worry might throw everything off because she would then need to have the plasterers come twice—once after the plumbers and before the tile workers and again after the electricians finished blasting access points into the thick walls so they could rewire the palazzo.

When anything ran close to schedule—too close to schedule—she began to panic, wondering if the whole elaborate, delicately-balanced plan, budgeted to the lira and to the hour, would come crashing down around them. On these days, Louis—who stopped by nearly every day—would beg her to accompany him to Café Tramonta, to Harry's, or farther afield to one of the cafés across the Giudecca Canal for a short break.

"You've got to get away for a few hours, have some prosecco or a cocktail," he urged.

But what she most needed when the entire project appeared to be in jeopardy—and what he eventually came to understand—was to work twice as hard, twice as fast, and sometimes late into the night to get ahead in one area if they appeared to be falling behind in another.

They couldn't afford to pay the workers extra to work faster, or longer, so she tried to balance flirting with them and cajoling them while taking care not to divert them too much from their work. The entire enterprise gave her headaches and anxiety at first, but as the weeks passed, she grew to enjoy the challenge, and she vowed she would open the hotel on time and at budget. One of her key strengths, which surprised herself as well as Louis, was her ability to persuade the artisans to lower their prices or to work longer.

"We're just like you," she reminded them. "We're not a big Swiss hotel chain, we're Italian, and we're simply trying to bring back a bit of Venetian history. Did you know Marco Polo's sister lived here? And that there are remains of a Roman bath and temple beneath the foundation? It has a very good feeling, don't you think? And it's got to be good for a person—any person—to help with such a project, eh?"

The workers mostly agreed, managing to get the project back on schedule whenever things fell behind. She promised other things, too, like invitations to the opening night party—an event like Venice hasn't seen for years—and for each of them to bring a guest and stay the night.

"And you can always stop by in the morning before work for a free cappuccino," she would add, casting an appreciative look at Louis if he was in the room.

After she'd turned down Louis' invitations to go for cocktails several times, he looked at her with an impish grin. "Who are you?" he asked. "And what have you done with my friend Claudia?"

One by one, the second and third floor bedrooms neared completion. Some of the rooms remained oddly empty, though, as it made little sense to bring in furniture that would only get dirty with all the plastering, drilling, refinishing, and painting still underway in some sections of the palazzo. But some pieces did arrive—eight creaky, walnut armoires for the third floor rooms, old armchairs and ottomans they'd purchased from a hotel that was closing in Verona and had been reupholstered, and table and floor lamps. The tables for the dining room had arrived, which she immediately covered with sheets since the only task remaining in that room was to paint.

Together, she, Sacci, and Louis chose the colors for each room deciding on rich, deep hues that evoked the Renaissance. The dining room would be burgundy-red, which would highlight the dark brown carved beams and the faded, but still colorful pastoral designs. And the lower sala, which would have a bar and wine cabinet in the corner, would be royal blue.

Sacci came through with more incredible furniture—an enormous stone fountain for the terrace from the decrepit villa of an elderly uncle, oversize wingback armchairs for the lower sala, urns for the entrance, and the highlight, an antique, elaborately carved oak counter that would serve as the reception desk.

This time, when she peppered him with questions about how much he'd paid for the items and how he'd found such unique pieces that hadn't been accounted for in the budget, he made it sound as if they'd come from a friend of a friend. She was suspicious again, but what could she do? If he had additional money to spend and wanted to use it on the hotel, why should she be bothered?

When she'd shaken her head upon seeing the reception desk arrive, she realized the deliverymen looked familiar—perhaps the same ones who had delivered the espresso machine. One of them shook his head back at her, only more emphatically.

"It's bad luck to question good luck," he'd said, clucking his tongue. "The gods smile on you."

Perhaps she was being cynical, paranoid even. Why should good fortune arouse so much suspicion? Because she'd never encountered such good luck, had never known such contentment, did that mean she should question it? Still, she wasn't one to believe in a god who acted in mysterious ways. No, her informal schooling had drummed all of her childhood superstitions (many imparted by her mother) out of her head.

"But you act as superstitious as someone who believes in the Father, Son, and Holy Spirit," Sacci had observed. "Your beliefs are simply the reverse. If good things happen, it's not to be trusted. You believe just as much as old church ladies that there are forces at work."

She protested, but wondered later if he might have a point. Just what did she believe, anyway? Perhaps if she were tested, forced to pray for something as if it were life or death, maybe the life of a daughter or something having to do with Louis, then would she believe?

The first week of August, early in the morning before the heat rose from the cobblestones, the warm waters of the canals, and the brick and stone walls of the palazzi, houses and buildings, another delivery boat pulled alongside the canal door of the hotel. (A gray granite stone with *PALAZZO SPIRITO* etched into it had recently been embedded in the wall next to the gate). Claudia had risen early to greet the boat and open the gate and doorway. She'd arranged and expected the delivery, so this time she knew exactly what was contained in the hulking crate on the flat boat.

Even though she'd been living there by herself for only a few months, she'd grown accustomed to the building and no longer felt alone. The deliverymen must have thought her strange, especially after she showed them into the cavernous entry hall and down its length to the dining room and finally the kitchen. The palazzo lay completely silent.

"There, against that old tile," she'd said, pointing to the empty space in the kitchen that would house the new stove and ovens. "Everything's ready for it to be hooked up, so it shouldn't take long."

She followed them back out to the door, watched the five men heave the stove and then the ovens onto the stone doorstep, and eventually onto flat dollies, which they rolled all the way to the kitchen.

They were just finishing installing and testing the ovens when the entry bell rang.

"Scusi," she said to the workers, rushing out of the kitchen for the front door. "Ah, Louis!" she beamed, motioning him in with a quick wave. "Hurry, you're just in time to see the new stove and ovens!"

They rushed into the kitchen just as the deliverymen were finishing.

"Signora, they work *perfettamente*."

"*Bravvissimi*," she cheered. "Now I just need to learn how to cook and bake."

The men looked at her strangely again, as they had when she'd led them through the giant palazzo by herself. No doubt, women who remained in Venice cooked and cleaned. They didn't open hotels.

"Come by for a cappuccino and breakfast when we're open," she urged as the men reboarded the boat. "*Mi dispiace*, but that's the best I can do for a tip."

As soon as she was back in the palazzo, she turned to Louis.

"Dai, what am I to do now?" she moaned.

"It's not so bad that you didn't tip them," Louis lied, wondering if they would deliver things late and without much care the next time. "They'll understand to return for breakfast."

"No, no," Claudia sighed. "It's time now for me to start thinking of when this place is open—not all the plumbing, electrical, plastering, and painting. The end's in sight."

Louis stared at her blankly. "I don't understand."

"Who's going to make breakfast?" she asked, eyeing him meaningfully.

"Don't look at me, *cara*," he protested. "I don't cook or bake. I can make espresso and cappuccino, that's all."

"Why can't you master the oven and stove the way you did the espresso machine? You made that thing come alive and you taught yourself. Couldn't you do the same for the hotel—just 'til we find someone who can do it?"

"You know I can't do it—I have to work. I'd do anything to help with the hotel; you know that, but this I can't do."

"It's only breakfast—it would be easy. You just bake the bread, pastries, and cornetti early in the morning, then when the guests come down to eat you cook ..." She trailed off, sounding uncertain. "Okay, so what do I do? I need someone who can cook and bake—just basic items, but they have to be done beautifully. We have to serve the tastiest pastries in the city. But I can't pay a chef or baker—I can hardly afford to hire a cook."

Claudia's brow furrowed, her eyebrows tickling her forehead. Her eyes bore into her friend's face.

Louis waved his hands as if to erase the image she'd created.

"I'd have to get up *every* morning," he said. "Think about it—can you imagine me rising by four o'clock every morning, baking and then cooking for hotel guests until, what, ten or eleven o'clock? And then when would I do my work?"

Claudia sighed. He was right: her idea would never work. But she would have to have bread and pastries from someone. Buying dried-out, flavorless baked goods from one of the established suppliers would never do.

"There have to be plenty of part-time bakers around, maybe a mother who can't bake full-time because of having kids to watch. Or maybe someone doesn't want to work full-time. Certainly you could find someone like that, and then just hire a line cook to prepare eggs and French toast," he suggested, relieved when she began nodding.

She liked the idea, but how would she ever find such a person? The odds seemed remote.

"So how do I find one? And what if I get one and their pastries aren't good enough? I mean, if they haven't sold commercially or they don't have clients or customers, how would I know if they bake anything exceptional?"

"Try an ad in the paper, or some flyers," Louis suggested. "I'm at the fish market every couple of days and I could distribute some flyers there. In fact, I'm friendly with the owners of the bar there and I bet they'd put up a flyer if I asked them. And determining whether they make stuff that's any good is easy—they have to try out."

"Try out?" she asked, perplexed.

He too often took for granted that she understood his American English given all the time she'd spent in New York, but every once in awhile he used an expression that confused her. He stood up, moved next to her, and began to prepare coffee for them. He pulled the lever for the steam and the machine came to life, gurgling and hissing.

"They have to bake you some samples. You get to try them out before you hire them, understand?"

Claudia's head nodded again. "Sì, sì, I could do that," she said. "That would work."

"I can do the flyer for you, if you want. I'll just put your number and name on it, and I'll make sure to include something about the fact that you're not looking for an average baker, but someone with some flair, maybe an old way of doing things. I'll think of something," he said, feeling relief that his contribution no longer had to involve learning to bake or rising early every morning.

Claudia paused, a worried expression clouding her face again.

"But what if we don't find anyone?"

"Don't worry," Louis said. "You'll find someone. Remember what Sacci said, okay? And don't be so pessimistic. So far everything has gone your way, so this will happen, too."

He couldn't believe he was philosophizing, advising her to be optimistic. Did he sound like a Hare Krishna?

Two days later, he'd posted flyers at Café Tramonta, the fish market, the library, the train station, and on walls in the neighborhood that had anything affixed to them. Within another day, Claudia had received half a dozen calls. He stopped by in the morning to make their coffee and find out if she had any interesting prospects.

"No one I talked to makes everything—they either do bread or pastries, or they do just simple things," she said, looking perplexed.

"No one sounded possible?" Louis asked.

"Except for one," she said, hesitating.

"Except for one? Why do you sound troubled?"

"She told me she had once owned the best bakery in Venice, that she'd been asked to make cornetti and pies for General Patton when he visited during the war after the liberation—"

"What? Snatch her up. Tell her yes! She sounds exactly like the person you're looking for—though maybe a little old."

Claudia leaned on the counter, fidgeting with one of the polished levers on the giant espresso machine, which had begun to hiss loudly. Studying the spreading wings of the angel, she ran her hand back and forth across the smooth marble counter.

"She sounded odd," she mused. "Strange, I mean."

"You don't need to be best friends with her," he countered, placing two cups beneath the espresso spouts. "Just find out if she can bake and if you can depend on her. What did you tell her?"

Propping her chin in her hands, she told him, "I lied and told her we'd already found someone."

"Why did you do that?" he asked, sounding angrier than he'd intended. It was just that her response sounded so irrational, more like the old Claudia. Sacci and the deliverymen were right: why did she have to question everything?

"I wasn't certain, and there was just something strange about her. I don't know. So I thought maybe it wasn't a good fit, if I felt uncertain about her, I mean." She frowned and pulled locks of her dark brown hair in front of her eyes, studying the uneven ends.

"Maybe you could have met her first, or tried her baking. Who knows, maybe she's just awkward on the phone," he sighed, pulling two shots into one of the hotel's cups that had just arrived a few days earlier. *Palazzo San Spirito* had been printed on the side in flat, gold script.

"I know, I know," she muttered, observing his eyes on the misprinted cups. "I've already asked them to redo the order—this time with the correct name on them."

Louis placed a demitasse spoon on a saucer, along with a few anise-flavored cookies. He figured they might as well get used to having their coffees the same way all the guests would. And he had a feeling he'd be working the machine from time to time—at least until she found someone she could afford to pay to work it. After he finished steaming milk and mixing his cappuccino, he carried the two drinks out of the bar, setting them onto one of the dining room tables draped with a white sheet. Though the dining room was finished, the well-applied plaster smooth, the polished beams aglow, and the refurbished mosaic tile floor glossy, Claudia was keeping the furniture covered—or as much of it as she could. She thought that everything should remain hidden behind closed doors, or covered until the last possible moment.

"The woman sounds intriguing," Louis said, returning to the subject of the baker.

"But that's not all," Claudia started to explain. "The other odd thing was that she sensed that we were somehow connected, though she couldn't say how. She told me she'd passed the palazzo a hundred times since the work started and yet had never seen me, as if she ought to have."

"That's how all Venetians are," he observed, noisily sipping his drink. She sounded interesting, probably the perfect baker for the palazzo. The hotel ought to have a baker that had a story, some character, and not someone fresh out of culinary school who baked only for money.

She nodded her head reluctantly. "Still, she made me feel uncomfortable. She acted like she'd been waiting for this job for years, telling me that she'd not baked since the war. Can you believe that? She must be around eighty."

"If she can bake, who cares? But what does it matter—the opportunity's lost now," Louis said. "So who else sounded possible—even remotely?"

"No one," Claudia answered, gulping the last swallow of her espresso. She wiped the corners of her mouth with her index finger, looking back at the machine. "I guess I should call her then."

"Call her? Call who?"

"The woman. She left her number in case I changed my mind."

"What's her name?"

"She didn't say. See, isn't that strange? I didn't realize until I'd hung up the phone that she'd never even told me her name."

"I'd call that lucky," he chuckled. "I'd call her and have her send some samples over. If you think you can count on her, and her stuff is good, then I'd hire her. That's what I'd do, anyway. You can find out her name later."

He stood up, taking both their cups and walking back to the machine. While he prepared four more shots, he peeked over the side of the machine.

"You're not at all superstitious, are you?" she asked.

"I didn't think *you* were," he chided. "What do you think is bad luck about this woman?"

"It's just a feeling, that's all," she shrugged.

"A feeling that this woman is dishonest, that she's bad? I don't understand."

The machine started hissing, the steam rattling the metal chamber. The angel's wings atop the tank vibrated, shaking imperceptibly as the steam built up inside.

"It's just that there's something about her, that's all, and I can't figure out exactly what it is. Don't you think it's strange that she acts like she knows me, that she was expecting this job?"

"Maybe she has a point. She sounds perfect," he shrugged, thinking of the conversation he'd had with his mother a few months ago. "You could just go with that."

"Okay, okay, I'll call her," she said, waving at him to bring the coffee over quickly. "Just as soon as we finish painting the second floor sala. It's the third and *last* coat."

He brought over the refilled cups, the steaming espresso topped with caramel-colored crema, and his cappuccino capped with a creamy-white crown, a nut-brown swirl of color twisting through its center. She wondered if he missed the days when they would meet at Café Tramonta and he would order his two drinks at once, such an impulsive, American thing to do. Had she really ever ordered prosecco in the mornings? Now all she wanted was coffee—and lots of it. And then perhaps a glass or two of prosecco or wine in the evening to gently nudge her into a deep sleep after a long day of painting, sanding, polishing, cleaning, waxing, and sweeping.

"I was going to translate today—I'm behind," Louis explained tentatively. He ran his finger across the edge of his cup, avoiding Claudia's eyes.

"Please, please, for just a few hours," she begged. "Then I promise to let you go do your work."

"I'll be up so late tonight getting everything done. I really shouldn't," he said, looking genuinely sorry.

"Sacci's coming," she said, her face brightening. "And he's going to help, too. We can paint together—the three of us."

Louis studied his friend's face. What did she mean; did she

somehow know about his months-long crush on Sacci? But she smiled innocently, leading him to think he was simply being paranoid. How could she possibly know, he hadn't said a word about the crush to anyone—and for good reason. The relationship was going nowhere, and he knew that, but just couldn't get rid of the nagging, love-struck feeling that surged every time he saw the guy.

The more he saw of Sacci, the more he felt drawn to him. All the work on the hotel, the daily visits, the weekends, the all-consuming transformation of the neglected palazzo into a hotel, made his feelings for Sacci that much stronger. As much as he fought it, his crush remained, settling into his insides. It was as if the three of them, he, Claudia, and Sacci were all partners, though he was merely Claudia's best friend. But what was he to Sacci?

Maybe, just maybe he could ask him for a drink, or make some sign that might make it clear to Sacci that he liked him. But if he did and Sacci wasn't even gay, then what? What if the man was repulsed, if he didn't want Louis hanging around the hotel? Of course, he would still have his friendship with Claudia—he would always have that. But what if it made things awkward, and this while Claudia was so stressed with opening the hotel. The time couldn't be worse to pursue his crush. That he'd somehow been able to sustain it—or more accurately, that it had been sustained in him—was bad luck.

This crush felt different, though. Deep within, he had the understanding that he should be patient and wait to see how things played out, not attempt to force anything this time. Just as he urged Claudia to trust and believe that things would turn out, so he told himself that he should do the same with Sacci.

Though he couldn't place his finger on it, he felt certain that there was something to this crush—something different was going to happen this time.

When Louis rang the door chime, the hour was seven o'clock. Every once in a while, he saw clearly how much Claudia had changed.

When he'd first met her, she was the type to rise late, having spent much of the early morning hours at one of the cafés, nightclubs, or bars. Now she rose before he did, forcing him to adopt her strange hours. If his parents had imposed such demands on him, he would have called them uptight, puritanical. But things seemed different now, and as much as he wanted parts of the old Claudia back, he enjoyed watching her come alive. There was certainly more to her than she had let on, perhaps more than she'd known herself.

Claudia opened the door quickly, as if she'd already been heading toward it when he'd rung. She looked excited, her cheeks colorful and her eyes bright. They kissed on the cheeks before she waved him in.

"Please, I need my coffee," she cried, walking quickly toward the dining room and motioning him to follow. "They've arrived—and they smell incredible."

"What time did they get here?"

"Exactly at six-thirty," she smiled, looking impressed and hopeful.

"Good sign—see, I told you she sounded good to me."

Louis ducked behind the bar, turning the steam lever, and preparing two portafilters with ground espresso. The smell of the freshly ground beans wafted toward Claudia who stood in the dining room.

"I'll get the milk," she said, heading into the kitchen.

A moment later, she returned with the milk in her hand and two baskets covered with checked cloths. Setting the baskets on the nearby table, she removed the cloths revealing golden rolls, flaky cornetti, mini baguettes, and mini crostate. She handed the milk to Louis, then leaned against the counter, smiling.

Despite the heady scent of the espresso, Louis detected the sweet, yeasty smell of the breads and pastries. "Where are they?" he asked. "I can smell them—I want one!"

"As soon as you finish the coffee we can try them. There are two baskets, so we've got a lot of eating to do."

Louis quickly finished preparing the coffee before they took their usual spots at one of the smaller tables.

Claudia had placed small white plates with the incorrect hotel name on them at the table, and she ripped the pastries in half, setting a portion on each plate. In moments, both plates were full.

"Cheers!" she chuckled, and tapped her tiny cup against the side of his larger cappuccino cup.

"Cheers!" he echoed, picking up his cup.

Then as if a gun had gone off at a horse race, the two started devouring the sweet-smelling contents of the baskets. Halfway through their feast, Sacci appeared in the doorway.

"Sit down!" Claudia called. "You've got to try these pastries and bread. They're incredible."

"Can I get a cappuccino to go with them?" he timidly asked.

Louis popped up and hurried behind the towering machine.

"Claudia, this baker is incredible—she's the one you need to hire," Louis assured her, steaming a cup of milk.

Claudia took another bite of an apple crostata. Brushing away flakes from her chin, she nodded. "I don't know that I've had such pastries or breads—anywhere, not even in Rome."

The machine thumped and hissed, echoing through the room and threatening to drown out Sacci and Claudia's voices. Working quickly, nervously, Louis made Sacci's cappuccino and brought it to the table. Lately, Sacci had been arriving at the palazzo just as Louis was making a second round of coffees, and he had started sitting with them at the littlest, simple wooden table in the hushed, cavernous dining room.

The week before, Sacci told Louis that he had operated the machine like a true barista, like an Italian. Louis had blushed, hiding his face behind the steaming, metallic behemoth, hoping he would somehow make a perfect coffee that would express what his tongue could not.

"Try the pastries," Louis suggested, sliding the half-full basket across the table.

Sacci tore a piece from a mini baguette, pushing it into his mouth. He chewed the bread thoughtfully. "Oh, Dio, this is perfect bread."

After they'd eaten nearly all the bread, including a petite round loaf, cocoa-colored and encrusted with seeds, minced herbs, and specks of sea salt, Claudia slapped the table.

"I'm going to hire her," she announced, eyeing the baskets, which now contained only a few crusts of bread, the flaky end of a crostata and crumbs. "I'll call her right now."

"You can cross that off the list ahead of schedule," Sacci joked. "I couldn't even think about it, didn't know where we'd find someone or how it would turn out. But like everything else, it just fell into place."

Jumping up from the table, Claudia grabbed the phone. "Louis was the one who made it happen," she admitted. "I wasn't sure about the woman, but he convinced me. And now I'm certain she's the one."

Sacci nodded, as if what she were telling him sounded familiar, expected even. "He has good judgment," he remarked.

Louis blushed, this time without the machine to hide his face. He smiled sheepishly, scraping a remnant of milk froth from the bottom of his cup with a spoon. He could feel Sacci's eyes on him, both of their expectant gazes on him, actually, so he awkwardly pushed himself up from the table.

"You call, and we'll get to work upstairs on the sala walls," he announced a little too loudly. "I mean, we'll just start to get things ready to go."

"I don't even know what to tell her we'll pay," Claudia said appearing self-absorbed. "What do you pay for boxes of baked goods, for such a variety of things?" she asked, her face falling in embarrassment. "I completely forgot to check with other hotels to see what the going rate is."

"Don't worry about it," Louis advised. "I think you can trust her. See what price she quotes and if sounds too high, tell her you'll get back to her to see if it's within your budget."

"Bravo," Sacci said, causing Louis to blush again.

Louis gripped his arm, digging his nails into his wrist just enough that it took his mind off Sacci.

"Okay, then, that's what I'll do," Claudia said, sounding more confident.

"We just apply the last coat of paint, right?" Louis asked.

"Exactly," she answered, pulling the woman's phone number from her pocket. "I'll join you two in just a minute."

Louis looked at Sacci. "Shall we?"

His friend nodded and the pair headed out of the room toward the upper sala. Louis felt strangely aware of each step they took down the long hallway. They climbed the grand marble stairs to the upper sala, which was still cluttered from the previous day's painting, its floors covered with tarps and three ladders in varying heights standing at the parameters.

Louis sensed Sacci following close behind. Why did things have to be so complicated, why couldn't he develop a crush on someone he could have? He relished the thought of spending the morning, perhaps the whole day with the man, but at the same time felt depressed.

He should tell him, or give him some sort of sign that would be unmistakable. And what would it hurt to be open and honest? Yes, maybe he'd be spurned, but knowing would be better than the constant doubt and uncertainty that so often colored his mood from bright to dark.

"You seem bothered," Sacci said as they stood in the sala. "Do you feel okay?"

"It's nothing," Louis lied. "I'm just a little tired."

Could he really tell him what he was thinking? No, Sacci would have to sense it, and how could he not? Why would Louis be spending all of these hours with him, even Friday and Saturday nights, which he used to spend in cafés or at Harry's?

But no, he must already know. And in typical Venetian fashion, he maintained a polite facade. Of course, wasn't he Catholic, too, just like the contessa? Didn't he subscribe to the pope's views? Sure, he was modern enough to accept gays, to tolerate them—even be friends with one, perhaps—but that was likely as far as it went. Even if deep down he harbored gay tendencies.

Of course, Louis had been wrong before, having a string of unrequited crushes on guys who turned out to be straight—or at least uninterested in being gay. That was the problem with liking guys who acted and looked straight—most of them *were* straight.

Since he was the taller of the two, Louis volunteered to climb the ladder to paint the upper parts of the walls.

"You're a good friend to Claudia," Sacci said, loosening the lid of a paint can.

"I do it for you, too," he answered. "You're both good friends to me."

Louis loosened the lid on another can of paint, collected a rag, some brushes, and a roller, and climbed to the shelf at the top of the ladder. He could feel his face growing warm as he raised high above Sacci's bent head.

"Watch the floor, okay?" Sacci warned. "The parquet's uneven."

Louis nodded silently, cutting in where the wall met the molding, taking care to go slowly and not mar the refinished molding. The paint, a dusty green, contrasted with the warm brown of the trim, the intricate molding, and the pillars framing the doorways. Already, he could envision the room when it was finished. The sala would be a good place for a visitor to read a book, to sit quietly in a quiet city.

Just one more coat in that room and the major painting projects would be complete. The summer had flown by with only a month left until the hotel opened, and Louis' shoulders, arms, and neck ached from all of the painting. He would be glad to be finished, to turn his efforts toward something else—anything but the repetitious motion of a roller or a paintbrush.

After he'd cut in the top of the wall, he began rolling the final coat, which turned the walls a darker, more solid green. He liked looking across the room, even glancing out the windows. With the right art and some comfortable pieces of furniture, the room would be the perfect place to unwind and soak up the city. Mesmerized by the light spilling through the doors and striking the walls, he didn't realize he was leaning well forward on the towering ladder and it suddenly lurched, tilting toward the wall.

For a moment, he hovered between falling against the wall and righting the ladder, but his weight had gone too far toward the wall. As he and the ladder tilted ominously toward the wall, he yelled.

"Dio!" he heard Sacci shout.

The top of the ladder struck the plaster with the force of his weight. Louis' feet slipped off the step and he slid down the wall, his rear end striking the tarp-covered floor with a thud, knocking the breath out of him. A large swath of plaster crashed down around him, raising a cloud of dust. Most of the plaster fell between his back and the wall, but still, dust covered his hair and his clothing. Beneath the pile was the can of spilled paint.

"What the hell?" he muttered.

Sacci rushed over. "Are you okay? What happened, did you lose your balance?"

Louis rubbed his knees, shaking his head slowly. His ass still hurt and a cloud of plaster dust hovered in the air, dirtying the room, which moments before had been so close to being finished, so close to perfection.

"I think I'm okay," he answered, leaning forward should more plaster loosen from the walls. "It looks terrible—what have I done?"

Claudia would be pissed. Now the plasterers would have to return, and the upper sala wouldn't be finished on time. Why hadn't he been more careful? He dreaded seeing her walk into the room, and her instant realization that something had gone wrong.

Sacci leaned over him, brushing bits of snow-white plaster off his shoulders.

"Strange that the whole section fell like that," Sacci said, standing back and eyeing the wall.

As he studied the wall, the expression on his face turned, his eyes opening wide. "What can that be?" he muttered, stepping back.

Louis turned to look. There was still a lot of dust in the air and the wall was also covered in dust, but a pattern emerged from the white cloud.

"Dio, I think it's a fresco," Sacci exclaimed, leaning forward to brush lightly the dust-covered wall with his sleeve. "By the looks of it, I'd guess it to be an old one."

Louis lurched forward to get to his feet. Sacci sprang forward to help him, pushing his hands under Louis' arms, and pulling him up.

"Are you sure you're okay?" Sacci asked, looking worried.

"I'm just stiff—and have a sore rear," he said, rubbing his butt.

The ladder still leaned against the wall, and stretching beneath it on both sides was a wide mural that looked as if it might cover the entire stretch of wall. Louis saw figures. What were they doing? He reached forward to brush off the dust.

"Careful," Sacci cautioned. "The whole fresco might come off if you brush too hard."

Leaning forward, he blew softly on the wall, creating another cloud of dust.

"I'll get some damp towels—wait for me here," Sacci urged and raced out of the room.

Louis moved down the wall to see if any more of the plaster might be loosened. By the time Sacci returned, he had righted the ladder, and then carefully picked at a few plaster pieces that sent more small sections crashing to the floor.

"The whole panel must be a mural—and what about the other segments of the wall?" Louis asked.

Sacci shook his head. "There's no way to know without busting off the plaster covering them."

"And if there's nothing there?"

"Claudia will kill us."

Sacci leaned forward, softly brushing the wall with one of the damp rags. "Here, take one of these," he told Louis, handing him a rag. "Go lightly, *very* lightly," he cautioned.

Louis eagerly took the rag and very lightly brushed the wall in front of him. How many mysteries did the palazzo hold? And how many did Venice hold? As he brushed the lower parts of the wall, figures and forms came more distinctly into view. There was a king-like figure, columns in the background, even a temple. There were soldiers and men in brightly colored Renaissance robes and hats all approaching the king. In the background, maidens danced on conical hills or hung in the background, smiling suggestively at the king.

As they continued brushing the wall, the colors came alive, and posing figures came into colorful view. There were rich Venetian blues, sea greens, lustrous oranges, and fiery reds.

"Is it real?" Louis asked, moving closer to inspect the dusted section of the wall. "It looks so new."

Sacci laughed excitedly. "Of course, it's real!" he said, sidling up to Louis and pressing his shoulder into him. Moving his face closer to the wall, he clucked his tongue, smiling broadly. "It's been covered for years and that's what's preserved it. And some sort of sealer was put on it to protect it when this layer of plaster was put over it. I can't believe it."

"Why would anyone cover this up?" Louis asked.

Sacci shrugged. "Maybe a wife didn't like it—look at the nude maidens in the background, and there are likely to be more elsewhere. Or perhaps my grandparents did it because they didn't want to have to register it with the government, to be bothered with taking proper care of it."

"That's crazy," Louis remarked, lightly slapping his mouth in regret. Had he just insulted Sacci?

"There's so much of this stuff in the city, like the bathroom you saw upstairs, and some of it can be bothersome to take care of. In some ways, you don't really own it—the government does. And people try to break in, steal it, destroy it, and scholars come knocking. Or maybe it was covered up during one of the plagues, when the religious people of the city tried to pin the diseases on those who strayed too far from the church. Anything too risqué was destroyed or hidden."

"But your grandparents never said anything to you about it?" Louis asked, lightly brushing his fingers across the mural, as if by touching it he might understand its significance.

"Not a word."

"Who do you think it is?" Louis asked, pointing at the figure in the center of the scene. Above the figure, eagles soared, and below his feet, porpoises frolicked.

"Nearly every figure in it would be the likeness of someone, some family member, neighbor, friend, or patron," he explained.

"But who's that?" Louis repeated, moving his finger so close to the figure that he nearly touched it.

"Maybe a Roman figure—or the duke, the one who lived here in the early 1500s," he suggested uncertainly. "I don't really know—and only a scholar might be able to say for certain."

"But you don't want a scholar coming around here, do you? And you don't want to announce this."

Sacci winked at Louis. "One of our many secrets, okay?"

"But, Sacci, this'll be a hotel, with guests coming in and out every day. Don't you think someone will figure it out?" he asked, shaking his head.

How could they uncover such a work and not report it to anyone? And wouldn't it be good for the hotel, a little free publicity before they even opened?

"Figure what out? You and I can't figure it out—even after we remove the rest of the plaster," he explained, shrugging while he continued pacing along the expanse of the mural. "And so we have a beautiful, old mural in very good condition here. No one needs to know that it's original, or that it was probably painted in the 1500s instead of the 1600 or 1700s. And if some scholar or art historian recognizes it for what it is, they'll assume it's not significant and that the government already knows about it."

Squeezing Louis' shoulder, he glanced at the walls surrounding the mural.

"I guess I don't really need to tell anyone," Louis said. "I'll just tell my parents or anyone who comes to visit that it's a nice mural, but no big deal."

"Perfetto," Sacci said. "It's just like the bathroom—just another little secret, okay?"

Fidgeting, Louis avoided his eyes, turning back toward the mural.

"So do we remove the plaster layer ourselves or do we call someone to do it?" he suddenly asked.

Sacci laughed.

Before he could even begin to explain, Louis stopped him. "That's right; there's no money in the budget for a worker to remove the plaster. So the answer is no."

Nodding, Sacci slapped him on the back softly, kneading his shoulder lightly. "Bravo," he smiled. "We can just do it ourselves if we're careful."

"What happened?" Claudia boomed, striding into the room with her hands flying. "What is *that*?" she shouted, frantically pointing at the piles of plaster on the floor.

She looked stricken and on the verge of tears.

"I decided to paint you a mural," Sacci teased, winking at her as he swept his arm toward the mural.

Claudia's eyes moved up to the mural, a smile creeping across her face.

"*Bellissimo*!" she gasped. "I can't believe it! How did you find it?"

"It found us," Sacci chuckled, his gaze fixed on the fresco.

"It's really, really old, isn't it?" she asked.

"I think it is," Sacci agreed. "Not a masterpiece, but something unique."

Throwing her arms around Sacci, and then pulling Louis into her embrace, too, she laughed deliriously.

"Isn't Venice wonderful?" she gasped. "Crazy, wonderful and full of so many wonderful secrets!"

"Sì," Sacci replied, "*É bella*."

"I wonder what's next," she said, grinning.

"I wonder, too," Louis said, hoping fervently that everything would continue to go so well. *Every*thing.

Because if Claudia could start to believe that only good things would happen, then maybe he could, too.

Chapter Fifteen

The ringing phone was jarring, unexpected. The dogs barked, running in circles around Sacci's legs as he ran to pick up the heavy, black handset.

He picked up the phone, out of breath. "Mother?"

A strange voice on the line corrected him.

"No. I'm sorry it's not your mother. And I'm sorry to bother you like this."

It was a woman's voice. She had a voice like a patrician, with long, drawn out vowels.

"I want to help you," she said. "And I'd like to ask you at the same time if you can help me—it's nothing big at all, just a small favor that will be helping yourself at the same time."

"Who are you?" he asked, wondering if he should be frightened. Was it the mafia? The government? Had a wealthy collector heard about the mosaic or about the fresco and now wanted to buy them?

"I promise to tell you everything if you'll meet me. I need you to meet me right away, though, because I'm very late."

"What if I say no?" he asked, still wondering who was on the other end. Weren't these the sorts of meetings that got people into trouble?

"Your hotel opening will be a little less grand. And you'll miss a wonderful opportunity. Trust me. You don't know me, but you can trust me."

He stared at the dogs that seemed to be waiting for him to do something, react to the call.

"How do I know I can trust you?"

She laughed; a small, confident laugh that was nearly a giggle. "I see," she said. "I can understand your fear. But I'm not a murderer—"

Sacci felt stupid, paranoid. "Of course, I didn't think you were—"

She laughed again. "Do I sound so frightening? Anyway, I'm amused—flattered that I could frighten you, as I'm completely harmless."

For some reason, she suddenly sounded not completely harmless, though in different ways than he'd originally thought.

"If I told you that I'm a very close friend of your manager and partner, Claudia Baggi, would you feel better about meeting me?"

Why hadn't she said that initially? Well, what would it hurt to meet her if she knew Claudia? To find out at least what she wanted. Maybe she was telling the truth, and maybe this was another piece of the puzzle falling into place. He rubbed the small *San Francesco* medallion hanging around his neck, giving quiet thanks as he hung up the phone.

There were obviously bigger currents tugging at him. It was useless to fight such things; the best approach was to swim *with* the current. So that was what he would do. And if he needed to, he could outsmart fate. He wasn't one of those people who lacked insight, that couldn't see or sense the inevitable. He would know if the woman was trying to do damage, he reasoned.

Many dramas had a surprise visitor, didn't they? He smiled, leaning down to pat the dogs on their heads as they spun frantically at his heels, hungry for his affection.

Sacci didn't read the newspapers, hardly even watched television, so he didn't realize whom the woman was until well into their conversation. He'd agreed to meet her at a strange place, Il Cane, a small café he'd never heard of in a sleepy piazza all the way over on

Giudecca, one of the smaller islands across the *Canale della Giudecca*, so wide it resembled a lagoon. Of course, once he put the pieces together, the reasons for her choice were obvious. No one could possibly have spotted her at Il Cane.

She told him she would be standing at the bar—not sitting outside at one of the little tables crammed next to a narrow canal. It was odd that a woman who spoke like a patrician would stand up to have her coffee. Or whatever it was she intended to have.

He walked into the narrow bar, its walls lined with sepia-toned photographs of turn of the century Venice. An attractive, older woman stood at the bar, sipping vin santo, and nibbling on a biscotto She nodded at him, smiling serenely. He walked up, extending his hand.

"I'm Sacci."

The woman nodded. "Of course, and I'm Claudia's mother," she said, as if it were the most natural pronouncement.

Claudia's mother? The contessa who had disowned her daughter? What could the woman possibly want? Was she attempting to ruin the hotel's opening, persuade Claudia to leave just as everything was about to come together?

"I can tell by your expression that you know about my daughter and me, and you're wondering why I'm here, aren't you?" she asked casually.

She met his eye, studying him without a trace of embarrassment. To her, whatever Claudia had told Sacci didn't seem to matter. She didn't appear flustered, but calmly took another sip of vin santo and another small bite of biscotto which she'd dipped in the spirit.

"Exactly. It does seem rather odd, er, unusual given what Claudia has told me," he admitted.

"But then maybe she's told you I'm also capable of change."

"She didn't mention that—but I believe you," he said, wondering if perhaps she had changed in the past half year as much as Claudia had.

She looked like the sort of person who wouldn't lie. Maybe he was wrong about that, though. He'd have to ask Claudia. Was there a bartender? Though no one else stood at the bar, he hadn't been approached.

"Life is full of things to learn—about yourself and the world," she added, sounding philosophical. "No matter your age."

Sacci nodded. So she had figured out some things, even as a contessa—and one who could no longer count herself as young.

"I was wrong I guess, at least that's how things look at the moment," she announced, raising her voice an octave. "And perhaps you would think I'm unhappy because things have gone well—"

"I can't say either way. It's just surprising that you're here given what little I know about your relationship with your daughter. And I suppose I'm curious—and a little fearful," he said, glancing nervously around the bar. Where was the bartender?

"You've nothing to fear from me—really. I'm not here to lure Claudia away—though I admit to still preferring that she were in Rome. But I've no intentions of meddling—at least with malice in mind."

She eyed him again, turning her face toward him fully as if to invite him to find any trace of deceit. She gazed around the room with a satisfied expression.

"So what are you here for then? It can't be a coincidence that you're here just before the hotel is to open," he asked, trying not to sound overly suspicious. After all, she was bound to tell him.

"It's no coincidence. As you can imagine, I have my contacts here who keep me apprised of what's going on with my daughter and anyone involved with her."

Not surprising. He'd overheard conversations that Louis and Claudia had had about her mother having lived for a short while in Venice when she was a young woman. And that there was some mystery about that time. So, it wouldn't be strange for her to still have contacts.

"She's worked very hard," he said. "I'm assuming you already know that the hotel opens in just a few days and that there will be a grand opening party. Something really spectacular that will show off the restoration of the palazzo."

"My friends here tell me that it looks like it will be very unique—a stellar boutique hotel. She's made good use of the money her grandmother gave her."

She gazed at Sacci, looking smug that she knew so much.

"What else have they told you?"

The contessa smiled again, seeming to enjoy letting him know just how much she knew. "There's a loggia, twenty sleeping rooms, I think, and Claudia has been living there—by herself. And she's been working very hard, as you say."

"She has been," he nodded. "You should be very proud. You have a smart daughter who's also a very hardworking individual."

Did his compliment sound like a reprimand?

The contessa nodded, her smile fading. Maybe she didn't want to be lectured or reminded that she had been wrong about her daughter. Or did the realization that it was a complete stranger who had helped her daughter annoy her? Still, he shouldn't be worried that much. After all, she wanted something from him—not the reverse. If this was a game of cat and mouse, he was the cat, despite her title and reputation.

The contessa motioned for the barista who had finally appeared at the end of the bar. He acknowledged the two of them and walked slowly down the length of the bar. She ordered Sacci a cappuccino and another glass of vin santo for herself.

"I feel like I want to do something," she abruptly announced, picking up her glass and taking small, measured sips. "I thought it would be a nice gesture. And to show that, well, I was mistaken about her decision."

Sacci tried to contain his surprise. The woman seemed to be begging him to treat the whole conversation as natural and expected. He nodded, eyeing the barista who stood in front of the giant, old coffee machine fiddling with the controls. He wished he had his cappuccino, craving the sharpness of mind the caffeine would provide.

"I've walked by the hotel already, seen it myself," she announced casually, as if he shouldn't have been surprised.

"Do you think she saw you?" he asked.

"I don't think so," she said, sounding vaguely condescending. "I was careful and didn't spend too much time around it. And I wore strange clothes, very unlike me. I'm sure she didn't spot me, though I did see her."

"How did you see her? And how can you be certain that she didn't see you?"

Contessa Baggi frowned, annoyed with his doubts. "I hired a gondola—of all the quaint things to do in Venice! I nearly jumped off the boat because he started to head out to the *Canale della Giudecca*—I *hate* that canal. It's so wide it reminds me of a lagoon."

"But you crossed it to get here. And you chose this place," he mused.

She shrugged.

"I had my reasons for wanting to meet in a quieter part of town, as you can imagine. And maybe the canal is less odious than it used to be. An old woman can change, can't she?" she said, her voice sounding shrill, defensive.

Sacci studied his coffee, which the barista placed in front of him. The caramel-colored foam, edged with creamy, marshmallow white milk on the sides, looked too perfect to drink.

"How did you see her?"

"I had the gondolier take me along the backside of the palazzo—and what an exquisite building it is that your family has had all these years."

"Grazie."

He thought it strange to have a contessa from Rome compliment a crumbling palazzo in drowsy, dowdy Venice.

"Yes, it's beautiful and would cost an absolute fortune in Rome. *Ma Venezia non é Roma*."

"It's not—and thank God for that," he shot back. So she really did despise Venice—just as he'd heard.

Smacking her lips, she seemed to ignore his tone. "There were some rooms with wonderful old windows that look half-hidden, hardly visible even from the canal," she observed, eyeing him over her glass.

She really did have a gift for observation. But he would ignore the innocent-sounding statement that appeared as much like a question as anything she'd asked him.

"So how was it that you saw Claudia?" he said, noticing a slight flicker in her eye, probably annoyance that he'd ignored her remark.

"She was out on the loggia, directing some painters and workers. And I heard her talking about how everything would be set up for the opening party. I was amazed listening to her. She sounds utterly changed. I told the gondolier to stop and sit there for a moment so I could listen."

"Eavesdrop, eh?"

"Exactly. It makes me nearly Venetian, doesn't it?" she laughed, more pleasantly than earlier.

"I see Venetians aren't the only ones who enjoy the sport," he teased, surprised at finding her interesting—though difficult to talk to. Even though she seemed friendlier than he'd imagined she would be, even contrite, she made him nervous.

Sacci studied her face, but she didn't seem sad. Perplexed, maybe, but not sad. It must have felt strange to eavesdrop on a daughter. Did she sense the peculiarity of her behavior or did parents treat estrangement from their children as a natural occurrence?

She sounded vaguely proud, almost maternal when she mentioned Claudia. But she seemed to avoid saying anything too complimentary, as if that would be revealing something to him. So his perception about the contessa being a difficult person to understand and deal with was true. He thought of his own mother who had given up the idea of title before he was born. She spurned parties or any events that the town's bluebloods favored, preferring to live quietly away from the city in Trieste where no one knew her.

An only child, as soon as she married she left the palazzo to other family members and renters, preferring the anonymity of Trieste. And so the decline of the family palazzo began.

"You can see easily onto the canal from up on that loggia," he warned. "Are you certain she didn't see you?"

The contessa waved his worries away with a brush of her hand. "She was engrossed in planning the party. In that way, she's not changed a bit. But can I tell you what I've come to ask? The favor that I need from you?" she said, suddenly impatient.

"So what is it? I can't think what I can do for you," he said, realizing that maybe *she* was nervous, too.

"It's really not that great a favor, but I want to do something for the opening—for the hotel," she said soberly.

She smiled then, leaning toward Sacci. She moved her face so close to his that he could smell the vin santo on her breath.

"I'd like to make the opening party really fabulous—over the top incredible," she said, her voice trembling slightly.

"How do you mean? What would you like to do?" Did she mean to take control of the opening? Was that her way of insinuating herself into the project, of taking control behind her daughter's back?

"You don't need to look so worried," she said, diverting her gaze from his. "Whatever you've heard about me isn't so true. I want to help, that's all. I was mistaken about Claudia, that's all. And to make amends, I just want to help a little. In fact, I've already—" she started to say, stopping herself abruptly.

"Already what?" Sacci asked, wondering what she'd nearly said. Had she already done something?

"Nothing," she countered. "I was just going to say that I'd already thought of things I could do to help."

"How would you help?" he asked. "What exactly would you like to do?" He didn't know whether to sound worried or excited.

"I overheard Claudia, and as luck would have it, I overheard her talk about what would *not* happen at the party—what you all couldn't do because you've sunk all your money into the hotel."

She looked pleased, suddenly confident in her ability to contribute.

He wondered if her plans approximated what Claudia had originally wanted—had she learned of the plans from someone? They'd reasoned that there was little sense in hosting a blowout opening, only to close the doors of the hotel weeks later for lack of funds, so they'd scaled back their party plans.

"Claudia talked about muslin curtains lining the perimeter of the loggia, catching the breezes from the sea, torches and servers fanning out across the loggia—the whole hotel—with trays set with champagne, cocktails, Bellini's—fabulous drinks, a fully-stocked bar, great—not mediocre—antipasti. Staff to serve everything—enormous flower arrangements. How can you say no? *That's all I want*," she whispered. "Just to provide these things. Not much of a favor, is it?"

He was afraid to say yes, but equally afraid to deny her. Not that she could really do anything to him, but everything seemed so tenuous with the hotel, and denying her request would cause a sudden conflict when things had been going so smoothly, drifting right up to the opening without delays or any major problems. If he said no, it would feel like he was spurning a generous handout that had seemed to fall from the sky.

He recalled the advice of one of the deliverymen, wondering why he should resist good fortune.

Still, he had a nagging doubt. What would Claudia think? She would find out eventually. Would it spoil the project for her, ruin the opening if her mother were involved? And she'd been worried from the beginning that her mother would somehow mess up things, working behind the scenes to make certain that she didn't succeed.

But Claudia's mother was standing before him, delicately sipping her drink, and appearing candid and honest. No, she didn't appear at all to be plotting or malicious.

"I don't know," he said, avoiding her gaze. "Something scares me about it."

"That's ridiculous," she said sharply, coming closer. "There's nothing to worry about. I won't even show up—I'll simply arrange to have workers set everything up. And pay the bill for the servers and drinks. You can even arrange for them if you wish and then send me the bill."

She looked frustrated, annoyed with his uncertainty.

"I'll pay in advance. No strings attached," she added.

"I just don't want to upset Claudia. This has been her project—especially the opening. And maybe with the way things have been—"

"Yes, we haven't been speaking, but that could never be permanent," she scolded, her voice rising. "I don't hate her—Dio, she's my daughter. I know we both always shared the knowledge that one day we would speak again. And what I'm asking of you is really *nothing*—she doesn't even need to know that I did it. You can claim it as *your* surprise, eh?"

She set her glass on the bar significantly, as if they were beginning to wrap up their conversation.

"Then what's in it for you? Why do this for her and not ever tell her that you did it?" he asked, sipping his cappuccino.

She nodded, acknowledging his point. "I suppose that I'd like to tell her at some point—when we talk again, which I hope is soon. But what if I promised not to tell her until I knew that she was okay with me again? I could wait until the hotel is open and going strong—long after the opening. Whatever terms you want."

He couldn't give any good reason for not wanting to accept her offer, but it still didn't feel right.

"Look, it's what she wants. I heard her say it herself. This would be giving her the opening she's dreaming of but can't afford to buy. I can buy it for her—for all of you. And I'm happy to do so—it's a trifle for me."

She leaned back toward the bar, away from his face as if she'd just realized she was crowding him. She smiled, picking up her glass and sipping the vin santo.

"Come on, won't you say you'll help? What could go wrong?" she asked, lightly touching his arm.

He couldn't think of a good reason to say no, only an irrational, nagging uncertainty. But if Claudia didn't know who had paid for everything, what did he have to fear?

He started to nod when the contessa leaned into him, the corners of her mouth twitching back slightly.

"And there's one other thing," she said, avoiding his eyes. "One other reason that I suppose I should mention—not that it has any bearing on what I'd like to do or how things would proceed at the opening."

Was she going to confide in him? He wasn't sure how to respond, but nodded slightly.

"Maybe you know—maybe Claudia has told you—that I don't care for Venice?"

"She'd mentioned that, yes," he said.

"I have my reasons, though they're nothing that I'd want to talk to a stranger about." She looked up at him, seeing him avert his eyes. "Don't be offended," she added. "I haven't even talked to my husband about it. You see, doing this—allowing me to do this—is a way to exorcise past demons, if you will. To try to give myself some better memories of this city. Maybe I've been irrational, unfair, but something happened to me here and it turned me against this place."

So there *was* truth to the vague stories he'd heard. Exactly what had happened to her in Venice so many years earlier?

"I've never been able to get past it, and when I come here I feel claustrophobic, like everything is rotting and sinking. Sometimes I believe I can feel this ancient city sinking right into the sea."

She looked down at her glass with a vague frown.

"But Rome is old, too. I don't understand," he said quietly.

"Yes, but not sinking. Venice seems somehow ancient. The air smells of rot—can you not smell it?"

Her eyes flashed, but then she quickly dropped her gaze to her hands, shooting Sacci a smile.

"At any rate, what I mean to say is that I mean to give it another chance. This will help me. If my daughter is going to live here—which I've come to accept—then I'd like to do something for her."

He nervously ran his fingers across the edge of the saucer,

wondering what it was that had happened to poison her to the city that millions found so alluring.

"Will you help me, *please*?" she asked.

As if warming to the idea, he slowly nodded. "I can't think of any good reason to say no, so I guess I have to say yes."

Claudia wouldn't know until after—not until he deemed it safe to tell her, and the contessa wouldn't even attend the party. So what could go wrong?

"I wish you'd be more excited about the prospect of my help, but I'll take a yes—even if it's timid—over a no," she said, relief washing over her face. "Salute!" she toasted, clicking the base of her glass against the lip of his cup.

"Salute," he echoed. To avoid bad luck, he sipped the cold remnants of his cappuccino, some grounds, and the remains of the nearly formless foam clinging to the bottom of the cup.

Then a thought struck him. How did she propose getting into the hotel with Claudia living there?

"I've already got a plan," she said, noticing the concerned look, which had crept onto his face. "The night before the opening—"

"That's only two days away," he interrupted, forgetting that she would already have a plan.

She nodded. "It's best if you get her to take a sleeping pill that night—I know her and she'll be restless and awake."

"How do I do that?" he asked.

"Have her finocchio friend get her to take it. Have him tell her it's good for her nerves."

So Louis *was* gay—just as he'd suspected. And the contessa was not so broad-minded.

"He's not finocchio," he said, the words slipping from his mouth like some sort of challenge. What was it that made him want to say that, to defend Louis when the contessa was actually right? Was it simply that she'd used the demeaning finocchio to describe him?

The contessa looked at him with narrowed eyes and a mouth that was perfectly round. It was the first time he'd seen her look genuinely surprised during their conversation.

"I don't mean to argue," she said diplomatically, but he could tell she didn't believe him. "I'm sure I'm mistaken. At any rate, what I was saying is that her friend Louis could encourage her to take the sleeping pill. And I suppose it doesn't matter whether he's gay or straight, does it?"

Sacci nodded, still annoyed.

"I'm sorry if I offended you—a second time in such a brief meeting. You must think me rather hard-edged." She looked him directly in the eye, as if searching for something she hadn't seen earlier.

He was only half engaged in the conversation, preoccupied with the confirmation that Louis was gay. Why did he care so much and why had he so quickly tried to protect him?

"Signore, I've lost you," the contessa said, reverting to extreme politeness. She smiled conspiratorially, as if she knew what he'd been thinking. "Just a moment more of your time to arrange the details—would that be okay?"

He wished he could ask her how she knew, but he couldn't.

"Va bene," he answered. "There's just so much on my mind the past few days."

"I understand," she said, pausing a moment to catch his eye. "So I would suggest that after awhile, after you've waited a little while to allow the pill to take effect that someone lets in the workers. And they'll work setting everything up for the party. I'll have everything prepared at a nearby warehouse and everything can be delivered and set up within hours. Easy, isn't it?"

She smiled again, her teeth white and straight like an American's.

"What do I need to do?" he asked, standing straighter while rolling the bottom of his coffee cup on its saucer.

"Just arrange to have someone let in the workers—that's it. They'll do everything, unless you don't trust me and want to make the arrangements for the workers yourself."

"What would they do?"

"Just what we talked about—and anything additional that'd you'd like done yourself. We might be able to add those at the same time. You can talk to them directly or just let me know what you'd like." She shrugged as if the task were as easy as ordering a dry martini.

Sacci was pensive for a moment, thinking about what he might want done. In the end, he thought of nothing additional, she seemed to have thought of everything. "Okay, then. Sounds easy enough. I can let in the workers—and get Claudia to take the pill. What else can I do?"

"That's all, Signore Sacci. You don't need to do anything else. You could be home in bed while the final touches are applied or you can stay and watch. As you wish."

She slid a thick, cream-colored business card across the bar, tucking it into his hand. "I'm staying at the Palazzo Reale," she said. "When you know how you'd like things to proceed, just call me. If I'm not there, you can leave a message at the desk."

"Va bene," he said, sliding the card into his shirt pocket.

"Just don't take too long, okay? There's not much time."

As if he might have forgotten that the hotel opening was a mere two days away.

"Sì, sì, sì," he replied, tapping his fingers on the table.

"I'd recommend that the workers arrive at midnight," she suggested, sounding impatient. "If that sounds good to you."

So, she wanted to simply plan for him, he realized. Well, she had the money, and he was certain she would hire only the best, so it would be one less thing for him to worry about. All he would need to do is open the door at midnight—and to get Claudia to take a sleeping pill. Easy enough, he thought.

"Perfetto," he chirped. "And you'll get the curtains for the terrace; ones made of muslin or light silk that blow in the wind?"

"Certo," she said. "I'll ask the events people to make sure everything is done as if the event were at the Reale itself—including the curtains."

She smiled, lifting her glass and tilting it toward him.

"Salute," she toasted. "To *San Spirito*."

"Salute," he said, furrowing his brow. "To *Spirito*," he corrected, returning the toast.

She drained her glass and then dabbed the corners of her mouth with a cocktail napkin.

"I hope to see you sometime after the opening," she said brightly, stepping away from the bar. "And in the meantime, *buona fortuna*."

"I hope so, too," he said, wondering if the next encounter would be as easy. "And thanks for the good wishes—I've a feeling that we'll have plenty of luck."

Her smile turning to a frown, she shook her head. "Don't trust life. It's not always predictable, eh?"

He shrugged, noticing the old square photographs of Venice from a hundred years earlier. Had the people in those photos trusted life, had they known a Venice so different from the one he knew that he wouldn't even recognize it? They probably hadn't even known their homes and city were sinking, slowly dissolving into the sea and mud.

"Grazie," he decided to say, accepting her advice though he didn't feel unlucky. If anything, he'd been feeling just the opposite.

"Thank you for helping me," she said genuinely, her eyes appreciative.

"You're helping me as well ... I mean us," he clarified, trying to sound grateful. "So I should thank you."

"It's not always that things work out so," she said, nodding and stroking the sides of her thin arms. "And I'm glad for it."

"*Anch'io*," he responded.

"Arrivederci," she called, smiling and waving as her slim figure glided toward the door before disappearing into the glow of the sun-filled day.

Should he have felt guilty for meeting with the woman, for allowing her to play such a role in the opening of the hotel?

But he was happy and optimistic, despite some pre-opening jitters. Perhaps the afternoon's meeting would lead to reconciliation between mother and daughter. A good start, an event that really established the place as uncommon and special was exactly what they needed. And now they would have it, so why should he feel bad about that?

No, the contessa had had a change of heart, and so would Claudia.

He could sense it.

Chapter Sixteen

Claudia's feet felt tender, as if she'd been walking on sharp river stones without shoes the whole day. The small of her back ached, the exact spot she'd seen middle-aged women grab toward the end of the day. But she was too young to be so sore and worn out. Months of madness were nearly over.

A thought suddenly occurred to her. What if after the hotel opened things were just as frantic and stressful? What if the pace that had marked the past few months, the long days, the incessant phone calls, and the constant hard work, were merely the beginning?

She didn't know if she could continue. All she wanted was to sleep. But that night wouldn't be a good night's rest, and perhaps she would be awakened again by thoughts of random details that might have been left undone. Were all the phones in the rooms working? Who had tested them? Were there hangars in the armoires? Where were the bedsheets? What if no one showed up?

Such questions could continue for hours, and that night more than any other she needed her sleep.

She thought of the little blue valium Louis had slipped into her palm after dinner.

"This will help you sleep, make you relax. But don't take it the day of the opening and don't have anything to drink with it. You should take it tonight, okay?"

Didn't some old movie star die from mixing valium and alcohol? Was it Marilyn Monroe? Maybe some others, too, but she couldn't remember their names. She planned to have one little cocktail with dinner, or maybe a glass of wine. And what could the harm be in that? Stressed and bone-tired, she had worked harder than she'd known was possible. And the opening was the following day, so maybe she could—maybe she *should*—relax a little.

Oddly, Louis had made her promise she would take the little pill.

"I've taken them before and they're just the cure for stress. You'll have a great night sleep and wake up ready for the opening," he'd explained. "But you might need an extra espresso in the morning."

She nodded, slipping the pill into her pocket.

And then it was odd, too, that Sacci had hinted that she should take something, as if he'd known that Louis had given her the pill. Had they discussed it?

"Do you have anything you can take to sleep tonight?" he'd asked. "You'll need it—better to take it to be sure."

Instead of making her suspicious, the coincidence persuaded her that she'd be wise to take their advice.

Sacci had assured her that everything was ready. The catering staff knew their way around the kitchen and dining room. Extra bartenders were hired and bars set up on the loggia.

She peeked in the kitchen, where only a work light atop a metal counter shone, giving the room a warm, occupied feel. The lounge was completely dark, but she could make out the massive armchairs and sofas. In the corners, giant potted palms threw haphazard shadows, their shiny leaves catching silvery bits of light from the hallway.

Everything was in place, ready for the opening, but she was too tired to look in the other rooms, too weary to explore any room upstairs but her own. The loggia would be a wonderful place to be now, bathed in a little moonlight and cooled by a breeze from the sea. The thought of sitting there in a T-shirt and underwear, sipping a glass of wine, made her body ache. It would be her oversize bed instead—that night, anyway. She would quickly undress, falling between the cool cotton sheets—if she could get up the enormous stairs. The stairway seemed to go forever, but she assaulted each wide marble step as if it were a separate challenge. When she finally arrived at the top, the door chime rang, making her jump.

Who could have stopped by? Maybe it was a delivery.

But it was eleven o'clock!

She hated the thought of walking back down the stairs—and then back up again. If she did, she would have to talk to whoever was there and she was too tired to talk to anyone, let alone walk back down the stairs and undo the two sets of heavy doors.

"Who's there?" she hollered down the stair hall.

But her voice couldn't be heard, not down the long hallway lined with carpets, and through the new glass doors fronting the enormous wooden doors.

The bell rang again. She wished there were staff working already so they could answer the door. She moved a foot toward the first step, but felt a sudden wave of exhaustion. No, whoever was ringing would have to return—she was going to bed. She was expecting no one and no deliveries, except for the food, which would arrive early the next day. The wine and prosecco, though not the best, had already arrived by the caseload. And she'd seen both Sacci and Louis hours before, so it couldn't be them—and they had keys, anyway.

She flicked off the hall light, plunging the lower hallway into darkness.

Enjoy the darkness, she told herself, because thereafter the corridors, the salas, and the dining room would be illuminated every hour of the day. She thrilled at the prospect of being on the cusp of so much change. The sweet silence, heavy shadows, and perfect darkness seemed the calm before the storm. On the following day, the palazzo would become a hotel, beginning a new life. And on that same day, she, too, would begin a new life.

She marveled that they'd been able to pull it off, transforming the dirty old building into a series of rooms that charmed, thrilled, and seduced. Theirs would be one of the most unique, beautiful small hotels in the city.

If only her mother knew—well, who was she kidding? Of course, her mother knew. She was probably aware of her every move.

She shuddered, wondering if her mother would make an appearance at the opening. Claudia had a sudden vision, a fantasy actually, of her mother showing up at the end of the evening, jazz wafting in from the loggia, filling the hotel with its silky sound, and her mother tentatively creeping through the front doors, awestruck. She would search for her daughter, taking in all the rooms (except for the bathroom with the mosaics—Claudia would never allow her to know about that), seeing the guests and her friends and new family—yes, they honestly felt like family—enjoying the party, basking in the warmth of the beautiful hotel. And she would finally find her daughter on the loggia, surrounded by Sacci and Louis. Sacci's dogs would be sitting on a nearby bench, observing everything with their wise faces and even noticing the one woman who walked onto the loggia with an expression of purpose. Or atonement?

Claudia stood on the threshold of her room savoring the soft stillness. The building seemed to sense the swirling changes down to its massive, five hundred-year-old beams, its stones shipped from the mainland, and its thickly plastered walls. The building seemed to sigh, settling easily into its latest incarnation. She thought about all the other things it had been—a store, a palace, an office, a warehouse, and all the people who had known it.

When they'd pulled down the multiple layers of plaster on the ceiling of the lounge, she'd glimpsed thick, seasoned beams that probably hadn't been viewed since they'd first been hoisted in place hundreds of years earlier. Who had carved those beams, putting them in place, and who had last seen them? What were their lives like?

Yes, the building was a living, breathing thing, having far more stories to tell than she did. She listened to it creaking and groaning, as if the structure was even now settling into the sea. At more than five hundred years old, was the palazzo tired of standing?

But that couldn't be. As they'd restored the rooms, bringing life back into them, something had happened, something she couldn't quite put her finger on. Did buildings have a soul, *un spirito*, because that's what it felt like—as if the building were coming alive again. Had the restoration of the building brought back bits and pieces of all the people that had once lived there? If there were such a thing as ghosts, she imagined that they would be comfortable in such a place.

They'd somehow figured on the right name for hotel, *Palazzo Spirito*. Had that been as fateful as everything else that had happened to bring her to that very moment?

Undressing in her giant room, which she would eventually have to give up to guests (the door to the bathroom and study would always remain locked, but reachable for her and Sacci via another passage); she listened for all of the familiar sounds of the building. The snaps and sighs, the lapping of the canal waters on the moss-covered entry step and foundation stones. Thinking back to her first few weeks there, she remembered that all of the noises had frightened her. She'd even gone so far as to beg Louis to spend nights there, sleeping on a downy sofa between two of the enormous windows looking out over the canal.

He'd done so much for her, she realized. How would she ever repay him?

As for sleeping there so often at the beginning, he'd told her just being in the place, and taking a bath in the giant marble tub in the center of the tiled room or having a few hours to work in the light-washed study with its inspiring views were enough. He claimed he'd never been as quick or efficient with his translating and copywriting as he was while in that room.

Now the palazzo's sounds felt like the sighs and whispers of a mother lulling her to sleep and giving her the feeling that she was never alone there.

She examined her image in the large mirror in the dressing room. Did she look different? She decided that she must, that she certainly wasn't the same person she'd been half a year earlier during the lunchtime meeting with her mother. She found it difficult to believe that the event hadn't occurred years earlier and that it seemed so long ago.

Her stomach was still flat—was possibly even flatter after all the running around and working. She wondered what her now ex-husband Pietro was doing in New York, whether he found himself happier, too. What if she had remained married and in New York, having had children, and probably not ever working? The thought made her feel queasy, claustrophobic. She would have been another person completely, probably an unhappy, bitter one, gliding through life seemingly content, but deep down experiencing a gnawing resentment that life wasn't as she felt it should have been. Venice and the life she'd built in the last six months felt more like home than any place she'd been.

The palazzo was merely a small hotel, but it felt much bigger. She'd helped bring the place back to life, joining herself to a city in the process. She'd never been that attached to Rome or to New York. She'd never belonged anywhere, but she recalled the art teacher of her youth who first introduced her to the ancient, watery city that turned out to be the best place to be.

From cats wandering the tiny, meandering streets—that someone told her were inhabited by the spirits of deceased Venetians—to the current generation of Venetians who were the descendants of those who had first fled the mainland, building an impossible city from the marshy sea, she loved the city. She'd found a place she liked, that even seemed to like her back. Things had fallen into place, an experience she'd heard other people describe, but had never encountered. Suddenly she knew the feeling, a faith in a deeper current carrying everyone and everything, even the brick-heavy, waterlogged city itself.

The city was sloppier than Rome or New York, more mystical and mysterious and not all that it appeared. So much lay hidden below the surface, drifting along in the canal currents, which glided through the ancient waterways. Would she ever really know it, really feel like a Venetian?

After a cursory brushing of her teeth—she could do a more thorough job in the morning—she fingered the small blue pill Louis had given her, laying it in the palm of her hand.

She felt tired enough to sleep for days, but knew it was wise to take it. Otherwise, she might awaken at three or four o'clock in the morning, restless and anxious. It was better to take the thing, to have a guarantee of a night's sleep. She would need every ounce of energy the following day, and at that moment, she felt like she had none. Placing the pill on her tongue, she took a swig of water to wash it down.

Crawling beneath the sheets, she flicked off the light, plunging the room into inky, humid darkness. She wished for a little breeze from the sea to push out the still heavy September air hanging over the city. The air felt damp, brooding. Not right at all for her mood or for the opening of the hotel.

After that night, everything would change. She would never sleep alone in the palazzo again and eventually, would no longer even sleep in this room. At first, she'd refused to stay there alone. Now she didn't want to share it, wanting to keep the place and its secret moods to herself. She'd been content to glide through the rooms, taking in the exposed beams or restored frescos and plasterwork, breathing in the history, the spiritual residue of everyone who had passed through the rooms since they were built.

She shivered, her head sinking deeper into the down pillow. The following day would begin a new phase of her life.

Until that moment, the palazzo had seemed all hers. She'd never thought about that, but it was okay because she'd been wrong about everything from the start. Sacci and Louis had to cajole her into taking the job, and she'd doubted that she could succeed or that the ruin of a building would ever successfully make the transition from dusty, drafty rooms to a cozy hotel.

It was frightening to think of what would come next, but she had newborn faith that things would go well. Her fading thought as she fell asleep was that her mother had been wrong, too. Wrong about her and wrong about Venice.

Hers was not a city of tragedy and death, but a city of life.

Chapter Seventeen

Giovanni stared out across the rooftops of the city, struck at the darkness and quiet. Here and there, waxen mounds of light rose from clusters of streetlamps in the small piazzas. The sky nor the city couldn't have been darker if it had been a foggy November evening. If he'd been superstitious, he'd have taken the darkness for a good omen. But he would leave the superstitions to all the other Venetians, friends like Paolo who was as suspicious as they came.

Everything was happening just as he'd planned, except for the annoying wind, which had risen and would make poling the gondola more difficult. But he'd maneuvered boats in stronger winds. The only thing left was to board the boat and pole it toward the opera house.

"You want more wine?" Paolo asked him, holding the bottle in the air. "You need a little more before we go?"

At such times, he realized that he and Paolo were fundamentally different. He didn't need any wine to do what they'd planned, whereas Paolo greedily drank from the bottle they'd opened, searching for courage.

"No, I'm finished. No more for me."

His friend shrugged, pouring himself another full glass of the Barolo—fancy stuff for two odd-job guys about to commit a crime, but Giovanni had figured it was a special occasion and when did he ever buy a Barolo? After opening the bottle, Paolo had leaned out a window in Giovanni's apartment and tipped his glass, pouring a little into the canal below.

"Why'd you do that?" Giovanni asked.

"To return a little to the earth. For good luck."

Giovanni clucked his tongue, looking confused. "That's good wine, you know."

"Sure, I know," he'd answered, emptying his glass before pouring himself another.

"What's the matter?" his friend asked, worried that Paolo intended to finish the bottle.

"I'm nervous," Paolo announced. "You sure we won't get caught?"

"No, we won't get caught. Finish your wine, and then let's get going."

His friend guzzled another glass of wine, spilling the red liquid down the sides of his cheeks and chin. Giovanni was glad that the job wasn't too complicated because Paolo wasn't too bright. And right now, that seemed self-evident by the squeezed, anxious expression in his eye and the rivulets of wine running down his face. Paolo set his glass down and wiped his face with his shirtsleeve,

"*Pronto*?" Giovanni asked him.

"*Pronto*."

"I'll carry the stuff," Giovanni said, picking up a zippered canvas bag sitting beside the door.

"Is everything in there?" Paolo asked, eyeing the bag.

"Sì, I checked already—double-checked. Everything's there."

Before Paolo had arrived, he'd gone through the contents of the bag, making certain they had everything they would need: three working lighters, rags, gasoline, and duct tape.

They left Giovanni's apartment, flipping on the dim, timer-operated lights in the stair hall. The building stood completely still, a middle of the night quiet that comforted Giovanni but made Paolo uneasy. He felt just like one of the characters in one of the many operas in which he'd sung. How many times had he watched others seek revenge onstage? Now it was his turn.

"We should be in bed," Paolo said, nervously rubbing the palms of his hands against his trousers. "No one's awake now."

Giovanni stopped and turned to face his friend, saying gruffly, "Look, if you don't want to do this, if you're going to get there and decide you're too afraid to do it, then tell me now."

"No, no, I'm just nervous," his friend protested. "But I'm not going to let you down. I'm going to help. Trust me."

Giovanni eyed him suspiciously, wondering if he should have done the job on his own.

"You don't have to go, you know. I can do it on my own."

"I know," Paolo said, extending his fingers in front of him and looking down at them, avoiding his friend's eyes. "But it's better if I come with you. You need help."

"You promise?"

"I promise." Paolo moved his gaze from his hands to Giovanni's face.

His friend nodded and started walking down the stairs again with Paolo right behind him. The stair hall was eerily silent, but toward the first floor, a muffled sound came from under the stairs. A rat maybe? Or one of the city's tens of thousands of cats? Giovanni stopped short.

"What is it?" Paolo asked, looking worried.

"Shhh. I don't know."

Giovanni crouched and cocked his head in the direction where he thought he'd heard the sound. There it was again, but what he'd thought was muffled squeaking was actually crying, sobbing.

"Someone's crying?" Paolo asked.

Giovanni nodded, straining to hear more. The crying came from the other side of the wall, not from below the stairs. He pushed his ear to the wall, but the thick wall blocked the sound—it must have been coming from a vent somewhere.

"It's bad luck to listen to someone crying," Paolo said suddenly. "Let's go, okay?"

"You're typical Venetian," Giovanni smirked, clucking his tongue. "Full of superstitions."

"I don't deny it," Paolo said, licking his lips. "But I'm in the majority, not you nonbelievers."

The crying made him nervous, conjured up images of something gone wrong. It seemed like bad luck or a bad omen, and he didn't want to linger in the hall listening to the mournful sound. Better to pretend he hadn't heard it at all.

"Who do you think it is? That young American—do you think he's homesick?" Giovanni laughed, his ear pressed against the wall.

"I don't care who it is. Leave the person to cry. You don't need to borrow anyone's pain, do you?" Paolo said. "Leave misery to sort itself out. It doesn't like to be watched—or listened to."

He pushed past Giovanni and walked heavily down the stairs.

"Hey, wait for me, Mr. Superstitious," Giovanni called, hurrying after him.

Just before arriving at the foot of the stairs, the American strolled in, pushing open the heavy wooden door and nearly hitting them. Paolo looked back at Giovanni, his eyes wide.

Just act natural, Giovanni wanted to tell him. Why was he acting so suspicious in a situation that could have seemed so natural? He wondered again if he'd made a mistake by involving his childhood friend. But he had to have someone to look out, a second pair of eyes. And the thought of doing the job on his own gave him the creeps. After all, he wasn't really a criminal.

"Buonasera," the American said in that cheerful, confident manner that betrayed his nationality.

"*Sera*," Giovanni said. Paolo just nodded, raising his hand and arm slightly in a half-formed salute.

When they were both into the soft Venetian night, Paolo whispered, "I think he looked at us suspiciously. Do you think he'll call the police?"

Giovanni laughed softly. "He looked embarrassed—that was the look you saw on his face."

"Embarrassed? Why would he be embarrassed?"

"I don't know," Giovanni said, walking toward the boat. "But he sure looked embarrassed about something."

Paolo shrugged, studying the dark sky. "He seemed to be looking at us."

"Of course he was. And we looked at him. But you don't need to worry. He was as surprised to see us coming out late as he was to be heading into his studio so late."

"Still, he makes me nervous," Paolo said.

"Everything makes you nervous," Giovanni clucked. No moon shone and the sky above the hulking buildings appeared as soft as black velvet. Giovanni's boat was tied to a mooring at the end of the little street. The canal was completely still, the boat scarcely moving in the shallow waters.

He grabbed one of the mooring lines. "Let's just get in the boat and get going."

Paolo jumped in, carefully setting the canvas bag at the bottom of the boat. "Should I cover it?"

Giovanni shook his head. "It's a bag," he whispered tersely. "No one knows what's in it. And it's pitch black—no one can see it."

Paolo sat back silently, watching his friend untie the mooring lines and then hop in the boat. Giovanni carefully extricated a thick pole from the bottom of the boat and moved carefully toward the stern. Standing toward the back, next to the motor, he spread his legs wide enough to obtain leverage and began pushing the boat away from the ancient stones that formed the canal bank. He pulled the motor up out of the water, the metal blades of its propeller glowing dull gray in the inky darkness.

"If anyone asks, the motor's dead, right?" Giovanni whispered.

"I thought you said we wouldn't see anyone."

"We won't, but just in case we do, okay?"

"Sure."

Paolo sat fidgeting, watching Giovanni pole the boat down the canal. He was surprised at how well his friend knew the canals, how he navigated the narrow corners. Giovanni had been a gondolier, but that had been years ago. Paolo figured maybe it was one of those things like riding a bicycle, one never forgets, and maybe Giovanni remembered every corner, bridge, and bend in the canals. Paolo walked everywhere, rarely even boarding a vaporetto, so riding on the canals—especially in the dark—made him feel lost, as if he were in a strange city instead of the only city he'd ever known.

After fifteen minutes of poling, Giovanni, breathing heavy, stopped for a minute and stood quietly in the half-light cast from yellow lamps that shone from the streets into the shadowy canal. The boat's wake lapped against the walls, the soft sound of water sloshing against the old brick and moldy-stone foundation walls seemed loud. Other than their whispering voices, it was the only sound echoing down the narrow, watery passageways.

"We're getting close," Giovanni announced.

Paolo smiled nervously.

"Look at that place," he hissed, motioning with the end of the pole. It was an old palazzo, its upper shutters open, and the giant windows inside emitting a soft light.

"Maybe a party?" Giovanni asked. "But I can't hear any voices or music."

Craning his neck, he peered up as they drifted slowly forward. Somewhere above, he thought he saw two shadows on the loggia looking down at them. But there was no way anyone could see them in the thick darkness. He couldn't hear voices, just the sound of water lapping quietly against the buildings they glided by, their wake gently licking the old foundation stones.

"Look at that," Paolo said, pointing at a row of windows set back slightly from the side of the palazzo, as if hidden. A few of the casement windows were turned open completely to catch the evening breeze. From within, a soft, amber light glowed.

"I bet there are some nice things in that old place," Giovanni laughed. "Too bad we're not thieves, too!"

As quickly as they'd appeared, the windows disappeared behind rooflines as the two men drifted down the canal.

"My nonna used to talk about an old palazzo around here—not too far from the opera house. I remember her telling me that it was built right on top of a Roman temple. She said that the palazzo had a secret door and staircase that descended into a secret chamber, an ancient Roman purification room that the city's remaining pagans still crept into from time to time. I don't know if I would like to live in such a place. There must be lots of lost spirits wandering around. And then pagans probably want to get in there," Paolo said, his voice tremulous.

"You listen to old people too much," Giovanni complained, dipping the pole into the water and pushing them closer to their hulking destination just a few minutes away.

The canal curved slightly, the old palazzo and the golden light emitted from its enormous windows disappearing behind them. The canal once again sat immersed in darkness, seemingly void of life.

As they approached the opera house, that eighteenth century jewel of the city, Giovanni felt excitement growing in his chest. He would really do this, seek revenge, and set his life back in order. And he and Paolo would get away with it easily because who would suspect that a member of the chorus would turn arsonist, setting the exquisite building on fire? Better, who would imagine *anyone* setting the building on fire? People didn't set landmarks or architectural jewels afire in Italy, so no one would ever suspect.

His plan, though, wasn't to burn the theater to the ground—the old fire curtain would prevent that. Besides, the enormous, thick beams that helped support the structure, if they happened to catch fire, would take forever to burn.

He figured that little fires set in the prop room would do some damage, scaring the hell out of anyone who loved the theater, but not destroying much. The alarms would go off, and the fire department would arrive in minutes. Then everyone, particularly the patrons and government, would be looking at the management for an explanation.

What he longed to destroy was the management, and the horrid choral director, in particular. With her gone, he felt certain that he could return to the theater and go back to singing in the chorus as he'd done for so many years.

If they caught him, would they find it strange that he actually loved the opera house? He'd given his life to the place, singing year after year for twenty years, but once management decided they had no use for him because his voice had changed, he turned bitter. Instead of jockeying for small roles, he was desperate to get even.

Giovanni's voice had hardly changed, but something else *had* changed. Ever since the new choral director arrived, he'd slowly been pushed out of the house. The new director, Silvia Morasso, was visibly annoyed with him—she hadn't even tried to hide it. And as quickly as a full moon tide rushes into the city, he found himself with no real place in the opera house. After spending so many years as one of the oldest and most respected of the company's members, he wouldn't stand to be humiliated and pushed out by someone who'd only recently arrived.

He could blame *Direttore* Morasso. He'd tried to make her understand that he was part of the company, a fixture of the old and traditional opera house, but she only stared at him blankly. When he'd confronted her, asking if she was trying to force him out, she'd clucked her tongue and told him, "Change happens. And with a changing of the guard come a lot of changes that are not pleasant to everyone," she'd lectured. "But they're essential for the continued life of the organization, eh?"

She may as well have been German, and he knew she was from the little mountainous corner of northern Italy that had once been part of Austria, the Tyrol. Maybe he was too relaxed, not serious enough for her Teutonic sensibilities. Whatever the reason, her dislike of him was thinly disguised.

"It's nothing personal," she'd told him, gazing at something of interest over his shoulder. "An opera company is like any other—it has to hire the most qualified persons for the jobs. Or it doesn't survive."

"But my singing used to be fine. Last year I was in ten operas—*ten*!" he argued, sensing that she was lying. After all, the Venice opera was hardly going anywhere with its long, storied history and gem-like house.

He'd hated sounding so desperate and self-promoting, but more than anything, he wanted to continue singing at the opera. Single and a one-time gondolier who had turned to renting his license and boat to a thirty-year-old from London, he'd never had much of a life aside from La Fenice.

"And things have changed this year, so you need to adjust to the change," she'd further lectured, as if he were a child! "Life is like that—always changing. You can't expect things to stay the same."

She gave him a wan smile and turned back to her computer to read her e-mail.

He felt that she wanted him to leave, resonating smugness about her handling of the situation. But he also sensed that she was uncomfortable. Yes, she disliked him for some reason, maybe because he represented what she could not: a full-blooded Venetian with a lifetime of experience at La Fenice, where she was from the Dolomites, a virtual mountain Heidi, who didn't belong.

"But I've been here for years, helped this company in so many ways," he'd continued, feeling foolish but unable to stop himself. "I've been an integral part of La Fenice for most of my adult life."

He knew his voice sounded desperate, plaintive, but he refused to give up.

She swiveled around in her chair, a vague frown of annoyance marring her thin, Teutonic face. "And I've been told by many that your work has been appreciated. But to be quite frank, there are other singers out there who are just more talented. Stronger voices or better styles. And I must do what is best for the company—you are not the only one who loves La Fenice—"

"But you've just arrived here. I've gone to this opera house since I was a child. And I've worked here for twenty-five years. You've only just arrived," he repeated, his voice rising.

Waving her hand, she dismissed him.

"I love this opera house and company as much as you," she snarled.

"I came here as a child, too, though only on the rare occasion when we would travel here from my small town. You can love La Fenice as much as any Venetian, even if you didn't grow up here."

And that was when Giovanni realized that she was jealous, that she must have felt like an outsider in the old, cliquish city.

"But you can't push me out of the company like this. You *can't*," he'd insisted, leaning forward in his chair. "It's not right."

She clucked her tongue, smirking. "As I told you, it's nothing personal. And I *am* making the decisions about the choir and these are decisions you have to abide by and accept. You can go above me if you like, but I've not been overruled on any of my decisions."

She turned back to her computer, opened an e-mail, and began to read.

He had stomped out, slamming her office door so hard he was afraid he might have cracked or broken the window in it. He turned to see if anything had broken, but the thick glass had been fine—it was his life that had been shattered.

He deftly poled the boat up to the opera house landing where a streetlight cast long, difficult to distinguish shadows. Well, he thought, she would be sorry.

Giovanni smiled broadly, shaking in anticipation of what they were about to do. He'd planned this for a night without a moon, of course, and they found themselves well hidden. They'd be back off down the dark canal before anyone knew a fire had even been set.

"Tie us up—not too tight, though, remember?" he told Paolo.

His childhood friend nodded, quickly tying the boat to the heavy wooden posts rising from the quay. When he'd secured one rope to each of the two posts, he looked expectantly at Giovanni, whose face was scarcely visible in the dimness.

"I'll bring the bag," Giovanni whispered. "You ready?"

"*Pronto*," Paolo whispered. He was glad his face was in darkness, for if his face were visible it would have given him away. He wished he hadn't come. He knew why Giovanni was here, but why had *he* come? To help his friend or merely for a little excitement? Or maybe for the simple reason that he could do something big enough to get in the papers—maybe in the papers around the world. Then he might not feel like such a small guy living in such a sleepy-small place, stuck in a sinking, smelly city.

And, he felt a sense of loyalty to Giovanni who'd found him a job and had always watched out for him in their neighborhood when they were growing up. Paolo had been small; always the object of derision for the bigger boys, but Giovanni had kept the bullies away as if he'd been an older brother.

Paolo followed Giovanni along the small via heading away from the boat. The streets, just like the canals, were completely deserted, eerily quiet except for the occasional sucking sound of water in the canals. Scientists said that the city was sinking, and on quiet nights when the water made strange sounds, it was easy to believe.

For a fleeting moment, Giovanni doubted himself, wondering if their act might bring about calamity. Maybe the whole opera house would burn; maybe the whole city would catch fire. Could this one act be the end of everything?

Some of his superstitious friends—apart from being appalled at his actions—would think he was tempting the gods, even *playing* the part of a god. These friends saw the world in strange ways, as if every action, every human, was placed on giant scales that tipped the balance of fate toward goodness or evil. They thought there were forces—a god or *gods* they sometimes called them—that stuck their fingers in the stew called humanity and stirred.

These seemed to him the same as religious beliefs. He believed in nothing of the sort. "You're an atheist," a friend had scolded. Giovanni had shrugged in response. He didn't even like the label because he wasn't certain how to categorize or align himself. He believed in life, believed in taking charge of his own fate, so that was something wasn't it?

And that's why he'd vowed to set fire to La Fenice. If he was not good enough to sing there, then he should strike back, hit the very people who had decided arbitrarily that the one thing in his life that he could call a passion was to be no more. And maybe something, somehow, would give him another chance. The fire would be like cleaning house, wiping the slate clean. And he would make sure that the thick-skulled manager, Signore Cavaltini, would be fired, taking with him the choirmaster, Signora Morasso. And Giovanni would be there, prepared to help in any way he could, cleaning ashes and smoke from the walls, putting himself in the position of having the opera house indebted to him. And that would surely give him a second chance.

He smiled, an idea so perfect coming to him that if he believed in a god he would think it was divine inspiration.

Paolo noticed his friend's sudden smile and furrowed his brow.

"Why smile?" he asked, slowing their rapid pace. "That worries me. You seem drunk with revenge."

Giovanni laughed, slapping Paolo on the back. "Don't worry, my friend," he said. "I've just had a great idea, that's all. Nothing to worry about."

Paolo didn't look convinced.

"You'll see when we get there—I'll tell you all about it," he promised, regretting that he would have to explain his thoughts.

He tapped Paolo's elbow, prodding him to walk faster. "Let's go and you'll see when we get there. I promise."

They rounded a curve and Paolo stopped abruptly for just ahead of them, bathed in soft, glowing light was the Baroque facade of the opera house.

"Let's not stop—no time," said Giovanni, cupping Paolo's elbow. "We want to get in and out quickly, and it's getting late."

Paolo followed him down the narrow via alongside the high walls of La Fenice, gripping the zippered bag with one hand and dragging his hand along the wall with the other. They arrived outside the stage door, under a small light bulb, which cast a weak, jaundiced pool of light. Giovanni removed a key and quickly unlocked the deadbolt. Then they were inside, enveloped by thick darkness that smelled of old wood and mildew. He felt along the doorway, finding a switch and flicking on an overhead light.

"It's a dump in here," Paolo whispered, looking around him. "Not at all what I thought it would be."

"This is backstage, and everything backstage is for working, completely utilitarian, and just simple beauty. Inside you'll see the grand opera house you're thinking of."

He marveled that Paolo had never been to an opera, not even in the cheap, nearly free seats offered for every performance. Anyone could go to the opera in Italy, after all. And he thought all Italians had been to a performance at least once in their lives.

"So I'm changing the plan, by just a few minutes. I just want to make a short stop," Giovanni announced, signaling for Paolo to follow.

They walked quickly down a narrow hallway lined with pipes, ropes headed upward, the ends disappearing into black holes. Giovanni flicked on lights as they walked, each bulb casting a pool of weak light on the worn, dusty wooden floors. A line of varnished wooden doors with cutouts for windows shone in the dull light. Giovanni stopped in front of a door with a name on the window.

Sra. Silvia Morasso

Direttore del Coro

Giovanni laughed. He covered his hand with his shirt, grabbing the doorknob and turning it with a flourish.

"What are we doing here?" Paolo asked.

"Helping my cause," he explained. "This is the new part to my plan, the inspiration I mentioned outside."

He flicked a thick, old switch, bathing the small office in bright light. Paolo touched the computer keyboard and laughed when the screen came to life.

"She never turns off her computer," Giovanni grinned. "Fool."

Paolo watched as Giovanni opened the e-mail, selected a message, and read it quickly. He closed that one and then opened another. Then another. Finally, he opened one that prompted a triumphant smile. The message read:

> *Sra.* Morasso. Thank you for the recent tickets. I would also like to attend one of the upcoming shows of Il Trittico. Can you please advise me of ticket availability for the press? *Grazie.*

The e-mail was signed:

Signore Facci, *Editore Musicale, La Repubblica*

Giovanni hit reply, quickly typing:

> *Sr.* Facci. Thank you for your inquiry. We appear to have plenty of tickets available for all performances of Il Trittico, so please forward date availabilities and I'll be happy to accommodate you. *Grazie.*

He then closed the e-mail with:

Signora Morasso
Direttore del Coro
La Fenice

"This is what you had to do? I don't understand," Paolo said, eyeing Giovanni with suspicion.

"Don't worry. You'll come to understand later. I'm finished now, so let's get to work."

Giovanni stood up quickly and moved toward the door. Paolo slowly followed, looking back at the computer.

"But I read what you wrote," he puzzled, pointing at the computer. "And it doesn't make sense."

Giovanni flicked off the light in the small office, wishing he didn't have to explain everything.

"Like I said, never mind. You'll understand later. I promise."

Stepping into the hallway, he tugged at Paolo's sleeve, coaxing him along.

"Aren't you going to turn off the computer?" Paolo asked, closing the office door.

"No."

Turning, Giovanni reopened the door and then flicked the light back on.

"What is it you're doing? I don't trust you," Paolo said, blocking Giovanni's passage in the doorway.

Giovanni shook his head. "Come on, we don't have time for this—"

Then the shrill sound of an alarm broke the air.

Giovanni jumped, pushed past Paolo, and raced down the hall with Paolo following.

Then Giovanni stopped, unzipped the bag he'd been carrying and spilled the contents onto the floor. "We won't have time to do what we planned, so just light anything on fire!"

"But the fire curtain is open," Paolo said, pointing onto the nearby stage and the dimly lit view of boxes and seats ringing the theater beyond it. "Won't the whole place burn?"

"We don't have time," he exclaimed. "They'll be here right away—the alarm's already ringing. Just hurry! Light something on fire."

Giovanni tossed Paolo a lighter, rags, and gasoline. He felt numb, strangely disconnected as he poured gasoline on the rag as if he were watching someone else start the fire. It was better that he didn't have time to think about it anymore, but had to hurry before the police arrived. If they failed, what sort of a life would he have? No, the choral director had to go, and this was the only way to ensure her dismissal. Maybe she would even be prosecuted. He smiled recalling the e-mail he'd sent in her name, the luck he'd experienced in hatching the simple plan. He'd never considered that she might have the arson pinned on her so easily, but this only made things better. As with everything else, things were falling into place as if the outcome had been intended. He wasn't religious, certainly didn't believe that there was a sweet-faced god above or even a trident-sporting bearded figure who picked sides and meddled, yet he experienced the undeniable feeling that things were turning out as intended.

A nagging voice derided his naïveté. What if he was wrong and the whole place burned? Well, that was preferable. If he couldn't have his little, rightful share of the opera house, then no one could. The thought of Silvia Morasso working there for years into the future made him tremble.

As he watched a tongue of fire lick its way up the curtain, he smiled. Silvia Morasso was mistaken—she would *not* be working at La Fenice. Maybe no one would work there for a while, but she would certainly not work there again.

He looked over at Paolo who stood motionless, his mouth agape.

"I can't do it," he pleaded. "Sorry. I thought I could, but I can't."

Paolo looked out into the theater, then at the backstage fire behind them. He shifted his weight between his legs, back and forth, back and forth, looking nervous. He paced like an animal; his eyes took on a worried look as he watched the growing flames.

The fire grew, moving quickly up the curtain, making little sighing noises as it consumed the thick red fabric. Smoke started pouring upward and Giovanni knew that in a moment the fire alarm would add its shrill buzz to that of the burglar alarm already ringing.

He'd have been better off without Paolo. It was stupid of him to have ever mentioned his plan or that he needed help. Now there was someone who knew what he'd done, though he'd hardly been an accomplice.

"We'd better get out of here," Giovanni said, grabbing the bag and gas can.

"Can we close the fire curtain?" Paolo asked timidly.

"There's no time," Giovanni said. "And I don't think you need to worry anyway. We only set this one small fire—look how big this place is. And with the alarm already going off—which is another reason not to spend a minute more here—and the smoke about to set off the fire alarm, this place isn't going to burn down. The fire fighters—*and police*—will be here momentarily."

Giovanni gently prodded his friend, pushing him down the hallway.

"Let's get the hell out of here, okay?"

Paolo looked up at the flames and back into the theater, but followed Giovanni down the hallway and out the side door. When they reached the small via at the side of the opera house, they could hardly hear the alarm.

"But I'm certain it's rigged to the police station, right? It must be," Paolo said, glancing over his shoulder at the dimly lit facade of the opera house.

In front of La Fenice, they scanned the piazza, but Venice was as dead and as void of life as it had been when they'd passed through on their way into the theater.

Giovanni tried to walk casually, without looking too hurried, though his legs longed to break into a run. This was Venice, after all, and anyone could be watching or listening.

Then the fire alarm sounded, piercing the air with its wail.

"See, you've got nothing to worry about," Giovanni said to Paolo, patting him on the back. "They'll be here in minutes."

Paolo smiled, looking relieved as they turned the corner. Ahead, in the shadows, the two could see the outline of their boat riding higher in the water than it had been. The tide was creeping into the city, spilling into the lower piazze and onto some of the sidewalks. Giovanni knew it would be a slower ride back against the tide, but they were no longer in a hurry.

The men boarded the boat quietly, each one untying a rope. Before picking up the pole, Giovanni methodically emptied the remaining contents of the canvas bag, placing the rags that Paolo hadn't used into the glove box of the boat, the lighters into his pocket, and the gasoline near the motor. After everything was put away, he walked carefully to the stern and began leaning into the pole, pushing the boat back into the canal, and away from the street and La Fenice.

Was it his imagination, or was the canal quieter—hushed even—than it had been on the trip there? He listened for the fire alarm, but heard only the soft splash of the water on the bow of the boat and the hollow plunk of the pole striking the water as he planted it on the canal bottom.

They rounded a slight bend, and were once again in sight of the palazzo with its doors and windows still open, some shedding light into the night sky. As they neared the palazzo, the wind started blowing from the north, pushing the boat forward. Eager to get home, he was relieved for the help.

In the distance a siren sounded.

"They're going now!" he whispered to Paolo, who nodded in the dark.

Directly above them, the breeze carried giant panels—curtains, they seemed to be—out over the canal. Fluttering above them, pushed by the suddenly strong wind, the material looked like ghosts, something alive.

Giovanni could smell rain in the air and realized why it was so dark. The skies must have clouded up after sunset, closing off the stars and gibbous moon. Rain would be good, helping the *pompieri* to fight the fire.

Behind them, the windows of the palazzo suddenly went dark, the lights inside flickering off, extinguishing the golden squares of glowing light. Despite the dark, he could still see the panels of white fabric dancing in the breeze, waving good-bye like the handkerchiefs his mother used to wave at the train station platform when his father traveled out of the city to visit his parents. Then he strained against the pole, pushing his weight against it and propelling the boat around a corner. The ghost-like curtains disappeared, replaced by deep shadows and the faintest outlines of buildings. He would have to feel his way through the smaller canals, moving slower than he would like because of the darkness.

"I don't feel right about it," Paolo announced, his face invisible in the thick darkness.

"Shhh," Giovanni scolded. "Sotto voce, sotto voce!" he hissed.

Whispering, Paolo continued. "I have a bad feeling. I think it was a mistake."

Breathing hard now from poling, Giovanni slowed for a minute, but the wind began pushing the boat off course. He pushed back against the wind, whispering unevenly. "You think too negatively, like a cursed Venetian. Why can't you think more positively, eh?"

In the distance, a chorus of sirens from fireboats rose.

Giovanni was glad for the dark, thankful that he didn't have to see his friend's pursed mouth or his darting, nervous eyes. Why had he included him when he could just as easily have done the whole thing himself? Paolo had agreed that the new director had violated a tradition that probably originated with the guilds of the Middle Ages. He'd seemed just as angry and insulted as Giovanni had been which is exactly what he'd hoped for. Maybe he was too clannish, but the fact that the new director was an outsider only made her plan to fire him even more insulting.

What did she know of La Fenice? What did she know of Venice?

She would learn, though he wished his lesson could have been more direct, less subtle. She would regret coming to Venice. In that, he was certain they had succeeded.

Still, he wished he had left his friend out of it.

"I can't help it," Paolo's voice said darkly.

"Well, what can we do about it now anyway?" Giovanni said, irritation flooding his voice. He pushed the pole especially hard against the canal floor, not caring that making the boat go so fast in the dark was reckless. Maybe he would scare Paolo, shut him up.

"Go back and help," was the surprising answer from Paolo.

"What?"

"Let's go back and help fight the fire. If things are going fine and the fire is under control, then we can turn around and go back—"

"And what do we tell the pompieri, that we were just out on a late night canal ride in an old motor boat, thumbing our noses at the rising storm? And we heard a commotion and thought we'd come by and help?"

He wished he could see Paolo's face because he didn't respond, at least not immediately. After a few moments slid by, marked by the sloshing of water against the boat's bow and the nearby sides of houses, Paolo sighed heavily, barely audible given the gusting wind and sloshing water, and the hardness of Giovanni's breath from the exertion of pushing the boat through the water.

"You can do what you want, but I plan to walk back over there when we get to your apartment," Paolo announced. "Maybe you're right that it would be suspicious to show up in the boat, but I can tell them I couldn't sleep and then followed the sound of the sirens. I bet I won't be the only person."

He was right about that. Because people lived so close together, Venetians only had to open their windows, run down some stairs, or walk to the end of the street to find out firsthand what was happening when there was a commotion. And a fire at La Fenice was certain to draw a crowd. So maybe he didn't need to worry.

"And you won't talk to anyone while you're there?" Giovanni asked.

"Not anymore than I need to. I'll just offer to help, that's all."

"Okay," Giovanni said, trying to sound encouraging. He worried, though, that his friend would talk to someone, say something that drew suspicion to him. "Maybe I'll go with you and help, too."

The thought made him feel better. He could help fight the fire, which would assuage his guilt and keep an eye on Paolo at the same time, which would ease his worries. He strained harder against the pole, suddenly anxious to return to La Fenice, to see what he'd done.

Of course, things were going according to plan. How fast could a fire burn? Why did he let Paolo's pessimism infect him? Better to assume the best. Let Paolo think the way he wanted; he wouldn't let it bother him.

When he gently nudged the boat up to the wooden pilings next to the apartment building, he noticed light coming from one of the windows on the third floor, the American's studio. If the man saw or heard them coming in, what of it? How would he ever connect two friends going out on the canals at night with a fire that had happened halfway way across the city?

Hopping out of the boat, he noticed that Paolo had jumped out even quicker. They each tied a rope to one of the posts, and then hurried along the narrow gangplank along the building. When they reached the street, Paolo nearly started running.

"Are you trying to lose me?" Giovanni asked, catching up to and running along beside him. "Let's first get the stuff out of the boat and stash it upstairs."

"No. I just want to get there quickly to help," Paolo replied, breathing heavily.

"And have someone find the stuff in the boat?" Giovanni asked in a terse whisper. "Come on—it'll take just a minute."

"Okay," Paolo said, turning. "Quickly, though. I feel like I've done a bad thing."

They raced back to the boat, retrieving the bags, the rags, and the lighters. Why hadn't they just tossed all of the gasoline-soaked rags? What would they do with them?

"These stink!" Giovanni whispered. "Good thing no one's around."

Heading back down the narrow passage, with Paolo right behind him, they reached the door of the apartment building and Giovanni quickly turned the key in the lock. When he opened the door, the timed stair hall light was on.

"Someone's in here!" Paolo hissed.

Giovanni brought his finger to his lips, gesturing for his friend to be quiet. They stood silently for a moment, but heard nothing.

"Maybe the light's stuck on?" Paolo suggested.

"Or someone was just returning or leaving rather late—that's all. Nothing unusual about that," Giovanni whispered.

They stood a moment longer before they detected it, the muffled sobbing they'd heard earlier.

"Oh, no, it's that crying again," Paolo whined, shaking his head. "Bad, bad sign."

"It's nothing, *means* nothing," Giovanni said, speaking softly. "We heard that earlier."

"Shhh. What was that?" Paolo whispered, raising his finger to his lips.

"Just the crying," he answered loudly, ignoring the gesture.

"No, no, it was something else, I heard something else."

Giovanni shrugged. "You're as superstitious as old Signora Crespi who sits in her window observing everyone on the street and believing in spells and prayers. What's done is done; we started La Fenice on fire. If we'd been cursed we would never have succeeded."

Faintly, through the thick walls of the building, they heard the sound of distant sirens.

Paolo glared at his friend. "Why did you say that? Why do you have to talk so loud? Can't you whisper?" he hissed, angrily waving his hand through the air.

"Okay, okay," Giovanni said, whispering again, his voice dripping with sarcasm. "You want me to whisper, I'll whisper."

Paolo raised his fist. "I should never have agreed to help you—I was a fool to do this."

"I should never have asked you to help me—what little you helped. Your type is as sunk as Venice, more medieval than modern," he smirked, turning his back on Paolo and starting to climb the stairs.

"*Stronzo*!" Paolo shrieked, bounding after him.

Giovanni raced up the stairs, leaping the wide steps two at a time.

Staying just ahead of Paolo, he laughed maniacally. "Why don't you ask the gods for help, eh?" he shouted.

"You always were *senza vergogna*—you deserve to be cursed! You've no respect for anything! Burning the opera house—you're an animal!"

As Giovanni reached the second landing, he turned onto the second set of steps and nearly fell into the lap of the young American who sat crouched on the stair. Wincing, his forearm shielding his head, the American yelled as Giovanni tripped over him. Following just behind, Paolo pounced on the cowering man, roughly clamping his hand over his mouth.

"Shut up! Shut up!" Paolo hissed, his voice an angry whisper. "Not a word, nothing!"

Giovanni sat up from where he lay sprawled across the stairs, rubbing his shins with a grimace. With a puzzled expression, he looked a few steps below him on the landing where his friend sat atop the other man's chest, his hand covering his mouth. Shaking his head in disbelief, he clucked his tongue.

"What are you doing, Paolo?"

"*Shhh*!" he hissed. "Don't say my name—don't *ever* say my name again, okay?"

Giovanni smirked. "What do you propose doing now?"

"He heard *everything*—don't you know—he's an eavesdropper? He just heard the conversation we had because *you* weren't whispering. Because you wouldn't *listen* to me. Because you know it *all*!"

Paolo's eyes darted nervously between Giovanni and the man pinned beneath him. Breathing unevenly, his chest heaving as he panted, he struggled to catch his breath.

"Let him go," Giovanni said. "He doesn't know anything."

"*Magari*! Of course he does! How could he not? And besides, by tomorrow morning, he'll have figured it out if he doesn't already know."

The man beneath him shook his head feebly, his eyes small and fearful.

"Don't worry, we won't hurt you," Paolo whispered. "We're not *assassini*. We're simply arsons who set La Fenice afire. You know La Fenice, the opera house?"

As the American nodded weakly, his eyes fixed on the peeling ceiling far above Paolo's head, Giovanni sighed, a long, drawn out release of breath that echoed in the silent landing.

"Va bene," Giovanni said with resignation. "What do we do now?"

Paolo looked at his friend with disgust, shaking his head as if it were obvious. "Tie him up. We'll tie him up and flee."

Chapter Eighteen

Sacci inserted a large key into the deadbolt and slowly turned the key. The workers stood idly behind him, shifting their weight from one leg to the other. He felt nervous, as if he were breaking in. He'd checked the windows and no lights appeared to be on. Claudia would certainly be in bed by this hour.

"Signore, there's no alarm to be worried about is there?" one of the workers asked.

"Good thinking, but hotels don't have alarms. And starting tomorrow, the hotel will be open every day, all day until it goes out of business. So an alarm would do no good."

He wondered what the workers thought, sneaking into a hotel led by a man claiming to be a co-owner. Then why sneak in, they must have been asking themselves? Maybe they thought he was mafia. Thankfully, though, they didn't ask a lot of questions, they merely stood reticent, with eager expressions on their faces. They wanted to get their work done and head home.

A worker approached Sacci as he listened to the turning of the bolt.

"Signore," he said accusingly. "We were here an hour ago and rang the chimes, but no one answered."

"What did you do?" Sacci barked, his voice shrill. Had Claudia answered the door?

"Did you talk to anyone? Did anyone come to the door?" Sacci asked, wondering if the plan was ruined.

"No, no one answered," the man said, still sounding suspicious. "And the hall light went off right after we rang a few times."

"Didn't the contessa warn you *not* to ring the bell, to wait silently outside until you were let in?" he hissed.

Maybe he'd been wrong to trust her. Was this the first of many missteps?

"We weren't certain. I do remember hearing that, though. Seemed odd to me, though, and we saw a light on so thought that it might be the person who was supposed to let us in, so we thought we might as well ring the door chime," he said, sounding annoyed. "Hey, who are you, anyway?"

"I'm the owner of this palazzo, signore," he shot back, annoyance evident in his own voice. "And while the contessa may be paying for you, I can cancel the contract at any time."

He was surprised at how severe he sounded, unlike his manner at any other moment in his life. Was he sounding a little like an American? Or had he taken his cue from the contessa?

"Spiace, signore," the man apologized.

Unaccustomed to unlocking the door, Sacci proceeded slowly, deliberately. When the lock sprang open, it seemed as loud as a brick striking the pavement. They all froze, cocking their heads toward the door and the upstairs windows. But no light flickered on and there was no sound of scampering feet.

Sacci slowly pushed open the massive door, waiting for a creak of tremendous proportions. None came, so he waved the workers inside.

"You'll want to set up a bar in this first lobby, and then one upstairs on the loggia," he instructed, motioning for them to follow. "*Quiet*," he whispered. "Please be *quiet*."

They nodded, following him around the hotel like lambs. When he finished a quick tour of the rooms in which they would work, he watched as they hurriedly unloaded boxes of glasses, liquor, and wine, and began setting up the bars. He was struck at how quickly and quietly they moved, probably motivated by a bonus provided by the contessa.

He was tempted to peek in on Claudia to see if she was sleeping, but decided he might wake her. It would be better to avoid her bedroom door completely, which he'd also told the workers to do. He closed the doors into the upper salon, which had become a lounge with a pool table, a library nook, and a small bar. With the doors closed and her room down another small passage, she was unlikely to hear them.

He felt a surge of confidence. Things would work out perfectly. The hotel, even with only a few lights on, looked magical, like a Venetian palace ought to look. From the beginning, everything had fallen into place. It had seemed unlikely, crazy even, to trust a complete unknown like Claudia, but his gut had told him she was the one to oversee the renovation and run the hotel. And so far, he'd been right.

When his siblings had asked him who would manage the project and run the hotel, he'd lied a little, telling them that Claudia had a lot of experience. And in a short time, they'd come around, too, seeing what a natural she was.

Sitting at one of the tables in the loggia, he watched the transformation of the already comfortable space. Two workers brought up giant bolts of creamy muslin and began unrolling and cutting the fabric into panels twenty feet long. They then attached the curtains to enormous window-like box structures made of metal. Within an hour, glowing curtains, which fluttered faintly in the nearly still night, surrounded the exposed half of the loggia.

Other workers brought up cases of prosecco, wine, champagne, and liquor, followed by box after box of champagne, cocktail, and wine glasses.

No, the contessa certainly wasn't all-bad, he decided. When he'd met her, she'd been surprisingly friendly. He realized, of course, that she'd wanted something from him, and that that had probably affected her manner. Still, he'd been taken aback when she'd revealed some deeper, almost vulnerable side, and it had become obvious that she intended to spend quite generously for an event she wouldn't even attend.

Recalling the way she'd mentioned something happening to her in Venice when she'd been young, he wondered why she'd been so mysterious. He made a mental note to ask his mother and an aunt if they remembered anything about an Anna Baggi, but realized he didn't know her maiden name. He would have to ask Claudia, discreetly.

After the hotel opened and was running smoothly, he would ask around and discover the answer to this odd little mystery.

The workers moved in near silence setting everything up quietly. They whispered, using hand gestures and shakes or nods of their heads, as if they'd rehearsed the whole evening. While one group of workers had erected the frames to hold the curtains, others set up tall-cloaked bars fronted by potted palms with blooming orchids at their bases.

Claudia couldn't be angry when she discovered what he'd allowed her mother to do—the hotel would be enchanting, unlike any he'd seen in Venice or glimpsed in magazines. For the first time, he wished the opening were upon them, that he could speed up time and quickly zip through the remaining twenty hours or so until guests started arriving.

He knew the minute Claudia awoke and saw everything she would start asking questions. In the past twenty-four hours or so since he'd first launched the plan with her mother, he'd rehearsed what he would tell her countless times. A dying uncle had won the lottery, he would tell her, and so he'd given him the money to spend on the palazzo. The sole remaining question was whether Sacci would sleep in one of the rooms that night, or go home. If he slept here, he'd be present to explain what had happened overnight. But then, shouldn't she have the palazzo to herself for one more night and morning, before she could no longer savor it by herself again? He could explain everything when he arrived in the morning.

He'd seen right away how she'd taken to the place, just as he had as a child. She noticed every molding, each mosaic tile, soaring pillar, giant door, piece of wooden or plaster trim, sturdy shutter, and wavy glass window. While at first she'd hesitated to live here on her own, she'd eventually seemed to belong here, just like the old stone columns in the entry and the eternally colorful, Venetian Gothic windows.

Every decision she'd made, about where to place the baths for each of the guest rooms or where armoires should stand, seemed predetermined, as if she could sense how to place each piece of furniture to maintain the spirit of the place. Though it was altered from when he'd visited as a child, the palazzo possessed essentially the same feeling. The difference was that the place seemed to have come alive. That was how the building had changed the most, he realized. Like Claudia herself, the palazzo was vibrant and breathing.

He decided to leave the palazzo to Claudia for one more peaceful, dark night and another bright, serene morning. She might call him first thing, but he decided to let her discover by herself what they'd done during the night.

Two younger workers slowly entered the loggia, struggling to carry two wooden crates bursting with straw. The contessa hadn't mentioned many of the things that were emerging from boxes and the carts parked outside the entrance. He realized that she'd misled him in a way, doing far more than she'd told him about.

He watched as the lids of the crates were carefully removed and the straw pulled aside. One of the workers reached in and slowly pulled out small, brightly colored glass lanterns, each one with *Palazzo San Spirito* in scrolling letters running up one side. He recognized the glass immediately as Murano, marveling at the contessa's deception: there was no way to make lanterns in twenty-four hours. Even her money couldn't have created two crates of lanterns specially made for the hotel just since they'd met a day ago.

But there it was again, even the contessa making the same mistake. The wrong name for the hotel seemed to follow them like an innocuous curse, trying to bring a conscious sacredness to the hotel that no one seemed to want. Had it been intentional, was that the contessa's way of reminding them of her religion, that the only type of spirit worth naming a hotel after was a holy one?

Years ago, he might have cared, fearing that they tempted fate by dropping off the traditional "San." But he no longer believed strongly in anything. He attended Mass on occasion, mostly when visiting his mother, but when he went it was more out of habit than fervent religious desire. It wasn't that he didn't believe, he just didn't believe strongly enough that he would let religion color his decisions.

He watched as the workers carefully and silently dusted the lanterns, filling them with oil and setting one on each table already covered with a snow-colored cloth. He wished they could light the lanterns so he could see how the loggia would look the following evening, but the workers were hurrying, and he needed to get to bed as soon as they finished. Claudia wasn't the only one who would be exhausted the following day.

From the canal below, he heard the sound of a boat and hushed voices. Peering over the edge of the loggia, he barely made out the outline of a small boat and on its bow, the faint outline of a man standing, poling the short vessel forward as if it were a gondola. In the back of the boat another form hovered. What were two men doing on the dark canal so late?

He strained to hear their conversation, wondering if they were burglars or in the pursuit of mischief. Being good Venetians, they kept their voices low, probably wary of eavesdroppers.

"*Eccola la Fenice*," he heard one of the voices exclaim.

Sacci wondered if their destination was the famed opera house, or simply a landmark they'd recognized.

The boat disappeared around the corner, headed in the direction of the hulking building down the street.

"Signore, we're finished now," a hoarse voice whispered over his shoulder. It was one of the men who'd led the team of workers. Even in the half-light, Sacci could see that the man's face was sweaty and pink from rushing up and down the stairs, racing from one side of the loggia to the other.

Sacci pulled away from the balustrade, forgetting the boat.

"And you'll be back tomorrow or on Sunday to pick everything up?"

"No, signore," the squat man said, shaking his head looking perplexed. "The client made no arrangements for us to return to pick up anything."

"It's not a rental—except for the lanterns?" Sacci asked, beginning to realize just how generous the contessa had been.

"Everything here was purchased. Nothing's been rented," the man explained, appearing surprised that Sacci didn't know.

Sacci nodded, lost in thought, while the man shuffled from the loggia, the last to leave. The hotel was silent again except for the murmur of a slight breeze beginning to stir.

He admired the loggia, wishing again that he could light all the lanterns and pillar candles so that he could get a preview, enjoying his family palazzo come back to life, as the city slept. Following a short distance behind the workers, he descended the wide steps slowly, noticing the shadows of the men clustered around the distant entryway.

The contessa must have paid the team of men a lot of money. She'd probably spoken to her friends in the city and hired the best men available. Sacci realized that none of the workers was familiar—he hadn't seen one around town. Yet, he'd grown up here.

"*Buona fortuna* with your opening tomorrow," one worker said sotto voce, shaking Sacci's hand as he approached. "I'll tell all my friends—it's a beautiful hotel. And the loggia—perfetto!"

"I think so, too," Sacci said, feeling relieved. "Thank you—and come to the opening party tomorrow—at eight o'clock."

Sacci glanced around, noticing that newly potted palms and sweet-smelling lemon trees flanked the entry hall. More carts had apparently arrived while he'd been on the loggia because he hadn't seen any with six-foot palms or citrus trees spilling out of them. The lemon trees were in bloom, their intoxicating, and Elysian-sweet fragrance already settling and wafting through the wide corridor. With her keen sense of smell, Claudia would probably detect the blooming trees before she even left her room the next morning.

"I would be happy to come," the man replied. "I think your palazzo must be one of the most charming hotels in all of Venice."

Sacci and the head worker stood on the threshold, wearily surveying the dark street. Nearly a dozen carts lay empty, clustered around the front entry stairs. There was no longer any room to pass in front of the hotel, but Sacci didn't care. No one was up, anyway. And the hotel looked even better than he could have imagined.

Before he went to bed that night, he would toast the contessa, and then toss a full glass of port into the canal. He might as well play it safe and follow the old tradition, which he'd heard came from the ancient Romans. He wasn't certain what he'd be honoring by following the tradition, but what could it hurt?

Though it was late, he planned to take his time walking home along the darkened and silent streets. After locking the massive doors, he crossed the street and turned to view the transformed building. Having placed the two keys to the palazzo in his pocket, he felt the larger skeleton key—the one that opened the enormous outer door—digging into his thigh. He pushed the key deeper into the pocket, placing it vertically, but the old key wasn't meant to fit in a pocket. No doubt, his ancestors had had someone to carry it, or they'd fastened it to a belt.

"Dai," he muttered.

Thankfully, he wouldn't need to carry the keys again—just this one night. After that, the doors would remain open and he could keep the keys at home or in a back room of the palazzo. Marveling at their size, he tucked both keys deep into his shallow jacket pocket.

The keys no longer digging into his thigh, he looked back toward the palazzo where dim lights in the first floor reception and lounge shone through the wide slats of the shuttered windows. Upstairs, a pale golden light poured out of the large upper hall balcony windows, the shutters having been left open. Looking toward the loggia, he sighed. A breeze had sprung up, carrying the curtains out above the street, making it look as if the walls of the upper story were undulating.

Claudia had been right about those curtains—she'd been right about all of the little details that he had sensed she would know intuitively. He'd been right, too, and it felt as if fate were playing itself out. Who would have guessed a year earlier that he would ever be inspired to do something with his family's crumbling palazzo, to pursue something more creative and interesting than being a simple landlord?

He felt genuinely lucky. The gods, fate or whatever seemed to be smiling, looking favorably on Venice, and stirring the air with powerful, breeze-producing fingers. What an evening—and the weather forecast claimed that the following day would be the same: breezy and warm. He couldn't stop himself from feeling grateful already, and in awe at how things had come together, right down to the weather. Could he have asked for a more perfect evening?

Moving farther down the street, he spun and gazed at the building again, marveling at its transformation and the way it seemed to glow. The discreet, vaguely orange-hued blemishes of the old architectural elements, the capitals flanking the front door, the coat of arms on the side of the loggia, and the gargoyle drain spouts—Louis' brilliant idea. Larger areas of diffused light illuminated the whole building, casting a soft glow on the old brick and stone walls, which appeared sturdier and seemed prepared to withstand another hundred or more years. He'd arranged to have the stones and brick tuck pointed, plastered, cleaned, and repaired, and they seemed the perfect amalgamation of old and new.

Why hadn't he thought to renovate the palazzo years earlier? Of course, had he done that he wouldn't have had Claudia or Louis, and maybe it came down to timing—and the feeling that it was meant to be. He hadn't had so much energy, felt so content or excited about anything for years. In the course of imbuing the palazzo with new life, he'd found that he'd been given new life as well.

Had that been meant to be, too?

He felt a sudden appreciation for being Venetian, inspired by the city's ability to overcome its swampy setting to become not merely an inhabitable city, but one of profound beauty. He remembered an Asian saying that beautiful and sacred things such as the lotus sprang from the mud. And so it had been with this ancient, improbable city that he called his own.

He told himself that if he crept slowly and quietly, rushing less and inhabiting the quiet corners and crumbling bridges, that he could better listen for the sounds the universe made—or maybe just the ones that his very own city made.

At any rate, he was lucky that things turned out the way they did.

Sacci walked an indirect, random route home, assessing other palazzi and comparing them to *Palazzo Spirito*. There were plenty of larger, grander palazzi, but none as interesting—none with such a unique combination of Gothic and Renaissance elements. And he seriously wondered if any other hotel had the painted beam ceilings, simple frescoes, or perfectly preserved wood floors that his did.

The hotel they'd created was truly unique, not only physically, but in some other intangible way, too. If he possessed a spirit, then maybe a building could, too. After all, it had survived longer than the lives of people. It had sheltered so much life, and ultimately, wasn't it made of things that had once been living?

Such thoughts could only visit on a quiet, dark night while wandering the narrow, meandering vie of Venice. He'd never entertained similar sentiments before, having never given too much thought to such things. Why did he experience a sudden rush of ideas, the sense that his life was more than a simple, prescribed path?

His heartbeat quickening, he decided to veer away from the via that would take him home, choosing instead to head to the old heart of the city, Piazza San Marco, figuring there might be others like him, or at least mesmerized tourists with whom he could share what remained of the evening. On such a night, there might be Venetians drawn from their stuffy flats and palazzi by the refreshing breeze. The streets leading up to the piazza lay silent, though, dimly lit by puddles of yellowy light cast from the occasional streetlamp, which illuminated gossamer webs tucked into the tenebrous corners of alleyways and passages. It seemed that the city was his alone, with no one awake or stirring to challenge his claim.

When he was a child, there had never been such moments because the city seemed always alive, its cramped streets never abandoned or empty. In those days, there must have been twice the number of inhabitants, and he would have had to walk to the edge of the neighborhoods to find an abandoned calle. Now a person merely needed to avoid the tourist areas, San Marco, and the Grand Canal. He enjoyed the complete and utter silence, the absence of the whine of vehicles, wondering how anyone lived with the noise of the buses, cars, and streetcars that he imagined were omnipresent in Milan or Rome.

Passing Tramonta, the café and bar at which he first saw Claudia and Louis nearly a year earlier, he paused, hearing laughter and singing wafting from the cracked windows. With the muffled laughter, singing, and voices, the faint smell of tobacco smoke and stale wine crept out, too.

Turning a corner overseen by a dimly illuminated, badly faded fresco of the Virgin Mary, he nearly ran into a neighbor, Signore Guarda.

"Ah, Signore Sacci," the old man said, exhaling breath redolent of wine and garlic. "You're out celebrating, eh? I've heard your new hotel opens tomorrow. S'that true?" The man smiled sloppily.

"It's true," Sacci answered. "And I hope you'll come to the opening—you received an invitation?"

"I did," the man said. "Can't come, though. My wife's having a dinner. Maybe we can stop by after—if it's going late?"

"It's sure to be going late, so stop by," he urged.

"You're getting married then, eh? I never thought you were the type to marry." The old man leaned in, smiling conspiratorially.

What was he referring to? Did he mean Claudia?

"No, she works with me, that's all," he said, trying not to sound annoyed. "And she's too young for me, anyway."

Sacci didn't like his old neighbor asking, even if he'd known the man since he was in nursery school. That was the one thing about the city he didn't like—the constant gossiping, the prevailing thought that anything about a person's life was open for discussion. If one didn't yield some information, neighbors, and schoolmates simply created scenarios and intrigues or labored incessantly to find out secrets as best they could. Sacci chose to keep to himself, not having much of life or many secrets to share anyway. Whatever people made up would be far more interesting than the truth, he figured.

"No, no," Signore Guarda laughed. "That's not what I meant at all."

He slapped Sacci on the back, giggling. "You're marrying the palazzo, eh? That's your new wife after tomorrow. We've never expected you to marry."

Sacci sighed, laughing a little, too. "I guess you're right. I've heard it's like getting married—running a hotel, or running a restaurant. So I guess in a way you're right."

What did he mean, though, that no one ever expected him to marry? Did they think he was the same way as Louis?

"Sì," the man said. "That's the old saying, open a restaurant or hotel, and gain another wife. Or in your case, a new one. Well, congratulations then, eh?"

"Ah, it's bad luck to congratulate before the hotel's even open, isn't it?" Sacci exclaimed, slapping his neighbor on the back.

"You're right—*scusa*," he said more soberly. "But I've heard wonderful things about the palazzo. I've walked by a few times—what a job you did. It'll be a great hotel, beautiful, too. And right near La Fenice—that'll bring all the tourists. Smart!"

"Grazie," Sacci said. "Things have turned out wonderfully. Better than I could ever have expected."

"And it must be nice to have the old family palazzo back in working order again, eh? That's good for your ancestors, good for you to bring it back from the dead."

"It was never really dead, signore," he protested. He'd never thought of the building as dead, just sleeping, dreaming of waking up maybe.

The old man slurred his words, his face a sloppy grin.

"No, no, you're right," the man agreed. "*Scusa ancora.* Still, it's nice to see it restored. Makes me think Venice is not dead after all."

"Why do you think that?" Sacci asked, sensing already what his neighbor of so many years might say.

"It's so quiet now—"

"It's always been quiet," Sacci countered. Why was he opposing him for saying what he'd been thinking earlier?

"*Quieter* now. Always quiet with no cars, but now quiet with no people. Unless you count the tourists at Carnivale and the summer. But you know that's not the same."

The man grinned again, shrugging his shoulders. "You remember, eh? Remember what the calle was like then, don't you?"

"I do," Sacci answered, smiling vaguely. When he'd been young, he'd thought the city would always remain like that, full of people, men on the streets playing cards, women gossiping while hanging laundry on clotheslines that zigzagged overhead.

"The calle was the living room," said the old man. "That's where everything happened, everything but lovemaking, and sometimes even that." He grinned. "Now nothing happens. You can buy a ceramic Carnivale mask made in Taiwan—or pay a sackful of lire for one of the few made here."

"No, it's not the same, I guess," Sacci said.

He'd been so happy just moments before, optimistic, too. Signore Guarda was right, but who knew. The city wasn't dead yet, though it was hard to believe it had ever been a center of anything, let alone the entire Mediterranean.

"What to do, what to do?" the man muttered, shaking his head again, his voice trembling. "I suppose nothing. Can't stop things from changing, can you? Can't go back and undiscover the New World, do away with the automobile. Can you?"

Sacci grimaced, thinking how lost the old man must feel in a changed Venice, a changed world. Venice had not changed so much in his lifetime as it had in Signore Guarda's life. The city must seem a different place entirely. Would Sacci recognize his city in another thirty years when he was the same age as his stooped-back neighbor?

The oceans could rise, as he'd read in the papers and heard on the radio, and Venice, along with other parts of the world, might be no more—just a memory, a shipwreck of sorts. Centuries into the future, the people might speak of Venice the way people today talked of the lost city of Atlantis. But then maybe Venice had always been lost.

He looked up at the old man who studied him with glassy, drunken eyes. He was waiting for an answer, gazing at Sacci expectantly.

What was it he'd even asked: whether a person could stop the world from changing? And that's what led his train of thought, all the way to a Venice that might be no more. The thing was, he didn't know. Just like no one but a few hundred people knew about the atom bombs before they were dropped, or when Vesuvius would erupt again, Sacci stood on the cusp of a change he could only guess at. He used to think nothing would surprise him, that he'd managed to take all the surprise out of life, but the fates would have their way, and they often surprised.

A cloud of despair settled around him as he looked at his neighbor. The yellowy glow cast from a nearby streetlight, its panels dusty and laced with cobwebs, lit the corner feebly, barely illuminating the mossy, cobblestoned patch of street.

"No, I guess you can't," he answered slowly. He should have said something hopeful, reassuring, but what could he have said to an old man who knew more about the world than did he?

Signore Guarda shook his head slowly, the smile fading from his lips. He paused, gazing up at the glowing Virgin Mary ensconced in the thick peeling wall above them.

Would the man make the sign of the cross, settle all of this ponderous unknowing and latent sadness with the comfort of a simple, archaic gesture?

The man's face moved up and down, taking in the glowing orange lights meant to mimic candles. He thought back to when he was a child, when someone had placed real candles there, lighting that shrine and every streetlamp, and every other shrine in the neighborhood each night. When did electric lights replace the candles? Did anyone even care anymore for all the ancient shrines on doorways, arches, and corners tucked into the twists and turns of the calles and vias?

"The city exists today, so there's that," Sacci said. "And my hotel opens tomorrow—er, tonight," he corrected himself after glancing at his watch.

Signore Guarda smiled; his eyes heavy-lidded.

"Maybe it is. What do I know? I'm just an old man, eh?" He sighed, releasing a hiccup that surprised them both. "And that's something, isn't it?"

"What's that?" Sacci asked.

"That you're opening that hotel, restoring that palazzo. Good for you. Stay defiant, eh?"

He gently patted Sacci on the back, squeezing his neck.

"Grazie," he answered, wondering what the old man meant. He embraced him. The old man felt thin, fragile.

He'd never hugged Signore Guarda before, never even shook his hand, or kissed his cheek. Sacci thought it odd how some people you saw nearly every day of your life you never embraced or kissed.

Was the old man religious? He'd never known him to go to church, so what had he meant by his staring at the Virgin Mary? He'd seen some people grow more religious as they grew older. Perhaps his old neighbor feared death, seeking comfort in the easy religion of his childhood.

"I hope it's not dead," Sacci said referring to the city. "I know it's changed a lot, but maybe it's still Venice—still a little different from other cities. We still have the fish market; still don't have a subway or cars, right? And we're still sinking!" he added. "But I suppose we've always been sinking, so that's nothing new."

His neighbor studied him, narrowing his eyes.

"*Allora*, what is it that you want, *ragazzo*? What is it that you really want?"

Sacci thought the man was certainly drunk, but seemed serious.

"To open this hotel, to complete the restoration of the palazzo," he offered timidly, uncertain what the man meant.

The man scowled, shaking his head. "No, no, no. What is it that you really want? That you *want*?" he scowled, emphasizing the last word as if it had greater meaning. Was he looking for him to say something religious?

"I'm not sure what you mean. I suppose I want many things—"

"No, *ragazzo*," he interrupted, grasping Sacci's arm with his bony fingers. "What do you want that maybe you can't have? That's what I mean. What do you *want*? What do you hunger for?"

Sacci shrugged. He thought of his dogs, his mother in Trieste, his flat in a good building. He would never marry, was never interested, and didn't miss it, so he could never say that he *wanted* that. At that moment, he just wanted to open the hotel, start a new life with the restored palazzo. That would be enough.

"Signore," he started, hoping that by speaking formally the man would sober up. He liked the man better when he was the reticent neighbor who waved or sang a simple greeting to him. He'd never had much of a conversation with him, just an exchange of niceties, but this night the man was drunk and making little sense.

"I can't think of anything I want that I don't have," he murmured. "Really. If the palazzo is successful, I'll be happy."

His old neighbor studied him, frowning. "That's not what you want, *really want*, is it?"

Did he think he was in love with someone, wanting to marry or have children? That he had some secret love or that he'd always harbored some suppressed desire to be a writer, an artist, or a politician? Whatever did he mean? Had there been gossip, did his neighbors think him in love with some neighborhood woman?

He shook his head in response, avoiding the man's gaze. "That would be enough for me. I don't have a great love—I don't have any love—and I don't need a love, if that's what you mean. I'm satisfied with what I have right now. It's enough."

"You are asleep, *ragazzo*," the man slurred, sniffing the air. "You live in Venice, which does the sleeping for you, so you don't need to sleep. Why don't you wake up, eh?"

He squeezed Sacci's arm again, a tight, grasping squeeze. The man had surprising strength.

"You should go home, Signore Guarda," Sacci said finally, growing impatient. "You're not making sense," he said, feeling defensive.

The man drew back, leveling his eyes at him. "You don't listen. *Che vergogna. Che lamenta.*"

He pushed his shoulders back, stepping away from Sacci.

"You should think about what I said," he said, his voice petulant. "Maybe tomorrow, or better yet, the day after when the hotel has opened. I know I'm drunk," he sniffed. "But I'm serious. This is the talk of a philosopher, the kind of talk everyone should have sometime—the sooner the better. The kinds of talk people have with their *psicoterapeuta*, right?"

He laughed and sighed, lapsing into silence.

"I don't know," Sacci answered. "I'm not sure at all about that. But you should go home, okay?"

The man lowered his eyebrows, lost in thought. "I thought you'd understand, but you really don't."

"Sorry. I'm not sure I do. But I'm okay, I'm happy, so you don't need to worry about me, okay?"

"I'll worry about you just the same. And everyone else in this crazy, sinking city."

Signore Guarda turned away to continue his walk down the street, rounding the corner where they'd almost bumped into each other.

"Happiness isn't everything," he called out, turning onto the via Sospiri.

"Do you want me to walk you home?" Sacci shouted after him. The man seemed to be walking okay, but what if he stumbled, falling into a canal? He would hate to be partially responsible, to have been the last to see Signore Guarda.

"No, no," he said hoarsely, waving Sacci away. "I'm not so drunk I can't walk. Just drunk enough that I can't make you make sense of me, that's all."

Sacci crept to the street corner, spying on the man who walked without stumbling, humming loudly as he picked his way carefully across the uneven cobblestones. He would make it home, if not for another twenty minutes, at least alive.

Sacci headed toward Piazza San Marco, hoping he would encounter other Venetians out for a stroll, proof that Signore Guarda's prophecy wasn't true. But the streets were quiet, cloaked in shadows and marred by bits of paper spun in circles by the strong southern breeze.

He'd never noticed the absence of lights in the upper stories of the buildings he passed. It must have been the hour, for he knew that that part of the city was almost fully occupied, though many other neighborhoods seemed nearly abandoned. What was anyone to do in the city? You could fish; do something with tourists like open a hotel, but little else.

He couldn't understand why the young would leave the city, couldn't forgive them for turning their back on their *patria*. How could they leave that most beautiful and mysterious of cities? He'd heard Signore Guarda's sons wanted him to move to Milano where they were, to reunite the family. How sad that they'd all left their parents to slowly die alone in the decaying city, remnants of a passing epoch.

Even before Sacci reached the piazza, he could see the soft glow of the lights on Il Duomo and the Doge's Palace reflected in the sky. When he entered the enormous space, he saw immediately that it was empty.

The tower stood at one end of the square like a bold punctuation mark, regal and imposing. Café tables and chairs stood stacked and bundled, covered with canvas and vinyl tarps. They looked like hulking monsters, distinctly out of place in the unmarred, classic perimeters of the piazza. There were lights on in some of the palazzo windows, and the monumental buildings all bathed in the soft glow of carefully positioned spotlights, but there was no life in the piazza aside from blowing newspapers and rattling dried leaves. He strolled around the perimeter of the square, glancing in a few of the shopwindows, shops that had been there when he was a child and didn't cater exclusively to the tourists. There was the old linen shop, where his mother used to buy her handkerchiefs, and the wine store that now carried only Barbarescos and high-priced Barolos. What about simple Chiantis from farther south, or jugs of everyday wine? A person had to leave the area to get those.

The wind blew harder, throwing stinging bits of cinder into his cheeks and sending pieces of newspaper sailing like flapping, wayward spirits. As he approached the little via from which he'd entered the piazza, he heard the nearby wail of a fireboat.

Bad night for a fire, he thought, pushing his body into the wind. The firefighters wouldn't have it easy.

As he rounded one of the corners, he caught a glimpse of wavering golden light and shadows cast against one of the walls of the portico of the Zecca. Clustered around a haphazard stand of beeswax church candles sat American college students, talking quietly as they cupped their hands around the small flames to keep the blustery wind from blowing them out. There were peace signs, and a few bottles of wine placed near the candles. They drank the wine out of plastic cups.

Were they fearful they'd be asked to leave if discovered?

The Americans somehow reminded him of Louis, introspective and drawn to candlelight instead of neon. They were enjoying what he enjoyed about Venice—it's beauty and atmosphere, the quiet little corners that invited reverie.

One of the students held up his opaque cup of wine. "Signore, do you want to join us?" he said in decent Italian.

"No, no, grazie," Sacci answered, smiling.

"*Perché* no?" one of the others asked.

They were seemingly the only ones awake in the city except for the firefighters racing to their boats to the call. He could still hear the siren wailing; only suddenly, there was more than just one.

"Okay, then," he answered, shrugging as he approached the warm circle of candlelight. He could smell the beeswax and wine, the scent of youth and testosterone.

A smiling milky-brown girl, her hair in tiny braids, poured a cup of wine and handed it to him. Her manner was familiar, yet respectful. How was it that Americans acted more generous and hospitable than the Venetians who actually lived there? Maybe they didn't act the same at home. Was it being in a strange, new place that enabled a traveler to come outside of himself, to approach the world and everyone in it with a broader spirit?

"*Saluti*," the girl called, sitting up straight and raising her small cup in his direction.

"*Saluti*," he echoed, raising the plastic cup to all of them.

The wine was cheap, but tasty. Maybe it would make him feel drowsy; help him unwind so that he could get a few hours of sleep before the opening.

"*É molto tranquillo a Venezia,* no?" the girl said to him.

"Sì," he said. "*É molto tranquillo.*"

"What are the sirens for?" one of them asked in clumsy Italian. "A fire or is it something else?"

"Probably a fire," Sacci answered, glancing at the little flames of the candles that danced in the breeze, sending flickering shadows across the old gray walls of the Zecca. The building's cracked, worn, and faded walls had witnessed centuries of candles, torches, and even bonfires, all the while absorbing smoke and heat into their ancient skins.

"It's good that you're enjoying the city," he said. "Good to have the piazza to yourselves. You know that normally you must share it with thousands of other—tourists, er, people."

None of them seemed offended by his remark. He'd been momentarily thoughtless—they too, were tourists. He sat down, occupying a little opening in the haphazard circle. It was warm with the candles and the bodies huddled together, so he took off his jacket, tossing it on the cobblestones behind him. The winds raging across the sea pushed away the warm, humid air that had occupied the city earlier.

"We've seen it during the day," one of them said, nodding. "We prefer it at night. We're going to school here for a semester and come here a few nights a week—mostly weeknights, though, when it's quieter. Tonight's very strange, though—there's no one here."

"It is strange," Sacci said. "Not very typical. But maybe it's the wind and the promise of rain. You know a wind like this can bring a storm."

A chorus of "*sis*" answered. He didn't want to sound like a concerned mother, but was that how he'd suddenly sounded, as if he was warning them about the coming rain?

"It stays pretty dry under here, even if it's better to be out in the open," the brown girl said. She smiled at him. "Do you live here?"

"I do—I've lived my whole life here."

They studied him wide-eyed, looking impressed. "That's cool," one of the guys said in English. "You're so lucky."

"Why lucky?" he asked.

"To live in such a cool city, such an old place," the girl said.

He shrugged. "I am, I suppose. And I like Venice, but why do you like it so much? I thought Americans like things new—to come and visit the old, but to want to live in the new."

Most of them shook their heads. "Where I live, in the suburbs of San Francisco," one of the other girls said. "Things seem so phony. Everything is new and plastic-like. It doesn't seem natural. Here, things seem real, a combination of new and old, and something else that I can't quite put my finger on. There's something else that makes it seem more alive."

"What do you think it is?" Sacci asked, curious whether they could put into words what he'd felt his whole life.

One of the young men placed his wine on the cold stone floor of the Zecca. "In America, the only places that seem to have soul are churches and cemeteries. Here everything seems to have it."

A girl with tight blonde curls and an accent different from the others leaned forward, her face hovering above the candles. "That's just your impression—I think you're giving the place characteristics it doesn't possess," she countered, her voice rising. "Like a ghost, it's all in your head."

She leaned back, massaging a large crucifix that hung around her neck. Even in the dim light cast by the dull streetlamps and candles, Sacci could see that she was flushed.

Everyone seemed to want to speak at once, and he was reminded of all he'd read and heard about Americans being uninterested in conversation or any of the big questions of life. Maybe these kids were different.

"If it's my impression, if it's the way I feel, then maybe that's reality," one of the other girls said angrily. "How is that different from your belief in Christianity? You can't prove he existed, and you say he makes you feel different, fills you with something, so how is *that* any different?"

The light-haired girl leaned back into the candlelight, her blonde curls trembling in the wind.

"That's religion—it's completely different," she said. "Having faith in another world—in a god—is *completely* different from saying that a *place* fills you with something. It's just this sort of thinking that gets man into trouble. That's why we're so full of sin. We can't be trusted to do right by him—instead worldly things distract us. And Venice is just another of these."

A chorus of boos sounded from around the cluster, and Sacci could see that most of the students appeared united against the blonde girl. She reminded him of the daughters of missionaries he'd occasionally seen on a tour of Venice before they left for Africa or the Middle East. He felt sorry for the girl, as she would never be liked except by people just like her, and would only condemn, judge, and alienate with increasing frequency, as she grew older, until she could only interact with people from her church or family. Like the monks and nuns of the Dark Ages, the girl and people like her cloistered themselves—without ever building drafty and cold monasteries and retreating to the tops of mountains. Was that the future, to return to the past?

So many of the Americans spoke at once, arguing with the girl or trying to answer the question Sacci had posed, that he could scarcely make out what any of them said. Then more sirens howled and a gust of wind summarily snuffed out the candles, interrupting their conversation.

The girl who'd first offered him wine jumped to her feet. "Let's find out what's going on, it sounds like a big fire or something. And it's not too far away."

There was a chorus of *sis* and the group moved quickly to pick up the blankets and wine bottles—except the blonde girl.

"I think I'm going back to the flat," she said quietly, her voice shaking. "I need to do some studying tomorrow and should get to bed."

No one attempted to persuade her to join, to convince her to postpone going to bed. In fact, no one seemed to take notice of her announcement. Sacci wondered that maybe she'd not been with them at all. Maybe someone in the group had felt sorry for her, seeing how she would never fit in, always be on the outside, and had asked her along. Or perhaps she'd invited herself.

"I think I'll go along, too, if you don't mind," Sacci said. "There are so many sirens that it must be really serious." He got up grabbing his jacket, but decided to carry it instead of putting it on since the night air wasn't yet cool.

Except for the blonde girl who dawdled, perhaps waiting for an invitation to join them, the students quickly had their belongings collected and headed toward the opposite side of the piazza near the duomo. The sirens seemed to wail faster and higher, prompting the group to run along zigzag streets, and up and over footbridges large and small. Twice they headed in the wrong direction, only realizing that the sirens were growing fainter after they'd gone a hundred feet or more. Venice had no straight streets, so they ran with almost blind faith, as if in a maze.

"It must be *huge*," the brown-skinned girl said, sounding almost pleased. "I hear so many sirens!"

It was an adventure for them, Sacci realized. It was not *their* city burning. Still, wouldn't most youth—and certainly children—be awed by a big fire, by the sirens, the firefighters, and the boats? They were only behaving naturally, though their excitement at the fire and their resolve to get to the scene quickly made him uneasy. If he could've been spared their eager expressions and whispered urgings to run faster, he might have thought them all pleasant enough. But following along, he was seeing an ugly side to the Americans he hadn't first imagined.

They all headed through a section of town full of ancient palazzi, some divided into still grand apartments and others closed up and uninhabited like his family's had been for so many years. Though he'd momentarily lost track where they were in the darkened city, having taken small, crooked streets with only the sound of the sirens to guide them, he realized they were heading toward the palazzo.

It couldn't be, he thought, but after they rounded another corner, he realized the sirens were not coming from next to the palazzo, but to the north of it. They rounded another corner and saw the sky glowing orange from the fire. Lights blazed in the *piano nobili* and the higher floors of neighboring buildings, and he saw figures in the windows or heads hanging over the street. The ground floors, mostly stores and offices, remained dark and closed. Everywhere people peered out of windows, staring at the ominous glowing sky.

Passing the Doge's Palace Reale Hotel, he could see tourists standing on their small balconies, pointing as they looked and gesticulated toward the west.

When they passed the turn for *Palazzo Spirito*, he felt a wave of relief when he saw that the fire was to the right—not to the left and toward the hotel. But what was afire?

They ran along the curving street, followed by other tourists and locals, and even some firefighters. He could smell the fire; maybe even feel the heat from the flames. As they rounded the curving street, La Fenice came into view—but not the opera house that he knew.

Flames shot from its immense windows, giving the night sky a yellow cast, while bands of firefighters frantically aimed arcs of frothy white water at the building.

"It's La Fenice!" he shouted to the students, shaking his head in disbelief.

"Wow!" one of the students said, stopping at a line of wooden barricades. "What is it?"

"The opera house," Sacci moaned. "It's hundreds of years old. Very historic. Beautiful on the inside, like a jewel box."

"Was there a performance tonight?" one of the students asked. "We were just trying to get tickets for a performance, but we weren't able to because it was closed."

"I don't know," he answered. "I know opera season is over, but maybe there was a concert. I can't believe it's burning!"

As they watched, flames shot out of more windows. The fire climbed floors—both up and down, and across the enormous building. Firefighters trained hoses and huge arcs of water on the blaze, but seemingly with little effect. Made of wooden timbers and floors, the old building was burning like a tinderbox, crackling and snapping as the fire consumed its interior.

Sacci felt the heat from the fire pushing down the street toward them, carrying an occasional spark and ash with it. "I wish we were on the other side of the opera house!" he said. "We should be upwind so we're not in the path of the heat and ashes."

But no one wanted to move, eyes and bodies fixed on the opera house. Police were everywhere, and roadblocks were erected on any street that headed toward La Fenice.

"Back, back, move back!" an officer shouted, picking up a side of the barricade and pushing it toward them. "You've got to move back—the fire's getting too big. It's not safe for anyone to be so close. Dai! Dai!"

Sacci grabbed the other side of the barricade, helping the officer move it another twenty feet down the street and then helping him move the other two that spanned the street. More firefighters poured through the barricades, some obviously roused from bed.

The fire sighed, creaked, and roared, as it ate its way through the structure. In the background, the tinkling sound of fire alarms barely rose above the din created by the thundering fire, and the hollering firefighters. The crowd pressed against the barricades. Arcs of water splashed against the sides of the building, probably from fireboats on the nearby canal. Despite all the hoses trained on it and the ladders thrusting toward its sides, the hulking building was no match for the fire.

Had the firefighters arrived too late? Was the old place simply too much of a tinderbox? How could such a landmark, an enormous building that had survived for a few hundred years, suddenly catch fire? And was there no sprinkler system, no caretaker, or security guard to prevent such a calamity? The building seemed to moan, sighing horribly, as firefighters scurried around its base.

Occasionally, the sound of something falling or breaking inside the building traveled down the street. One by one windows burst, sending shards of glass onto the street and peppering the helmets and shoulders of firefighters. The old wood popped, hissed, shrieked, and groaned. A few centuries' worth of phantoms escaped into the murky Venetian air, carried upward by the heat and across the city by the strong, buffeting wind that coursed across the island.

Why, thought Sacci, why did it have to be so windy?

Firefighters darted back and forth in front of the building, some rushing through the open doors with hoses in tow, while others stumbled back out, black with soot and sometimes with steaming or smoldering jackets. There was a flurry of activity, a large number of firefighters rushed through the doors on the right side. Streams from the hoses arched onto the roof, but no flames were visible there—the fire seemed to only dart out of the windows and doors like a hungry tongue.

Sacci couldn't stand to watch and averted his eyes. How many operas and concerts had he seen at the historic house, attending his first one with his grandparents in their cramped, overheated box? Now the building might disappear from the city, merely another shell of a structure that had once been something magnificent.

And here he'd thought Venice was sinking, that water would ultimately destroy the ancient place. Had he once considered what fire might do?

Steam began rising from the rooftop where the water was being sprayed, enormous, billowing clouds of it, solid as thick cream against the dark sky.

A television crew arrived, set up a camera, and trained it on the fire. A reporter stood in the foreground, and almost immediately, she started speaking into the microphone while the harsh light above the camera illuminated the chaotic street, fire, and police officers rushing around behind her.

But who was watching the news at such an hour? Sacci had meant to be home himself, and had he made it, he would never have bothered to switch on the TV. It would have been better not to witness the old landmark slowly eaten by a fire that seemed intent on consuming the entire structure, leaving nothing but a blackened shell. At least he would have had a peaceful night's sleep, and wouldn't have wondered what sort of an omen the fire might be.

But did he believe in such nonsense, in omens or the superstitions of the church and his childhood?

What a grim day it would be to have a party. At least Claudia was sound asleep, knocked out from the sleeping pill. Otherwise, she would be pacing the floors, worried despite her lack of faith.

If he moved back thirty or forty feet to where the street curved, he would be able to see the facade of his own palazzo jutting into the street. On the side of the curve where he stood, madness seemed to reign. Sacci felt his throat tighten; feeling as if perhaps the event somehow spelled the beginning of Venice's demise.

He chided himself for the silly, nonsensical thoughts swirling through his head. Claudia wouldn't think such a thing; she would chalk up the disaster to the vicissitudes of an imperfect planet. And he knew he should think so, too, and banish these creeping, baleful premonitions.

Could he will himself to be at peace as she was, dozing in the dark of her high-ceilinged bedroom with its wall of murals, shutters and French doors shut tightly against the restless breeze? He hoped she wouldn't awaken from the noise of the fireboats and the roaring fire. If she did have one of the shutter doors ajar, at least the view she would glimpse, if she happened to open her eyes, would be the cobalt sky to the south.

Sacci glanced around, realizing that at some point the American university students had disappeared, either working themselves deeper into the crowd or deciding to head to the other side of the opera house. He'd never even asked their names, yet after witnessing the fire and talking to them at the piazza, he felt he should have.

The wind gusted even harder, pulling, and pushing the flames in and out of the opera house windows.

"Why, wind? Why blow so hard?" he muttered, watching it fan the flames.

At that moment, he felt he would have done anything for a calm night, one that the city so often experienced. Even a still, humid night in July, one that seemed to suck the air from his lungs, or a damp and chilly February day that pierced his bones, would be better than this. If the fire had happened on such a night, it wouldn't have burned so furiously. Why, oh why couldn't they have one of those nights? And why couldn't the miserable, gusting wind stop blowing?

If he'd been a person who said prayers, he would have sent petitions skyward, but the heavens didn't appear to oppose the burning of the opera house. And whom would he pray to anyway? If he still had his childhood beliefs, maybe he could find some comfort and pray to a god that the Enlightenment had killed. But he possessed only half-beliefs, and while feeling the urge to pray, couldn't bring himself to utter the words.

The firefighters in front of him were apparently taking breaks. They grimaced, gazing at the upper floors of La Fenice and then to the swirling darkness of night sky. The wind gusted, carrying more sparks out the windows and down the narrow, winding street. The sparks seemed to blink out before they traveled far, likely snuffed out by the buffeting wind.

He wondered how much larger the fire could get. Based on the pure orange and red emanating from the doors and windows, he couldn't believe there was much left inside to burn. Glimpses of the building's interior through the windows and lower doors, reminded him of the inside of a furnace, a mass of orange and red flames and white-hot glowing embers.

Every few minutes he heard something crash inside, maybe the old seating boxes, or the stairways. Who knew exactly what was falling, resigning itself to the raging fire and returning to the earth. At every crash, the spectators cowered, as if the sky were falling.

Venice wasn't sinking, he thought, it was burning.

The firefighters darted from one side of the building to the other, but they no longer ventured inside. They moved back from the building, training more hoses on the inferno, the white, watery arcs from the hoses shooting gracefully onto the building. Some hoses pointed at the windows, others through the open doorways, splattering against the already smoke-stained facade. But it was as if there were no hoses trained on the fire at all, so fiercely did it continue burning. The firefighters paid particular attention to the roof, pointing hoses from the tops of tall ladders that allowed them to aim the water with more precision.

The top of the opera house steamed even more, sending up billows of rolling white clouds of vapor that glowed against the dark sky. The steam turned dark and then an angry orange. The flames were almost certainly eating their way through the roof.

Would the building collapse? Was there nothing else to do to save the place? Sacci ran his hands along the barricade, back and forth along the smooth wooden edge.

The winds gusted, driving the fire and shooting sparks into the street. Almost immediately, Sacci saw flames shoot through the roof.

Shaking his head, he knew there was no saving the building. The firefighters would be lucky if there were even a blackened shell remaining, but he was beginning to believe there would be nothing left at all. With the prodding wind and raging core of fire in the building's interior, the firefighters could do nothing to stop it until, having nothing left to consume, the fire burned itself out. Some firefighters stood weeping, shaking their heads, and catching their breath as they gazed at the burning building. Were they upset at their helplessness, the realization that they existed to put out fires, yet couldn't extinguish one that was claiming one of the most cherished landmarks of the city?

The shouting crowd bumped against the barricade as flames shot ten and twenty feet above the rooftop. The wind carried the flames toward them, high overhead and well down the street. Softball-sized, glowing sparks and bits of blazing debris flared into the sky like shooting stars. The firefighters began to push the barricades and surging crowd farther from the fire. They shook their heads worriedly, watching as the wind carried more sparks and embers into the sky. Most of the glowing, fiery pieces winked out, but as the flames on the rooftop grew larger, there were more and more burning pieces in the air blinking brightly, dancing far above the crowd's heads.

With a sudden roar, the flames jumped completely through the roof, carrying high above the rooftops of the city and tearing at the sky. Sacci stepped back, his heart thumping against his chest. Would the fire spread, could they control it?

More boats arrived. Firefighters jumped off the decks and sped toward the blaze. More hoses pointed toward the fire, but still it grew larger. The firefighters hurried about like hornets stirred from their nest, switching positions and relieving one another on the hoses.

Another gust of wind took the tower of flames southward, snipping off bits of flame that melted into the air. The next gust carried sparks upward and along the street, scattering them across the cobalt sky.

Firefighters rushed toward the crowd, reaching for the barricade.

"It's dangerous—move back," one of them shouted. "*Vai, vai*! You should go home. It would be better if you were at home."

"Is there anything we can do to help?" someone called. "We can help!"

"Go home," a burly firefighter snarled, pushing the barricade into the line of spectators, forcing them farther down the street. "And if you're downwind, watch your house and your neighbor's house."

Was he serious? Could the fire be carried so far as to ignite tile roofs?

"But the fire is dying, look!" a man a few feet away shouted, pointing toward the fire barely visible at the very end of the cobblestone street.

It was true. The flames, which might have been thirty feet high minutes earlier, had dropped, still consuming the roof and whatever remained inside, but much smaller in size, hardly visible as they licked at whatever remained.

"Yes, but it won't die down completely for hours. Maybe a day," the firefighter muttered wearily. "So you should still go home. And the wind is still blowing, so it's dangerous." Turning to Sacci, he asked, "Where do you live?"

"I live in the Dorsoduro," he said. "But I have a hotel just down the street."

"You'd be more of a help there than here," the firefighter said. "Keep an eye on the roof."

"The roof?" he cried. "What can catch fire on the roof? It's all tiles."

"Leaves, grass, dust. Anything can collect on a roof and catch fire. Trust me, signore, I've seen it," he said, clearly annoyed.

Sacci remembered the curtains that the workers had finished installing only hours earlier. Could a stray spark catch them afire? And if they did, wouldn't they burn so fast they wouldn't have time to ignite anything else?

He spun, running from the firefighter and pushing his way through the crowd.

"The government should have taken care ..." he overheard a

voice start to say. "How could they let such a thing happen?" another muttered.

"It's punishment," he heard another say. "Years ago they started allowing nudity and all sorts of illicit scenes ..."

Sacci ran faster, so fast he couldn't hear the voices anymore. He had only a block to go, but as he neared the corner where the street curved toward the palazzo, he almost ran into one of two men who had just sped around the corner toward him.

"*Scusami*!" they shouted at each other.

Sacci nearly fell, his shoulder having clipped the other man's shoulder. He felt a flash of pain, then throbbing.

"There's a fire on this street, too!" one of the men panted. "A roof is burning."

"Dio," Sacci swore, his heart sinking. "What's the building—what does it look like?"

"It's a palazzo," the man exclaimed, still breathless.

"The one that was just renovated?" he virtually screamed, his voice like a wail.

"*Sì*!" the man exclaimed. "That's the one, but we've got to hurry to get the firefighters—we phoned but couldn't get through."

"Gesù Cristo," Sacci moaned. "Why this? What have I done?"

Claudia would never wake, drugged because of the sleeping pill he and Louis had urged her to take.

"It's your building?" one of the men asked, incredulous.

"*É mio*," he gasped. "Please hurry and get the firefighters, will you? I've to get a friend out of the palazzo—will one of you come with me, help me?"

The taller man nodded, and Sacci raced away toward the palazzo, the footfall of the short, fat one echoing behind him. He rounded the curve and saw immediately the imposing facade of the palazzo standing a few feet into the street, just a little bigger and bulkier than the buildings around it. The lights he'd admired earlier still shone warmly on the centuries-old ornamentation, highlighting the gargoyles and family shields. The palazzo looked perfectly normal, serene even and for a moment, he thought the men must have been mistaken. Then his eye was drawn upward toward movement and bright light peeking over the terrace. As he ran closer to the building, more of the terrace came into view.

"Oh, no," he cried.

The curtains and terrace were blazing, like a miniature version of the fire he'd just been watching.

"Cristo, Cristo!" he shrieked. "My friend's in there asleep!"

"It's not so bad yet," the man assured him, placing his hand on his shoulder. "Don't worry, we'll get her out. There's still time."

They ran across the street, approaching the giant wooden doors that he'd locked so carefully merely hours before. He'd hoped the sirens might have awakened Claudia and that he had seen the lights on and heard the massive door open, but he knew that was unlikely. If only she hadn't taken the sleeping pill. He should have known the contessa was bad luck, he should have sensed it from everything Claudia had told him.

Reaching into his pocket, he panicked.

Where were the keys?

He remembered placing them in his jacket that he'd been clutching all along. He fumbled with the jacket, reaching into the wrong pocket first. He thrust his hand into the other pocket—nothing there either. Trying the other pocket again, his heart sank.

"You don't have the key?" the man asked.

"I know I do. I *have* the key," Sacci said firmly, shaking the jacket. "They didn't fit in my pants pocket and I remember distinctly putting them in my jacket pocket."

He felt the jacket again, running his hands down the arms and across every inch of the light fabric. He felt nothing as large and as hard as the oversize skeleton key. For the second time in minutes, his heart sank. How could he be so unlucky?

"Claudia!" he screamed up at the windows, throwing the jacket on the street. Her room faced the canal, though, so he knew his cry would be in vain. He had to do something, but what?

"Claudia, Claudia!" he screamed again.

The man shouted, too, looking up at the mostly shuttered windows dubiously. He nervously glanced at the still-blazing fire on the terrace.

"Dio, it's getting larger!" Sacci swore.

"I don't think you should wait for the firefighters, or to see if she wakes up," the stranger advised, grasping Sacci's shoulder and shaking it. "Is there a back door?"

"Just the canal door, but that must be locked, too," he said, studying the palazzo as if it were a puzzle. He knew its shape and form so well, but could think of no way to get in.

"Why not phone her?" the stranger said excitedly. "I have a phone you can use."

"Yes, yes!" Sacci agreed, grabbing the man's phone quickly retrieving his phone from his hand and dialing Claudia's number with trembling fingers. The call went through quickly, but after five or six rings, her voice mail picked up. "Damn!" He disconnected, dialed again, this time the main hotel number. Could he hear the front desk phone ringing from where he stood on the street? He was certain he could—if only he were on the other side of the doors!

Why did old palazzi have to be built like fortresses, nearly impossible to break into? Of course, the palazzo had been a fortress five hundred years earlier, just like every palazzo in the city and across Italy. Regretting that he'd never changed the original floor plan and windows, never making it easier to enter during an emergency, he kicked the stone foundation. He began pounding on the massive front doors, but his fists barely made a noise against the thick old wood, and his thumping didn't move them at all.

"Claudia! Claudia!" he shouted again, beginning to despair.

Could the palazzo burn as quickly as the opera house had, and turn it into an impenetrable mass of flames that was certain to doom her?

"Don't worry," the man reassured. "The firefighters are sure to be here shortly."

"Claudia! Claudia!" he echoed, nodding at Sacci as if to convince him it was a sound course of action.

But Sacci knew she wouldn't wake up. Above them, the fire popped and snapped, eating whatever was constructed of wood on the terrace. He could see the firelight reflected on the building across the street, the light growing brighter.

"Dio!" he heard someone shout. "Cristo! Scusi, scusi! Have you called the fire department already?"

Where was the voice coming from? He looked both ways down the dimly lit street, but he and the stranger were alone.

"Up here, up here!" the voice called urgently.

Across from the terrace, he saw open shutters and a dark form leaning out of a window. The sound of sirens—new ones—echoed in the distance.

"Sì, sì! We've already called the *vigili di fuoco*. Maybe they're coming now—I hear more sirens," the stranger yelled.

The wind gusted again, carrying sparks from the terrace into the dark night sky. Before heading upward, some nearly blew into the man's window.

"Dai, dai!" the man screamed. "Curse this wind—it'll catch my building on fire! I'm shutting these and heading down to the street." The man started to pull on the heavy shutters.

"Wait, wait!" Sacci yelled. "Can you help me?"

"I don't have time—sparks are blowing in!" the man screamed, frantically pulling on the enormous shutters, batting at the occasional spark that blew past him.

"Someone's in that building—please!" Sacci yelled, running toward the open window.

The man ignored him, continuing to tug on the shutter, but something wasn't releasing and the oversize shutter only moved a foot or so forward. "Dai, dai!" he yelled. "*Madre di Dio*!"

Sacci was directly under the open window now, the stranger beside him.

"We'll help you close the shutters if you help us," the stranger yelled.

"No, no! No more delay. It could cost me my building. What do you want, anyway, to jump across the street onto the terrace?"

"Exactly!" Sacci yelled. "Please, please, we don't know when the firefighters will arrive. And there's a friend sleeping in the palazzo."

The man gazed skeptically down at the two of them, his expression illuminated by the fire across the narrow street and lights from inside his apartment. "You'll never make it. You can't jump across this street—it's too wide."

"Not enough time to explain," Sacci yelled, trying to sound patient. Why couldn't the man just let them in—it would take minutes?

"*Please*—we'll help you close the shutters. You can't get them closed anyway, and maybe I can start to put the fire out after I wake my friend."

The man scoffed. "Ha! Maybe you'd better come up and look at this fire on your terrace. There's no way anyone but the fire department will put it out."

"Signore," Sacci pleaded. "It's a friend in there. She'll die."

The man jerked his head and looked at Sacci. "Okay, I'll ring you in. Hurry, though."

His form disappeared from the window, but not before he gave the shutter a last tug. Sacci and the other man rushed to the doorway and pushed their way into the entry vestibule. The door hadn't closed behind them when the entry release clicked. They yanked open the giant door and raced up a worn marble stairway.

"Up here, up here!" a voice from the next landing urged. "Hurry!"

They rounded the first landing, leaping two stairs at a time. Halfway down the hall, the man stood in a bathrobe in front of his door.

"Here, here," he motioned, waving frantically. "Quickly!"

They raced into an entry hall of thick wooden floors and carpet, the walls crammed full of oil paintings. The man shuffled hurriedly down the hall through a doorway to the left and into an enormous salon. Like the hallway, the room was full of paintings and watercolors, even brightly colored frescoes on a few of the walls. Random floor lamps illuminated the walls and an eerie, flickering orange light shot through the windows—the fire! The man stopped in front of one of the enormous windows, the exact one he'd been standing at, and motioned them over with frantic waves.

"See, see! You'll never jump that far! It's crazy," he said, his voice shaking.

Sacci's heart sank. The street was wider than it had seemed from below and the terrace was ablaze. What was burning? Maybe if he stood on the iron railing of the window he could get far enough above the terrace of the palazzo, which was probably five or six feet lower than the floor they were on. He would have something sturdy to push off from. The edge of the terrace just opposite wasn't on fire, the curtains having already burned away. He had a perfect landing spot.

"Do you think you can leap that far?" the stranger asked, looking skeptically out the window.

"I've got to. And if I don't, I'll have a broken leg at worst." To not try, to have something happen to Claudia would be worse.

The man who lived in the apartment nodded vigorously. "Exactly. I had a burglar who scaled the corner wall and tried to open one of these shutters—they're rusty and difficult to move—and he fell to the street. He broke a leg."

Sacci eyed the distance again, judging it eight or ten feet. And if they could push him, that would help a little. The terrace glowed with fire, but there were pathways through it, and he couldn't see any flames from within. He hoped the fire hadn't spread inside.

"Okay, I'm going to climb on this railing," he explained, his voice quavering. "And then when I say push, shove me as hard as you can."

"It's crazy," the man who lived there said. "I don't think it can be done."

"I'll do it. I don't want to, but how am I supposed to get my friend out of there?" Sacci asked, pointing across the street.

Both the stranger and the man nodded. "Okay, we push," the man said. "But, hey, you promised to help with the shutters!"

"I'll help with the shutters as soon as we push him," the stranger said.

"I'm going," Sacci said, pulling himself onto the railing. His legs shook a little, despite his will. How would he jump with such shaking legs?

"Don't look down," the stranger said. "Just look where you're jumping, where you want to be. Think about that and nothing else."

Sacci smiled; a small, relieved smile. He'd grown accustomed to having such decisions spread out over time, to living a measured and calm life. Suddenly, life seemed to be moving so quickly, before he had time to react or absorb events. It was as if he'd been awakened from a deep sleep, unable to grasp fully what was happening, what he should do, though he would run through the motions almost blindly.

Grasping both sides of the window frame, he leaned forward, keeping his eye on the terrace ledge that seemed so close. Fearing he might think about it too much and lose his nerve, he yelled, springing from the iron railing and into the whispering air above the street.

His first sensation after his foot gave a desperate push from the metal railing was heat and the realization that instead of fleeing the fire, he was moving quickly toward it. He never looked down, but felt vividly aware of how everything below and to the sides of him looked. It was as if he had eyes everywhere, though his gaze remained fixed on the terrace.

"Go!" he heard the voices behind him echoing.

Airborne for what seemed minutes, he struck the side of the terrace so hard he nearly bounced off. His chest had slammed against the thick old wall with such force he'd had the wind knocked out of him. One arm locked over the parapet wall, the rest of his body dangled down the flat, rough side of the building. He almost fell immediately, but then he started breathing again, realizing he had to turn his body and his other arm up and over the parapet wall. He pulled with his left arm, straining against the weight of his thin, but long body. If only he were stronger.

"You've got it, you've got it!" voices called from behind. "Pull, pull up!"

He could hear the fear in their voices.

"I'm running down to the street—I'll be right back," he heard one of them say. The stranger.

Then his arm gave out, flipping skyward and sending him plummeting down the coarse and uneven exterior wall of the palazzo.

Chapter Nineteen

The bell shocked them both. Sacci, his eyes red and burning from the smoke, his ankle sore, but not broke from his fall, slowly rose from the sofa.

"I'll get it," he said, motioning for Claudia to stay where she was on the sofa, her feet propped on a pillow.

He followed the dogs that had already raced down the hall to the door where they spun in manic circles.

"Who can that be?" Claudia moaned. "I don't want to see anyone; I just want to climb into a hole."

She pulled a blanket over her head, exploring the darkness under the thick blanket. Even the generous sunshine pouring in through the giant windows was blocked in the little world she'd created. The thought of staying cocooned or at least staying here in Sacci's apartment, for days, weeks, or months appealed to her.

Here in the dark beneath the blanket, she could vividly recall being pulled out of bed sometime very late the night before and lifted from the soft wrap of thick cotton sheets. At first, she'd wanted to panic, to kick and fight back aware that she wasn't dreaming and that she was really smelling and seeing thick clouds of smoke drifting through her bedroom. And the firefighters, whom she hadn't recognized at first, wore masks, and so her sleeping pill-addled mind had seen the masks and distorted faces of kidnappers. She recalled the helpless, panic-inducing realization that as much as she wanted to rouse herself and run, or at least kick and pummel her abductors, her limbs wouldn't respond.

In the light of day, after coming out of the somnolent haze caused by the sleeping pill, when she'd been told that the hotel terrace and the upper stair hall had burned, she'd recalled the firefighters and felt a wave of relief that she hadn't been able to fight them.

When she'd awakened, Sacci filled her in on all of the unreal events of the previous evening—his frightening fall from the neighbor's window, the fire at the opera house, the partial burning of the palazzo. He told her too that though only a small part of the building had burned, so much smoke had poured into most of the rooms that almost all the linens would have to be washed or replaced and the walls scrubbed—again.

Her heartbeat frantic, she felt like a hunted and trapped rabbit that lay prone, awaiting the inevitable.

Oh, where was Louis? Why hadn't he called or come by? Certainly, he'd heard about the fire.

Given all that had happened the night before, a small, nagging voice somewhere within warned that something terrible had happened, that the opera and hotel fire were only part of the complete, awful picture. She shook her head as if to dislodge the disturbing thoughts, pulling the blankets away from her face, and popping her head into the cool, fresh-tasting air of Sacci's living room.

She could hear Sacci open the creaking wooden door, but she couldn't hear any voices. What was he doing? She detected whispering, deliberate, measured voices coming from the entryway.

"Who is it?" she called, wondering if she shouldn't just stay quiet. He might be telling whoever it was that she wasn't here. If he didn't, they would barge in, wanting to console her, asking her a hundred annoying questions. Didn't people know that what a person most wanted after experiencing defeat, having something dissolve that you'd worked on nonstop for six months, was to be left alone?

"Sacci!" she called again, raising her voice.

She turned to find her friend standing in the doorway wide-eyed, another person standing beside him.

At first, she didn't recognize the person, or maybe she did, but couldn't believe it was really her mother.

If things had been different, if her mother had been a different person, Claudia might have raced into her arms and buried her head in her chest as she'd been allowed to do as a young girl. Lately, she'd turned to Louis for such comfort, and since last night, Sacci. She sat up awkwardly, pushing away the blanket.

She was uncertain what to say. With a mother like hers, who had comforted her only when she'd been utterly devastated and never after she grew as high as her mother's shoulders, she didn't know how to act. Her mother had stopped her from doing what she wanted for as long as she could remember, attempting to curtail nearly every natural impulse she'd had.

But she'd also just learned from Sacci that her mother had crept into town to fill the hotel with plants, lanterns, wine, bars, and waiters. And with that bit of information, Claudia grew to suspect her of orchestrating other occurrences, like the espresso machine and the umbrellas that she'd ascribed to good luck.

How would she make sense of it?

"*Cara*," her mother said, her voice strained, sounding unlike her mother at all. "Come here—no, better yet, I'll come to you."

She strode over to the sofa, leaning down to awkwardly place her arms around Claudia's shoulders. Clasping her tightly, she whispered in her ear.

"*Dispiace*," she said consolingly. "I'm so, so sorry."

Claudia tentatively hugged her back. Even after so many years, her mother's embrace felt familiar.

"Mamma," she whimpered, hearing with dismay how her voice cracked. "What are you doing here?"

"I'm not sure. I wanted to help," she answered, standing to study her daughter.

Did her mother look changed? Was there something unfamiliar in her eye despite the sadness? Claudia detected a flinty shine to her expression, even if a frown covered her face like a mask.

"What, Mamma, what is it?" Claudia asked. Had she come to judge, to crow now that her daughter was even more hopelessly lost than she'd been since the last time they'd seen each other? Her mother looked different—what was it? Gone was the domineering gaze, the air of certainty. Did her mother, the contessa, look vulnerable?

"I meant to surprise you, to be a help, but I'm afraid I've caused something terrible to happen. I'm to blame for the fire—in a way. You see …"

For perhaps the first time, Claudia felt sorry for her mother. The look of pain she saw on her mother's face had always been there, if only in the corners of her eyes or on certain days. Why had she never noticed it?

"I know, Mamma. Sacci explained everything," Claudia said.

"If you disliked me before, I can't imagine how you feel now," her mother said, standing crooked, no longer upright, as Claudia had always pictured her.

"No," Claudia responded, shaking her head.

How strange life could twist and turn. Her mother had sneaked into town, attempting to make the best thing to happen to her even better and now worrying about how her daughter felt about her. And she looked sad. Sad, but calm and resigned, no longer rigid and stern. What had happened? Certainly, it wasn't the hotel fire—that couldn't have affected her, too.

"I'm bitter about it, Mamma, crushed and broken, but I don't blame you."

Was she angry because, in a way, her mother had warned her?

"But maybe in a way you were right. I can see now that you possibly saw more than I did. Not that *this* would happen, of course, but just that things might not turn out well for me here," she admitted, biting the inside of her cheek.

Claudia would have liked to blame her mother, to blame anyone, but there was no one to fault but perhaps the cursed city itself. Venice did seem unlucky, after all. Things had looked so different, so hopeful just twenty-four hours earlier, but how quickly it could all change. Maybe she should abandon the city as so many others had done. Even if a person tried to create something, establish a future, the dream could so easily crumble. Maybe it was inevitable that things sank, people and dreams succumbing to the spirit of Venice. In the end, how could a person evade whatever it was that characterized a place? Why had she thought herself immune, as if by being an outsider and coming to the city she could flaunt its rules?

Sinking back into the sofa, she looked at the clear blue sky outside the window, the strong winds of the night before having swept away the smog, the smoke, and the summer haze. It would have been a perfect first day for the hotel, an auspicious one, even.

"You were right about Venice—I should have listened," she said quietly.

Then Claudia remembered her friend still standing there. She glanced up at Sacci and saw him wince as if she'd struck him.

"I'm sorry, Sacci. I don't know what I mean or what I think anymore," she murmured.

He shrugged. "I'm sorry, too," he said abjectly, limping out of the room. "I'll let you two talk."

How hateful she was! Sacci had lost a lot, too. He and Louis had devoted as much to the restoration of the palazzo and the opening of the hotel as she had. If her fate intertwined with that of the hotel, then his did too. In fact, hadn't they all started living as if the hotel had given them a new life, a focus for their lives?

She wished now that she'd never entertained the dream. If she could change the past, she would have stayed in New York or wandered to a different city.

But she realized that then she would have never met Louis and would never have known that she could be successful. Now, the loss of the hotel and her blossoming life was too much, and she merely wished to have never gotten into such a position. Perhaps it was better to have never known happiness at all.

The contessa sighed. She remained silent, staring at her daughter.

Yes, this was Venice, the city of the tragic. She was back on Vittorio's boat, spirit buoyant and youthful. Why was it that she never understood then that the abundant optimism about all aspects of life was a characteristic of youth, never to be enjoyed again? Oh, she had cried, too, and had felt as dead inside as if she'd sunk to the bottom of one of the deepest canals thick with the mud and rot of centuries. Not until she'd been long gone from Venice, and even begun dating other men who approached her tentatively as if she were half-ghoul, half-porcelain, did she appreciate what she'd been through. And perhaps not until this moment—more than thirty years later—did she begin to understand.

"Don't blame the city, carina," she sighed, shaking her head slowly. "Don't make the same mistake I made. And don't commit a sin even worse than blaming Venice."

The contessa walked slowly to the enormous window overlooking the orange-tiled rooftops of the city, punctuated by antennas poking skyward like haphazardly placed, bent hairpins. She'd never studied the city so closely, never seen it from an upper story window. What she had to say would be easier if she didn't look at anyone, especially her daughter whom she realized was more like her than she'd ever thought possible.

"You can't blame anyone," the contessa said slowly. "This didn't happen because you were in Venice. Or because you did anything wrong. If anyone is to blame, it's me."

"How can that be?" her daughter asked, lifting her head listlessly. "What did you do?"

Claudia could still smell smoke, even after a long shower and bath. The smoke reminded her of defeat, death, and ruin. She had somehow failed, been taken in by everything—by the city, by Louis, by Sacci.

"I put the idea in your head. Maybe taught you what I was taught—that bad things happen because of God or the gods. But now I see that it's in the nature of things that bad happens—as well as good."

"Why didn't you tell me this before?" she asked. "I didn't know you thought such things."

Claudia leveled her eyes and studied her mother as if she were someone she'd never met. What had happened to her? Something seemed to be changing her even as she stood with her back to her.

"I'm just figuring it out right now. As I watch you, I understand better what happened to me," she said, turning from the window to look at her daughter.

Claudia thought her mother's expression suddenly honest and open. Had she ever looked at her this way before?

"What exactly happened to you, Mother? What happened to you here that made you hate Venice so much?"

Right then the contessa decided to tell her, realizing it would be a new story for herself, too. Why had she held back all those years? Had she feared poisoning her daughter or giving power to the bad feelings and bad luck? Or was it that she didn't want her daughter to know that things hadn't always gone her way, that she wasn't a Pucci after all?

So she revealed her tragic tale. With the passing of so many years, the story no longer seemed quite so awful. There was the remembered pain in her chest, her limbs jelly-like, but the story felt familiar, no longer accompanied by disappointment, the gnawing awareness of what might have been.

She knew as she told the tale that she would always look at water as something to be mistrusted, keeper of secrets and hidden danger. The problem was that one could never know exactly what lingered below the surface, what might reveal itself. And as much as she had changed her mind about Venice, she still couldn't bear viewing the yawning expanse of the *Canale della Giudecca*, where Vittorio had drowned.

The contessa recited each memory, from meeting Vittorio and their awkward romance, to the boat ride, her tongue rolling over the words as if she were a storyteller. She'd never recited the story to anyone, not even her husband, no, especially not him nor to a priest.

And she'd never actually told herself the story either, never allowing herself to dwell on the details or stitch the events together, forming a pattern, a story.

Still, there was one other person besides her daughter that she would have liked to tell about this seminal event—her grandfather. He would have understood. He'd known life the way she had, though he was no Maledetto. For years, she had wondered if he were still alive, would he somehow blame her? Would he think less of her for having failed him in some way? How silly she'd been. In some ways, she hadn't really known the man at all. Now though, with the passage of time, she felt she understood him better than when she was a child.

She hoped Claudia would understand so that she might view life differently than she had. It remained to be seen whether Claudia was destined to make the same mistakes, whether such was the fate of everyone or just those who were Maledetti. She now realized that the penance for her sins wasn't found in church, after all, but in the passage of life.

After so many years of living a suspended life, she vowed that she would now change. She felt as if she was on the cusp of a new beginning, a curious mix of penance, unburdening, and hope. She had made many mistakes, allowing Vittorio's drowning to infect her life like a cancer. While his death hadn't killed her, it had crippled her.

The contessa paused frequently in the telling; trying to recall some details, though other minutiae that she hadn't recalled in years came flooding back. Like the color of the setting sun reflecting on the water as they were leaving the dock at the russet-colored palazzo, and the little neighborhood boys, wide-eyed and thrilled hanging over a bridge watching the boat. Where were those boys now, she wondered. Still in Venice, walking the twisted, mildew-scented alleyways? Or had they left like so many others, carried by an ebb and flow that pushed and pulled people across the globe, influenced by the machinations and currents of history or perhaps something deeper. Maybe one of those boys had waited on her at the restaurant that she had dined at the night before. Maybe another one of them had driven her water taxi from the train station. Maybe one of the boys had drowned in the canals. And maybe others had died regular deaths—cancer, auto accidents, anything really. Death reached into the world every day. One just didn't always realize that it was forever present, lurking in the shadows or moving to the fore, ebbing and flowing just as life did.

She'd had a misplaced belief that the world was opening up to her when she'd first visited Venice with Vittorio, like her first time at the circus when she was a child. Everything had seemed possible then, and life was simply a thrilling and endless, enchanting possibility. The second time she'd had such a magical feeling, she wasn't merely a spectator at the circus, but fully immersed in life.

But the feeling hadn't lasted, and she'd shamed herself for her pride and conceit in the years that followed. How had she dared believe that she'd been blessed over others? That she would get what she'd wanted because fate had decreed it, because she somehow deserved happiness and all the things she'd dreamed of? In the course of the years she'd gone from one extreme to the other.

"When the boat flipped, I flew through the air and couldn't even remember that detail for years. I have fragments of memories of what that looked and felt like. And what happened to Vittorio? We were right next to each other—scarcely a foot apart. How can a foot make such a difference?" she asked, averting her eyes again to the pale blue of the sky outside the window. "For one person to fly out of the boat and for the other to get caught by the gunwales—maybe knocked on the head—and then pulled under a capsized boat? How does that happen?"

Claudia stared. Her mother was crying, stiffly, quietly, her tears rolling down her cheeks, the wet streaks glistening in the clear, late September sun that fell through the windows.

"That was your first love, Mamma?" she asked in a whisper.

"My first and only real love," she admitted. "I love your father, but it's different—a different kind of love."

She dabbed at the corners of her eyes with the edge of her sleeve, leaving a blot of mascara on her cuff. She shrugged her shoulders and rested her arm on a table.

"Why so different?" Claudia asked, though maybe she already knew.

The contessa tilted her head, looking away. "First loves are always different, of course. And that's one reason. You're young so you don't know. And you're naive. You believe that love can save you, make you, be the world. And in some way, just because you're so naive, so optimistic, and sanguine, maybe that is really so. For a while, anyway."

"Of course," Claudia murmured. She'd never felt pity for her mother who always seemed the sort to scorn it, anyway. Besides, she'd never really seemed vulnerable or hurt before. Why had she never guessed that there must be something beneath her mother's icy facade? After all, Claudia shared the blood flowing through her mother's veins. Were they that different?

"And then the accident took away my optimism," she sighed, straightening the sleeves of her blouse. "All these years I've thought it worse to have what you want within reach, almost in your grasp, and then to see it slip away. Makes you think it would be better to never have seen and tasted it, eh?"

Her eyes pink and swollen, she looked across the table at her daughter.

Claudia nodded, unable to take her eyes off her mother. Did everyone walking down every street in every city in the world have their own sad story, their own heartache to tend like a secret garden, which they visited from time to time or perhaps not at all? If her mother who had always seemed so cool and remote had her story, then maybe everyone did. Only, couldn't some people get through the whole of life without ever letting on, never submitting to the disappointment, sadness, or loss that occupied some remote corner of their insides?

The hotel was Claudia's taste of what could have been. She'd divorced, but until the previous six months, she hadn't loved. Did loving a hotel count? Did loving your whole life, every little piece and second of it from the frayed bedside rug to the corner café, to Sacci's bug-eyed, panting pugs, to the crooked Venetian streets and all the dying, thick-ankled Venetian widows shuffling through the fish market, to dear Louis, and the hundred-year-old wisteria climbing outside her window count? Hadn't all these things and every other detail constituted a life plenty big enough to savor, to elicit a chorus of contented sighs?

Maybe it was a love of a sort, the coming together of life in a pattern that she had recognized, taken on, and worn like a familiar, favorite sweater. Not until her mother had cut her off, had her life opened up. Sure, there were those first few frightening weeks, but in retrospect, even those had been livelier and more genuine than any she'd experienced previously.

And just when she'd thought that her life was somehow unexpectedly coming together after months of hard work, coming to fruition, her hopes were dashed. Was it punishment? Bad karma? The gods? The priests? Why did such things happen?

In the end, in her very young life she'd *had* all these experiences. She had loved these things, loved her life, and now it was broken. Maybe *she* was to be broken, like the old woman dressed in black who haunted the fish market and side streets, supposedly mourning a daughter lost in one of the canals. Well, if her own loss wasn't the same as losing a daughter, still she had lost all she had.

"I don't know why, Mamma, but I have this sense that this was it," she said carefully, tiptoeing through her words. "And that maybe this is all anyone gets. Maybe I was lucky to have had some months of bliss, some very real hopes. I think some people don't ever even have that."

She pushed her hair behind her ear, smelling the smoke again. She wondered how long the smell would haunt her, reminding her of what she could scarcely stop thinking about.

"I guess I'm your legacy," Claudia sighed.

"I think I've learned that it's really better," her mother said quietly. "At least I had a little taste, got a look at what might have been. And a taste of bliss is better than no taste at all."

"But then you knew what you didn't have, and isn't that what's made you so unhappy all these years?"

She thought of her mother's moodiness, her sometimes-cold embrace. Certainly, these were the signs of an unhappy person. Now Claudia had her own disappointment to tend. Maybe she would be as bitter as her mother was, becoming caustic and world-weary, opinionated, and imperious. It made sense to her now why her mother was the way she was.

The contessa shrugged. "It didn't have to make me unhappy. That was what I chose."

She blinked slowly, gazing out the window through which she could still see a smudge of black smoke marring the sky. The old timbers of La Fenice would smolder for hours more. There was a lot of life and history to burn, not like a building made of new, fresh timbers lacking the soundness and density that came with age. On the news, opera house authorities had already said that they would rebuild the landmark, a better version—and fireproof.

Claudia sniffled, wiping her pink, watering eyes with a tissue.

"It makes no sense to me, though. Why be allowed a taste, why know happiness at all if in the end it's taken away?" she asked, her voice wavering. "That seems more like a world governed by an awful brute of a god, a trickster, or worse—"

"*Cara*, you shouldn't speak like that. Life's a mystery. God's a mystery, if there's a god at all. And how Venice exists, how it's survived all of these years is proof that the unbelievable exists."

"If there is a god, I despise him," Claudia declared, her voice steady again. "And if he gave me a mouth and a mind, why shouldn't I use them? Why would he give them to me and expect me to neglect them? If he even exists, he's cruel. *Awful*."

The contessa shook her head, tears appearing at the corners of her eyes. She dabbed them with a linen handkerchief and looked sadly across the table.

"Maybe God didn't *do* any of this. Think of that for a moment. Perhaps he's not responsible," she said.

"But he must have *let* it happen, didn't he? He stood by, allowing us to put all of this work into the palazzo, and then lets it burn. He lets me be truly happy for the first time in my life, to know what it feels like to create and to work and for what! To have it all taken away—or to stand idly by while it's destroyed? No, any such god doesn't deserve my prayers."

"Do you think that God gave you the palazzo, arranged for you to meet Louis and Sacci, or even to have you run to Venice after you left New York?" her mother asked, leaning forward.

The contessa had stopped crying, her voice becoming steady. She slowly stroked Claudia's hand, noticing the small calluses and scratches. Her own hands had never had such blemishes. She'd always considered herself a hard worker, but her labor had been something entirely different from her daughter's.

"Give yourself some time. But do your mother a favor—even if you owe me none—and think about the possibility, okay?"

"The possibility of what?" Claudia asked, gazing at her mother quizzically.

"That there is a god who exists, but that he controls nothing."

"Nothing? But that goes against what I was taught—what you and Papà taught me, not to mention the church, and all the priests and nuns."

"If I taught you that, I'm sorry. I'm not sure I believed that," the contessa said, gazing at her daughter regretfully.

"What's the point in a god who controls nothing?" Claudia asked, her voice high and nearly cracking.

Her mother shrugged and glanced out the windows wistfully. "Does he have to be?"

It was Claudia's turn to shrug. How were they talking about God, when the more pressing matter was that her newfound life was no more, and perhaps more than anything, she longed for reassurance—even if it came from her mother. She couldn't imagine it coming from the religion of her childhood.

The contessa cleared her throat, brushing her thin, manicured fingers across her throat.

"I didn't fully realize a lot of things until right now," she explained.

"Watching you go through this has sharpened my understanding of a lot of things about my own life. I see and understand for the first time."

"What do you mean?" Claudia asked, observing her mother's calm expression. Her face no longer looked hard. Were her eyes smiling?

"I blamed life—and God, too—for Vittorio's death. I hated for a long time after that, and marveled that his mother hated me. But you see, his mother blamed me for his death. Maybe a lot of people need to find someone to blame for a death or for bad things. So it's God, a lover, a mother, a father, a husband—whoever. It fulfills the need, does the trick. So we blame."

She nodded her small head, the French-like mole on her cheek rising slightly.

"But what do you think is the truth then?" Claudia asked, pulling her hand away from under her mother's and hugging her own ribcage lightly. Her insides hurt; a dull, constant ache that squeezed her breath.

"I don't know for certain," her mother shrugged. "But blaming gets you nowhere and brings you nothing. What exactly do you ask of blame, and what does it give you?"

"I don't know either. Don't know what to think," Claudia murmured. She felt empty, uncertain. Even her mother wasn't knowable, familiar. In a way, though, she liked her mother now. How had she known her for so many years without ever suspecting she harbored such a secret? She thought her mother was one-dimensional, like one of the fashion photos in magazines she had pored over as a teenager.

"I realize that blaming helps nothing at all," her mother said. She sighed. "Blaming brings nothing, least of all peace. I wish I'd known that so many years ago. I could have had a hell of a life."

Claudia scrutinized her mother for the first time, it seemed. Had she ever really known her? Or had this woman she'd observed all her life transformed herself, like one of the goddesses she'd read about in grade school mythology? The way she'd carried herself, even talked about herself had never led her to believe her mother saw herself as other than regal and entitled. To learn that this more complicated woman might have any misgivings, any regrets, surprised her.

"Let's go on the terrace, can we?" her mother said, standing and turning toward the enormous door. "I need some fresh air."

Claudia rose slowly, deciding she'd like to get outside, too. There didn't seem to be enough air in the flat, and she felt like it was hard to breathe. Maybe getting outside, with the bright sky above and maybe a little sea air, if she was lucky, would make her feel better.

"Maybe the breeze will take the smell of smoke out of my hair," she said hopefully, running her fingers across her head.

"It'll take days, at least," her mother said casually. "You've got the smoke in your nose and lungs, not to mention in your skin and hair. You won't get rid of it as quickly as you'd like."

She opened the door casually, as if she'd visited Sacci's apartment many times. Claudia followed, pulling the door closed behind her.

"What to do, what to do," Claudia murmured. "I haven't a clue what I should do now."

Her mother turned from looking over the balustrade onto the red tile rooftops of the city, the church towers, and palazzi. A giant, gnarled wisteria vine climbed out of an oversize terra-cotta pot sitting in the corner of the terrace, twisting around the balustrade, framing the doorway and shooting pioneering tendrils onto the roof above.

"What do you think you should do?" her mother asked, her voice flat.

Claudia wondered why her mother had asked her this instead of making suggestions, seizing the opportunity to inject her with advice.

"Run," Claudia said soberly. "Run or hide, and quite possibly sleep. I would like to sleep this off and wake up in a week, months even, and have forgotten all the work we did. I thought things were going to be different. That my life had taken a turn."

"You don't mean that," her mother sniffed, waving her hand dismissively, as if swatting at flies. "And you'll find that your life is now different. There's no going back."

Her mother looked across the city's rooftops, the radiant blue of the sea in the distance. Something caught her eye just below on the street, a bent elderly woman walking with surprising agility and steadiness, followed by an elderly man—her husband? The man wore old clothes, a sport coat that must have been twenty or thirty years old. His clothing didn't look threadbare, just dated. However, from three stories up, she couldn't tell for certain.

The woman seemed almost familiar, her slow plodding taking her gradually down the street like a snail with no seeming sense of destination. She wore a baggy, gray cardigan—and the same dull colors as the man following her. But the way they walked didn't match the way they looked. The woman looked bitter, agitated, and the man looked troubled in a different way, as if he was seeking something—something from the woman he followed. They both walked so quietly that not even a soft murmur of their footsteps floated up the narrow street to the terrace.

If they were a couple, thought the contessa, might one of their children have been one of the boys who'd watched the boat as it departed the Lunardini palazzo on that fateful summer late afternoon? Certainly, they were in the city on that day long ago. She would have liked to talk to them, to know what their lives had been like, where they'd been in those slow-moving, uncomplicated years after the war.

"Look at that old man and woman," the contessa whispered, pointing below. "What do you think?"

Claudia walked to the balustrade, leaning beside her mother and allowing her shoulder to rest gently against her mother's shoulder. Claudia saw the elderly man and woman walking methodically down the street, the man trailing the woman by five or ten feet. She looked at her mother in surprise: there was nothing remarkable about the two, dressed in drab colors and making their way down the calle like countless other people across the city, across Europe.

Leaning farther over the balustrade, Claudia watched the couple as they approached the building, noticing that in a moment they would be directly beneath them. Her mother leaned over, too, tipping a terra-cotta pot of geraniums off the railing. Claudia moved clumsily to grab the pot before it toppled over the edge.

The two women, mother and daughter, shouted at the same time, warning the couple and anyone else below, but the pot had hit the street at the same time, shattering and skidding across the cobblestones. The old woman jumped, lost her balance, and nearly fell, but the man raced up from behind and steadied her by planting one hand on the small of her back and the other on her shoulder. Before she looked to see who had kept her from falling, the woman looked upward and spotted Claudia and her mother.

"*Ci spiace, ci dispiace tanto, signori*!" Claudia shouted, her hands clasped together in a sign of contrition.

"Are you all right?" her mother shouted. "I feel awful. I'm so clumsy!"

The woman pulled away from the man without turning to look at him.

"Niente," she said, shaking her head. "It was an accident."

"I'm sorry to frighten you, but I'm relieved that you aren't hurt," the contessa said, her hand tightly gripping the balustrade.

"Poor *fiore*," the old woman said, shaking her head and looking at the pieces of terra-cotta planter and the scattered potting soil and bits of geranium. Shielding her eyes from the brightness of the sky, she returned her gaze to the terrace.

Claudia noticed the woman study her mother, as if puzzling about something.

"Do I know you, signora?" she called up at them.

"Do you know her?" Claudia asked, wondering if it was some woman who'd figured into her mother's short stay in Venice so many years ago.

Her mother returned the woman's gaze, scrutinizing her face and withered figure, shrugging in response to her daughter's question. She had been in the city such a short time so many years ago, who could it have been? The contessa twisted her mouth thoughtfully, gazing at the old woman standing squat-legged, apart from her husband.

"No, I don't think so," she murmured uncertainly. But the woman did seem familiar. How could she? When she'd been in Venice last, she'd known only the Lunardinis and Vittorio. The woman looked unlikely to have been a friend of either. Had she met her at a party or at a dinner somewhere?

Still, she looked simple, common, and how would she have made her acquaintance? When she'd visited Vittorio, he'd brought her to dinners at other palazzi and to the old restaurants in the cramped quarter near San Marco. Where could they have possibly met?

The old woman continued gazing, a smile appearing on her face. Nodding her head slowly, she seemed to grow more certain.

"You have come back, haven't you?" she called, chuckling good-naturedly.

"Who is she?" the old man asked. He turned his head up toward the terrace, his eyes squinting.

"Oh, not even an acquaintance," the woman explained. "I knew her name once, I believe, but now I just know her as having stayed at the palazzo of the Lunardini family."

So it was at the palazzo. Maybe the woman had worked there when she'd been young, or perhaps her circumstances had changed in the many years since they'd last met. But she felt certain the woman couldn't have been mistaken, even if she had no memory of her. They must have met.

"I'm sorry, signora," the contessa called down. "You must be right, as when I was here last I did stay at Palazzo Lunardini, but I can't place your face or how I would have known you. Can you tell me, please?"

The woman smiled, shading her eyes with one of her hands. Her whole face seemed to exalt, contrasting with her gray, drab clothing. She stood still and silent, studying the two of them from three floors below.

"Is that your daughter?" the woman asked after a moment.

"Sì, it is," the contessa said, smiling at Claudia. Maybe they did look alike after all, she thought.

"I'm happy for you," the woman said. "So very happy for you."

The old man's hand flew to his wife's back, as if to catch her, but she didn't seem to have stumbled. Swatting away the man's hand, she shielded her eyes again, the smile fading from her lips.

Still puzzled at how she might know the woman, the contessa asked, "Are you from Venice? Are you Venetian?" She noticed that the man's squinting eyes sparkled in the sun. Was he crying? Was his mouth trembling, shaking so that either he was about to break down or was he speaking, mumbling something to the woman? The woman ignored him, not turning to acknowledge him.

The woman seemed to ponder the question, studying the building and even taking a quick look down the street as if to see where she was.

"Yes, I'm Venetian," she answered hesitantly, as if still pondering the question. "I'm from Murano, but this is my city I suppose."

The contessa nodded, still uncertain. "I'm not sure how I know you, how we met," she explained.

The old woman shrugged. "It doesn't matter."

Then the woman began laughing, pulling her hand from her forehead and waving at Claudia and her mother, the sun illuminating her wrinkled face.

"Maybe not," the contessa said uncertainly, so quietly that she wasn't certain the woman could even hear.

"Buonasera," she abruptly called in a louder voice, noticing that the woman had begun making her way down the street again sure-footedly, seemingly aware of the man, her husband, probably, shuffling along a few feet behind.

"Buonasera," the old woman called back, turning slightly and waving up at the contessa and her daughter.

"Will I see you again?" the contessa called after her, wondering what she was proposing.

The stranger stopped, shielding her eyes from the sun again and shrugging.

"It would be my pleasure," she called, her voice faltering. Then she and the man turned, moving more quickly down the street.

Wordlessly, the contessa and her daughter watched the couple shuffle down the street and disappear around the corner, lost in the maze of Venetian alleyways.

"How did you know that woman, Mother?" Claudia asked, tenderly fingering a late-blooming wisteria blossom.

"I've no idea, *cara*," she said. "But I think when I met her last I didn't like her. Now she seems so harmless, no different from me in some fundamental way. I cannot imagine what it was about her that I didn't like, but that part of me is gone."

Claudia studied her mother's face, watched her study the city spreading out below them, each alleyway and canal filled with a jumble of houses and buildings, small and large and in a multitude of colors.

"I think I've seen that woman around in the markets," Claudia offered, wondering if that would help her mother figure out how she knew her.

"It would have been many years ago," her mother said. "And perhaps some mysteries are better left unresolved. If all the answers were revealed, life wouldn't be that interesting, would it?"

"No, I suppose it might not be," Claudia said, furrowing her brow.

"I'm ready to go for a prosecco or an espresso, carina. Are you?" the contessa asked, moving away from the balustrade and straightening her skirt.

"Sure, Mamma," Claudia said, feeling a sudden urge to squeeze her mother's arm, to lead her down the stairway, and out into the maze of Venetian streets.

Chapter Twenty

It seemed natural that they should meet at Café Tramonta. Louis arrived first, a little before the agreed upon nine o'clock meeting time. He felt nervous. Why? Twirling the demitasse spoon, he ran a finger from his other hand along the rim of his empty cappuccino cup. Rubbing his red, swollen wrists, he marveled that after all that had happened in the past few days, they would be together at Tramonta as if nothing had happened at all.

Or would Claudia have changed?

Despite being assaulted, tied up, and left for nearly twenty-four hours, he had decided he would stay in Venice. But with the bizarre burning of the old opera house and the palazzo, what about Claudia? What would she decide to do?

He'd always been early and Claudia late.

But that had no longer been true, had it? Not since the palazzo. Once she'd started working on the hotel, then habits like tardiness had melted away.

When Claudia arrived, he would order a second coffee. He would need all the caffeine he could ingest without making himself sick. Then, if he drank too much, he could follow the former practice of ordering an early prosecco to take the nervous edge off the caffeine buzz. Could they fall back into their old routine, maybe just for that morning? And if they did, would they be stuck there, unable to move forward again? He wanted to be in both places: back in time before he'd been tied up and the hotel nearly burned down, and in the present, when maybe the fire had left a truly clean slate for all of them.

Things—life—had been leading up to something during the past six months. He'd been so misled, believing that life was opening up, changing. Scarcely aware of the change in himself, he realized that he'd started acting and feeling different some months ago. He awoke in the morning feeling content, full of wonder, almost as he did on the first balmy days of summer when he'd just gotten out of school and had full, unstructured days strung out in front of him. As far as he could comprehend, he'd thought at the time. Now they were gone. Not unlike his idea of where things were going in Venice.

How had things gone so woefully off track? He was a sucker for not having seen that something might go wrong, that things just couldn't go as well as they had without some hitch.

Things were often clearer when viewed after the fact. Maybe he should have skipped out of town the minute he'd been discovered at Harry's Bar, that fateful night more than half a year ago.

Then, his mother would never have found him, and he would still need to run. Maybe that was why he hadn't run; he no longer needed to.

The nearby church tower began striking nine o'clock and Claudia walked through the door of the café. Her eyes, glazed with a pinkish caste and swollen, darted around the room, quickly finding Louis. She smiled with a warmness and ease that surprised him. Not an expression of relief, her smile seemed to encourage, and to hold within it some other emotion.

"You're on time," he said, as she made her way over to his table.

He rose, kissing both of her cheeks, and then they hugged. Her face glowed pink, freshly scrubbed, but a strong aroma of soap and perfume only masked an acrid scent of smoke.

He thought she might cry—or that perhaps he would. But she only gripped the whole of his upper body firmly.

Maybe he was the one bound to cry. He felt the realization of all that they'd been through manifest itself in his body, emanating from his very core. Was everything lost, was life bound to change? She and Sacci had probably lost the palazzo, and she'd lost something more, perhaps, for he knew that the hotel had breathed new life into her. But what had he lost?

Claudia pushed him away from her, maintaining her grasp on his forearms and searching his face.

"Luigi," she said, calling him by his Italian name, which she rarely used. "I can't believe what happened to you? Are you okay?"

Grabbing his wrists, she examined the red marks created by the rope, and she dabbed them softly with the tips of her fingers. She sighed.

"Good enough," he replied, trying to smile. "For having been pounced on and tied up for twenty-four hours. But how are *you*?"

He hadn't meant for his question to sound so ponderous, with a hint of an expectation of a certain sort of answer. She didn't seem broken, though, didn't look as if she'd given up on anything. But she had no money, and she and Sacci had both told him before the fire that they'd had no money for anything but liability insurance.

"Let's get coffees, okay?" she suggested, tugging on his arm. "Then we can catch up. I want to hear *every*thing. How it happened, how Sacci found you, how you learned about the hotel and the fire. You know, I thought you'd left for some reason, just decided to move on. It was so strange to me that all day long yesterday after the fire, you never called or stopped by. I couldn't figure it out. Little did I know."

She smiled at Louis, squeezing his arm.

"I'll get another coffee and fill you in. And I want to hear how you were rescued—Sacci told me about how you'd taken a sleeping pill, how he lost his keys and was locked out of the palazzo, and then how he fell trying to jump onto the terrace knocking himself out in the process," he said, shaking his head in disbelief.

"If only he'd known the firefighters were right around the corner," she chuckled. "How he fell a whole story with nothing but a slightly twisted ankle I can't understand. I feel like we're all lucky."

Louis stared at Claudia as if he'd been struck.

"Somehow I thought you'd look at it differently, that you might see all of us as unlucky, might be ready to leave Venice," he admitted as they approached the counter.

"Yesterday was different. Twenty-four hours ago I was exactly as you describe," she said, nodding at the barista. "Despondent and hopeless, looking for a rock under which to hide for the rest of my life. I wanted to be anywhere but here in Venice."

At the counter, they both saw the beautiful simplicity of the place. Louis wondered if Claudia had the same feeling as he that the place could disappear at any moment. They'd come to take it for granted, as if there were such a coffee house on every street, in every city in every country. But like the ancient coffee house at the fish market, there was no other.

Giant beams—at least three or four hundred years old—crisscrossed the low ceiling. The walls and ceiling, a smoky shade of ochre, had seen the curling, bluish smoke of centuries of cigar, cigarette, and pipe smoke. The long, battered, and dimpled zinc bar had been doing service for probably a hundred years. And best of all, the baristas and owner of the café, who smiled and would gossip if invited to, made working at a coffee house seem a noble profession. Though he and Claudia had only been going every once in a while since Sacci had bought the giant espresso machine at the palazzo, he was happy to see that the same regulars were still there, sipping espresso at the counter, or slugging shots of vin santo.

"Espresso doppio?" the owner's son asked, waving and nodding, as if they'd still been coming in every morning.

"Sì," she smiled, turning to Louis. "And then my mother showed up at Sacci's door yesterday afternoon—"

"Your mother? Had she arrived to take you back to Rome, to kidnap you or something?"

Claudia smiled reluctantly, as if she couldn't yet believe it herself.

"No. She apologized."

"For cutting you off, for trying to make you leave? But she was right, the hotel ended in disaster, so I thought she'd be lording that over you," he said excitedly, nearly tripping over his words.

A lock of hair fell into her eyes, which she pushed back tentatively, tucking it behind her ear after sniffing it and frowning.

"I suppose you'll be leaving now? Venice is no good anymore, is it?" he asked hesitantly.

"I'm staying," she said emphatically. "We'll reopen the hotel."

"But I thought the hotel burned to the ground?"

Claudia laughed, her eyes lighting up. "The terrace, the curtains, the umbrellas, the plants, and just a few things in the upper sala burned. Luckily, though, none of the beams caught fire. The structure's just fine."

"I didn't realize," he said, sounding more hopeful. "I heard on the news that there was considerable damage."

"There's a lot of smoke damage—the rugs, furniture, and curtains that caught fire created a lot of smoke," Claudia explained, looking more somber. "Everything but the furniture needs to be replaced. And the terrace looks awful—charred and empty."

"But you didn't have any insurance, how will you replace it all? And what curtains—you said there were curtains on the terrace?"

She shifted her gaze, grinning crookedly. "We have a new partner," she said sheepishly.

Louis paused, studying her face. "Your mother?" he asked, furrowing his brow.

Claudia nodded.

"Won't she try to get you to move back to Rome, to control you as she always had?" he asked, confused at her sudden turn.

What had happened to change her mind when she'd sounded so certain about her mother after her last visit? So much had changed in only twenty-four hours, and they hadn't even gotten to his misadventure. He felt like he'd been tied up and gone a full year, not merely a day.

"How can that be? And what about the curtains, what are you not telling me?" he asked, incredulous.

"I can hardly explain it myself—"

"Cappuccino?" the barista interrupted, smiling at Louis. "The second always comes in ten minutes, no?"

Louis nodded, smiling.

Claudia continued. "With Sacci's permission, my mother arranged to have workers come in the night before," she began, sliding lire across the counter as she accepted the cup of double espresso. "You won't believe it—I couldn't. Her workers set up bars, brought in boxes and boxes of liquor, carted in enormous palms and lemon trees—most of which are wilted, burned, or dead—boxes of glasses and the curtains, *they* hung the curtains on the terrace."

"And it was the curtains that caught the sparks from the fire at La Fenice?" he asked, remembering the news accounts he'd heard on the radio while tied to a chair in his studio.

"Exactly."

"So it was indirectly your mother's fault that the palazzo burned?" he asked.

"That's the way she looks at it. Who knows whether it would have caught fire or not if the curtains hadn't been there? Doesn't matter, though. When I was revived by the paramedics in the ambulance and they explained the fire to me, I kept thinking there'd been some sort of mistake or that I was dreaming because they told me that the curtains on the terrace had caught fire and that they'd taken me out of the palazzo to rescue me."

Sliding more lire across the counter for Louis' drink, Claudia picked up her espresso, and walked to a nearby table. Louis followed.

"'What curtains on the terrace?' I kept asking. And because the paramedics couldn't explain it to me, I didn't believe them. And I was groggy, well, really out of it from the sleeping pill I took the night before. So until Sacci told me, and I saw the pictures on the news, I didn't believe it."

"Did you go to the hospital?"

"*Si*. And that's where I found Sacci—in the emergency room."

"What was Sacci doing in the emergency room? Oh, did they take him there after he fell?"

"Exacto," Claudia nodded. "The minute he awoke, he started raving like a lunatic, they told me, screaming that he had to save his friend in the burning *Palazzo Spirito*. That's when they wheeled me over to where he was. I'd heard someone screaming elsewhere in the hospital, but didn't realize it was Sacci. Poor, Sacci."

"He looked okay when he found me last night, except for a little limp," Louis said.

Sipping her espresso, Claudia shook her head in disbelief. "He's so lucky he didn't kill himself, really. I mean, what was he thinking jumping from that window across the street to the terrace?"

"It almost sounds like something a lover would do, doesn't it?" Louis asked, averting his eyes as he took a sip of his cappuccino.

"Louis," Claudia said, reaching across the table and lifting her friend's chin so that he was forced to look at her. "I've gotten this sense, from comments here and there, and from your occasional sulking, that you think there might be something between me and Sacci."

Louis swallowed hard, realizing that he was often so transparent. How long had she suspected?

"Maybe … I might have thought that a little," he mumbled.

"If there were, why would that bother you?" she asked.

Why couldn't he simply have admitted why it bothered him? Wasn't that the lesson he'd learned just months earlier from his mother, not to skulk around harboring secrets? And hadn't Claudia confronted him for being too secretive? Yet, what if he was wrong, and what if Claudia turned out to be interested in Sacci, too? While his feelings toward her wouldn't change (he'd been through plenty of triangles that ended similarly), what might she think? No, perhaps one didn't need to tell a person everything. There might be some secrets worth keeping.

"Oh, I'd feel like a third wheel, that's all," he half-lied, popping a finger in and out of the coffee cup handle.

Claudia stared him down. "And that's it? That's all you'll tell me?" she said, her voice rising.

"Is there something you've seen?" he asked, deftly thinking he'd turned the tables on her.

"Okay, then, yes there is," she answered, holding his gaze. "You don't spend as much time together as the three of us have without noticing things. You know, looks and comments, gestures, and well, behavior."

"What are you saying?" he asked, coyly.

Shaking her head, a lock of hair falling from behind her ear and across her face, she seemed to change her mind. "Let me just say that I might be able to help you, okay?" she smiled. "I'm on your side."

Louis nodded, grinning sheepishly. "Okay, then, you're right. It's *true*."

"What's true?" Claudia asked, leaning across the small table, causing the cups and saucers to tremble.

"What you thought might be true," he mumbled, avoiding her gaze.

"Just say it, Louis. Why don't you just say it?"

"It's stupid, crazy, I know. He's Italian!"

Claudia pursed her lips. "What's that supposed to mean? *I'm* Italian."

Waving his hands, as if to clear the air, he explained. "With Italian men, it's hard to tell if they're gay—you know, there just aren't that many gay men here."

"Go on," she said, leaning back in her chair.

"Well, there's that whole macho thing here, it's different from in Latin countries, but similar, don't you think?"

"Sure," she said, nodding. "But what does that have to do with Sacci? Do you think he's like that?"

"You don't find him inscrutable? Mysterious?"

Claudia laughed. "You *are* in love with him, aren't you? He seems that way to you because you've got a crush on him, not because he's Italian."

Louis blushed. How long ago had she figured it out? She said it as if she'd long suspected.

His heart pounding against his chest, he leaned forward, clearing his throat that suddenly felt tight. "So do you think … would you guess that Sacci is … *gay?*"

Claudia paused, studying his face.

"Yes, I think he is," she answered matter-of-factly. "But I'm not certain that he knows it."

"What?"

"I think he's asleep in a way," she explained, frowning. "And I don't want to discourage you, but I wonder if he'll ever wake up."

So maybe he hadn't made it all up this time, perhaps it wasn't merely his imagination. He wanted to cry, but from what? Relief? Joy? Fear? His insides, having hardly settled from being tied up for a day, and then learning about the fire and Claudia suddenly had something new he must digest. And was she right? Could he *be* gay?

He grew aware that Claudia was looking after him, trying to get him to talk to her, and yet, she hadn't told him enough about her mother's visit and how her mother had become a partner in the hotel.

"*Amica cara,*" he said, letting his tongue pause on the last syllable, observing her eyes as they sparkled and her face brightened. "I want to talk about this more—I'm dying to, in fact. I want to know what you think, how long you've thought it, and what I should do. But right now, I want to find out more about you. What happened with your mother? How is it that you're still here in Venice?"

"Well," she started, pushing away the empty espresso cup. "While at first I was tempted to flee, I realized that I still don't want to return to Rome, and there's nothing more for me anywhere else. I'd just be starting over again."

"I just thought you'd think you were unlucky, that this place was cursed. I kind of started to think that myself," he admitted. "I wondered if you might come around to your mother's way of thinking about Venice."

"No, I don't think that, though at first I did," she said gravely. "It's all in how you look at it. I did some reading when we were restoring the hotel. Venice was an improbable city from the start—malaria, wars, tides, and floods. And it's still here."

"But it's just strange how many bad things happened at once, all in a row like this," he said, wondering how she couldn't be wondering if she were cursed.

"This could have happened anywhere—really. Just open a newspaper or turn on the news," she said, playing with the espresso cup.

"So nothing's changed?" he asked.

"Oh, everything's changed," she gushed, leaning toward him and smiling. "I've been baptized."

She gave Louis a quick glance and then looked back toward the immense clouded window and the quiet, shaded street beyond.

"I hope you don't mean that you found religion again," he said.

"No, better than that," she said. "It's just a different way of looking at things."

"Aren't you worried about your mother being a partner?"

"You don't need to worry—really. I don't blame you, but my mother's changed. She was maybe always this way somewhere on the inside, less controlling and generous—with more than just her money—and has only recently figured out how to be *that* person."

"So she'll live here?" he said, patting the tabletop marred with coffee stains.

"No. She's just like an investor, but she tells me an undemanding one. I think she'd like to give me the money, but she's hesitant for some reason, not quite ready to give up control completely."

"So she could come in and take over or close it down, force you back to Rome somehow or to marry some idiot? I mean, what if she changes back to the person she was?"

Laughing, she slapped her palm on the table.

"You've gotten quite an impression of my mother—worse even than mine when I disliked her most." she said, shaking her head. "No, I'm confident this time that my mother means no harm and wants to help. I think her days of meddling—unless it's purely for the good—are over."

"So that's settled," Louis smiled. "You're staying, there's money to reopen the hotel. And Sacci, will Sacci stay as a partner?"

"He has to," she said. "Most of his money is tied up in it. And then, maybe he has other reasons to want to be around. And it's his palazzo," she said with a grin.

Blushing, Louis tried to change the subject. "How long do you think it'll take to clean it up and get it ready to open again?"

"Months, I hope. The hardest work's been done. Now we just need to clean, paint, toss out everything that smells of smoke or scrub it furiously. I know it's a lot to ask, but will you help again?" she asked, leaning across the table. "Or at least stop by in the mornings before you go do your translating and make me a coffee?"

"The machine survived?"

"There's not even any smoke damage on the first floor, so the machine's fine. Doesn't even need to be cleaned. And the faster we get the machine going, the sooner the smell of coffee will replace the smell of smoke."

"Sure, I'll help again," he agreed, wondering what a second round of helping might hold.

"Good!" she exclaimed, and then clearing her throat, she lowered her voice. "You haven't told me yet. What happened? I mean, Sacci gave me the overview, but I want to hear it from you."

"After leaving you at the palazzo, I wanted to do a little work because I was all excited about the opening and had some chapters to finish, so I went by the studio."

"That must have been about the time I was contemplating taking a sleeping pill!" she calculated.

"So I'd been working awhile, and though I had plenty of energy, I didn't want to be ruined for the opening. So, I turned off the light and headed down the stairs to go home. "

"If only you'd left earlier," Claudia sighed. "I'm so sorry."

"Now this gets embarrassing because sometimes I hear someone crying in the stair hall," he continued. "And something always draws me in, makes me stop and listen."

"That's a very respectable Venetian pastime, you know. Nothing to be ashamed of," she smirked.

"That's what Signora Crespi told me when she caught me once."

"She's not the crier? So who's the crier?"

Playing with his cup, he narrowed his eyes thoughtfully.

"I think I know, but am just not certain. When I know, I'll tell you. Anyway, I'm sitting on the stair listening to the crying, thinking about the hotel opening and other things and suddenly the door downstairs opens—"

"The guys who burned La Fenice?" she interrupts, her voice trembling.

"I don't know at first, but I hear them downstairs. They start arguing, and I start to get up to sneak back up the stairs into the studio, but decide that'll make more noise, so I just sat still hoping they'd leave."

"But they didn't."

"No, they didn't. They began arguing again and that's when I started to figure out they'd done something criminal. It's as if they *wanted* me to hear what they'd done. Suddenly they're racing up the stairs. I couldn't figure out anything to do quickly enough before one of them landed on top of me."

"They knew you were there?" she asked, looking confused.

"No, they'd begun fighting and one of them came up the stairs so fast he didn't even see me and just fell right over me. I think he ran right into me because the other one was chasing him. Then the one admitted what they'd done right in front of me because the other one thought I didn't know anything. He wanted to let me go."

"Too bad he didn't get his way," she sighed.

"Yeah, the one was suspicious of me from the start. I guess he was right since I'd heard what they were talking about even before they came up the stairs. I froze, though. Guess I'm not very good under pressure."

Claudia giggled. "You've become a true Venetian. All ears, aren't you?"

Louis nodded sheepishly.

"So they just decided to tie you up? You must have been scared to death."

"They didn't seem like killers to me. In fact, they didn't even seem like criminals. I guess they just had to get me out of the way temporarily while they made their escape. My heart was racing and I was shaking—I think they could see how frightened I was. But I never had the feeling they'd kill me. At least I didn't fear that."

"You know the one guy worked there, at the opera house, did you hear that?"

"No, but it doesn't surprise me. While they scared me at first, especially the one who wanted to tie me up right away, they seemed pretty normal. The whole time I was thinking that I couldn't believe these two guys lit the opera house on fire. I'd even seen them earlier that evening—probably on their way to light the fire. They just looked so normal, just like they have any other time I've seen them, like regular, quiet neighbors."

"How long did the police question you?"

"For hours. You'd have thought I was a friend of the guys—that I was the one who'd done the tying up. One police officer kept thinking that I knew them—I had to have known them—otherwise, why did they choose me to tie up?"

"That's the *carabinieri*," Claudia deadpanned. "At least in the end they didn't keep you."

"Hell, I'd already been tied up for twenty-four hours. I don't know if I could've taken any more time than that. They would've had to arrest me to keep me there."

"So the guys dragged you into your studio?"

"Yeah, and they had some rope in a bag—which I think was lucky because there was nothing in the studio they could have used. I was afraid they might take me with them, kidnap me. The shorter, meaner-looking one tied me up and did a pretty good job. My thumbs and the sides of my hands are still a little numb."

He stroked the sides of his hands, his fingers feeling the puffy, swollen flesh where the rope had bit into his skin.

"The taller one seemed to feel guilty about the whole thing. He turned on the radio so it would keep me company, and then they stuffed a sock in my mouth and left."

Claudia grimaced.

"That was the worst part, absolutely horrible to have that thing in my mouth. Sometimes I thought I might gag or choke. Or just go crazy. I tried to concentrate on the radio. First, there were news reports on the opera house, which seemed even more degrading somehow. I mean, here the guys who'd done it were escaping and I knew it, but could tell no one. And they left me to listen to the unfolding of their crime. Unreal, isn't it?"

Claudia tapped the rim of her empty cup, nodding. "Everything's unreal these last few days. Did you ever see a movie called *The Year of Living Dangerously*?"

"Yeah, that was with Mel Gibson when he was young, handsome, and not yet a freak?"

"That's the one. This has been our year of living dangerously, the year of bad and good things almost happening, including things worse than actually happened. I'm just relieved, unbelievably relieved that you're okay. When I think that you were tied up for a whole day, I feel sick—"

"Signori!" the barista interrupted, appearing over Claudia's shoulder. "Two *prosecchi*—on the house."

The man smiled reassuringly, as if he knew what they'd been through.

"Of course he knows," Claudia said, reading his mind. "*Grazie tante, signore*."

Neither knew what to propose for a toast, so they timidly clinked glasses and said, "*Saluti.*"

"When did you start to figure out something might be wrong?" Louis asked.

Claudia took a sip of the prosecco and then bit her lip. "Well, it wasn't actually me."

Louis looked at her with a confused expression.

"Don't have such hurt feelings about it—are all American men so sensitive? It's just that I always had a little bit of a suspicion that one day you would up and move on—you know—disappear. And I couldn't tell what was going on with you and Sacci. Or what you thought was going on between Sacci and me. And then there was the whole hotel business. And though you played off your mother's surprise visit as if it turned out well, I always wondered if it spoiled Venice for you."

"So you thought I'd left, on the day the hotel was to open? Without saying anything?"

"I wondered—I mean, how would I have guessed that you'd been tied up? It never entered my mind, of course, that anything like that would have happened to you in Venice."

"Yeah, I suppose, but I was the one who feared that you would leave. I was always thinking in the back of my head that I might want to leave after you left, and until the hotel, I wasn't certain that you'd stay."

"Ha!" Claudia laughed. "Me? You thought *I* was the one who would leave?"

"Well, that's what I thought—same as *you*."

Sipping from her glass, she shrugged dismissively. "Funny, eh?"

"Yeah," Louis nodded. "So who thought to check on me in my studio? Was it Sacci?"

"That was all his idea. In fact, I didn't even know he was going over there. And who knew that he even knew where your studio was!"

"I don't think I ever mentioned it," he said, a grin slowly spreading across his face.

Claudia nodded. "I think he checked your place first. Maybe he phoned a few times, I'm not sure, I was with my mother. And then a few hours later I got his call telling me you'd been tied up!"

"I would have called," said Louis, "but Sacci called the police first, and got me something to eat and drink. I thought I might pass out. And that sock dried out my mouth, made me so damn thirsty, I thought I might go crazy. So after they rushed me to the hospital and examined me there—all the while with the police asking a million questions—Sacci told me about the hotel. That's when I knew I needed to call. So, before the police took me to the station to ask me another thousand questions—most of them a repeat of what they'd already asked me—I told them I had to make one call."

"And that's when you called."

"Exacto."

"And here we are, you with sore wrists, me with a half-ruined hotel."

"But you've got money now."

She was changed. He suddenly saw so clearly how she'd been transformed. He'd seen hints of it after she'd been working in the palazzo for a few weeks, when her eye had first started to hold a glimmer that he hadn't seen before. Her mother must have seen the change, too.

"You're so changed, Claudia."

She turned; her eyes looked hurt. He smiled then, wanting her to know that he liked the new Claudia.

Smiling back, she said quietly, "I think you've changed, too. Neither one of us is the same person we were when we met a year and a half ago, are we?"

"I'm not sure I've changed so much."

"No, you have. I can see it," she said, leaning in. "Think about it," she said in a near whisper. "Do you want the same things you wanted a year ago? And what are you afraid of now? Did you even know what you were afraid of when we met?"

She was right. Maybe they were both in the same space, like fledglings.

"You seemed so secretive when we met."

"Secretive?"

His mother had been right. Odd how people could be so unaware in how they came across to others.

"I didn't mean to be—I didn't even know."

He wondered how others had perceived him in college or when he'd dated Greg. They'd never even talked about it. Had he seemed secretive to him, too?

"Things changed after your mother paid that surprise visit. Don't you think?" she asked, sipping her prosecco slowly.

Louis chuckled—she didn't even drink her prosecco the same way.

"Yeah. She made me realize some things about myself. Funny how you can live for so long in the dark, not even knowing why you're doing the things you're doing."

"That's how *most* people live, Louis."

Louis noticed the barista approaching their table again. He looked around; the café had almost not customers.

"Another prosecco or coffee?" the barista asked. "On the house and to celebrate your good fortune."

So, the barista had heard. They were in Venice, after all.

They ordered two more *prosecchi*, and then slouched in their chairs as they used to do.

Staring at the old timbered ceiling, Louis said, "I think I need to go back home for a while, to Chicago."

Claudia was quiet for a moment, studying her friend. She shook her head slowly, a vague frown forming.

"I'm afraid you'll go and not come back. Just moments ago, I thought maybe I'd been silly to have that fear that you'd leave at any time for the next place. I never thought about you ever going back home because you never talk about it. What is it that makes you need to return there?"

Louis leaned forward across the table.

"I just left there—abruptly," he explained, shrugging. "I took my backpack for an extended tour of Europe, maybe knowing in the back of my head that I wouldn't return for a long time. But I never told anyone it would be years before I returned."

"You were so unhappy to run away like that?" she asked. "As unhappy as I was?" she quickly added.

Louis frowned.

"I didn't like much about myself, or my life. So I didn't like where I was, not my family or my friends, not really anyway. It wasn't necessarily anything they did—just my take on things. Well, except for Tad, the neighbor we saw at that lunch with your mother, and a few others like him. Everything seemed tainted to me, so I just wanted a fresh start, a new place, and new people. Figured I could do better that way."

Claudia nodded, pushing a Lavazza sugar packet across the table with fingers no longer perfectly manicured.

"Sounds familiar. But why go back? I don't need to return to New York—or even Rome. I'm finished with both of them. This is the first time I feel like I'm where I'm supposed to be."

Pulling a strand of hair in front of her face, she sniffed again, frowning.

"Ugh—smoke," she groaned.

"We both smell, I think," he said.

"What do you smell of?" she asked, sniffing again.

"Fear, I guess. Uncertainty. But maybe not as strongly as I did a little while ago."

Claudia shook her head. "I don't smell it at all."

"Well, I have to admit that I can smell the smoke on you," he said, leaning forward with his nose pointed toward her.

The barista appeared above the table, clicking his heels together and announcing the drinks.

"*Prosecchi per due.*"

"Grazie, signore," they gushed, lifting the glasses toward the waiter.

"You'll come back … stay?" the barista asked with a hopeful expression, his eyebrows arched.

"I'll be here," assured Claudia. "And I'll come in more regularly—as soon as the palazzo is cleaned up again. I'll need a break from it now and then." She turned to Louis, allowing him to speak for himself.

"I'll be back, too. I'm just going to head out of town for a short while. But not until I help at the palazzo."

"*Bravi,*" he said, bowing slightly. "We missed you."

He turned quickly and headed back to the bar.

"Oh, this smell of smoke," Claudia muttered. "I can't stand it. I soaked in the tub for an hour—and washed my hair twice."

"It's not every day you get caught in a fire. I think you may smell like smoke for a while. And maybe that's not such a bad thing."

She gazed at him thoughtfully.

"Maybe," she admitted, "but I'd still prefer not to smell like smoke. It reminds me of destruction, death. It doesn't smell like a fireplace on a damp, cold day or a campfire. This is a smell of something very different. I don't know if I'll ever get it out of my nose." She paused."You haven't told me why you need to return to the states. And I only ask because there's a part of me that's afraid that you'll go—it's home, after all—and decide to stay there."

Claudia picked up the glass of prosecco, taking a slug as if it were grappa or a shot of whiskey. "And you know how mothers can be."

Unable to help herself, she brought another strand of hair in front of her nose and scowled again.

"My mom thinks I should come home, though I don't know all her reasons for it," Louis began. "I'm sure she'd like me living there, or at least closer. But she also said things about just wanting me to be honest, and to stop running. I need to go through my things—throw away stuff I don't want and put the rest in storage. As far as I know, all my belongings are in my old room and in the attic where I left them when I moved out of my apartment. And I said good-bye to no one—not my grandparents who are getting old—or my friends. I didn't think I owed anyone an explanation. I thought they somehow deserved to be snubbed—or that I didn't deserve a proper send-off."

"And your mom's visit made you realize this—or did she tell you these things?" Claudia started toying with the sugar packet again, sweeping up crumbs, and stray pieces of sugar.

"Her visit made me realize, but she didn't say anything close to what I figured out by myself. And I don't know what I'll find when I get there. I haven't been home for so long, and I suddenly feel so different."

"Sorry if I'm sounding possessive, but now that I've decided that Venice is the place for me, I don't want to lose my best friend or have him discover that Venice isn't the place for him. I guess I'm getting greedy—and possessive. Just like you-know-who."

Louis smiled, thinking back to when he'd first met Claudia and thought her fun, but shallow. He could remember specifically thinking that she would make an ideal companion to spend some lonely days with in a foreign city—not a friend as close as any he'd had. He had the sudden realization that it was as if he'd been playing a game of musical chairs and when the music had stopped, he'd found himself in Venice. If he'd been somewhere else, would he have the same feeling? Was it timing, the convergence of people and events, or just fat chance? Was there ever a place for anyone, that chosen place of all places around the world where a person fit as snugly as a puzzle piece? His mother had said that place didn't matter, but maybe in this case it did. If he'd been anywhere but Venice, would things have turned out?

He felt certain that he'd end up back here; he just needed to return home—if that's even what he would call it anymore. He'd clean up the messes he'd left with friends and family—and with Greg. If he were to have any chance at all, he would have to start with a clean slate.

Claudia squinted, scrutinizing his face. She picked up her glass, taking another sip of prosecco. "Sorry to be acting like a regular Hemingway, but I didn't realize how much I needed this until the barista brought it over. It tastes wickedly good, doesn't it?"

"Tastes good to me, too," he said, taking a sip.

"When do you think you'll go?" she sighed, looking out the window at a lone old man wandering down the street.

"The sooner the better, but I want to help you and Sacci get the clean-up started, and I've got a few assignments that I need to finish," he said, though anxious to buy the ticket and be on his way. Until he went, he would feel stuck, unable to have the clean start he suddenly craved. And with Claudia and Sacci starting fresh, he felt the drive to put his past in order so he could get started with the future, whatever that might be.

Claudia frowned, suddenly looking uncertain, the same look he'd expected she might have when she first walked through the worn oak door of the café.

"Don't worry," he said, grabbing her forearm. "I'll be back."

At least he was no longer afraid to want something. And even if it came with no guarantee that he would return to Venice or that Sacci would even be gay or like him back, he would follow that thread of desire. If it petered out into nothing, unraveled or snapped, well, at least he had followed something.

And that was better than waiting idly and restlessly for the unexpressed or unknown things he wanted to come to him.

Chapter Twenty-one

Louis felt frightened, yet optimistic and excited. How many years had it been since he was last in Chicago, since he last stayed in his parent's house on tree-lined Alta Vista Terrace? A visit home seemed far less frightening after all he'd been through. Funny how a few events could transform a life.

While he would be gone from Venice for barely two weeks, he already missed the city. Somehow, the ancient, tucked-away place resonated with him, the shadowy canals, labyrinthine streets, and jumbled-up piazzas. Nothing would happen while he was away or nothing much, anyway. Claudia could catch him up on everything over a few coffees at Café Tramonta. Or maybe they could have a cocktail at Harry's, or even one of the old hotel bars on the Lido—if she could pull herself away from the hotel.

He'd been helping clean the palazzo, scrubbing away smoke stains, removing curtains to be aired, cleaned, or thrown away. Painters had come and gone, and still there was more to be done. He could see that once again the hotel was nearly ready to open.

It seemed a perfect time to leave, to clean up his past life before jumping into a new one. Claudia had the money she needed to open the palazzo, and even had the blessing (and financial support) of her mother.

Sacci seemed hardly the timid, reclusive landlord he'd encountered when Louis had first arrived in the city and answered an ad in a giornale for a tenant. The thought of the man stirred his insides, making him restless and sleepless, but he finally knew better, feeling his crush finally fading. He felt confident that it would be his last improbable crush.

If things had worked out, it might have seemed too much like a Hollywood film, especially with all that had happened to him the night the opera house burned. When he'd jumped at the sound of someone knocking at the studio door, wondering if the men who'd tied him up had returned, he couldn't have imagined that it would be Sacci.

Hopping up and down in the wooden chair he was tied to, he'd made enough noise for Sacci to hear. And when the lock on the door was picked a few minutes later (he would never have imagined that Sacci would know how to do such a thing), he took it as a sign that things with Sacci were meant to be, that finally he would have what he wanted. Sacci was rescuing him, after all.

When his wrists were untied and the sock removed from his mouth, he was scarcely able to speak his tongue was so dry, but he decided he would no longer remain silent, wouldn't skulk around the perimeters of his life waiting for something to happen. But it wasn't until he met and received Claudia's encouragement the following day that he walked up the three flights of stairs to Sacci's apartment and knocked on his door, his fingers trembling.

"I'm gay," Louis had announced hoarsely, gazing at Sacci when he answered the door.

"I know," his friend had replied, nodding his head.

"And I love you, I think," Louis added quickly, suddenly fearful that he'd lose the resolve he'd only just discovered .

Sacci nodded, smiling at him. Louis' heart expanded in his chest, making him wonder why he'd waited so many months to say anything.

Then Sacci had gripped his shoulder and bit his lip. "I can't," he'd said quietly. "I'd like to, had even begun to think that maybe this was what I've been waiting for, but I realize it's not. I'm too old, too much like my old mother, I think. And too influenced by the church."

"The church?" Louis asked, his arms and insides going numb. "But you never mentioned that you were religious."

Sacci shrugged. "I'm not," he said dryly. "But somehow all the teachings from all those years and more than forty years of living with it have made it impossible to throw it all off. It's as if it's part of me now, part of my insides, even though a lot of it I just don't accept."

Louis thought his friend looked pained, but relieved at the same time, as if he were coming to a conclusion as he spoke. "It's somehow too late for me."

"You could have loved me?" Louis asked, still confused.

Had he met someone he thought he could love, traveled so far for that? What was the point in having had his hopes raised, only to have them dashed? Unlike Sacci or the contessa, he had no god to lash out at, no one at whom he could direct his anger. He'd believed that things happened as they were meant to happen. There was no omnipotent being directing his life or the lives of others, only that some sort of energy existed, and that like mountain brooks eventually making their way to the sea, his life and those of every person were somehow directed, flowing in a natural, but not exactly prescribed direction. But he didn't want to believe there could be a reason for that unanticipated turn.

"I do love you," Sacci confessed, nearly whispering the words. "But maybe like Ficino, or Michelangelo. I didn't grow up with the possibilities that you did, so this life that you live I don't know—*can't* know—"

"But you could," Louis interrupted, growing annoyed at Sacci's stubbornness, unbelieving that his hunch had been true, only to find himself denied in the end. If he believed things happened, as they should, why was he fighting Sacci's decision?

"I'm sorry," Sacci murmured with downcast eyes. "I can't offer you more than friendship."

After two months of endlessly replaying the memory of refusing to accept his friend's disappointing and perplexing pronouncement, that both satisfied his heart in a fundamental way while deceiving it, he had begun to feel that maybe things would be okay if he didn't get what he wanted. He felt loved by, and loved, Sacci. More than that, he felt stronger and more determined to stop running from his past, whatever that was. For that reason, he felt even more compelled to return home to make his move from Chicago final.

All his plans had seemingly toppled in months, though it had actually been more than half a year. The hotel had burned—and much of Sacci's and Claudia's money with it. And hadn't he encouraged the project, been responsible for getting Claudia involved in the hotel? But she had hardly been to blame for the fire. Ultimately, the arsonists were to blame, and then maybe Claudia's mother who had arranged to have the spark-catching curtains hung on the terrace. And who had sent the winds, the unusually strong, blustering winds that had carried the sparks from the opera house fire to *Palazzo Spirito*? Certainly the weather had played a role as much as anything else.

Everyone was to blame and no one was to blame.

Claudia had very nearly left, which might have set him adrift again. Only after they'd talked for hours and hours, weeks after the fire did he realize how close she'd come to leaving Venice, to starting another life somewhere else.

But there had been other things, a half-year stuffed with more meaningful events than it seemed he'd encountered his whole life. His mother had tracked him down, confronted him, and found him out. In the end, that had been a good thing.

After the fire and being tied up, Louis had experienced the familiar desire to pack up his few bags. He would sell the collection of belongings he'd somehow acquired during the past year and head somewhere else, maybe a quiet corner of Cairo, or a soporific Greek isle.

But then things had turned out, after all.

Life had caught up with him, or he'd allowed it to catch up. In Venice, an improbable, hidden, slow-as-a-snail city, he'd found his life. Maybe he could have found it in Chicago, or possibly in Paris or even

Prague. But things had come together in Venice, for whatever reason—if for any reason at all.

The plane would leave at noon that day from the little airport on the mainland and set down in Milan where he would catch his flight to Chicago. Then he would take the rattling El home to see his parents, his siblings, and maybe even some of his neighbors and friends. If he saw Tad or Irene, he wouldn't even care. He didn't even know who was left in the city. Had they gone in search of something as he had?

His favorite place to be in the mornings—other than in bed or at the café—was the fish market. So he rose early, like a good Venetian housewife of decades past, and wandered along the crooked, quiet streets immersed in early morning shadows. The streets seemed different somehow, the air thick and fragrant with the awakening city. Maybe it was the musty, damp smell hanging in the air in the tight corners and narrow streets that the morning sun normally burned off, or the murmuring from the restless waters of the canals usually covered up by the sounds of street noise.

The sun's rays wouldn't strike the streets for another hour or two, and except for the fishmongers, bakers, newspaper deliverymen, and café owners, the streets would remain relatively untraveled for a while yet.

In twenty-four hours, he might be on Lake Shore Drive or walking by the chaotic streets of his parents' neighborhood crowded with Victorian row houses and courtyard apartment buildings made of bricks and stones in many different colors. But that morning, he had Venice nearly to himself. Others had likely experienced similar moments for centuries, believing they had the city to themselves. But in reality, hadn't the reverse been true, hadn't the ancient city possessed each of them who caught a thrilling glimpse of its spirit in the morning calm when its windows were still tightly shuttered against the growing light in the eastern sky?

He felt sorry for those who would follow in another hundred years or so, when Venice ultimately succumbed to the sea like a modern-day Atlantis. For the city gave him the idea that the improbable cities of his dreams, the ones with bridges soaring through clouds or inhabiting giant bubbles built undersea or occupying impossible craggy mountaintops, might exist somewhere after all.

Rounding via Pescatori, he smelled fish mingled with the bracing scent of the nearby sea, the coffee makers, and the bread bakers. He wondered if Chicago would still have its own smells, some he'd no doubt forgotten. Venice always smelled a little of water, mold, decay, and bread and coffee. If he ever did leave, he would never forget its early morning smells.

Others were hurrying to the market in front of him, a man in his trademark white chef's uniform, and two middle-aged sisters, dressed in drab grays and browns, brightly colored silk scarves twisted around their necks. In small or big ways, Venice would have its way with you.

Had he changed, or was it the city? Had he finally found his place, his right place in the world, or had something within him changed? After all, Marco Polo and others had seen this same eastern sky beckoning, drawing them away instead of bidding them to stay. For him, the same sky sheltered, like an umbrella or talisman writ large.

As he passed under the massive old, peeling columns and arch, the market was just coming alive, with vendors still setting up their stalls. Piles of different size shrimp, and half a dozen different sizes and colors of crabs lay dazed on beds of ice, sometimes with legs or whiskers still twitching.

Taking a direct route toward the bar, he decided he would wander the market after having his coffee. He could spend at least an hour there, plenty of time to sip some coffee, eat some pastries, and maybe, like the fishmongers, slug a glass of vin santo. Then he'd stop by his *appartamento*, grab his bag, and catch a vaporetto for the airport.

As he approached the bar, the owner spied him, nodded, and began to prepare his cappuccino. Other shoppers and vendors crowded the bar, sipping espresso, vin santo, or wine. Louis found a spot toward the end of the bar, and his cappuccino in its cream-colored, embossed cup and saucer arrived a moment later, the owner offering a quick, but cheerful "giorno."

"Worst year I've ever seen," Louis overheard one of the fishmongers saying. "Twenty years ago, I thought the problem would be the pollution in the Mediterranean—now it's the over fishing. There's less and less to catch. Less and less to sell."

The middle-aged man who'd just spoken, sipped his espresso, shaking his head.

"Venice will always have seafood—langoustine, clams, mussels, squid, sardines—they'll always inhabit the Adriatic," one of the other white smock-cloaked vendors countered. A simple, sanguine expression covered his face like a mask.

"With global-warming, half the earth will be ocean," an older man added. "So there'll be plenty of space for even more fish."

"But the oceans will be polluted. If New York is underwater, the whole Atlantic will be polluted," another vendor claimed. "Then no fish for nobody."

"If New York is two meters underwater, then Venice will be ten meters underwater," the bartender said. "And we'll all be dead with no city to call our own, let alone anything to eat. It's all over then."

Silence invaded the bar, settling heavily on the dozen vendors and a street cleaner who sipped their morning beverages as they pondered the bartender's point.

"Maybe the city's time is up, anyway," an older gray-haired vendor mused, pursing his lips. "Maybe we just need to let it go, let it sink into the sea under its own weight."

"You're too deep, so *serio*!" one of men remarked.

A few others laughed and took hurried sips from their glasses or cups.

I've just got here and decided it's my city, Louis thought to himself. I just made it my own.

The older man chuckled, playing with his demitasse spoon and then, as if he'd read Louis' mind, said, "Nobody owns Venice—if the city belongs to anyone, it belongs to the past and maybe the sea. The whole place is borrowed from the sea."

"All cities everywhere are borrowed, *carino,* if not from the sea, then from the mountains, the rivers, or the earth—and maybe all are borrowed from time, eh?" the bartender joked, wiping the bar. "Nobody's owed anything and anything can be taken away at any time."

"I agree, signora," the older man said to the bartender with a shrug. "What will happen, will happen, and doesn't matter what you or I think. Venice—the whole world—has a mind of its own. What we think doesn't matter. I think Venice is a city that's had its time. Now it slowly sinks, but what do I know?"

The man shrugged again, as did a few others at the bar.

"The city sinks every year. The tide grows higher. More people move away," the middle-aged man said. "The only industries are taking care of tourists and fishing. You can't even make wine here."

"Like I said, it doesn't matter what I think—or what you think," the old man repeated. "We're just guessing, but maybe Venice knows and maybe she doesn't. I think she's dead—dying. Maybe I'm wrong. But I think I'm right. In the end, does it matter who's wrong or who's right? Does it change anything?"

"Of course it does," Louis said suddenly, the men all turning to face him. "Why should it die? It doesn't have to die."

The man gave Louis a nod of encouragement, as if he recognized him, though Louis was certain he'd never seen the man.

"That's the optimism of youth," said the man. "You think that your thoughts and ideas can change fate," he said. "Maybe they can change people for a while, but you can't change the earth. Not really. So I'm happy for you that you want to stop Venice from dying, but if Venice must die, it will die."

"And what would be the shame in that?" a gravelly voice from the end of the bar asked. "We'll all die. And if Venice lives, we won't be here to know about it. So who cares? Let's just get about the business of dying."

Louis couldn't see who was speaking, but he recognized the voice. Others around the bar studied their glasses and espresso cups, as if looking for patterns in the foam. Louis leaned forward, craning his neck to see who had spoken.

He recognized the woman—the crusty baker who grumbled at everyone as she walked around the city, the one he'd seen wandering the market before. She cleared her throat and left some lire next to her empty cup. She extended a steady, but wrinkled hand to retrieve a shopping bag nestled at her feet.

"Giorno, signora," the bartender called, her voice having a falsely casual sound.

The old woman grunted, but returned the bartender's quick nod. She hesitated a moment, then set her bag back down and pushed up to the bar once more.

The mood in the bar was more somber than Louis had ever seen it. The woman seemed to poison the air every time he'd seen her there, but perhaps it was the conversation. Patrons downed their drinks, paying and leaving, scattering like children released early from school. He'd learned to recognize the subtle reaction the old woman had on the bar—no one seemed to stay very long when she was there. But why did she even come when she talked to no one and seemed pained to greet the bartender? Why did she subject herself to people who knew her, nodding her head and issuing a deadpan "giorno" if she despised them all?

Why had no one told her to get lost, to go away, and leave everyone in peace? In Chicago—in the states—they would let her know she was unwelcome; maybe even force her out of the place.

"You're bad for business," they'd have said.

But at the market, they allowed her to make her rounds, spewing her venom as if it was to be expected, as normal as the water in the canals rising and falling.

The sounds of the fish market interrupted the momentary silence. A small tractor turned a corner, carrying a load of silvery, glistening dorado, eyes frozen and listless, but shiny like marbles. A fresh tide of bleary-eyed workers and shoppers approached, once again filling the small corner bar. He noticed they avoided the old woman until there was no space at the bar left but right next to her. They nodded politely, their faces as expressive as the slack-eyed fish lying on ice behind them.

He felt a change in the air, the quiet conversations that had sprung up falling to a murmur. The bartender jerked, moving uneasily from one task to another. She set a cappuccino on the counter with an indelicate bang, a tide of frothy beige steamed milk slipping onto the saucer.

"Spiace," she shouted, but didn't offer a napkin and turned back to the machine to make another drink.

Louis looked to his side and spotted a figure approaching the bar. It was the same old man he'd seen there before, his neighbor, possibly the crier? With his mother's visit, the hotel fire, and his trip home, he'd raced to and from his studio, forgetting completely about the crying, which he hadn't heard recently.

He turned slightly, maintaining his space at the bar, but casting a smile in the old man's direction. But the man didn't see him, focused as he was on the bar and the old woman. Was he going to speak to her again?

The man waved at the barista. "No drink today," he croaked.

The men and women at the bar cast cursory, stolen looks at the man. Like the previous group, they finished their drinks quickly, leaving coins on the counter before they hurried back into the market and disappeared.

Louis had thought he would have a vin santo, too, but decided he should leave as well. Waving toward the bartender, he failed to get her attention. If he left a thousand lire, that would be enough for his cappuccino. There were only two customers remaining at the bar—both of them on his left, leaving the old man and old woman next to each other.

Louis should have turned away like the barista, but he pivoted, watching the man reach for the woman's elbow.

"I know it's you," she croaked in her tired voice, still facing the bar. "Like a cold front or thunderstorm, I can sense you."

"Consta … I … came on purpose," he stammered, his face twitching while nervous eyes darted around the bar.

"Don't call me that," she said in a near whisper. "You have nerve, seeking me out today. Any day is bad, but today—why today—no, no, I know. I've suspected you would come one day and why not today?"

"I'm sorry—"

"You know what today is?" she said bitterly.

"Yes—I'm sorry. Of course I know what today is," he whispered. "You're not the only one who suffers."

"Is this what you've come to tell me—*again*? I know you're sorry. You, you have always told me you're sorry. Is that all you have to say?"

The woman's voice sounded weary, only slightly caustic. Not quite the hard-edged way she'd sounded when Louis had first seen her in the market.

"Enough is enough, isn't it? Can't it be? I'm old and you're old. My life is nearly over, and it has been miserable, not a life I would wish on anyone—a half life," the man said, his voice trembling and rising as if he wanted others to hear.

"I made a promise to myself that I would never forget," she said with resignation. "Why should I?"

"Never *forgive* you mean," he suggested, moving next to her at the bar, his words tinged with bitterness.

The woman turned to look at the old man—her husband? Louis wondered who he was and how the couple knew each other. They looked alike—were they siblings?

With the woman's face turned toward the man, Louis couldn't see her expression. She would treat the old man harshly, probably, despite her softer voice. Upbraid and belittle him again for whatever he'd done. That's what she'd done every time Louis had seen them together. But what had he done? He didn't seem so bad. In fact, he looked rather innocent, harmless.

Maybe he'd cheated on her? Ruined the family business? It must have been something terrible, but not criminal. And the man seemed nice enough, just marked with the ponderous, hangdog look of the wretched.

"Last night I had a dream, a nightmare actually," the man said, wringing his hands.

Turning back to the bar, the woman pulled her hand over her face, sheltering her eyes. "I don't want to hear it. Please don't tell me."

"She was in it. And you know what she told me?" he asked hoarsely, leaning toward her.

"No, don't tell me. Please," she sighed.

But she didn't move away, didn't wave him away with the hand that stayed above her eyes, as if shading them from the sun.

"She told me to tell you—that's why I came."

"You should go to church—speaking blasphemy like that," she said angrily, removing her hand and turning to him. "And on top of it bringing me more pain." Pulling her cardigan closed, she took a small step away.

"She made me promise—promise to tell you," the man said, stepping closer.

"Tell me what! I'm old now, too. Why do you want to torture me with this now? Let's allow each other to die with what little peace we're able to enjoy, no?"

She covered her eyes again, leaning on the cool, scratched surface of the old zinc bar.

"She asked me to tell you. Made me promise," he explained, talking more quickly. "Maybe it was just a dream, maybe it was something more. Maybe it was my hopes. Still, it makes no sense."

"What makes no sense?" the woman asked sounding bitter again, her voice hardly more than a whisper. Her chin pushed into her sunken chest, her eyes closed.

"It was odd," he explained. "But she said, 'Tell my mamma Venice is sinking.' That's all she said."

"Venice is sinking?" she asked, her voice trembling.

"Sì," he said, shaking his head. "Strange, isn't it? I awoke crying. And I don't know why."

Resting her head on her hands, the woman started sobbing, her small shoulders shaking.

"I'm sorry. I don't want to make you cry. Don't want to hurt you again," he said soberly. "I'm just so tired."

The man reached his hand toward her back, deciding to withdraw it just before his palm touched her. The bartender stopped making an espresso, glancing distractedly at the old woman.

"What does it mean? Does it mean anything at all?" the man asked, leaning into the woman's ear.

But the woman continued crying, her shoulders shaking and hunched over the bar. She acted as if she hadn't heard his question at all. After a few long minutes of sobbing, the woman looked up at the man.

"It must mean something. Tell me," he said, reaching for her shoulder, but stopping again before he touched her. His hand dropped to his side.

"Maybe it means it's time to forget all this—before we're both dead," she laughed, her voice sounding tired and false. "Maybe it means to start living again—ha!—now that I'm older than eighty? Possibly, it means nothing at all. Just a strange dream you had—your own wishes to see your daughter again invading your dreams, allowing you a taste of bliss that you'll be forever denied in your waking hours."

The man's eyes grew red-lidded, heavy.

"Tell me it means something. Can you?" he said, running his shaking hands along his lapel. His lower lip trembled, his mouth attempting to form words that wouldn't come.

The woman shrugged, gazing at him innocuously.

"I don't know if I believe in such things," she sniffed. "I used to think I did, that spirits might visit, or that prayers might work. If I still believed all that I used to, then I might think she's giving me some advice that I gave her so many years ago. But how can that be? Why would she visit now, after so many years of hell? Only now after my worthless life begins its slow fade to nothingness."

The man shrugged. "Who can say?"

"Who can say?" she asked sarcastically, waving her hand through the air and dropping her eyes to the counter where she traced the outline of coffee rings on the cold metal surface of the bar.

"I don't know. I just feel that—no, I have a strong feeling that she meant something *specific*—that my dream wasn't random, or the result of a lifetime of longing. I could just as easily ask, why visit now, and give me a message that doesn't have *some* significance?"

The woman started sobbing softly again, hiding her eyes behind her gnarled hands. "I'm afraid that now that I've started crying I'll never stop. Not until I break and sink into the swamp that is this city."

The man pushed his handkerchief into her hand, awkwardly leaning toward her. "Tell me, Consta. Please. What does it mean?"

The woman nodded her head slowly, fixing her gaze on the counter.

"There was a day when Breva told me that her nonna had warned her that Venice was sinking. I was angry then, wondering why that old woman would tell a young child such crazy things, such frightening things. I suppose, though, she would have heard such tales soon enough."

"So what did you tell her?" the man asked, dropping his head closer to her face.

Sniffing, the woman said, "That we would simply swim, that it was nothing to worry about. The thing is to live, that's what I told her. I didn't want her to worry, you know, to live in fear. Maybe I meant to take things as they come. Maybe I don't even know exactly what I meant myself," she sobbed, her voice cracking.

"Maybe it does make sense," the man said.

Shaking her head, the woman continued to cry softly. "I'm not certain of anything anymore. I haven't been for many years."

"Venice is dying; just like us. Maybe I'll die before you; maybe Venice dies before both of us. The city could sink tomorrow, buried in the sea from the weight of all these bricks, stones, and mortar, or drowned by melting polar ice caps."

"What are you saying?" the woman asked, looking confused. "They were just talking about that before you came in."

"Never mind," he said shaking his head. "I've been dead, as dead as Breva for all these years, for most of my life. I lost twice, lost my whole life. First my art, my livelihood, then my daughter, and then—" he stopped, hanging his head as his shoulders drooped. "Life has been a torture to me."

The old man shook his head slowly, his hands clenching and unclenching, as if grasping for something.

The woman rested her cheek on the zinc counter, gazing at some far-off point while tears rolled down over her nose and onto the bar.

Tentatively, the man raised his thick-fingered hand toward her back again, this time not dropping it, but pushing gently but firmly into her spine. His other hand sat nearly a foot in front of the woman's face, awkward and solitary, a dark reddish scar marring the inside of his wrist and disappearing up his shirtsleeve.

A sudden rush overtook the bar, with customers ignoring the elderly couple, casting only occasional, cursory glances and gulping their espresso or vin santo before heading back to work or shopping. Louis could no longer hear or see the couple, only the top of the woman's head, her cheek pressed against the zinc bar top and the man's outstretched hand. Conversation around him drowned out whatever the couple was saying, though only two stall workers squeezed between them and only a few feet separated them.

He felt certain the old man's sobs were familiar, the same ones he'd heard in the stairwell. So they'd lost a daughter. How, he wondered?

Despite having been estranged for an unknowable, but undoubtedly considerable amount of years, the two still seemed like a couple, as bound to each other as Venice was to the canals, water and sea, and the tiny bits of land it clung to. Louis leaned forward, gazing past the customers next to him who observed his interest in the couple with shifty, disapproving looks. Did they protect their own, preventing some secrets from ever being revealed, even if on the surface they didn't seem to like the old woman?

The pair stood silently as customers came and went. The man gazed intently at the woman as she continued to cry with the slow and gentle rhythm of a late autumn rain. Customers—many of whom certainly recognized the pair—cast an initial discreet look their way upon approaching the bar, often turning their gaze to the bartender for affirmation that a remarkable event was in the offing, that their eyes were not in fact deceiving them.

The bartender nodded, pouring drinks and pulling espresso from the scratched and dented old steam coffee machine, moving even faster than usual and whistling. The polished eagle crowning the machine stared absently at the customers lined up at the bar, and past them into the crowded market. There was more conversation than usual, which served to fill the otherwise heavy air. Everyone except Louis turned away from the couple, as if allowing them their privacy.

Stealing glances, he saw that the couple hadn't moved. Had she finally stopped crying? He couldn't see.

There was a rush to pay bills by the latest wave of customers, most of them already knowing exactly what they owed. Patrons left lire coins next to espresso cups and wine glasses and hurried away from the bar, disappearing down the aisles of the market. They scattered across the uneven, damp halls of the fish market like spilled marbles, spinning away quickly and smoothly.

Before he stole another glance at the couple, Louis studied the bar, noticing little things he hadn't seen before, the way the glasses were carefully stacked on shelves and the few photographs of children—the bartender's?—taped to a mirror behind the bar. He gazed at the framed certificate on the wall.

This bar hereby proclaimed
a Landmark Institution
of the City of Venice
Owned by the Turco family since 1862

When he turned his gaze back toward the couple, the old man's once-solitary, idle hand tightly clasped the hand of his wife.

The old woman's tears formed a small puddle on the zinc counter, which reminded him of the sheen of the Adriatic on an overcast day, silvery-gray, flinty, and hard.

Constanza, eyes closed tightly and still softly crying, wore a whisper of a smile on her wet and creased face.